Joan England
Pemberton. N.J.

The Countess Angélique

NOVELS BY

SERGEANNE GOLON

Angélique
Angélique and the King
Angélique and the Sultan
Angélique in Revolt
Angélique in Love
The Countess Angélique

SERGEANNE GOLON

The Countess Angélique

TRANSLATED FROM THE FRENCH

BY

MARGUERITE BARNETT

G. P. PUTNAM'S SONS

NEW YORK

FIRST AMERICAN EDITION, 1968

Originally published in France by Editions de Trévise, 1967
as Angélique et le Nouveau Monde

© Opera Mundi, Paris, 1967.
English translation © William Heinemann Ltd.,
London, and G. P. Putnam's Sons, New York

Library of Congress Catalog
Card Number 68-21162

SECOND IMPRESSION

PRINTED IN THE UNITED STATES OF AMERICA

PRINCIPAL CHARACTERS

Angélique, Countess Peyrac. An aristocratic French lady of the seventeenth century; after leading the people of her native province, Poitou, in their uprising against Louis XIV, she was condemned to death and obliged to flee France with her youngest child Honorine. She reached America, where she was reunited with her long-lost husband and her two sons, Florimond and Cantor.

Honorine. Angélique's illegitimate daughter, aged four at the time of the action.

Joffrey de Peyrac. A high-born Frenchman. His great learning and considerable fortune aroused the envy of King Louis XIV, who contrived his ruin and had him condemned as a sorcerer. After many adventures, he was reunited with his family and disembarked in America on the shores of Maine, where he planned to found a colony. The Indians called him Tekonderoga.

Florimond. Angélique's eldest son by Count Peyrac, aged 17.

Cantor. Second son of Angélique and Count Peyrac, aged 15.

Servants and followers of Count Peyrac on his expedition:
Hervé le Gaën: a Breton sailor.
Enrico Enzi: a Maltese diver.
Porguani: an Italian gentleman.
O'Connel: an Irish merchant.
Lymon White: an English Puritan, dumb as the result of having his tongue cut out.
Sam Holton: an English Puritan.
Clovis: a French blacksmith from the province of Auvergne.
Octave Malaprade: a French cook.
Jacques Vignot: a French carpenter.
Nicolas Perrot and François Maupertuis: French-Canadian trappers.

French Huguenots who fled France with Angélique:
Monsieur Jonas: a watchmaker from La Rochelle.
Madame Jonas: his wife.
Elvire: a baker's widow, whose husband was killed on the crossing
    to America.

French-Canadians:
Count Loménie-Chambord.
Lieutenant Pont-Briand.
Romain de l'Aubignière.
Baron Eliacien de Maudreuil.
Robert Cavelier de la Salle.
The Duke of Arreboust.
Eloi Macollet.

Iroquois Indians:
Swanissit: Chief of the Five Nations.
Outakke: Chief of the Mohawks.
Tahoutaguete.

Algonquin Indians:
Mopuntook: Chief of the Metallaks.
Piksarett: Chief of the Patsuiketts.

French Jesuits:
Father Masserat.
Father Sebastian d'Orgeval.
Father Philip de Guérande.

PART ONE

Early Days

CHAPTER 1

'So we're together, then, he and I!'

This was the thought that kept on fluttering around Angélique's head. She could not have said whether it came from within her own mind – for at that moment she felt herself quite incapable of forming any thoughts whatsoever – or whether it was rather something from outside herself akin to the buzzing flight of the mosquitoes and insects all about her. It came and went, began again, grew louder, then flitted away....

'So we're together, then, he and I!'

Her whole attention was focused on the task of keeping her horse safely pacing up a steep track, and Angélique could not have said that she was taking the slightest interest in the meaning of this buzzing sound which kept nagging at her.

'We're together! We're together!'

The phrase was repeated on two tones. One held a note of doubt, the other of affirmation. One was fearful, the other joyous. It formed a soothing accompaniment, a kind of a leitmotif, to the weary tread of her mount.

The young woman who rode beneath the overhanging crimson maple leaves on this American autumn day, was wearing a man's big felt hat with a feather in it; in the shadow of its brim her eyes looked as limpid as fresh spring water. To protect her hair from the dust of the trail, she had bound it up in a linen coif. She had given up riding side-saddle, and her long skirts revealed her legs in their close-fitting riding-boots right up to the knee. She had borrowed the boots from her son Cantor, who had been very willing to help her out. Her fingers, as they gripped the leather reins, warm and almost spongy from the pressure of her damp palms, were white at the knuckles from the strain of holding the horse's head turned towards the top of the hill, and preventing it from jibbing away towards the edge of the gorge on their left, whose deep shadows and rumbling echoes seemed both to fascinate and terrify the animal. Was it the void or the roar of torrential waters tantalizing the thirsty beast that made it so jumpy?

Her mount was a hardy mare, and very handsome too, but from the time they had set out, it had seemed utterly bewildered by what was

3

being asked of it. That was hardly surprising either, when you came to think of it, for nothing could have seemed less suited for the noble pace of a horse than these twisting trails that snaked up and down the slopes and valleys, scarcely visible beneath the trees, losing themselves on scorched heathland or in swamps, vanishing into rivers along which the travellers had to splash for hours on end when the forest became impenetrable, clambering over crests and plunging into the abyss with a recklessness common to all paths which a man on foot will follow when he seeks the quickest possible route and when he has only his own bare feet to consider, and not the precious hocks of a horse.

The trail they were now following was carpeted with dry, slippery grass, burnt almost reddish brown by the sun. The horse kept on flattening it down, and its impatient hooves found nothing to grip on. Angélique held it with a firm hand, exercising careful pressure on the animal to keep it calm and force it to go on. She knew her mount by now, and even if it required a constant effort from her, she no longer feared that it would disobey her commands. It would do what she wanted it to do, and if, when evening came, she was left aching in every limb, that was another matter.

On and on they went. They were reaching the summit. The shadowy depths of the gorge, frothing with yellow and red foam tinted by the trees that leaned over the rushing waters, dwindled away below the trail, seemed to draw itself in between two slabs of enclosing rock and disappeared from view; then they found themselves on a kind of plateau over which there wafted a gentle resin-impregnated breeze.

Angélique breathed deeply.

Before her lay a forest of conifers: pine-trees, blue cedars, and shaggy spruces formed a dark army, shimmering with sombre, soft emerald green and blue-grey hues, embroidered by clusters of needles in tufts, posies, rosettes, and garlands which made up a finely stitched tapestry, tint on tint, green on green.

The ground had become stony again, broken by outcrops of hard shale, over which the horse's hooves clattered.

Angélique relaxed the grip of her hands on the reins and her knees on the horse's flanks. The persistent little thought fluttered about her again, mingling now with the welcome breath of the breeze.

'So it really is true, we're together!'

She halted and, as one does on waking from a dream, listened to the echo of it. She gave a start, raised her head, and her gaze sought out a familiar silhouette at the far end of the company of riders.

4

There he was at the head of the cavalcade, Count Joffrey de Peyrac, the great wanderer in the eye of the Eternal, adventurer of the two worlds, the man of dramatic destiny, who, having tasted of all life's glories and privations, today pressed forward, a grim horseman, drawing his company on behind him day after day, in a haughtily casual manner that occasionally appeared reckless, but always proved reliable.

How many times had Angélique said to herself when they came face to face with some obstacle: 'We will never make it. Joffrey shouldn't have risked it.'

Yet, even as she spoke, they would make their way one after the other, riders following trackers, porters following riders, through some burrow-like hole in the brushwood, through the tunnel of a mountain gorge, across the fast flowing current of a river, the shifting no-man's-land of a swamp, or the unknown fastness of a rocky hill across which the shades of night were falling. And they got through, they moved on, light appeared at the end, there was the shore, the shelter for the night. Each time it happened it seemed to have been neither possible nor predictable, and yet it happened. Joffrey de Peyrac never warned anyone of these surprises. He presented them as if they were the most natural thing on earth. Angélique still wondered whether he really knew where he was going or whether it was mere chance that kept bringing them through safely. They ought to have been lost and have perished a hundred times over, but the fact remained that no one had perished. And for three weeks now, those who made up the little caravan that had left Gouldsboro during the last days of September, had bowed to their destiny, carried along and intoxicated by the forest through which they were journeying, like pebbles swept along in the flood of a torrent, their complexions brown and roughened at the angles, their eyes faded by the brilliant light, the dazzling blues, the blue of the sky seen through the coloured kaleidoscope of the leaves, and the folds of their garments redolent with the scent of wood fires and autumn, resin and raspberry. In the autumnal heat the mist that hung over the lakes would evaporate in the early hours of the morning, leaving the surface of the water dazzling and limpid, and the undergrowth so dry that it could be heard crackling at a considerable distance.

In the evening, the temperature would suddenly fall almost unexpectedly, bringing a sudden chill that was a foretaste of winter, but there were still many trees decked in green, only just beginning to turn yellow. Then, as if by a miracle, a camp site would appear, just a little off the beaten track, to avoid the sandflies and the mosquitoes. Fires were lighted. The Indian women deftly cut long poles from the undergrowth, and in less than an hour the clearing was dotted with tepees covered with sheets of birch-bark sewn together or with great patches of elm-bark overlapping like rooftiles. At first Angélique had wondered how they had managed to strip these sheets of bark from the trees in such a short time. Later she noticed that Joffrey de Peyrac used to send a party ahead whose job it was to clear a path and sometimes even to blaze one, and also to prepare the camp site. On some occasions, there was no one waiting for the cavalcade at its destination, but in that event the men would dash off in various directions, and, as lively as a dog unearthing a bone, they would lift up big strips of moss in various places in the wood, or roll away rock from the entrance to same cave, to reveal an abundant cache of elm-bark piled up ready for the traveller and supplies of buried maize.

It was primitive but adequate. For the three white women, Angélique, Madame Jonas, her niece Elvire and the three children accompanying them, a drill tent was erected. The ground was covered with pine branches and bearskins, which also served as blankets. It was very cosy in these tents and a good night's sleep could be had provided one was not accustomed to feather-beds and eiderdowns, which was certainly not the case for Angélique and her daughter, who had experienced many far less comfortable lodgings in the course of their adventures.

The unchanging fair weather made their journey easier. At least they did not have to dry out rain-drenched garments. Hunting and fishing provided them with tasty food every evening, to supplement their commons of dry biscuits and bacon which they had brought with them from Gouldsboro.

But, as the days, then the weeks passed, their cautious advance disguised extreme lassitude. Angélique felt it especially this morning, when her horse's hooves began to clatter over the stony ground. The noise seemed to be amplified by the grey trunks of the pines, and by contrast emphasized the silence in which they were advancing. She noticed that for several days now Cantor's guitar had been silent, as had the cheerful voices of Maupertuis and Perrot bandying jokes or swapping advice. The company kept steadily on but no one spoke any longer. It was weariness perhaps, or the instinctive cunning of those in peril, who at every step are on their guard and try to be as inconspicuous as possible. That morning, Honorine had asked to ride behind Angélique for the first time since they had set out. Up till then she had foisted her company on each of the riders in turn, and indeed she had been much sought after, for she was a most entertaining companion. She had even got herself carried on the greasy shoulders of some of the Indians, with whom she claimed to have had some very interesting conversations.

But today she wanted her mother. Angélique could feel her asleep against her back. When the terrain became difficult the child ran the risk of slipping off, but Honorine had been brought up on horseback, and had been rocked all her childhood by the stride of horses making their way through dense forests, and in her sleep she instinctively tightened her grip around her mother's waist.

The trail vanished into a patch of grey sand, intermingled with pine needles, and the velvety surface deadened all noise once more. The sounds of breathing, the creaking of the saddles, the snorting of the horses as they drove off the flies, all mingled with the sighing of the wind that whispered softly through the pine-trees like the distant roar of the sea. The trees were very big now; straight, pale-grey trunks shot high up in the air, stretching out their horizontal branches with architectural precision. These were trees worthy of having been planted by the hand of man. They reminded one irresistibly of the cathedrals, and of the great parks on the Ile de France and at Versailles.

But it was only a park created by untamed nature, sown spontaneously at the wild will of the winds, the soil, and frail seeds, and which today, for the first time since the dawn of the world, was echoing to the sound of horses' hooves. The tall American pines watched the horses go by. They had never seen one before.

The animals sniffed the fragrant air. Their senses told them there was something unusual about this first meeting with the giants of an unexplored world, but, like the civilized creatures of noble English and Irish blood that they were, they overcame their apprehensions.

A pine-cone came tumbling down from branch to branch, one of those round bristly fruits, open like a water-lily and rimy with white resin. Angélique started at the noise, her mount shied and Honorine woke up.

'It's nothing,' said her mother.

She spoke softly. There were squirrels up there in the trees, watching them as they went by.

They had been walking now for nearly an hour on this flat ground amidst the grey colonnade of pine-trees.

The land began to slope down gently towards the valley, and with it went pines then firs then, as they slid down the slope, birches appeared

7

again, and aspens with their leaves still almost green, then elms, already golden brown, rugged oaks with clusters of huge brown or wine-coloured leaves, and finally the entire gamut of the maple family, of which Angélique had never encountered so many different varieties. It was these maples that gave the autumn its loveliest colours, ranging from honey via hectic red to burnished gold.

Shortly before plunging into undergrowth hung with purple, they caught sight on their left of a vast horizon rimmed with dark mountains. These were the first mountains they had seen, for although up till now they had appeared to be constantly going up- or downhill, since they had left the coast, the travellers had merely been crossing a vast peneplain, furrowed by sudden gorges, watercourses and lakes.

The mountains they saw did not seem very high, but there were many of them and they seemed to go on for ever, rolling away into the distance like a long, gentle swell, with blue upon grey and grey upon blue, until they melted into banks of similarly coloured clouds that crowded the far sky.

At their feet, in the foreground, spread a valley, pink-tinted beneath a light mist. It was vast, calm, serene, and devastatingly empty.

Angélique suddenly felt overwhelmed by the panorama she had glimpsed, for it had brought sharply home to her the scale of the world in which she found herself. It represented, so to speak, the discovery, all illusion past, of the true extent of a virtually impossible task. She began to doubt whether she had ever lived anywhere else, whether she had ever been amongst a crowd of people, amidst other women, at Court, at Versailles, whether it were possible that, somewhere in the world, there were cities thronged with people and the busy hum of men, nations where human beings lived huddled together, overcrowded and turbulent. It all seemed inconceivable. They were now transported back to the beginnings of the world, the pride of silent matter: water, earth, rocks, swamps and clouds, leaves and sky. And for her, everything had fallen silent. Gone now were the noisy scenes of the past, where she had played out her brilliant but solitary destiny as a beautiful young woman hemmed about by desire and peril. It was as if a red theatre curtain had fallen, from behind which she could hear laughter, sniggering, and cackling.

Angélique shuddered and drew herself up in her saddle, with a sensation of nausea:

'I almost went to sleep. How stupid of me, I could have broken my own ribs and dragged Honorine with me. You're all right, aren't you, Honorine, my love?'

8

'Yes Mummy.'

'It's all this red too. . . .' '

They were moving forward in a blaze of scarlet, through a grove of maples that the autumn had turned red from head to foot, for the fallen leaves already formed a thick carpet and made it almost impossible to pick out, in the midst of the foliage, the black trunks and branches that supported all this panoply. The light filtering through the leaves took on all the brilliance of a blacksmith's forge, the radiance of stoned glass. Three bold, rapturous black-and-white magpies hopped from branch to branch, chattering clamorously.

'Oh, that's all it was! It sounded like Madame de Montespan.' Her rival at Versailles was far away, and the thought of her was like something out of a colourful nightmare. All that was no more real and substantial than an empty fruit-skin crushed between one's fingers. The Court, King Louis XIV's passion for her, Angélique. The curtain had come down. All that lay behind her. That was how she felt about it. And before her lay the desert and the man she had found again. Everything was beginning once more.

She had felt something analogous to this a long time ago, when she had crossed the desert of Mahgreb with Colin Paturel: a transformation of her whole being, a break with herself. But it had not been at all the same thing; for then she had been fleeing from the desert, and Colin Paturel had merely crossed her path. Whereas now the desert to be crossed would never end, and she was tied to the man she loved.

They were together.

And this thought around her and within her suddenly raged with conflicting feelings, an unspeakable joy and then a sudden chill of fear, as if a chasm had suddenly yawned beneath her feet. A feverish shudder ran through her body, leaving her feeling inwardly shattered. The fear sprang from the words she had uttered almost unconsciously, speaking of herself as 'tied', or saying that the desert was never-ending. She looked down at her hands as they held the horse's reins, and found them familiar. They were slender and long, and many a man had kissed them without suspecting their hidden strength. It was that strength, practised over the years, which now made it possible for her to handle heavy arms, to knead dough or to wring washing as she performed her heavy household tasks, and to master a restive horse.

They were clean-cut, those hands, very much her own, and they bore neither dress rings nor a wedding ring. They were her hands!

Angélique trusted them, they were her most faithful friends. But as for the rest of her, at times she felt a weary, childish weakness. Her

9

heart and her mind were in a turmoil, she felt so highly-strung, her laughter was close to tears, a single word could cause her dismay, joy, plunge her into uncertainty, perplexity, and she felt a feeling of oppression mounting within her, nameless and without purpose, that began to overwhelm her just as the clouds across the plain, piled above the valleys, had begun insidiously to swell and invade the clear sky.

Everything had gone too quickly, and now everything was going too slowly.

It had been too swift, too staggering, the joy she had felt that morning when he had taken her hand in front of them all and said: 'I would like to introduce to you my wife, the Countess of Peyrac.' It had been too dazzling, too painful, like a flash of lightning, that moment when she had caught sight of her sons, alive, and had realized that they were really there.

It had all been too violent, too exhausting, the joy of those nights when her body, restored to life again, had rediscovered the urgency of desire.

It had been like a whirlwind that gripped her and ravished her. The red-hot brand of joy and happiness had touched her, had penetrated her, but she was not yet capable of severing herself from all that she had been for too long, that other woman born in travail, that woman branded with the seal of the King, the Rebel. That was why she sometimes found herself a widow again, alone with all her old irrational reflexes.

It was at times like these that the reality of her situation would strike her like a gunshot, leaving her in a state of shock and stupor.

'But it's true. He is here. We are together.' Joy and fear mingled within her, and she would almost faint.

Rather than face these moments of awareness that burnt or froze her in turn, Angélique found it preferable in the end to allow her mental energy to lapse, to sink into a kind of torpor favoured by the slow laborious progress of her horse. There was nothing really dangerous about the journey, but everything was unexpected. Attention remained on the alert, thought slumbered, grew vague, and seemed unwilling to consider anything beyond the narrow track, its winding course, its rise and fall, its signs and smells, refusing to dwell on anything beyond tangible and immediate marks, stones, leaves, grassy patches to cross or skirt, and what lay all around them . . . and that was nothingness, nothingness, nothingness, as far as the eye could see, nothing but silence and a dead earth wrapped in a shroud of crackling leaves

'But I've always had too much imagination,' Angélique told herself.

'I would dream . . . I would settle down among the pictures of my own imagination, and find that I liked it so much there that I had great difficulty in coming back to a different and often disappointing reality. If I begin to let my imagination play on the idea of a vast hostile desert behind those interminable clumps of trees, I will wear myself out before we get there. . . . Much better for me to wait till I find out what this country really is and not to think about it. Oh, all this red! . . .' she murmured with a shake of her head. 'How could one ever dream of such splendour? Could one have dreamt that such colours existed?' she asked herself, with a feeling of sudden exhaltation, drawn out of herself by an impulse of admiration that plunged her into a state of almost supernatural bliss, eyes wide open, gloating on the rippling colours, in which light and shade vied with one another to give to each subtle shade all the splendour of a jewel. Red, saffron and pink stood out against the bronze sackcloth of the undergrowth and blackberry bushes from which emanated a warm perfume of blackberries and honey. Angélique thought she saw something move beside a near-by tree-trunk and discovered two black bear cubs climbing up the tree, the claws of all eight paws gripping the bark. As the horse went by they turned their snouts curiously to watch, with a look that was both artful and guileless.

She nearly woke Honorine to show them to her, for they were so funny.

But she reflected that the mother-bear might well be in the offing, and she checked the pocket of her saddle to make sure that the pistols Joffrey had given her were still there.

Some distance behind her Master Jonas's horse came out from under a double scarlet archway. As if bent double beneath the weight of the incandescent leaves, the watchmaker's back had grown round. He too must be half-asleep, and Angélique kept an eye on him as he set out across the track covered with dead leaves. If the mother-bear were to make a movement over there in the undergrowth, the horses would certainly take fright. But nothing happened; Master Jonas and his horse passed under the gaze of the bear cubs, which took considerable interest in watching this apocalyptic animal whose four-footed lower half looked like the original and whose upper half, surmounted by a kind of black cone – the baby bears did not know it was called a hat – gave out a loud snoring noise as it went by.

Master Jonas and his wife had asked the Count de Peyrac if they might join his expedition rather than remain in Gouldsboro. With their niece Elvire, the baker's widow and her two young children, they formed the Huguenot contingent of the company, Angélique's personal acquaintances. The rest of the party, among whom were Italians, Germans, Englishmen, and possibly Scots, she still did not know properly and even found it hard to distinguish one man from another. She reproached herself for this uncertainty, which was by no means her way; for she had always shown a degree of curiosity about her fellows which inclined her to get to know them quickly. But they were Peyrac's men, not hers, and both sides were biding their time.

The only one to stand out from the crowd was still the Canadian trapper, Nicholas Perrot, more generally capable, useful and indispensable than ever; he had a way of appearing at the opportune moment whenever she needed something done. He walked, by choice, with the tireless, silent gait of the Indians, his gun resting butt upwards on his shoulder. He often went on ahead to clear the trail and prepare the site for the evening camp. Angélique had the impression that this calm, mysterious young man could well have familiarized her with everything that frightened her, but he would no doubt have been astonished to know her thoughts since his surroundings were so everyday to him: a tree was a tree whether red or not, a river was a river, a redskin a redskin, the important thing being to decide very quickly whether one was dealing with friend or foe. A friend was a friend, an enemy an enemy, and a scalp a scalp; one of the best things in life was a halt round a well-packed peace-pipe, one of the most disagreeable an arrow through one's heart.

In this respect he was a simple man, and the mystery in him derived only from knowledge he possessed of strange and unaccustomed things. He was quite unconscious of it himself.

She was sorry that he was not near her now. She would have asked him the names of some of the plants she saw along the track; for she knew some of them but not all. She would have asked him how they managed to feed horses in a land with no fields, no clearings, with nothing but the dense undergrowth, dead leaves, fallen branches, and no grass. She sensed that this problem of the horses must be worrying him. He had already explained at considerable length to her that in this area, the only means of communication were the rivers, and the only means of transport little Indian birch-bark canoes which one carried on one's head over the rapids and refloated on calmer waters farther on. 'But of course, with horses and women! . . .' he would say with a shake of the head.

The forest was coming to an end in a blaze of sunset hues between the walls of rock which widened out to form a sort of gorge. Water came bounding down the hillside to meet them, but this time the slope was not difficult to climb. Before going on her way, Angélique halted this time and turned round to look back over the cavalcade emerging one by one from the ravine, some on horseback, others on foot, as if they were climbing out of a well.

She noted their weary demeanour; all of them, even the young men, seemed to be overcome by fatigue and heat.

Honorine, the little three-year-old, was sleeping with her arms around her mother's waist, leaning against her back. At the spot where the child's plump cheek rested on her, Angélique could feel a hot damp patch. The slightest point of contact was almost unbearable in this intense heat, for the air was bone dry and quivering.

Sweat ran down the back of her neck and made her clothes stick to her skin. In spite of her broad-brimmed hat the back of her neck was sore.

One of the men in the party came up to her and greeted her with a vague salutation as he went by. He never even raised his head, and his dragging footsteps raised a little trail of dust behind him. Angélique looked back again. She could not see her younger son, Cantor, and felt slightly anxious about him.

The men filed by one after another, bent double beneath the weight of their burdens.

Some of them, strangers to her, were speaking English together. They glanced briefly as they went by at the young woman sitting on her horse at the edge of the path; some of them greeted her, but none stopped.

During the course of those three weeks, all Angélique had managed to gather as she watched these men, chosen by Count Peyrac to accompany him on his expedition into the backwoods of the American continent, was that they were not a talkative lot, that they were shy, unsociable men, of tremendous stamina and passionately devoted to their leader. They were rough fellows and it did not take much penetration to suspect that each one of them had his secret to hide. Angélique was not unfamiliar with this breed of men, and she knew that they are not easy to tame.

Later on she would see about establishing some contact with them. Meanwhile her task – and it was such as to demand all her strength – was to dominate a restive horse and to look after her little daughter and the handful of Huguenot friends who had accompanied her.

In spite of the fact that she had long been accustomed to riding through forests, up hill and down dale, she had had some anxious moments. She remembered her husband's dubious expression when she had begged him to take her with him, and now she was beginning to understand. The life of adventure that awaited them in the backwoods of the province of Maine, where Count Peyrac had decided to work the gold and silver mines, would be full of unknown, unforeseeable difficulties, like the trail they had been following for so many days.

Indian men and women passed her too, leaving a musky smell behind them in the sweltering atmosphere. They had joined the caravan when it had reached the banks of the river Penobscot. They were members of a small tribe of Abenaki Indians, the Metallaks, who, after a trading expedition to the coast, were returning to their normal hunting grounds beside Lake Umbagog. They had asked for Count Peyrac's protection on their journey, fearing possible encounters with the Iroquois, their cruel hereditary enemy, who often ravaged their lands during their warlike excursions in the summer season.

Monsieur Jonas, the watchmaker from La Rochelle, stopped beside Angélique, holding his horse by the bridle. He took off his hat, carefully wiped its brim, then his forehead, then his glasses.

'Goodness! What a steep slope! And to think that there are twenty more like this to climb every day!'

'I hope your wife is not finding the going too hard?'

'I asked one of the men to help her during the climb. One false move and I fear my poor wife might well break her neck in one of these cataracts. Ah, here they come!'

The worthy lady from La Rochelle caught up with them. The young Breton Yann le Couennec, one of the men from the *Gouldsboro*, was obligingly leading her horse. Madame Jonas was crimson in the face, but cheerful.

So far they had stoically faced all risks involved in their decision to go with the Count, and Madame Jonas, a strong sprightly woman in her fifties, had shown great endurance as a horsewoman.

'What a change it is from the back shop in La Rochelle,' she would say. And she had gone on to explain to Angélique that, as the daughter of a farmer, she had been brought up almost entirely in the country.

'Have you seen Cantor?' Angélique asked her.

'Yes, he's giving Elvire a hand; she's not especially good on a horse. Poor child! I wonder what on earth induced her to ask to accompany us, with those two sons of hers, rather than remain at Gouldsboro. Of course it's true that she is our niece and that we are all the family she has left!'

Cantor appeared at the edge of the ravine and Angélique felt a glow of pride on catching sight of his sturdy youthful figure leading with a firm hand the horse to which a young woman and a little boy of six were clinging.

Elvire seemed frightened and admitted that it was above all the noise of the waterfalls that upset her. Now she would be able to continue unaided. She thanked Cantor politely and asked whether anyone had seen her elder son Bartholomew, who was eight. Angélique reassured her, saying that Bartholomew had gone ahead with Florimond, who had taken charge of him, and that the child refused to leave his side.

The group from La Rochelle set off again and Cantor stared after them, shaking his head as they walked off.

'If it wasn't for me, I don't know how that poor girl would get on,' he said in a tone of scorn tinged with pity. 'To encumber oneself with women and children on a trip like this is sheer madness. I don't mean you, Mother . . . you are my father's wife, and it is only natural that you should come with us. But you must admit that to travel in a caravan in an unknown land is a very different thing from dancing in the salons at Versailles!'

'Yes indeed, Cantor, yes indeed . . .' Angélique agreed suppressing a smile, for the boy spoke so earnestly, 'and I admire your endurance; you're carrying a heavy load and are on foot, whereas we women and children are on horseback!'

'Pooh! It's just a question of habit! We are no milk-sops!'

'Aren't you feeling a bit weary nevertheless in this dreadful heat?'

He straightened up, refusing to admit the slightest trace of fatigue. She guessed that he was not being entirely open with her; for even the toughest of the men in the party occasionally complained of the length and severity of the day's march. She noticed that he had grown thinner, and that he had rings under his eyes, which were the same shade of green as his mother's. Once again she asked herself why Joffrey was forcing them to keep up this almost inhuman pace. Was he putting them to the test, trying to find out what he could expect from each of them? Was he trying to prove to himself that the women and children in no way hindered his plans? Or did he have some secret reason that forced him to press on towards a goal which to Angélique was still vague and unprecise?

'What about you, Mother, how are you? Is that horse still playing you up?' Cantor inquired, forcing his chapped lips into a smile.

He already had the solid frame of a young man, but beneath the layer of grime and sweat, his soft pink cheeks were still those of a child. And it was these fresh, beardless cheeks that reminded Angélique of the chubby little page he had once been, singing for the Queen at Versailles, and she wanted to stroke his curly hair, to smile tenderly at him, to draw him to her and press his head against her hip, the head of her boy restored to life again, the son she had at last re-discovered, and who now stood before her, miraculously alive. . . .

But she restrained herself, knowing that adolescents feel shy about expressing emotion, and after many years of separation, her son's heart was a closed book to her. She was longing for the time when the caravan would finally come to a halt beneath a permanent roof, when the weariness she now felt would vanish and she would be able to establish closer contact with her family, to gather them about her, her husband and her two sons, and get to know them better once more in the tranquillity of everyday life.

This journey was a barrier separating them from her, she felt. Each one of them had to fight his own separate battles, obsessed by the thought that he must not be the one to slow the others down.

In answer to Cantor's question she said that everything was going fine, that Wallis seemed to have calmed down and to have grown more obedient.

'It was asking an awful lot of you,' Cantor said anxiously. 'Flori-mond and I could see that the mare was a handful, and we were worried when we saw that you had taken her over. We kept on think-ing that she was going to hurl you down a precipice or that you would never manage to force her through a difficult bit of the way. . . .'

'And do you boys think that I have not managed too badly?'

'Oh yes, you have managed very well,' said Cantor patronizingly, in order to conceal his surprise.

'You ride very well,' he admitted, stressing each word.

'Thank you very much. I needed that encouragement to help me to keep it up. I was very nearly going to give up this morning. It's so hot.

'Would you like a drink of water?' he suggested helpfully. 'I filled my flask at the foot of the cascade and it's still cool.'

'No thanks, but I'll give Honorine some.'

'It's not worth it. She's asleep,' said the lad quickly, withdrawing the flask he had held out.

He fastened it and hung it on his belt again.

'I'm going on ahead. Once we're through this wood, we'll have another shelf of rock to cross and I must help poor Madame Elvire,' and he strode off.

16

Angélique guided her horse back on to the path. She was watching Cantor, thinking that he was handsome, that he was being kind and thoughtful towards her and that she would have no difficulty in winning his confidence again, but she had been aware for some time that he did not like Honorine.

She gave a sigh and bowed her head a little.

Would she ever have the courage to talk to her two big sons about Honorine? What would she say to them? It was perfectly understandable that the two lads should wonder about the half-sister their mother had brought them from the Old World!

Which of their mother's lovers was her father? This thought must have sometimes crossed their minds. How had they both reacted in their heart of hearts to these disturbing revelations? What did they think of their father who had forgiven her and made the child welcome?

Honorine represented the essence of everything they wanted to forget; the cruel past with its separation and its inevitable betrayals. . . .

'Should I have left her at Gouldsboro?' Angélique asked herself. 'Abigail would have looked after her with loving care.'

'No, I could never have done that! I know that you would have died if you had been separated from me, my poor little bastard child,' she told herself, looking over her shoulder at the little round head pressed up against her so trustingly. 'And could I ever have forgotten you, could I ever have lived happily after once again casting you out of my life? Poor little child of fate, thrown on the world with such violence and horror!'

'No, I could never do that.'

Why was it that Honorine, that very morning, had absolutely insisted on returning to her mother? Wasn't it revealing? Whenever the child felt anxious about something, she would always seek out Angélique.

Up till then, she had been gay and very sociable. What manner of danger might they have to face today that made her feel the need for protection? Would there be difficulties along the trail? Would there be a thunderstorm? A tornado? Would they run into Iroquois?

For the entire duration of the trip, the Indians, whether friend or foe, had been almost invisible. Perrot and Maupertuis explained that the tribes had gone off to the coast to sell their furs, and that ships lay waiting for them loaded with brandy, hardware and pearls. The travellers passed abandoned camp sites full of purple willowherb and

17

honey-coloured pumpkin flowers with bold-shaped leaves cupping the morning dew.

These were the last traces of a semi-settled way of life which would soon disappear altogether as the trees closed more and more around them. The numerous Abenaki tribes, the indigenous race in Maine, had nomadism in their blood.

At the beginning of the journey they had first encountered Metallaks, who had joined the white man's caravan.

But apart from these they had seen no one, neither Iroquois nor Abenakis. And this absence of human contact, which for a long time had seemed a guarantee of safety, now began to weigh heavy on their weary hearts.

On their right, the mountains came into sight again across a wide stretch of scorched ground where fire had destroyed the trees, thus opening up a wider vista.

Angélique glanced hopefully towards the mountains, for she knew that at the foot of the Appalachians lay the outpost of Katarunk which belonged to Count Peyrac and was the destination for which they were heading. They were to spend the winter there, before going on in the spring to the mines which lay farther on. The mare went on across the soot-coloured plateau. A strong smell of burnt wood and resin hung in the air like incense.

In the crackling drought of this Indian summer fires broke out easily. It only took one spark to unleash an army of roaring flames that devastated and devoured the forest with the insatiable appetite of a ferocious dragon, driving before them the panic-stricken animals, and only coming to a halt when they reached the edge of a cliff or a stream, with an infernal hiss. For a long time after they had passed, the clear air still smelt of smoke which gave the vast forest spaces their characteristic and specific savour.

Here the fire was of recent origin; for the horses stirred up warm ashes with their hooves. Branches left black marks on anything that brushed against them, and the stumps of trees and tree-trunks that were still standing were burnt-out and dead. Through their bristling spikes, the valley glittered with the pink and mauve of its innumerable lakes. They reached the edge of one of these lakes to find that the fire had burnt right up to the water's edge and that there was not a single blade of grass left for the horses to eat.

They skirted the lake through the ashes until they came to a ford which the horses crossed, picking their way gingerly over a dam of boulders. The land rose steeply on the other side, and they climbed up the banks in the cool of firs and other trees untouched by the fire. These were not yet the foothills of the mountains, but a kind of island that rose in the middle of the valley, a rampart of rocks left stranded amidst the lakes, that must once have been rivers or formed a single fresh-water sea. After crossing this spur dark with pines and cedars, they began to descend again and soon another shimmering lake appeared, through the garishly yellow branches of a clump of young birch-trees.

Beneath a pearly sky, the mirror-like expanse of water sparkled in the noonday sunshine. Opposite them lay a hill steeped in gold and blood, its leafy masses reproduced in the depths of the waters.

The lake was extraordinarily limpid, unlike those they had encountered up to now, which always seemed to be thick with algae and moss. Here the grey sand was visible through the luminous water.

'I would like to paddle in that water,' exclaimed Honorine.

There were signs of an impending halt. Some way ahead, behind the willows, men were shouting and horses snorting. One of the trappers who had gone ahead reappeared and waved an arm to tell those who were still on their way down that there was to be a short rest. For those who might have missed his sign, he gave a guttural cry, to which the Indians who were bringing up the rear and were still some distance off among the trees, replied.

Angélique slid off her horse and helped Honorine to clamber down.

The little girl immediately removed both shoes and stockings and, drawing up her skirts, ran into the water.

'It's very cold,' she called, laughing with delight.

The horse had had a drink and had begun to crop the grass which, although scant, was still green along the little beach. As it grazed with lowered head Angélique stroked its neck, which, in the brilliant sunlight, resembled the sumptuous colours of the forest.

'Don't you worry, old girl,' she said softly. 'Look, there is plenty for you to eat. One day we shall find some big wide-open spaces for you to gallop over. We shall soon reach our destination.'

The mare twitched her ears as she ate and one had the impression that her breast was heaving with great repressed sighs. Horses do not like forests. Angélique remembered the war in Poitou and the long rides she had had to make with her supporters through the farthest corners of the Druidic forests. It was not the sense of danger, of a lurking enemy, that had made their horses so nervy, but rather the silence peculiar to the forest, a silence made up of numberless sharp, menacing sounds, and of the play of light and shade amongst the tree-trunks and the branches, giving rise to phantasmagoric visions, unleashing superstitious imaginings and adding to the real perils men face the fear of spirits and demons.

The great forestlands of North America were perhaps less grim and forbidding than those in which Angélique had spent her childhood. These forests were studded with vast blue lakes, and the crystal-clear atmosphere, vibrant with a dryness that even the winter mists could not dispel, made all outlines so clear-cut that they lacked mystery. This was no haunted forest.

Angélique was standing beside the lake. She did not want to let go of Wallis's bridle, for once, when left to graze, the mare had suddenly rushed off into the undergrowth as if to break out of some magic circle. She might easily have impaled herself on broken branches or broken her legs in potholes, and it had taken the Redskins, who knew the thick undergrowth like the back of their hands, all their skill to find her again.

The young woman felt the blood beating through her temples, and the back of her neck ached. She was deafened by the strident calls of cicadas.

Seeing that the mare appeared perfectly calm, Angélique took the risk of tying the end of her bridle to a branch of a young tree, then walked down to the water's edge to scoop up a little water in her hand and raise it to her lips.

An exclamation behind her stopped her in her tracks. The great Sagamore Mopuntook, Chief of the Metallaks, was making signs to her not to drink. Still in sign language, he explained that higher up there was a spring whose water was better to drink and that his braves had stopped there to quench their thirst. He invited her to join them there. She pointed to her horse, signifying to him that she could not move away from where she was. He understood her and with an imperious gesture told her to wait. Shortly afterwards he returned with a squaw bearing a wooden bowl full of water from the precious springs. The only trouble was that the bowl had contained a maize gruel and possibly other concoctions as well, and had only been cleaned by being scraped with fingers and nails; so the water in the bowl was already beginning to grow unappetizingly cloudy.

Angélique nevertheless forced herself to put it to her lips and swallow a few mouthfuls. She had already had occasion to notice that the Red Indians were extremely quick to take offence.

The great Chief waited solemnly, watching her drink, and undoubtedly he expected her to express lively appreciation of the remarkable water he had taken the trouble to offer her.

She found his smell, the strong smell of a male animal, covered from head to foot with bear grease, decidedly off-putting.

His smooth chest was tattooed in blue and black. Two serpents outlined his powerful pectoral muscles and a bear's-tooth necklace cast spiky shadows across it.

He was a chief, a Sagamore, as one could tell from the eagle feathers and the bushy racoon tail he wore in his hair that was pinned up in a bun at the back of his head.

From all along the edge of the lake came the noisy splashes and the happy shouts of men enjoying the diving and the cool water.

Florimond came up to greet his mother as he did during each halt along the way. He almost burst out laughing when he saw the delicate situation she was in; he intervened tactfully:

'I am terribly thirsty, Mother. Might I be allowed to drink some of that wonderful water you have been fortunate enough to taste?'

Oh, Florimond! What a thoughtful boy he was!

Angélique passed him the calabash with a sense of relief, but once again Mopuntook stopped her with an exclamation of horror. There followed a discussion to which they summoned Nicolas Perrot to act both as interpreter and diplomat.

'If I understand correctly,' said Florimond, 'a greenhorn like me is not worthy of the privilege of drinking from the same spring as his honourable mother?'

'Yes, that's part of it. . . .'

'It is not rather that there is a certain element of contempt for women in this ban our great chieftain has just mentioned?' Angélique asked.

'No, on the contrary. In offering you the best water he could find, the Sagamore wanted to pay tribute to the Woman, the Mother in you. Women are greatly revered among the Indians.'

'Really?' replied Angélique in surprise, glancing at the slave girl standing with lowered eyes behind the Chief.

'I know this seems too difficult to grasp, Madame. You have to have visited the sacred valley of the Iroquois in order to understand . . .' the trapper replied.

He handed the bowl back to the Indian with a great flow of words which seemed at last to satisfy him.

'And now, my boy, what do you say to a plunge in that cool water?'

'Hurray!' cried Florimond.

They vanished behind a curtain of willows and alders whose long leaves drooped down towards the surface of the water, and shortly afterwards they were swimming vigorously, their heads breaking the surface of the shimmering lake.

Angélique would have given anything to have been able to do likewise.

'I want to swim too,' said Honorine, beginning to strip off her tiny garments.

Madame Jonas and Elvire joined them with Elvire's two little boys, Thomas and Bartholomew. They agreed to allow the three children to splash in the water.

They danced about naked near the bank making great splashes and shouting for sheer delight.

A group of outraged wader-birds rose up out of the bushes with a noisy beating of wings.

Some tufted ducks with flame-coloured and violet crests on their heads, showed their annoyance by cackling loudly as they swam off leaving a wake behind them across the shimmering surface of the lake.

Angélique gave a sigh of envy as she looked at the cool water. But she remained beside her horse, a victim of her duty. And that was how Joffrey de Peyrac found her when he appeared on the little beach at the edge of the lake.

CHAPTER 2

HE WAS still holding the sextant with which he had just taken their position. He handed it to Octave Malaprade, the sailor from Bordeaux, who had escorted him carrying his leather writing-table and parchment. The man sat down beside a rock to put away the instrument and the maps in the portable desk that had been entrusted to him.

Angélique watched her husband as he strode forward through the brilliant light that was made even harsher by being reflected back from the water. His tall figure seemed to look even more solid. Amidst these almost too lovely evanescent surroundings, in which everything seemed dulled by the heat, he stood out hard and real. He seemed to move across this fascinating landscape unconcerned by the disturbance he brought into it. The utter indifference, even latent hostility of the countryside which Angélique did not like, seemed to make no impression on him.

The gravel crunched beneath his leather boots, as he strode across it with heavy tread.

'He still limps a little,' Angélique thought to herself. 'Aboard the *Gouldsboro* one noticed it less, because of the movement of the ship, but here on land one does.'

'What sudden thought made your eyes sparkle like that?' asked Joffrey de Peyrac.

'I just noticed that you still have a slight limp.'

'And you are pleased?'

'Yes!'

'Women really are an unpredictable lot! All the efforts I made to give you back a husband in presentable shape have only succeeded in stirring up regrets for the past! Or even arousing suspicions! I wouldn't put it past you to wonder whether this is not a case of assumed identity. . . . They tell so many entertaining stories of that sort, during those long evenings in the country districts, back in France. It is never easy to play the part of a man brought back from the dead! In the end I shall begin to wish I had my short leg back again.'

'It is only that I loved you the way you were then!'

'And you are not quite sure that you love me the way I am now?' he said with a roguish smile.

Then, without awaiting her reply, he greeted Mopuntook.

He always treated the Indian Chief with ceremonious politeness. He had removed his feathered hat and his thick hair glistened in the sun with a metallic sheen. Steely lights shone on his tight curled, typically Gascon hair, still almost jet black although beginning to shine with silver at the temples. His southern ancestry, with its admixture of Spanish and Saracen blood, made his face look as dark and sun-baked as that of the Redskin he was addressing. There was a paler area over his cheekbones left by the mask he sometimes wore. His bushy eyebrows had an easy graciousness above his magnificent eyes, but his profile was still sharp, broken by the sinuous curve of his lips, which stood out provokingly aggressive and sensual.

His lips were strong and wide, like fine silk but scarcely tinged with pink beside the tanned skin of his face. They trembled, they tightened, or parted over his shining teeth. They seemed to lead their own life in his extraordinary face in which every element seemed to contribute to the total aristocratic impression. He had the vast strongly-lined forehead of the man of intelligence, the delicately arched browline of the man of birth, and there was fire of spirit in the depths of his dark eyes. His nose and chin were strong and rugged, those of a conqueror, a man from the mountains, accustomed to hold his head high, to watch the eagle in his soaring; and between them lay that slightly Moorish mouth, imperious, demanding so it seemed, even when silent and impassive, the mouth of the man of this earth, a sign of materiality amidst the sublimated features, which enhanced its ambivalent and disquieting strength. It was such a mouth that the sculptors of ancient times gave to the images of their gods, without realizing that their chisels were thus expressing all the lust for life and pleasure of those early Mediterranean civilizations.

Whenever Angélique looked at that vibrant and sensitive mouth set in that often severe and formidable face, she felt suddenly overcome with the desire to lay it on hers.

She was now, for example, as he stood answering the Chief of the Metallaks with gestures and a few Indian words. Then he turned and gazed away into the distance towards the other shore, trying to fathom who knew what mystery of this untamable landscape.

For a moment he seemed far away, perhaps anxious after their exchange of words. He was thinking and his mouth quivered. As she watched him, Angélique felt her heart beat faster. She longed for those lips on hers, their tenderness then their passion. She devoured him with her eyes.

The heat of the ride had left his brow damp and a few drops of sweat ran across his temples and, without his being aware of it, trickled down the scars on his face. Angélique would have liked to wipe that lined face tenderly, but she did not dare. There were still spontaneous gestures she found it impossible to make, held back as she was by a kind of fear. She told herself that he had lived for so long without a woman at his side, completely unhampered. That he had been accustomed to considerable sexual and emotional freedom. Might he not find the daily attentions of a wife importunate?

Here, even more than on board his ship, she sensed the man's independence. It radiated from him like a halo. He was a man who had lived many lives.

A complex man beneath his apparent simplicity. And she must find her place in the complexities of this superior mind.

In the dazzling light she saw him as he was, a man who had reached the peak of his existence, in full possession of his strength, of his faculties and of his experience of life. He was a complete, close-knit personality, a man without uncertainties, his character forged by his life of adventure, wars, death, torture, and passion. When he stood motionless like this, his breathing was almost imperceptible. She could see no tremor in his chest, held tight in a black velvet doublet, no movement of his waist tight-buckled in a wide leather belt, and the impression was mildly disquieting. She did not remember ever having noticed in him in the past this resemblance to the great cats when immobile just before pouncing. But in the past it had never occurred to her to observe him, to notice every detail about him, apart from the scar that had so frightened her. That was why she had so quickly forgotten his features after he had disappeared. What a scatterbrain she had been in those days! Life had taught her to read people's faces, to examine their physiognomy, to catch a fleeting thought in an expression. When one's life has hung by the thread of other men's decisions, these are things that one learns.

Once upon a time she had lived two years of her life beside this man, but she had never examined him as she did today. She did it with singular avidity. She found him even more compelling than she would have wished. His gestures, the inflection of his voice which she was beginning to find more familiar again, intrigued and fascinated her; she could neither explain nor resist her fascination. But perhaps there was nothing to explain. It was a case of an overwhelming natural attraction that draws a woman towards her predestined mate.

Her heart would beat faster when he came near, his attentions gratified her, she grew anxious when he went away. But above all she had still not grown used to not losing him any more, not having to wait for him.

'How I love you, oh man that I fear!'

She stood and watched him, motionless. After his discussion with Chief Mopuntook he raised his telescope to his eye and examined the surrounding countryside. Then he folded it again, handed it back to Malaprade and again turned towards Angélique.

With his inimitable courtesy, that contrasted so sharply with his *condottière*-like appearance, he took her two hands in his, turned them over, lifted them to his lips, and gently kissed the hollow of her palms, a furtive gesture accompanied by a glance full of complicity from his warm eyes, which had suddenly filled with a great tenderness as they rested on her.

'These lovely hands seem to me less sore than they were yesterday. Am I to understand that your steed is proving more docile?'

'Yes indeed. She is growing tamer. My wrists are no longer stiff from holding her.'

'I entrusted her to you because I knew how strong you were. You were the only person who could have managed her. I myself have tamed the stallion, who is of the same breed as her. We have a couple of other English horses, and the rest come from Mexico.'

'Is this country suitable for horses?' she asked, allowing her anxiety to show through.

'It will become suitable! Wherever man lives, there must horses come. That is one of the cornerstones of a well-established civilization. Did not the Huns bring their horses with them? Did not Alexander the Great conquer India on horseback? And what about the Arabs in Africa? And the Iroquois in South America?'

Mopuntook had gone off. He came back with some more water and offered some to Honorine, still in the same questionable calabash. The child was quite unconcerned and laughed and joked with the Indian as if they could understand each other. As she paddled in the lake she splashed him and the proud Metallak, far from being offended, crouched down at the water's edge to be on a level with the child, and went on chatting animatedly to her.

Joffrey de Peyrac had taken one of his pistols and was loading it. His patrician hands had a precision and swiftness of movement that stemmed from years of practice.

'Are your guns loaded too?'

'Yes. I checked them this morning and replaced the powder in the primer which had been spoilt by damp.'

'Good. In these parts it's just as well to have one's guns always at the ready.'

'But the countryside seems completely deserted, and wild animals would run away rather than attack us.'

'It isn't only wild animals I am thinking of. And deserted country can be misleading.'

He changed the subject.

'Not one of the ten horses we have brought with us from the coast has died. That is one victory already and we can count ourselves lucky to have managed the journey so successfully. It was something no one had ever dared to undertake, travelling across country instead of following the rivers.'

'I know. Nicolas Perrot told me so. But I had already realized that the horses were not here to carry us, but rather that we were here to get them successfully to their destination. And likewise the Indians are not escorting us, we are escorting them.'

'That's right. The Metallaks are frightened of meeting Iroquois, whose war parties are permanently on the prowl in their lands during the summer months. They have put themselves under the protection of our muskets, and reluctantly agreed in exchange to carry some of our baggage. And incidentally it's their womenfolk who do the carrying. America is not the Africa you knew, my love, swarming with slaves. White men are here on their own, their own masters, but also their own servants.'

'But there are black slaves in the English colonies in the south.'

'Yes, but not in the north. And that, incidentally, is why I chose the north. . . . And also because of the gold and silver mines,' he added as if suddenly remembering the true reason for his choice. Slavery has its advantages . . . especially for the masters.

'I am sorry, my love, not to be able to offer you all the comfort I would have liked, for lack of domestic help. But here we have to do without either servants or slaves. For the Red Indians are anything you like but not slaves. If a Red Indian is forced to work for a white man he will die.'

'I am not concerned with comfort.'

She plucked up the courage to move closer to him, touched his sleeve and rested her cheek for a moment against his shoulder. She was frightened to show him much tenderness in front of his men.

'I am longing to have you to myself for a while. I always get the feeling that when I sleep far from you I have lost you again. When shall we reach Katarunk?'

'Perhaps soon . . . perhaps never!'

She questioned him sharply:

'Are you expecting something to happen?'

'Nothing, darling! Just my old cautious habit! I shall not believe we have reached Katarunk until the gates of the palisade have closed behind us, and my flag is flying at the top of the mast to inform everyone that I am at home. My love, the more I look at you, the more wonderfully beautiful I find you. You cannot imagine how disturbing you are, when your eyes shine like that out of your reddened face, when your eyelids are ringed a little with weariness, when you are hot, and when you do your best not to appear tired. . . . I adore you.'

'How right you are! I am worn out and I am hot!' Angélique replied. 'And, believe me, the object of the exercise was not to seduce you; I would give my life to be able to take a dip in that cool water.'

'That shouldn't be difficult.'

He beckoned to Nicolas Perrot, who had come out of the water and dressed again.

'My good friend, may I ask you to watch over the reputation of the

27

ladies? I have discovered a small creek near by in the shelter of the willow-trees where they could enjoy the pleasure of a bathe. All I ask of you is that you stand sentry at the mouth of the path that leads down to the creek and head off anyone indiscreet or unsuspecting who wanders that way. Place another sentry at the end of the promontory to keep the swimmers away too. We shall stay here for an hour or more.'

CHAPTER 3

ANGÉLIQUE was absolutely delighted with the little cove, which was indeed as quiet and sheltered as could be wished. Her two companions hesitated. Bathing with nothing on, out in the open, no, really they never would dare! Angélique did her best to assure them that they could not be seen and that sentries had been sworn to guard them, but they could not bring themselves to bathe. But they decided to make the most of the privacy and removed their stockings and their headdresses to cool themselves a little. Angélique left them and moved farther along the shore, where she threw off her clothes behind a clump of trees and looked out jubilantly across the smooth surface of the lake all golden in the sunshine.

As soon as she was undressed she stepped cautiously down the sloping shore. The water was indeed very cold and it took her breath away. But after a while she began to feel the full benefit of the icy water on her burning skin. She walked on until the water came right up to her neck, letting herself slide backwards into it with a sigh of satisfaction. The water covered the sore skin on the nape of her neck. She shut her eyes. The sensation of cold reached to the very roots of her hair, and she felt herself come to life again.

She kept herself afloat by moving her hands slowly. She could swim a little; for, during the summer months in Paris, she used to swim in the Seine, at the quayside. She had also bathed at Marly with the Court.

But the Seine was far away.

Angélique opened her eyes. A whole new world of light and shade, fresh and beautiful, appeared to her now, a world that was all hers. She rolled over a little and began to swim gently, her hair trailing out behind her in the water like pale seaweed.

She swam away from the bank, round a promontory, and on the

other side discovered a bigger creek which no doubt formed one of the ends of the lake.

At the far end of this cove, beside a little beach, a huge red maple spread its great roots along the surface of the sand, amidst a bed of mauve asters. Above the maple-tree stood a cliff crowned with round grey rocks set above sumac bushes glowing red like hot embers. Then still more maples, but yellow this time, forming a veritable fortress of pure gold, glittering in the sunshine.

On her right, where the cove widened out, lay some little low islands covered with thick-leaved alders, glowing wild cherries and black firs, giving a silken sheen to the opaline surface of the waters in which they were reflected. The low bank on the opposite side was topped with a colourful army of conifers and deciduous trees.

The scarlet cherry rubbed shoulders with the blue cedar, the purple beech stood out splendid against the emerald green of the great tufted pines, and the bushes ran like flames along the banks.

Near the shore, rounded rocks broke the surface of the water, which was now pale, now blue.

Angélique swam over to one of these rocks, hauled herself, with the water streaming from her, up on to the granite block, and examined the deserted landscape around her. Then slowly, as if in a drowse, or waking out of an enchanted sleep, she stood up, offering her white body, made golden by the light, to the warmth of the sunshine. She took her hair in both hands, wrung it out, and lifted it above her as if in homage, then, throwing her head back, her gaze lost in the seraphic blue of the sky, she raised her voice and chanted rather than spoke the words of rapture that rose unbidden to her lips.

'Thank you, O Creator, for this moment. . . . Thank you for the scarlet of the maple and the gold of the poplars, for the scent of the stag in the undergrowth, and the perfume of the raspberry. . . . Thank you for silence and ice-cold water. . . . Thank you for keeping me alive and well. . . . Thank you, O Creator, thank you for the fact that I am in love. Thank you for my body. . . . Thank you for your gifts of beauty, youth and life, O Creator.'

She dropped her hands again and held them open at her sides while her eyes drank in the beauty of the day.

'Glory be to thee, New World! New World!'

Then she slid swiftly down into the water again, supple as a siren. . . .

Torn suddenly from her rapture, she felt her heart beat wildly.

She looked up towards the golden foliage above the grey rock in an attempt to solve the mystery.

29

'WHAT IS UP THERE? I heard a sound. I saw something black move.... Who is it there? WHO SAW ME?'

She stared intently at the dazzling fringe of trees against the deep blue of the sky. There was no sign of movement save the slow convulsive shudder of the trees in the light wind. But this apparent calm could not rid her of the sense of anxiety that had so abruptly assailed her.

'There were eyes up there just now; yes, eyes that pierced to my very soul.' And she shuddered violently. She suddenly felt desperately faint and was frightened that she was going to sink inertly under the clear water. But somehow she managed to swim to the bank, then, clinging to the bushes, made her way back to the cove where she had left her clothes. She dragged herself up on to the sand and lay there for a while to get her breath back. She found it hard to understand what had happened to her, but she was trembling all over.

Was it some unusual noise she had heard? Had she seen or thought she had seen something moving through the branches, as she stood naked on the rock, while the smooth surface of the lake sent back the reflection of her white body?

Whatever it was those could not have been human eyes. It had been something supernatural.

The members of the caravan were gathering over on the right side of the lake, where she could hear them laughing and shouting. The rest of the countryside was deserted.

Then she suddenly remembered some of the stories that Perrot and Maupertuis had told round the camp fire when they halted for the night, stories about strange happenings in the great forests of the New World, from which dark furies had not yet been exorcized, where missionaries, travellers and traders had often sensed the presence of evil spirits and felt the breath of dread and black magic upon their faces. The wild monster lurking, the cruel soul of pagan peoples, that roamed at large and took on unaccustomed forms the better to lure men into its snares.

She told herself that it was probably the effect of the ice-cold water on her overheated skin that had made her feel so faint. But she also knew that something inexplicable had happened and that it had struck a chill to her heart. At the very moment when she had felt her whole being overflowing with love for this new land which was to be hers, a contrary force had intervened, casting her back once more into the darkness. 'Get you gone!' was its cry. 'You have no right to live here. You cannot be a citizen of this land.' This was the mysterious message that had struck her like a hurricane blast, only to disappear as swiftly as it had come.

She lay motionless on the bank, then suddenly sat up and stared fixedly again at a point in the forest beyond. Nothing stirred. Everything was still.

She got up and dressed quickly. She felt better now but her anxiety and distress remained.

This land had rejected her, this land was her enemy. She told herself that she possessed none of the qualities needed to face it, nor to face the life awaiting her beside an unknown husband.

CHAPTER 4

SHE RETURNED to the beach where the young Breton, Yann, was looking after her mare. Those with horses were already in the saddle and the caravan was beginning to get under way. Honorine was half dressed and still paddling. She held something in her hand, examining it with undivided concentration. It was the skin of a white ermine, that had been so beautifully cured that it looked like a supple, little live animal.

'Mopuntook gave it me.'

And she added as she came out of the water:

'We did a swop. He gave me this little animal and I gave him my diamond.'

'The diamond your father gave you at Gouldsboro?'

'Yes! That was what Mopuntook wanted. He is going to wear it in his hair when he dances. He'll look very handsome, you'll see!'

Angélique was already in such a state of nerves that this announcement of her daughter's made her feel the urge of hysteria.

'I really don't know what to think,' she said to herself, finding it very hard to keep calm. 'Joffrey did say that the diamond was less valuable than a head of corn, but all the same! And he gave it to her that evening when he said: "I am your father." She can be infuriating at times!'

She hauled her daughter unceremoniously up into the saddle, settled herself there too and, gathering up the reins, steered Wallis away from the water and its green banks, and back on to the arid path under the flaming archway of the trees.

She rode on for a long time, quite unaware of how much ground she had covered. The end of the lake narrowed into a valley, and as they entered it through the open gates of the raspberry-tinted gorge, the deep blue dome of a distant mountain came into sight. The travellers began to pass through the valley, at first following the bed of the river, its crystal-clear water strewn with rocks; then bit by bit they were obliged to make their way up the steep side, as the river became a torrent and outcrops of rock appeared all round them.

They climbed up a path that still held a certain amount of clay, and on which the roots of the trees formed steps. A mule would have managed it comfortably but the aristocratic Wallis showed some apprehension.

As they rounded a bend, they came upon three snowy waterfalls whose roar filled their ears. The water spilled over three steep ledges in the black rock, crashing down into the bed of the deep-set river. Trees clustered along the precipice, almost covering it. It was like a well from which rose a ceaseless rumble and clouds of smoky, iridescent spray that wet the elm and ash leaves and made them glitter like a thousand tiny metal spears. The sky was invisible, the shadows sepulchral, and yet light seemed to penetrate everywhere, pitilessly, stinging their eyes, etching the lines of the undergrowth as if it were copper, shining in ever-changing facets through the thicket, and further complicating with its deceptive patterns of light and shade the inexplicable tangle of trees through which the path wound its way. Angélique could no longer pick out the Indians ahead of her. The noise of the waterfall cut her off from the few echoes which, until then, had kept her aware of the presence of the others, even when the forest had grown too dense for them to see one another: the crackle of dead leaves, the dull thudding of the horses' hooves, someone calling or a murmur of conversation borne to her on the wind. The thunderous roar of the waters seemed to shut her up in an uneasy, leaf-enclosed world in which she felt utterly alone. It was as though she were moving through a nightmare on the border of realms of dread, impenetrable forests watched over by dragons, fallen gods or monsters, in which she could not even hear the sound of her own horse's hooves.

The noise grew deafening. Angélique saw the leaves dripping wet through an emerald light, and felt the damp exhalation of the chasm on her lips.

A huge stone, a great round mass, broke away from the slope in front of her without a sound – which made its slithering fall all the more unnerving – and came to rest full in her path. As it lay there, this inert, hard block seemed to come to life under the spell of the greenish light. It swelled, it puffed itself up, like a big grey bubble, split open like a hideous fruit, with the slow movement of a blossoming plant. Then, out of the mass that was both rock and living creature, a cruel reptilian head reared itself and stretched out towards her wavering sickly from side to side.

Panic-stricken, Angélique's horse reared up to its full height. She did not hear its terrified whinnying but felt its fear in the spasms that coursed through the animal's body. She gave a cry, but her cry was lost. Honorine must have screamed too, unheard. The horse beat the air with its hooves and backed away. It was going to fall, dragging down both Angélique and the child, and together all three of them would roll in a tangle of saddle-bow, reins, and harness before plunging in a huddled mass headlong into the abyss.

With a superhuman effort, Angélique threw herself on to the horse's neck, and pulled herself forward almost up to its head, to force it back on to its four feet by the sheer force of her weight.

But this was not enough to save them; Wallis still continued to back down the fated slope.

Angélique knew perfectly well that the creature that they had seen was only a giant tortoise. But how could she convey this to her frantic mare? The shocking din of tumbling water was all around them and all other sounds seemed to have ceased to exist. She could not even hear the branches snapping, but she could see them breaking and the splinters flying. She saw the racing white torrent raging below her, coming closer and closer, rising to meet them, a dancing mass of foam spewed forth by some mythical monster, but she was no longer aware that the din that deafened them came from the unleashing of these rabid waters. For an instant, a large gory patch loomed beneath her gaze, the inverted reflection of an archway of leaves in the waters. For a fraction of a second she imagined she heard the sound of their fall, a confused tumble down to the bottom of the ravine. She even thought she felt herself falling, caught up in the roaring torrent.

A twig struck her across the forehead and tore her from this deadly sensation. The rocky ground was crumbling beneath Wallis's hooves, a few inches from the precipice, but it was still within her power not to yield to death. The thought of Honorine, whose tiny hands clung to her, galvanized her into action. It seemed to her that her whole consciousness and lucidity were centred in those hands. She knew what she must do. She relaxed the grip of her clenched fists on the reins and let them hang loose, giving the horse its freedom. Thus freed, the animal shook its head, astonished at the sense of relief. Then she dug

33

her spurs into it until she drew blood, and the horse took a leap forward, slightly closing the gap between her and safety. She managed to steer the animal firmly back on to the path, where it stood, its legs quivering. They had been saved from their imminent fall, but the giant tortoise was still there, blocking the path.

'It's a tortoise! It's only a tortoise!' Angélique shouted, as if hoping her steed could understand her.

She could not hear the sound of her own voice and became aware of the pain in her wrists and legs, whose muscles had gone into spasm with the effort she had had to make to dominate Wallis.

Would no one come and help her to hold the animal, or at least get rid of the horrific creature that blocked their way? The Indians stood motionless around her. She might have taken them for statues, had it not been for the glitter of their almond eyes, which seemed to form a sombrely glinting mass about her. They watched her fighting, struggling within an ace of death, watched her with a wooden impassiveness which, even in such mysterious people, seemed decidedly odd. Then suddenly she thought she detected a hint of fear and wonder in their attitude. But they themselves did not seem altogether real, separated from her as they were by this solid wall of sound which made deaf and dumb ghosts of them. Nevertheless, their pungent smell of warm fat and carrion reached her nostrils, almost as if it were the smell of the tortoise, of the forest, or of the abyss.

Honorine was still there!

Angélique managed to turn round towards her daughter, and shouted to her to get off the horse. And in the end the child understood her.

With a sense of relief her mother saw her tumble down on to the dead leaves, then pick herself up and run towards the nearest Indian.

Now it was her turn to leap off the horse, but it was no easy task; for Wallis was doing her best to get away and bolt off through the bushes. She reared again and only just missed striking Angélique with her iron-clad hoof. Angélique sprang to the horse's head; holding it firmly with one hand and slapping it hard across the nostrils with the other, she gradually managed to force the animal back under the overhanging trees. Above all she wanted to get it away from the object of its terror.

The bit crunched between the mare's teeth. Angélique's neckerchief, her hands, and her sleeves, were drenched in froth from the horse's mouth, but she took not the slightest notice and went on striking the animal harder and harder.

At last Wallis appeared to calm down. Trembling, covered with froth, the mare allowed herself to be firmly tied to a tree; she ceased her agitation and rebellion, and her delicate head suddenly drooped towards the ground in a movement of surrender. Angélique almost felt like doing the same. There she stood, unspeakably dishevelled, her clothes covered with stains. But above all she must escape from this infernal noise, she must somehow get away.

She went back to the path and approached the tortoise. The Indians did not move a finger. They seemed rooted to the spot for all eternity. The tortoise's shell was as big as a small table, and its feet, covered with reptilian scales, were as large as a grown man's hand.

Angélique's anger was even stronger than the repugnance she felt towards this antediluvian monster, which, as she approached it, began to draw back its hideous head into its shell. Wedging herself against the shell, she pushed it with one heave out of the way. The huge thing began to slither down the slope, tipped over then rolled in leaps and bounds down to the bottom. And it, and not they, finally plunged into the river with a great splash.

Angélique sat down and, somewhat dazed, wiped her hands on some dead leaves, then went back to fetch her horse. She led the horse by the bridle up to the top of the slope, until they had at last emerged from the hollow in which they had almost died. She came out on to a plain covered with red bilberry bushes and small blue fir-trees. As if by magic, the roaring of the waters ceased, swallowed up in the depths of the gorge. They could hear the chirping of cicadas again and the song of birds and the wind. Now the travellers found themselves in a tall deserted valley at the foot of the mountains, the domain of a thousand lakes. A little river full of grey and pink stones meandered by on their right amidst its escorting throng of fiery red bushes. The Indians appeared again, talkative once more, and began to argue together with bird-like squawking noises.

Angélique could hear Honorine sobbing her heart out. She remounted her horse. She would have given anything to have been able to lie down among the bilberries and fall deep asleep, even if only for a short time. But Wallis would have been quite capable of taking advantage of her and making a final dash for freedom.

'Come on,' she said to Honorine. She lifted her up in front of her in the saddle, blew her nose for her, wiped her swollen face, kissed her and hugged her close. She felt stunned. Then she suddenly caught sight of Count Peyrac on horseback only a few paces away, with her son and most of the menfolk who had turned back.

'What's going on?'

'It's nothing,' Angélique replied, as pale as death. The twig that had struck her across the forehead had left a red line. With her filthy clothes, her snivelling daughter in her arms, her steed with blood coming from the corners of its mouth, she was acutely aware of how distressing a sight she must be to a man unaccustomed to being burdened with his family on his expeditions.

'I was told we had run into some Iroquois!' Joffrey de Peyrac went on.

Angélique shook her head. Fortunately the wind was dispelling the nauseating odour of the savages who had moved in close and were busy explaining in detail what had happened. Florimond and Cantor joined them, making full use of their knowledge of the Indian dialect.

'Mopuntook is absolutely convinced that there are Iroquois in the offing.'

There was a clicking of muskets being cocked at the mere mention of the name, and the Spanish soldiers took up position around the group of travellers.

Angélique was incapable of getting a word out, then at last she managed to speak.

'It was only a tortoise . . . a tortoise blocking the trail.'

And she briefly related what had happened. Count Peyrac frowned and gave the mare so angry a look that Angélique felt guilty herself.

Honorine's sobs redoubled.

'Poor tortoise!' she wailed. 'It was so stupid and so clumsy. And you pushed it over the cliff. You're horrid.'

Angélique nearly burst into tears herself. For on top of everything else she had just noticed that Honorine's feet were bare. She must have left her shoes and stockings beside the little lake where she had paddled. This was a disaster. Wherever would they find more shoes and stockings for the child in this wilderness? It was the last straw. Had she not needed both her hands to hold her daughter and her horse, she would have looked for her handkerchief in which to bury her misery. As it was, she had to turn her head away to hide her over-brilliant eyes.

The Indians now seemed to be seized by a kind of hysteria and were noisily acting out their explanation to the whites, who plied them with questions in a babble of different languages, trying to understand what had happened. The Spaniards were demanding a chance to get at the enemy.

The Count drew himself up slightly in his saddle and called for silence.

36

The tone of his voice produced an immediate effect. The Indians obeyed him. When there was a certain expression on Joffrey de Peyrac's face, there was no choice but to obey. 'He would be capable of striking a man down on the spot,' thought Angélique with a shudder.

Joffrey de Peyrac laid a soothing hand on Honorine's head.

'Tortoises can swim,' he said gently. 'This one that frightened you has already climbed out of the water and is wandering along the edge of the river eating flies.' The child was consoled as if by magic.

Then the Count dismounted and approached the Sagamore to hear what he had to say. He was as tall as the Indian, and listened attentively to his explanations. The advent of Nicholas Perrot finally cleared up the misunderstanding.

Joffrey de Peyrac smiled, climbed back into the saddle and rode over beside Angélique.

'This is another example of the way their superstitious minds interpret things,' he said. 'For them the tortoise symbolizes the Iroquois. Meeting a tortoise was an evil omen to them, an almost infallible sign that their most redoubtable enemies are prowling in the neighbourhood. Hence their dismay and fright when they saw the harmless creature, which is common enough in these parts.'

And Nicolas Perrot added:

'They also say that the emblem of the Iroquois rose up in front of the white woman in an attempt to kill her, but that she fought against it and refused to let it overcome her. The Metallaks consider, Madame, that from now on none of the Five Nations of the Iroquois will be able to prevail against you.'

'I accept their omen,' she replied, forcing herself to smile too.

'Come and ride beside me, the path we are on now is wide enough. We are coming out on to an Indian "trail" as the English call it, that runs along the crest of the Appalachians for hundreds of leagues. Don't leave my side, my love.'

Her husband's calm voice made her feel better. And she was happier at the idea of riding beside him. And yet she still felt intimidated by him, and wondered whether he were not angry at heart about an incident that had almost ended disastrously, although with his customary self-control he revealed nothing.

At the end of a huge pale-green lake that turned and twisted like a river, and whose shimmering surface ran between promontories bristling with straggling pine-trees like so many regiments of lancers, another deep, narrow valley opened up at their feet. The mountain opposite them was a mass of pink, red and orange-tinted crests, stippled here and there in blue and mauve by clusters of trees that had already lost their leaves, with an occasional patch of startling green. Something on the flowery mountainside, this embroidered and brocaded dome, caught Joffrey de Peyrac's eye, and he called a halt at the edge of the wood. They had reached a small open patch of bare rock from which they could scrutinize the surrounding country before plunging back under cover of the endless trees.

He called for his telescope.

A thin haze blowing up from the valley had softened all the colours, which looked washed out and appeared to melt into one another. The sky, now filled with clouds, was coming down to meet the mists rising from the land.

'In a few moments, we shall probably not be able to see any more,' said the Count. And swiftly he handed his telescope to Angélique.

'You have a look and tell me what you think you see.'

At first she was surprised by the brilliant image that appeared in the circle of the lens. The trees looked so close, larger than life, and as if drawn one above the other with a bold brush, aiming at perfection of detail.

The tree-trunks, some black some white, seemed to bear aloft the brilliant masses of their foliage in accord with some rigidly fixed artistic convention. In the shadowy gaps for which provision seemed to have been deliberately contrived, she was astonished to see human figures moving. There was no mistaking the shimmering of the feathers that decked them in spite of the fact that from a distance they would escape notice, melting into the background of the autumnal hues of the forest.

'What do you see?'

'I can see savages; two or three? No, more! In fact there seem to be a lot of them.'

'Do you notice their hair?'

'Their heads are shaved and they have left a tuft of hair in the middle into which they have stuck their feathers.'

She lowered the telescope.

'Joffrey, the Cayugas wore their hair like that. . . .'

'Yes indeed!'

And slowly he closed the telescope.

'Does this really mean that your encounter with the tortoise had a hidden significance after all? I don't want to appear credulous, but it certainly looks as if we have run into a band of Iroquois. . . .'

Two or three of the men began to mutter among themselves, and slowly the members of the little caravan drew together, the escorting Indians mingling with the whites and staring with the same weary resentment in the direction of the low multicoloured mountain where lurked unseen dangers.

'What rotten luck!' said the steward, Malaprade. 'We were almost within sight of Katarunk, and would soon have been greeting good old O'Connell, and enjoying all the blessings of civilization. Monsieur de Peyrac, I was going to cook you some *quenelles de volaille aux choux* as soon as we arrived, but it looks as if we're going to end up in quenelles ourselves now.'

'Nonsense!' said Florimond, 'don't be so gloomy, my good friend. We will live to eat your hash, Malaprade. The Iroquois rather take advantage of their reputation in the north: people run away before they even set eyes on them. But I have seen some of them in New England, where they are known as Mohawks, and they don't seem any worse than the Mohicans. In the New York region they even lent a hand to the English against King Philip, a Narraganset Indian who from time to time massacres the white inhabitants of the frontier-lands.

'It all depends whether the Indians over there on the other side of the ravine take us for French or English. Either way, they won't have much time for the Metallaks accompanying us. Any member of the Algonquian race is, to their way of thinking, only fit either to become a slave or to be roasted alive. And the Metallaks know it. Look at them!'

They were indeed preparing for battle under the orders of their Sagamore.

Swiftly they laid the baggage on the ground. The Indian women and children vanished, as if swallowed up in the depths of the scarlet-leaved forest. The men hastily made themselves up with red, black and white powder, but mainly red. The bowmen checked the tension of their bow-strings, then the three feathers on each arrow, to check that they were accurately set.

Each man was equipped with an enormous tomahawk hooked over his left arm, and with his right felt for his scalping knife, which he then held between his teeth in order to put the finishing touches to his bow.

Several scouts slipped away like serpents into the yellow and red undergrowth, where, even when still close at hand, they became invisible although moving about.

The Chief and the main contingent of the braves formed up in close ranks in front of the whites.

All the Indians were aglow with a savage joy, as if the prospect of battle was what they most ardently desired.

The Europeans, with the possible exception of the young men, like Florimond, could scarcely be said to share their enthusiasm for the forthcoming battle. Their faces, dark tanned by long days on the march, wore expressions of weariness and anxiety. If it was indeed true that only a few more hours' march lay between them and the outpost where they would find the security of a palisade and the welcome if simple comfort of a few basic necessities, it was a bitter disappointment to be held up by an ambush, and to run the risk of being killed or wounded. Angélique glanced at her husband, awaiting his verdict.

'Let us wait,' he said. 'When the scouts come back, we shall know what is what. If these Iroquois look like attacking us, we shall dig in and defend ourselves; if they decide to ignore us, we shall treat them in the same way! I have warned Mopuntook that if he shows any sign of beginning the battle, without evidence of hostility from the other side, I shall not come to his assistance.'

They stood waiting, arms at the ready,

When the Indians returned they seemed disappointed, for, not only had the Iroquois not shown the slightest desire to attack the caravan, but it seemed highly likely that they had not even seen it, for they had literally melted away without leaving a single trace.

The Metallaks turned their stolid, grotesquely painted faces towards Angélique and shook their heads. The white woman had put the Iroquois to flight.

CHAPTER 5

'THERE'S THE Wolf, the Roebuck, the Bear, the Fox and the Spider, but above them all is the Tortoise.'

Thus spoke Nicolas Perrot that evening at their encampment. The cold was beginning to edge over the top of the ravine and they all clustered round the camp fires.

A saffron-coloured haze had turned everything about them to gold; in the distance the mountain seemed to sink to rest, to settle down like a beast brought to heel, and at its feet they caught the glimmer of a long liquid path, the gentle, languorous waters of a broad river. . . .

Joffrey de Peyrac had pointed it out in the distance as they reached the encampment:

'That's the Kennebec.'

Like the Hebrews contemplating the promised land, so did de Peyrac's men rejoice, each in his own way. Some of them, the Jonas family for example, said a devout prayer of thanks to the Lord for granting them a glimpse of the end of their wearisome trek. Some exchanged great friendly thumps on the back, or threw their caps up into the air. . . . They were all the more delighted at the prospect of soon being in the shelter of a good strong palisade because of the glimpse they had caught of those frightening Indian shapes among the trees, and still more because the strange, though fortuitous, incident of the tortoise had left the whole caravan with a vague feeling of apprehension.

Mosquitoes buzzed all round them. Angélique sat with Honorine clasped sleepily against her, wrapped round with her heavy woollen cloak. From time to time her eyes would turn towards the shining line of the Kennebec winding its way gently across the plain. That was where Katarunk lay, their haven of safety!

'The Wolf for the Mohawks, the Roebuck for the Onondagas, the Fox for the Oneidas, the Bear for the Cayugas and the Spider for the Senecas, but the Tortoise stands for all of them, the Five Nations of the Iroquois; it is their password and their Spirit Commander-in-Chief.'

Whenever Nicolas Perrot was deep in thought, the tanned leathery surface of his forehead wrinkled up and made his fur cap wriggle.

'The tribes in this region, the Abenakis, Etchemins or Souriquois are accustomed to a nomadic existence. They have no sense of order or custom, no bread or salt. But the Iroquois . . . they are a superior people, a great farming nation.'

'Anyone would think you were fond of them,' Angélique remarked.

The trapper gave a start.

'God forbid! They are demons, the scum of the earth. The Iroquois are the Canadian's worst enemy. But it is true,' he went on after a moment's reflection, 'that I have lived among them, and I cannot forget it. Anyone who has shared the life of the Iroquois will understand what I mean. For I have seen the Sacred Valley where reign the Three Gods worshipped by the Five Nations.'

'Three Gods?'

'Yes! The Maize, the Pumpkin and the Bean,' Nicolas Perrot replied without a smile.

Honorine had fallen asleep. Taking care not to wake her, Angélique rose and walked over to the drill tent that was pitched every evening

41

for the women and children. After wrapping up her daughter snugly in the furs, she went back outside again to help Madame Jonas who was busy cooking with Octave Malaprade.

The Appalachians were glowing purple in the light of the setting sun. They were mountains of gentle yet lofty lines.

The wind swept across the headland where they had pitched their camp in the hope that the continuous breeze would protect them from mosquitoes and sand-flies; another reason for selecting this promontory had been so that they could keep a better watch on the surrounding country.

Florimond and Cantor were busy cooking in the embers some fish wrapped in leaves which they had caught with their hands at one of the bends of the river.

Several haunches of moose were roasting on a spit, and the tongue, the choicest portion, simmered gently in a stew-pot with vegetables and herbs. There was boiled maize in another pot which Madame Jonas had taken off the fire and was beginning to serve out.

She was still slightly shocked to see the dirty Indians mixing shamelessly with the whites, and being the first to hold out their dirty bowls to her.

They were constantly interfering with everything, handling everything, meddling with everything with a quiet insolence; for was this not their home and were not these Palefaces after all under their protection!

The good woman pursed her lips and cast what she hoped were eloquent glances in the direction of Count Peyrac. She could not begin to understand how so fastidious a gentleman could tolerate the close proximity of these smelly people, a matter which also perplexed Angélique herself on occasion.

Now a cold blue light spread over the landscape, and the sentries walked back and forth along the edge of the forest. For a long time the only thing visible in the valley was the sparkling Kennebec.

It had been a day full of excitement, and one further stage of their journey had been completed. What did the following day hold in store for them?

Angélique looked around for her husband and caught sight of him standing a little way off, looking into the distance. He was alone.

She could tell from the way he stood that he was deep in thought.

Angélique had already noticed that when he withdrew from them all in this way no one ever dared interrupt his meditation.

A strange respect surrounded the leader in whom these very different men, most of them not at all amenable to discipline, had placed their trust.

The majority of them had observed with some jealousy and anxiety Angélique's advent in the life of the man they worshipped.

'Women! Everyone knows what they do to a man worthy of the name,' said Clovis l'Auvergnat, screwing up his little narrow eyes. 'They take the guts out of him!'

'Not him though,' Yann le Couennec, the Breton, protested.

Then, with an admiring glance towards the young woman, he went on:

'Nor her either!'

'Oh, you're an innocent, you are!' replied the man from Auvergne with a shrug. His drooping black moustaches gave a sardonic twist to his mouth.

Angélique had no difficulty in guessing what they were talking about. She herself had once been the leader of an armed band. And these men were not 'her' men.

A life of shared dangers and triumphs had brought them together round the Count de Peyrac. Personal, highly prized, indissoluble bonds, of which their manly reticence would never allow them to speak openly, bound each and every one of them to the man whom experience had taught them to consider their lord and their sole hope. Together they had fought Saracen and Christian, explored the Caribbean, and rode out storms. They had shared the booty with him and, with his encouragement, had caroused and revelled, living like lords whenever they put into port. Wine had flowed freely, there had been women for the asking, and their leader had distributed gold-pieces to them with open-handed generosity.

Angélique sometimes tried to imagine what kind of a life her husband had led during their years of separation.

More often than not she imagined him surrounded by his scientific equipment.

She saw him leaning over a globe or a map as his cabin swayed with the movement of the ship; or else he stood at the top of some Moorish terrace beneath the Cretan sky, examining the stars through a priceless telescope. But in that past, the moment would always come, of an evening, when a servant would enter and bring in a veiled woman, a Spanish beauty when they were in the Caribbean, or a half-caste Indian or Negress.

He would leave his work and welcome the woman with his inimitable charm, and would dance attendance on her, laughing and joking with

43

her to coax from her all the sensual pleasure she had come to give him.

He was an individualist, a lone figure.

He was a complete man, in full possession of his powers and his faculties, entirely self-sufficient. And now she, Angélique, was claiming her place at this man's side. But when he stood motionless thus, absorbed and far away, she dared not approach him.

The night grew dark. As he sat by the fire Cantor began to play a Tuscan cantilena on his guitar. He had a delightful voice; for although it was already rich and firm, it still retained the soft inflection of youth. When he sang he seemed happy. But as far as her boys' inner thoughts were concerned, Angélique had simply not had enough time to talk to them and win their confidence. . . . That would have to wait until they reached Katarunk.

She felt a sudden pang of anxiety about her mare again, and before rejoining the others she walked down to the bank of the river where the horses had been put out to pasture.

Wallis had escaped! Her broken halter hung from the tree to which she had been tethered.

Angélique had a feeling that the horse could not be far away, and after climbing up the slope again to collect a bridle and bit, she walked along the bank of the river calling softly.

A misty moon was rising over the top of the black firs. A tawny owl screeched. Dormice coughed in the thickets, and the river, running almost dry, babbled over the stones.

She heard a snapping of branches and, turning in the direction of the sound, she caught sight of the mare in a patch of moonlight, cropping the grass in a small clearing; but when she reached it, the flighty animal had moved farther on.

By the time Angélique finally caught up with the creature at the top of a hillside, she realized that she had lost sight of the camp fires. But this was of no consequence; for she would make her way down to the river-bed again and follow the river downstream. After fastening the bridle firmly over the horse's nose she kept a tight hold on it and listened for the sound of running water from below.

As she stood there all alone in the depths of the dark night, she no longer felt afraid. The scent of this unknown virgin forest enveloped her in its pungent perfume, and once again she tasted the fleeting yet intense sensation of being alive, full of youth and strength, on the threshold of a new life which it was for her to build up from its very foundations. But she would find an ally in the great unmapped open

44

spaces which they had reached after so many dangers. And she felt her heart swell with the same feeling of love towards this untamed land that she had felt earlier when bathing among the magical shimmering waters of the lake. It was at this moment that the strange noises began.

She could hear the distant call of a moose, the whispering of the wind, the dull roar of waterfalls in the depths of the forest, and, mingling with all these sounds, she heard the sound of hymn-singing.

CHAPTER 6

Ave Maris Stella
Dei Mater Alma . . .

THE WORDS of the hymn rang through the primeval night. Angélique stared up at the treetops as if expecting the sky between their branches to open and reveal a choir of angels.

A shudder ran down her spine, and she turned round warily. Behind her a pinkish glow like an anxious dawn showed over the edge of the cliff, casting dancing shadows among the pines.

Holding Wallis by the bridle, Angélique crept towards the edge of the ravine from which the sound of men's voices rose in a hymn.

Angélique found it hard not to imagine that she was back again in the forest of Nieul where the persecuted Huguenots had taken refuge to pray and sing psalms.[1]

She moved still closer to the edge and, leaning over, discovered a strange, incredible scene.

At the bottom of the gorge, the rocks were red from the glow of two great fires that had been lit by the river. A priest in a black soutane, his arms held aloft in benediction, stood facing a group of kneeling men.

He was standing with his back to her, but she could see the men's faces; some were dressed in suède and fur, while others wore blue uniforms with gold frogging, and Angélique noticed two noblemen among them with lace collars and cuffs.

They reached the last lines of the hymn and the singing stopped. Then the priest's voice rose up alone, clear and fervent.

'Queen of Heaven.'

'Pray for us,' the congregation murmured in response.

[1] See *Angélique in Revolt.*

45

Angélique started back.

'They are French!'

'Tower of David.'

'Pray for us.'

'Arc of the Covenant.'

'Pray for us.'

'Refuge of sinners! Comforter of the afflicted.'

'Pray for us! Pray for us!' they replied in chorus after each invocation. There they were, trappers, soldiers, and noblemen, kneeling together, heads piously bowed, telling their beads.

'They are French!'

Angélique's heart began to beat wildly.

She would have thought herself in the grip of a nightmare in which she was reliving all the horrors of the Poitou war, had she not noticed, behind the French, the copper-coloured figures of some half-naked Indians. Some of them were praying and singing with the white men and women, while others sat around a second fire scraping the last of their meal from the bottom of their wooden bowls with their fingers. The smell of food still hung in the air, and a medium-sized cooking pot had been laid to one side of the fire after its contents had been doled out.

The tall figure of a strapping, shaggy-haired Indian all glistening with grease bent over the glowing embers. As he stood up, he took an axe from the flames, and its red-hot blade flashed. Holding the weapon with care, the savage moved a few paces away from the circle of men. It was only then that Angélique sensed the presence of another naked Indian in the shadows, tied to the trunk of a tree.

Slowly and deliberately, as if he were doing the most natural thing in the world, the man with the axe pressed the red hot blade against the man's thigh. Not a sound passed his lips, only the sickening smell of burning flesh reached Angélique a few moments later.

She started in horror, choking back a cry, and Wallis shied, making the branches snap. Realizing that she would be seen, Angélique leapt astride the horse.

The savage, who had just replaced his axe in the fire, looked up and lifted his sinewy arm with its feathered bracelets towards the top of the cliff.

In a flash they were all on their feet, and glimpsed the figure of a woman with long hair, on horseback, outlined against the moonlit sky.

Then a terrible cry went up from their breasts:

'The She-Devil! The She-Devil of Acadia!'

46

CHAPTER 7

'DID YOU say they shouted: "the She-Devil of Acadia"?'

'That's what I thought I heard.'

'Good God! Heaven forbid that they should have taken you for her,' Nicolas Perrot exclaimed, crossing himself. And Maupertuis did likewise.

'I do not know whom they took me for, but whoever it was they gave chase like madmen. One of them, a giant of a man, almost caught up with me just as I headed Wallis into the river.'

'Did you kill him?' Peyrac asked sharply.

'No. I fired at his hat and he fell backwards into the water; they are French, I assure you, camping in the ravine on the other side of this very mountain where we are encamped.'

'If you would allow us to, Monsieur de Peyrac, we trappers, Maupertuis, his son Pierre-Joseph and I, could go and meet them,' said Nicolas Perrot.

'It would be a very odd thing indeed if we did not find some good friends and acquaintances among these people from Quebec, and we would be able to reach an understanding with them.'

'But don't forget, Perrot, that we have been condemned to death by the Government of Quebec,' Maupertuis objected, 'and even excommunicated by his Grace the Bishop.'

'Pooh! That's all nonsense. People from the Saint-Lawrence always enjoy meeting old friends.'

So the two trappers, followed by Maupertuis's son, a half-caste of twenty by an Indian woman, disappeared into the dark bush.

The whole camp had been under arms since Angélique had returned and given the alert.

The soldiers and the other men were all at their stations, muskets in hand.

When the three trappers had gone off into the woods, Angélique turned towards Peyrac.

She found it hard to suppress a trembling in her voice and when she spoke to Peyrac her tone was a little sharp.

'You did not warn me that we might run into the French where we are going.'

'One always risks running into the French when wandering about North America. I've already told you that, although there are not many of them, they are very active, and travel about every bit as much as the Indians. They were bound to take an interest in us. . . .'

'Come closer to the fire, darling; you are frozen. This unfortunate encounter has upset you. And once again it's the fault of that blasted mare of yours.'

Angélique held her hands out towards the flames. Frozen she was, frozen to the bottom of her heart.

Question upon question rushed to her lips. She wanted both to be reassured and to find out exactly how great the danger was.

'That was what you were frightened of, wasn't it? That was the reason you made us hurry so? You were frightened the French might make a raid into the land you want to settle, where you have already built your outpost.'

'Yes. Not far from Gouldsboro, my nearest neighbour, Baron Saint-Castine, from Pentagoet, who is in charge of the French outpost in Acadia, a man with whom I have always been on good terms, came to warn me that the Catholic Missionaries who are busy converting the Abenakis in Maine were concerned about my arrival near the source of the Kennebec, and had asked the Government of Quebec to send out an expeditionary force against me.'

'But what right have the French to object to your settling in these parts?'

'They consider this land part of Acadia and, as such, their territory.'

'Who in fact do all these uninhabited lands belong to?'

'To whoever shows the greatest enterprise. It's a no-man's-land. The Treaty of Breda, to which France was a signatory, gave it to the British, but they consider the forestlands too dangerous and don't care to leave the coastal strip to enforce the provisions of the treaty.'

'And supposing these Frenchmen from the north discover one day who you are, and who I am . . .'

'That isn't going to happen tomorrow . . . and by the time it does I shall be a great deal stronger than this wretched group of colonists the King of France has abandoned in the Antipodes. . . . No, have no fear, the arm of Louis XIV cannot reach us here. And in any case, even if he still dared try to get us here, we could fight him. America is a big country and we are free . . . so take heart, my love, and get warm . . .'

'What did they mean by the name they shouted out when they saw me: the She-Devil of Acadia?'

'They must have thought you were a vision. Castine and Perrot had

48

warned me that New France has been greatly disturbed by the visions of a saintly nun in Quebec: she dreamed that a female demon was snatching the souls of the Acadian Indians, whether baptized or not, from the Church. This would explain their suspicion and excitement. And it may well also be the reason for their present expedition. . . . They say that the She-Devil, riding a mythical animal, a unicorn . . .'

'Ah! I understand,' Angélique exclaimed with a nervous laugh, 'when they caught sight of me: a woman, a horse . . . something unthinkable round here . . . and it fitted in with their vision . . .'

Peyrac seemed annoyed:

'It's stupid . . . but it's pretty serious. This confusion in their minds could well cause us further bother. These people are fanatics.'

'But still, they can't attack us if we show no hostility towards them. . . .'

'Wait and see! Time will tell what they have in mind. This morning Perrot sent his Indian scout Mazok out on a reconnaissance. When he returns, he will be able to inform us about all likely movements in the area: the French, the Iroquois, or the Indian allies of the French who accompany them on their expeditions, Abenakis, Algonquins or Hurons. Come to think of it,' he said suddenly, 'the savages we saw earlier on were in all likelihood only Hurons following the French. For, although the Hurons are sworn enemies of the Iroquois, they belong to the same race and observe the same customs, among others the way of doing their hair up in a single twist on top of their heads. But we did hear that there was also an Iroquois war party on the prowl in the region, and the French may only be here on their account, and we might . . .

'You see, that's America for you. Wastelands which suddenly come to life and swarm with a vast number of different people, all sworn enemies.'

They saw some torches shining through the undergrowth, coming towards the camp. They could hear the sound of muskets being cocked and the smell of the tinder that some of the men had lighted.

But it was only the three trappers returning empty-handed.

Farther up the river they had indeed found traces of the French camp, as well as a half-roasted Iroquois prisoner tied to a tree, but not a sign of soldiers or Hurons.

In vain had they called at the tops of their voices:

'Ahoy there! You men from the Saint-Lawrence, where are you, cousins? Where are you, brothers?' Reply came there none.

And as for the Iroquois prisoner they had set free, burned as he was, he had managed to take advantage of a moment when their attention was diverted, had leapt up and vanished into the dark undergrowth.

Henceforth they would be surrounded by a varied throng of shadowy figures: French, Algonquins, Hurons, Abenakis, Iroquois, while the mysterious forest continued to murmur serenely in the sighing wind, with no other sound save those of distant waters and the belling of a rutting moose.

Joffrey de Peyrac left some of his men under arms and organized a twenty-four-hour watch, for he had no intention of being taken by surprise.

He advised Angélique to take some rest in the women and children's tent. He accompanied her to the tent and, as it was very dark, took her in his arms and tried to kiss her lips. But she felt too agitated and anxious to be able to respond.

She also felt resentful towards him at times like these for having journeyed apart from her and for not letting her spend the nights with him. But Angélique realized that the discipline of the caravan and the recent arrival of women in this world of men made this essential.

She remembered that when she had escaped from Meknes with the Christian slaves in Morocco, Colin Paturel, their leader, had banished her from his company in the same way, saying, 'This woman belongs to no one; we'll have no dalliance before we are safe and sound in Christian territory.'

There was a touch of the same severity in the way Joffrey de Peyrac insisted on mustering the women and children in the same tent, while the men were made to sleep apart, in threes, on mounds of bark.

He, the Chief, remained alone too, without special privileges, feeling that he owed it to the men under him.

He took and made his own the law of ancient primitive tribes which says that a warrior, on the eve of battle, or when faced with some particular danger, must shun women to keep his mind clear and his strength intact.

But Angélique did not share this strength. She was weak, she sometimes told herself, and needed him terribly. She never felt entirely secure when she was far from him, fearing lest she lose him again. The miracle of their reunion was still so recent.

Of course she knew that behind Joffrey de Peyrac's self-control and coldness lay a keenly sensual, passionate nature, and there was no mistaking his feelings where she was concerned. But sometimes she feared that she was nothing more to him than an object of pleasure, who charmed him no doubt, but whom he kept apart from his inner life, from his joys, his ambitions and his cares. As the days went by she realized that she was bound to a man about whom she knew little, to whom she nevertheless owed submission and devotion, and also that she would often find herself pitted again his iron will; for he had an unyielding, secretive, matter-of-fact side to his character, and had grown even more astute than he had been before. You never knew what he had up his sleeve.

She slept badly, expecting at any moment to hear shots or, at the very least, a noisy invasion by the French.

At dawn she heard a sound and slipped out of her tent.

Mazok the Indian loomed up out of the mist; on reaching the shores of America, after his voyage to France, he had resumed his loincloth and his leather moccasins. His plaited hair was full of feathers again, he carried his bow in one hand, and had a quiver full of arrows across his back.

He greeted his master and Joffrey de Peyrac who came forward to meet him.

Angélique joined the men and they told her the Indian's news.

For two days now the outpost of Katarunk had been occupied by a small detachment of French, accompanied by their allies the Algonquins and Hurons.

At first light, they broke camp. It was still cold, and a rainbow-tinted mist hung over the land, making it impossible to see more than three paces ahead.

Moisture hung in drops on all the leaves, and the whole forest was dripping.

One behind the other, leading their horses by the bridle, they left the clearing and plunged into the damp thickets. Messages were passed along the line in a whisper and the soaking wet children told to try to control their coughing. The dew was raining down on them and their stealthy march was wrapped in mystery. Little by little the mist grew less damp and, when the sun appeared, a pale yellow disc that burst into blossom above an invisible land, it was only a matter of minutes before the fog vanished, revealing a glistening, wet landscape, shining in the full radiance of its brilliant colours.

They were crossing an open space at that moment and orders were given to make haste for the shelter of an oak-grove a little below the trail, where they were instructed to regroup and halt for a while.

It gradually grew warmer beneath the branches of the great twisted oaks, with their sombre violet, almost black leaves. Acorns fell without a sound on the dry mossy ground. The horses had been grouped to-gether and were tethered to low branches, and all continued to observe the strictest silence.

The four Spanish soldiers began to climb down to the bottom of the ravine, moving rather heavily and making the undergrowth crackle as they went, whereas Mopuntook's Indians seemed to melt into the bushes and reached the bottom first, quieter than ghosts, each man standing behind a tree of which he seemed almost a part. They appeared delighted at the chance of putting a hole or two into the skin of some French or Indian enemy. Hidden behind a dry brushwood hedge, the soldiers stuck their forked musket-rests into the pebbles of the river-bed and rested their arquebuses on them. These guns were far more powerful and carried three times farther than muskets, although they were less accurate, and more like portable culverins.

Angélique was wondering what she should be doing since it seemed evident that they were preparing to give battle, when Count Peyrac came towards her.

'Madame, I need to call on your skill as the best shot I have in my company; we're going to need it.'

He told Honorine to stay like a good girl with the Jonases and the other children and two men were detailed to watch the horses.

Then he took Angélique right to the edge of the cliff, where big rocks formed an overhang. It was an excellent look-out point from which they could see quite a long way up and down the river, as it ran below them in a deep cleft. The river was broad and in torrential flow even at this time of the year. There was a ford across it, but apart from the rocks that stood out of the water, allowing people to cross easily, almost without wetting their feet, the surrounding river was deep, and full of whirlpools that betrayed a treacherous river-bed. This was another of the ledges, or 'saults' as the trappers called them, which brought the level of the river down step by step to the lake, which they could see shimmering farther down the valley through the purple leaves.

'Sakoos Ford,' whispered Nicolas Perrot.

The ford was divided in the middle of the river by a small sandy island with a spinney on it.

The Count pointed this out to Angélique, and he showed her too the dark tunnel in the hedgerow on the opposite bank through which anyone following the forest path would come out on to the shore.

'Soon some men will come out there and begin to cross the ford;

they will probably be the Frenchmen you saw yesterday evening and their Indians. . . . You will recognize them since you saw them face to face. When they reach the little island, but only when they reach it, I want you to fire to stop them crossing the second half of the ford.'

'The island is too far away for accuracy,' said Angélique with a frown.

'That is what the others said when I asked them to do this, but there is nowhere else we can stand. There is a cleft in the rock that prevents us from taking up a better position opposite the island, and we have not got time to cross the cleft; it would take several hours. So we must shoot from here and stop the head of the convoy so that no one can go to the outpost to raise the alarm. We must stop them, but you must not hit anyone, for I want no bloodshed.'

'You are asking something well-nigh impossible.'

'I know, my love, Florimond himself said he could not do it, and yet he claims to be a good shot. . . .'

The lad was there, looking dubiously at his mother and father, tempted to show off his skill, but honest enough to have doubts about his own capacities.

'Firing at the tip of the island, Father, that's impossible,' he cried. 'If you wanted it done as they started to cross the ford, that would be different. . . .'

'But at that stage some of their party would still be in the forest. I don't want anyone to escape. Some of our men are posted up-river on the bank, to catch anyone who does try to get away, but if there are too many of them, it will turn into a real battle and there will always be one or two who manage to escape. No, I want to get them all, or almost all, out of the wood, either in the process of crossing the ford or on the island, before we fire. Our Spaniards down at the bottom can then cut off their retreat completely on this side and they will be well and truly encircled.'

'But the island stretches right out in front of us. Stopping the head of the convoy at the very moment when it begins to cross the second half of the ford, at this distance, and without wounding anyone, would seem to me a very tricky business.'

'Do you think you can do it, Madame?'

Angélique had been examining the situation in minute detail, and she turned towards him.

'And what about you, Joffrey? . . . Are you not a skilled shot too?'

'At this distance, I am convinced your eyes are better than mine. . . .'

'If that's how it is ...'

She hesitated. What he was asking her to do was extremely difficult. Sunshine flooded through the gorge.

On the other hand, she was pleased at the confidence the Count was showing her by this request, and pleased to be able to do something at last. Her sons and the men who had been posted near by looked at her in perplexity, astonished at the Count's action, and she welcomed the chance of proving to them that, when it came to wars and gunfire, she had seen as much, if not more than they, for all that they were pirates.

And as Joffrey repeated:

'Will you take up the wager, Madame?'

She replied:

'I will try.... What weapon are you giving me?'

One of the men handed her a musket which he had loaded, but she refused it.

'I want a gun I have loaded myself.'

They handed her Monsieur de Peyrac's own gun, which the Breton, Yann le Couennec, carried for him and kept in order. It was a flint musket which could fire two shots without being reloaded. It had a walnut butt, inlaid with mother-of-pearl. It was both light and strongly made, and Angélique put it to her shoulder with a feeling of satisfaction. She examined the powder, the bullets, and the primer they handed her, cleaned the double barrel, rammed the charge home once, slipped the bullets in and rammed again. Eyes full of curiosity followed her every movement.

When the primer was in position, she leant back against the stony ledge.

The slight feeling of excitement she knew so well was beginning to steal over her, the scent of guerrilla warfare! Down below in the sunlight, she could see the tip of the island, and the sparkling heap of stones at the beginning of the second half of the ford.

Her heart beat faster. That was what happened before the fighting began. But when the moment came, on the contrary, she would feel strangely calm, empty, petrified. She stood up.

'Have two loaded guns ready to pass me in case the first shots are not enough to stop them.'

Then she waited.

Less than an hour later the screech of a nightjar rang through the forest. It was so familiar a cry, that and the cooing of doves, that no one took much notice of it any more. But Nicolas Perrot seemed to read a particular significance into this call, for he leaned over a little towards Angélique and whispered:

'That's Marok's signal.'

An Indian was the first to appear at the river's edge, a Huron, followed by a trapper whom Angélique had seen the day before in the ravine. Then followed an officer, several Indians and a very young Frenchman, a mere golden-headed boy, dressed in the blue frock-coat of an officer of the King beneath a miscellaneous collection of arms, an axe, a cutlass, and a powder-horn. His lace cravat was rather rumpled and carelessly tied, while his hat, which was all dented, was adorned with black and white eagle feathers which had absolutely nothing in common with the regulation plumes, even though the frogging of his revers, his cuffs and his buttonholes did give his get-up some semblance of a uniform. He wore leather leggings and moccasins.

They saw him rush gleefully into the water at the edge of the river, give his face a splash, and shake off the foam. His commanding officer, the colossus whose hat Angélique had put a bullet through the day before, called him to order:

'Take it easy, Maudreuil! You're kicking up as much din as a charging moose.'

'Well, we are only half a league from Katarunk,' the young man replied cheerfully. 'Are you frightened of another meeting with evil spirits like last night? ...'

Their voices were carried, clear and distinct, to the watchers by the echo in the valley.

'I don't know what I fear,' the lieutenant replied, 'but I don't like the look of this place. I always have thought it a real death-trap.'

He glanced up at the cliffs and his eyes seemed to be trying to penetrate the secret of the leaves moving gently in the breeze.

'Can you smell the Iroquois?' the young soldier asked with a laugh. 'You seem to have a particularly sharp nose for them.'

'No, but I do sense something else, I don't quite know what. Let's get a move on. The sooner we are on the other side, the better for us. Come on now. . . . I'll go first. L'Aubignière,' he called to the trapper, 'bring up the rear, will you?'

And he began to cross the ford, springing with great supple strides from stone to stone.

Up on the cliff-top, where they were hiding in the trees, Nicolas Perrot touched Angélique's shoulder.

'For heaven's sake don't kill them,' he whispered. 'That one, the big fellow, is Lieutenant Pont-Briand, my best friend. The other is Three-

Fingers of the Three-Rivers, and the youngest is young Baron Maudreuil, the finest lad in all Canada.'

Angélique blinked to show that she had understood. Yes, of course she would take every care of such precious enemies, but all these recommendations did not make her task any the easier.

The colossus whom Nicolas had called Lieutenant Pont-Briand had reached the island. There, he stood motionless once more, hands on hips, looking up, examining his surroundings like a suspicious dog. He appeared to be literally sniffing the air. He wore no hat, and his dark brown hair blew free round his head and shoulders. With the light behind him he seemed to be wearing a small reddish halo. He did not seem to sense anything odd, and with a shrug of his shoulders began to cross the island, followed by the Hurons who had already crossed the ford.

Angélique concentrated hard and steadied her gun against her shoulder. Then she began to follow Pont-Briand's silhouette with the tip of the gun-barrel as he moved on down the beach.

L'Aubignière, the trapper, known as Three-Fingers, was nearer to her, he was still on the shore urging on the savages who continued to pour out of the forest.

Pont-Briand had just reached the farthermost tip of the little island. He stopped for a moment and looked at his men, now engaged in crossing the river. Without realizing it, he was playing into the hands of those who watched him from the cliff-top; for soon the entire contingent of men would be assembled in the gorge, and that was exactly what Joffrey de Peyrac had wanted.

Then at last the lieutenant made for the second half of the ford.

The moment had come.

Angélique's entire concentration was fixed on that one point: the flat stone on which the man was about to place his foot.

Her finger pressed the trigger. The edge of the stone shattered, and the gorge echoed with the sudden roar of the explosion.

The French officer sprang backwards.

'Get down!' he shouted, as the Indians and the French on the island fell to the ground and crawled into the shelter of a few scant bushes.

But the lieutenant, instead of doing likewise, made a dash for the ford again. Angélique fired. He was already half way across. Once again a stone exploded at his feet. They saw him lose his balance and fall into the water. It occurred to Angélique that this was the second bath he had to thank her for in two days; he had also fallen into the river the previous evening, when he had been chasing her through the ravine. She was sure she had not hit him.

'The other gun!' she snapped.

The lieutenant's head reappeared. He was struggling in the current and moving still farther off. Angélique put the gun to her shoulder again, aimed, and fired. The bullet ricocheted on the surface of the water, passing so close to him that it must have splashed him.

'Don't kill him,' Nicolas Perrot begged in a whisper.

'The devil take you!' thought Angélique, all on edge. Could he not see that the man would not be stopped, and how was she going to prevent this madman from reaching the bank unless she killed him?

She fired again. This time, the French nobleman seemed to get the point. Caught between the dangerous currents in the river and the running fire a few inches from his head, there was no longer room for hesitation. He swam back to the island, clambered up and, like the others, dragged himself into the shelter of a stunted alder.

Angélique was able to relax a little, while still keeping an eye on the ford. But no one else appeared keen to imitate the officer's reckless example, and it seemed very unlikely that anyone would now risk his life across so well guarded a stretch of water.

She relaxed and half sat up. Sweat poured down her brow which she wiped instinctively with her powder-blackened hand; then she took another loaded gun from the hands of one of her amazed sons, re-assumed her firing position and continued her watch.

It was just as well that she did, for once again the lieutenant tried his luck, springing up like a jack-in-the-box....

A bullet ricocheted off the sand at his feet, and he promptly took shelter again. Meanwhile the surprise attack had been going forward on all fronts. When Angélique's first shot stopped the convoy, the Hurons who were half-way across the first half of the ford had tried to retreat into the cover of the forest, but shots rang out from the shore they had just left. L'Aubignière dived behind a tree and began to shoot back in the direction of the cliff.

The Hurons, encircled as they were by heavy fire on all sides, stood in the middle of the first ford, daring neither to advance nor to re-treat. Even so one of them, with the customary audacity of his race, hurled himself into the tempestuous river, but as he reached the bank further downstream, a little above the rapids, one of the Spaniards shot at him, wounding him in the leg.

Another of them managed to break away into the thicket, but the invisible enemy posted there by Peyrac was waiting for him, for there was the sound of a struggle followed by an exclamation of fury.

Then silence fell again, so complete that the strident chirping of the cicadas seemed to drown every other sound, even that of the rushing river.

The acrid smell of gunpowder filled the gorge.

Angélique gritted her teeth. She had forgotten where she was. It seemed to her that she was once again on the watch above some canyon in Vendée, in the heart of the forest of Poitou, and that the King's men were falling beneath her fire. Behind her clenched teeth there rose that ancient cry from her heart, which had so often risen to her lips: 'Kill! Kill!'

She began to tremble.

A hand was laid on her shoulder.

'There, it's all over!' said the calm voice of the Count.

She sat up a little, her face drawn, her gun smoking in her hand, looking at him as if she did not recognize him. He helped her get up, then gently wiped the black powder marks from her forehead with his handkerchief.

There was a smile in the depths of his eyes and something indefinable, half-way between pity and admiration, as he looked into her face, a woman's face of such rare beauty blackened with the sweat of war.

'Bravo, my love,' he said softly.

Why had he said bravo? What was he applauding? Her immediate success? Or was it her erstwhile struggle? Her frantic, despairing struggle with the King of France? Or was he applauding everything that lay behind the fantastic skill of those hands, resting on that weapon of death?

With great respect he took her lovely powder-blackened hand and kissed it.

Her two sons and Peyrac's men stared wide-eyed at Angélique. The trappers fired from the bottom of the gulley. Pont-Briand had guessed where they were from the movement of the leaves. A piece of the overhanging rock exploded right beside them.

'Now then, that's enough!' Perrot shouted at the top of his voice. 'Enough damage done already, my good folk! Stop this little game, will you? Pont-Briand, my cousin, calm down or I'll make you wrestle with me and I'll force your shoulders to the ground as I did on the famous feast of Saint Médard that you won't have forgotten!'

The trapper's stentorian voice echoed back and forth across the gorge hung with acrid smoke.

There was a silence, then a voice from the island:

'Who is that?'

'Nicolas Perrot, from Ville-Marie, on the island of Montreal.'

'Who is with you?'

'Friends, French friends!'

'And who else?'

Perrot turned to the Count with a questioning look, and Joffrey replied with a nod.

Then the trapper cupped his hands round his mouth and called:

'Hear me, good people of the Saint-Lawrence, hear my proclamation. Let me introduce Monsieur le Comte de Peyrac de Morens d'Irristru, Lord of Gouldsboro, of Katarunk and other places, and his company.'

Angélique thrilled to hear the Indian forest ring with that name which for so many years had been condemned to the silence of disgrace and death. Joffrey de Peyrac de Morens d'Irristru! Was it written that this old Gascon name should be born again, should dare to live again, so far from its native place? But was this not dangerous?

She turned towards her husband, but the expression on his face revealed nothing.

He was standing at the tip of the promontory, hidden by the drooping branches of the pine-tree against which he leant, still observing the site of the encounter with the same attention, as if indifferent to all the shouting.

The smoke took a long time to clear, and sounds were deadened by the powder-laden atmosphere. Visibility was poor and prudence demanded that both sides should remain on the alert. Joffrey de Peyrac kept his loaded pistol in his hand.

At last someone stood up behind the bushes on the island. It was the tall man, Pont-Briand.

'Come down here unarmed, Nicolas Perrot, if it's really you and not your ghost!'

'I'll be with you in a moment.'

The trapper handed his gun to his servant and clambered down the slope to the edge of the river.

As he made his appearance on the narrow bank, in his suède clothes and fur bonnet, he was greeted with exclamations of enthusiasm. Both the French and the Hurons ran forward to welcome him. He shouted to them to go a little farther up the river, round the next bend where they would be able to cross by a simple bridge made of tree-trunks which the Spaniards had thrown across at a point where the two banks were only separated by a narrow gap. This crossing was rarely used, since the ford alone spared people several hours' detour by enabling them to avoid a very deep chasm in the rock. As soon as they had all joined forces, there was a great deal of strenuous back-slapping and noisy congratulations. The trapper and his compatriots greeted one another with great slaps on the shoulders and thumps in the ribs.

'Oh, brother! Here you are, as large as life! We thought you were dead!'

'We thought you had gone for good!'

'Gone back to the Iroquois!'

'We thought you had got used to living with savages and would end your days there!'

'That is in fact what almost happened to me,' Nicolas Perrot replied. 'I had intended to return to the Iroquois after I left Quebec three years ago. But I met Monsieur de Peyrac and changed my mind.'

The Hurons were very pleased to see Perrot. But some of them looked a bit sour and demanded blood-money, since one of their men, Anahstaha, had been wounded.

Perrot spoke in the Huron tongue:

'My brother Anahstaha should not have tried to slip like a snake between our fingers when our musketeers ordered him to stop. Let him who knows not the language of gunpowder not meddle with making war. . . . Come gentlemen, if you please,' he concluded, turning to the French officers, while the Hurons, subjugated by this familiar manly voice, sat down for a pow-wow and finally decided to let the Palefaces sort things out for themselves.

CHAPTER 8

THE THREE men who followed Nicolas Perrot up the steep side of the mountain were not lacking in curiosity in spite of the discomfiture they had just suffered. For the name of Count Peyrac had already acquired some renown in North America. Few had seen him, but people talked a great deal about this enigmatic personality, from the coast of Massachusetts and Nova Scotia up to the borders of Canada.

Furthermore, since they had occupied the fort which the Count had built on the Kennebec with a military garrison, the French were in an embarrassing situation, and, had it not been for the presence of their friend Perrot, they would not have given much for their chances. As they went by, they caught sight of men posted behind the bushes, true buccaneers' faces from the four corners of the globe, who glared at them as they passed.

On reaching the top of the slope they came to a sudden halt, overcome with fear and astonishment.

In the shadows dappled with patches of light falling through the leaves, they had just caught sight of a rider, wearing a black mask, and seated on a jet-black stallion, as motionless as a statue.

Behind him they saw other men on horseback, and a group of women.

'Greetings, gentlemen,' said the masked rider in a muffled voice. 'Please come closer.'

In spite of their courage, they found it hard to recover their self-possession.

They greeted him nevertheless and, as the tall lieutenant seemed incapable of uttering a single word, it was the trapper Romain de l'Aubignière, known as Three-Fingers of the Three-Rivers, who spoke up. He introduced himself and added:

'Sir, we are here at your disposal to parley with you, although your method of opening the discussion seemed to us a trifle . . . explosive.'

'Was yours any less so? I have heard that you took it upon yourselves to occupy my outpost on the banks of the Kennebec.'

L'Aubignière and Maudreuil turned towards Pont-Briand.

The lieutenant ran his hand over his brow and came back to earth. 'My lord,' he said with spontaneous deference – a fact which later was to astonish him – 'my lord, it is indeed true that we have been instructed by the Government of New France to proceed to the source of the Kennebec in order to find out all we can about your movements and your intentions; we had expected you to arrive by river and were awaiting you in the hope of being able to open discussions with you with a view to reaching an understanding.'

A slight smile appeared at the edge of Peyrac's mask, for the lieutenant had said: 'we were expecting you to come by river.' Their arrival overland, on horseback, had taken the French unawares.

'What about my Irishman, what have you done with him?'

'Oh! do you mean the fat red Englishman, the funny one?' exclaimed little Baron de Maudreuil. 'He led us a fine dance. Although he was all alone up there, anyone would have thought there was a whole garrison inside the fort. The Hurons wanted to scalp him, but our colonel said they weren't to, so we just put him in the cellar to cool his heels, after stringing him up like a sausage.'

'God be praised!' said Peyrac. 'I could never have forgiven you the death of one of my men, and the issue between us would have had to be settled by fighting. What is the name of your colonel?'

'Count Loménie-Chambord.'

'I have heard of him. He is a great soldier and a very worthy man.'

'Are we your prisoners, sir?'

'If you can guarantee that no treachery awaits us at Katarunk, and that the sole purpose of your expedition is to parley with me, I shall be happy to treat you as friends rather than hostages, as my adviser, your countryman Monsieur Perrot, suggests.'

The lieutenant bowed his head and seemed to reflect for a time.

'I think I can guarantee that, Monsieur,' he said at last. 'I know that, even if your movements were causing anxiety in certain circles which viewed them as an incursion of the English into our territory, there were others, and in particular Governor Frontenac, who were interested in the possibility of an alliance with you, that is to say, with a compatriot who would not seek to harm New France.'

'If that is the situation, I will agree to meet Monsieur de Loménie before embarking on pointless hostilities. Monsieur de l'Aubignière, may I ask you to go to your colonel and tell him of my arrival with the Countess of Peyrac, my wife.'

He beckoned to Angélique to step forward, and she urged her mare out of the shade and came and stood beside her husband. She did not feel much inclined to show any particular friendliness towards them after the fright they had given her the previous evening, but the expression that came over their three faces when they noticed her and saw her coming towards them brought a smile to her lips.

All three recoiled as one man and their lips formed a strange word which could be easily read although it remained unspoken: 'The She-Devil! The She-Devil of Acadia! ...'

'Madame, may I introduce these Canadian gentlemen?'

'Gentlemen, Countess Peyrac, my wife....'

With an ironic expression he watched the varied emotions in their faces.

'The Countess told me of your encounter yesterday evening. I think you must have given one another quite a fright. I can understand that the appearance of a white woman on horseback in these parts must have caused you some surprise, but as you see, what you saw was no vision....'

'But it was,' exclaimed Pont-Briand with true French gallantry. 'Madame de Peyrac's beauty and grace are such as to make us wonder

62

whether our eyes are not deceiving us and whether we are not in fact witnessing a vision or apparition.'

Angélique could not help smiling at this amiable retort.

'Thank you for your courteous words, Lieutenant. I regret that our first meeting was a somewhat rough-and-ready one. I owe you a hat, I believe!'

'Almost a head, Madame. But what matter! I would have welcomed death from so lovely a hand.'

And Gaspard de Pont-Briand, bending his knee, bowed with courtly elegance. It was quite obvious that Angélique fascinated him.

The caravan had set off again in some disorder.

Now that they had reached agreement, they fetched the wounded Huron so that he could be carried on horseback, but he was afraid of the strange animal.

Baron Maudreuil introduced their chief, a man called Odessonik, resplendent with his bears' teeth trappings and with feathers stuck in his top-knot. For those unfamiliar with Indians it was difficult to tell one from another, but Angélique felt sure that this was the warrior she had seen the previous evening torturing the Iroquois prisoner with such thoroughness. The Hurons had grown friendly and curious now, and thronged about them, anxious to see the new Palefaces. Their tufts of hair and feathers rising from their shaved scalps danced a saraband around the riders.

'They frighten me,' said Madame Jonas. 'They look far too like the Iroquois. They are all so much of a muchness.'

The Protestants were terrified. They felt, possibly even more than Angélique, the unfortunateness of this meeting with the French Catholics and soldiers, the very people they had fled from in La Rochelle at such risk. They kept quiet, hoping that the two officers would not notice them.

Actually, the interest of the latter was centred on two things: Peyrac's masked face, which they found utterly intriguing, and Angélique's. In spite of the fact that she was weary and dusty in the shadow of her big hat, Pont-Briand kept on asking himself whether her face was not in fact the loveliest in the world. She-Devil or not, her eyes shone with a strange light, and he found himself obliged to look away suddenly whenever he met her glance.

The emotional shock he had felt on seeing her astride her horse, a creature of flesh and blood and no vision, still made him catch his breath, and he showed a complete lack of interest in his present situation, which was in fact a rather delicate one. The farther they went, the more convinced he became that this woman who had loomed up out of the forest was the loveliest creature he had ever met.

Lieutenant Pont-Briand was a colourful colossus, a solid mass of muscle, to which his aristocratic ancestry alone was able to lend a certain elegance. Born to be a soldier and, what was more, compelled to be one on account of his position as youngest member of the family, he had a ringing voice and a hearty laugh. He was a brilliant swordsman, a man who could tear the end off a cartridge with a single rapid bite, an indefatigable marksman, a warrior of fantastic endurance; but although he was a man in his prime, having passed the age of thirty, he seemed still to have the mentality of an adolescent.

This explained his relatively subordinate position for a man of high birth, since, while he could perform wonders under the orders of an enlightened leader, his impulsive nature often made it extremely dangerous for him to act on his own initiative. He had, nevertheless, been given the governorship of one of the most important French fortresses, the outpost of Saint Francis, and was extremely popular with the natives of his area. In spite of his strength and huge stature, he could walk through the forest as silently as an Indian.

Angélique was aware of his attentions and found them irritating. There was something about this sanguine man with the surprisingly feline step that immediately put her on her guard.

There were moments when she regretted the fact that they had not fought it out that morning. Her husband wanted to settle things by negotiation but her whole instinct and all her memories rejected the notion of conciliation with the French.

Meanwhile the flame-coloured mountain was subsiding and settling down like a tamed beast, and suddenly in the distance, set in the pass the mountain no longer defended, they caught sight of shimmering blue water. In under an hour they had reached the river.

From close to, the Kennebec looked a deep, metallic blue, like armour, and they were surprised to find themselves looking up into the pale sky to see what it was that caused the reflection in the water.

The clouds that had been heaped on the horizon had melted into mist; and the mist, joining with the river haze, had risen towards the heights, where, warmed by the sun's rays, it gave the sky the gentle hue of flax blossom. It was impossible to tell whether the wind would not once again blow the little puffballs into heavy, scudding masses.

But there was one piece of open sky, a limpid, brilliant blue, through which the sun shone in dazzling rays.

Angélique was delighted to catch the whiff of man-made fires.

Then, quite suddenly, she saw the fort.

Her face grew radiant and she stood up in her saddle.

It was set back from the bank in the centre of a clearing from which had been cut the heavy stakes for the palisade. This was rectangular in shape, and nothing appeared above it save the shingle-boarded roofs of two buildings with quietly smoking chimneys. All around the palisade, the land looked rough and chaotic, although green. It had not the symmetry of a garden, nor the rolling lines of a meadow, which was easy to understand once one realized that the stumps of the felled trees had not been cleared from the ground and that the few crops planted outside the palisade were coming up in the midst of gnarled roots and sawn-off stumps. Still, these were the first crops they had encountered during their long trek through the forest, and Angélique's dry lips broke into a smile. She liked the place. After so many wanderings she would be pleased to have a settled home at last.

Pont-Briand was looking at her.

She was oblivious of his stare. She was completely engrossed in what she saw from the top of the hill, an area over which seemed to hang a golden mist composed of mingled smoke and dust.

It was only a remote outpost, without clear boundaries, and looking ridiculously small in the heart of this limitless forest, but for one who had travelled for many a long day without seeing the slightest trace of any human handiwork save a few wretched wigwams, and one or two birch-bark canoes left to rot in some creek, the sight of this piece of land brought promise to the traveller of many missed comforts in a less primitive world.

The river widened out in front of the outpost to form a kind of big peaceful lake across which canoes glided swiftly, light as dragon-flies, some making for a small near-by island, others skirting the banks, while still others set off to join a whole flotilla of light skiffs that lay motionless, side by side, at the southern extremity of the semi-circular beach.

It was still hard to make out the men paddling the canoes, and those who must be moving about on the shore, but the impression was one of movement, like the agitation in an ant-hill which tells one, when still some distance away, that it is inhabited and not deserted.

Farther down, Angélique could see a beach of grey sand and big pebbles, on which had been erected a number of birch-bark tepees, from whose cone-shaped tops white wisps of smoke rose sleepily. The site had clearly been chosen because it was protected from the unpredictable mountain winds.

A long cry heralded the arrival of the caravan, and the Indians, scattered about the outpost, converged in their direction, chattering loudly and uttering ear-splitting whoops as they began to climb the slope to meet them. L'Aubignière must have warned them of the arrival of strange Palefaces, mounted on horseback.

After calling a halt, Joffrey de Peyrac examined the outpost and the beach from his horse.

'Monsieur de Maudreuil!'

'Sir?'

'Is that not a white flag I see flying at the central masthead?'

'Yes indeed, sir! It is the oriflamme of the King of France.'

Peyrac raised his hand to his hat, removed it, and held it at arm's length in a respectful salute, which, for those who knew him well, had a hint of exaggeration about it.

'I bow before the Majesty of him you serve, Baron, and am honoured that he should visit my house in your person.'

'And in that of my superiors,' young Maudreuil retaliated, looking anxious.

'I am delighted at the prospect. . . .'

He put his hat on again. His manner was so lordly that even his friendliness seemed dangerous.

'Nevertheless, custom demands that when a lord returns to his own land, it should be his flag that flies from the masthead. Perhaps you would run ahead, Baron, and give orders to this effect; for it would seem that nobody has thought of this. O'Connell will know where to find my flag.'

'Certainly, my lord,' the young Canadian replied, dashing off along the stony track.

He raced past the Indians as they came up the hill, dived into a spinney and ran on to the fort. Shortly after, the gates were opened, and a blue flag with a silver escutcheon was hauled to the top of the flagpole.

'The arms of Rescator,' Peyrac said softly. 'Theirs may be an obscure glory, perhaps even a dubious one, but surely, Madame, the time has not yet come to strike them without a battle?'

Angélique did not know what reply to make.

Once again she was disconcerted by her husband's attitude. For her part, she felt that the French had not been entirely straightforward in saying that they had come to Katarunk without hostile intentions. The occupation of a military outpost had never been regarded as evidence of great friendship. But theiir position had been reversed. Peyrac had arrived, taking them by surprise. And among his friends he numbered Perrot and Maupertuis, men who had been long years in Canada and were held in the highest esteem.

But for all this they were standing on a powder-keg. Angélique was horrified to see the host of Indian warriors, the allies of the French troops, who climbed up the hill towards them giving blood-curdling whoops; although, for the time being at least, these were merely cordial manifestations of amusement and welcome.

Joffrey de Peyrac continued his examination of the port and the esplanade through his telescope.

Facing them, the two big gates in the palisade stood wide open.

The soldiers had lined up on either side of the gates as if for an inspection, and a little in front of them stood an officer in full dress uniform, no doubt Loménie-Chambord, whose name had been mentioned to him.

He folded his telescope, bowed his head, and appeared to be deep in thought.

He knew that this was his final opportunity to answer force with force. Once this moment had gone he would be in the lion's mouth.

He and his men were about to mingle with a changeable band that could from one moment to the next turn into ferocious enemies.

Everything would depend on the good faith of the colonel, and on his influence over his men, in a word, on the wisdom of the man with whom Peyrac was about to find himself face to face, the man who represented the King of France.

He looked again. Through the telescope he saw the distinguished figure of a man who stood, hands behind his back, apparently waiting fearlessly for the arrival of the master of Katarunk announced to him by Maudreuil.

'Let's go,' said Peyrac.

He asked those on horseback to line up behind him, placed the Spaniards in their breast-plates at the head of the column with their arms, followed by Florimond and Cantor bearing his banners, then his men, each carrying his musket and a piece of lighted touchwood.

Indians loomed up on all sides, intensely curious. Nicolas Perrot, struggling with every language he knew, greeted them, and at the same time asked them to be a little quieter, for the horses, alarmed by the sudden din, the hurly-burly of plumes, painted faces, bows and brandished tomahawks, had begun to neigh and to shy. At last the procession got under way, and soon Wallis's delicate hooves were treading along the river's edge between a double line of soldiers. Peyrac had asked Angélique to remain beside him. She felt embarrassed by Honorine's bare feet, and would also have liked to tidy her own hair, but it was as much as she could do to keep her horse walking slowly in parade step. After the loneliness of the vast open spaces, they were now the cynosure of the eyes of a noisy, feathered, brown-skinned crowd of strong-smelling people, all wanting to see and touch them.

Perrot, the trappers, and the Sagamores, chieftains of the various assembled tribes, shouted in vain to keep the more frenzied members of the crowd away from the horses. Wallis of course reared up, her hooves lashing out at some of the greasy heads. Then she bolted at a gallop down to the river's edge. Angélique managed to bring her to a halt and force her back, quivering but docile and magnificent before the astonished gaze of the hysterical mass of Indian spectators, who were whooping with delight. Apart from this incident, which was clearly regarded as a welcome interlude, the arrival of Count Peyrac and his followers at Katarunk took place as protocol demanded.

He sat motionless before the open wooden gates, his wife beside him, his companions behind, while the two Canadian drummer-boys, in their blue military uniform, came forward to meet him, drums rolling. Behind them at a slow march came six soldiers and sergeants to form a guard of honour, immaculately turned-out in spite of its small size and the speed with which it had been organized.

The colonel came forward, dressed in the blue frock-coat with gold frogging worn by the officers of the Carignan-Salière regiment, adorned with chamois-leather revers on sleeves and collar, and big guilloched buttons.

He was a distinguished-looking man of about forty; he wore knee-boots, and his sword at his side was tied with a white sash, which, for a soldier in the field, showed a determination to keep his turn-out up to regulation standard. His short pointed beard, a trifle old-fashioned, suited his distinguished face with its fine, handsome features; his tanned cheeks and forehead made his calm, grey, penetrating eyes look pale in comparison.

What struck Angélique about him was above all the gentleness that seemed to emanate from him, like a kind of diffuse, inward light.

He was not wearing a wig, but his hair was well cared for.

He saluted, one hand on the hilt of his sword, and introduced himself.

'Count Loménie-Chambord, leader of the lake Megantic expedition.'

'A great name!' Peyrac replied, bowing his head. 'Monsieur de Loménie, am I to understand that the position of my modest outpost here has simply served as a secure place to bivouac? Or must I consider your presence here, along with your native allies, as a seizure of my territory?'

'A seizure! Heaven preserve!' the other man exclaimed. 'Monsieur de Peyrac, we know you are French, although not a representative of the King, our master; but no one in Quebec would dream of considering your presence here as damaging to the interests of New France – far from it! At least, that is before you have given us cause to think so.'

'That is precisely my view of the matter, and I am delighted that we have removed any possible misunderstanding between us. I shall in no way harm the interests of New France, neither by my work, nor by my presence beside the Kennebec, provided no one tries to harm mine. That is an undertaking that you may give in so many words to your governor.'

Loménie bowed again without replying. Although his career brought him considerable experience of delicate situations, the one in which he found himself involved on this occasion seemed to him the most astonishing of all. People had indeed begun to tell all sorts of tales throughout Canada about this French adventurer, of obscure background, who was prospecting for precious metals, manufacturing gunpowder, was a friend of the English to boot, and who, for more than a year, had decided to stake out claims somewhere in the vast, undeveloped depths of French Acadia. But their actual meeting had proved a far livelier event than could ever have been imagined.

This fantastic story must be reported to Quebec and was indeed of unusual interest. A group of Europeans had arrived from the south, on horseback, not by water, travelling through regions which had never before heard the sound of a horse neighing. There were women and children among them. And their leader was a masked rider, slow-spoken and gruff-voiced, who from the very outset had adopted a position of command and authority – as if two hundred armed savages, allies of the French, and ready to rush into action at the slightest sign, had not been there at all, bearing in on him and his tiny party on all sides.

Count Loménie liked courage, he liked the grand manner.

When he looked up again, there was a respect and a sudden, spontaneous warmth in his eyes. 'Perhaps this is what falling in love at first sight is like, if it can apply to friendship....' he thought.

He wrote these words many years later to Father Daniel de Maubeuge in a letter dated September 1682, which was in fact never finished. In

69

it he described his first meeting with Count Peyrac, and, in spite of the lapse of time, he remembered every detail, with admiration tinged with sadness.

'That evening,' he wrote, 'beside a wild river in the midst of the wilderness we have tried in vain to win over to civilized Christian thought, I knew that I had encountered one of the most extraordinary men of our time. There he sat, on horseback, and I do not know, Father, if you appreciate just what the words "on horseback" signify, unless you have ever dragged your boots through the cursed, majestic country of the upper Kennebec. There he was, surrounded by his wife, children, young men, all of them having undergone great hardship, the women unaware of their own courage, the children contented, the young men daring and passionate. He did not seem to realize what a feat he had just accomplished, or perhaps he did realize it but cared little. I had the feeling that this man lived his life on a superior plane, but with all the simplicity that people bring to their daily actions. And I began to envy him. All this took place in a flash as I tried to penetrate the secret of his black mask.'

The drums continued their muffled rolling, which beat an accompaniment to no one knew what potential drama.

Loménie walked up to the horse and looked up at the masked rider. His simple greatness had made him loved by all around him. One could see from his calm, honest eyes that cunning and fear were unknown to him.

'Monsieur,' he said, coming straight to the point, 'I think that you and I shall never need many words to understand one another. I also think that we have just become friends. Would you be willing to give me a token of your friendship?'

Peyrac examined him carefully. 'I might. What kind of token do you have in mind?'

'A friend has no need to hide his face from his friends. Would you show us your face.'

Peyrac hesitated slightly, then a ghost of a smile flitted across his face and he raised his hands to the back of his head to untie his leather mask.

He took it off and put it away in his doublet.

The French showed considerable curiosity and stood silent examining his face, the face of a *condottière*, marked with the scars of battle. It was a face that told them they were up against no mean adversary.

'Thank you,' said Loménie gravely.

And he added with a trace of humour:

'Now that I can see you, I feel convinced that it was a good thing we reached an understanding with you.'

Their eyes met, then Peyrac burst out laughing:

'Monsieur de Loménie-Chambord, I like you.'

He leapt down from his horse, throwing the reins to one of his servants. Then he took off his glove and the two men shook hands vigorously.

'I too anticipate that our friendship will be to our mutual advantage,' Peyrac went on. 'I trust you found everything you needed here in Katarunk to refresh you after your campaign?'

'More than enough; your outpost is undoubtedly as well equipped as anyone could hope for. I must confess that my officers and I have . . . er . . . made some inroads into your stocks of excellent wine. Let it be clearly understood that we will pay you back, if not in wines of such high quality, which we would be unable to send you, at least by the advantage of our presence here in case of any threat from the Iroquois. They are said to be on the prowl in the region.'

'We took a prisoner yesterday, a Mohawk, but he escaped,' Lieutenant Pont-Briand interposed.

'We too ran into a party of Cayugas in the south,' said Peyrac.

'That treacherous tribe has infiltrated the whole area,' Count Loménie sighed.

As he spoke his glance fell on Nicolas Perrot, and it became apparent that his eyes, which to Angélique had appeared so gentle, could also take on a look of great sternness. The look he gave to Peyrac's right-hand man would have made anyone other than this easy-going trapper wish the earth would open and swallow him up.

'Is that you, Nicolas, or am I dreaming,' Count Loménie asked coldly.

'Yes it's me, my lord,' Perrot replied cheerfully, his face lighting up in a broad smile. 'Delighted to see you again . . .'

And with a spontaneous gesture, he went down on one knee in front of the officer, took the hand that was not being offered him, and kissed it.

'I have never forgotten the marvellous battles you led us in in the past against the Iroquois, sir. How often have I thought of you during my travels . . .'

'You would have done better to think about your wife and child whom you abandoned in Canada, without giving them any news of your whereabouts for the past three years.'

The unfortunate Perrot hung his head in confusion at this reprimand, and stood up with an expression on his face like a scolded child.

The French soldiers had broken ranks and hastened to hold the ladies' horses. They were now able to dismount, and to the accompaniment of much hat raising, they made for the gates of the outpost.

Seen from close to, it was in fact, as Peyrac had said, more a trading post than a fortified position to defend a strategic point. The palisade was scarcely taller than a man, and the only artillery it possessed consisted of four small culverins set at the corners facing the river.

Inside, the place looked more like a sheepfold, it was so crowded with people and miscellaneous objects. Merely to walk across it was quite an adventure. The first thing Angélique noticed were the carcasses of two black bears, slit open and hanging like monstrous scarlet watermelons, which the Indians were beginning to carve up skilfully.

'There, you see, we shall not need to touch your stocks of venison,' said Monsieur de Loménie, 'hunting went well today and our savages have decided to hold a feast straight away. There are two more animals already cooking in the cauldrons. And with a good bag of bustards and turkeys, everyone will be able to eat his fill, and tomorrow too.'

'Could you tell me if the cottage is available?' Peyrac asked. 'I would like to put up my wife and daughter there, so that they can get some rest, and the women and children with them as well.'

'My officers and I had taken up quarters there, but we shall vacate it. If you can wait just a few moments. . . . Maudreuil, go and check over the cottage!'

Young Baron Maudreuil dashed off, at the double as usual, while Peyrac informed the colonel that one of the members of his escort was the great Sagamore Mopuntook of the Metallaks. Loménie knew him by reputation, but had never met him, and congratulated him warmly, expressing himself in the Abenaki tongue with great fluency.

This great crowd of people moving around began to stir up the dust, which mingled with the smoke from the many fires. The breeze was so gentle here that it did not blow the smoke away. Angélique longed to get away from the noise. At last they managed to cross the courtyard, taking it stage by stage, little by little through a confused jumble of pots and pans, the guts of animals lying around in pools of blood, ashes, glowing fires, kegs and quivers, animal skins and feathers, muskets and powder-barrels. Angélique accidentally stepped on a kind of blue greasy substance which the Indians apparently used to paint their faces. Honorine almost fell into a cooking-pot, Elvire slipped on some slimy entrails, while her two sons were kindly invited by the savages to partake of some raw bear's brain, a delicacy reserved exclusively for men.

They finally reached the door of the house that had been set aside for them. Baron Maudreuil was just coming out, while an Indian of indeterminate race finished sweeping the floor with a broom of leaves. The young ensign had worked hard, and the room they entered was small, but cleared of all unnecessary clutter, and only the merest trace of the inevitable smell of tobacco and leather remained. A big pile of juniper wood had been placed in the central fireplace over a handful of bark, ready to be set ablaze as soon as they began to feel the chill of the evening.

CHAPTER 9

ANGÉLIQUE could not help giving a sigh of relief as soon as the door shut behind them. She collapsed on to a wooden stool standing near by, and Madame Jonas sat down on another. The place was poorly furnished.

'I hope you are not too worn out, my dear?' Angélique asked, thinking sympathetically of the fact that the plucky woman was over fifty.

'Well, you know, the journey itself was all right, but my head is splitting with the noise all that mob made. In this country you seem either not to see enough people, or too many....'

'How do you feel, Elvire?'

'I'm scared, I'm awfully scared!' the young widow replied. 'All these men are going to slaughter us.'

Master Jonas took a peep out of a crack in the window by lifting one of the pieces of hide serving as a pane, which had come unstuck. His serious, good-natured face revealed that he too was frightened.

Angélique kept her fears to herself, in an attempt to reassure them.

'You must not worry. Here we are under the protection of my husband. The French soldiers have nothing like the power here they have in France.'

'Still they gave us some very queer looks. They must have discovered that we are Huguenots!'

'They must also have noticed that some of our men are Spanish and some even English, whom they regard as far worse enemies than you. But we are a very long way from France, as I said.'

'Yes, that's true!' the watchmaker agreed. He was watching the Indians swarming round the house.

'Don't they look just like the masked carnival figures that you see at home at shrovetide. Some of them have their noses painted blue, their eyes, eyebrows and cheeks black, and the rest of their faces red. What a masquerade!'

The little boys went over to the window and looked out too. Angélique took off her right boot and scraped the sole with a penknife to remove the remainder of the blueish paint clinging to it.

'I wonder what ingredients they use to make these paints. The colour is very fast. It would be wonderful to paint one's eyelids with before going to a ball. ...'

Then she took off her stocking to look at a bruise on her ankle which had been hurting her for some days.

The door burst open and there stood Lieutenant Pont-Briand on the threshold, petrified as he realized that he had forgotten to knock.

'Please forgive me,' he stammered, 'I was bringing you . . . some candles.' In spite of himself he could not take his eyes off Angélique's bare leg and foot resting on the hearthstone.

She pulled down her skirt and gave him a haughty look.

'Please come in, lieutenant, and thank you for your kindness.'

The lieutenant was accompanied by two men carrying the baggage. As they deposited the bags and the tawed leather trunks in a corner, the lieutenant himself placed candles in brass candlesticks on the table, with a pitcher of beer and some drinking mugs, talking incessantly to cover up his blunder.

'Do take a little refreshment, ladies. I have no doubt your ride must have been long and difficult. My comrades and I are full of admiration for your courage. Do not hesitate to tell me if there is anything I can do to make you more comfortable. I will bring you anything you ask for. Monsieur de Loménie-Chambord has instructed Monsieur de Maudreuil and me to place ourselves at your disposal, while he receives Monsieur le Comte de Peyrac. I would advise you, if possible, not to budge outside this evening; there are a lot of Indians here and they have decided to hold a celebration. They could be a nuisance. To-morrow, most of them will be going on their way and you will be able to get to know the place better. In any event, do not let any of them in here and keep your eye on your possessions. It is not so much on account of the Abenakis or the Algonquins that I say this, but be-cause there are a lot of Hurons among them and, according to a well-known Canadian proverb: who says Huron says thief.'

As he spoke he gave an occasional bold glance towards Angélique. But she was paying little heed to his words and was waiting impatiently for him to leave them. She was weary. She ached all over. Although primitive, the outpost of Katarunk would have delighted her had they been able to arrive as masters of the place. As it was, notwithstanding the protestations of friendship they had received, their situation was far from agreeable. The place was still not their own, and she could see what turn events were going to take. Her husband would be entirely taken up by his self-invited guests and forced to keep an eye on them. For a start, she would not see him that evening, and she would indeed be lucky if he did not set off the following day on some reconnaissance goodness knows where, leaving her in this stinking hole full of cheeky Indians whose language she could not even speak.

With a sudden unconscious movement she threw off her big hat which felt too tight across her forehead and, throwing back her head, she closed her eyes and ran her hand over her brow, which was beginning to ache.

Pont-Briand fell silent and his heart rose into his mouth. My goodness, she was lovely! So lovely she took your breath away.

Angélique looked at him, thought he looked thoroughly stupid and had to restrain a shrug.

'Thank you for your kindness, sir,' she said somewhat coldly, 'and please believe me when I say that my companions and I have not the slightest desire to mingle with these savages, nor any intention of losing our few possessions to gratify their acquisitive instincts. My daughter is already without shoes. She left them beside a lake. And I cannot begin to imagine how I shall ever get hold of a pair of shoes to fit her.'

Pont-Briand stammered out that he would take care of that. He would ask one of the Indian women to make some moccasins for the child and tomorrow she would be shod. He backed over towards the door, snatching up some items of uniform that had been left lying on a bench, and found himself on the doorstep with his mind about as sharp and unsteady as if he had drunk three glasses of Canadian rye brandy.

'By jove!' he muttered between his teeth, 'what's up? Is something actually going to happen in this god-forsaken country?'

Love began to stir in him like a serpent. He felt it stealing over him with an inner shudder. It was like the excitement one felt when hunting or fighting, and he could not understand it. But life had acquired a new savour for him and, as he crossed the courtyard, he lifted his

75

face to the sky and gave a wild whoop, an explosion of sheer uncontrolled delight.

'Why are you giving your victory cry?' asked some of the Indians near by.

He launched into an imitation of their syncopated dance round the camp fire, their war dance, with brandished tomahawks and arrows. The Indians laughed. They in their turn began to dance too, interspersing their movements with sudden strident whoops that rent the air above them.

'What a din!' Angélique sighed.

The noise sent horrible shudders down her spine, and she took Honorine in her arms and clasped her wildly to her. The threat of violent death hung everywhere, infesting the very air they breathed. She could taste it on her tongue. How could she explain what she felt? That was America – violent death surrounded you wherever you went but you had the right to live and defend yourself.

'Madame,' Elvire called, 'come and see. There are two rooms beside this one, three in fact, with beds in them, and each one has a fireplace. We shall be very comfortable here.'

The tiny bedrooms had been built around the central chimney as if round a pillar, which made it possible for each room to have its own fireplace. The chimney itself was pretty rough, and appeared to have been constructed with stones from the river bonded together with mortar made of sand, lime and gravel. The rustic beds, some with posts made of logs, which had not even been stripped of their bark, had moss-filled mattresses but were made with comfortable-looking woollen blankets and furs. The bed in the room on the right was a well-made piece of furniture, elegant but solidly built, with a tester and curtains of coarse brocade held back by cords. There was another less elaborate bed in the room on the left, also with curtains round it. The rooms at the back contained several low beds with logs for legs, but they were all covered with woollen blankets or furs. Elvire decided that she would sleep here with the three children.

The two Jonases would sleep in the room on the left and Madame de Peyrac in the one on the right. As a matter of fact, they had already automatically placed her trunk in there. There was something about the furnishing of this little rustic room, which was more akin to a woodcutter's hut than to a room in a farm-house, with its walls made of great logs that had hardly even been squared up, that told Angélique that this was the room that Joffrey de Peyrac had used himself the year before when he had stayed at Katarunk. As she drew back a curtain that covered some roughly-made shelves she discovered a collection of leather-bound books with titles in Latin, Greek and Arabic.

The other rooms must have been intended for his sons or for his right-hand man whom he always took with him. He regarded this place only as a camp, a road-post, a place for men to live among men; but she recognized his touch in the details, in his love of comfort, in a certain felicity he had always shown in his choice of the objects that surrounded him. The chandelier that stood on the vast table in one corner was of wrought brass. Its delicate curves were a pleasure to look at, although its beauty seemed strange and somewhat out of place in this hut in the depths of the woods. Unfortunately, no one had bothered to remove the mountains of wax which had trickled down on to it, as candle after candle had burned low during the past few evenings. The hearthstone was furnished with handsomely forged fire-dogs, but the floor was strewn with ash, and pieces of charred wood. Everything was in the usual untidy mess characteristic of the military. Young Maudreuil had obviously not had time to arrange for the cleaning of the bedrooms as well as the main room.

Angélique realized that the first thing to do was to set to work with a broom. There were some besoms, made of leaves or twigs, standing in corners, and the women set about trying to purge their quarters of all traces of the barrack-room. When they had finished, they decided that they liked their little well-sheltered house with its four fireplaces, in which the logs were soon crackling merrily. They were anxious to leave their mark on the place, to make it their own, to impress on it their personal habits of tidiness and cleanliness, so that they could feel well and truly at home, and no longer wanderers and vagabonds as they had been for the past three long weeks.

Once the door was well shut, and the latch well latched, they began to feel more and more at ease. Master Jonas sat down in front of his fire and set about drying out his shoes and stockings, which had been soaking wet ever since they had crossed the last marsh. Elvire undressed the three children and washed them.

After finishing her sweeping, Angélique looked round to see if she could not find some sheets for the beds. Leaning the lid of a chest back against the wall of her room she discovered a large mirror fixed to the inside. This too, she thought, was the hand of Joffrey de Peyrac. It was a friendly surprise, a mark of the unspoken bond between them.

'Oh, how I adore him,' she thought.

She stayed where she was, kneeling in front of the chest, looking at herself. She was resting. There was no linen in the chest, only some men's clothes. After looking them over, she stood up again and shut the lid of the chest. Those few moments in front of a mirror had made her long to change into something more elegant. She opened her own trunk. First of all she found a clean shift for Honorine. Fortunately, the children were sleepy, and they were able to put them to bed in the little back room where they were less likely to be disturbed by the noise from the courtyard.

Madame Jonas had found a big cauldron in the shed to hang from the pot-hook. Someone would have to fetch water, but not one of the three women felt she had the courage to face the crowds in the court-yard which they would have to cross to reach the well. Master Jonas said he would go, and he returned accompanied by a swarm of Indians who crowded round the doorway to see the white women. They would never have thought of carrying his load for him; for they considered it scandalous that a 'tcheno', an elderly man, should be given this chore to perform while his womenfolk stood idle. The little house came very near to being invaded by an excited horde of evil-smelling natives who refused to be put off.

'I have never met a more brazen lot than these barbarians,' said the watchmaker, dusting himself down and wiping his brow when at last the door had been closed and barricaded. Once they've decided to pick on you, there's no shaking them off.'

To avoid having to send him on a second expedition, the ladies decided to share out the precious water between them for their ablutions.

They hung the cauldron over the fire which was crackling merrily. And as they waited for the water to get hot, they sat round the fire and poured out some beer.

This time there were several light taps on the door, and Nicolas Perrot appeared with a large loaf of wheat bread, some cold meat, and some blackberries, raspberries, and mulberries in a small basket. His Indian servant carried in a supply of logs.

They were cheered by the food and took some to the children, who fell fast asleep almost before finishing the last mouthful.

'But what's all this about your being married and having a child, Nicolas?' Angélique asked. 'You never told us anything about it.'

'I didn't know,' the trapper replied hastily, growing very red.

'What, do you mean you didn't know you were married?'

'No, I mean I didn't know I had a child. I left immediately after-wards.'

'After what?'

'After the wedding, of course! You see, I was forced into it. If I had not got married, I would have had to pay an enormous fine and at the time I was hard up. The trouble was I had been condemned for trading without a permit from the Governor of Canada, and they threatened to excommunicate me into the bargain for selling brandy to the Indians. So you see, I preferred to get married. . . . It was easier.'

'What had you done to the poor girl to be forced into that?' Madame Jonas asked.

'Nothing. I didn't even know her.'

'Really?'

'She was one of the King's Girls, and she had only just landed in Canada. I understand she is a nice respectable sort of a girl.'

'You're not sure?'

'I didn't have time to find out.'

'Do explain yourself a bit better, Nicolas,' said Angélique. 'We can't understand a word of what you are saying.'

'It is simple enough. The King of France wants to build up the population of his colony, so from time to time he sends over a boat-load of young women and all the bachelors in the place are forced to marry within a fortnight, under pain of paying a large fine, or even being sent to prison. So you see, when I was asked, I did it. But afterwards, off I went back to my savages. . . .'

'Did you find your wife as bad as all that?' Elvire asked.

'I've not the faintest idea, we didn't have time to get acquainted, as I said.'

'Enough time, though, to become a father,' Angélique remarked.

'But I had to. If she had complained that the marriage had not been consummated I would have been in for another fine.'

'So, the very next morning after your wedding night off you went without a backward glance. And have you never had any regrets these last three years, Nicolas?' Angélique asked, with feigned severity.

'As a matter of fact I haven't!' the trapper admitted with a sigh. 'But I must say that since Monsieur de Loménie gave me that old-fashioned look earlier on today, I do feel a bit uneasy. That man is the most saintly person I know. It's a pity he and I are not more alike,' Nicolas concluded with a wry smile.

In spite of the shortage of water, Angélique enjoyed her wash in front of the fire in her bedroom. She had brought with her two dresses which might have seemed unnecessarily elegant for these wild regions, but she had decided that, even if there was no one to admire her, she should still be able to take pleasure in her appearance. What was more, she did have her husband, her young sons and even Honorine to think of; in short it was a matter of prestige! Why should she not from time to time give them a glimpse of an elegant woman, like those in the faraway cities, where coaches pass along the streets, and where, behind every window, eyes peer and mouths exclaim 'have you seen Madame X's new dress?'

So she put on her silvery-grey dress, with the silver braid outlining the seams of the sleeves and shoulders, and a lawn collar and revers edged with fine silver lace. She freed her hair from her headdress and gave it a thorough brushing with the gold and tortoiseshell brushes from the exquisite toilet set her husband had given her before they left Gouldsboro. It gave her a sense of well-being to feel these luxurious articles in her hand.

Before they set off on their journey, Angélique had asked her friend Abigail Berne to trim her long hair.

Now she wore it at about shoulder length, where it made a golden frame round her face.

It was thick silky hair, that fell in broad waves and curled lightly at the ends, and she wore a slight fringe over her sunburned forehead.

There was something a trifle coquettish and provocative in the way Angélique de Peyrac made the most of her hair. For, although she was only thirty-seven, a few premature white hairs mingled already with the dazzling gold. But this did not worry her; she realized that their silver sheen gave an elusive charm to her astonishingly youthful face.

She bent over the mirror in the chest to fix a little pearl-studded diadem in her hair.

As she did so a shadow moved across the yellow parchment of the window and fingers came to rest on it, their tips making small round spots ringed with light, while the nails scratched lightly on the surface.

CHAPTER 10

AFTER A moment's hesitation, Angélique lifted the wooden latch and drew one of the roughly-made shutters of the little window towards her.

A man stood leaning forward with an air of mystery and looking all round him as if fearing to be noticed. She recognized young Yann, the Breton lad who had been a member of the crew of the *Gouldsboro*

and whom Monsieur de Peyrac had brought along with him as a
skilled carpenter and a man capable of standing up to fatigue and
hardship.

'Madame la Comtesse.'

'Yes?'

He smiled, looking a trifle embarrassed, as if about to make a joke,
then suddenly he blurted out:

'Monsieur de Peyrac wants to shoot your mare Wallis. He says she
is vicious and that he made up his mind yesterday to get rid of her.'

Then he disappeared. Angélique had scarcely had time to hear what
he said, let alone to grasp its implications. She leaned out and called:

'Yann!'

He had vanished! The window was at the back of the house,
near the palisade, and the space outside served as a storage space for
a whole arsenal: muskets, arquebuses, bows and quivers, along with
fur cloaks, leather jackets and uniforms. There were enough savages
wandering around for her call to attract their unwelcome attentions.
She saw them turn at the sound and quickly shut the window again.
Then, leaning on the frame, she began to think of what the young
Breton had said, and the implication of his warning began to sink in.
Almost at once, she felt the full force of the blow and her eyes blazed.
So angry was she that her heart began to pound in her breast and she
almost choked. She stumbled round the room looking for her coat, for
it had grown quite dark. The very idea of killing Wallis, her mare,
whom she had brought through to safety after such incredible difficulties!

It was by this sort of behaviour that men gave women the impression
they did not exist, that they did not count! And it was a feeling that
no human being worthy of the name, even if she were of the weaker
sex, could endure without protest.

So Joffrey wanted to put down Wallis, did he, and without even telling her! Wallis, the mare Angélique had ridden until her back and her
wrists were nearly broken, ridden with her life sometimes at stake!
After all the work she had put in to calm her, break her in, force her
to accept this uncivilized land, every square yard of which seemed to
cause this hypersensitive animal insuperable terror and repulsion!
There were some smells which neither the mare nor Angélique could
stomach, the smell of the Indians, for example, or of the undergrowth
in the eternal forest untamed by the hand of man. The mare was
suffering in both body and spirit from the strange, unfamiliar world
it had been compelled to face: the vastness of the country, its un-

cultivated wildness, the latent hostility of nature turned in on itself, and it almost seemed to suffer physical pain in setting its delicate hooves on the virgin land. How many a time had Angélique asked the blacksmith from Burgundy who was travelling behind her, to take a look at its shoes. But he could find nothing; the agony was all in Wallis's mind. And yet her mistress had succeeded, or almost. . . .

She was about to sweep like a whirlwind through the other room, when she halted.

She must control her violent impulses a little in order not to get the young Breton into trouble. He had shown considerable courage coming to tell her what was going on when he had not been instructed to do so. Joffrey de Peyrac was a master whose decisions no one ever questioned.

Lack of discipline, and even mistakes, were dearly paid for under his command. Yann le Couennec must have hesitated a great deal before he acted.

He was a lad who showed a certain delicacy of feeling compared with his coarser companions. During the trek he had frequently made himself useful to Madame de Peyrac, by holding her horse's bridle on a slope, or by rubbing the mare down when they halted for the night, and the two of them had become firm friends.

So that evening when he heard that the Count had given orders to destroy the mare, he had decided to come and warn her. Angélique resolved to remain calm when she discussed the matter with her husband, and not to mention the young man's name.

She quickly picked up and wrapped around herself a purply-pink taffeta cloak lined with wolfskin which she had not yet had occasion to wear.

Madame Jonas threw up her hands when she caught sight of her.

'Are you thinking of going to a ball, my lady Angélique?'

'No, I am only going to visit the gentlemen in the other building. I have something of the greatest urgency to say to my husband.'

'No, you must not go,' protested Master Jonas. 'All those Indians! . . . It is no place for any woman to be alone in the midst of all those savages!'

'I only have to cross the courtyard,' said Angélique as she opened the door.

The din outside struck her like a blow in the face.

CHAPTER 11

THE SUN had not quite set, and a golden glow from the West bathed the scene in a diffuse, powdery radiance, a tinted haze of mingled dust, smoke, and steam.

The insipid sweet smell of boiled maize rose in a cloud from huge black cooking-pots suspended over the three fires. The soldiers were doling out the mush in big wooden ladles, and the natives crowded round the stewpots holding out their birch-bark or wooden bowls or even their hands cupped together to receive their steaming portion, without appearing in any way troubled by the heat.

Angélique reached the door of the main building, which was guarded somewhat casually by a sentry who was busy swapping tobacco leaves with the Indians for half a dozen black otter skins.

She did not bother to ask his permission to enter the room in which she hoped to find Count Peyrac. He was there, as she had expected, making merry with a motley crowd of men among whom she found it hard to pick out Count Loménie and his lieutenants. The main room of the outpost was so thick with smoke that it seemed almost dark inside, although they had already lighted the oil-lamps on the walls. But through the swathes of smoke their light was yellow and flickering like that of distant stars.

Opening the door helped to clear some of the haze, letting in a bit of fresh air and some light from outside. Angélique noticed that the room, which was fairly big, was occupied from the threshold, which consisted of two steps, right to the fireplace at the back, by a long solid wooden table, which was laden with steaming dishes, brass goblets and a few flagons of smoked glass, as well as a big pot-bellied earthenware jug running over with white froth and smelling of beer. After the smell of tobacco this sour smell was the strongest, followed by that of hot fat and boiled meat, and the more diffuse and complex scent of leather and fur; and over and above everything else, mingling with the other scents like a delicate, piercing counterpoint heard through the sounds of many other instruments, hung the subtle aroma of brandy.

The men had their pipes in their mouths, and a glass or goblet stood within reach of every hand. Their knives were being busily plied, cutting up pieces of meat, and their jaws were actively at work. Their tongues too; the noise of conversation in the raucous Indian tongue mingled with the smacking of lips as they seized their food, to form a continuous uproar in the background which, from time to time, was broken by a burst of laughter like a thunderclap. Then the eating and talking would rumble on again.

In the middle of the table she caught sight of Sagamore Mopuntook wiping his hands on his long plaits, and not far from him, the Huron Odessonik wearing the gold-braided felt hat belonging to Lieutenant Fallières. Angélique almost had the impression that she had burst right into an Indian camp. But the Indian chieftains were only guests, as was the custom, at the Palefaces' table, and it was in fact the Palefaces, however odd they might appear, who were busy feasting as dusk fell on that October day. They were celebrating a meeting all the more accidental for having taken place at an almost unknown spot on the continent, between people who, coming from different directions, had each secretly hoped to avoid the other party or to give it a thorough mauling. Beneath their apparent cordiality they were watching one another. Their inner tensions and conflicting ideas were not apparent. Count Loménie-Chambord was possibly sincere in saying that he considered himself fortunate to have encountered Count Peyrac under such peaceful circumstances, but Don José Alvarez, Peyrac's Spanish captain, looking sombre and disdainful as he sat between an Indian and a Frenchman, was irritated by the presence of these intruders in a land which the decisions of the Pope had, since the year 1506 and for all eternity, assigned to their Most Catholic Majesties the King and Queen of Spain.

The Irishman O'Connell, as ruddy as a tomato, was considering what sort of explanation he would give his master Count Peyrac when he asked him later about the invasions of the post. The two or three French trappers who had come with Peyrac from the south of Dawn-East hoped they would not have to give any account of what they had been up to during the previous year to their trapper friends from the north; some, like L'Aubigniere, had made their way to the trading post on the Kennebec with the vague idea of meeting the new fur dealer, not with the idea of running into soldiers and officers of his Majesty Louis XIV's army.

As for Eloi Macollet, a very old man who, a couple of months back, had escaped from the loving care of his daughter-in-law in the village of Levis near Quebec, and had paddled off into the depths of the forest with the firm intention of never setting eyes on another human being, no, nothing but bears or moose, or at a pinch a few beavers, he was busy telling himself that America was no longer a country for folk with a taste for solitude. The land had been completely 'spoiled'. With his red woollen hat decorated with two turkey feathers pulled right down to his bushy eyebrows, the old man mulled over his grievances as he chewed away at his briar pipe; but the alcohol helped and by the time he had reached the third glass his eyes had regained their merry sparkle and he told himself that at least his daughter-in-law would never find him here, and that meanwhile it was quite enjoyable to find oneself among friends at a well organized 'napeopounano', or 'bear festival', which is celebrated, according to rite, exclusively in male company, after blowing tobacco smoke down the animal's nostrils and throwing a mouthful of meat and a spoonful of fat on the fire for luck.

Pont-Briand, who had killed the bear, had been the first to taste it, cutting himself a piece from round the neck and distributing the rump, which was considered a real delicacy, amongst his friends. It was autumn, the season in which bears, having gorged themselves on whortleberries, are particularly tasty.

No sooner had the old man come to the end of this train of thought than he almost choked on a small bone and spat it out with an oath. He thought he had seen his daughter-in-law suddenly appear through the smoke. No, it was not Sidonie! But it was a woman standing on the threshold looking at them all.

A woman in a 'napeopounano'! What sacrilege! A woman in the heart of the wildest territory south of the Chaudière, a region no one likes to drop down to when coming from Saint-Lawrence, and up to which those who come from the shores of Acadia on the Atlantic never go, where in fact no one would go were there not from time to time a few heretics to scalp in New England.

The old man began to bellow inarticulately and to wave his arms about amid the wreaths of smoke and thick steam rising from the maize gruel. His neighbour François Maupertuis – can you believe it? That feller had disappeared the year before, and everyone thought he had frozen among the Mistassins – pushed him down on to his chair again, saying 'calm down, Grandad!'

The Sagamore raised a hand and, pointing to the woman, began to speak in solemn tones. He started to tell an involved story about a turtle and the Iroquois, saying that this woman had overcome the turtle and had the right to sit amongst the warriors.

So it was not a 'napeopounano' any more, the men's feast, but a

85

'mokouchano', and old Eloi needn't have bothered to come so far just to avoid meeting a piece of skirt, and in any case these Metallaks from Lake Umbagog were the most idiotic of all the Algonquins. Yes, of course they were hunters, for the region was a hunter's paradise, but they were still the most stupid of all Indians; for one could not even teach them to make the sign of the cross.

'Oh shut up you old dotard,' François Maupertuis bawled at him, pulling his hat down over his eyes. 'Aren't you ashamed of yourself, insulting a lady?'

Maupertuis's beard was trembling with indignation and excitement. He found Angélique tremendously impressive as she appeared through the blue haze of tobacco smoke, with her fair, shining hair gilded by the evening light as it streamed in through the open door. He scarcely recognized her. And yet he had come all the way from Gouldsboro with her, in the caravan. But she was no longer the same woman, with her hair hanging free and wrapped in that huge cloak that was the colour of the sky at sunrise. She looked as if she had stepped right out of a picture frame, one of those pictures you see in the home of the Governor of Quebec, with her hair over her shoulders and her white hand peeping out from a lace cuff and resting on the rugged wood. She appeared delicate now, no longer the tough horsewoman of the past week.

The trapper tried to go to her rescue, tripped over his stool and fell headfirst on to the cobbled floor. Clasping his battered nose, he swore at O'Connell's treacherous brandy, saying that the Irishman must add fermented barley and boiled roots to it to make it so strong.

Angélique, hesitating between laughter and fear, told herself that, all things considered, she had never seen so handsome a collection of men, even back in the days when she ran the Red Mask Tavern. And among these men, her own husband was by no means the least formidable!

He had not yet noticed her coming in, but was sitting at the far end of the table, smoking his long Dutch pipe as he talked to Monsieur de Loménie. Whenever he laughed, she caught the flash of his teeth clenched round the stem of his pipe. His profile stood out clear-cut and black against the dancing flames in the hearth.

There was something about the appearance of the room which reminded Angélique irresistibly of the past: the great Count of Toulouse entertaining his guests in the Palace of Gay-Savoir in the midst of gold plate and exotic dishes. There too, he had sat at the head of the table while behind him the flames in the vast chimney with its

86

armorial plaque and sculptured pediment cast their cheerful, dancing light over velvet, crystal and lace.

This scene was like a parody of those happy days. Everything seemed to have conspired to make Angélique aware of how low both her husband and she had fallen over the years. Their table was no longer graced with elegant lords and ladies, but with all manner of men – trappers, savages, soldiers, and even amongst the officers one was aware of a strain of coarseness produced by the lives they led – harsh, dangerous lives, lives given over entirely to the vicissitudes of warfare and hunting.

Even the distinction of Count Loménie seemed diminished in this unduly masculine atmosphere of tobacco, leather, game, alcohol and gunpowder.

She noticed that he too had sunburnt skin, the teeth of a meat-eating animal, and the dreamy, fixed gaze of the tobacco smoker.

She realized that Joffrey de Peyrac had also become attuned to this rough world.

Life on the ocean with its tempests, unending battles, struggles to the death, daily fighting with sword or pistol in hand, for the success of one's ambitions, for the control of one's men, for the achieving of some object, or the conquest of nature at its most extreme – desert, ocean or forest – had emphasized the adventurous side of his nature which, in the past, she had sometimes glimpsed beneath the elegance of the great lord and the measured gestures of the scholar. He had led men into battle through sheer necessity, but also because he enjoyed it, and he had made his life among men.

Angélique made as if to withdraw.

But Pont-Briand had leapt to his feet in his turn, and managed, unlike Maupertuis, to remain on his two feet and walk over to where Angélique stood. In any case, he was not drunk, having imbibed a mere two glasses of brandy to liven himself up.

'My compliments, Madame.'

He offered her his hand and helped her descend the two steps, then led her towards the middle of the table to find her a chair. She hesitated, resisting a little.

'Monsieur, I fear that my presence may offend the Indian chiefs. I am told that they do not welcome women at their banquets.'

The Sagamore Mopuntook, who was sitting close by, raised one hand and said something, which Pont-Briand immediately translated for Angélique's benefit.

'You see, Madame, the Sagamore is saying that you are worthy of a place among the braves for you have vanquished the emblem of the Iroquois. . . . So please do not hesitate to grant us the pleasure of your company.'

With a few vigorous shoves, he cleared a place in the middle of the table. Finding himself unable to catch Corporal Jeanson, whom he had pushed a little too roughly to one side and who was struggling to get up from under the table, he found a handsome young colossus, pushed him down beside Angélique on her right and seated himself on her left.

Pont-Briand's intervention and Mopuntook's speech had attracted everyone's attention; the buzz of voices ceased and everyone turned in Angélique's direction.

She would have preferred to sit beside her husband and tell him immediately why she had come. But she found it difficult to escape the peremptory welcome the lieutenant and his friends had given her. Her neighbour on her right leaned forward and tried to kiss her hand, but he was seized with an uncontrollable fit of hiccoughs and missed his aim, excusing himself with a smile.

'Let me introduce myself; Romain de l'Aubignière! I think you must have seen me already. Forgive me, I am a little hazy. If you had come a trifle earlier . . . but don't worry, I am still sober enough not to insult you by seeing double and thinking that there is another woman on this earth as lovely as you are. I can see one and that is enough. I assure you that you are the one and only . . .'

Angélique began to laugh, but her laugh froze on her face as her eyes lighted on the young man's hands. The left hand had the thumb and middle finger missing and the right lacked the fourth finger. His remaining fingers were all swollen at the ends, some of them had no nails, only horn-like blackened skin in their place. When he had been introduced to her in the forest she had not noticed this disfigurement.

'Pay no heed, lovely lady,' L'Aubignière said gaily. 'Those are only a few mementoes of the friendship of the Iroquois. It's not pretty, I must admit, but it doesn't stop me from using my gun.'

'Did the Iroquois torture you?'

'They caught me when I was sixteen, one autumn when I went out duck shooting on the marshes around Three-Rivers. That's why I am also known as Three-Fingers of Three-Rivers.'

And, as Angélique could not help looking sympathetically at his terrible hands, he went on:

'They began by cutting three fingers off with some sharp shells. The remaining thumb was burned in an Indian pipe, and as for the others, they tore off the nails with their teeth, and burned some of the other fingers.'

'And you didn't break down?'

It was Florimond's voice. His tousled head appeared over the soup tureen, and his eyes were glistening with excitement.

'Not a whimper, young man! Do you think I'd have given those wolves the pleasure of seeing me writhe and twist in pain. What's more, I should have been condemning myself to death, and by the hands of the women as well. What shame! When they saw I had the endurance of a brave, they adopted me and I spent over a year with them.'

'Do you speak Iroquois?'

'Possibly better than Great Chief Swanissit of the Senecas himself. . . .'

And he added suddenly with a glance round the room that seemed to take in more than met the eye:

'It's him I am looking for here.'

He had black eyes set in a brown face. His hair was brown and curly and hung down on his suède Indian jacket with its leather fringes. Round his head he wore a headband embroidered with tiny beads and with two feathers fixed at the back. It must have been the ribbon in his curls which gave his face an effeminate and almost childlike look, in spite of his burly shoulders and above-average height.

'If it's Swanissit you are looking for, my lad, anyone would think you were trying to dodge him; for last month he was up in the north on Lake Mistassin, with some of his tribe,' said Count Loménie. 'We heard that from two savages from the mountains who fortunately managed to escape from them before they reached their village.'

'And I assure you he is here,' replied L'Aubignière striking the table with his fist. 'He has come down to join Outakke, the great Mohawk leader. We captured an Iroquois the other evening. We made him talk . . .

'Wherever Outakke is you will find Swanissit. Scalp those two heads and that's the end of the Five Nations of the Iroquois.'

'You're out to avenge your three fingers,' said Maupertuis with a laugh.

'I'm out to avenge my sister and my brother-in-law, and the relatives of my neighbour Maudreuil here. For the past six years now we have been on the trail of that old fox Swanissit to do his hair for him.

'Patience, Eliacien,' he said, turning to the little Baron beside him.

'Some day you will hold Swanissit's scalp in your hand, and I shall hold Outakke's.

'When I was with the Iroquois,' he went on, 'Outtake was my brother. He is the most eloquent man I know, the most cunning and the most vindictive. He is something of a medicine man and in close touch with the Spirit of Dreams. I both love him and hate him. Put it this way: I respect him for his courage, but I would gladly kill him because he is far and away the most vicious animal a Frenchman could ever run into.'

'Are you ever going to give this lady anything to eat, cousin?' Eloi Macollet interrupted crustily.

'Yes, yes, Grandad, keep your hair on. Madame, I do apologize. Pont-Briand, couldn't you do something about it too?'

'Yes I am, I am looking for some morsel in this revolting stewpot which would be fit to grace the fork of a pretty lady, but ...'

'What about this, the bear's foot? It's the tastiest bit. You've no idea at all, Pont-Briand, my friend. It's easy to see you're a new arrival.'

'Me? I have been fifteen years in Canada!'

'Are you or aren't you going to give her something to eat?' the old man asked again in a threatening growl.

'Yes, yes, here it is.'

They drew the enormous dish towards them with its gelatinous dark rounds of meat swimming in amber-coloured grease. Romain de l'Aubignière thrust his mutilated fingers into the dish without fear of being burnt. He skilfully removed the boiled meat from the sharp claws, each one resembling a tiny, cruel, curved stiletto, which had been slightly softened by cooking, but still clinked as he piled them on the table.

'Our friend Mopuntook would make himself an elegant necklace with these, to wear round his hips or round his neck. Here, Madame, is a piece you will be able to taste without the risk of Maskwa – his lordship the bear – leaving one of his defensive weapons stuck in your throat.'

Angélique carefully examined the piece of bear meat her neighbours had insisted on placing so courteously on her plate, covering it with the greasy sauce. She had come here to discuss the question of the mare with her husband and found herself caught up in an almost official banquet. She kept on glancing towards her husband, who was sitting quite a distance from her at the far end of the long table, but because of the smoke and the movement of the guests, she was unable to catch his eye and could scarcely make out his expression. She was aware that from time to time he seemed to look somewhat enigmatically at her. She decided she must make an effort of politeness towards the somewhat tipsy Frenchmen who had invited her to sit beside them and who might take offence if she disdained their offering.

She did not feel hungry, but after all she had done more difficult things in her life than eating bear meat; so she put a piece in her mouth.

'Have a drink!' said Pont-Briand. 'You must have something to drink to wash all the fat down.'

Angélique took a drink and nearly fell over backwards.

The entire table was following her every gesture in complete silence like hunters on the watch.

Fortunately Angélique had learnt to drink at the French court and was able to put a good face on things.

'I am beginning to understand why the Indians call your alcohol firewater,' she said when she had regained her composure.

They all burst out laughing and filled her glass again in delight. Then suddenly everyone turned back to his food and the roar of conversation broke out again.

Angélique caught sight of Octave Malaprade, the cook, who had appeared at the end of the room with some roast poultry. Remembering her friends the Jonases, she made as if to stand up, with the intention of asking him to take something across to the little house. But Pont-Briand held her back with such force that her forearm was quite bruised.

'Don't go,' he said in a voice full of urgency. 'I couldn't bear it.'

At the other end of the table Count Loménie noticed Peyrac, who had half risen from his feet in anger. He intervened.

'With your permission, Count,' he murmured, 'I shall set Madame de Peyrac free and bring her to the place of honour. Don't worry, I shall look after her. Let us avoid a scene. . . . They are drunk.'

Angélique suddenly saw the French Colonel bowing before her.

'Madame, allow me to lead you to the place which is rightly yours as lady of the manor.'

As he spoke he gave Pont-Briand a brief but peremptory glance, ordering him to release his grip. Taking Angélique by the arm, he led her most gallantly to the far end of the table, which was unoccupied, seated her there and sat down himself at her right hand. Angélique now found herself still farther from her husband, but she could see him at the other end, facing her, and it was just like their Gay-Savoir days. The Colonel was very attentive towards her and had her brought some roast turkey with a few braised vegetables.

'This food is more to the taste of a young woman freshly arrived from France.'

She protested for, all things considered, she had not found the stewed black bear so unpleasant a dish. She could see that she would have no difficulty in getting used to it.

'But there is no need to force nature pointlessly,' said Loménie. 'You will see, here in the autumn we have a great deal of the kind of game to which our European palates are accustomed. We might as well make the most of it. Monsieur,' he said to Malaprade, 'Madame de Peyrac would like a nice supper taken over to her friends in the little house. Would you be kind enough to see to it?'

And he told the cook to put in a flask of good wine with the food.

However drunk Lieutenant Pont-Briand might have been, his Colonel's intervention was enough to sober him up again.

'I don't know what came over me,' he whispered woefully to L'Aubignière.

'You must be mad!' the other replied uneasily. 'Mad or under a spell . . . you watch out! The She-Devil of Acadia may not be a myth after all! . . . This woman really is too beautiful. . . . What if she were the Devil? Remember what Father Orgeval said?'

Sitting beside Colonel Loménie-Chambord, Angélique was beginning to relax.

Her husband was facing her, as of old. She could see him at the end of the table, through a haze, and, as in days gone by when he had begun to fall in love with her, she could feel his searching gaze upon her. It gave her a feeling of euphoria, a desire to shine and to join in everything that was going on around her. She felt happy. The alcohol was beginning to make her feel slightly hazy, and she was forgetting why she had come. The courtly charm of the Colonel was having its effect on her, and the instinctive attraction she had felt towards him from the first was changing into a feeling of confidence.

The simplicity of his manners and his clear-cut precise gestures went hand in hand with a gentle, winning grace in which Angélique's observant mind could not help seeing the man accustomed to talking with women. This did not, as people all too often think it does, take the form of paying elaborate compliments, but he possessed that rarer quality of knowing how to talk to women in a way that is familiar to them and puts them at their ease, and which, in brief, without any attempt to charm them, reassures them and wins them over. He intrigued her, for there was something uncommon about him.

He told her all about the northern territories, the three French cities on the Saint Lawrence, and of the many tribes that swarmed around them; and when she asked him about the Hurons, he confirmed that they were in fact of Iroquois origin. They had broken away from their kinsfolk in the Sacred Valley a long time ago, after some dispute or other, and had henceforth regarded the Iroquois as ancestral enemies. It was from the mouths of the Hurons that the first French explorer Jacques Cartier had learnt the name of the Iroquois, a word signifying 'cruel vipers'.

The talk always came back to the Iroquois. Angélique's immediate neighbours were happy to join in a conversation on a subject they knew something about and which seemed to interest them. They were tremendously impressed by her manner, which was that of a great lady. Even here everyone had a feeling that she had once sat at the King's table. They had not the slightest doubt that she had ruled at Court amid an admiring throng of men. They sensed that she had been the darling of princes....

They watched her every movement, the way she crossed her supple hands, and rested her chin on them, the way she would look the person who spoke to her straight in the eyes as she listened to him, or, on the other hand, lower her long eyelids reticently; the way she nibbled absent-mindedly at her food, grasped her goblet and emptied it unceremoniously in one draught, and suddenly burst into irrepressible laughter that stirred their vitals.

That evening the motley specimens of mankind gathered together at Katarunk had a glimpse of an unfamiliar paradise.

This woman sitting at their table represented heaven on earth, spring in midwinter, beauty come among them, rough as they were, smelling of leather and grease. She was a ray of sunshine piercing the fog of tobacco smoke, and her smile fell like balm on their hardened hearts.

They felt like heroes, strong in resolution, nimble of wit, and words came effortlessly to their lips to describe the lands they had known, or to express their point of view.

Romain de l'Aubignière spoke of the Sacred Valley of the Iroquois, of the pink light that bathes the hillside covered with rows of long bark houses with rounded roofs, and the smell of green maize: '... Few are they that come back alive from that valley. . . . Few are they that come back with all their fingers. . . .'

'I did,' said Perrot spreading out his hands.

'Oh you, they treat you as if you were a medicine man. You must have made a pact with the devil, old chap, to get away unscathed. . . .'

'It is a strange fact that the mere mention of Frenchmen sends the Iroquois into a furious rage, which surely proves that they are especially prone to possession by evil spirits,' said one of the trappers called Aubertin. 'They seem above all to fear the power of the religion the French bring with them. Look at the way they treated our missionaries! We can never consider ourselves safe from them, even in the depths of winter. Wasn't it in the middle of February that they attacked your domains, Maudreuil, and yours, L'Aubignière, and scalped your parents and your servants, setting fire to everything? Those who were left wounded died of exposure....'

'Yes, that was what happened,' confirmed Eliacien de Maudreuil.

A sombre glow came into his blue eyes, as if grief lay heavy in them like molten lead.

'It was Swanissit who did that, with his Senecas, and ever since he has scarcely stopped ranging the countryside spreading terror wherever he goes. I am not going to let him go to earth again before I have his hair.'

'And I shall have Outakke's scalp,' said Romain de l'Aubignière.

Mopuntook raised his hand and stood up to speak, and everyone listened to him in solemn silence.

The Palefaces had learnt from the savages never to interrupt a man when he was speaking and to listen to one another respectfully. Everyone present appeared to understand what the chief of the Metallaks was saying. Loménie, realizing that Angélique was interested, leaned towards her and quietly translated what the Sagamore was saying.

'We are surrounded by the Iroquois, who prowls the land like a ravenous prairie wolf. He wishes the destruction of the children of the Dawn. We encountered him on the borders of our lands, and he spoke to us of war. But the white woman faced him without fear and hurled him down into the waters. Now the Iroquois has lost his strength. He knows it, and will seek peace with us.'

'Pray God you're right,' Perrot replied.

'The old tortoise story again,' Angélique said to Loménie. 'At the time, I must admit I was frightened, but it never occurred to me to see such mystical significance in the incident. Was it really as important as all that?'

She took a sip of brandy and got a whiff of apples from the bottom of the glass.

Loménie watched her with a smile.

'I think you are beginning to feel less anxious already,' he said. 'You have reached the stage when the horror stories you hear every day have little more effect on you than the latest titbits of local gossip. You will see, you get used to this life very quickly.'

'It may be due to this excellent brandy, and to your kindly encouragement,' she said, with an affectionate glance. 'You know exactly how to handle women. . . . Oh! please don't misunderstand me. I mean that you have a particular manner, which is rare in a soldier, of building up a woman's self-confidence, of reassuring her, and giving her the impression that she really matters. Where did you acquire these skills, Monsieur de Loménie?'

'Well,' replied the Count, not in the slightest embarrassed, 'I suppose it was during the years I worked for Monsieur de Maisonneuve.'

And he told her how he had come to Canada at the time that gallant nobleman was founding Ville-Marie on the Isle of Montreal. At that time young couples were arriving from France along with the King's Girls sent over to marry the colonists. He, Loménie, had been given the task of meeting them on the banks of the Saint-Lawrence, advising them and helping them to get used to their disconcerting new way of life.

'At that time we were a constant object of Iroquois attacks and there was not a man amongst us who did not run the risk of losing his scalp on his very own doorstep. The settlers harvested their crops with their guns at their side. The King's Girls they sent over to us were for the most part nice, agreeable, well-behaved girls, but they knew very little about running a house or working in the fields. Mademoiselle Bourgoys and I were responsible for teaching them.'

'And who was Mademoiselle Bourgoys?'

'A saintly young woman who had come over from France for the sole purpose of teaching the settlers' children.'

'All alone?'

'Alone at first under the protection of Monsieur de Maisonneuve. Our Governor did not consider it possible at the time to bring over an order of nuns to so remote an outpost. More often than not we all lived together in the fortress. Mademoiselle Bourgoys tended the wounded, did the washing, taught the women to knit and mediated in their little squabbles.'

'I would like to meet her,' said Angélique. 'Is she still in Canada?'

'Yes indeed! Over the course of the years she has found companions to help her in her task and she is now head of a small group of women who teach about a hundred children in Ville-Marie and in the outlying villages around Quebec and at Three-Rivers, and for my part, since Montreal is now self-sufficient and Monsieur de Maisonneuve has been recalled to France, I re-enlisted under Monsieur de Castel-Morgeat, the military governor of New France. But I shall not easily forget the time I turned master cook in order to teach the new arrivals from France some recipes to keep their husbands happy.'

Angélique laughed at the picture of this army officer wearing a blue overall, busy teaching the rudiments of family cooking to the village lasses or orphans from the poorhouses whom the Board of Administrators had been generous enough to get off their hands by sending them overseas to get married.

'It must have been marvellous for them to have you to welcome them and to enjoy your company. The women must have been mad about you, weren't they?'

'No, I don't think so,' said Loménie.

'You surprise me! You are so charming!'

Loménie laughed, realizing that she was becoming a trifle tipsy.

'Didn't it all lead to a great deal of jealousy?' Angélique asked.

'No, not at all, Madame. You see, we were a very pious community with a strict code of behaviour. Had it been otherwise, we should never have been able to live as we did on the frontiers of Christianity. I myself am a member of a religious order; I belong to the Knights of Malta.'

Angélique gaped in utter astonishment.

'Oh, how silly I am!' and then she added rapturously:

'A Knight of Malta! How wonderful! I am so fond of the Knights of Malta. It was they who tried to buy me back when I was sold as a slave in Crete. . . . At least, they did their best to. But the price went too high for them. I shall never forget the fact that they tried, though. And when I think of all the stupid things I have said to you! How will you ever forgive me!'

And she threw back her lovely neck and burst into peals of laughter.

Everyone including Loménie looked at her, enchanted. Her teeth flashed through the semi-darkness of the smoke-filled room and her eyes were like two stars. Her laugh made them disturbingly aware of a female presence among them.

Peyrac clenched his jaw. He had watched her, fascinated, overcome by her charm, but now he felt anger welling up inside him at the display she made of her charms, the way she looked at people and giggled, and the somewhat coquettish manner she had adopted towards Loménie. It was quite obvious that she liked him, and in any case she had had too much to drink.

But, by Jove, how lovely she was!

The laugh made men's hearts turn over with happiness.

No, he could not possibly be angry with her for being so beautiful and attracting everyone's attention. She had been born to dazzle. . . .

But, damn it! he would know how to remind her tonight that she belonged to him and to him alone!

Clovis l'Auvergnat, the sinister gnome in the woollen cap, suddenly appeared beside Peyrac with a musket under one arm.

'I am off to shoot the mare, sir,' he whispered.

Peyrac took another look in Angélique's direction. Even if she was behaving a trifle giddily he could certainly trust Loménie.

'Right, I'll come with you,' he said standing up.

CHAPTER 12

ANGÉLIQUE gave such a start that Loménie, caught by surprise, put out a hand as if to support her.

'It's nothing,' she stammered, 'but, I wonder . . .'

She had just noticed that her husband's place at table was empty and she sprang to her feet.

'Forgive me, but I must go . . .'

'Already, Madame? We shall all be heartbroken, could you not stay a little longer?'

'No, no, I must have a word with Monsieur de Peyrac . . . and I see that he has gone. . . .'

'At least allow me to accompany you.'

'No, thank you very much all the same. Please stay with your friends. I can manage perfectly well. . . .'

But Loménie behaved as any gentleman should towards an attractive woman whom he suspects to be slightly inebriated. Without hesitating, he nevertheless helped her to the door, opened it and left her only once he felt sure that the outside air had helped her, that she could stand on her two legs and was only a few yards from her room.

As soon as he had left her, Angélique rushed away across the courtyard. It was even more crowded than before. Night was falling, mingling with the thick smoke, and in the blue misty cold the red flowers of the camp fires blossomed beneath the cauldrons.

But the sky above the fortress was limpid and cloudless like a great golden dome.

Angélique pushed her way roughly through the crowd to the gate in the palisade. She caught sight of her husband walking down the slope towards the lower fields beside the river and at his side she saw the stocky shape of the blacksmith from Auvergne carrying a musket.

She rushed after them.

It was no easy matter to pick a way among the treacherous tree-trunks, which were themselves all entangled with runner beans.

Angélique tripped and tumbled to her knees, swearing like a trooper. But the shock of her fall sobered her up a bit. Once back on her feet again she was careful to keep an eye where she trod. She was trembling all over with impatience, fearing to arrive too late.

She could see the silhouettes of the horses, black shadows against the dazzling sunset, as they cropped the scant grass where it grew through the dried mud.

At last she was within earshot.

'Joffrey! Joffrey!'

The Count turned round.

Angélique was panting when she reached him.

'Are you going to kill Wallis?'

'Yes! ... Who told you I was?'

Angélique refused to reply. She was beside herself, choking with rage. The darkness of the earth and the brilliance of the sky both hurt her eyes. She could not see Joffrey de Peyrac's face, for he had the light behind him, and she felt as if she hated this black, opaque figure of a man as it stood there before her like a rock.

'You have no right to do it,' she cried. 'No right. Without even warning me. I brought ... Yes, I brought that animal here, I put up with all sorts of difficulties and exhaustion. And now you are going to destroy it all at a single stroke.'

'I am astonished, my dear, that you should come to the mare's defence. She has proved herself to be both vicious and intractable. By panicking in front of the tortoise, she nearly killed you and your daughter. And by breaking her halter in the evening she forced you to go and look for her under circumstances which could have involved us in a nasty incident....'

'What does all that matter? It's for me to decide. It's nothing to do with you. ...'

Her breath still came in gasps and her voice trembled.

'You gave her to me to see if I could get her here and I did. It was only because the noise of the waterfall prevented her hearing my voice. And she can't stand the awful smell of those Indians. Neither can I, incidentally. I understand Wallis. It's not her fault, it's the fault of this country. And you were going to kill her without even telling me! Oh, I shall never be able to get on with the man you have become. . . . It would have been better if I'd . . .'

Angélique choked. She felt as if she was going to burst into tears, and she turned away and ran off as fast as her legs would carry her in such a state of nerves that she managed to cross the dark, uneven field without tripping once.

She finally came to a halt through lack of breath, and found herself beside a small stream glittering with the reflection of the sunset.

She had run off instinctively in the direction of the light, where the plain and the mountains still glowed with the red of the now set sun. She had turned her back on the night and the noise of the camp, and now in the silence the sound of her own breathing seemed disproportionately noisy to her, as if amplified. It seemed as if the entire grandiose and taciturn landscape had suddenly stood still to harken to this solitary woman regaining her breath.

'I really must be completely drunk,' she told herself .'They'll never catch me drinking their wretched Canadian brandy again! Whatever did I say to Monsieur de Loménie just now? I even think I told him I was sold as a slave in the market in Crete! How absolutely dreadful! And what about Joffrey? How could I have spoken to him like that? And in front of one of his men, too. It had to be Clovis too, the worst of all! Joffrey will never forgive me. But why, why is he so . . . so . . . ?'

Words escaped her. She still could not see quite straight. She breathed deeply and her heart began to beat fast. Her great purple cloak billowed in the wind.

On the horizon small pearly-grey clouds stretched out to form a mass that melted into the summits of the Appalachians. Towards the west the mountains were gradually disappearing in a saffron haze, while the plain stretching out at her feet was growing darker, but it was a darkness steeped in light reminiscent of the fugitive glint of quicksilver; it stretched out, mile upon mile, dotted with a thousand lakes of unbearably brilliant gold. Beneath this cloth, beneath this veil spread by the approaching night, Angélique caught a glimpse of the true nature of this land, abandoned to trees and waters, everlastingly renewing itself yet sterile, and the slow panorama of the mountains as they vanished into infinity made her want to groan like a soul in pain. Not a single puff of smoke made its way slowly skywards to betray the presence of a human being somewhere in all this wilderness! It was a dead land!

She fell to her knees, overwhelmed by it all.

Close beside her some leaves beside the stream gave off a mild, slightly bitter smell which she recognized. She seized one of them and crushed it in her hands.

'It's mint, wild mint!'

And she buried her face in her hands, breathing in the heady, familiar perfume which reminded her of the thickets she had known in her childhood. She felt a kind of exultation as she revelled in the smell and sighed as she ran her sweet-smelling hands over her cheeks and her brow.

She threw her head back. The wind caught her hair and rustled interminably through the woods with their crackling autumn leaves. The earth was growing darker and darker, and the sky had become pale yellow. A star appeared, white and trembling.

Angélique looked round slowly and tasted the wind on her lips.

But when her eyes reached the edge of the wood, a few paces from where she knelt, she turned her head away quickly, and went on examining the distant mountains, her mind a blank, wondering whether she was dreaming. What was it she had seen sparkling through those motionless tree-trunks?

Was it a pair of eyes?

She glanced twice again in the same direction and each time looked back at the dark plain whose lakes continued to sparkle like great sheets of gold interspersed with brown islands.

When she looked the third time her eyes no longer returned to the plain.

There was no doubt about it. There was someone standing just a few feet from her. A tree had become a man, a column of flesh and blood amidst the tree-trunks, but of the same dark impassive colour.

A Redskin stood there looking at her, mingling so intimately with the shadowy forest and standing so completely motionless that it was well-nigh impossible to pick him out from the surrounding trees. He stood amongst them as if amongst his peers. He lived the same vegetable life, with its unseen pulsations, born of the earth, a prisoner of their roots and, like them, the secret, silent, and proud witness of wind and weather. A tree with living eyes. Two agate eyes in the smooth bark.

The sulphur-tinted light filtering through the branches fell on his shoulders, his arms and his hips, throwing his powerful muscles into relief.

He wore a glistening white bear-tooth necklace around the base of his extraordinarily long neck, which was broad as well and very muscular, hung on either side with spherical scarlet-coloured earrings.

His face was short and round, but sharply angular, and his nose, his cheek-bones, and deep-set eye-sockets stood out strongly above a broad sardonic mouth.

His ears were wide-set, large and pointed at the top, and seemed not to belong entirely to the rough-hewn head, but to have been added as an afterthought, with their pendants as ornaments.

Out of the middle of his forehead grew an enormous tuft of hair that thickened until it reached the top of his shaved skull, there to sprout into a tuft of eagle feathers, and black and white skunk tails.

He wore his hair like a Huron.

BUT HE WAS NOT A HURON!

Of this, Angélique was certain. It was this chilling conviction that made her scrutinize the Indian, who was a mere six paces from her, with all the attention one concentrates on a dangerous animal.

But at the same time something inside her refused to accept the face as human, since it did not stir. It was as motionless as a rock, and even the brilliant eyes lost their life, so fixed and motionless they were.

She suddenly felt convinced that the face did not exist, and that her eyes had deceived her.

Then the wind brought his smell to her, the animal smell of an Indian smeared all over with rancid bear fat, impregnated with tobacco and blood, possibly hiding half-dried scalps in the folds of his leather belt.

That smell was certainly real and made her leap to her feet in horror. Still the Indian made no move and she began to back away slowly. Soon she could see him no longer for dusk was falling and darkness had spread over the earth.

Then she turned and ran back towards the fort, fearing that she might feel an arrow strike her between the shoulders.

Astonished to find herself still alive, she reached the outpost without difficulty and found herself back in the midst of the Indian encampment. She was about to give the alarm, 'Iroquois in the offing' but refrained from doing so; she no longer felt certain about what it was she had seen. And yet it had not been a Huron. The Hurons had lived for too long under the shadow of the French, following in their tracks, participating in their wars, camping on the outskirts of their townships, eating their leftovers, praying to their God. . . . They were like jackals, always in groups. They never prowled through the woods like that, as solitary and wild as wolves.

Here were the Hurons, dancing, with their little bells, their plumes and their medallions all a-quiver and, as she went by, they thrust out their dirty hands in an attempt to touch her cloak.

She crossed the threshold of the camp, then the compound, and soon shut the cottage door behind her.

The entire excursion outside the palisade, her meeting with the Indian, all the comings and goings through the shadowy silence, broken by the soughing of the wind and other unidentifiable noises, had had the incoherence of a nightmare. Angélique felt like a person in a dream who, while conscious of certain events, has forgotten who he is and what he seeks. She remembered that she had run first to the right, then to the left through the dusk, as if trying to escape some intolerable menace, that she had thought she had found peace on plucking the wild mint, that she had looked at a tree and had seen that it was not a tree but an Indian, then, on examining the Indian, she had seen that he was not human but the very epitome of hatred, and now she was no longer sure that she had really seen any of these things at all. In the big room the embers were dying in the grate. There was no one there. The impression of unreality continued and for a while Angélique could not remember exactly what it was she had hoped to find. A sound rising and falling hypnotically, going on and on endlessly, brought her back to herself again. She gave a shudder, unable to understand what was producing the noise that broke the heavy silence at regular intervals. Then at last it dawned on her – it was merely Master Jonas snoring in the next room.

Angélique took a deep breath and laughed at herself. Her friends had gone to bed, making the most of their well-earned rustic comforts after weeks of trekking. Everyone was fast asleep, including Honorine, no doubt. On the table she saw a pile of bowls that had been washed up, a witness to the Protestant housewife's concern to leave her house tidy before going to bed. The washing-up bowl was drying in one corner of the room and they had carefully mopped up the water spilled on the floor and cleared away the remains of the meal from the rough wooden table.

A candle set in a candlestick had been placed ready for her with a stick of touchwood beside it. She struck a light and, candle in hand, entered the room on the left. This room, which she had left several hours earlier, was also empty, but someone, possibly Elvire, had discreetly removed her travelling clothes and her boots to clean them, had tied up the curtains of the rough bed and turned down one corner of the blanket as if in preparation for a restful night. Angélique mentally blessed the helpful young woman and knelt down before the fire to stir it into a blaze again.

Her nimble fingers, skilful at all manner of tasks, snapped the twigs and piled up the logs automatically, avoiding the long juniper spikes as she threw a handful into the flames to produce a pleasant smell. The fire crackled and roared up the chimney.

Angélique thought about the man she had glimpsed through the trees beside the stream. She thought about the French who had come from the northern territories, from the cold waters of the Saint-Lawrence, to lie in ambush for them, maybe to strike them down. She thought of her two sons and of their youth so difficult to understand. She thought of Honorine. Would there always be this insurmountable barrier between her daughter and herself which neither of them seemed able to cross? She thought too of her husband and was torn between her desire for him to come to her and her wish to be left alone.

She continued to feel a sense of oppression, but was unable to say precisely why. She held out her hands to the flames.

The flames danced and crackled, and Angélique clung to the things she knew, the things she could still bend to her will, like fire, and wild mint. . . .

The latch lifted and, seeing Joffrey de Peyrac's tall form on the threshold, she was overcome with joy and a hunger for him which sent the blood coursing through her veins, as she said to herself:

'He has come back. He won't leave me. . . . He knows that I need him. . . . And he needs me. . . . How lucky that our bodies understand one another. . . .'

CHAPTER 13

ON ENTERING the cottage, Joffrey de Peyrac had felt a sudden fear that she might not be there. Earlier beside the river she had run away from him so tempestuously; at the time he had considered running after her but had feared that might make her still more angry.

In any event, before joining her he had to post his sentries for the night, sentries of his own to keep an eye on the French sentries. There was to be one of his men to each group of Frenchmen or Indians. Throughout the night, Cantor would play his guitar for the soldiers and sing them some of the local songs.

'*Alouette, gentille Alouette . . . Alouette, je te plumerai . . .*'

The question was, who would pluck whose feathers! Florimond would come and relieve him in the early hours of the morning and, if the soldiers finally decided to go to sleep, Florimond could do likewise, but he was only to doze. These were the orders.

Octave Malaprade was to put himself at the disposal of the officers after they had gone to bed, and Yann le Couennec would take over from him, ready to spring into action at the slightest move on the part of these gentlemen.

Throughout the night Perrot, Maupertuis and his son were to go from wigwam to wigwam amongst the Algonquins, Hurons and Abenakis, chatting with the Indian chiefs, smoking a pipe or two with them, and reminding them of old times.

For they were all good friends, were they not? But it was just as well not to lose sight of one another for a single moment.

At last Count Peyrac was free to return to the cottage and the thought had suddenly flashed through his mind that she might be there no longer.

He had lived so many days, so many years, without her, with the pain of her absence eating into his heart; now they were reunited the idea sometimes seemed incredible to him, and he would begin to doubt whether she was really there or had disappeared once more.

She had become a shadow, a memory, a bitter, torturing memory as in the days when he had thought of her in another man's arms or dead in the Moroccan desert.[1]

He contemplated the empty first room with dismay. Then, seeing a light through a crack in the door on his left and hearing the crackling of a fire, he strode across the room and found her there, kneeling before the hearth, her golden hair spread over her shoulders, looking at him with those unforgettable wide eyes.

He pushed the door to silently and turned the clumsily-made key in the lock.

Then he walked slowly towards her and leaned against the hood of the pebble chimney.

Nothing could separate them, they were both thinking at that moment. Nothing, as long as the mere sight of one another filled them with so urgent a desire to be together, to make love.

She was thinking that she would accept anything in order to have the joy of knowing him there, beside her, standing firm on his long sinewy legs with their high black leather boots.

He was thinking that in order to have the right to take her in his arms, to put his lips on hers, to caress that full, supple form, he would forgive her anything....

[1] See *Angélique and the Sultan.*

She looked up at him and saw that he was half smiling.

'I think that what I had to drink made me very foolish tonight,' she said softly, genuinely abashed. 'Please forgive me for saying more than I really meant. You didn't shoot Wallis, did you?'

'No, I wouldn't dream of distressing you in that way. Still, she is a dangerous animal and I am very angry with her for the dangers she caused you. . . . But I admit that I blundered badly in not warning you of my intention to shoot her; that was a mistake unworthy of a man who once claimed to be a master of the Art of Love. I hope, Madame, that you in your turn will forgive me. For far too long now I have ceased to show women the consideration I used to give them in Toulouse. The Mediterranean teaches one bad habits in that respect; association with compliant, mindless courtesans makes one forget that women are thinking beings. One is tempted to despise them as playthings, objects of pleasure or slaves. . . . Where did you run off to this evening to cool down after you left me?'

'Up on the hills over to the west. I found a stream with wild mint growing by it.'

'Do be careful! It is extremely unwise to go so far from the camp. There is danger everywhere and I cannot be sure of anyone. Please promise me you won't do it again, my love!' Once again a pang of fear shot through Angélique's heart.

'I'm frightened,' she murmured.

Then, looking him full in the face, she summoned all her courage and went on:

'I am frightened. I disappoint you, don't I? I told you I would never be afraid, that you could bring me with you and that I would be strong and a help to you and now . . .'

She wrung her hands in anguish.

'Nothing is going as I expected it to. I don't know whether it is I who have got off on the wrong foot. . . . Everything appals me. I keep on wondering what we are doing in this frightening, dangerous wilderness full of enemies on the prowl. I feel that these enormous distances can only separate us, that this is no life for us, and that I do not have, or no longer have the necessary qualities to cope with it.'

And she repeated:

'I disappoint you, don't I?'

She hoped he would reply immediately, that he would accuse her, that he would unburden himself.

But he remained silent as she watched the firelight play over that tough, furrowed face in which she could read nothing.

'No, you don't disappoint me, my love,' he replied at last. 'On the contrary, I am pleased to know that you are neither gullible nor oblivious of the true nature of things. But what precisely are you frightened of?'

'I don't know,' she replied with a helpless gesture.

For there were too many things and, had she been asked to put them into words, would she have been able to say that the things that made her so uneasy were vague, imprecise things, like the sensation she had had of someone looking at her through the trees? And would she have told him about the Indian she had glimpsed that evening?

She shook her head.

'It's a pity,' he said, 'it might have helped us both for you to know precisely what it is that is frightening you.'

He drew a leaf of tobacco rolled into the shape of a cigar from a pocket in his jerkin. He occasionally relinquished his pipe in favour of something else. She liked to see him smoke as he had in the Gay-Savoir days, and she hastened to pass him a piece of burning twig.

Slowly he puffed the smoke out from between his lips.

'The thing I am frightened of above all,' she went on hesitantly, 'is to find that I have been completely mistaken, and that I am incapable of ever getting used to this land, or to its people. . . . Or even to you,' she added with a smile to soften her words. 'Wives are a nuisance, aren't they, my lord?' And in the smile she gave him he could read the full weight of her passion for him.

He gave a little nod:

'Yes, indeed, a wife can be a nuisance when one is unable to look at her without wanting to make love to her.'

'That is not what I meant.'

'But I did!'

He paced up and down the room in a cloud of blue smoke.

'It's true, my love, you are a terrible nuisance to me. I must keep cool headed and yet when you come near me, no matter what time of the day it is, your nearness excites and disturbs me. I have a terrible urge to go off alone with you, to take you in my arms and kiss you and kiss you, to listen to you speaking to me alone, to look at you. But I have other things to do and I find it very hard not to regard them as of secondary importance whenever you appear. Your voice sends shudders down my spine, and the sound of your laughter leaves me quite distracted. I forget where I am . . .'

In spite of everything he had succeeded in making her laugh, and her cheeks were beginning to recover their colour.

'I don't believe you. You are talking nonsense.'

'Nonsense, perhaps, but it happens to be true, and I take none of it back. What is more, I haven't finished yet. Yes, a wife is a nuisance when not a single man can look at her without marvelling at her beauty and when, however far into the wilderness you take her, she stirs up enemies around one. At Gay-Savoir in Toulouse, I was the master, I was known, held in high regard and feared. Few would ever have dared to set themselves up as my rival. Here, things are not the same at all, and I shall have to teach the people of Dawn-East and those of New France that I am no complaisant husband. I can foresee duels, ambushes and shows of force involving much bloodshed. But who cares! I would not exchange all the torments your presence causes me for the often bitter peace of my solitude.'

He came back and stood towering over her, leaning against the chimney; she sat with upturned face and hands folded in her lap, unable to take her eyes off his dark, admiring face.

'I am greatly impressed by your maturity,' Peyrac continued gently. 'You were an inexperienced little girl when I took you; your mind was as virginal as your body. How much you have been moulded by others since then! You are not the product of my love as I had dreamed you would be, a somewhat Utopian dream in any case, even if we had remained together. But time has passed, and today, you are yourself, that is to say a woman in the fullest sense of the word, a woman with all her mystery. A woman who no longer seeks her own reflection in another in order to know herself. A woman standing alone . . . who belongs only to herself, who has made herself what she is. And it is that fact that sometimes puts a distance between us.'

'But . . . I belong to you,' she said timidly.

'No, not yet, not completely. But that will come. . . .'

He drew her to her feet and, putting his arm round her shoulders, led her over to a map which he had pinned up on the rough wooden wall.

He pointed to several places.

'There . . . towards the north and east, that's New France. In the south you see New England. To the west we have the Iroquois. And I am there, in the middle, with a mere handful of men, do you see? There is only one way open to me, to make allies. As far as New England is concerned, it's already done. As for New France, our meeting with Colonel Loménie-Chambord was providential, because it may lead to an alliance. . . . As for the Iroquois, a year before I sailed for Europe I sent them plenipotentiaries and presents. The Cayuga attack

107

makes me fear that my efforts have been in vain, but, all the same, we must wait and see. Any declaration of war, any fighting would be disastrous to me at the present moment. We must bide our time, consolidate our position. If we manage to get out of this hornets' nest alive, I wager that one day we shall be stronger than the lot of them. And now come, my love, it is time to think of serious matters.'

Laughing, he turned her to face him, clasped her against his powerful chest, then gently let his hand wander over her shoulder, the back of her bowed neck, and the rich curves stretching her bodice, under her arms.

'The Iroquois won't come tonight, my love. And the French will sleep, for they have been drinking, singing and making merry. Their plans to massacre us can wait till tomorrow. One night! Who cares about tomorrow provided we are granted one night more. . . . One night is a whole lifetime!'

He tilted her chin up with his fingers and kissed her proffered lips insatiably. Then he buried her proud, lovely head in his shoulder, and clasped her tightly to him again.

'We are new-made creatures, darling. And so is the world around us. In the past we lived in our palaces, surrounded by riches, and we thought ourselves free. Yet our every act was judged by a thousand cruel, pitiless eyes, the eyes of a petty, jealous society that had run its course and whose bonds held it fast on every side. I was the living proof that it was no easy matter to be different from others in the Old World. Here it's another matter.'

Then very softly, with his lips in her hair, he added:

'And even if we should die, maybe tomorrow, maybe in dreadful torment, at least it would be together and no longer for some futile, pointless reason.'

She felt his hand on her hips, through the stuff of her dress, then suddenly she felt it gliding over her naked breasts, and she saw stars everywhere. Yes, he was right, nothing else mattered, even if they were to die tomorrow, even a terrible death. . . . She was his, subject to his male strength. He had undone her dress, and pulled the top of her shift down over her arms.

'Let me undress you, my darling. One needs to be able to breathe freely when one's heart is gripped with fear of the French and the Iroquois. Now, isn't that better? . . . Let me . . . It is so long since I had the pleasure of unlacing these complicated European clothes. In the East, the women offer their bodies without giving a man any sense of mystery.'

'Oh, don't talk to me about your slave-girls any more!'

'But you only stand to gain by the comparison.'

'That's as may be! But I hate them.'

'I adore you when you're jealous,' he said, tumbling her on to the rustic bed.

And a thought flashed through his mind as it had through hers earlier, about how lucky they were that their bodies were so well adjusted to one another.

CHAPTER 14

IN THE enclosed darkness of their bed where, surfeited with delight, their bodies lay resting, Angélique dreamed a dream. The Iroquois she had glimpsed that evening rose up out of the forest and fixed her with his cruel eyes. The dusk had given way to day and the sun, glittering on his oily chest, transformed it into a brilliant gold breast-plate. His face stood out sharply in the light and the tuft of hair on his scalp, decked with feathers and blown upright by the wind, looked like the crest of a strange bird. He was standing over her brandishing a toma-hawk, about to bring it down on her head. He struck her a furious blow but she felt nothing; then she suddenly noticed that she was holding the dagger that the Polak – the woman who had been her friend at the Court of Miracles, when she had lived among thieves and outlaws – had given her. 'I know how to use it,' she remembered, and she in her turn struck out at him, a swift, sharp blow. And the Iroquois melted away like a cloud.

She tossed about so much in her dream that the man lying beside her woke.

'What is the matter, my love?'

'I killed him,' she murmured.

And she fell back to sleep again.

He struck a light from the flint, and lit a candle on a little shelf above the bed. They had drawn the linen curtains round the bed to protect them from the chill of the night.

In the impenetrable darkness, under the cold pall of mist that had formed over the remote little outpost, presaging the coming of winter, they were alone, as alone as if they were the only people in the world.

Leaning on one elbow, Joffrey de Peyrac lowered the candle to look at his sleeping wife.

She seemed to have fallen back into a deep sleep again. Her outstretched hand had fallen back on the bed and her lips, which a moment before had murmured 'I've killed him', were slightly parted over her light breathing. Cradled in the hollow of their coarse mattress of moss and dried grasses, her body took on a new fullness. As she lay beside him in the abandon of her superb nakedness, the curves of her back appeared more opulent, her breasts heavier, and her beauty had a statuesque quality that her liveliness of manner prevented one from noticing during the day.

In her sleep, she had the full, fruitful curves of an ancient goddess. Her smooth face kept its secrets. Not a trace remained of the expressions which it sometimes wore, appearing as suddenly as flames, revealing for an instant Angélique's secret soul. Nothing of that infinite variety of astonishing feelings: hatred, for example, like that she had felt when she raised herself up that afternoon, her musket smoking in her hand, and he had seen her delicate jaw thrust forward as she repeated in a kind of incantation through her clenched teeth: 'Kill! Kill!'

Nothing remained either of the seductive charm she had displayed that evening, laughing with the men. During the feast, silent and apparently detached, he had allowed jealousy to eat his heart out, wanting as he did to know everything about her; for he had the scholar's obsession with the truth and had never refused to face the facts.

Might it not be better to be a little blind when love with its imperious demands had crept into his very heart?

For his part, what more did he want than what he already possessed? Nothing. He had everything, danger, the struggle, victory and success, and every night this woman's body was his and his alone, in all its lush sensuality.

One of his Angélique's arms was thrown half back like a pale flexible stem opening out above the dark, heady calyx of her armpit.

What more could he ask for himself? Happiness? But this was happiness! The earth had given him all it had to give. But what about her? Who was she? What innocence, or what calculation lay hidden in this fleshy envelope, which seemed the quintessence of every feminine charm? What open wounds lay concealed behind the serenity of her face?

Peyrac brushed her still cheek with his hand, brushed her soft skin. If only with the same caress he could reach her unquiet spirit, he might soothe the hurt he sensed within her. He might make her well again. But she confided so little in him, and when she slept, she seemed still farther from him. She was alone. It was as if the veil that hung over those fifteen years of separation were parting, revealing her as she had been, passionate and vulnerable, swept along by the turbulence of a broken life. Separated from him she had become a flower uprooted by the wind, the wildly oscillating needle of a compass that has lost its North, a heart bereft. He was beginning to understand how true had been her protestations when she had said: 'When you were not there I did not live, I merely survived. . . .' Her life of adventure had served merely to stifle her hunger, to enable her to defend herself.

Although constantly besieged by men, although sometimes carried away by her own emotions, the lengthy periods of continence she had suffered as a woman without a husband, had made of her a woman whose body had grown solitary and often frustrated.

The violent repugnance she had felt over the past few years for love in any of its physical manifestations had changed her without her knowing it, had left a strange mark upon her. They had to begin all over again, to start afresh. But he was the lover she needed. She lay there beside him, a woman who had known many a lover, and yet she seemed possessed of a kind of virginity which he found most attractive, an incorruptible amazon whose unapproachability made her conquest all the sweeter.

He kissed her soft shoulder tenderly, almost religiously, and as she gave a little shudder, he drew away and buried his face in her hair as it lay spread out, smelling of wind and forest.

Her scent was the scent of the lands they had travelled through and, by that adaptability to circumstance so many woman have, she already seemed completely different from the woman he had known in La Rochelle.

The sun had turned her skin golden, and her gestures had taken on a primitive languor. These wild lands had already enfolded her in their mystery.

What would come to pass between her and this wild country?

True women are incapable of remaining outside things; they must enter into them, become involved in them, make them their own.

For his part, neither the Mediterranean, nor the Atlantic, nor the Caribbean had affected him. He would leave his mark on North America, but America would leave no mark on him. . . . Very little at any rate.

But what about her? What would be Angélique's reaction to the New World?

Sleep, my mysterious darling. Sleep! I shall not leave you. I shall stay beside you to defend you.

Outside, a night bird hooted, and its lugubrious velvety cry rang out several times through the night. There was an answering bark of dogs, and Peyrac heard the Indians calling to one another from their birch-bark wigwams. Then silence fell again.

Joffrey de Peyrac sat up. His arms were ready beside his bed, a loaded pistol on the table and his musket leaning against the foot of the bed.

Then he lay down once more, stretched an arm out towards his sleeping wife and drew her to his breast.

One night is a whole lifetime.

In the chill mists of the night in which the great round orb of the moon looked like a watery silver sun, up there on the hillside, in the heart of the dark forest, the Iroquois stood naked and alone, watching the fort, and his catlike eyes glittered between the branches.

CHAPTER 15

THE DAY dawned and the previous day seemed a long time ago. That autumn day in Upper Kennebec which might have echoed to the sound of fratricidal musket shots between the Palefaces had ended peacefully.

This morning, all round the little outpost, smoke rose from all the birch-bark shelters in pure white arabesques into a blue sky.

Angélique, with that recuperative capacity women have, awoke happy, her fears gone. The bed in which he had slept beside her still held the shape of his beloved body and reminded her of the moments of forgetfulness and intensity of living that he had given her. It was like a miraculous dream, and she reached out her hand to touch the empty place beside her to convince herself of its reality.

She remembered that she must busy herself about the house and have an excellent meal prepared.

Angélique was a wanderer. Ever since her days in Toulouse life had driven her from one place to another until she had grown accustomed to feel at home anywhere. She needed very little to create the homely atmosphere she needed around her: a good fire, warmth, a few odd-ments in a bag, a few comfortable clothes, and Honorine's box of treasures. She had liked all the different places she had lived in, but had grown attached to none of them. The tiny room in the rue des Francs-Bourgeois where she had lived with her two little boys held more pleasant memories for her than the Beautreillis mansion where she used to hold such elegant receptions. She had not as many happy memories of her suite of rooms at Versailles as she had of the chimney-corner in La Rochelle, where she used to sit with old Rebecca of an evening, 'picking' a crab they had cooked in the ashes. She even remembered with contentment the stable in the Abbey of Nieul where she had slept with her child, and where the singing of the monks had brought her an extraordinary peace.

Yet, ever since she had found her husband and sons again she had developed a nostalgic desire to have a house of her own, in which she could make them at home and look after them. The natural urge that women have always to go on rebuilding their nest after it has been destroyed was not dead within her. So this morning her head was full of ideas, which she had decided to put into action without even waiting for the French to depart.

She found the Jonases in the next room, peering through the cracks in the little window to see what was going on in the courtyard.

'Dame Angélique, we are not at all happy,' they said, lowering their voices and glancing all about them as if expecting to see the devil himself rise up through the floor. 'It appears that a missionary has come to say Mass for the French soldiers.... A Jesuit....'

As they uttered this last word their eyes nearly started out of their heads and Angélique found it difficult to repress a smile.

There had been a tragedy in these people's lives. As Huguenots of La Rochelle they had sent their two little boys of seven and eight off to school one morning and the children had never come home. They had heard later that the two Protestant children had been imprudent enough to stop and watch a Catholic procession as it went by; for they were curious to see the embroidered chasubles and the gold monstrances. Some worthy souls had seen in their interest irrefutable proof of their desire for conversion and had taken them off to the Jesuits. At that very moment a cart-load of Protestant children who had been removed from the care of their parents was on its way out of the city, and the two little lads had been loaded on to it along with the others. All attempts to find them or even to find out what had happened to them had proved fruitless.

It was not hard to understand the Jonases' fright today. Angélique herself had shared the countless dangers the French Huguenots had lived through, forced as they were to flee a kingdom in which persecution of their sect was growing worse with every day, although she herself was a Catholic, had been brought up in a convent, and one of her brothers, Raymond, belonged to the Society of Jesus.

'You must not get all upset,' she told them. 'We are not in La Rochelle any more. I shall go and see what is happening, but I am quite sure that there is nothing very sinister about this worthy missionary.'

In the courtyard she found something which she certainly had not expected, but which in itself was in no way alarming, namely a portable altar in carved wood gilded over.

Some tall Indians covered in medallions were busy securing it in a wooden packing-case which two slaves lifted up on to their shoulders. Their chief was a tall, thin, supple man, draped in a black bearskin and holding a lance in his hand. His sharp profile with the upper lip standing out over two prominent front teeth gave him the appearance of a sarcastic squirrel.

As she went by, Angélique thought it wise to greet him but he did not return her greeting. Shortly afterwards they left the outpost.

After their departure the courtyard appeared almost deserted. There were still a few traces of the feasting of the night before: ashes and cold logs lay where the three fires had been, and a yellow dog sniffed at some scraps of meat, nibbling at them without much sign of appetite. There was not a bone left behind and every container from the big stewpot down to the bark bowls had been cleared away.

With his red woollen cap pulled down to his eyebrows old Eloi Macollet was sitting smoking on a bench in the sunshine, leaning against the wall of the cottage. He gave her a sidelong glance, like an Indian, and he too appeared not to have heard her greeting.

In a corner down by the store, she found Honorine and Elvire's two little boys rapt in admiration while the youngest of the drummer-boys practised on his drum. He was a puny-looking lad who could hardly have been more than twelve or thirteen, and he literally disappeared beneath his three-cornered hat and his blue military capote. But his skinny wrists seemed to be uncommonly strong and agile, and when he began one of his impressive rolls you could no longer see his drumsticks.

'He has promised to teach us,' said Honorine in great excitement.

The drum was taller than she was but she had not the slightest doubt that she would rapidly master the instrument.

Angélique went off again and shortly bumped into Octave Malaprade.

'Madame, we are not savages,' he told her, 'and we cannot go on living on bear fat. I must think up a menu to include some good Christian food. Could you help me?'

He had been the cook on board the *Gouldsboro* and behaved more like a steward than a run-of-the-mill cook. The inhabitants of Bordeaux are great gourmets. His sing-song Médoc accent which gave his speech a slightly southern touch, called forth memories of *agapes de cèpes à la crème* and succulent steaks coated with the famous *sauce au vin rouge et aux échalottes*, as it is eaten in the taverns of Bordeaux.

In this barbarous country there was no question of their being able to create such masterpieces, but with the imagination of a true artist, Malaprade was already beginning to see how he could make the best of what local products there were.

Angélique and he entered the storehouse together. He told her that he had already taken an inventory of the little cellar, which held only barrels of wine, beer and flasks of brandy.

Angélique would have been astonished to learn that, while she was busy inspecting the stores, she was at the same time irresistibly and quite extraordinarily filling the thoughts of two men as different from each other as Loménie-Chambord the Knight of Malta and his lieutenant, Monsieur de Pont-Briand.

The latter, accompanied by Romain de l'Aubignière and Second-Lieutenant Fallières, was walking back from the esplanade where Mass had just been celebrated.

He caught a glimpse of Angélique before she vanished into the doorway of the storehouse, and stopped dead in his tracks.

'That woman! Oh! that woman!'

L'Aubignière gave a sigh of exasperation. 'Are you still at it? . . . I had hoped that after you had slept off your brandy you would stop making such a bloody ass of yourself!'

'Shut up! You don't know what you're talking about. Are you incapable of seeing that you only meet a woman like that once in a lifetime? Granted, she's lovely, but there's more to her than that. To put it bluntly, one has a feeling with her that she enjoys a good lay and does it well.'

'And you saw that all in a flash, did you?' replied the trapper ironically. 'What do you want to go and fall for a white woman for? You've got Chief Faronho's daughter, and all the savages you want at Fort Saint Francis, where you live like a king!'

'I like the Indian women,' said little Fallières. 'It's funny . . . they've no hair! They're smooth all over like children.'

'Well, I'd jolly well like to feel some hair again . . .'

'Shut up, you lewd lout. You're out of your mind.'

'I've had enough of savages. I want some white skin! A woman who reminds me of the ones I used to lay in the Paris brothels when I was a young man. We didn't half have fun!'

'Well, get back to your Paris then! Who's stopping you?'

L'Aubignière and Fallières burst out laughing; for they knew perfectly well why Pont-Briand kept on re-enlisting with the colonial regiment instead of returning to France. He suffered from sea-sickness and his first crossing had left him with such terrible memories that he had . sworn never to set foot on a ship again.

'No need to go back to Paris if I find what I want here,' he growled, looking defiantly at his two comrades, who had grown serious again. The trapper laid a hand on his arm.

'Listen, Pont-Briand, it's no go, old chap. You're forgetting Count Peyrac. Believe me, he has his reputation too; Castine tells me that he is pretty fond of women and can have Indian women or whoever he wants whenever he feels like it. He is a man who likes a good lay as well, and who does it well. Anyway, well enough to keep a woman happy enough not to care much about others. You only have to see the rapturous way she looks at him. Believe me, you have no chance in that direction. And as for him, he's not going to give up his handsome wench!'

'Wench! But she's his wife,' young Fallières protested, shocked at the coarse, off-handed way the two men had spoken about a woman whom he, from the moment he set eyes on her, had regarded as a great lady, as fascinating as she was inaccessible.

'His wife! That's what *they* say! For a start, they're neither of them wearing wedding rings!'

Pont-Briand was one of those men capable of a total disregard for the obvious, which enables them to bend the facts to suit their purpose and keep their conscience clear. He managed to convince himself more and more strongly that Angélique was free, only too ready to think of her as one of those lovely creatures condemned by common law that the Kingdom of France was accustomed to unload on the colonies, and who could always be picked up in the Caribbean islands. If Peyrac had appropriated her, why shouldn't he? His friends left him and he remained leaning against the palisade, smoking, his eyes glued to the door of the storehouse through which she had vanished.

On the other side of the courtyard Count Loménie-Chambord, seated in front of an upturned barrel he was using as a desk, was reading a letter from Father Orgeval. For it had not been the head of the Acadian mission who had celebrated Mass that morning at Katarunk but one of his assistants, Father Lespinas, and he had brought the Colonel a letter from his superior.

The sun blazed down from a pale-blue sky. It was a day that was to be filled with a multitude of small happenings, which, added together, became something like the light mists of a summer's day building up little by little into thick storm clouds or even a hurricane.

Anxiety and uneasiness lay just below the surface; people haltingly sought contact with one another without daring to come out into the open. Count Loménie, the leader of the Canadian mission, read his letter:

My dearest friend,

It is a great source of sorrow to me not to be able to see you. As I was about to set out to meet you, something unexpected – I might almost say supernatural – happened, which so upset me and brought on such a raging fever that I had to break off my journey and make for the little village of Mobedean, which I reached with considerable difficulty. I am still unable to leave my bed and I still lie here shivering. But I must find strength to write to you.

Our faithful Abenakis, the Patsuiketts and their Chief have come down from the upper reaches of the Connecticut to this village, and are only waiting for a sign from you to join your troops in your holy campaign to exterminate not only the Iroquois in the region but the group of undesirable foreigners who are trying to settle there. You could wind up your campaign with a double victory, and today, which is the feast of the Archangel Raphael, I could not help thinking of you as I read the words of the gradual: 'Raphael the Angel of the Lord took hold of the demon and put him in chains . . .'

When strength is sustained by grace, it has no need of a thousand wiles or a thousand battles to achieve its ends.

Loménie understood full well what his childhood friend, the Jesuit, meant. Peyrac in Upper Kennebec was 'a contemptible, heretical Englishman penetrating in the heart of our land once the way is opened up for him'.

'Now he is chained and powerless,' Father Orgeval wrote, 'thanks to you.'

Loménie tugged thoughtfully at his beard. There was a misunderstanding. . . . It did not seem to have occurred to the Reverend Father that Count Peyrac and his men might not have been arrested. Apparently he couldn't imagine that they might have come to some sort of understanding.

But why had he not come to Katarunk himself, after meeting Pont-Briand, Maudreuil and L'Aubignière two days before? Did the incident of the woman on horseback, whom, in the darkness, they had taken for the apparition of a she-devil astride her mythical unicorn, justify his sudden departure?

It was he, Father Sebastian d'Orgeval who, in the spring of the previous year, had asked for help against the foreigners settling in Acadia.

Loménie almost decided to embark and visit the Jesuit lower down the river. He could be there that same evening and would come back two days later. But he thought better of it, realizing that he should not leave his men nor his Indian allies. Their situation was unstable, explosive, and his presence here indispensable to avoid any incident which might touch off the powder barrel.

'I am anxious to hear your news,' the Father went on. 'If only you knew how pleasing it is for me, my dear friend, my dear brother, to know that you are near....'

Beneath the deliberately cold, peremptory tone of the Jesuit, one had a glimpse at this point of the warmth of affection which was his great charm and the delight of those he counted as his friends. Loménie was one of them, their friendship going back for many years, in fact to their school-days. It was the friendship of two children who had grown up close to each other beneath the dark vaults and the miserable cold of the dawn with its smell of ink and incense, the murmuring sound of the Mass and the recitation of lessons. Sebastian d'Orgeval, a quiet sensitive boy, had found the hardships of life as a boarder hard to bear. Loménie was a contented, gentle, happy lad, and he supported and protected his friend, driving away the shadows that weighed on his childish soul which might well, without this friendship, have been broken. Many a young child goes into a decline and wastes away in the infirmary of a boarding-school.

Then came adolescence and their roles were reversed; Sebastian d'Orgeval developed magnificently, burning with a sombre fire, enduring every manner of mortification and hardship with unshakeable courage, and encouraging Loménie, who was as strong but less fervent, to follow him along the path to saintliness.

Their theological studies had separated them, but the two friends had met again years later in Canada. Loménie-Chambord had been

118

the first to disembark, with another Knight of Malta, Monsieur de Maisonneuve, and they had founded the settlement of Montreal. Indeed, this had influenced his friend the Jesuit's decision to come to Canada. Loménie's letters had aroused a passionate vocation for the conversion of the Indians in d'Orgeval, who at the time was teaching philosophy and mathematics in the Jesuit college at Anneçy.

Father Orgeval had done wonders in the ten years since he came to New France. He knew the whole country, every tribe, every dialect, and had experienced everything, even the torments of martyrdom. Loménie considered his own colonial service to be of little merit and relatively unimportant beside that of his friend. He felt inferior, and sometimes reproached himself for having allowed his passion for a military career to overshadow his religious vocation in which he believed he should have been more single-minded. So he was always touched to the bottom of his heart, when, in the letters they exchanged, a word or a phrase brought him closer to the friend whose exceptional qualities had come to inspire him with a kind of veneration. Now, as he leaned on his desk, he thought of Orgeval's high forehead with its thick tuft of auburn hair. Orgeval had an immense forehead, which was an indication of his extraordinary intelligence.

'This child will never live with a forehead like that,' the teachers in the seminary used to say. 'His intelligence will kill him.'

Blue eyes shone out under his bushy eyebrows, astonishingly clear and deep-set; his features were nobly cut and his nose, which had been broken by the Iroquois, in no way detracted from the impression they made; his broad, full mouth was framed by a beard like that of Christ. This impressive looking man bore the most crushing of burdens with the utmost serenity.

Loménie imagined his pen running swiftly across the piece of birch-bark which he used as parchment, although the hand that held it was shaking with fever. This hand was strangely swollen and pink, the result of terrible burns, and some of its fingers were too short, like those of a leper, while others were blackened by flames and still others stubbed at the ends where the nails had been torn out. His courage under torture had so impressed the Iroquois that they had allowed him to live. When he had recovered from his terrible burns, Father Orgeval had escaped and, after a journey fraught with peril, had reached New Holland and set sail for Europe. In spite of his mutilations, the Pope had granted him permission to celebrate Mass, and the great Jesuit had preached at Versailles and in Notre-Dame de Paris, to a congregation reduced to tears among whom ten ladies had fainted.

On his return to Canada he had been sent to Acadia, a province hitherto neglected on account of its remoteness and the dangers it was exposed to from its proximity to the British territories. On reflection, it would have been hard to find a man more suitable and better prepared for this difficult mission which had so many hidden facets. The presence of Father Orgeval on the banks of the Kennebec and the Penobscot, which were both important waterways, took on a political significance. He had received his instructions from the King in person.

'Without you, without your help, my task would be an intolerably heavy one, and I will not disguise from you the fact that for many a long week now I have been troubled by a terrible sense of foreboding....' the Jesuit's letter went on.

Loménie himself had also been troubled by a sense of foreboding. The weather, which was dry and, when the sun shone, scorching hot against the icy background of winter, accounted for much of his anxiety. For sparks would sometimes flash from the ends of a person's hair, and run crackling over his clothes, irritating like an infestation at the slightest movement. There are certain times in certain seasons when everything seems ready to burst into flames. Towards the end of winter or at the end of summer, one has a feeling of being surrounded by evil spirits. It is the time of sunspots, a time of tragedy, of petty meannesses or bloody disasters. In the towns, a husband whose wife has deceived him will kill his rival, and in the depths of the forest a man will slay his best friend for the skin of a beaver or an otter.

The Governor of Quebec remonstrates with the Bishop because he has not burned incense to him on the feast of Saint Louis, alleging that it was not only his own feast day, but also that of the King of France whose representative he is. A wine merchant empties a whole crate of expensive bottles out of a window on to a sailor who owes him money; little Indian boys in the seminary leap over the walls and run away back to the forest; nuns in their convents are tormented with passion, while at night a devil wanders at large, twitching the feet of the most saintly among them, banging the shutters and raising up before their appalled gaze visions of naked women with flashing eyes, mounted on apocalyptic unicorns....

Count Loménie-Chambord himself remembered one of the phrases in the prophecy of the she-devil of Acadia.

'A very beautiful naked woman rose up out of the waters astride a unicorn...'

A very beautiful woman...

He became aware of the fact that he had never stopped thinking about Angélique de Peyrac. It was as if her face, her presence, were stamped like a watermark over the entire letter he was reading, and he felt intuitively that Father Orgeval, as he had written, had also had her constantly in his mind, although he had never met her. The martyr missionary knew everything from a distance.

Count Loménie-Chambord slipped his hand quickly into the pocket of his military cloak where he encountered his rosary beads. Their contact did him good and he felt calmer again. He must not lose his head. Sitting down at his barrel, he wrote his reply to Father Orgeval:

. . . For the moment a temporal rather than a religious policy seems to be indicated. Let me explain. . . . Warfare does not seem to me to be the only desirable course of action when what one is seeking is peace and it seemed wise both in the interests of Canada and in those of the King. . . . Monsieur de Peyrac has already given us proof of his goodwill by supplying French outposts along the coast of Acadia during the winter. . . . Furthermore, as L'Aubignière, Pont-Briand and Maudreuil had fallen into his hands yesterday, we were forced to parley and to give an undertaking. We should certainly not have succeeded in overcoming his company except with great bloodshed and this in any case did not seem to me essential . . . I am confident in the good faith of this man. . . .

When he had finished he swiftly sanded the wet ink. His orderly blew on the end of a touch-stick to melt the red sealing wax with which the Count closed the folded letter. While the wax was still soft, he pressed his seal into it: two sable towers on a field of gules, surmounted by a sun of or.

Absorbed and preoccupied as he was, he paid no heed to the Indians who were running hither and thither, for he had grown accustomed to their childish excitability.

CHAPTER 16

ACCOMPANIED BY Octave Malaprade, Angélique was finishing her inventory. In the stores at Katarunk there were ample supplies of maize, and salted meat in two well-stocked largish wooden chests; there were also pieces of dried meat hanging from the rafters and even some hams that did not look like wild pig. O'Connell had been going in for pig-breeding, Malaprade said:

'The Irishman in whose charge Count Peyrac left the outpost during his last journey, told me that he raised some pigs brought over from Europe. Four or five of them are still grazing in the forest and we must bring them in to the camp before the first snows. We shall fatten them up for a while with scraps and kill them for Christmas. We should get about five hundred ells of sausages from them, three hundred pounds of pickled pork, with luck ten good hams and a hundred ells of black and white blood-pudding. That should be enough to see us through the winter even if the game gets thin on the ground.'

'That all depends on how many we have to feed, Monsieur Octave. If we have to keep a whole garrison going as we are now . . .'

The man pulled a face:

'That is not the intention of Monsieur le Comte. He told me so only this morning. If I am to believe the information I was kindly given this morning, the gentlemen from Canada and their savages will be leaving us tomorrow at crack of dawn.'

'O'Connell is the big fat red-head, isn't he? He never seems to be there when he's wanted and when one does see him he always looks a trifle bewildered.'

'Yes, he gets a bit bewildered by the intense activity of the Canadian gentlemen and above all of the Jesuit Father who called here this morning. O'Connell has gone off down the river with the Abenaki Indians as far as the mission, where he hopes to go to confession and receive the blessing of the great missionary himself. Now I am a good Catholic, Madame, but I reckon that just at present the most urgent task is to find out how we stand for stores. Winter is coming on and it's no joke wintering in these latitudes even when one has considerable supplies in hand.'

'Have you already spent some time here?'

'Yes, I strung along with Count Peyrac last year.'

As she chatted on with her newly-acquired steward, Angélique continued to list the stocks of food. There were large quantities of dried berries and even some dried mushrooms. The berries were only supplementary items, but by no means negligible when, towards the end of the winter, their weary bodies had grown tired of salted foods and preserves. She remembered the theory propounded by old Savary the traveller, who maintained that there were fewer cases of scurvy on long sea journeys if, failing fresh fruit, a handful of dried fruits was eaten daily.

'We shall soak some in water and put them into tarts or pies. Oh, I

122

know what I need, Octave; I would like some white flour to make a cake or, at least, a good cob of bread. We haven't had any for days.'

'I think there are a few sacks,' Malaprade replied.

Angélique was delighted with her find. But Malaprade frowned when he examined the contents of the sacks.

'We have no more than twenty pounds of white flour left. The rest is barley or rye flour. And, what's more, this was bought in Boston, so it's poor quality badly-ground wheat. Nothing but dust . . . the British, really, they haven't a clue.'

'Never mind, we shall still have a good loaf of bread tonight and we'll use some spruce beer to raise it. . . .'

Octave Malaprade took a calabash and put enough flour in it for their luxurious project. As he went along he wrote down the list of supplies on a piece of birch-bark stretched between two pine twigs. He noted three big round cheeses, barrels of sauerkraut, kegs of oil and pots of fat, dried peas and beans, and on some swinging bails a whole array of neatly stocked marrows and pumpkins.

'We must eat those quickly,' said Angélique. 'These vegetables, which are apparently plentiful in America, soon spoil.'

'That's where you are wrong, Madame. Here, marrows will dry without losing any of their flavour and they can be used far into the winter months, although as food they are rather insipid and none too easy to digest.'

Their tour of inspection had cheered them both, and Angélique felt she would be able to make herself useful in the days to come in dealing with problems of a familiar nature.

But alas! The very next moment she was brought face to face with the realities of her new life. As they left the stores they encountered a crowd of Indians clustering round the door in silence. They had some difficulty in forcing their way out. Malaprade, thinking the Indians might be bent on pilferage, quickly closed the wooden door behind him and fastened the latches.

'If they manage to get in here they will eat us out of house and home! But what do they want? What's got into them?'

He knew a few words of the native language, but his questions received no reply.

Lieutenant Pont-Briand elbowed his way through the crowd to reach them, grabbed Angélique by the arm and set his impressive frame as a rampart between her and the evil-smelling onslaught of the Indians.

'Don't be upset, Madame. I noticed that you were in difficulties. What is going on?'

'How should I know? I don't understand what they want.'

The Indians turned to the lieutenant, shouting all at once with looks that spelt either anguish or ecstasy.

'The legend of your encounter with the tortoise, which is the sign of the Iroquois, has been passed on from wigwam to wigwam during the night. They want to know from your lips whether the Iroquois is really vanquished and whether you have reduced him to bondage. . . . You see, in their eyes, symbols and dreams are more important than life itself. But have no fear, I shall make sure that you are spared their curiosity.'

He spoke firmly to the Indians and they consented to wander off, still talking animatedly among themselves.

Pont-Briand was glad of this opportunity to approach Angélique and to assume the role of her protector. He was aware of the scent of her skin, but she saw through him and disengaged herself from the hand on her arm.

'Madame, I should like to ask you a question.'

'Ask away then.'

'Were you really the infernal marksman that gave me such a rough time yesterday? They tell me it was you, but I find it hard to believe.'

'Well, it's true. Believe me, never have I had to deal with so pig-headed a man. I really thought I would have to break your arm to get you to stop, since I had orders to stop you reaching the other bank. You know, lieutenant, I think you find it very hard to grasp my precise status,' she added with a meaningful look. He gathered that she found his attentions too pressing, and out of place. But he could not bring himself to leave her. Since he had after all come to rescue her from an awkward situation, she stayed to talk for a few moments more, then, with a reserved nod and smile, she left him.

He felt shaken and giddy, as if he were drunk. The air before him trembled and her flashing smile danced before his eyes. What a lot had happened during the past two days! His whole world had been turned topsy-turvy; everything seemed to have a different flavour, a different colour. But why had Loménie refused to fight Peyrac? He, Pont-Briand, would have been the first to lay hands on her, thus acquiring the right to take her as his captive to Quebec . . . to convert her. Have I not also the right to lead a lost soul back to heaven? . . . That way, I could have installed her in my house.

What evil spell had that great black devil with the masked face cast on them all to make them, French Canadians, as gentle and docile as a lot of sheep?

Beware, old chap, beware of evil spells! And what does it matter after all, he told himself, if she is the She-Devil of Acadia and if she does come from hell! I'd be happy to join her there!

CHAPTER 17

WHATEVER APPEARANCES may have suggested, the day dragged slowly on and everyone remained tense.

'What is to become of us?' moaned Madame Jonas tearfully. The arrival of the Jesuit had proved too much for her courage. 'Fetch your children inside, Elvire, they will slaughter them.'

Over the past few days Angélique had developed a considerable admiration for Peyrac's companions. The men showed an admirable spirit of discipline, and by remaining calm as they did, they manifested their confidence in their leader. Yet there were foreigners amongst them: Englishmen, Spaniards, Frenchmen on the run, men who might well have expected to be treated as enemies by those who awaited them at Katarunk. Even so they had entered the fort, heads held high, behind Count Peyrac, and the French had not protested. They had even all made merry together, laughing and singing companionably.

But they kept a constant wary eye on one another. Peyrac had a talk with Monsieur de Loménie, then went and greeted the chieftain of the Algonquins and the Hurons, taking them gifts of tobacco and beads.

The men worked together, and swopped stories.

'I wish they'd go! My goodness, how I wish they'd go to the devil!' Angélique thought.

Meanwhile, one must keep up the little game, keep a wary eye on everything and show no trace of fear or impatience.

She tried to create an everyday, humdrum atmosphere, making a show of settling down among her possessions. But it was difficult, for everyone's nerves were on edge.

Once when she had gone over to the well and was busy hauling up the big wooden, iron-banded bucket, she called Cantor who was standing near by.

'Would you give me a hand, my son?'

To which he replied arrogantly:

'What do you take me for? That's women's work!'

Angélique felt herself turn pale and, reacting automatically, seized the bucket and hurled the entire contents over him.

'That should freshen up the ideas of a great warrior like you, who considers himself too high-and-mighty to help his mother carry a heavy load.'

She hooked the bucket on to the chain again with a clatter and let it down the well, tight-lipped with anger. Cantor was soaked from head to foot and his eyes flashed angrily at her, but Angélique gave him as good as she got.

This furious exchange of glances appeared to strike old Eloi Macollet, who alone had witnessed the scene closely, as wildly funny. He came up with a great toothless grin on his face.

'Bravo, that's the way to bring up the young!'

A crowd of Indians, who had been lolling around doing nothing, rushed up roaring with laughter at the young man in his wet clothes, telling one another what they had seen from a distance and coming to take a closer look at Angélique; they hooted with laughter as if she were undoubtedly the funniest animal in creation. . . . They hustled so close round her that she almost let the full bucket fall down the well and nearly fell in herself.

'Back! Back!' said Macollet. He thrust them back with a few sharp words. 'I'll give you a hand, ma'am. I like to see women with spirit, I do. Oh, these youngsters nowadays, they have to be teached, and that's a fact. They don't know nothing, they don't. I'll carry your bucket for you. There's no shame in that when it's for a lady of your station. And I'm good deal more of a warrior than that little whipper-snapper. . . .'

'Hey, just look at him paying court to a lady,' Cantor shouted at him, his voice breaking in fury. 'You giving lessons in manners, that's a nice one! You who can't even take your cap from your skull, even with ladies present or even at Mass. I saw you this morning, when the priest was saying Mass.'

'My cap is my cap,' the old man replied. 'But if you're as easy to please as all that, I'll take it off for you, my lad.'

'No, don't,' L'Aubignière and Perrot shouted simultaneously. They had been passing by and rushed towards the old man, grabbing his two arms. 'Don't you look, Madame. He has the most hideous skull in the whole of New France.'

'He was scalped when he was a young man,' Perrot explained.

'Near Montreal,' added Macollet by way of explanation.

'It's a rare thing for anyone to survive such an operation. But he did! It was Mother Marguerite Bourgeois who saved his life. But the result is not nice to look at, and he is better with his cap on. Keep still, Eloi.'

'No, I want to give that little varmint a lesson.'
But Cantor had run away to hide his vexation and change his clothes.

The day dragged slowly on under a brilliant sky, and still more slowly a few of the Hurons and the Algonquins began to leave the camp. They had been told that there would be no war and had been given handsome gifts by way of compensation for their disappointment.

Peyrac kept an eye on them from a distance and every time one of the canoes left the shore and began to paddle up-stream, he felt a sense of relief. His shrewd glance travelled from the black wall of fir-trees in the north, to the meandering curves of the river that flowed like a golden snake through the kingdom of the trees then went on its way towards the south-east. For the time being the spectre of war was departing, leaving these vast uncivilized lands to go back to their customary daily round of hunting, fishing, sleeping, and smoking.

The beach was humming with activity again, but this time it was the harmless hustle and bustle of a market day. The natives of the small local tribes, Metallaks, Narrandsouaks and Sokokis, were also preparing to leave, unmindful of the events that had passed them by so closely and of which they might well have been the victims, like all small neutral nations that lie between two opposing, powerful forces.

A thin, happy shout rose through the clear evening air and Joffrey de Peyrac turned in the direction from which it had come. It was little Honorine playing with her friends Bartholomew and Thomas, the little Huguenot boys from La Rochelle.

Peyrac watched her for a moment. She seemed happy, her cheeks were pink and covered in dust, and she had that look of health and rapture seen on children who are left to their own devices the whole day long.

His heart stirred with tenderness towards her. He felt strangely attached to this little illegitimate child, an attachment arising out of the rich complexity of feelings that lie concealed in a manly heart, feelings which they rarely have occasion to bring into play, and among which one would find first and foremost a sense of justice.

Looking at this tiny creature, so particularly weak and unprotected, that had received nothing when she came into the world, not even her mother's love, he felt that in exchange, since she had been placed under his protection, he must give her everything.

He always kept an eye on the child, and could see that Honorine was delighted, now they had reached Katarunk, to be in her own home with her own family, among people who did not merely tolerate her, as they had in La Rochelle where her mother had been a servant. Here she took first place, first place of all, as she had decided in her little head with its bulging forehead, for was she not the daughter of Count Peyrac?

She was the daughter of the man they called my lord as they bowed before him, of the man who was the arbiter of life and death, of peace and of war. Therefore, since she was the daughter of so great a leader, she must be the most important person after him, and her pride in her high rank was apparent in her exhilaration and the little shrieks of joy she gave, for all the world like an inebriated swallow.

All was well. He smiled. Yes, she was the daughter of his choice, for she had been free to choose, had chosen him, and her faith in him was unshakeable.

PART TWO

The Iroquois

CHAPTER 18

THE SMOKY evening had come, with its accompaniment of red fires and lights shining through the cold blue darkness.

The little cottage was suddenly rent by a piercing, hysterical scream.

Angélique was busy setting bowls on the table for the children's supper.

The scream came from the room on the left, her own room, which Elvire had entered a few moments before to turn down the bed.

Angélique thought:

'Here we go, the massacre is beginning!'

And she rushed in with her hand on the butt of the pistol that never left her side.

In the middle of the room stood an Indian holding by one wrist Elvire, who was half-crazed with fear. The Indian was even more hideous and terrifying than the one she had seen the day before on the hillside. His pitted face, disfigured by smallpox, was daubed with soot, as were his naked limbs and body. A scrap of dirty red cloth held his hair so high on the top of his scalp and made it look so dishevelled that he looked just like a porcupine. You could smell him throughout the room.

She thought: 'He's an Iroquois!'

He had placed his other hand across Elvire's mouth and, after a struggle, she fell to the floor in a faint.

Angélique slowly raised her gun, hesitating. The Indian's eyes flashed and he uttered a few stifled words which she did not understand, but which she guessed from his gestures meant that he wished her to be quiet.

'Don't move,' she said to the Jonases who were standing in the doorway.

Seeing that they were not raising the alarm and that silence had fallen on the cottage again, the Indian put his hand to his filthy loincloth and took out a small object which he held out towards Angélique. He signalled to her to approach him, realizing that if he made a move towards her she would be frightened. She stepped carefully forward. The object he handed her was a cornelian ring and she recognized the seal engraved on the red stone as that of Rescator, her husband's seal.

Then something he had said the previous evening came back to her.

'I've got some of the Iroquois leaders on my side.'

She looked questioningly into the savage's slanting eyes.

'Tekonderoga, Tekonderoga,' he repeated in his hoarse, monotonous voice.

'Peyrac?'

He nodded vigorously.

'Nicolas Perrot?' she asked again. He gave a further nod and a glow of satisfaction lighted up his horrible face.

'I will take him this ring . . .'

The Indian clamped his greasy hand down on her arm.

He kept on repeating a certain word on a threatening tone, and she understood that he wanted her to remain silent.

The Jonases were clinging to her.

'Don't leave us alone with this devil. . . .'

'Well, you go then, Monsieur Jonas. Tell my husband that . . . someone wants him. When he sees the ring he will certainly understand. Don't speak to anyone. It seems to me that this Indian is trying to tell us to keep his visit a secret.'

'He's an Iroquois, I am sure he's an Iroquois,' Madame Jonas stammered, falling to her knees beside her unconscious niece.

The Indian, tense and on the alert, still held Angélique by the arm.

When Count Peyrac and Perrot appeared in the doorway, he released her and greeted them with hoarse welcoming noises.

'Tahoutaguete!' exclaimed Nicolas Perrot.

And after a warm exchange of greetings with the savage:

'It's Tahoutaguete, the deputy Chief of the Onondagas,' he said.

'Then he's not an Iroquois!' Madame Jonas asked hopefully.

'Yes he is! and one of the most ferocious too . . . he's a very important man among the Five Nations. Ah, good old Tahoutaguete, how good it is to see you again! But how did he get in?'

'Down the chimney,' said Elvire in a quiet voice as she came round. 'I was in here turning down the bed-cover when he just landed in the fire as silent as a devil out of hell.'

'Yes indeed! I can see that from here.'

Peyrac seemed pleased as he looked at the Iroquois.

'He has brought me back the ring I entrusted to him. It was intended to help me recognize their messenger if one day their Council agreed to parley with me.'

'It looks as if the day has come,' said Perrot, 'but they've chosen their moment badly. If ever any of those Hurons, Algonquins or Abenakis, or any of the French wandering around out there suspected that there was an Iroquois here, and especially if they knew it was Tahoutaguete, I wouldn't give a bean for his scalp.' Then turning to the Jonases, he went on: 'Now listen, you others, you are to go into the next room and get on with preparing your meal. If anyone should come in, say nothing and try to forget you have ever seen this man.'

'That will be difficult,' Elvire murmured as she got up.

Angélique had fetched a bowl of stew and Joffrey de Peyrac handed it to the Iroquois with a twist of tobacco as a token of hospitality, but the savage backed away, refusing vigorously to touch the gifts.

'He says he will neither eat nor smoke before we have conveyed our decisions to the Grand Council of the Five Nations.' The Iroquois went over to the hearth and knelt down. He gathered together the glowing embers that he had scattered in his fall and threw a few small twigs on top of them. Then he took a pouch from his belt that contained some very finely ground yellowish flour and, after tipping a little into the palm of one hand, he uttered a single word as he held his hand out towards Nicolas Perrot.

'Water,' said Perrot.

There was a jug of fresh water standing in one corner and Angélique handed it to Perrot who poured a few drops into the savage's hand.

The man stirred the water into the flour with his forefinger, producing a not very appetizing-looking, transparent dough which he ate in tiny mouthfuls. When he had finished his frugal meal he gave a belch, wiped his hand on his moccasin, and began to speak.

Nicolas Perrot crouched down in the same position opposite him, and listened to him, patiently and amicably, without revealing any of his feelings, as he translated word for word what the savage was saying. Joffrey de Peyrac sat on a stool between them both.

Angélique sat down on the bed in the shadows. These were the words that Tahoutaguete spoke, apparently heedless of the dangers that surrounded him, a lone Iroquois, in the very heart of the enemy camp, to the man his people had nicknamed Tekonderoga, that is to say Man of Thunder:

'Ten moons ago you, Tekonderoga, whom we call Man of Thunder because it appears you can cause mountains to explode, you sent us gifts and two necklaces of wampum. It escaped nobody's notice that these porcelain beads were of inestimable value, the kind one exchanged between great nations, on the occasion of great treaties. So Swanissit made some investigations concerning the Paleface who sought alliance with the peoples of the Long House and cared enough to pay a considerable price for it, such as had never been paid before.

'You had also given me your ring and I spoke on your behalf. And what about the other presents, I asked Swanissit, were they to be disregarded? There were gunpowder, bullets, lengths of red cloth which neither rain nor sun could fade, and cooking-pots that rang beneath your fingers, made of metal so black and so strong that we did not like to use them for our everyday food, but kept them for our dead; there were axes and cutlasses so glittering that one could see one's face in them, and finally, a handful of shells so rare that I know not on what solemn alliance wampum we would ever dare to sew them; and finally, a gun that needs no touch-stick, that hides its spark in its entrails, with a butt inlaid with mother-of-pearl; Swanissit has carried it with him ever since, and it has never betrayed him.

'Furthermore, you promised us a magic powder to fertilize our crops, and you invited us here to Katarunk, to conclude a pact of alliance.

'When he had seen all these things, Swanissit pondered in his heart, and he called together the Council of Mothers and the Council of Ancients and told them that they must reach an understanding with a Paleface who took orders neither from the English, the French, nor the Black Robes, and who was, furthermore, a generous man.

'For Swanissit is very old, as I am myself, and we both know that the peoples of the Five Nations are not alas! what they were. Interminable wars have weakened us, and we spend too much time on fur-trading to the neglect of our crops, so that when winter comes, we are decimated by famine. The young men are for ever longing to be on the warpath to avenge their dead and the insults suffered, but Swanissit said, "Enough of death, or the Iroquois people will cease to be a great people held in awe. Thanks to this heaven-sent, powerful Paleface, we have an opportunity of a breathing space to gather our strength again; for one day he will be stronger than the French in Canada and will unite all the people in peace, as it is sung in our Song of Hiawatha."

'Thus spoke Swanissit and the greater part of the Nation harkened to his words.

'We therefore came to meet you, O Man of Thunder, but what did we find at Katarunk? Our enemies waiting to kill us!'

Nicolas Perrot was not at all impressed by this show of indignation. Sending a delegation to the Man of Thunder had not been the sole purpose of their voyage.

'On your way to Katarunk, did you not make a little detour to the east?' asked Perrot mildly.

'Yes, indeed, we had a small account to settle with some of the Iroquois on the Saint-John river.'

'And did you not also burn down some of the villages in that area and massacre their inhabitants?'

'Pooh! Only a few of the red scum the French make such a fuss of but who in fact don't know how to plant an ear of corn or a grain of sunflower seed.'

'Right then! Let us say that on your way back from your campaign on the Saint-John river you decided to come via Katarunk to meet the Man of Thunder....'

'And what did we find?' Tahoutaguete repeated in anger and despair. 'Was it you, Tekonderoga, who prepared this trap for us to fall into? All our worst enemies assembled here! And I don't mean only those Huron and Algonquin traitors who covet our scalps so that they can sell them at considerable profit in Quebec. But there is also that Colonel Loménie who has made a promise to his crazy God that he will kill us all before he dies, for it is true that nothing can harm him in battle; then there is Pont-Briand who walks silently on the warpath, a Paleface whose approach one cannot hear, although he is as heavy as a bison on the plain; and who else is with them? Oh, how can I bear the sight of those scoundrels? Three-Fingers who was my brother among the Onondagas, and Maudreuil who was a son to Swanissit. They are there, talking of vengeance, they who acted with such treachery! Did not Three-Fingers kill two of our brothers when he escaped from our village, after we had shared the same cooking-pot for over a year. As for Maudreuil, he was a little boy when Swanissit took him in. He was handsome, and a good hunter, and our hearts were filled with sadness when we were forced to exchange him for two chieftains the French had taken prisoner. And now he too has forgotten the kindness we showed him, and the warmth of our hut, and here he is today telling everyone that he seeks to avenge the death of his family, his father, his mother and his sisters whom Swanissit had killed. Nor is this true, for Swanissit has never scalped either a woman nor a child with his hands; and Maudreuil knows this better than anyone else. It was the Palefaces who taught us to kill women and children and what can we, the Elders, do if our young warriors have begun to imitate them? As for me, I am old, and I too shall die in the tradition of my forefathers, without ever having killed a woman or a child.

'When I went to Quebec, how many a time did I hear the French say: "as two-faced as an Iroquois" ... but who has been the more two-faced, us, or those who, like Maudreuil and Three-Fingers, betrayed the laws of adoption by which we had given them security instead of death? Vakia Toutavesa!'

Several times he repeated: 'Vakia Toutavesa', which means: 'It makes me shake and quiver to the very marrow....'

'And what about Black Robe Etskon-Honsi who is at Mobedean with all his preachers and his altar of gilded wood? Why did he come? Did he come to do the Magic?

'And what of Piksarett, the chief of the Patsuiketts, one of our worst enemies, who has the scalps of at least thirty of our brothers hanging on the door of his wigwam? What did he come here for?'

'The Abenakis have made peace with the English and with the Paleface Tekonderoga,' said Perrot.

'But not Piksarett. Piksarett is not an Abenaki like the others. He would break any treaty for an English or an Iroquois scalp! He hears only one voice, the voice of Black Robe. He proclaims that baptism is good for the Abenakis and that it is the God of the Palefaces that brings them victory. Black Robe has him in his power, and Black Robe seeks the destruction of the Iroquois.'

'But Black Robe is not in command of the armies. It is Colonel Loménie's decision whether we fight or not. And the Colonel also wants to make peace with Tekonderoga.'

'But will he manage to hold back his friends the Abenakis? They have been after us now for several days. . . . They even captured Anhisera, the chief of the Oueiouts, and they half cooked him the other evening. He managed to escape and make his way back to us. We are living in holes in the ground and dare not approach your house, for it has been made foul by the presence of these jackals and wolves. Was it you, Tekonderoga, who laid this trap for us?' he repeated in solemn tones.

With Nicolas Perrot acting as go-between, Peyrac explained briefly that he himself had been caught unawares by the French incursion, and that at the moment he was trying desperately to get them to return home before any trouble occurred.

Contrary to what one might have feared, the Iroquois plenipotentiary appeared not to doubt his word in the matter, although he still seemed worried. He had already sensed the truth but the situation was none the less serious for his people.

'We could escape from them more easily if we were on the other side of the river, but we can no longer cross the river. There are too many people around between Katarunk and Mobedean.' Then he crouched even lower and plunged into meditation.

'We are being hunted in the forest,' he went on. 'Do you think we shall be able to escape the dogs on our heels for long?

'Tekonderoga, if you are truly powerful, give us a guarantee that we can cross the Kennebec in safety. . . . Protect us against those coyotes.'

'I think I can get Colonel de Loménie to agree to that,' said Peyrac. 'You haven't done anything reprehensible in the region, have you?'

'We were coming to see you.'

'Be patient until the day after tomorrow. The allies of the French are beginning to take to the river and heading up north. Most of them will have gone by then and you will be able to send a peace delegation to Katarunk.'

Tahoutaguete's face, which looked like a great earth-covered tuber, wrinkled under the effort of reflection. Then he stood up.

'I think that will be well,' he said. 'If our peace terms are rejected and we are unable to cross the river, at least we shall have fewer enemies to fight. Did you say that the tribes are heading north?'

'At least we can hasten their departure as much as possible,' said Perrot.

'Now my hardest task yet remains,' said the Indian. 'I have to convince Outakke, the chieftain of the Mohawks, that he must come to terms with you. You know that every one of the chieftains of the Five Nations has to give his consent before any action can be taken. Well, Outakke will hear none of it. He says that one can expect nothing but treachery from Palefaces, and that not a single exception to this rule exists. He is for war and war only. He wants to launch an attack with his braves on the Patsuiketts, while we attack here.'

'That is madness, and you know it, Tahoutaguete, and Swanissit knows it too. Can't he convince Outakke?'

'You know Outakke,' the man replied sceptically, 'his skull is harder than granite. And he said a terrible thing to Swanissit, which was that he had learned in a dream that you, Tekonderoga, Man of Thunder, would bring about Swanissit's death, Swanissit the great chieftain of the Five Nations.'

'I?' exclaimed Peyrac half standing up, in a burst of anger worthy of the best Indian tradition. 'Is that wretched Mohawk chieftain whom I have never even seen accusing me of treachery?'

'How could you possibly be the cause of Swanissit's death since you are seeking alliance with him? That was Swanissit's reply to Outakke. But we are not easy in our minds, because we know full well that Outakke is friendly with the Spirit of Dreams. . . . We also know that

137

he is a great liar for he told us that he had overheard the Algonquins saying at one of their camps that your wife had triumphed over the symbol of the Iroquois at the Moxie waterfall, thus proving that you are planning our downfall.'

Tahoutaguete's little bloodshot eyes went from Peyrac to Angélique where she sat in the shadows. They felt that he was hoping for some kind words of hope, but that the two serious objections that chief Outakke had presented had gravely shaken his own confidence in the Paleface, the Man of Thunder, whom he had warmly supported at the Council.

'Do the Iroquois want my wife to die?' asked Peyrac. 'Had you and Swanissit and the others decided suddenly to appear before her so that her frightened steed might hurl her and her child into the abyss? No, you did not seek that. But that was what the tortoise did. So you see, I don't hold you and yours responsible for what the tortoise did any more than you should consider my wife, who moved it out of her path to save her own life, responsible for wishing to harm the Five Nations? You know as well as I do that the tortoise is a capricious, dreamy animal, and that the spirit of your ancestors that slumbers within him does not always guide his actions.'

This piece of subtle logic seemed to please Tahoutaguete who, after passing it back and forth several times through the convolutions of his Indian brain, gave his approval by nodding his head several times.

'I always did think that Outakke was a little mad. His hatred leads him astray. Now Swanissit, he is a wise man. He wants to save the Five Nations and has seen that you could help him.'

'I shall help him,' said Peyrac, laying his hand on the Indian's.

He thought it pointless for the moment to ask for explanations of the Cayuga attack in the south.

'Return to the forest and tell Swanissit that he must continue to trust me. I shall do my best to hasten the departure of most of the Indians who are camping around my outpost, and I shall try to obtain a truce from the French officers to enable your braves to cross the river. In two days' time we shall let you know whether the French agree to the truce and whether your chieftains can come to Katarunk in safety.'

The Iroquois messenger rose and, after applying more soot to his face with a piece of charcoal; for his disguise had enabled him to move unseen through the night, he pushed the burning logs to one side with his moccasin and swung himself lithely up into the chimney.

They stood motionless for a long while, waiting for the shouts that would have told of a band of savages hot on the trail of the enemy. But nothing happened.

'That's odd!' said Nicolas Perrot, scratching his head beneath his fur cap. 'What a business! I have the impression that there's going to be one devil of a mess-up before long.'

'I thought that the hostile chieftain Outakke had been seized by the French during a banquet to which he had been invited and that he had been sent to France and sentenced to penal servitude!'

'Yes, he was! But he came back. Monsieur de Frontenac obtained his release and permission for him to return.'

'How ridiculous!' Peyrac burst out. 'Will people in high places never learn that you pay dearer for a mistake than for a crime, and that when one has gone so far as to commit such a crime as that of kidnapping a guest invited to one's table, and of sending a great Iroquois chieftain to ply an oar in a galley on the Mediterranean, one might at least have enough political courage to carry things to their logical conclusion and let him die there. How could they ever have been so naïve as to imagine that once he was back in his own country he would not immediately become their most implacable enemy? How could one ever expect him to forget the way he had been treated?'

'Who is this man Outakke?' Angelique asked.

'A great Iroquois chieftain, of the Mohawk nation,' Perrot explained. 'He has led a most unusual life. As a child he was adopted by Monsieur d'Arresboust, who paid for him to be educated at the seminary in Quebec. Unlike the other Indian boys he was a serious lad and good at his studies. Even now he still speaks excellent French, which is a rare thing among the Indians. But when he grew up he disappeared and it was discovered that he had become one of the most ardent instigators of hatred for the French among his people. He himself tortured some of our missionaries with almost unbelievable refinements of cruelty. The fact is that this man Outakke is a wild animal.'

Angélique recalled the impassive face with the scarlet earrings which she had glimpsed at the edge of the wood, from whose eyes had shone such fierce hatred.

'What is he like?' she murmured. 'I mean what does he look like?'

But no one heard her. . . .

CHAPTER 19

OUTAKKE, chief of the Mohawks slipped through the sunny forest, treading silently between the branches.

Heedless of brushwood, roots, or intermingled branches, he strode on through the thick rampart the forest ereects against living creatures, passing through it as a spirit might pass miraculously through a wall; nothing halted his progress, or the rapid pace of his tough, close-knit calves, the skin of which he had once slit open in order to remove fat so that only his tireless muscles might remain to thrive and develop alone.

He was crossing the Abenaki forest, an enemy forest, but one he knew, for he had ranged all the forests, ever since he was a young brave, tracking down Hurons, Algonquins and Frenchmen.

On he went, crossing streams, rivers, skirting lakes, climbing abrupt cliffs, following the crests of the mountains with their jutting rocks and stunted pines. Then he came down again into the darkness of the overhanging leaves where the trees glowed purple and gold.

He thought of his brothers, the chieftains of the Five Nations, whom he had left behind, crouching like frightened rabbits as they listened to the words Tahoutaguete had brought them from Katarunk. No, never would he join them in making peace with the Paleface. . . . For he was not to be taken in. He could be deceived no longer. It was in vain that he had tried to warn them. Oh foolish brothers! The Palefaces had made a mockery of him, even though he, Outakke, had seen them in a dream, their heads covered in blood.

They laughed at him when he reminded them that Tekonderoga's wife had pushed the sign of the Iroquois out of her way. And yet he, Outakke, had seen her in flesh and blood, in the falling dusk, seen the white woman kneeling, doing homage to the God of the Earth. No, she had not been praying as the Palefaces pray, shutting up their fervour within them and not allowing it to escape. She had prayed by crushing leaves of mint in her hands, lifting her hands to the sky, then rubbing them over her face, while she closed her eyes and her face was aglow in the setting sun. Ever since he had seen her he had felt a heavy weight of dread on his heart. Then he strode rapidly across an open space devastated by fire, and his eyes wandered over the wilderness of forest lands, mountains, strings of lakes and winding rivers that made up the bleak yet splendid landscape of Upper Kennebec. He wondered if this area had ever known such traffic as in the past few days, in which the Man of Thunder had arrived with his pack of horses and his women-folk, his soldiers dragging their cannons, and had joined the Canadians from the north with their red allies armed with bows, lances and tomahawks, while from the south had come the Patsuiketts from Connecticut and the Etchimins, all of them Abenakis, and enemies of the Iroquois, along the blue-black Kennebec river. And at their head, leading their flotilla, had come Black Robe with the eyes of fire, the Jesuit Etskon-Honsi.

And finally this great crowd had converged on the outpost of Katarunk. What could be their object, if not to destroy the Iroquois?

Outakke plunged into the forest again.

He thought of the white woman who had encountered the tortoise along her path and who had not turned away.

And as he lifted his eyes towards the sun which darted its burning shafts between the tree-trunks he felt a kind of dizziness and a pain in the pit of his stomach. It might only be due to the fatigue of hunger, of long marches, and of warfare which, for the past three months, had formed the fabric of his life; but the pain might also have come from the memory of what he had experienced when, hidden among the trees, he had seen her approach, a strange, disquieting spirit, decked in her flame-coloured cloak. It had given him a horrible sensation in which he thought he had recognized fear and uneasiness at some strange, new thing that defies understanding.

Hunger made his head swim slightly, giving him a supernatural and sublime insight. His mind became detached from his body and floated before him. His spirit was like an intoxicated bird that went before him, wailing in despair. This must be how the lost souls wailed. His soul wailed because of the everlasting temptation created by the Palefaces, the eternal seduction that brought the Indians to the feet of those treacherous, coarse brutes, with the ever-living hope that this time it would be He, the Ancestor-with-the-white-face, bearer of the torch of glory, whose coming was foretold by every Indian priest and by the most ancient legends of the Cult of Birds.

How much longer must you go on, before you realize that it is not He, that it never is He?

Instead it is the False Messiah, as the Black Robe would say. The Ancestor-with-the-white-face did not exist, he would not come. . . . What weakness was it that brought Swanissit back to the feet of an illusion, there to seek greatness, strength, victory, and protection, and to receive nothing but poison?

Have you not received enough musket shots, O Indians, have they not let you swill enough of their fire-water that destroys the forest? But Swanissit the wise man, Swanissit the hero, still hopes against all evidence, and against all experience. He still hopes in the Man of Thunder.

And Outakke himself, making his way to spy on the Paleface outpost, did he not hope too? He too, alas!

To escape from the temptation of the Palefaces one would have to kill them all, to kill their soul. But they had no soul! Their soul was a beaver skin....

The sun was beginning to go down, shooting great golden shafts between the trees. The Iroquois stopped, and sniffed the surrounding air.

He hid behind a tree and soon caught sight of two Abenakis. They were Patsuiketts, members of a tribe that had come from the upper reaches of the Connecticut, who had tricked their way into the land of the Children of Dawn. They had long noses, protruding rabbit teeth, and short chins. Their skin was the colour of red clay, they wore their hair in plaits, and their topknots were so badly tied that it was hard to know where to grab them to 'do their hair' for them.

The Iroquois stayed hidden, looking at them with scorn as they passed by a few paces from where he stood. Their long hooked noses were inclined towards the ground; they were following a track.

That track would lead them to the place where the five Iroquois chieftains had recently held their pow-wow. Although Tahoutaguete had taken care to destroy his tracks from time to time, the Abenakis would undoubtedly see them, for they were even better trackers than coyotes, probably thanks to their long noses. The two men would find the place where the pow-wow had been held, and would certainly notice the scent of their enemy.

The Iroquois glided after them like a furtive shadow, slipping from tree to tree, and, when he had come up behind them, stove their heads in with two blows of his tomahawk, so perfectly aimed and so deadly that the two redskins fell to the ground without a sound, their skulls split open. Heedless of their bodies, even of their scalps, the Iroquois went on his way.

As he reached the approaches to Fort Katarunk, the sunset was casting a red, powdery light across the open space that men had wrested from the forest, at the river's edge.

He heard the neighing of horses and was so startled by the unfamiliar sound that a great shudder ran through him, shaking him to the roots of his being. He stood there for a long time, as if in a trance, listening to the distant sounds through which he could now make out a new one.

Without ever having seen him, he hated the Paleface who had just come, for he was yet another to hold out to the Indian people the promise of support and hope, a new venture that could be their salvation. And yet he knew that all that was nothing but a mirage.

How could he reach the soul of the Paleface, if he could not get rid of him by force, before he deceived them yet again?

At the risk of being discovered by one of the Abenakis, or a Huron, or of being dislodged from cover like some common animal by the dogs that stood yapping over there at the river's edge, the Iroquois remained where he was, as if under some spell.

This was where he had seen the white woman kneeling among the sweet-smelling plants, with her hair flying free like feathers in the shades of the night.

'Oranda! Oranda!' he murmured. He was calling to the Supreme Spirit who lives so closely intermingled with created things and communicates his strength to them.

He could hear the stream sobbing and the heat intensified the warm scent of the mint.

Then he reached his decision:

'Tomorrow I shall come back here. I shall call the white woman, and when she comes, I shall kill her.'

CHAPTER 20

A HALT had been called to the exodus of the Indians. A message had been drummed out, telling them that two Patsuiketts had been found in the forest, their skulls split open.

There was no doubt that an Iroquois was responsible.

Nicolas Perrot waxed eloquent in an attempt to prove to the Hurons and the other Algonquins that the affairs of the Patsuiketts were no concern of theirs. They were not even Abenakis like the others, he explained, for their name meant those-who-have-come-by-trickery. They were in fact strangers, who had come from the other side of Connecticut, and had infiltrated amongst the Children of the Land of Dawn to raid their hunting and fishing grounds.

Let them sort things out with the Iroquois, he told them. Their numbers were so small that there was no point in the fearless warriors from the north setting out to chase the offenders on their behalf. The Iroquois themselves were lying low at present, not daring to attack the powerful tribes gathered together at Katarunk. It was not even worth digging up the war hatchet that had been buried by Onontio, the Governor of Canada, for the sake of a handful of squabbling Iroquois and Patsuikett scum.

As he orated, poor Perrot could not help having an uneasy conscience with regard to the Patsuiketts; for they were in fact the best fighters and the best Indian converts in the whole of Acadia. Although to some extent intruders, they were nevertheless one of the tribes that showed the greatest devotion to the Catholic missionaries.

Count Peyrac had spoken to Loménie and told him that the Iroquois were in the forest asking for a safe passage across the Kennebec.

But the incident of the two murdered Patsuiketts put the whole issue in the balance again.

Nevertheless, Peyrac's orders were categorical:

'Let the Patsuiketts fight it out with the Iroquois farther down the river if they want to avenge their dead. As far as I am concerned, I don't want Katarunk involved in anything, neither my own people nor the others who are here at the moment. The French have a deplorable habit of getting involved in the endless inter-tribal quarrels of the Indians with disastrous consequences to their schemes of colonization,' he told Loménie, who was still hesitant.

Loménie agreed, and confined himself to sending a small group of Etchimins south in case Father Orgeval required any help.

All the white men made the most of the hatred the other Abenakis felt for the Patsuiketts, and towards the end of the afternoon the atmosphere had grown less tense. Laden with gifts, the Indian chieftains decided to go home, leaving the Patsuiketts and the Iroquois to their fate.

Only Baron Maudreuil disagreed and wanted to launch an attack on the enemy.

'And what if Father Orgeval and his catechumens are attacked?' he asked passionately.

'The Iroquois have said that if we allow them to cross the river without hindrance, they will undertake to return to their own lands without causing any trouble amongst the people they encounter on the way,' Peyrac replied.

'And to prove it they've started by killing two Patsuiketts.'

Peyrac had to admit to himself that he could not explain this act of violence after the conversation he had had with Tahoutaguete on the previous evening.

'You'll get to know them,' said Maudreuil sarcastically. 'There is nothing but double-dealing and treachery in the mind of an Iroquois.'

Loménie called him to order. The Canadians were too prone to forget that their Governor had signed peace treaties with the Five Nations....

'Treaties mean nothing to scum like that,' the other man replied.

And he went on, his blue eyes flashing: 'War, war to the bitter end! There can be no other solution between the French and the Iroquois.'

In spite of all this the army of redskins went on with their plans for embarkation, and in the evening the women and children who had gone off to hide in the woods in preparation for the fighting, returned to the camp and hung their stewpots over the fire for the evening meal.

It was then that someone noticed Madame de Peyrac's absence.

They searched everywhere for her, hunting high and low through all the buildings and the compound. They shouted her name across the burnt-off clearings and along the banks of the river.

A sense of disaster seized upon them all.

Angélique had disappeared.

CHAPTER 21

THE FEELING had crept over her in the strangest way when she had been alone in the cottage; an uneasy feeling that weighed heavy on her heart.

Then she had suddenly felt an urge to go back to the hillside behind the fort and pick some mint.

She had to put the persistent feeling out of her head several times, then in the end she began to feel a little better.

She had nothing special to do and seemed incapable of settling down to any particular task so she leaned up against the window and looked through the little parchment panes, although she could make out nothing but hazy shadows coming and going across the courtyard.

She was thinking about her younger son Cantor's character and his moods, for he had been in a sulk with her ever since she had thrown the bucket of water over him. It had never been easy to know what he was thinking, even when he had been a curly-headed cherub. But now that he had grown into a strong, sturdily built young man, with that healthy, somewhat rustic good looks that she had known in some of her brothers, he had become still more difficult to deal with.

Angélique tapped her fingers automatically against the small parchment squares as she remembered the way Cantor had looked at her. His eyes were those of a girl set in the body of a young athlete.

'What is wrong, my son? What is wrong, young man?' she said softly to herself. 'Have we already nothing more to say to each other? Do we mean nothing to each other any more, although we are still mother and son?'

This thought echoed a question which she had often asked herself without knowing how to answer it, ever since she had found her two sons again in Gouldsboro.

'Of what possible use is a mother to two grown lads of fifteen and seventeen, who for so long have learnt to do without one?'

There was a loud bang on the door followed by the appearance of a happy, smiling, and sun-tanned Florimond.

Angélique, whose hand had leapt to her heart, asked him whether he remembered that he had been the best-mannered page boy in Versailles, and if he could not manage to adopt less military habits when he came to see a lady, even if only to spare her pointless distress.

A bang on the door so often meant soldiers and heaven knows what, bringing nothing but trouble to people.

Florimond agreed good-naturedly that his travels, and in particular his life as cabin-boy on a merchant vessel had rapidly put an end to the good manners of drawing-room and court which his tutor the Abbé had inculcated into him. It was not his fault; he always had been a scatter-brain.

And if the manners he had encountered in New England had been more formal than on board ship, they still lacked grace.

Here at least people didn't add to life's difficulties by silly bowing and scraping. He pointed out shrewdly that the thickness of the wooden doors in a forest outpost made it impossible for one to scratch with one's little finger nail like a well educated damsel brought up according to the principles of honourable civility, because one would risk having to stand on the threshold for a very long time before being heard.

Angélique laughed and agreed with him. She watched him with pleasure as he moved back and forth through the room, thinking what a splendid lad he was now, and remembering all the worries she had had about his delicate health when he had been small.

He had done his hair like Romain de l'Aubignière and Baron Maudreuil, and wore it long, held by a pearl-studded headband, topped with feathers and fur tails, which suited him extremely well.

He too was handsome, as handsome as Joffrey de Peyrac would have been had he not been disfigured by a sword-cut in his youth.

Florimond was almost as tall as a man now, but his smile was still the smile of a child.

He told her he had come to have a talk about Cantor. He admitted that his brother was pig-headed, but that he was kindly and plucky, and that just at present, he was 'having difficulties'. Florimond did not elaborate on this point.

Angélique felt touched by the concern showed by Florimond both for his brother and herself.

She assured him that she had nothing whatever against Cantor, but that they must both try to reach some kind of understanding.

After this they had a friendly chat together and Florimond told her of the plan he had in mind. He said he wanted to take advantage of the advance his father had made into the hinterland of America to take an expedition still farther towards the west where he hoped to discover the China sea passage for which men had been searching for so long.

He had his own ideas about the matter, and had not yet mentioned it to his brother.

It was better to wait for the spring.

Evening was falling. As she began to prepare the lamp and fix candles in the candlesticks, Angélique went on talking with her son. Then suddenly the memory of the dream she had had in which the Iroquois had stood brandishing his tomahawk over her, came back to her so vividly that she thought she was going to faint.

Seeing her grow pale, Florimond stopped short and asked her what was wrong.

She admitted that she did not feel well, she felt stifled. She would go out for a bit and enjoy the cool of the evening air. She would go and pick some mint up there by the spring, for soon the frost would blacken the delicate leaves and they would be no use for making potions. Angélique spoke like one in a dream. It seemed essential to pick the mint and she was surprised to find that she had forgotten to do so, and only to have remembered it at this late hour.

She threw a woollen cloak over her shoulders and picked up a basket.

On the threshold, she had a feeling she had still forgotten something, and stood looking at Florimond for a while, who, quite unperturbed by her abrupt departure, was pouring himself some beer.

'Florimond, would you lend me your cutlass?'

'Certainly, Mother,' he replied, with no sign of astonishment.

He handed it to her; it was a blade as well cared for as you could hope to find in the possession of a boy of seventeen who already considered himself an experienced hunter and a practised trapper.

The double-edged blade was razor sharp, and its polished handle, the grip of which was carved, fitted comfortably into the hand.

'I shall give it you back presently,' Angélique said, and she hurried out of the room.

When they began to search for her a little later, Florimond was playing the flageolet in the kitchen, and watching Monsieur Malaprade making a cake with wheat flour, sugar and vanilla, a cake such as he had not tasted since his childhood. A bit of elk fat had to be used instead of butter, which was something unknown in these parts.

When Florimond was questioned he told them that his mother had gone to pick mint up on the hillside near the spring, and that she had borrowed his cutlass.

He was surprised to see his father give a start and look at him in horror.

'Quick,' he said to Nicolas Perrot. 'Let's get up there. I am sure she is in danger.'

CHAPTER 22

Angélique had climbed up the hillside between the rows of felled trees.

She had crossed the de-forested zone and continued on up the grassy slope.

Then at last she saw the spring. It was just like in her dream, as the sun was still shining brightly up on the slope.

And she knew that there was a presence there, as there had been the day before, still invisible, though undoubtedly there, even though on this occasion she could see nothing between the tree-trunks. The undergrowth hummed with swarms of flies, the stream babbled and everything was calm.

But the Iroquois was there.

She also knew that it was too late to turn back and that her dream must become reality.

The slightly strained feeling of nerviness that had brought her this far now left her, and she felt an old familiar strength welling up inside her, the strength that came before the fight. Many a time had she felt it, particularly when she had had to defend her children, dagger in hand. She had experienced on these occasions such a sense of inner calm that afterwards she would remember these moments as some of the most exalting in her life.

She took Florimond's blade in her hand, and, hiding it in the folds of her skirt, went on to the edge of the stream, where she knelt down.

And the hidden watcher, seeing her with her back towards him, apparently unsuspecting, had not expected to see her suddenly turn to face him as he leapt forward.

She saw him, a dark shadow, thrown into relief against the setting sun, with tomahawk raised, his tuft of hair transformed into a brilliant crest like that of a huge bird of prey, immense and silent as he plunged down upon her. She twisted out of his path and he tripped, missed his aim, and fell heavily into the leaves at the edge of the stream, brought down by her hand on his ankle. His tomahawk fell from his hand and almost immediately he felt the sharp point of the knife against his throat.

All this had happened with such extraordinary speed, without a sound, without even a noticeable change in their breathing.

Yet, as she was on the point of killing him, Angélique hesitated. Her full weight bore down on the prostrate Indian, and through the slanting slits of his eyelids his brilliant black eyes were witness to his incredible astonishment.

The Iroquois could not understand how so strong, so skilled, and so invulnerable a warrior as he could possibly find himself at the mercy of a woman, and a white woman at that! The spirit was utterly knocked out of him, and only began to revive when he considered the possibility that it was not a real woman, but a superior, doubtless a divine being. Then he began to breathe again, for in this case he could admit his defeat, which was no longer a disgrace.

His voice came hoarse and low:

'Woman, spare my life!'

During her moment's hesitation before slitting his throat, he could have attempted to struggle, but he seemed to have given up all idea of doing so.

'If I spare your life, you will take mine,' she murmured.

Her soft musical voice trembled and went straight to the savage's heart. He was overcome by an almost mystical feeling of jubilation.

'No,' he replied fervently. 'That I swear by the Great Spirit. If you are an incarnation then your life is sacred, and henceforth no one can destroy it.'

She noticed that their exchange of words had been in French.

'Are you not Outakke, the chief of the Mohawks?'

'It is even so.'

Then Angélique released her hold on him and stood up slowly. The Iroquois rolled slowly over on to one side, never taking his eyes off her, then he too stood up, as supple as a cat. He made no attempt to pick up his tomahawk, but stood there empty-handed, motionless, looking at her.

'And you, you are Tekonderoga's wife, are you not?'

And, as she appeared not to understand, he went on:

'The Man of Thunder. The man who blows up mountains, the man the outpost of Katarunk belongs to?'

She nodded in affirmation.

'Then take me to him,' he said.

The men who strode swiftly up the hill, guns in hand, rushing to Angélique's rescue, saw two silhouettes coming towards them, not very clear at first, for night was falling on that side of the mountain.

They recognized the young woman, but their feeling of relief was rapidly mixed with suspicion of the man who accompanied her. They stood still, alert and wary. Many of them experienced that strange feeling of fear and awe that men must have felt, in days gone by, who witnessed some legendary saint returning from the mountains trailing behind her some monster, some dragon, some Tarasque in chains, finally rendered harmless.

For it was evident that the man who followed her was no common creature; there seemed to be in him the daunting heat of the vanquished monster.

It was indeed the breath of the fire-breathing, all-devouring dragon that swelled his tattooed chest and made his dilated pupils glow like red-hot coals.

And the scent of the savage that emanated from him, the reek of the lair and of guilt seemed more pungent and more stifling by contrast with the lithe figure of the woman who walked before him. Some of Peyrac's men, for all that they were hardened sea-dogs, started back in dismay. The Metallak Indians, who had joined the party, turned on their heels and ran off as fast as their legs would carry them to seize their weapons and position themselves for an ambush. Back at the camp, the women, warned of his approach, snatched up their children, cooking-pots and food, loaded them on to their shoulders and made off once more for the forest, with their dogs, which did not even bark.

'This is Outakke, chief of the Mohawks,' said Angélique, introducing him. 'He is alone and wishes to parley with you. I have guaranteed his personal safety.'

They stood in silence looking at the indomitable leader of the Mohawks.

Outakke wanting to parley. . . . This was inconceivable.

But those who had already met him, recognized his thick-set body, that seemed to be inhabited by a fierce, controlled passion giving an impression of vast strength.

It was indeed he.

They recognized him by his way of making his hair and plumes quiver spasmodically, as if they had been set on end by a series of terrifying lightning flashes, and were as stiff and hard as the fur of an enraged or terrified animal. Outakke the Mohawk always created an atmosphere of drama around him.

Young Baron Maudreuil spoke a few words in Iroquois, to which the Indian replied with a grunt. Maudreuil gave a start:

'He says that Swanissit is with him. . . . I thought as much. I followed his tracks. There's no mistaking the smell of that fox. We've got them at last, these Indian savages!'

'Hold your tongue,' Nicolas Perrot snapped, 'you are forgetting that you must never insult a plenipotentiary.'

'Him, a plenipotentiary! Not him, he's God's worst enemy about to enter our camp, and I would not trust a single word from his mouth.'

The Iroquois remained impassive, then he spoke, and they were surprised to hear him express himself in guttural but almost perfect French.

'Where is Tekonderoga, the Man of Thunder? Is it you?' he asked, turning towards Peyrac. 'Yes, I recognize you. I, Outakke, chief of the Mohawks, greet you. Swanissit, the Seneca, chief of the Five Nations, wishes to have peace with you. I have come in his name to ask for your alliance, and to ask you to prevail upon the French to allow us to cross the Kennebec.

Count Peyrac raised his hand to his hat, whose black and red plumes were bending in the wind, removed it, and bowed low to the savage as a token of respect and welcome.

'I knew,' Outakke was subsequently to relate, 'that the Palefaces reserved that kind of greeting for their King. And yet that was how this white man greeted me, and my heart began to glow as if the fires of friendship had been kindled within it. . . .'

Some hours later Outakke set off again, bearing proposals for an agreement to Swanissit. If the party of Iroquois were allowed to cross the river without hindrance, the chiefs must undertake not to molest any of the Abenaki or Algonquin peoples they might encounter on their long journey home.

'But why should you Frenchmen be concerned about those red foxes?' the Mohawk asked scornfully.

Maudreuil remained adamant, and even the two lieutenants Pont-Briand and Fallières wholeheartedly supported him when he protested:

'You'll see, they will give undertakings, and will keep none of them.'

The allied leaders were also displeased.

'We came to make war,' said the Huron chief, 'and now that the enemy is at hand, there is talk of nothing but treaties. . . . What will our people say when we return without a single scalp?'

Loménie stood firm. To obtain an undertaking from the Iroquois that they would go home without causing any devastation on their way was far better than letting one easy victory reopen the series of bloody feuds which had been going on for nearly a hundred years and which Monsieur de Frontenac had been very anxious to see ended.

'Don't forget that the hatchet has been buried between Outakke and the Five Nations,' the Colonel repeated.

'We do not forget it,' the Iroquois replied. 'We have not attacked the French for a long time now.

'But you have attacked the tribes friendly to us. . . .'

'We have not buried the hatchet with any other tribes than the French,' the Indian replied craftily. 'What concern is it to the French?'

When the men had begun to parley, Angélique had wanted to withdraw, but the Mohawk chief had lifted his hand to stop her.

'Let her remain!'

His tone was peremptory, angry, insistent. No one could guess what prompted him to demand the presence of the white woman at the war-council. There was some mystery here, and people were left wondering whatever could have happened up there on the hillside, and surreptitious glances were cast in Angélique's direction, with more than a hint of trepidation in them.

She was beginning to think that things were getting complicated and that on balance she would have preferred to stick to her cooking and household tasks. A sick headache throbbed in her temples and she ran her hand over her forehead in a vague kind of way. She could not begin to see how she would explain to her husband what lay at the origin of her encounter with the Mohawk chief.

Occasionally her eyes fell on Outakke's tomahawk, which now hung from his belt, and the sight of this terrible weapon which had been raised against her made her shudder in retrospect with a fear she had not felt at the time.

When the Iroquois had gone off in the direction of the forest, she went to her own room; for she did not wish to join in the buzz of comment on what had happened; there she got into bed and fell into a deep sleep.

When she woke the following day, she felt better.

She saw that her husband had slept beside her, but he had already gone. She had been totally unaware of both his arrival and his departure. She still kept wondering what she would say to him, coming first to the conclusion that she should say nothing and then that she should ask him to give her the benefit of his experience in an attempt to understand all the strange and disturbing things that had happened. After seeking to kill her, why had the Mohawk manifested this sudden desire for loyalty and alliance that had led him to follow her.

As soon as she was ready she went out and ran over to the small corner bastion from which one could survey the surrounding country-side while remaining in the cover of the palisade.

The gates of the outpost were closed, but as soon as the arrival of the Iroquois was heralded by smoke signals from the neighbouring hills, they were opened again, and both Count Peyrac and Loménie-Chambord went out on to the esplanade with Peyrac's soldiers and armed men behind them.

Their Indian allies came out of the forest where they had been hiding, armed with bows and tomahawks, and gathered round the out-post, but in silence, like a reddish tide.

The Jonases and the children had joined Angélique on the platform, where they all stood looking with interest between the points of the rough-hewn stakes.

At last the Iroquois appeared round a clump of willows beside the river. There were six of them, half naked, and they moved slowly along the stony bank, apparently heedless of the armed throng that awaited them; then, when they reached the beach, they lined up in front of the outpost. They were the Iroquois chiefs.

Angélique had no difficulty in recognizing Outakke the Mohawk with his earrings made of inflated bladders painted vermilion.

Beside him stood an old man. His hair was grey and full of eagle feathers. His body was spare and his strong muscles stood out like strands of knotted rope beneath his leathery yellow skin. His long face, with its little wrinkles round the eyes and mouth, wore a haughty, intimidating expression. Innumerable tattoo marks outlined his ribs, his breasts, and his collar-bones.

Angélique guessed that he must be Swanissit, chief of the Senecas, the supreme leader of the Iroquois league. They moved forward a little, then all sat down on the ground beside the water, except Outakke, who began to climb slowly up towards the Paleface outpost.

When he reached Count Peyrac and Count Loménie he stopped, lifted both his arms and handed them something that looked like a kind of fringed scarf, close-set with tiny beads embroidered to form geometrical designs in purple on a white background.

After the presentation of the scarf, he laid it on the ground, then, taking a red stone pipe decorated with two black feathers from his belt, he put this down likewise beside the scarf. Taking two steps back, he crossed his arms across his chest and stared fixedly just above the heads of the assembled crowd, remaining as motionless as a stone statue.

By now everyone seemed to be perfectly calm, even the Abenakis and the Hurons, and even Maudreuil, who wore a vague smile, his hair, like that of an archangel, blowing freely in the wind.

Nicolas Perrot once more acted as interpreter.

He conducted the pow-wow according to the time-honoured ritual. Lengthy, solemn sentences were accompanied by broad gestures to indicate the sky, the earth, this person, or that, and every question and answer patiently repeated. Angélique was astonished at the subtlety of the Iroquois in confusing his interlocutor. But Nicolas Perrot was no easy game. He knew every lakeland tribe and all their dialects; he had acted as go-between hundreds of times in their wars and during the French military campaigns. Besides, he had spent a year as a prisoner among the Oneiouts. Not a single subtlety in the speech of the Iroquois escaped him.

There came a moment when the Iroquois warrior lost his impassivity and let slip a somewhat sharper remark, which brought a noisy and hilarious response from his Canadian interpreter.

'He says that had he known that I was here, he would have preferred not to come, but to have grabbed his tomahawk instead.'

After a while Chief Outakke returned to the lakeside amongst his own people and the Europeans went inside to talk things over. The sun shone high in the sky and the time had come for a drink.

Angélique noted in passing that the officers seemed anxious, and she went forward to greet them.

'Monsieur, how do you feel things are going?' she asked Loménie. 'Are you pleased with your parleys with the savages? Shall we be able to avoid fighting as Monsieur de Peyrac hopes?'

'What am I to say? It's always the same with these Iroquois,' said Loménie. 'Even when they are outnumbered ten to one they always consider they are doing their enemies a favour in sueing for peace. This alone seems to them to justify every sort of concession from us. In the present instance, they are unwilling even to undertake not to molest other tribes, arguing that if they withdrew under those conditions, everyone would regard it as a defeat and scorn them for it.'

'Let's charge and exterminate them all,' urged Maudreuil fervently.

Pont-Briand was quiet, for he was watching Angélique, unable to take his eyes off her pure, perfect profile.

Joffrey de Peyrac was also silent. He looked at each of them in turn but no one could read his thoughts. Loménie-Chambord turned towards him:

'And you, Monsieur? Are you not afraid they are laying a trap? Supposing all their protestations about wanting to make an alliance with us are nothing but duplicity. Once we have gone, they will swoop down on your outpost and ransack it – and as for you and your people....'

'I'll take that risk....'

'We don't even know how many there are of them. . . . There may not be enough to stand up to all of us, but there may be plenty to deal with you and your party.'

'Don't be so concerned about my fate,' said Peyrac, while a subtly ironic smile lit up his eyes. 'Suppose I were backing the wrong horse in counting on the good faith of the Iroquois. Well, that ought to be a welcome prospect to those who, only yesterday, would have liked to see the end of me! But for the moment that is not the problem. We have to decide whether hostilities are to be reopened between New France and the Five Nations, whether violence is necessarily the answer, and whether you are prepared to accept responsibility for it.'

'I say, look who's coming!' said Fallières.

The Mohawk chief reappeared in the doorway. To come to them like this before they had finished their deliberations could hardly be regarded as according to the rules.

'Did you forget to transmit some important message to us?' Perrot asked.

'You have guessed aright! My brother Swanissit instructs me to tell you this. In the forest not far from here my braves have a child of your race, who is your sister's son, your nephew,' he said, turning to Romain de l'Aubignière. 'The great Notable of the Senecas is prepared to hand the child over to you if the French and their allies agree to allow us to go on our way towards the valley of the Mohawks without molesting us.'

Surprise was on every face.

'Little Marcelin, my nephew!' cried L'Aubignière. 'So he escaped the massacre!'

'The dirty swine!' Maudreuil growled. 'He must have realized that there was opposition among us and that his mission had failed. They have decided to play their last card.'

Turning towards Loménie, L'Aubignière entreated:

'Monsieur le Comte, we must do all we can to save the child! We must get him back from these wretches who are bringing him up to hate God and his ancestors!'

Loménie bowed his head gravely.

'I think we must accept,' he said after a glance at Peyrac.

Then, turning to the Iroquois, he went on:

'So be it; give us back the child and you can proceed without hindrance across the Kennebec.'

Young Baron Maudreuil contained himself until the messenger had gone, then he exploded.

'No, they can't! Those miserable wretches can't leave this region with impunity. Let it never be said Swanissit had come so close to me and that I had failed to get his scalp. . . .'

'Do you care so little for my nephew's life, and the saving of his soul?' shouted L'Aubignière, seizing him by the scruff of the neck.

'It wasn't Swanissit who scalped your family! He's here and I can't let him get away alive. I have promised his hair to Our Lady. . . .'

'Quiet now, you two,' said Loménie as he separated the two young men.

With a wild glint in his eyes Eliacien de Maudreuil dashed off to his hut to pack his kit.

These young men were decidedly hot-headed, and Angélique found herself admiring Loménie all the more with every day that passed, for managing to retain his graciousness of manner in spite of so long a stay in Canada.

Realizing that it was necessary to get rid of young Maudreuil, who was a man of the region, the Colonel made no objection to his departure.

He summoned him, gave him something of a dressing down, and then decided to turn the young baron's impulsive action into an official mission. First he gave him a message for Father Orgeval, then a letter for Baron Saint-Castine who was Governor of the outposts of Pentagoet at the mouth of the Penobscot river. The long journey would calm Maudreuil's ardent Canadian temperament.

'The outpost of Pentagoet is near the Gouldsboro post where Monsieur de Peyrac has settled a party of recently arrived French Huguenots, and I want to give the Baron instructions concerning them. If, when you arrive there, you find one of the company's ships which hopes to reach Quebec before the ice sets in, get aboard her; if not, you are to spend the winter at Pentagoet with Castine. One last thing. Don't take any Hurons with you, or you will work one another up with ideas of vengeance. I shall give you my Outane friend, Massonk, as a travelling companion.'

CHAPTER 23

THE SURRENDER of L'Aubignière's nephew took place early the following afternoon.

This time the Iroquois came by the river. They appeared downstream, paddling against the current in some reddish canoes they must have stolen from the river tribes. They disembarked on the gravel shore and walked up towards the outpost.

As on the previous day, the Palefaces stood in a group round the entrance, the Hurons, Algonquins and Abenakis standing to one side in a compact, silent mass. Angélique stood slightly behind the others with Honorine and the two other women. True, the spectre of war seemed to have been averted, but such was the reputation of the Iroquois that their appearance invariably caused considerable apprehension.

There were only some ten of them and they carried no firearms, advancing in a scornfully off-handed way, and pretending not to notice the other natives, whose hatred of them found expression in angry grumblings.

The wampum necklace placed half-way between the river and the outpost guaranteed the safety of the enemy spokesmen.

At their head came Swanissit and Outakke with a little boy of seven or eight trotting between them, holding their hands. His clothing consisted of a single band of leather between his legs and a pair of moccasins on his feet. Although his hair was plastered with grease, they could see it was as golden as corn, and the eyes that looked out from his sun-tanned face were as limpid as lakewater. There was no doubt about his likeness to the trapper with the mutilated fingers; they were certainly kith and kin.

The sight of him wrung Angélique's heart with pity and apprehension, and she clasped Honorine to her. Elvire, the young widow, looked at her two boys sitting quietly on the grass a few yards away. The same thought struck both of them: would fate ever cast their children into the hands of these barbarous Indians, to live half naked in the forest? They had before their eyes living proof that such things could occur, and the two women were moved by pity and distress at the sight of the unfortunate little boy. Their minds were already busy planning the bath they would give him, in a few hours time, when at last he was restored safe and sound to his own people.

That day the two parties sat facing one another across the wampum necklace. The negotiations did not go off without incident.

'Why,' asked Nicolas Perrot, 'why have you not brought your peace-pipe with you? Have you come with your minds made up to reject any possibility of peace?'

'We have come for the sole purpose of exchanging the child in return for your promise of a safe passage. We shall smoke our peace-pipe later with Tekonderoga, the Man of Thunder, when you others have gone and we are sure that he has not betrayed us to the other Frenchmen, and above all to the jackals who are with you,' Swanissit replied bluntly.

'Why did you take a young child like that on a war-party with you?' Romain de l'Aubignière asked in turn.

The Seneca screwed up his eyes craftily.

'Because I love him, and I am all he has in the world. He did not want to leave me.'

'Shouldn't you rather say you wanted to have him with you if things turned out badly for you, when you found that the time of reckoning had come for all the crimes you have committed amongst our people and the friendly tribes. . .?'

Florimond went backwards and forwards, keeping the ladies informed of what was going on. At last he was able to tell them that it looked as if a general amnesty was about to be declared. The French seemed willing to state that they were not interested in this wretched band of Iroquois who had allowed themselves to be cornered between the river and their way back to their native valley. Onontio, who had been Governor of Quebec since the treaty of Michilimackinac, was prepared to treat the Iroquois as his children, and the French here present would forget their grievances, following the example of their father Onontio, remembering only the satisfaction Swanissit had given them by handing over the little boy.

A barrel of brandy which Romain de l'Aubignière himself handed over to Swanissit put the seal on this new era of peace as well as on the transfer of the tiny hostage.

It was then that things began to go wrong.

They were all standing now and Swanissit and Outakke brought the child to within a few paces of his uncle. Then, letting go his hand, they called out: 'Off you go!' with a sweep of the hand that returned him to his own people.

But the little boy, after glancing in terror around him, began to howl, and rushed back to Swanissit, clutching the chief of the Senecas round his long skinny thighs, and looking up at him with tear-stained face as he whimpered, terror-struck, in Iroquois.

Consternation seized the Iroquois braves forthwith; their impassiveness vanished and their tattooed faces revealed their dismay and perplexity. They crowded round the child, entreating and admonishing him volubly.

'What's going on?' Angélique asked anxiously, turning to old Macollet who stood smoking his pipe in the shade of the palisade as he followed the scene with ironic gaze.

He shook his red woollen cap.

'What was bound to happen, heavens above! The lad doesn't want to go to his uncle and refuses to leave the savages! Ha! Ha! Ha!'

Then, still laughing, he gave a fatalistic shrug.

'What was bound to happen, after all. . . .'

The bawling of the child continued to rise over the general uproar.

With their high-pitched voices, and their eloquently onomatopoeic words, and the swaying of their feathered headdresses, the Iroquois looked like a group of delirious parrots.

Without the slightest thought for his dignity, Outakke knelt down to be at the same height as the child so that he could explain things to him better, but the little French boy clung to him as well, with one arm round his powerful neck and the other grasping the leather straps Swanissit wore round his hips to hold his loin-cloth.

The French, extremely vexed, took council.

'We must stop this!' said Count Loménie. 'L'Aubignière, go and fetch your nephew whether he likes it or not, and get him away from here quickly. Put him somewhere where we can't hear him crying any more, otherwise we'll end up with everyone in a fine state.'

L'Aubignière walked over to the Iroquois with the intention of firmly grasping the object of dispute, but no sooner had he put out his hand then the savage braves turned menacingly towards him.

'Don't touch him!'

'Looks like trouble,' Eloi Macollet muttered to himself. 'Well, couldn't expect anything else! Couldn't expect anything else! They say that everyone knows the French are cruel to their children, but that no one's going to lay a hand on this particular child. . . . You've got to be patient, they say. That'll get us a long way. If the lad's as pig-headed as his uncle L'Aubignière, we'll still be here tomorrow. In any case, all the L'Aubignières are as obstinate as mules!'

Angélique moved forward a little, and approached her husband.

'What's your impression?' she whispered.

'That things could take a very nasty turn.'

'What shall we do?'

'Nothing for the moment. Just be patient! That's what these Iroquois gentlemen wish us to do.'

He remained calm, apparently standing aside from these negotiations which did not yet directly concern him. Angélique realized as he did that it was essential to keep calm, but tempers were growing frayed.

The child was purple in the face and bawling louder than ever, with eyes tight closed as if refusing ever to accept the terrible fate that awaited him, that of leaving the savages and returning to these monsters with pale faces! His nose was running and his eyes streaming.

Angélique was seized with pity for the child in his despair and felt she must do something. She went back into the fortress and ran over to the storehouse, where, feeling her way, she managed to find what she was looking for – a loaf of white sugar from which she broke off several lumps. Then she dipped her hand into a barrel of prunes, grasped a handful and ran back to the scene of the trouble.

Loménie had called his lieutenants to one side.

'Let them go off with their insufferable brat, then we'll fight it out with them, get him back, and have them at our mercy.'

'Supposing they killed him to get their own back,' said Maudreuil.

'They wouldn't, they're too fond of him.'

Peyrac intervened.

'If we were to break off negotiations at this stage, we should have to face not only the difficulties we have been trying to avoid but still worse ones. I beg you to keep calm and be patient.'

Angélique bent down to talk to Honorine.

'Look at that poor little boy who's crying over there; he's frightened by all these grown-ups he doesn't know. Take him a piece of sugar and some prunes and then take his hand and bring him back to me.'

No one ever appealed to Honorine's kind heart in vain. Completely fearless, the little girl made straight for the Iroquois, whom she seemed to regard as familiar friends.

She looked like a little doll who had stepped straight out of a picture-frame, with her broad pleated dress and her green linen pinafore. Her green bonnet, from which her copper-coloured curls escaped, shone bright in the sunshine. Her feet were shod in moccasins, their turnovers embroidered with beads. An Indian woman had brought them to her the day before as a gift from Lieutenant Pont-Briand.

In a sweeping, spontaneous gesture, she held the offering out to the little boy. Swanissit and Outakke immediately joined in the game, enthusiastically singing the praises of these wonders that Honorine was offering to their young charge, who, for all his despair, actually managed to open his eyes. He sniffed spasmodically as he examined the presents. Had he ever seen white sugar before? He preferred to grasp the prunes, which were more familiar to him, but his eyes stayed glued to the piece of white stuff they told him was edible. Then Honorine took the little wild child by one hand and made her way slowly back towards Angélique.

All nations held their breath.

That short distance covered by those childish feet would decide between peace or war.

Angélique knelt down, and watched the child's approach, taking care not to make any movement that might frighten him.

When he reached her, she spoke softly to him.

'It's sugar! Taste it. You'll see.'

He could not understand her but seemed to like the sound of her voice. He looked up at her with his big blue eyes in a kind of fascination that seemed to make him forget his fear or even where he was. Did this white woman's face, with her fair hair held back in a coif, remind him of the young Frenchwoman who had been his mother and who had been scalped one terrible night? It almost seemed as if he was trying to remember something.

She went on talking reassuringly to him. Then old Macollet came to her rescue and, speaking as gently as his gruff voice would allow, repeated what Angélique was saying in Iroquois.

'It's sugar. Taste it....'

The child made up his mind to lick the piece of sugar, then he took a great bite of it, and his dirty little face lighted up in sudden wonder, and he broke into peals of clear laughter.

Everyone breathed a great sigh of relief.

The Iroquois delegation relaxed again and everyone crowded round Angélique and the two children.

Angélique had called Elvire's two boys to her.

'Haven't you anything in your pockets that might interest him?'

It was a wise guess. Any self-respecting seven- to ten-year-old boy has pockets full of hidden treasures. Bartholomew found two agate marbles, left over from the last game he had played in the streets of La Rochelle.

They were all that was needed to win the little boy over completely.

The women and children formed a tight group round him and managed without any trouble to get him into the compound, then over towards the house. At last they found themselves with their captive safe behind a closed door.

Angélique was afraid that, once he felt himself shut in, he might begin to scream again. But after glancing at the walls around him and giving an almost imperceptible start of surprise, he seemed to resign himself somewhat unexpectedly and went over and sat down on the hearthstone in front of the roaring fire. She felt sure that his surroundings must have reminded him of happy days gone by in his Canadian farmhouse. He was being worked on by the memory of things he knew, and he nibbled at his piece of sugar as he watched Bartholomew rolling his marbles across the floor. Occasionally he would say something in Iroquois, so, to win him over completely, Angélique sent for the old trapper with the red cap, and settled him too before the fire with a glass of brandy.

'Do me a favour, Monsieur Macollet, and act as "go-between", as you call it here, for this young savage. I am worried in case he grows impatient if he feels that we don't understand him. . . .'

She gave each of the children a lump of the precious sugar by way of thanks for their help.

'Without your help, children, we should have been in trouble. You were very useful.'

And that was also Monsieur de Loménie's opinion, when he came over in person a little later to thank Madame de Peyrac.

He informed her that the Iroquois had left peacefully, satisfied that their charge was in good hands.

'We owe you a thousand thanks, Madame. Had it not been for you and your charming children, we should have reached a deadlock. We soldiers forget all too easily that there are certain situations which only a woman's tact can handle. We should have all got ourselves massacred over this bit of a lad, whereas all you had to do was smile. . . .'

Then, turning to the children, he added imprudently:

'I want to gice you something to thank you. What would you like?'

The youngsters, intoxicated with success and a week spent in the open air, showed no hesitation. Bartholomew was the first to speak:

'I want some tobacco and a pipe.'

'I'd like a gold Louis,'[1] said young Thomas who still retained his Old World sense of values.

'And I,' said Honorine, 'I'd like a scalping knife . . . and to go to Quebec.'

The Count showed considerable astonishment at the variety of their wishes.

'A scalping knife for a young lady? And who are you going to scalp?'

Honorine hesitated. Angélique was on tenterhooks.

But fortunately Honorine decided that she did not yet know and that she would think about it.

'And you, my lad, what do you want to do with a pipe?'

'Smoke it of course!'

Count Loménie laughed heartily. He gave Thomas his gold piece, and told Bartholomew he would get his pipe but only to blow bubbles with.

'And as for you, Mademoiselle Honorine, before I give you the knife, I shall wait till you have decided who your enemies are. But I can

[1] French twenty-franc piece.

already say on behalf of his Lordship Governor Frontenac that he extends a most cordial invitation to you to visit his worthy city of Quebec.'

CHAPTER 24

REALIZING WHAT a trial this complete change in his way of life would be to a small child, Angélique gave up all idea of trying to bath her new charge.

'But he smells absolutely awful,' Madame Jonas and Elvire protested. 'And look at his hair! It must be full of vermin.'

'Yes, I can see. But we might scare him if we put him in the bathtub today, so let's be patient and hope that perhaps tomorrow we may be able to attempt this delicate operation.'

Things began to settle themselves, and for the rest of that day the child was only difficult for short periods. He would occasionally cry and Eloi Macollet managed to calm him very effectively.

'I've told him that, if he is good, Swanissit and Outakke will take him off to hunt and fight tomorrow.'

Later, when he saw the other children splashing about happily in a tub of warm water, the little boy decided to join them. But the women only managed to get the top layer of filth off him, since the bear-grease and dust together had formed a resinous coating all over his skin.

Angélique managed to get him to take a warm drink to which she had added a few drops of some poppy-seed decoction which she had found in the rather inadequate medicine cupboard of the outpost.

O'Connell the Irishman could hardly have been ill very often, and whenever such a misfortune did befall him, he must have treated himself with brandy. She thought of all the bags of herbs she had left behind in La Rochelle, of the ointments, the syrups and the elixirs that it had given her such pleasure to make for the Berne family, using recipes she had learned from the witch Melusine and the good advice she had received from Savary the apothecary.

All these would have been very useful here, but it was already too late in the season to pick the plants she needed most . . . even supposing they could be found in this new hemisphere. Still, some of the bark and the rhizomes she needed might still be available during these later autumn months. She would see about it tomorrow.

. . . . .

164

That evening, Romain de l'Aubignière came over to see how his nephew was.

The little boy was just going off to sleep, rolled in a blanket on a litter they had prepared on the floor, as he had refused to be put into a bed.

The trapper looked glumly at him.

'I know exactly how he feels,' he murmured, shaking his head. 'I too was a prisoner of the Iroquois, over there in the valley of the Mohawks. How can I ever forget that time? How shall I ever forget that valley?'

'But in heaven's name,' said Angélique with a certain impatience, 'are the Iroquois your friends or are they your enemies? Did you enjoy the life you led with them or was it intolerable? For goodness sake make up your mind!'

He seemed surprised. Like Perrot, he saw nothing illogical about mingling his nostalgic feelings with his bloodthirsty intentions. He agreed:

'Yes indeed, I was happy with the Iroquois. But I still cannot forget that they slaughtered my entire family and Maudreuil's too. My sworn duty is to scalp them and scalp them I will. I know we have just reached an agreement with them today, and that that was the price of my nephew's life. But, never fear, we shall meet again face to face!'

She asked him softly:

'What do you intend to do with this little lad?'

'I shall send him to the Jesuits! They have a seminary in Quebec for orphans and Indian boys they want to train up to be priests.'

Angélique looked again at the sleeping child. With his funny little face all smudged with dirt, and his pouting expression, he seemed so innocent and vulnerable. What would the walls of a seminary in Quebec seem like to this forest-bred child? Like a prison, she guessed. She lifted her head to tell young L'Aubignière of her doubts.

Had it been worth setting such store by the child's freedom, if it were only to shut him up again? Their sole concern seemed to have been to snatch him away from the savages in order to save his soul. A worthy motive no doubt, but she wondered whether any thought had been given to the child's happiness and well-being.

As she was about to open her mouth she noticed that the trapper had vanished. These trappers came and went like shadows.

In the next room Elvire was helping the other children prepare for bed. Monsieur and Madame Jonas were in their room, busy tidying things away. Eloi Macollet had gone off to fetch some tobacco. Angélique was alone for a few moments beside the child's bed in the main room. He kept on moving and giving sudden moans, and seemed to be looking for something beside him which he could not find. To calm him, Angélique gently stroked his filthy, unkempt hair.

Then she softly drew the cover up over his thin naked shoulders.

There was no sound in the room save the crackling of the fire.

Yet, as she went to stand up, she discovered the two great Iroquois chiefs, Swanissit and Outakke, standing so close behind her that the fringes of their loin-cloths brushed her shoulder.

She looked up at them in stupefaction. How had they got in? The Mohawk chief's hand rested at about the height of her own eyes on the handle of his polished wooden tomahawk, tipped with a great, pointed, shining ivory spike. A single blow from this weapon would cleave a skull through to the brain, and especially when held by such a hand, equally broad and smooth, an amber-coloured hand with prominent muscles.

Angélique had to make an effort to avoid giving a visible start. Outakke's eyes were no more than two black almost invisible slits, and the great Seneca was not looking at her but watching the sleeping child.

After a few moments, he leant forward and laid a little bow and quiver containing some arrows on the makeshift bed, the weapons the French boy had learnt to use under his tutelage.

Then he pulled himself together and appeared to recover his self-possession. He began to pace round and round the room, followed by Outakke, looking here and there with an insolent stare, touching everything, and still pretending not to notice the young woman. They went into the next room.

Angélique heard Madame Jonas cry out in terror at the sight of the two grimacing, feathered men, as she stood up after poking the fire. The two Iroquois burst into noisy laughter. So far they had been silent, but now they began to talk volubly, exchanging impressions in a mocking tone. Madame Jonas cried out a second time when they laid their dirty hands on a lace scarf which she had just spread out on the bed to get the creases out. What a pity the poor woman had chosen this day of all days to take out her precious things!

The two chieftains made a great hullabaloo in the children's room, and while Elvire huddled in a corner shaking from head to foot the children looked on them as if they were masked figures from a carnival. Disappointed at not finding anything interesting, the visitors went into

Angélique's room, where their curiosity seemed at last to be satisfied. They opened the boxes, took out clothes, and seized books off the shelves, thumbing through them before putting them back again in complete disorder.

Angélique had followed them, trying hard not to lose her patience. She prayed to heaven someone would come and get them out of the place, someone who knew their language.

It seemed to her that Outakke's feelings towards her were questionable. While Swanissit had apparently come to take a last look at his adopted son, it seemed clear that the other wanted to try to pick a quarrel with her, the woman who had humiliated him.

'Should I throw them out?' the watchmaker whispered to her.

'For goodness' sake don't! You'd get your head split open.'

Although they had spoken so quietly, the two savages suddenly swung towards them as if to catch them out in some guilty secret; but they could read nothing but calm in Angélique's expression as she leaned against the door-frame.

They were visibly amused by the frightened Europeans. And they left everything higgledy-piggledy around them, like over-excited children.

Then Swanissit suddenly discovered Angélique's dressing-case full of precious things. He seemed dazzled, and began to handle the comb, the brush, the candlestick and the seal, finally settling his attention on the hand mirror, in which he pulled funny faces, guffawing with laughter. But the gold and tortoise-shell frame and the handle made of the same precious material delighted him even more than the clear reflection in the glass.

Outakke did not seem to share his enthusiasm, and made some rather sharp remark. Was he reminding the chief of the Senecas that the Palefaces were not lenders, that their gifts had to be bargained for, and that this woman belonged to the same tight-fisted race?

Abruptly Swanissit became the great chief again, cold and hostile. He froze, tall and thin in his leather loin-cloth, and put the looking-glass back into its case. With lowered head, he fastened on Angélique the grim gaze of a wounded eagle. His furrowed face wore a sombre frown, as it had earlier, when he had stood looking at the little Canadian boy. Then he seemed to change his mind and reach a decision; a flash of triumph lit up his face, and he grasped the mirror again, tucked it into his belt with a possessive gesture and throwing a defiant glance in Angélique's direction. But his look was very much that of a naughty boy, crafty and provocative.

Angélique went over to him, looked in the dressing-case and took out a red silk ribbon. She lifted the mirror out of Swanissit's belt, placed it against his chest just below his bear-tooth necklace, and, tying the red ribbon round the handle, added this new and exotic ornament to his barbaric finery. The two chieftains had followed her every movement, intrigued.

'You can speak and understand the tongue of the French,' she said to Outakke; 'will you translate my words to the great Seneca. I, wife of Tekonderoga, in the name of my husband, make him a present of this looking-glass he likes so much.'

Outakke repeated her words with a certain reserve. Swanissit looked down at the mirror which now glittered on his breast, and spoke rapidly:

'Does the white woman seek to deceive the great chief of the Senecas?' Outakke translated. 'Swanissit knows that the Palefaces reserve such beautiful objects for the service of their God alone. Black Robe has already refused to give him the mirror in which he looks at himself every morning and which he kisses with his lips, even though Swanissit has offered him a HUNDRED beaver skins in exchange....'

'What can they mean?' Angélique asked herself. 'I suppose the Jesuit father must have refused to give them his paten or some other object used in religious services; how can I explain to him that it is not the same. Oh well, never mind!'

'But why does the great chief of the Senecas fear that I am deceiving him?' she asked aloud. 'Is this object not worthy to grace the breast of the Great Considerable of the Five Nations?'

And she suddenly felt certain that Swanissit understood the meaning of her words, for an almost childish jubilation shone from the eyes of the grey-haired Indian. He radiated pride and joy, but in a heroic effort to regain his human dignity snapped out a few abrupt words which Outakke managed to make sound still more scornful.

'The Palefaces do not know how to make gifts. They are a vile race of merchants. What is the white woman seeking in exchange for what she has done?'

'The white woman has already received payment for her gift,' she replied, 'by being honoured by the visit of the great Swanissit, chief of the Five Nations, to her house.'

'Was the Frenchwoman not frightened by the visit of these fierce Iroquois,' Swanissit went on through his interpreter Outakke.

'Yes, I was frightened,' she replied. 'The arrival of the great Iroquois warriors took me by surprise. I am only a weak woman . . . quite unable to use arms in my defence.'

As she spoke, she looked Outakke full in the face, thinking that he would be the only one to understand the jibe in her remark, but Swanissit must either have had an inkling of the misadventure that had befallen his second-in-command – nearly having his throat slit by a white woman – or he must have been psychic, for he burst into peals of noisy, offensive laughter, slapping his thighs and casting mocking glances at the great chief of the Mohawks. Angélique feared she might have gone too far in humiliating Outakke and decided to pacify him by offering some kind of explanation.

'You see, once I had a dream,' she said. 'I was standing beside the stream up on the hill, towards the setting sun, while an enemy lay in wait for me and rushed out to strike me. So the following day, when I awoke, I armed myself with a knife before I went up the hill, for dreams are often a warning. . . .'

At the mention of dreams, they had grown serious again. All trace of hatred, irony, and distrust had left them.

'Tell us!' Outakke said in a hoarse voice. 'Speak, O white woman, tell us your vision.'

And they drew closer, leaning towards her like children awaiting the continuation of a fascinating, terrifying story.

At that moment, the door burst open with a crash, and a group of trappers and soldiers appeared on the threshold, led by Nicolas Perrot, Pont-Briand, Maupertuis and Three-Fingers. They looked at the floor and Angélique had the distinct impression that they had expected to see her lying there dead, her skull split open. Seeing her standing, alive and well, and apparently on the best of terms with the two redoubtable Iroquois, they stood aghast.

'Madame!' stammered Pont-Briand. 'Are you not? Have you not? . . .'

'No, I am not dead,' Angélique replied. 'What do you want?'

'We were told that Swanissit and Outakke were seen coming in here.'

'Yes indeed, and here they are; they came to see how their young ward was faring and to bring him his weapons. It was a thoughtful action that has made a very favourable impression on me.'

Nicolas Perrot gave a shudder on seeing her standing there so calmly with the two grim and revolting braves close beside her.

'You!' he exclaimed. 'You have never ceased to astonish me ever since the day I met you in La Rochelle. But never mind! Since all is well, we shall not be angry with them for breaking in so brazenly.'

He spoke to the two chiefs in their own tongue and Angélique vaguely understood from their gestures that he was inviting them to feast with the Palefaces. But they shook their heads.

'They say they will feast only with Tekonderoga, and only when all the French from Quebec have left,' Perrot translated.

'They give you their greetings and say that they will return.'

Then, with great dignity, the two chiefs allowed themselves to be escorted to the door and over to the gates of the fortress.

The gates were closed behind them.

CHAPTER 25

'WILL THEY leave? Will they all leave? When can we be alone again, alone with the silence and the wilderness?'

Angélique would not be happy until the welcome time came when she could be alone for a brief moment with her husband far from the eyes of strangers. Then she would let her head fall on his shoulder and would clasp him convulsively to her, avidly drawing strength from him to sustain her in her weakness; for she sensed that he was calm and free from anxiety. Anxiety was something he had never or hardly ever known in all his life, even in the hour of death or torture. Face to face with trials or dangers, he would summon up his strength to fight or bear them. He would never refuse to face the dangers of a difficult situation and would, as far as possible, take action to avoid them; but that which belonged to the future, or to the realm of the imagination, never had any power over him. All that mattered was the immediate tangible fact. During those difficult days Angélique discovered the secrets of a manly way of looking at things which her sensitive woman's mind found it hard to appreciate.

This discovery made him almost a stranger to her, but a comforting stranger; for, at the height of the storm, he remained truly, deeply calm, while she felt that, if this intense activity, this straining of every nerve and swift alternation of hopes or disaster that came and went like capricious gusts of wind, continued any longer her nerve would fail.

Ever since she had brought back chief Outakke from the mountain, nothing had been quite the same for her. The others behaved differently towards her.

Now she felt she was at the centre of things, deeply involved in lives and events that had hitherto been a closed book.

She began to realize that, little by little, she was becoming part of the New World, that she was becoming involved in its loves and its hates.

'They are going,' Joffrey de Peyrac repeated in so confident a tone that the matter seemed to be already settled. 'They are all going, and we shall be on our own in Katarunk.'

Gradually groups of canoes pushed off from the bank in ever-growing numbers.

Then the day came when Count Loménie-Chambord himself departed, the last to climb aboard the last vessel of the French expeditionary flotilla.

Things had not gone as they had expected when they had borne down on Katarunk to beleaguer it, but the Knight of Malta was not sorry.

He watched the couple standing on the shore and began to see them as the symbol of something he himself could not have been, but that he had always hoped to encounter.

In the distance the horses were cropping the grass, and the chirping of crickets filled the air.

'I am leaving you on your own,' said Count Loménie-Chambord.

'Many thanks.'

'And what if you don't manage to convince the Iroquois of your good intentions and they succumb to the temptation to fix your hair for you and carry off your possessions before they go back home?'

'Inch Allah!'

Count Loménie smiled, for he too knew the Mediterranean. 'Allah Mobarek!'[1] he replied. As he rounded the bend in the river he was still waving his hat.

CHAPTER 26

SUDDENLY SOLITUDE descended upon them, and their own adventure was about to begin.

They were alone, they belonged to no nation, they represented no king.

When the Iroquois came to seek alliance, they would negotiate with Joffrey de Peyrac, as if he were a king, speaking in his own name.

Hardly daring to believe it, they looked around at the outpost that was theirs once more.

[1] God is great.

That evening they held a joyous 'family' celebration to mark their victory and their independence. Goblets of wine were raised to Joffrey de Peyrac in honour of his skilful leadership, which once again had rescued them from a tight corner.

And that night Angélique experienced new bliss in clasping in her arms the man who supported them all and had not betrayed their confidence in him, feeling the urgency of his lips as they drank hers as if, now that the danger was past, he was seeking to take his revenge on fate.

To meet the Iroquois delegation, Joffrey de Peyrac put on his red velvet doublet, embroidered with silver flowers and black onyx beads. He had silver spurs on his black leather boots. With one hand resting on the silver hilt of his sword, he stood waiting in front of the fort.

The six Spaniards who formed his armed guard stood rigidly to attention on his left, wearing flashing armour and morions and holding their halberds; while on his right six of his sailors also stood to attention, dressed in a kind of uniform of dazzling colours: their jackets were half yellow and half scarlet, their breeches were scarlet and their leather boots fawn, a uniform he had had made by a tailor in Seville for his household livery.

It was a rare occasion indeed when he ordered his men to put on their full dress uniform.

The New World, except for the territories under Spanish rule, was no place for the pomp and ceremony of the Old. More often than not, men landed in the northern territories on hands and knees, with their shirts as their sole possessions, and poverty forced austerity on them for long periods.

Such was the case of all those who had fled from religious persecution, like the English Puritans or the French Huguenots, and the Jonases had trundled the same modest pack containing all their worldly goods all the way from La Rochelle.

Joffrey de Peyrac had come over with ships after he had grown rich diving for treasure in the Caribbean. He was therefore able to give his colony a more sumptuous turn, and even among the necessarily small amount of baggage they had brought from Gouldsboro he had seen fit not to leave out his soldiers' dress uniforms.

As they climbed up towards the outpost, the Iroquois wondered what could be the significance of all this brilliance, sparkle and glitter that stood awaiting them, adding its splash of colour to the autumn setting. The purple foliage of a giant maple beside the entrance to the outpost seemed to stand in welcome to them, like the escutcheoned banners which had been set up on the hillside as if to line a triumphal way.

The breeze was sharp and brisk, flattening the straw-dry pearly grass that bowed down and rose again as the wind whistled softly across it.

Swanissit was carrying his gun with the mother-of-pearl butt across his arms.

There were five of them: Swanissit, Outakke, Anhisera, Ganatinha and Ouasategan. Their breasts were bare, their stomachs empty, and their simple leather loin-cloths flapped in the wind.

Ouasategan was chief of the Onondagas, Ganatinha one of the bravest chieftains of the Oneidas, and Anhisera was spokesman for the Cayugas; for he was brother to their chieftain, although he himself was a Seneca. . . .

These men were therefore among the most important representatives of the Five Nations of the Valley of Maize, come to make alliance with the Man of Thunder. They had taken this risk for the sake of their peoples, but in their hearts there was more than a hint of suspicion, which they attempted to disguise beneath an attitude of arrogance.

Angélique wondered as she watched them advance from the top of the rampart what those wild hearts really felt, and she thought she could sense their suspicion, anxiety and sorrow. For Swanissit had told them: 'The Five Nations are no more what they once were. Now we must try to make peace with the Paleface.'

The fate of the Iroquois was becoming more and more subtly bound up with Angélique's existence. Was it because she had held Chief Outakke's life at the point of her dagger, or on account of that business with the tortoise that there still seemed to be a barrier between them?

That morning she and Honorine had sorted out the best of the beads from among the shoddy merchandise used for bartering.

'These are to give old Swanissit, if he comes to visit us again. He is a man worthy of great respect.'

'Yes, I like him too,' Honorine declared; 'he was nice to the little boy. Why did the little boy go away with the Frenchman? He could have taught us to use a bow and arrow.'

Angélique would also gladly have kept the Canadian child, but the question had not arisen.

Half-way up the hillside the Iroquois found the gifts Joffrey de

Peyrac had had placed there for them with a wampum sash of considerable value that he had taken from one of his chests.

When Swanissit and the others had worked out the meaning of the message drawn in white and midnight-blue porcelain beads, they appeared pleased, looked at one another, nodded and said: 'This is good! This is valuable!'

Swanissit reminded the others that the necklace had once been part of the treasure of the Mohicans. The fact that it had come into Count Peyrac's possession was an indication of the importance of his alliances and showed in what high regard he was held by the southern tribes. But the mere thought that he should present it to them made their hearts beat faster. They were feverishly excited at the idea that they might take it home with them, and Swanissit could already see himself entering the cities of the Long Houses, bearing the precious strip of wampum on his outstretched hands. The thought of his people's excitement when they saw it made him quiver inwardly like the skin of a tambourine beneath a merry musician's fingers.

They laid down their arms, their bows and arrows, the musket with the mother-of-pearl butt and the red stone peace-pipe. There was only one of these, a rather crude specimen, whose stone had grown cold from not having been smoked for many a long month....

They laid it down and gave a sigh when, among the gifts placed there by the Palefaces, they noticed some brown plaits of tobacco neatly set out on tanned hides; it was the best tobacco, from Virginia, and its delectable smell filled their nostrils.

How good it would be to have a smoke soon, sitting round the fire, with all the pleasure of promises exchanged.

But they must not succumb to the temptation of these pleasures and neglect the ancient complicated rituals of so important a pow-wow on which hung the whole future of the Iroquois League.

On this occasion Angélique had asked her husband if she could be excused from assisting at the ceremony. In spite of the part she had played, however unintentionally, in preparing the ground for this interview, she did not consider that her presence was necessary. This she deduced from what Nicolas Perrot had told her, namely that, in Iroquois society, although the women and above all the mothers have a right to be heard, their views are made known to the council of men only through their secretaries, who were usually chosen from among the young men. Besides since that morning she had been suffering from a terrible migraine and could not bear the idea of spending several hours listening to the noisy cackling of the Indians, and enduring their overpowering smell, their belches and snuffling noses, wiped with their hands or their hair. Joffrey de Peyrac agreed that, if the chieftains did not insist on her presence, she was free to stay away. Deep down she felt apprehensive at the thought of facing Outakke, the chief of the Mohawks again. She felt happier about the idea of seeing Swanissit and, by way of excuse for her absence, she got Nicolas Perrot to take him the collection of Venetian beads she had sorted out for him.

When she saw that the exchange of greetings was over and the parley about to begin, she retired to the cottage, feeling slightly chilly, and spent the afternoon with her friends and the children.

From time to time somebody would come over and tell them how things were going.

Out of conscientiousness and vanity, and because he was terribly hungry and the delicious smells coming from the outpost courtyard made him long to cut short some of the oratory, old Swanissit prolonged his speeches well beyond the limits of human endurance. But Count Peyrac seemed to be able to stand anything.

Swanissit exclaimed at great length that if there were only five of them today, this was because they had left Tahoutaguete in charge of the braves still in the forest and those who were beginning to cross the river a little farther down. There were a great number of them, a very great number, possibly a thousand of them, far more than the departed French had ever thought possible.

If he, Swanissit, had any reason to believe that the Man of Thunder had been trying to lull his suspicions, or that his promises had been false, and that he merely sought to weaken the Iroquois by making them bury the hatchet so that he could then help the French to deceive the Five Nations, let him beware, and straight away load his guns, for, before returning to their own lands, the Iroquois would derive much pleasure from roasting alive some of these impudent, deceitful Palefaces. There were some handsome heads of hair amongst them. Yours, for instance, Tekonderoga, and those of your sons. And that of your wife as well. 'Although I should not be the one to scalp your wife,' the elderly chieftain commented, as if seeing himself already faced with this situation. 'For I tell you, and I repeat, that never in all my life have I killed or scalped a woman or a child. I shall die before I ever take the life of a woman or a child, according to the ancient traditions of our people.

'But I cannot say the same of the new generation of braves,' he went on, with a scornful glance at the three other chieftains, although they were mature men; 'for they have learnt from the Palefaces no longer to respect those that give life, those that ensure our future, and they have hung women's hair on the doors of their wigwams. Ugh! The men of my nation will soon have become creatures as vile and ignoble as you Palefaces. But all the same I must defend them and lay the foundations for their future.'

Peyrac, calm and dignified, took little notice of Swanissit's remarks or threats, and managed to calm the suspicions which were apparent beneath this foretaste of ill-feeling. It was a lengthy process, and they would all have been there still at dusk if the weather had not suddenly clouded over. The wind dropped and a thick mist rose with astonishing speed from the river and the lakes, enveloping everything as it swept in like an irresistible sea over the tops of the fir-trees and the mountain crest.

So they had to gather up their gifts, their wampums and their peace-pipes, and shut themselves up in the outpost, where these humans made a refuge of heat and light that shut out the Land of Shades and the melancholy Kingdom of the Dead. They lighted two enormous fires in the hearth of the great hall, and there they feasted on fat meat, sweet-smelling maize and sour berries. They grew tipsy on tobacco, blue smoke, and colourless alcohol.

This paradise was only for those whose capacity for absorption and resistance had been proved by long experience of native banquets or piratical orgies.

Florimond and Cantor, among others, were sent off to the cottage, to eat their meal with the children, the womenfolk, those who preferred to keep sober and those with delicate livers.

Angélique was vastly amused at their discomfiture. The young Breton lad Yann had joined them too, explaining frankly that he did not enjoy drinking a great deal, nor eating endless boiled bear, and that the horrifying drunkenness of Indians made him feel sick.

Enrico Enzi, the Maltese, also sought their hospitality. He was the one with the delicate liver, which had been the shame of his life, but since he also had a reputation for being handy with a knife, scarcely anyone ever mocked him any more when his skin turned a shade more yellow and he refused a glass of wine or spirit.

The women helped to make the evening pass gaily. Someone played the guitar, and someone the fife, and they all sang. They ate fritters and aniseed-flavoured sweets that the children had made with sugar on the hearthstone.

Master Jonas told them all a story of a werewolf from the province of Saintonge. It was a very long time since he had last told it and he would occasionally lose the thread of the story. This was not because his memory failed him; on the contrary, he remembered the story very well, but he had not told it since his two little boys had been carried off one fine morning by the Jesuits of La Rochelle and had never been found again.

He went on pluckily to the end and was pleased to see how much they all liked the tale. Florimond and Cantor were not the only ones to ask him for another story.

Then they all went off to bed. Angélique suggested that the two boys should sleep there, since, if they went back to the hard mattresses in the other house where they usually slept, the noise of the festivities would keep them awake. So they rolled themselves up in blankets and lay down on the floor in front of the fire.

The fog made everyone sleepy without realizing it. It bore down on the world with a soft woolly pressure, its opacity shot through with damp, confused sounds, and heavy with an uneasy silence.

Sentries stood on the platforms at the four corners of the palisade, vainly attempting to catch any sight or sound, trying to make out the significance of the drips, the rustles and the lapping sounds that came to them as if dulled, more like sighs, woolly echoes sent back by the swirling fog. They could hear the croaking of frogs coming from the riverside, the call of nightjars and the hooting of owls in the forest.

The absence of the Metallak and Naraandsouak Indians who had left the camp made the night seem even darker. Had they been there, even through the fog one could have seen the glow of their fires, one could have smelt smoke as it seeped through the birch-bark wigwams, and one could have heard their babies whimpering.

But tonight there was nothing.

The outpost of Katarunk lay in the depth of the night like a wreck in the midst of the ocean.

CHAPTER 27

AT THE outpost of Katarunk there was mist outside the walls, and mist within. Icy mist outside and warm mist within. Outside the light made the mist look grey, and it sparkled with frost, whereas inside it was the blue mist of tobacco smoke. Outside it was the mist of the great open spaces with their stale, cold tomb-like smell, which came creeping across the dark land like a fearsome beast trying to thrust its way into the shelters of men; whereas in the hall it was a sweet-smelling mist, that rose in delicate spirals from the bowls of many pipes as men sat smoking to their hearts' content, their bellies full and their minds empty.

Swanissit was happy. The old Seneca had eaten fit to burst. He had not drunk much; for he dreaded the frenzying effect of brandy, and had never taken to it. He had likewise refused the beer and the wine they had offered him, whereas the water, with its earthy taste, drawn from a deep well, he had found delicious, and had washed down many a full bowl of 'sagamité' or maize mush. This excess of food and tobacco after a long fast, added to the weariness of warfare, had the same effect on him as alcohol, and he was every bit as drunk as the others. He thought of the band of wampum he would carry in his two hands before the Council of Mothers and Elders. He thought of the gifts they had received and the promises they had exchanged.

He thought of the great hunting-grounds that awaited the gallant brave when he reached the other side. There were certain festive evenings when the heart revelled in delight. And although he was still in this world, he found it easy to imagine that the pleasures of the elect must be similar to those he felt that night. There was nothing missing. And even, oh wonder of wonders! he suddenly caught sight of Baron Maudreuil, another child he had adopted once, standing before him, his teeth bared in a broad grin as he brandished his cutlass. . . .

CHAPTER 28

TOWARDS THE end of the night, but when it was still dark, the horses neighed.

Someone outside shouted:

'Bears!'

Joffrey de Peyrac stood up and hurried over to the door. In spite of his splendid powers of endurance, he was none too sure of himself as he made his way as best he could past bodies lying in a drunken stupor.

No matter what one's capacity may be to endure the manifestations of hospitality, there is no more gruelling experience than that of honouring an important treaty signed with Indian chieftains, and

178

especially with the Iroquois. Their appetite for speeches, food and drink is such that one begins to despair of a halt ever being called.

Fortunately his patience had long since passed its tests, and he could at least say that in a single night his knowledge of the Iroquois language had grown enormously.

The cold hit him like a blow. He was surprised not to be able to hear his own footsteps as he walked across the compound towards the fortress gates. He heard someone cry out again in a hoarse, strange voice and recognized it as that of the Spaniard Pedro Majorque, one of his sentries.

At the very same moment someone struck him a violent blow on one shoulder that sent him reeling. Actually the blow had been intended for his head, but an instinctive reaction had saved him. He had felt the blow coming and had moved to one side. Other blows followed, falling at random through the thick fog. Feeling his way, he grasped some slippery limbs, twisting them in one of the deadly holds he had learned in some oriental port, and heard the crack of bones. But whoever his attackers were, they seemed possessed of boundless energy, constantly renewed like the hydra with a hundred heads. Another blow – from an axe this time – almost struck him full on the forehead, but he dodged it once more and it just grazed his skull a little above the temple. The wound began to bleed and he tasted something sticky and salt on his lips.

He gave a bound and wrenched himself free from the knot of serpents that held him prisoner and sought to kill him.

He ran off through a strange silence he could not understand. His eyes were growing accustomed to the blackness, but he knew he could not see as well in the dark as the Indian. Nevertheless, seeing a silhouette coming towards him, a shadowy figure made still larger by the thick fog, he was first to hit out this time, striking the man full in the face with the solid silver butt of his pisol. The shadow fell, and disappeared from his sight, but through the darkness of the night still more shadows appeared, surrounding him in an attempt to seize him.

His wound was weakening him, and he ran towards the river to escape them, heading straight for the water. As soon as he felt the edge of the bank beneath his feet, he dived in.

This dark and icy haven seemed familiar to him, and he let himself go in the water, scarcely breathing, all thought suspended; and for a time, he knew not how long, he seemed to be reliving his escape into the waters of the Seine, fifteen years back, when he had slipped over the edge of the boat into which the King's musketeers had thrust him more dead than alive.

He struck against something, and stopped, clinging to some branches and wedging himself against some roots.

A cold pink light made his eyes ache, and he had the impression that someone was sending up fireworks in his direction. But then he realized that it was the pink sky of dawn and the glow of the rising sun. The air about him was full of tiny drops of gold and diamond, and a dazzling whiteness had replaced the black curtain of night; although he had not thought he had lost consciousness, he realized that he must have fainted for a time after clambering out on the bank.

Then he remembered: . . . Angélique! . . . Over there in the outpost. What had happened? . . . She was in danger! And what about the children?

His mind instantly became lucid and, in spite of the blood he had lost, the fury that filled him gave him a terrible strength. He was immediately ready, on the alert, with that kind of empty feeling that overcame him whenever the time to fight had come, a feeling that left him deaf and blind to everything that was not an essential part of the battle and an element in the peril he was facing.

Even the thought of Angélique was wiped from his mind now, and he was nothing more than a creature defending himself with all his skill, instinctive and acquired; his enemies had learned at their expense just how formidable a man in this state of mind he could be, even when he stood alone.

Slowly he got up and looked around. He was under the cover of a willow-tree, whose dangling leaves, golden beneath the snow, glittered like precious earrings.

It was this layer of snow everywhere that explained the dazzling whiteness, the silence, the sudden stifling of sounds and footfalls. Stealthily it had fallen in the middle of that night, mingling with the mist. It was characteristic of these very dry lands that, with the first shaft of sunshine, the thick veil of fog had disappeared as in a single breath, restoring the countryside to its dazzling clarity.

Count Peyrac realized that he was some way from the outpost: he could see the dark rampart of the palisade at the top of the hill, and spirals of smoke rising lazily from two chimneys, leaving a trail across the morning sky as white as the snow itself.

Carefully he came out into the open, holding his pistol by the barrel, ready to strike. His sharp eyes scanned the countryside, but he saw no human form. A little way up the hill he encountered some footprints, visible in the fresh snow, which led along the shore. As he drew nearer to the outpost, there were more footprints, going off to the right and the left. They must have surrounded the outpost before attacking it.

Attacking it? No, it seemed more as if they had entered the fort without difficulty, for he had been struck in the compound.

Then as he began to climb up the path that led from the river's edge to the main entrance of the fortress, still just visible beneath the thin layer of snow, he saw a human form spreadeagled on the ground.

He went up to it carefully and turned the body over. The Indian's head had been battered in, and his brains and blood poured from the gaping hole.

It was the man he had struck during the night with the butt of his gun.

He examined the man carefully.

Although Joffrey was not under cover and would have been an easy target for any enemy, he at once realized that he need have no fear of an immediate attack.

The Indian was one of those who come in the night and who make off with the dawn: one of those who do not fear to die in the dark since their souls thus escape their ancestral curse, those who alone dare. . . .

There was only one kind of Indian who would do this, and Joffrey de Peyrac's suspicions were confirmed as he leaned over the dead man. Something shone round the Indian's neck, and Peyrac gave a sharp tug to break the chain that held the amulet. After a quick glance at it, he slipped it into his doublet. Then slowly he continued on his way towards Katarunk.

CHAPTER 29

ANGÉLIQUE had been a long time getting to sleep. Her migraine gripped her temples and her eyes ached.

During the night some Abenaki tumblers whom Nicolas Perrot had persuaded to entertain the Iroquois chieftains with a little music had begun to shake their little tortoise-shell bells, to beat their drums and to blow their six-holed oak whistles. The fires cast pink dancing lights across the parchment of her little window.

Angélique was in a state of permanent anxiety lest threatening shadows appear at that window. The Indians were dancing in the compound with short, syncopated tread, and in the big hall she imagined their leaders and the Palefaces making merry together, passing round bowls full of Indian corn, steeped in bear-grease and sunflower seeds, hunks of boiled meat and many a goblet of brandy.

Every now and then a raucous cry would go up, rising above the piercing, strident sounds of the music, and Angélique would shudder uneasily.

She missed her husband's company and felt frightened.

'Oh, how I wish you were here,' she thought like a child. 'I do so need you....'

Then everything had grown hazy, and deep silence had engulfed her, the silence of the grave.

When she awoke the same silence reigned. The daylight had the special quality of light from an alabaster lamp.

Outakke the Mohawk was standing at her bedside. He was naked and deathly pale like a yellowed marble statue. He bowed his head as he looked at her and suddenly she noticed red blood running down from his shoulder or his chest, she could not quite tell which.

He spoke in a whisper:

'Woman, grant me my life!'

She leapt out of bed, and this sufficed to make the mournful shade of the Mohawk vanish. There was no one in the room.

'I am going mad,' she told herself. 'Am I going to start having visions too, like everyone else round here?'

And she ran her hand across her face in bewilderment.

Her heart was beating a wild tattoo. She listened carefully. What did this brooding silence mean? She knew it must be the result of something that had happened.

Something had happened!

Swiftly she dressed and, in her haste, seized the nearest cloak to hand, which happened to be the purply-pink cloak she had worn across her shoulders the other evening to go to the banquet. Little did she realize that this unpremeditated gesture would help her to save a life....

In the next room her two sons still slept the deep sleep of youth; after putting her ear to the Jonases' door and to that of the children's room, and hearing the light sound of sleeping people breathing, she began to feel easier.

But she still felt that the dead silence was very strange.

She walked quietly over to the main door and unlocked it, and was dazzled by the white light which, seeping through the tiny opaque panes that morning, had so intrigued her when she woke.

At the same moment an icy blast struck her and her dazzled eyes blinked as she stifled an exclamation.

SNOW!

Snow had fallen during the night, early, unexpected snow, which had fallen softly, enveloping the fortress in a fleecy mantle, stifling the noise of shouting, the rhythmical beat of chanting, and the crackling of fires, burying all life, sound and movement beneath it.

When morning had come, the snowflakes had ceased their stealthy dance, but the impression of surprise remained.

The wooden buildings seemed darker, more shut in under their immaculate white roofs. A rainbow-tinted mist hung about the edge of the palisade, softening its outlines and making them fade into the ghostly landscape. There was not a soul in sight, although the white-carpeted compound bore traces of many recent comings and goings.

Angélique saw that the porch stood wide open, and she could see something dark that looked like an outstretched body lying inside.

She was about to run over to it when a swirl of mist, thicker and lower than before, unfurled itself behind her, from over the roof top, in smoky grey rolls, dimming the light of the sun and plunging her almost instantly into a dense world of silence.

A strange piercing cry came from somewhere, but she could see nothing. She had to grope her way along the palisade to the gate, and once outside, she no longer knew in which direction she thought she had seen the outstretched form.

She shouted. Her voice echoed dully and did not carry.

Then, almost as suddenly as it had descended, the fog began to lift again, and became a watery mist, heavy with dazzling droplets. Above her on her right a tall scarlet form began to take shape. It was the solitary maple that stood near the entrance to the outpost. The snow had not managed to cover its glorious foliage. An edging of snow only served to heighten its scarlet splendour, while the diffused sunshine, struggling through the mist, glowed through the purple leaves as through stained glass.

Slowly the fog rolled away back to the river's edge.

A human form was climbing up the hill, from the river, through this first velvety snow that had flowered precociously, ready to melt as soon as the heat of the day touched it.

He was handsome and radiant like the Archangel Michael himself, that morning, little Baron Eliacien de Maudreuil. His golden hair shone beneath his Indian headdress of feathers and beads. His bare chest was visible through the open neck of his doeskin jacket, and three medallions hung there, shining and glinting from time to time, like the blade of the long cutlass he held in his raised fist.

He climbed the hill with his head held high, the snow deadening his footsteps. His blue eyes were filled with the dream of paradise.

What he saw through the mist, under the red maple with its stained-glass colours, was a vision of supernatural beauty, with a halo of light, a face as white as a lily flower and the most wonderful eyes.

She was waiting for him, watching him coming, serene and earnest, draped in the folds of a pink cloak.

Overcome with emotion, he fell on one knee.

'O Blessed Lady,' he murmured, his voice broken. 'O Mother of God, blessed be this day! I knew that I should see you in my hour of victory!'

Where he knelt, scarlet stars spangled the snow. It was blood! Blood falling drop by drop! ...

In his raised fist he brandished something black, and damp, trickling with pinkish droplets.

'Here is the demon's hair! Here is the spoil I promised you, O Mother of God! ... Here is Swanissit's scalp.'

A cloud blew across, wrapping them both around in cold mist and hiding the kneeling man from Angélique's gaze.

Once again she heard him cry out in the voice of a man demented:

'Swanissit is dead! Glory to God in the highest!'

Feeling her way, she backed away from him, seeking something to guide her. She walked in a kind of limbo across the compound, trying to find the main hall where they had all been feasting that night.

Suddenly she caught sight of the door a few paces from where she stood; it gaped like a black hole opening on to cold shadows. The heavy wooden door creaked on its leather hinges as the wind moved it back and forth.

A terrible fear gripped her heart.

'The banqueting hall!' She reached the threshold.

There were only four men sitting at the table. She saw immediately her husband was not one of them. They were the four Iroquois chiefs, Swanissit, Anhisira, Ouasategan and Ganatinha. They lay with their heads on the table, and seemed to be sleeping off their wine. There was a stale smell in the room where the fog had penetrated. The fires had gone out. Angélique noticed a sinister sound that sent shivers through the roots of her hair. It was the sound of something dripping slowly, like the trickling of slimy waters in the depths of a dark cavern.

What did it matter if the open door let in the cold and the fires had gone out! Those who sat there had no further need for warmth, for they lay there in a pool of blood, scalped. And the sound Angélique heard was the sound of their blood dripping from the table to the ground.

She suddenly felt sick.

And even her anxiety about her husband's fate seemed to give way to a sensation of sheer horror, the unspeakable shame of the sight before her.

The Iroquois chieftains had been scalped as they sat at their host's table, under Joffrey de Peyrac's own roof.

A shadow stirred behind her, and she wheeled round, grasping the butt of her gun.

She saw Nicolas Perrot, rubbing his head through his cap, staring vaguely at her. He too was looking at the scene in the room, and his lips mouthed oaths which he had not the strength to utter.

'Monsieur Perrot,' Angélique asked almost in a whisper, 'have you any idea who did this?'

He indicated that he knew nothing.

'Where is my husband?'

'We are looking for him.'

'What happened?'

'Last night we were all pretty drunk,' said Perrot. 'When I went out into the compound, someone knocked me out and I have only just come round.'

'Who struck you?'

'I don't know yet. But I'll wager it was that Sagamore Piksarett with his infuriated braves the Patsuiketts.'

'And Maudreuil! . . . I saw him just now near the gates.'

Perrot looked at the Iroquois and said dully:

'One of them's missing.'

He counted the dead men.

'One of them's missing. . . . Looks like Outakke. He must have got away.'

'But how could they have got in and taken you by surprise?'

'Someone opened the gates from inside. The sentries thought the French had come back.'

'And Joffrey? Where can he be? I'll go and tell my boys.'

Angélique crossed the compound once more; the dull grey fog had transformed it into a desert in which she might run into an enemy with every step she took.

She recognized the storehouse and stopped there, leaning against the wall with her pistol raised, thinking she had heard a slight rustle.

She heard the sound again, and something heavy slithered off the shingle roof in a shower of snow.

A body fell heavily at her feet. Outakke lay there motionless on the white snow; his body had the pallor of wax.

A moment passed and, seeing that he did not move, she bent over him. He was scarcely breathing. His open palms had lost their grip on the ridge of the room, from which he must have hung, wounded, for many a long hour.

The Iroquois opened his eyes, flashing a glance at her. His lips moved, and she guessed rather than heard the words he had already said once to her beside the stream and had repeated in her dream:

'Woman, grant me my life!'

She grasped him under the armpits, tugging and dragging him along. He was heavy, and Angélique's hands could not get a grip on his slippery skin.

She hunted through the pocket of her dress for the key to the stores, unlocked the door, pushed it open with her elbow, dragged the wounded man inside and placed him in a corner, covering him with a few old sacks to keep him hidden.

Then she went out and shut the door.

Behind her someone had come out of the fog and was watching her.

When she turned round she gave a violent start. An Indian stood before her and she recognized the tall chieftain with the bearskin whom she had seen a morning or two ago beside the gilded wooden altar. He was gigantically tall but very thin. His heavy greased top-knot had the wooden beads of a large rosary plaited into it, and on either side of his face wisps of braided hair were held in position by clasps made from the feet of red foxes.

He wore around his neck several rows of medallions and little cruci-fixes that hung on his tattooed chest.

He was watching Angélique, head on one side, his eyes screwed up in malice.

Slowly he came towards her.

He bared his teeth in a silent grin: they were white and pointed like those of a rodent, and his two protruding upper incisors made him look like a mischievous squirrel.

She could not think why but she felt no fear.

'Are you the Sagamore Piksarett?' she asked him.

Since all the Abenakis came into contact with the French, he must understand a little French even if he could not speak it.

He nodded his head.

She slipped between him and the door of the storehouse, determined to prevent him from getting in. Yet she did not want to kill him, only to send him away, to prevent him finishing off the wounded man, to strike a bargain with him.

She slipped her big purple cloak from her shoulders.

'Take this cloak.... It's for you.... It's something for your dead....'

The Indians had been dazzled by the cloak, news of which had already travelled far down the banks of the Kennebec. They dreamed of it, for ever obsessed with the problem of finding a shroud worthy of the bones of their ancestors. Many a Catholic priest had been martyred for refusing to give them his chasuble.

She had made the only gesture capable of diverting the Sagamore Piksarett's attention. He looked at the proffered garment in ecstasy as it lay there glowing like a piece of the dawn cut straight from the sky.

He made a grab at the cloak, spread it out, draped it around himself, then rolled it up into a ball and clasped it to his heart.

He looked once more at the closed door, then at Angélique, then at the cloak.

At that moment the sun, triumphant at last, spread abroad its rays, and the houses became visible again, and the palisade, while the snow began to melt in a whisper.

Nicolas Perrot, who was standing at the other end of the compound, saw Piksarett beside Angélique.

He ran over towards them. But the Abenaki took to his heels and, still clutching the cloak, bounded over the far wall of the palisade like the huge squirrel that he was, and vanished.

It was at this moment that Joffrey de Peyrac reached the outpost and entered the compound. Angélique ran towards him and threw herself into his arms, fearful to see him wounded, but wild with joy at finding him safe.

'God be praised! You are alive,' he said, clasping her to him.

'Are you hurt?'

'It's nothing. What about the children and the boys?'

'They're all right. I don't think we have any dead to mourn. At least, no one of ours.'

Peyrac's eyes had already lighted on the open door to the main hall, where some of the men had begun to form a crowd, and he went over, overcome, as Angélique had been shortly before, by a premonition of the tragedy he was to discover.

He stood on the threshold and looked at the waxen figures, grown stiff in an attitude of sleep or inebriation, with their blood-soaked heads reclining among all the dishes.

Then a wild anger shone from his black eyes, and he swore; teeth clenched:

'Damn them! Damn them! Accursed be the man to whom we owe this.' His fists were clenched and his blood-streaked face, framed with wet, mud-spattered hair, struck fear into them.

'It must have been the Patsuiketts,' said Nicolas Perrot.

'I know. I know who it was who came and betrayed us under cover of the night. I saw their sign.'

And from his soaking doublet he drew the object he had torn from round the neck of the dead Indian, and they saw a small gold cross glittering in the palm of his hand.

'The cross,' said Peyrac bitterly. 'Is there no place on earth where I can undertake anything without someone hurling a cross between my legs to trip me up!'

'Monsieur, I beg you, do not blaspheme!' Nicolas Perrot cried out, growing pale.

'What does blasphemy matter! It's actions that count!'

He looked darkly at them. Smothered violence made his voice shake. These blasphemous words he longed to utter, not one of the men standing round him, not even his brothers, his companions, would understand them. No one but her. For she had suffered with him, as he had, and for the same reasons. He put one arm round her and clasped her to him, passionately, looking with desperate intensity into her lovely face with its blue eyes.

She, like him, had been rejected by the world of believers and just men, and her love for him had branded her, when she was still only twenty, for ever to be cursed; and now, he realized in a flash, she had become his double, possibly the only person on earth who was like him.

'This must be the Patsuiketts' doing,' Maupertuis, who had now joined them, repeated, feeling he must say something. 'They can't set eyes on an Iroquois without getting their teeth into his throat. I suppose when they saw that these were going to get away from them ...'

'Yes, it was them. It takes a fanatically Christian Indian to risk fighting at night. Fanatical and fanaticized. The Patsuiketts are the only ones like that. Their faith is strong enough for them no longer to believe in the superstitions of their race that say that a brave killed at night will roam for ever in the outer darkness. They have been so successfully hypnotized by Black Robe that they trust in his mystical power when he tells them that the death of an Iroquois or an Englishman is a sure passport to heaven.'

'Are you referring to Father Orgeval?' Nicolas Perrot and Maupertuis asked. 'That's impossible, the man's a saint!'

'He's a saint fighting for his God. I've known all about him for a long time. The Pope and the King of France sent him to Acadia, for the sole purpose of encouraging the Abenakis to fight a Holy war against the English heretics and anyone else who might be considered an enemy of the Catholics or France.'

'It was he who sent for reinforcements from Quebec and got them to occupy our outpost. When he saw that I was beginning peaceful negotiations with Count Loménie, he believed Loménie had gone back on his word, and decided to strike a final, irreversible blow. This is not the first time he has sent the Patsuiketts out to fight on his own initiative.

'And now,' Peyrac went on, in a hoarse, broken voice, 'and now, through his fault,' and he looked down at the glistening gold cross in the palm of his hand, 'through his fault I have the blood of treachery on my hands. . . . Perrot, do you remember what Tahoutaguete said when he came here as a messenger. He had his doubts, for Outakke had told them that it was impossible to make an alliance with the Palefaces. But the Iroquois still clung to the hope of finding a Paleface who would not betray them. And now, what can I say to them? My house has been stained by an unpardonable crime!'

His voice trembled as he spoke, and at the same time, Angélique, whom he was still clasping to him with one arm, had the impression that this last phrase had, as it were, suddenly lighted up something within him, enabling him to catch a glimpse of a possible solution.

He grew calmer, regaining his habitual self-control.

He repeated softly:

'My house is dishonoured.'

He stared fixedly before him, as if in a dream.

'Outakke got away,' said Perrot.

'That only makes things worse! He will go back to his braves beyond the river and in a couple of days if not tomorrow they will be here. All we shall be able to do is to kill them down to the last man or be killed ourselves. Where are the sentries who were on watch last night?'

Jacques Vignot and two of the Spaniards stepped forward.

The Parisian related how at about two o'clock in the morning, as they were about to finish their watch, he had heard a French voice asking for the gates to be opened for Monsieur de Loménie-Chambord, who, the voice claimed, had been forced to turn back.

Reassured by the memory of their friendly leave-taking from Loménie's expeditionary force, the sentries had believed they were doing the right thing in opening the gates and letting him in. The foggy night was as black as pitch. No sooner had they opened the gate than they were knocked over the head and trussed up.

It was not Colonel Loménie. It was Baron Maudreuil at the head of a small party of Patsuikett Abenakis.

The cry of 'bears' having brought running outside those who, towards the end of the meal, were still sufficiently lucid and able to stand on their feet, the Indians took advantage of the darkness to knock them all out too.

It was then that the realization of a disturbing fact came upon Peyrac and his company: during the swift, silent scuffle in the night, not a single white man in the Count's service had been killed or even seriously wounded.

Some had been knocked out, most of them had seen nothing, for they had been sleeping either the sleep of the just or the sleep of the intoxicated.

It looked as if categorical orders had been given to spare the lives of the Europeans in the outpost. It seemed as if Maudreuil and Piksarett had been after the Iroquois scalps and nothing else.

The Patsuiketts had not reckoned with Count Peyrac's desperate fight to defend himself nor with his prodigious strength. One of them had been killed.

While Joffrey had been fighting in the compound, and plunging into the river to escape the blows of his assailants, Don Juan Alvarez, Maupertuis, Macollet, Malaprade, and those who were not already snoring, had witnessed the sudden appearance of Baron Maudreuil and Sagamore Piksarett.

'I realized what was going on straight away,' old Macollet explained, 'but what could I do? I couldn't get my backside off the bench. And even if I had . . . bit of a delicate situation, wasn't it? There's Maudreuil, a young lord, reeking holiness and money, and me, just a penniless old pagan. And the lad was right to come for Swanissit's scalp, since he had killed all his folk. When Swanissit saw them, he realized what it meant too, but he had gorged himself so much he couldn't budge. Anhisera and Ganatinha were equally incapable, and Ouasategan didn't see a thing as he was already snoring. Outakke was the only one to get up. And he fought like a devil before escaping through the window after smashing the frame with his fists . . . look.'

Joffrey de Peyrac ran his hand over his brow. He touched the sore spot and made the troublesome wound bleed again. This was the first blood he had spilled in his conquest of the New World. This wound would be called Etskon-Honsi, the Black Robe.

And it would not be the last.

The order to spare the Europeans had only been given for appearance sake.

They had been condemned all the same. For what primitive people, what people of any kind, could accept the outrage of these treacherous murders without seeking vengeance. From now on Katarunk would be an object of everlasting abhorrence to the Five Nations.

In spite of all the efforts made by Loménie and Count Peyrac, in spite of their reason, their wisdom, and all the patience and shrewdness they had exerted as men of honour to banish the spectre of a pointless war, it stood before them now, crazy, stupid and inevitable.

CHAPTER 30

ANGÉLIQUE slipped into the storeroom and stood motionless with her back to the door, listening for the slightest sound in the shadows.

Was the wounded Iroquois still alive? Was he dead? Was he about to spring on her? Anything was possible.

She waited. Nothing stirred.

She knelt down and crawled slowly over to where she had dragged him. The pile of old sacks she had thrown over him did not seem to have moved.

Shortly before, when someone had remarked that Outakke the chief of the Mohawks was not among the dead, she had chosen to say nothing yet. Before informing her husband they had a hostage, she must make sure that he was alive.

She ran her hand under the sacks and her fingers encountered a rigid body. He was still there, he had not moved, but had remained in the position in which she had left him, face downwards on the beaten earth floor. But Angélique felt that his flesh was warm and supple.

With a sigh of relief she got to work.

She had brought a lamp with her which she stood on a box and lit. She also had a flask of brandy, some ointment, and some pieces of lint she had found in the inadequately stocked medicine cabinet of the camp, and a calabash full of water freshly drawn from the well.

She removed the dusty sacks she had thrown over the wounded man to conceal him in the event of a search, and in the yellow light of the oil lamp his whole body was revealed, inert and marble-like. She turned him over flat on his back and held up the lamp.

Her practised eyes scrutinized him – the way he held his hands, the folds of his lips, the hollows of his closed eyes, and the pinched look about his nostrils.

It took her only a moment to decide that he would live. For she had nursed many a wounded man in her lifetime, both in Morocco and during the Poitou wars. She put down the lamp, and began to examine him more closely to discover the wound that had plunged him into this deathlike sleep.

When she laid her hand on a sick or wounded man, it was as if his body had become transparent. Invisible signs were revealed to her that lay beyond the sense of touch. She searched for her answer, her whole mind intent, scarcely touching him. Gently her fingers moved forward across the tattooed flesh. So light was their pressure that he remained unconscious, unaware of her presence. Then the Mohawk opened his eyes, and saw the white woman's profile with her hair hanging loose about her head, kneeling there in the light, like a moonbeam. He saw her lowered eyelids, and the grave line of her lips which gave her face an expression of utter absorption. And he felt the shock of her hands on him and the warm magnetic current that seemed to flow from those slender fingers with the glistening nails that shone like shells, and spread through his body to bring him to life again.

Then suddenly he saw her stiffen, like an Indian who has come upon the track of an enemy, and he heard her give a brief exclamation.

Then she nodded several times. She had lifted his bloodstained loincloth, and had discovered a wound on his right thigh, which extended almost up to the groin. A lance had been aimed at his stomach but the blow had been turned aside.

A piece of whipcord had been bound tightly around his thigh to stop the bleeding. As soon as he had broken out of the hall, Outakke had tied it himself, to prevent his blood leaving a track to show which way he had gone. It had been an effective though dangerous treatment;

for the edges of the wound and the leg itself had already swollen in an ugly way, and could have caused a fatal blood clot.

Angélique picked up the lamp again, and examined the wound with still greater care. She loosened the cord a little with great caution, and a small trickle of blood appeared. It was red, and should have gushed out in spurts. She could not understand it. The blood had stopped flowing. Within this rigid body, an impossible task of healing had already been accomplished. By what miracle, by what occult powers could it have happened? She looked up at the wounded man's face and shuddered to see that he was staring at her. Some strange power! Yes, indeed. Did she not know that Outakke, the chief of the Mohawks, had greater powers than any other? She had given much thought to the impulse she had felt the other evening to go up to the spring where he was lying in wait to kill her, and now she was sure that he had drawn her there by a spell.

She guessed that he must be capable of stopping his own blood from flowing and forcing death back step by step, by some supernatural yet acquired skill of which he held the secret. For all those hours while he had waited motionless for the white woman to return to help him, he had held death at bay as it tried to snatch him from life, by the sole strength of his secret, controlled willpower.

She began to examine him suspiciously. His catlike smell made her feel sick, and once again she had the impression which she had experienced several times in his presence, that she was not dealing with an altogether human being, but rather with a kind of animal, from an unknown world, and was almost surprised as she looked at him lying there naked and abandoned before her, to find that he had hands, feet with toes, protruding ribs, a navel, and sex organs like any other man.

She began to staunch the blood, cleaning the wound with fresh water and covering it with an ointment made from the emollient roots of the costus.

She fixed the dressing on tight hoping that the ointment would take out the swelling, and that this, coupled with the great Outakke's robust constitution, would turn his mortal wound into nothing more than a memory.

That was how the Iroquois were.

He knew that she knew. He also knew that he could harm her, but he had learnt that she was strong enough to frustrate his plans. He had 'called' her to the stream, but she had come with a dagger. She was a match for him. And it was probably because she too was on friendly terms with the Spirit of Dreams. But although it might not be a contrary power, at least it was a different one from his that animated this foreign woman, come from distant lands, and he had felt a strange shudder when she laid her hands on him.

Thus it was that Angélique and the Mohawk exchanged thoughts with each other through their glances. She wanted to convince herself that he was unconscious, and that in spite of that slanting glint that filtered from beneath his eyelids, he could not see her. She accused him of being an embodied spirit, dangerous, possessed and diabolical, and he on his side thought the same of her. And with every look, the things they learned about each other's powers, strength and character made their exchanged glances grow more and more fierce, but at the same time more and more understanding.

It was a magical duel, but a duel in which both sides were equally matched.

Who would have guessed it to see this white form kneeling at the side of a dying savage?

All they would have seen would have been a nobly born European woman devotedly tending a wretched wounded Indian, whereas they were really two creatures of equal strength, of close affinity, who were, without knowing it, embarking on an incredible adventure. . . .

With puckered brow, Angélique tied the last bandage, gave a last angry glance at the wounded man and stood up. She went across to a bale of merchandise and drew out three of the blankets intended for barter.

Trying hard not to disturb the body too much – it was as heavy as stone – she managed to slip one of the blankets between it and the ground. Then she covered him up from his feet to his chin with the second, and, rolling the third into a ball, placed it under his head.

Finally she allowed herself to look at him with satisfaction. Now at last he looked like a wounded man, like a well-behaved patient. Summoning up her courage, she slid one hand under his head, into the resin-impregnated hair of his bristling topknot, and tilted his head up a little as she held a calabash full of water to his lips. The Mohawk's impassive features came to life; he gulped the water down greedily like a child, and a deep sigh rose from his breast.

When she laid his head back on the pillow, his eyes had closed and she thought he had died, then realized that he was fast asleep.

CHAPTER 31

Angélique had to wait till the evening for the opportune moment Her husband was outside the camp for some of the day talking with Nicolas Perrot and Maupertuis, who, after some initial hesitation, seemed more and more disposed to agree with the ideas he expounded to them. One thing worried Angélique, which was that he did not seem to be feverishly organizing the defence of the outpost.

There was every indication that they could expect the Iroquois to appear any day, if not any hour. Yet the gates stood open, and Peyrac's men moved about the compound with no sign of haste. There was the odd brief discussion, a few orders were given and some of the men went off to carry them out. Some holes were dug outside the fortress on the hillside and beside the river, but they scarcely looked like fortifications.

Angélique found Florimond in one corner of the compound busy filling some stout cardboard tubes with powdered sulphur, potassium chlorate and copper oxide.

'What are you making there?'

'Fireworks.'

'Is this the moment to be thinking about fireworks?'

'Father told me to.'

'What for?'

'I don't know. Some idea of his.'

Angélique looked around. The snow had melted in a few hours, leaving a layer of shimmering moisture on the ground and the leaves, which made the sun's rays even more dazzling.

'Florimond, what is your father up to? The gates are wide open, although the Iroquois may appear at any moment.'

'Father has sent out scouts to reconnoitre and warn us about what they are doing and when they draw close.'

'What is he thinking of doing?'

'I don't know. But don't worry, Mother. I know our position is serious, but with our father things always work out.'

This was the magic formula they all used. 'With our father, with our leader, things always work out....'

When they saw certain expressions on Joffrey de Peyrac's face, his men and his sons knew that they must no longer ask any questions, but simply obey.

Well, she, Angélique, had learned the hard way that things didn't always work out easily, even with him. She had learnt at her expense that life is above all a snare set in the path of the human quest for happiness, and that, more often than one hoped, one falls into the trap. Deep down, she still found it impossible to forget or forgive the memory of the one and only time Joffrey de Peyrac seemed to have underestimated his enemy, or at least his swiftness to strike. Of course that enemy had been the most discreet, the most urbane, the most powerful King of France. Louis Deodatus, the fourteenth. It was also true that Count Joffrey de Peyrac had ignored the councils of prudence that warned him to escape immediately, in order to spend one last night with her, his wife, Angélique. And Louis XIV had struck like lightning. And both their lives had been shattered.

Even now there were still times when she felt she could only trust in her own strength, and how often, alas! she had found that strength wanting!

When something untoward happened, she found it easier to see the danger than to see what part chance or skill could play to turn it aside.

She mistrusted chance while Joffrey de Peyrac looked on the bright side and affirmed that there was always a way out from even the worst situations.

This quality in him made her envious, even a trifle jealous. He remained calm.

But he nearly lost his calm a second time in one day, when she at last caught him alone and told him that the Mohawk chief Outakke was alive, that she had saved him and nursed him, and that, far from being capable of rallying his brothers and urging them on to vengeance, he was at their mercy, in their hands.

'Why didn't you tell me about this earlier?' he exclaimed, almost banging his fist on the table. 'It seems to me it's pretty important news! This can greatly influence my plans! It strengthens my hand and makes me almost certain they will succeed.'

'What plans have you in mind?'

'That's my affair.'

'Do you intend to defend the fortress? Shall we have to fight?'

'Yes! . . . Perhaps. As a last resort. We are well armed and we could win. But if we wiped out this particular war-party it would be the end of our prospects in Upper Kennebec. Sooner or later we should be forced to depart as the Iroquois would never leave us in peace. I would prefer to try another way.'

'What way?'

'I can't talk about it yet.'

'Of course, I am too stupid to understand!' Angélique burst out. 'You seem to forget that I too led men in war! . . . But you want to send me back to my saucepans. You never tell me anything, it's infuriating!'

'And what about you!' Peyrac shouted. 'Are you so free with your explanations about what you do and what you feel? Did you ever tell me what it was, what piece of folly you committed to get hold of Outakke the other day, and bring him back, the dread enemy of the Palefaces, as if he were on a lead? . . . Do you think there's nothing extraordinary about that? Do you think that calls for no explanation, really? You come, you go, you risk your life just as it pleases you, you do fantastic, crazy things! And do you think it has nothing to do with me, your husband? Then today, after saving the Iroquois' life, you keep quiet about it for hours on end as if I were an unapproachable stranger. And what about all those Frenchmen staring at you the other evening, and the way you twisted them round your little finger. Do you think I enjoyed that? Do you think it's easy to have you for a wife!'

They glared angrily at one another, standing face to face and glowering.

Then suddenly their features began to quiver and relax, and they both burst out laughing.

'Oh, my love!' said Peyrac, drawing her to him. 'Oh my love, forgive my violence. I love you too much, that's the trouble. I am frightened of losing you and that some imprudent action of yours could be the end of you. You must admit that if you find me secretive, you give me as good as you get. But with every day that passes, I realize just how precious you are to me.

'Take this morning for instance! I would have choked with anger had you not been there, beside me, close to me. I could see in your eyes that you felt exactly as I did. It may be that you inspired me. We are very close, my love, much closer than we think, and I think we are very like each other. But I am still not going to tell you. Not yet, little lady! . . . I can only ask you to be patient. It's a shot in the dark, and a gambler needs to be alone and to concentrate his full attention on what he's doing. I have two wise advisers, Perrot and Maupertuis, to support me, and they approve of what I am attempting to do.'

He took her face between his hands and gazed into her eyes.

'Trust me, will you, my love?'

And such was the power of his loving, masterful gaze that all she could do was lower her eyelids as a sign of assent, and yield to his will.

Outakke opened his eyes. He saw two silhouettes standing beside his bed, in the bright frame of the open doorway. A man and a woman leaning against one another. Then he shut his eyes again in despair, for he already knew that his hatred would break against this rampart.

'My greetings to you, Outakke,' Count Peyrac said in even tones. 'I bring you news. Take courage, my brother! Swanissit, Ouasategan, Anhisera and Ganatinha were killed last night, struck down by the dastardly tomahawks of the Patsuiketts.'

'I know. I saw it.'

'Outakke, I remember the words that Swanissit told me in confidence. You are his heir. I therefore salute you as chief of the Five Nations.'

The Indian remained silent for a long time before replying in a dull voice:

'You invited us into your fortress, you made us enter your palisade and treachery awaited us behind those stakes!'

'But who was it who struck the blow? Tell me! Who was it who struck, since you saw it all?'

'It was Baron Maudreuil and his cursed allies, the Patsuiketts, children of Black Robe.'

'So you know it wasn't me. So you know that those who entered my fortress to strike you betrayed me too!

'Don't try to make my brow redden with shame, for it is already red with the blood those same Patsuiketts shed with their blows. Look!'

And he pointed to the bandage round his head.

Outakke seemed to hesitate, then raised himself up on one elbow, and a bitter grimace twisted his inscrutable features.

'What do I care about the Palefaces' quarrels,' he remarked disdainfully. 'They all stand by one another and I regard them all as one single enemy.'

'You are talking deliberate nonsense, Outakke, or else the fever is confusing your mind. I for one would never blame an Iroquois for a Huron's treachery, although Hurons and Iroquois are members of the same race, as I myself am a Frenchman.'

He was silent for a considerable while to give the Indian time to consider the comparison. Then he went on in persuasive tones:

'Outakke, take heart. Consider what I have said and, before you make up your mind, think about the fate of your people.'

'We have left braves on the other side of the river,' the Mohawk replied, 'and Tahoutaguete is in the forest. Soon they will learn what has happened, soon they will be here.'

And he fell back.

'You can kill me, Tekonderoga, but you will never prevent the Five Nations from avenging their dead.'

'And whoever said that I wanted to prevent them doing so,' the Count replied quietly. 'Yes, people of the Long House, come to Katarunk! Come, Five Nations of the Iroquois League! Come and avenge your dead! ...'

And he went off, taking Angélique with him, leaving the chief of the Mohawks puzzled and anxious.

The air was so dry and clear that the echo of the fierce battle between the Patsuiketts and the Iroquois lower down the river near Mobedean seemed to carry all the way to Katarunk.

They heard later that almost all the Patsuikett braves had been massacred. A few of them managed to escape and Piksarett was the last to remain.

Father Orgeval was struck in the side by an arrow. Piksarett, seeing him alone, lifted him on to his back and ran off into the thicket, where, although the Iroquois pursued him, they were unable to catch him. He carried the missionary to the Penobscot, where there was a French outpost on the island of Novumbega. It was a long time before anyone discovered what had happened to Maudreuil.

The victorious Iroquois, after setting fire to the village, roasted alive two Abenakis they had managed to seize.

And the following day they set out for Katarunk, where they had learned that their chieftains had met with an ignominious death.

CHAPTER 32

ANGÉLIQUE was kneeling, dressing the Iroquois' wound, as he lay on a pallet in the main room of the cottage, when an indefinable noise, both piercing and rumbling, rose up into the clear sky, grew until it drowned everything, then suddenly died away.

199

Angélique glanced out of the open window, looking for some sign of thunder or storm. But the sky was blue.

Outakke had sat up, his eye a-glitter.

Then she understood, and a shudder ran down her spine.

What she had heard was the Iroquois war cry.

But once again all was silent, and not a musket shot was fired in reply to the terrifying din.

Angélique finished dressing the savage's wound. She carefully tidied away the medicines and the lint, placing them all in the bundle she had prepared, for they had been told without further explanation to keep a small pack ready in case of need. Her pack contained one dress, a change of underwear, her tortoise-shell-and-gold toilet case, now lacking the mirror she had given to Swanissit, and Honorine's box of treasures.

There were moments when she began to suspect how Peyrac hoped to save their lives and still keep his influence in the area intact. Then she would shake her head, for it seemed impossible to manage such a thing without a terrible battle.

She checked that her pistol was ready on her hip. They all had to be armed; Madame Jonas stood holding a musket in her arms as if it were a child. On hearing the noise they had left their room and gathered with the children round Angélique, whose composure reassured them. There they waited with their weapons and their luggage, looking down at the Iroquois at their feet as if he were a poisonous beast.

When instructed, they were to cross the courtyard and leave the fort without showing any signs of fear. That was all they had to do. They had absolutely no idea of what was going to happen.

Maupertuis and his son came in, grasped the Mohawk under the shoulders, stood him on his feet and supported him so that he could remain standing.

Then Count Peyrac came in, magnificently dressed in scarlet.

'Your brothers are here,' he said.

Slowly he drew on his leather gloves with their silver-tooled gauntlets, and almost seemed to be smiling.

'They're here! Nicolas Perrot is watching them from the top of the hill and they are watching him. They don't know whether to pierce him through with their arrows, and they are waiting for you to come and tell them what to do.'

'What are you trying to get me to do, Tekonderoga,' asked the

Indian with a shudder. 'You know very well that if I open my mouth it will be to call my brothers to vengeance.'

'Against whom?'

'It was in your camp, beneath your roof that the treachery took place....'

'I know. I shall wipe out the shame. That's my business. But what about you? You asked the white woman of Katarunk, my wife, to grant you your life, and she granted it. That alone ought to tell you we do not seek the death of the Iroquois. But there is more....

'Remember, Outakke, why it was that Swanissit died. He risked everything to come here, and become my ally. Now you are the chief of the Five Nations. Where will you lead them? Towards peace, or extermination....'

He stood towering over the Indian and, just as the other evening he had bowed before him, now he did his utmost to dominate him. It was scarcely conceivable that he would be able to win over this restive soul. But it was a question of life or death.

All their lives depended on this flickering flame:

'Extermination,' cried Outakke. 'Yes! But you shall die first.'

'So be it, we shall all die!' said Peyrac philosophically. 'Monsieur Macollet,' he said, turning to the old Canadian who had entered the room with him, 'you know what you have to do. I entrust these ladies and their children to your care. Get yourselves in a position where you cannot lose sight of Nicolas Perrot. If he signals to you, as we have agreed, you will know that you must bring them back immediately into the shelter of the palisade and prepare for battle.'

'I'll keep my eyes open,' said the old man.

Peyrac looked at the Iroquois chief whom Maupertuis and his sons were holding erect.

His trump card! Thanks to Angélique....

'Give him a swig of rum,' he said, 'to help him to stand up! Then come along, everyone.'

As he strode across the compound, he tore the dressing from the wound on his forehead, and blood began to trickle slowly from it again.

Yann le Couennec was waiting for him, holding his black stallion by the bridle.

Peyrac leapt into the saddle, galloped off towards the open gates of the outpost and disappeared through the sunlit opening.

As he appeared, the Iroquois gave their war cry a second time and Angélique stopped short, her heart gripped with fear. But once again no shots were fired in response to their bellicose roar.

'Come along now!' said Macollet. 'When you are acting a part you must act it to the bitter end, ladies. Nothing will stop a wild beast in its tracks so effectively as a surprise, something it doesn't understand. Some of those savages have never even seen a horse! . . . And don't forget, ladies, if you feel a trifle anxious, that you never had, nor will you ever have again, a gentleman in attendance who's a patch on me.'

He went on in this vein and by the time they reached the gates of the fortress they were almost laughing.

There stood Nicolas Perrot, hands behind his back, the fringes of his doeskin clothes and the point of his fur cap flapping in the wind, as he looked out calmly down the hillside towards the river and the Iroquois army.

Joffrey de Peyrac was prancing up and down on his restive horse, and seemed to be inspecting his assembled men, who held banners in their hands.

The Spaniards' black breastplates sparkled in the sunshine.

Maupertuis and his son, supporting Chief Outakke, went and stood beside Nicolas Perrot.

A dull roar rose up from the foot of the hill.

Angélique looked in the direction from which it had come and felt the blood drain from her cheeks.

Both sides of the river and the beach were thick with a throng of filthy, feathered, blood-stained savages. The water was covered with canoe-loads of braves and more kept arriving in an endless procession.

Seen through the cloud of dust they raised as they disembarked, they formed a busy, moving mass, brandishing their bows and tomahawks, yet remaining almost silent.

They were all looking up towards the outpost.

They were looking at Nicolas Perrot, whose moccasins had so often trodden the secret valley and who had sailed across the five lakes of the Five Nations. In their eyes he was almost an Indian! . . . They looked at Outakke and no longer understood, for they had been told that all their chiefs had died at Katarunk! . . .

And the sight of Count Peyrac on that black, fabulous animal, quite clearly filled them with superstitious dread.

They went on congregating at the foot of the slope, but remained expectant.

Joffrey de Peyrac dismounted from his horse and took up his position towards the front beside Perrot and Outakke.

His cloak billowed in the wind, which likewise blew his hair, his lace jabot, and the streaming ribbons that hung from the shoulders of his doublet.

Angélique clasped Honorine's little hand in hers. She looked around for her sons, and saw them standing very straight, slightly back from the others, each holding one of the great banners embroidered in red, blue and gold, with their pennants flapping in the wind.

She did not know what the banners represented; she must ask them one day.

Everyone seemed so calm that it did not seem possible that anything terrible was likely to occur.

'What's going to happen?' Angélique whispered to Macollet.

'Well, for the moment, they're just looking at one another. Summing one another up! Counting the odds! They hadn't expected to find Outakke alive, and, what's more, those chaps there are frightened of palisades and open land. Then when in addition they find all the Palefaces gathered together outside, waiting for them, they don't know where they are any more. . . . They wonder what they should do! Look, some of them have begun to dance to give themselves courage. They are behaving like a cat trying to frighten a mouse. But at the moment no one knows who is the cat and who is the mouse. Careful now! They are going to give their war cry again. Don't move. . . . Don't show you are frightened. . . .'

An inhuman bellow rose from their hoarse throats and open mouths.

Madame Jonas and Elvire huddled close to Angélique, who held on to the frightened children saying: 'Don't be upset, it's only because they are all shouting together that it makes such a noise!'

The youngsters hid their faces in her skirt.

This time there was an answer. Two violent explosions were heard, one coming from the shore, not far from the spot where the advance guard of the Iroquois army was standing, and the other from the cliff behind the outpost.

Huge lumps of rock were hurled into the air, falling back to earth again with a crash multiplied many times by its echoes.

A breath of panic swept over the Iroquois, who began to waver in all directions.

A number of them surged back to the clumps of willows where they took cover while others hastily took to the water again. The bravest among them tried to form up again, lifting their arrows to their bow-strings. But a succession of explosions distracted them and they did not know which way to turn.

'What is it?' asked Outakke who had turned pale.

'Your brothers greeted me with a shout,' said Peyrac. 'That is my reply. Have you forgotten that I am the Man of Thunder? . . .'

And he added ironically:

'What are you frightened of, Outakke? What are they all frightened of? It's only some stones falling.'

The Mohawk chief stared fixedly at him.

'What do you seek from me?'

'I want to discuss the question of blood-money with you and your people.'

'What blood-money could ever pay for our chiefs?'

'Let us discuss it and you will hear.'

Outakke turned towards his braves and began to abuse them. But his voice had grown weak and did not carry. Perrot relayed his message for him and, with his hands cupped round his mouth, insulted them up hill and down dale on behalf of their chieftain.

'You dogs! You jackals! Come back! Show yourselves! It's only some stones falling. Let the chiefs come forward. We are going to discuss blood-money. . . .'

Eventually the braves calmed down and seemed to have decided to agree to a pow-wow, to discuss the question of blood-money.

They had already gained a respite.

The dictates of tradition were now going to allow enemies to sit down together with all the appearance of friendship, and meet the Indians' impulsiveness with a barrage of arguments, proposals and sober thought.

The leaders stepped forward. At their head stood old Tahoutaguete with his dark, hideous, pock-marked face. But the other Indians also climbed the hill behind them, settling in dense masses on the slope in reclining or sitting positions. In the sunshine the smell of these naked bodies rose in great waves, and hundreds of black, inscrutable eyes formed a kind of magic circle around Katarunk.

'They've not left us much of a retreat,' said Macollet. 'But never mind! Let's sit down too, ladies. We are in a good position here. If Perrot signals to me, it will mean that things are going badly and that there is no more hope. Then we shall have to take cover as quickly as possible, and hey ho for the big bangs.'

'What a lot there are,' said Angélique.

'Pooh! No more than a hundred. Their weapons aren't up to much and they're tired. You can see it. They must be war parties who agreed to meet here after their campaign. With weapons like ours we should easily get the better of them.'

'My husband hopes things will be settled peacefully.'

'And why not? In this country, Madame, until you are actually dead, you can never say that the situation is desperate. Of course, this time we mustn't lose sight of the fact that four of their big chiefs have been killed. But we can always try.'

And he waved a hand in the direction of one of the Iroquois who was seated not far from him, and called out something as he half lifted his red woollen cap.

'I told him there was no point in trying to scalp me, because it had been done already. Ha! Ha! Ha!'

'And you can laugh about it!' Madame Jonas said with a sigh, looking at him in admiration.

'That's the way it is here. You must always laugh, even if you're tied to the torture stake.'

Meanwhile Outakke, the two Canadians and Count Peyrac had seated themselves opposite the Indian leaders. Peyrac's other men had likewise taken up their positions behind him, and seemed calm, even casual, but Angélique, who was secretly keeping an eye on them, noticed that they were all on the alert, that each one had his allotted task. And their concentration never faltered for a single moment. Occasionally someone would enter or leave the fort, and everything that was done that day was done so efficiently, with such perfect discipline, that Angélique came to the conclusion that the men Peyrac had brought with him, although to her some had appeared unexceptional though not without use, had in fact been handpicked.

In spite of all their faults and failings, when danger threatened they turned out to be as cunning as serpents, unquestioningly loyal and unfailingly brave.

Count Peyrac began, through his interpreter, Nicolas Perrot, by reminding the Iroquois braves of the agreements they had reached with Swanissit before he had been treacherously murdered.

From where she sat, Angélique had no difficulty in following their gestures; she could hear bursts of conversation, as Nicolas Perrot tirelessly translated the French point of view to the Iroquois, and the lengthy speeches of the Iroquois which he repeated without leaving out a single word, even when these consisted solely of a flood of invective and threats to Peyrac.

Then Peyrac stood up, displaying his dazzling clothes, and fixing them with a fiery stare, so that he added the full weight of his personal magnetism to that of his eloquence.

He reminded them of the approaches he had made to the Five Nations and how Swanissit had thought them worthy of consideration. And how the other evening he and the wary old chief, who for more than twenty years had led his braves on the warpath, had made a peace treaty – there were wampum necklaces to testify to this – a treaty that covered all the Palefaces under Peyrac, or his allies, in fact all those who claimed the protection of his flag or of an alliance with him.

A secret sign would allow them to mingle with the Iroquois people with impunity, regardless of their nationality, whether they were French, English, Spanish, or Flemish, that is to say Dutch.

In return Peyrac and his people would undertake never to take up arms against the Iroquois, even if asked to do so by their French compatriots from Quebec or by the Abenakis, or the Algonquins, with whom they had signed peace treaties.

He had also added a promise, which the old chief had particularly insisted on, not to sell brandy to the people of the Long House, and not to encourage trade in beaver skins, thus preventing them from hunting the deer and the moose, or planting crops.

The old Seneca had been like a father to them until the moment of his death, seeking to protect his people from the two great temptations, fire-water and trading, that might bring about the rapid downfall of his people through degeneration and famine.

For, urged on by the white traders for ever to hunt beavers, and still more beavers, the Iroquois had ceased to hunt for food or grow crops, and a harsh or lengthy winter would wipe out whole tribes, who had not managed to gather enough food to see them through. The third temptation, the most crucial for the Iroquois people, was war, as Swanissit had explained to Peyrac. And here again the old chief had tried to save his people from this mortal danger by forcing them to live in peace with at least one Paleface, namely the Man of Thunder and his tribe.

To support these undertakings and to serve as a reminder in years to come to those who might be tempted to forget them, Count Peyrac had promised to make a gift each year to each of the five chiefs of the Five Nations, of a long-barrelled flint-lock gun, to which he would add two barrels of gunpowder and two barrels of lead shot for hunting, five fishing nets of English fibre, ten scarlet blankets of English wool, five scarlet or blue jackets according to choice, which would not lose their colour either in the rain or the sunshine, two hundred and fifty knives, two hundred hatchets, five saws for felling trees, five barrels of saltpetre, which is the wonder dust that makes the maize grow. And in addition a few of the cooking-pots which are known as cauldrons, of varied sizes, from Iron Mills, the best foundry in Massachusetts.

Should such agreements, so advantageous for the Iroquois people, be revoked without having given them a trial, if only for a year?

Tahoutaguete shouted something and Nicolas Perrot's voice repeated it after him.

'It is you, Paleface, who went back on your agreements even before they had been tried out. For we have never seen your gifts; but treacherous death and your attack, those we saw. It was you who provoked war between our peoples as soon as we had decided to set warfare aside.'

Peyrac showed no sign of dismay, but replied through Nicolas Perrot that Tahoutaguete was mistaken.

They would shortly be able to see all the presents Swanissit and his plenipotentiaries had received when they concluded the agreements, but first he would ask Outakke to give his brothers an account of the attack and tell them of the circumstances under which the Iroquois chiefs had met their deaths.

The Mohawk grudgingly agreed to do so.

Perrot, Maupertuis and all the other Palefaces who knew the Iroquois tongue listened carefully to what he had to say. Twice they forced him to admit that he had seen, with his own eyes, Peyrac's men struck mortal blows by their assailants; and he told how Baron Maudreuil and the Patsuiketts had used treachery to enter the outpost, and that afterwards the white woman, Tekonderoga's wife, had saved him from Piksarett who was hunting him down to kill him.

Then Peyrac threw back his hair to show them his red wound, and reminded them that it had been an Abenaki tomahawk that had caused it.

It was an exhausting duel of words. Not so much a duel in fact as a single-handed battle which he had taken on with the assistance of his interpreters. As far as the savages were concerned, the matter was already settled. He was to die. But the sight of the blows he had received seemed nevertheless to impress them.

It was very hot.

The discussions had been going on for hours. From time to time someone would walk down to the river to have a drink or to cool off. Angélique remembered that she had prepared a few slices of bread with a piece of fat pork and that she had them with her in her baggage; so she handed them out to the children to keep them happy.

They were all so exhausted that they had ceased to be frightened. Then suddenly things rose to fever pitch again and Peyrac's Spaniards imperceptibly moved in the direction of their weapons, ready to fire.

Outakke's statements had greatly disturbed the savages.

The fever of battle and of revenge was slow to subside in the heart of an Iroquois.

They all sensed that the savages had come to kill, and that they had no intention of being deprived of their pleasure, for incalculable pleasure it was to avenge a hundredfold the death of a brother, and still more so if he were a beloved and venerated chief. They were grief-stricken at the mere idea that they might not be able to assuage their thirst for blood, and they kept on muttering restlessly.

A young brave, more impatient than the rest, went up to Florimond, lifted his thick hair, and drew a circle in the air round his head with his knife. At the sight of this dumb show, Angélique found it hard to suppress a cry.

Florimond, imitating his father's composure, did not blench, and the Iroquois went off again, abandoning all attempts to frighten him. Angélique was full of admiration for her elder son. His delicate brown profile stood out like a medallion against the blue sky, and she thought with a quickening of the pulse that he was Joffrey de Peyrac's son. And because long, long ago, on the banks of the Garonne, under the star-spangled sky of Aquitaine, Joffrey had taken Angélique in his arms and had made her a woman, the sterling qualities that were his flowed through the veins of this young man. It was like discovering something quite new. But it had never seemed so clear before, and she thought: our son! ...

She was not really frightened on Florimond's behalf, but she considered Cantor too young to be exposed to danger like this, although he stood his ground pluckily and never flinched, banner in hand. Sweat was pouring down his round face, and she would have liked him to come and sit beside her with the other children, but he would never have forgiven her.

She also felt some anxiety for 'her' patient, Chief Outakke. How could a man, wounded as he was, stand up to so many hours of wrangling and agitation?

'Don't worry about him,' said Eloi Macollet, to whom she confided her anxiety. 'I know those critters, I tell yee. They've got several lives to spare, and so long as he can talk his head off he'll be all the better for it.'

'Couldn't you take him something to drink?' Angélique begged him.

'If he went and died there, right in the middle of the Council, that wouldn't do us any good.'

The Canadian did as she suggested and took a calabash of water over to the survivor of the Abenakis' bloodbath. This considerate gesture seemed to please him.

The murmurs had died down. The Iroquois were chewing over the account of the attack they had been given and their vivid imaginations could picture every twist and turn of it. From time to time they threw out a question then went back to their thoughts once more.

At this juncture, Joffrey de Peyrac stood up and began a long speech, which he interrupted at frequent intervals to allow Nicolas Perrot, who had stood up also, to translate his words in all solemnity so that they could be heard by those farthest away. 'Now hear me, all of you. I know that the sacred laws of vengeance forbid you to touch any food whatsoever before avenging your dead. You have attacked the Patsuiketts farther up the river and have killed and dispersed them. You might well consider that your duty towards your dead chiefs has been fulfilled, for the Patsuiketts alone are guilty. But I also know that your hearts are full of hatred towards me. Nevertheless, considering myself an ally of Swanissit, even beyond the grave, I shall treat you as friends. I welcome you without fear, as you see, since I do not wish to insult Swanissit by treating his sons as enemies before they themselves have given any sign of their hostility.

'I have therefore prepared a fitting welcome for friendly braves. Here are three piles containing the things I intend to give you.

'First there are supplies. You will not touch them until your hearts have grown calm and you have felt within you that your honour has been appeased. Then you will eat your fill. There are twenty earthenware jars of maize, four of moose meat, two of bear along with some vegetable marrows and some dried berries to give savour to your "sagamité". This will serve to strengthen the bodies of braves grown weary from a long campaign, to the point of giving way to the weakness of blind rage rather than thinking of the future of their race.'

Someone stood up and protested violently, but his neighbours reduced him to silence. It was evident that they were curious to know what gifts lay in the second pile.

'Hatchets and English knives to defend yourselves, two barrels of gunpowder and two of shot, three muskets and one flintlock gun.'

'You gave Swanissit a gun too....' someone shouted.

'And it shall not be taken from him. He will take it with him into his grave, so that he may catch his game the more easily in the Happy

Hunting-ground. As for the third pile you can make use of that immediately. No, do not make the sign of disdain and refusal, braves of the Five Nations. It is tobacco from Virginia, and there is no discredit in smoking before making up one's mind between peace and war, for tobacco will help you to act wisely when your spirits have been cheered.'

Outakke and Tahoutaguete consulted each other and agreed.

The temptation was too great for the exhausted Iroquois, who were swept by alternate waves of exhaustion and frenzy.

Nicolas Perrot, Maupertuis and Pierre-Joseph, the half-caste, handed out the strings of dried tobacco and a few pipes to be passed around from man to man.

'I'll be leaving you for a moment,' said old Macollet to the ladies, 'I must just go and chum up with them ruffians. Things look as if they've gone off the boil for a bit, and we'd better make the most of it.'

He went and sat down among the Iroquois, lighted his pipe from one of theirs and began to chat with them on the friendliest of terms. Maupertuis and his son, the half-caste Huron, went right down to the river's edge, noisily greeting those they recognized, and Angélique shuddered at their daring as she saw them alone and unarmed in the midst of these hostile savages.

The Iroquois smoked avidly. Thick blue wreaths of smoke rose from their lips and it was apparent that indulgence in the fragrant weed was calming their turbulent hearts and exchanging their grief and anger for a brief period of lethargy.

An hour went by almost in silence, occasionally broken by the cry of bustards or wild geese from the river's edge, whose V-shaped flight across the whitening sky was watched dreamily by all the savages reclining on the parched earth.

Fine dust mingled with the smoke and everything around them took on a hazy appearance through which colours glowed with heightened intensity.

Angélique felt a hand on her arm. Old Macollet had come back and was pointing to the sun, which had begun to descend towards the horizon.

She looked at her husband and saw him cough twice. For hours on end he had never stopped talking, and his aching throat must be torturing him.

She wished with all her heart that she could be close beside him, enveloping him with her tenderness and her passionate devotion. For hours now he had been fighting, he had been carrying them all on his outstretched arms. When, oh when, would victory be granted him?

Tahoutaguete rose suddenly and began to speak with great emotion.

'This is what Tahoutaguete says in the name of the Five Nations,' said Nicolas Perrot:

'Man of Thunder, do you think your gifts can bring our beloved chiefs back to life again? We have received presents and food, but they have received nothing but shame and death.'

A wave of commotion swept over the savages as he spoke. Once again Joffrey de Peyrac turned to face them. He seemed to be gathering all his strength together and spoke with such persuasive passion that he communicated it to Nicolas Perrot, whose voice rose firm and strong, alternating with Peyrac's.

'That is where you are wrong, braves! Iroquois braves! Your chiefs will not have received nothing but shame and death here, for, let me tell you, ever since the Sacred Valley took the Iroquois peoples into its bosom, not one of your chiefs has ever gone to his grave accompanied by so many riches and gifts and honours as these. . . . In your hearts you are saying: "They died far from their villages, and we are unable to drape their bodies with gowns and furs, neither are we able to give them cauldrons, nor weapons to use in the Happy Hunting-ground!" Well, look upon these things!'

And the armed Spaniards who had been standing in a close-knit group slightly in front of the outpost towards the left, solemnly drew apart and revealed what it was that Count Peyrac had wished to keep hidden up till now from the Iroquois army.

The moment had come.

At the foot of the great red maple sat Swanissit, Ouasategan, Anhisera and Ganatinha, cross-legged, their weapons in their arms, heads erect and eyes closed.

Magnificent plumed and tufted headdresses hid the ignominious sight of their scalped heads and a skilful hand had traced festive lines in ochre and vermilion across the cold livid skin of their dead faces. This too had been the work of the two Canadian trappers, who, bending low over the Iroquois faces, had recalled their memories of life amongst the Indians. These memories had been so closely woven into the fabric of their Paleface hearts, so inextricably bound up with their lives, that it would have been impossible to tell just how much of the Indian and how much of the European their hearts contained.

Maupertuis's thick finger had reverently outlined Swanissit's cheek-bones in red while Nicolas Perrot had drawn a long yellow line across

Anhisera's cheek, in memory of the first wound he received as a young brave.

When they had finished they had decked the Indian chiefs in sumptuous cloaks of fur or figured silk which Count Peyrac had brought with him in his coffers. They had driven a stake into the ground behind each figure and tied each by the neck and the back by way of support, enabling them to sit erect before their people; and these stakes had been decorated with ribbons and plumes that danced in the wind.

When the Iroquois saw the chieftains a muffled lament went up on all sides. Far from their own valley, in enemy territory, they saw their dead chiefs before them, and saw that the robes they had been decked in and the honours that had been bestowed on them were far in excess of anything their own people could have given them had they been slain in war.

They stood up and surged forward.

'Speak to them,' said Peyrac, laying an imperative hand on Nicolas Perrot's shoulder. 'Speak to them quickly! . . . Say anything to them! Show them the gifts the dead men have received!'

And Nicolas Perrot's voice rose up calm yet firm, dominating them because it was a familiar voice, as he began to run through the items like a merchant in a bazaar.

He held their attention, drawing their thoughts away from the horrible reality that faced them, the reality of their dead chiefs, and distracting them from their grief with all the skill of a medieval jongleur. He showed them the four silver bows with their multicoloured arrows encrusted with shells in leather quivers embroidered with thousands of beads, the scarlet blankets, rolls of tobacco, the ermine skins sewn together and the white bear skins, lynx and wolf skins which were to be thrown into the grave for the dead men to lie on. He counted out the jars of maize and rice, fat and meat, one for each dead chief so that he might eat during his long journey to the Happy Hunting-grounds. He explained the symbolic meaning of four unfamiliar objects, that looked like a kind of yellow flower and re-sembled touchwood; these were for wiping away their tears, for these huge light objects, known as sponges, came from distant islands, and were able to absorb water.

He took a calabash and demonstrated what the sponge could do.

Just as the pure water had suddenly vanished on contact with the sponge, so would their tears of shame and despair be wiped away, he told them.

He described the message inscribed on the two magnificent wampums, while the Iroquois' tears trickled down their smooth faces and they passed the damp sponges from one man to another, wiping the warpaint from their gaudily painted cheeks.

For the newly arrived Europeans, it was a strange sight to see the savages weeping and wiping their eyes with sponges, a grotesque spectacle, moving and tragic, a spectacle that brought laughter to their lips and tears to their eyes at the same time. Nicolas showed them the famous necklace the Palefaces had received as a token of faith from the Abenakis, a priceless treasure, ancient and venerable, showing a rising sun in blue on a white background and a procession of fish and sea-lions hand in hand – or flipper in flipper – a matter of personal opinion – two of the most handsome necklaces in all the treasures Tekonderoga possessed, which Swanissit could present to the Supreme Spirit by way of reparation for the treachery on the part of the Abenakis of which he had been a victim.

Then, growing still bolder, he described to them in detail the magnificent costume Swanissit was wearing, heavily embroidered with gold and silver threads, the very same costume that Hiawatha, the great founder of the Iroquois league, had told them should be worn by him who was to carry on his own work, by saving the Iroquois people from perpetual warfare, and keeping them at peace, to the benefit of their hunting and harvests alike.

The braves crowded round to look at and touch the magnificent gifts that had been made to their dead.

They were jostling one another with growing excitement, and they were dangerously close. While most of them manifested sincere admiration, it was obvious that some of them had grown covetous, and were casting glances towards the fort and arguing among themselves.

Angélique felt the change in the atmosphere; they had reached a turning-point. This was the moment at which Peyrac would either win or lose.

She noticed that those of Peyrac's men who had been standing farthest back, carrying the banners, had begun to slip away surreptitiously into the darkness.

Others, under cover of nightfall, had led the horses away into the forest, and Yann came over to Angélique and whispered that she and the other women and children were to move away too, and make their way quietly down towards the river-bank without making their movements too apparent.

The Spaniards covered the silent retreat, for they had loaded and prepared their weapons without the slightest sound.

'Look after Honorine for me, will you, and go down with Yann,' Angélique told the Jonases. 'I'll join you in a moment.'

Nothing could have induced her to leave until she saw her husband out of danger.

She noticed that the Iroquois were creeping up and peering through the gates at the interior of the outpost.

The blueish shadows grew thicker while a great red patch in the western sky continued to cast a coppery glow over everything.

She went up to the group of men which included Joffrey de Peyrac, Nicolas, Maupertuis and his son, Eloi Macollet, and a few of the men from the *Gouldsboro*, such as Malaprade and the Maltese Enrico Enzi who were standing guard behind their master.

Outakke stood in the midst of them, leaning on Pierre-Joseph Maupertuis's shoulder, but by now they were completely surrounded by Iroquois, who were growing progressively bolder and wanted to take a closer look at the fort.

It was not Joffrey de Peyrac that Angélique looked at, but Outakke. She stared so intently at him that, bit by bit, as if by some attraction, the Mohawk turned his head slightly to one side and his fearless, lustreless eyes met those of the young white woman.

'I granted you your life the other evening, by the spring,' her eyes cried out to him. 'When you were wounded I saved you from the hands of Piksarett who was after your scalp! . . . And now, you save him, save him! You who are able to, I beg you to save him!'

It was both an order and a supplication that flashed from her pale, staring eyes, and a wave of indefinable emotion swept over the Mohawk's yellow face.

A group of braves had drawn close to Peyrac and were talking to him insolently.

'And what about the firewater, the precious drink of the Paleface, where is it? We noticed that you refused to give any to our chiefs! . . .'

Their self-appointed spokesman sniggered as he casually balanced his tomahawk on the end of a brown hand.

'The brandy and the rum are inside the outpost,' the Count replied. 'They are gathered together in a single lot, which has been set aside as a tribute to the Great Spirit, and they are not for you.'

The man let out an ironical exclamation and shouted something in a mixture of rage and triumph.

Nicolas Perrot suppressed a grimace but translated in unfaltering tones:

'He says: we shall take it ourselves without your permission, Tekonderoga, you ally of the traitors who killed our chiefs.'

On hearing these insulting words, Peyrac took a step towards the man until he almost touched him, and stared fixedly into his eyes.

'And what is thy name, thou who darest to lay claim to something that has been offered as a tribute to the Great Spirit?'

The Indian leapt back a pace and raised his tomahawk but Peyrac neatly avoided the blow that whistled over his head then, standing up again, brandished his pistol and struck his adversary on the temple with the butt.

The Indian reeled backwards and collapsed stunned among his companions. Angélique's cry was lost amidst the roar that rose from the Iroquois.

But a still more imperious cry hushed the tumult. It was Outakke.

One arm raised, he placed himself in front of Peyrac, protecting him with his own body. Silence fell again, and all lowered their weapons. Outakke made a sign to a young brave to come and help him to stand, then, turning towards Peyrac, he spoke softly to him in French.

'I do not wish your death, Tekonderoga. The spirit of justice required me to grant you your life, for it is true that if vengeance is one of the laws of our people, that of gratitude takes precedence, and I would be false were I to forget that your wife Kawa, the Fixed Star, has twice saved my life. . . . Yes twice. . . . But will my braves agree to leave you alive and to retire without a fight? That I cannot answer! Nevertheless, I shall try to persuade them . . . and you will give me credit for trying, even if I fail.'

In moments of great stress, incongruous thoughts always seem to flash across one's mind. Angélique later remembered that the thing that had struck her above all at that moment was that the Mohawk, just like the Canadian trappers or lords he had mixed with in his youth, spoke French in a highly polished manner, and that nothing could have been more startling than to hear such choice phrases rippling over those barbarous lips.

'Our hearts are not quick to forget insults,' he went on. 'My authority will be weakened if I ask them to spare you.'

'I am not asking you to forget,' Peyrac replied.

Angélique could bear it no longer. Now she knew that even if Outakke intervened he could not save them. Only one thought remained to her, to take refuge inside the fort, to barricade the heavy log gates and to seize the muskets. Enough of this! She could no longer bear to see Joffrey exposed as he was, in constant danger of being killed. . . .

But he seemed in no hurry to leave, neither did he appear to be unduly wearied from the tensions of the day.

'I do not ask you to forget,' he repeated more loudly. 'In fact I intend to make it impossible for you ever to forget what has taken place at Katarunk. You are all busy asking yourselves: "If we spare these Palefaces, who will wipe out the shame that the renown of the Iroquois has suffered here?" And I reply: "I will.". . .

'Perrot, translate please. . . .

'You think that the pow-wow is over. But it isn't! Things are just beginning. You have seen nothing yet, heard nothing yet, men of the Iroquois nation. For it is now that I am about to speak. Listen well! For I want my words and my actions to sink like arrows into your hearts, for only then will you be able to leave this place without bitterness, your hearts satisfied. It is not true, my brothers, that the heart of the Paleface and the heart of the Indian are incapable of sharing the same feelings. For my heart, like yours, is filled with horror when I contemplate the outpost of Katarunk. Like you, I cannot help thinking that this place has seen the foulest of murders, the most loathsome of treacheries that I have ever seen committed in my many long years! . . . Like you, I believe that this place of treachery bears forever an indelible mark, and that the sight of it perpetuates that memory, and so all just men would wish to see it wiped out. . . . Moreover, are those who in future years might come to this outpost to say every time they come here: "That was where Swanissit was scalped, beneath the roof of his host, the Paleface Tekonderoga, the Man of Thunder"? No! . . . No! . . . That I could not bear!' cried Count Peyrac with a depth of violence and anger that awed them, and which on this occasion – Angélique could sense it – was not feigned. 'No, I could not bear that. Rather let everything be wiped out. . . . Let everything be wiped out! . . .'

He coughed after shouting these last words.

Nicolas Perrot slowly repeated what he had said, with a kind of exaltation: 'Let everything be wiped out! . . . Let everything be wiped out!' And now it seemed as if every eye in the dusk was glued to those two upright figures, the trapper and Count Peyrac, in his storm-coloured clothes, as they stood there still just visible in the last glimmer of the sunset.

'I know,' the Count went on, 'there are some among you who are thinking: "There are some good wares in that outpost!" Some of you would like to satisfy both your greed and your desire for vengeance! May those jackals cease their growling and sniffing around and go away, their tails between their legs. For I am telling you that from henceforth everything inside this fortress belongs to the shades of your ancestors. Thus, and only thus will they be satisfied!

'You have received your gifts. They are valuable gifts. And when you come to load them on your backs, you will realize that they are considerable gifts.

'But that which lies within this fort of Katarunk you have no right to take, any more than I have the right to make use of it. I have given it to the shades of your dead chiefs, in compensation for the treachery they suffered.

'Harken to me, and remember my words: in this fort lies food for several months, possibly enough to last years, venison, moose and bear meat, dried and salted cod, salt from the sea, ten barrels of sunflower-seed oil, whale oil and sea-lion oil. There is maple syrup and sugar from distant islands. There is rum and wine for the Palefaces and the Indian chiefs. There are twenty bags of wheat and maize flour. Two hundred tresses of Virginia tobacco. A hundred tresses of Mexican tobacco. Fifty bales of Dutch cotton goods. Ten bales of silk from China and the East. There are cloaks of wool and Egyptian cotton, carpets, guns, shot, and powder. There are fifteen traps for wolves, bears, foxes or lynxes. There is ironware: needles and scissors. . . . There are furs. None of this belongs to you, neither does it belong to me any more.

'All this belongs to your dead chiefs.

'You who say: "They have nothing but shame," this is what they possess. Everything. Everything except the barrels of brandy and wine, which I know that Swanissit would not have wanted and which has been set aside for the Supreme Spirit, who alone has the power to cleanse them of their harmful properties.

'And now, draw aside! Outakke, order your braves to go back as far as the river if they want to avoid being wounded or killed.

'I am going to make thunder!'

A stupefied silence fell on the assembled company after he had spoken. Then slowly the great throng of savages began to flow back towards the bottom of the hill to the bank of the river.

Their superstitious fears were mingled with avid curiosity. What did he mean to do, this Paleface with the clever tongue who claimed a better vengeance for them than that their arms could obtain?

Count Peyrac gave a few more orders to those of his men who were near him then, noticing Angélique, he put an arm round her waist and drew her away.

'Come quick! We must not stay here. Maupertuis, would you check that all our people are down at the river-bank and that there is no one left inside the compound!'

They found themselves mingling with the Iroquois on the river-bank where the evening mist was beginning to rise. Angélique felt Peyrac clasp her close against him before releasing her and quietly taking a tinder-box from a leather pocket on his belt. The Indians jostled one another like children at a play, for everyone wanted to see Peyrac and to know what he was about.

Angélique looked around for Honorine, the Jonases and her sons. It was impossible to see any more, but Maupertuis came and told her that everyone was there, gathered together beside a small coppice under the protection of the armed Spanish guards.

Yann Le Couennec came down the hillside unwinding a hempen fuse as he went. Under cover of the dark, some of Peyrac's men went back to the outpost, hastily laid the Iroquois chiefs in the prepared grave, threw their gifts in higgledy-piggledy after them, and rapidly shovelled the earth on top of them.

As they were finishing their task, the harsh sound of a bugle rose into the air, they broke up, and ran down to the spinney beside the river where the women and children had gathered.

Then for a second time the bugle rang out.

Then Count Peyrac took his tinder, struck a spark, and bending down lit the end of the hempen fuse which the Breton had unrolled to where he stood.

The flame caught on, swift and lively, and sped up to the hilltop, threading its way through the tree-trunks, the grass and the stones like a swift golden snake.

It reached the gate of the fortress and then they could see it no longer.

For suddenly a tremendous explosion burst up into the dark sky.

The whole outpost began to burn fiercely with vast flames fanned by the wind. All the woodwork of the houses and the palisade had been previously impregnated with oil and rum and sprinkled with saltpetre. It literally exploded.

In the dry, parched atmosphere of the end of summer, the whole outpost immediately became a roaring furnace, devouring everything, wreaking destruction amidst ferocious convulsions. The spectators had to retreat to the river-bank, scorched by the fierceness of the blaze.

Suddenly visible once more in the red glow from the fire, the up-turned faces revealed both admiration and terror, horror and delight, that mingling of complex emotions which man feels in the presence of the unleashing of natural forces in all their splendour and in-domitable power.

After a long pause, a voice rose up from the oppressed, panting crowd, the voice of old Tahoutaguete. He was asking a question.

'He would like to know,' said Outakke, 'if you had any beaver skins in your fortress?'

'Yes yes! there were,' cried O'Connell the Irishman, tearing his hair. 'Thirty bales of them! At least ten thousand pounds' worth of them in the loft. Oh! Monsieur de Peyrac, if only you had told me what you were going to do, if only I had known! . . . My beaver skins! . . . My beaver skins! . . .'

Such was the despair in his voice and so comical was he in the ex-pression of his grief, that the Iroquois burst out laughing.

Here at last was a Paleface who spoke from his heart! A Paleface like the others. . . . A true son of that race of merchants. They were back on familiar ground again. . . .

'And what about that skin there?' said Peyrac, pinching his great fat cheeks as they shook with grief. 'What value would you set on that? Ten thousand pounds, twenty thousand pounds? And that scalp they have left you with,' he went on, grasping the unfortunate trader by his red hair. 'How much for that? Thirty thousand pounds? . . .'

The braves laughed even louder. They clutched their sides as they mimicked the Irishman's gestures, pointing at him the while.

Their great bursts of terrifying laughter rang out like an echo to the noise of the flames.

'Are you laughing with us, Swanissit?' Outakke suddenly cried out, turning towards the blazing top of the hill. 'Are you laughing with your braves? Are you consoled by the riches and the presents they have left you?'

Then suddenly, like some fantastic answer to his appeal, a blueish white streak of light rose up from among the roaring scarlet wreaths of flame, higher and higher into the black sky, where it exploded several times and fell back again in a shower of silver stars.

No sooner had the shouts of surprise and fear left their lips, than another long red serpent unleashed itself across the blackness, bursting into a sheath of stars, which, in their turn, exploded into diadems of

219

rubies that slowly disintegrated, liquefying themselves and dripping like blood across the dark panoply of the sky.

The Indians fell to their knees. Others recoiled and tumbled into the river.

They were thrown into a state of utter confusion amongst themselves which mirrored the confusion in their minds.

Yet even those who found themselves splashing in the waters of the Kennebec were unable to take their eyes off this magical spectacle.

Now plumes of sparks and dazzling trails of fire seemed to fly in all directions in a display of fireworks that overwhelmed even the crackling of the last walls as they fell. The sky was full of green, red, and gold, falling back to earth as flowers, garlands, domes, long coils that crossed and recrossed, chasing one another through the darkness, forming weird figures, the shapes of animals, that would go out or vanish the very moment when they seemed about to leap. . . .

During an odd moment of silence, Angélique heard the children's delighted shouts. All fear had vanished in the general wonder, and with it hatred, anxiety and suspicion. . . .

And Florimond, who had made the fireworks, received the acclamations as if intended for him.

She heard his youthful voice saying: 'Well . . . what do you think of my skill? . . . It's every bit as good as Versailles!'

And Captain Alvarez and his men for a moment almost forgot the orders they had received to remain on the alert, one finger on the trigger.

But there was no longer anything to fear. The fearsome Iroquois stood there with raised heads, in utter fascination, like children. Their hearts were filled with delight. The intoxicating visions before them were like dreams, making them forget the reality of their bodies and the reason for which they were standing there on the banks of the Kennebec.

An immense emerald caterpillar fell squirming towards them. A fiery butterfly flew off into the darkness, and a giant glowing pumpkin exploded. . . .

When the last of the fireworks had flung their coloured powders out into the night sky, the outpost of Katarunk had vanished. Its ramparts had collapsed in showers of sparks and the place where it had once stood was nothing more than a vast glowing wound growing slowly darker as the minutes passed.

CHAPTER 33

THEN THE moon rose, a late moon rising towards the middle of the night. And its serene light, mingling with the shifting glow of the dying conflagration, gave a surprising brightness to the scene.

They waited. In the mingled darkness and brightness the half-naked braves were awaking as from an incredible dream.

Through the silence the murmur of the river at their feet grew louder.

Slowly Outakke came to himself once more; his glance, half-hidden between his long narrow eyelids, fell on the Paleface couple who stood before him, and he seemed to see them in a new way. There they were, a man and a woman supporting each other, waiting for him, a Mohawk, to give his verdict of life or death.

Then his heart swelled within him, carried away by the passionate, poetic incantations which so often swayed him, and he spoke privately to the man before him, the man who had mastered him.

'Are you the Ancestor foretold to us by the Bird, who is to come back to earth in the guise of a Paleface? I do not know . . . I still do not know who you really are . . . but I shall never forget what I have seen at Katarunk . . . never shall I forget it. . . . Speak, you . . .' he said aloud, turning to Nicolas Perrot. 'Repeat what I am about to say to my braves. I do not know who you are, Tekonderoga, but never shall I forget what I have seen at Katarunk.'

Nicolas repeated what he said, and the braves responded with a long-drawn-out cry that seemed to echo down the dark valley.

'Never shall we forget. . . .'

'I have also seen that you are not a Frenchman like the others, Tekonderoga,' Outakke went on in French in a voice that grew in clarity and firmness. 'I see that you are no Frenchman from Quebec, neither are you from the King of France. You really do stand alone and speak in your own name. Did it really mean little to you to lose all those beaver skins?'

'Of course I minded, but what I minded even more than losing the beaver skins was losing the instruments I had that enabled me to discover the secrets of nature, to see invisible things. I could talk to the

221

stars, but now Swanissit and your dead captains will use my instruments and will learn the secrets of the stars.'

'And happy may they be,' the Iroquois murmured.

'And as for you others, you know where their grave lies. It is in front of the fort, beside the ashes. No one will ever build here again, and you will be able to return here without shame and without grief to wash their memorable bones.'

'And you, Tekonderoga, what will you do? You have nothing but these horses and these clothes. The forest lies all around you, it is night, and the winter cold is drawing near.'

'That matters little since my honour has been retrieved and I have paid the blood-money.'

'Will you go back towards the Ocean?'

'No. The season is too far advanced and the journey too fraught with danger. I shall go into the mountains, and join forces with my four men who have a hut up there. May I tell them that you are still our allies?'

'Yes, you may. When the Council of Mothers and Elders has approved my decision I will send you a necklace of porcelain. Tekonderoga, do you really think you will triumph over all your enemies?'

'The result of a battle is in the hands of the Supreme Spirit. But I have made up my mind to fight and to win.'

'You have great courage and great cunning, and I foresee victory for you. But take a care, Tekonderoga, for you have many enemies still, and your muskets cannot vanquish the most terrible of them all, Etskon-Honsi, the Black Robe. He speaks for his God, he speaks for his King. He is invincible. Many a time have we sought to kill him, but he has always survived, he CANNOT die, do you understand? He wants to sweep you from his path, and he will hound you ceaselessly, for you come from the other side of his life. You belong to this world while he belongs to the world of invisible spirits, and for him the earth is unbearable. . . .

'I fear for you, now that you are my friend. I know he seeks your downfall. I know it, I have seen it – how often have I seen it in my dreams, seen his blue eye glistening! And I, a brave, I trembled, for I know of nothing on earth more terrifying than that eye. When he used to look at me like that when I lived with the French, I felt my soul and my spirit go out from me. . . . Beware, Tekonderoga,' he repeated in urgent tones, 'and take care, for you possess a treasure, you who possess nothing else, and that one last treasure he will try to snatch from you, especially that one.'

He pointed to Angélique.

'His hatred is already upon her. He will try to separate you. Will you be able to resist his powers? He is very strong, you know, and he cannot be killed.'

Suddenly Outakke seemed to have grown fearful.

And perhaps it was at that moment that Angélique's heart opened to love for the Indians.

It was a feeling that went beyond fear, beyond any repugnance one might have felt for these wild men, it was a feeling that took root in all the feelings of friendly, fraternal, and motherly love she felt for others.

Now she saw them naked, credulous, defenceless, with only their arrows to face the deadly fire of muskets, with no other defence against the mystical power of the Jesuits than their crude magic. Pity and respect for them made their way into her heart.

The broken voice of this Iroquois who, after so many words of hatred, was now offering them advice, revealed to her the human characteristics of these cruel people.

With all the passionate changeability of primitive creatures, here they were desperately concerned about the plight of those whom they had sought to massacre a few hours earlier, and for whom, since they had become their friends, they now felt more concern than for their own fate.

Joffrey de Peyrac went up to Outakke and spoke to him confidentially.

'I shall tell you something you can understand. My own guardian spirits are such that they fear neither the evil spells of the Redskin nor those of the Paleface. And Etskon-Honsi, in spite of his powers, remains a Paleface. Like me ...'

'That is true,' the Mohawk conceded, apparently reassured. 'You are a Paleface, and you can understand him, whereas our heads sometimes become confused, I understand. You will know how to get the better of him just as you knew how to outwit us when we sought your death. That is good! May you remain strong, Tekonderoga. We need your strength. And now, go where you will. However far you may wander, you and yours, if you meet a brave of the Five Nations, he will sing for you the song of peace. I have spoken! Farewell!'

CHAPTER 34

THE NIGHT wind blew over the ashes, and everything had grown dark and silent. The moon had vanished into the distant mist, leaving a faint diffused light that revealed the dark shapes of forest and mountain.

Joffrey de Peyrac was walking slowly along the river-bank. He was alone, and from time to time he halted and looked pensively towards the top of the hillside where, only a few hours before, the outpost of Katarunk had stood.

Angélique was standing some distance from him and could see him as he stopped, then took up his meditative pacing once more.

She too had returned to the same place, as if by some irresistible attraction.

The children had fallen asleep beside a fire in the cave to which, the previous day, the Count had had their blankets and some food taken. Most of the adults were exhausted and slept like children. Angélique had left them and had gone off quietly into the night where, for the very first time, she no longer felt afraid. The evil spirits seemed to have left the place, scattered far and wide by some tempestuous, tragic wind.

Now she found herself walking in the heart of a friendly forest, and every sound that reached her ears took on a new significance. They were merely the echoes of a living world, a world coming to life again under the branches, a tiny animal world, preparing for winter, busying itself with final tasks, singing its final song, nothing more. Mosses perfumed the air for the last time, squirrels scrabbled to bury their last nuts, and far, far away, beyond the ravines, like the blast of some melancholy horn, she heard the bellow of a moose.

Angélique no longer felt afraid. In doing what he had done, Joffrey de Peyrac had freed her from her anxiety.

It had been a crazy gesture! But it had been the only possible one. To burn down Katarunk. He was the only man who could ever have dared such a thing and carried it out. The idea must have occurred to him when he had said: 'My house has been stained by an unforgiveable crime!'

It was then that he had known what he must do. It was then that he had grown calm once more.

From now on no evil would come to them from the land of America. The holocaust had been consummated.

At first Angélique had felt something vaguely, then it had come to her like a revelation. And now she walked on through the trees, her heart light within her, for she felt that the rites had been accomplished and this gave satisfaction to her soul, steeped as it was in Christianity.

The sacrifice had been a good one not only because it had saved their lives, but also because it would bring them happiness. And the words that she had often murmured during the Mass came back to her: *Hanc igitur oblationem . . .*

'This is what we offer up to you, O Lord, we your servants, and our entire family with us. Graciously accept our sacrifice, O Lord, and dispose our days in Thy peace. . . .'

The land of America would no longer be hostile to them. Joffrey de Peyrac's sacrifice had touched its fiery heart. The Iroquois would never forget. But still more, Angélique thought of the utter destitution in which they both found themselves, and from her heart rose up the serene prayer: 'Dispose our days in Thy peace, O Lord. . . .'

Everything had gone up in smoke! What was left for men to strip them of now? Nothing remained save one marvellous secret treasure, their love. This must have been what fate had intended in giving them back to each other, so that they should recognize its value and not underestimate it. They had had to be able to recognize it without confusing it with other values. The pure love of a man for a woman, and of a woman for a man, two flames in one, burning in the arid desert, in the icy wastes, two hearts burning through the night of the universe, as at the time of the Creation. . . .

She stood and watched from afar as Joffrey de Peyrac's shadow moved meditatively along the river-bank.

The smell of fire still hung about the landscape, and in spite of the cold she still caught whiffs of the crowd that had so thoroughly trampled the ground here; now by contrast everything was so quiet that Angélique was overcome by a sense of well-being.

From afar she watched the lonely man who stopped from time to time and raised his head towards the hillside where the wind on occasion stirred the ashes to a red glow.

Then she walked towards him, without haste, sure she would find him in the night. When she was a few paces away she stopped once more. He caught sight of her, the shape of a woman standing out in profile against the blue shadows, her face a bright patch, then, after looking at her for a moment, he came towards her. Joffrey de Peyrac's hand touched Angélique's shoulder and she drew close to him as if to a source of warmth, placing her palms on his chest, then slipping her hands round his body and huddling against him as he tightened his grip round her and drew her to him, gathering the folds of his cloak around her to cover her, and drawing her ever closer and closer to him until they stood intertwined, clasped in each other's arms, feeling no passion, no other desire than the primitive need to be close, like two animals which fall asleep resting their heads on one another's necks, seeking mutual warmth and the reassurance of the other's presence.

Joffrey de Peyrac began to say something, but he refrained. What was there to say, he thought, that was not utterly banal? 'Were you frightened? Are you cross with me for burning down the house you already thought of as your home? For facing you with endless difficulties?'

These were banalities he could have said to any woman. But this woman, this woman who stood quivering against him, it would have been an insult to speak like that to her. She was far above it. She was far above anything he could ever have imagined her to be.

And he rubbed his cheek against her delicate skin as if to reassure himself of the presence of this living creature, warm and gentle, who was there in his arms and who was his wife.

She too had been on the point of saying something and telling him some of the thoughts that flooded her heart: 'How I admired you today, my love! Your courage saved us all! You were inspired. . . .'

But these words all seemed inadequate and did not exactly express what she wanted to say. Nor did she want to tell him what she had just discovered, that the sacrifice had been accomplished, that the gods were satisfied. . . . 'You and I are alone on earth, my love, you and I, penniless and alone . . . and I am happy. . . .'

But this he knew as well as she did. So they both remained silent. And they clasped each other still closer, in silence and in joy.

And from time to time she would throw her head back to seek the light of his eyes, that shone like two stars above her, and she guessed that he was smiling at her.

CHAPTER 35

TOWARDS THE north there lies a place where the waters spread out to form a vast silvery desert. Dead forests, their roots drowned beneath the waters, thrust their branches up into a pearly sky, like spiky candelabra, white as bone. A thin cloud of mosquitoes and sandflies lies like a haze along the shifting shores. The land is unsure and treacherous. But here and there, islands covered with black fir-trees standing up like so many distaffs, cast their long reflection across the unfathomable mirror of the waters.

This is the Lake Megantic region.

When the French soldiers reached it a few days after leaving Katarunk, autumn seemed to be much further advanced than on the other side of the mountains. Dry moss, the colour of old gold, covered the ground, and the leaves were falling from the sparse trees. They could already sense the atmosphere of Canada in the icy air they breathed and the wild desolation of the region. The soldiers, the Hurons, and the Algonquins all felt it and agreed among themselves that, on this side of the hills, they felt more 'at home'.

All they had to do now was to get their canoes back into the water, to cross the lake, and there they would find the good river Chaudière, which would lead them easily down to the Saint Lawrence, into which it flowed opposite Quebec.

For the last few miles, they would make their way past villages with vast stone farms built on the river's edge, while from the hillside the peasants, busy bringing in a late harvest of wheat, or picking a few apples, would wave their caps to greet the return of the war party. The white pointed spire of Levis would come into sight round the bend and then suddenly they would find themselves beneath the walls of Quebec.

Then they would look up to greet the lofty city, perched on the rocks, and the city would reply with all the bells of its myriad belfries.

Then it would be good-bye to the vast open spaces, good-bye to savages, to bowls of tasteless 'sagamité' and stewed dog. And heigho for Calvados, rum and brandy brought over by ship, for wheaten bread thickly buttered, for juicy steaks and ham cooked with cabbage, for cheese and red wine, and the pretty girls they would meet down town at Janine Gonfarel's. . . .

At Lake Megantic the sun shone dazzling and brilliant in a pale sky, the water had a metallic sheen, the trees were dead, and winter stalked the countryside.

The birch-bark canoes slid swiftly over the surface of the lake, hunting through the monotonous archipelago for the source of the Chaudière, for one had to know the area well to find it amongst all the islands and the endless meanderings of the water channels.

The Marquis of Loménie remained on the bank and watched his troops embarking. Fallières, L'Aubignière and his nephew, and one group of Indians were already far off, while others kept on arriving, their canoes on their heads, along the portage track.

An Indian, who had run the full length of the column of men, dashed up to the officer with one arm raised in a brief salute. He was a foreigner and Loménie-Chambord recognized him as the Panis slave, Nicolas Perrot's inseparable companion. He blurted out something, but nobody understood him for he belonged to a distant tribe, beyond the freshwater seas, a small group of Indians known as the Panis who had been dispersed and had then disappeared. He claimed not to understand any of the dialects of the Indian nations present, but agreed to use his lamentable French.

With the help of Pont-Briand, the Colonel managed to piece his message together. It appeared that at Katarunk, the Iroquois chiefs had been scalped by Maudreuil and the Patsuiketts. The Iroquois braves were marching on Katarunk to seek vengeance, and Count Peyrac and his family would be massacred.

'We must go! We must go straight away,' exclaimed Pont-Briand. 'We must go back. There are not enough of them to hold out against those hordes. . . .'

Loménie made no comment but immediately ordered those still with him to turn back. Most of the Hurons and Abenakis agreed to accompany him along with half the soldiers. There were always volunteers when a chance offered of having a go at the Iroquois.

When, a few days later, they found themselves beside the Kennebec again, they listened hopefully for the sound of shooting, which would have shown that those defending the fort were still holding their own. But the silence was unbroken, and the whole region seemed dead. Loménie was also concerned about the fate of Father Orgeval. Pont-Briand was plunged in gloom as if suffering some inner torment.

Before rounding the last bend which would bring them to the river-bank opposite Katarunk, the two officers halted the flotilla and ordered the men to draw the canoes up on to the shore amongst the willows. Each man loaded his gun in silence. Loménie and Pont-Briand climbed the rock face in order to take a look without themselves being seen. The air was clear and yet it had a tang of cold smoke. As soon as they reached the top and looked through the leaves they realized what had happened.

Katarunk no longer existed.

Before them lay an area blackened with ash and gutted tree-trunks, where once the outpost had stood.

And at the foot of the hill the Kennebec flowed on, its vivid, almost dark-blue waters rolling between the banks of scarlet sumacs, mountain-ashes and wild cherry-trees.

Not a human trace anywhere.

Pont-Briand gave a dull groan, and banged his head several times against a tree-trunk.

'She is dead,' he cried, 'she is dead; how can I have the courage to go on living? . . . You see, she was no devil. . . . She was only a woman! A beautiful, weak woman. . . . An adorable woman! Oh, my God, why must I remain here on earth now?'

'Tush, you are talking nonsense,' said Loménie, shaking him by the shoulder.

Then suddenly he too closed his eyes and bitter grief flooded his soul. Once again he saw the horseman in the black mask, surrounded by his oriflammes, facing Katarunk. And beside him the man's wife, such a lovely woman!

His heart was rent with pain and a searing sense of loss. Then he came to his senses again, thinking that it must have been Father Orgeval's hand that had planned all this. For was this priest not guided by God, for whom he had already spilled his blood? When Loménie had come from Quebec a month earlier at the head of his men, the Jesuit had given him an order.

'Get rid of them at all costs! Destroy them if you must, it will make things easier!'

He had been attracted by the strangers and had swerved from his duty. Heaven had taken a hand in the affair.

'Mission accomplished!' he thought.

And his heart flooded with bitterness. He stayed for a long time with Pont-Briand, unable to tear himself from the place. Then he gave orders to head north again.

When the French had finally departed, the Panis slave left the forest and he too came down from the mountains to the river-bank. His long black hair floated behind him in the wind. He moved stealthily down to the river-bank, stooping towards the ground as he walked. After following the shore to the little launching point, he climbed the hill to the charred area, wandered round the destroyed fort then returned to the river.

He had read on the ground the tale of an astonishing adventure.

Then he raised his head again, seemed to sniff the wind, and set off resolutely in a north-easterly direction towards the heart of the mountains.

PART THREE

Wapassou

CHAPTER 36

THE TEMPEST raged on. Rain mingled with melting snow lashed their faces and made their cloaks sodden with moisture. The party trekked on beneath the trees, dragging their feet heavy with earth and mud. The men carrying the two canoes they had used to follow the rivers upstream were at least protected from the rain. But they got their feet tangled in the low brushwood and had to be given an escort of two men with hatchets to guide them. Angélique lifted her head and saw, by the bluey-green light of the forest, waterfalls rising before her like white columns. These rumbling, frothing, white falls, these sparkling sheets of water with their heavy, liquid draperies, are the sentinels of the American forest land. They are to be found everywhere, roaring their proclamation: 'You shall not pass!'

These particular falls seemed taller and more inexorable than all the rest. Trees twisted in the wind contorted themselves in crazy convulsions all round them. . . .

Water was streaming off the leaves and a sudden torrential downpour struck Angélique's upturned face making her shudder violently.

She was soaked to the skin.

Water was getting in everywhere. Her heavy linen cape, for all its toughness, was dripping wet, soaked through, and no longer served to protect Honorine whom she had taken in her arms under its cover to protect her from the rain. She felt wisps of hair that had escaped from her headdress sticking to her temples.

But the others too presented a pitiable sight and they all stopped in front of the waterfalls with a feeling of discouragement, and stared gloomily towards the top of the cliff.

Joffrey de Peyrac joined the group, leading the black stallion by the bridle. He urged them all into the relative shelter of an overhanging rock, then, pointing to the waterfalls, said to them:

'Up there behind all that is Wapassou.'

'And what if we find no one there?' one of the men shouted above the noise of the waters. 'What if the French have gone that way too? Or the Iroquois? What if our friends are dead and their hut burned?'

'No,' Peyrac replied, 'Wapassou is too well-guarded. To reach it, you have to know what's to be found there and no one knows that yet.'

'Maybe they're dead, your "four" there,' Clovis went on. 'O'Connell said he hadn't seen them for a couple of months.'

'No, they are not dead,' Peyrac replied.

'Why not?'

'Because fate couldn't do that to us.'

He lifted little Honorine from Angélique's arms into his own, urged them all to move forward as cautiously as possible and began to climb the steep slippery slope beside the foaming water.

Some of the men had been detailed to watch over and lead the two horses they had kept with them. Angélique would have liked to volunteer to look after the mare, but she was exhausted and it was all she could do to keep going herself. The leaves, torn from the trees, whirled about her, striking her in the face and blinding her. One false move could have spelt death.

She looked round to see whether her companions or any of the children needed help. She noticed that Octave Malaprade the cook was supporting Elvire, almost carrying her. Monsieur Jonas, unruffled as ever, was hearty enough, although his broad face, streaming with water, was more like that of a triton newly risen from the waves than anything else, as he pushed poor Madame Jonas on in front of him, buttressing and supporting her as she climbed, utterly out of breath.

Florimond and Cantor had each taken charge of one of the little boys, and were carrying them on their backs, and she could see her two sons climbing slowly on, bent double beneath their burdens like the damned souls of Dante's Inferno, their hair hanging in a streaming curtain before their eyes.

It was a hallucinating scene of despair. Had it been completely dark, the blackness would have spared them the sight of the furious cataracts beside them. But in the muddy light that flooded everywhere, their very whiteness took on the aggressive appearance of a threatening monster trying to draw them on to its claws.

It was three days now since the party had left Katarunk after its destruction. They had taken only a couple of horses with them, while Maupertuis and his son Pierre-Joseph had been ordered to take the others back to Gouldsboro, and had set off towards the south-east.

Everyone who had decided to follow Peyrac on into the interior was aware of the fact that Wapassou was an outpost by name only. Before they had set out, he had not hidden from them the fact that it was nothing more than a rough dwelling place, without a palisade, a kind of burrow where the four miners he had left in occupation for the past year would not have made any special arrangements for the winter since the idea had been for them to winter at Katarunk. He nevertheless hoped that they would have time to make the place a bit more comfortable before the winter cold really set in.

On the first day of their journey, the two canoes had travelled upstream with some of the baggage and the children, who enjoyed the trip and found it restful. The others followed along the bank.

On the second day, they left the Kennebec, whose waters were growing more and more turbulent, and full of rapids, and headed east, following the course of a small blue, peaceful river that ran through what seemed like a parkland of prairies, willows and elms. They never met a single soul. For some mysterious reason it seemed to be a sacred river.

They had hoped to reach their destination early in the afternoon of the third day, but after a night during which the wind tore at the shelters they had made from branches, they were caught in a storm of icy rain that showed no sign of abating.

Wapassou, the Silver Lake, guarded by its sacred river and the spirits of the noble metals, defended itself fiercely against every approach.

Angélique fell to her knees. She had caught her foot in a root that lay close to the ground. She felt that she would never find the strength to stand up again and that she would have to finish her climb on all fours.

At last she summoned the energy to lift her head and almost cried out with relief. The dark pit was opening up at last to reveal a pale stretch of sky with tattered clouds racing across it.

Joffrey de Peyrac stood at the top, watching them all climb up. He carried her child in his arms. Her very own child. And even in her most outrageous dreams she had never imagined she would see that. Oh, my love, it was indeed you whom I saw in my dreams. . . . You were leading us on through the storm, farther, always farther. You are like Cain, fleeing with his people before the curse that lay on him. . . . And yet you have done nothing wrong. Why? . . . Oh why? . . .

He had seen that she had fallen, and the look he gave her from above urged her to get up again in one last effort to reach him. For that, she could find strength enough. It was like in her dreams, she hauled herself up from one branch to another and finally found herself standing beside him.

She saw Honorine peering through folds of his cloak, ecstatic with delight. Clasped to the breast of her father, whom she had found at the world's end, Honorine looked out on to a dark tumultuous world from which he protected her, and she was jubilant and happy.

Joffrey de Peyrac was unable to speak on account of the noise of the wind and the water but he nodded towards something and on her left she glimpsed, over the other side of the waterfall, some kind of construction made of planks with vanes that rose like great black wings.

This evidence of human labour gave them all renewed hope and courage.

But they had still not reached the end of their labours, for this windmill was only a beginning.

Somewhat farther on, the forest opened out and a broader landscape was revealed. A huge desolate lake stretched out before their eyes, pitted by the drumming rain and encircled by round-topped mountains, whose summits seemed to be blackened as if by wet soot, and crested with clouds that scudded swiftly across the sky, driven by the wind. Joffrey de Peyrac, still carrying Honorine, led his companions to the left bank of the lake, across a little wooden footbridge, and along a fairly well marked path which the rain had turned into a morass. Some of them were so weary that they slithered and fell constantly in the slimy mud. A single thought kept them going, the idea that soon they would find shelter and a roaring fire.

But they reached the end of the lake without seeing a light. Then they went through a narrow pass that led from the first lake to a smaller one, surrounded by precipitous cliffs. The steep banks crumbled beneath their feet, and they had to be careful not to tread too near the edge. They went through a further narrow gap in the rocks, and a third lake appeared, bigger this time and edged on the left with swamp-covered fields and low hills. The path across the swampy ground had been laid with duckboards to make it easier to cross.

Yet once again they reached the end of the lake without catching sight of any habitation.

The wretched people gazed around but could see nothing.

Then the sharp smell of a wood fire reached them through the rain.

'I can smell smoke,' cried little Bartholomew in a tremulous voice. 'I can smell smoke.'

His teeth were chattering and he was shivering so hard that he would have fallen had Florimond not held him firmly. Angélique's two boys in the normal course of events had thick heads of hair, but today their hair would have done credit to all the naiads of Ancient Greece. Nevertheless, Florimond and Cantor were standing up pluckily to the ordeal, bravely saying that they had seen worse. It was only a little shower!...

At his father's request, Cantor fumbled in his bag and brought out a great sea-shell, one of the conch shells that sailors blew into to make their presence known through fog.

The lad puffed out his cheeks and the cliffs echoed repeatedly with the hollow sound of the conch.

Shortly after, from a rocky promontory that stood out in the lake, covered with firs and larch-trees, a boat appeared through the blueish-grey mist, steered by a hazy figure.

The boat drew near.

An ashen-faced man with a glassy stare looked at them all in silence. The bark came to rest against the bank.

Count Peyrac spoke to the hazy figure in English.

The man did not reply. He was dumb. He was the boatman of the mists, as pale as a ghost, beneath a head of white hair. The women and children climbed aboard first, followed by Joffrey de Peyrac carrying Honorine.

The first group disembarked on to a boggy field and, while the boat went back to fetch the others, they climbed a gentle slope which led them to the tip of the promontory.

The smell of smoke was growing stronger. It seemed to emanate from the ground and mingle with the fog.

A hole opened up at their feet with log steps leading down into it.

They went down into the hole, down into this burrow, and pushed the door open.

The smells and sights burst upon them like the sun; the smell of cooked fat, of tobacco and hot rum, the light of lamps and candles, along with the cosy warmth of a blazing fire.

And against the scarlet backcloth of the cheery fire, a gigantic Negro watched in astonishment as they entered.

He was dressed in leather and furs, and golden earrings glittered at his ears. His woolly hair was as white as snow, and Angélique gave a cry as she recognized the black face from the past:

'Kouassi-Ba!'

CHAPTER 37

So she had encountered Kouassi-Ba again, the good, devoted, endlessly capable Kouassi-Ba, the huge slave who once, wearing figured satin and a sword, had stood guard over her door in the palace of Toulouse. Count Peyrac had bought him when he was still a young man, in Barbary, and had taught him everything he knew. Kouassi-Ba had remained faithful to him when he had been condemned, had followed him to the galleys, from which they had escaped together and had disappeared somewhere on the Mediterranean. . . .[1]

Why had it not occurred to her before to ask her husband for news of his faithful servant? . . . The fact was that they still did not dare talk about what had happened after he had been sent to the stake. And still the resurrection of the past went on!

The big Negro did not recognize her at first, and was astonished to see this dishevelled woman, soaked to the skin, rush towards him and clasp his two big black hands in her delicate frozen ones as she said:

'Kouassi-Ba! Oh my dear Kouassi-Ba!' While the rain trickled down her cheeks like tears.

Then the sight of those clear, unforgettable eyes stirred his memory, and he glanced at Count Peyrac, realizing that the miracle for which he had prayed with simple faith for many a long year had come to pass. He was filled with a radiant delight which he was quite unable to express adequately within the narrow confines of this room into which more and more people were now crowding.

At last he fell to his knees, and, kissing Angélique's hand, repeated like a litany:

'Oh Madame, Oh Madame, it's you! It's you! You are here at last! You! The Joy of my Master. . . . Now, I can die.'

There had been four of them, all miners, living in this smoky dug-out. A painstaking, solemn Italian, Luigi Porguani, a Spanish-Indian half-caste Quidoua from Peru, a dumb Englishman, Lymon White, whose tongue the Puritans of Boston had torn out for blasphemy, and Kouassi-Ba. All of them, even the Italian, seemed to possess some quality that made them different from the ordinary run of mortals,

[1] See *Angélique*.

something that smelt of sulphur and gunpowder; and as soon as Angélique set eyes on them, she recaptured something of the first impression she had had long ago when her husband had shown her over his mine in Salsigne. These were men of a different stamp, they had allied themselves with the hidden forces under the earth, and the master of them all was he who had just come in, the man they greeted with warmth and devotion, Count Peyrac, the sage of Toulouse. His presence here made everything fall into place.

The underground room was getting fuller and fuller as more and more miserable soaking people piled in. They could scarcely move inside; teeth were chattering, and convulsive sighs were forced from the lips of those who managed to hold their hands out towards the fire.

Once she was over her initial astonishment, Angélique set to work as fast as she could to strip Honorine and the little boys of their wet clothes.

'Give me a dry towel, Kouassi-Ba,' she said. 'Now some blankets. Quick, help me rub the children down! Wrap them up well!'

And he made haste to do as she bade him, as in days gone by.

She looked into the stewpot that hung over the fire and saw a kind of steaming hot broth, so she filled some bowls with it, and soon the children, fed and warm again, fell asleep on some little trestle beds, covered with furs.

Malaprade the cook touched Angélique's shoulder.

'Madame, the lass there's not well!'

'Which lass?'

'That one there.'

She saw that Elvire had half collapsed, almost hysterical.

'I can't go on! I can't go on!'

Angélique shook the young woman and made her take a few sips of some burning hot toddy.

'I want to die! I want to die!' Elvire went on. 'I can't go on. . . . Why didn't I die on board the ship, with my man. . . .'

'Calm down, my dear,' said Angélique, putting her arms round the young woman. 'Come on now, drink up. You have been very brave! Now we are safe. It's good here, it's warm, we've a roof over our heads and Kouassi-Ba is here. Can't you see how kind he is! Malaprade, get her shoes off. We must get these wet clothes off her. . . . Find me a blanket. . . .'

There was much activity in the room, but it was controlled. There was the sound of chattering teeth, then tremulous voices, then a smell of rum spread round the room and the voices grew louder and firmer. Steam was beginning to come from a little cubby-hole, where they were preparing a kind of turkish bath by throwing red-hot stones from the fire into a bucket of water. The four miners set to with a will, bringing out all the spare clothes they had, stoking the fire, adding more items to the soup, including their last piece of pork fat.

Bit by bit Elvire calmed down.

Then Malaprade the cook took her in his arms and laid her down beside the children, where she fell into a heavy sleep while he went on murmuring words of comfort to her. But Angélique took hold of him, saying:

'Now your turn, my friend.'

Octave Malaprade was not of a very robust constitution. He might well catch a chill in all those wet clothes. She poured him out a glass of spirits from a bottle that was being passed round, forced him to remove his sodden cloak, and even went so far as to rub him down herself in spite of his embarrassed protests, while making sure at the same time that Florimond and Cantor had also removed their icy garments. The clothes before the fire sent up clouds of steam, and piles of muddy shoes and boots began to accumulate, which they threw into a corner. Tomorrow they would see what they could do with them, for there was not enough room round the hearth to attempt to dry them now. By the light of the bear-grease lamps they huddled, shivering and naked before the single fire.

'We haven't made many inroads into the things we've got here for barter,' Porguani the Italian said. 'We've still got some blankets and some rum.'

'That's all we need for tonight,' said Peyrac.

The Italian handed round the scarlet blankets and they all wrapped themselves in them; they looked like a solemn conclave of berobed Indians as they began to relax a little and slowly come back to life again. Then with the assistance of the rum laughter broke out and they began thumping one another on the back as they told of all that had happened since the day before and during the past month. The children slept on like angels.

Angélique glanced contentedly about her. During the storm they had been among the most wretched creatures on earth, and she would never forget that then the only spark of humanity left to them had been in their coming first to the rescue of the weakest and thinking of their comfort. She had seen Malaprade comforting Elvire, and Yann the Breton passing a glass of brandy to the Jonases before taking one himself, and Clovis throwing his water bottle over to Yann, and Nicolas Perrot urging Florimond and Cantor to remove their clothes quickly instead of standing shivering before the fire. Joffrey de Peyrac had himself made sure that everyone had eaten his fill and was dry, before he himself removed his muddy cloak. Their eyes met and he came towards her, clasping her peremptorily to him.

'Now we must look after you, my love.'

His voice was vibrant with deep goodness and tenderness.

It was only then that she noticed that she was still shivering and trembling like one seized with epilepsy.

He made her take a draught of rum in some boiling water with some black sugar, enough to make an ox reel.

'I bless the man who invented rum,' said Angélique. 'Who was it? I don't know, but they ought to raise a statue to him.'

She only had a vague recollection of what happened after that. She remembered the little cubby-hole very clearly where the red-hot stones set the water in the bucket aboil, and she remembered the wonderful sensation of the scalding steam on her icy body, and two attentive, skilful hands that had helped her wrap herself in the blankets, strong, powerful arms that had lifted her like a child before helping her to lie down, and how he had covered her with soft furs, and how his face and his dark eyes had looked at her so eloquently as if through a mist, like a vision in her dream of old. . . . But this time the vision did not vanish . . . and she could hear him murmuring to her as he tended her and warmed her, gentle words like caresses, as if they had been alone in the world. . . . But that evening, it did not matter. They were all like animals crushed by the hostile elements, by the harsh hand of nature. . . .

When Angélique woke in the depths of the night she felt rested, and listened blissfully to the rain pelting down outside and the loud howling of the wind. Shadows played on the blackened beams of the low ceiling. She lay stretched out on the ground amidst all the others wrapped in their blankets, while loud snores rose from all four corners of the room. But she felt sure all the same that behind one of the walls she had heard the grunt of a pig. A pig! How wonderful! There was a pig in the house and they would be able to kill it for Christmas! And there were blankets and rum! What more could they want?

Her head felt both heavy and light as she raised it a little and she saw all her people sleeping heavily one against the other, and Kouassi-Ba, crouching beside the hearth, watching over them like some tutelary god, as he kept the fire going.

It was stiflingly hot, almost unbearably so. Angélique began to revel in the heat as in food after hunger, when it seems as if the appetite will never be satisfied.

The dark, icy wind howled over the promontory. And the evil spirit it bore on its wings knew nothing of the human folk nestling in their burrow. . . . They passed them by, not deigning to notice such pitiable creatures!

Angélique's happiness shone like a lamp in her heart. No doubt the warming rum from the West Indies had something to do with it too. God bless the man who invented rum!

It reminded her of the Court of Miracles, that fraternity of outcasts. . . . But of course there was no real comparison, for everything here was magnified by the presence of the man she loved; they had not come together on account of their wretchedness or their failures, but they and their companions formed a community that had undertaken a secret and important task which they and they alone were capable of tackling and bringing to a successful conclusion. Theirs was a beginning, not an end. Fortunately no one knew that and the evil spirits seeking them in the wind would not find them. . . . For a long time to come people would think that they were dead, thanks be to God!

It was a good thing that Katarunk had disappeared. As she lay only half awake Angélique lived certain scenes again. One that had impressed itself upon her even more profoundly than the feathered Iroquois massed beside the river as they shouted their war cry, was that first glimpse she had had of the French that night, kneeling before the Jesuit, while their Huron allies roasted a prisoner; she shook with horror at the memory of it, and the silence, the warmth and the cosy intimacy of this hidden dugout seemed by contrast to possess a very special and unforgettable charm.

She was going to like Wapassou. The spirit bloweth where it listeth. Katarunk was a place doomed to disaster. It was as well to have burnt it once and for all, to have got rid of everything. There she had been tormented by dreams. Here she would sleep well. To reach Wapassou, several passes had to be negotiated, like so many locks and bolts protecting the circle of mountains where, for thousand upon thousand of years, in the heart of the rock itself, unsuspected veins of gold and silver had lain. A stretch of the Indian Appalachian trail passed fairly close by, but the Indians who occasionally used it never thought of stopping in the area and hurried on, fearing the shadows of the cliffs and the forbidding solitude of the mountain. And who, especially in winter, would ever dare to climb the steep slope by the snowy water-falls that stood guard over the valley in which lay the three lakes?

Beneath her half-closed eyelids, the sequence of images went by, and at each new vision her heart filled with such ecstatic emotion that it brought tears to her eyes. There was Joffrey de Peyrac standing out against the stormy sky, with Honorine in his arms; there were Florimond and Cantor, bent double beneath the weight of the children as they stumbled through the mud, and Yann handing a glass of brandy to the old watchmaker as he stood dripping in the rain, and Malaprade rubbing Elvire's icy feet to warm them up. . . . And now! Heavens, how hot it was! Angélique drew one arm out from under the furs and raised herself on her elbow. Joffrey de Peyrac was asleep beside her. She remembered in a flash that it had been he, that evening, who had wrapped her in furs and laid her there, he who had been the last to lie down to take some rest. Now he slept, motionless, the sleep of the just, strong and serene. He had triumphed yet again, triumphed over war, over death, over the elements, and he was gathering strength to face another day.

She gazed down at him with adoration.

The mineral smell she had discovered once more on the clothes of the four miners, that she had smelt on their outstretched palms, all rough and pitted from handling powder and splinters of stone, this mineral smell hung about everything, like a special kind of incense that she had felt surrounding him in the past with a subtle, personal mystery. She did not know everything about him. She had discovered him bit by bit. He was the Count Peyrac who had dazzled Toulouse with the splendour and luxury of his way of life, but who could also sail a ship through a storm, who could stand up to kings and sultans, yes, he was all these at once. . . .

But beyond the soldier and nobleman, lay another personality, one almost unadmitted, since no one of his own day and age could have understood – the man of the mines, the man of the first of all sciences, the science that traces the gestation of the Universe by the revelation of its buried and invisible secrets. . . . Here at Wapassou he had returned to the bowels of the earth where slumbered gold and silver; he had come back to his own domain. She could already see, even from the way he slept, that he would feel better here than in Katarunk. And because he slept so soundly, so utterly unaware of any presence, even of his own, she dared reach out her arm towards him and stroke the scar on his cheek with a motherly hand.

CHAPTER 38

THE TWO carpenters never left their pit. From dawn till dusk one of them sat astride the beam they were sawing into planks while the other remained in the pit, and they worked the enormous saw like automata.

Some of the other men were felling trees, stripping their branches and squaring them up. They used poplars for the inside walls and the swinging bails, black oak for the outside walls and the bastions, fir for the guttering, the furniture and the roof shingles. They were working as fast as they could to enlarge the house and increase its height. First, the main living-room was doubled in length, and a big bedroom added to it for the Jonases and the children. A little cubby-hole, which, because of the rocky nature of the terrain, lay somewhat above the level of the rest of the house, was cleared of the tools and the barrels that had been stowed there and turned into a room for Count Peyrac and his wife. A window and a stone fireplace to link up with the central chimney were constructed.

A loft was added in which to store their food and, because it formed an air space above the house, it helped to keep the rest of the building warm. Count Peyrac also had a cellar dug in the rock for the barrels of drink, and a shed to stable the horses. The place echoed with the sound of axes on trees, the blows of hammers, the monotonous creak of the saw, and the clatter of planks and beams as the men piled them up.

There came a day when the whole roof was off the house and they had to camp once more in the open as they had done during the journey, surrounded by the croaking of frogs and the cackling of ducks among the rushes.

Fortunately, the sky had cleared again.

They had been granted the respite predicted by the Canadians. The end of October and the beginning of November brought a sudden miraculous dry spell and delightful warmth. Only the nights were cold, and sometimes in the mornings the mountains stood out blue beneath a powdering of frost.

From the very first morning Angélique had seen that her first impression had been right. Wapassou, meaning 'the Silver Lake', was a hidden spot, miles from anywhere, a place people would hesitate to approach. Their most urgent task was to prepare for winter. The stores they had found at Wapassou, apart from maize and the pig they had been fattening throughout the summer, were almost all used up, and the four miners had been about to set off for Katarunk when the party had arrived. Now Katarunk was no more, and thirty odd people and a couple of horses had to get through a winter beside the Silver Lake.

They needed shelter, warmth and food. They had to build, hunt, fish, and bring in supplies of wood and food.

Winter would make off with it all. Angélique fought with the birds for the last red berries of the mountain ash and some black elder-berries. She would use these to treat fevers, bronchitis, aches and pains, sore kidneys. . . .

She sent Elvire and the children off to pick anything edible they could still find on the bushes, in the thickets, or on the open ground, any kind of berry, bilberries, whortleberries, little apples or stunted wild pears.

It all seemed very little when she thought of the number of people she would have to feed, but even this small amount of fruit had a considerable value, since once it had dried, a mere pinch might well save them from scurvy towards the end of the winter. Scurvy, the scourge of seafaring men, but also the scourge of long winters in un-known lands. That was why sailors called it the scourge of the land. Savary had taught Angélique, during the course of her travels, to value the merest scrap of fruit peel. There was little enough of it here and it would be many a long month before they saw any more ripen. But the dried berries would be a help.

Next the children picked caraway seeds, mushrooms from moist hollows, hazelnuts and mast for the pig. Then they were given the task of gathering round pebbles from the moraine above the lake for the masons to increase the height of the central chimney with its four fireplaces, and build a second at the far end of the main room.

They were asked to watch the edge of the lake to prevent migratory birds settling on it, to protect the grass and the other plants the horses needed. They paddled along the shore all day long, shouting at the birds, and digging up a kind of tuberous sweet potato from the sand, a delicacy snatched from the wild geese.

Madame Jonas had undertaken to cook for everybody. Day after day she put the pots on to boil with maize, boiled marrow, meat and fish. . . . It took both her arms to hold the wooden ladle which was as big as she was and to stir the three great cauldrons hanging over the primitive hearths. She got her husband to make a megaphone out of an old powder horn to call everyone for meals. The rest of the time she spent rushing hither and thither among the wood shavings and the tools, taking brandy or beer to the carpenters, the woodcutters in the forest, or the men working about the house. Her cheeks were ruddy and glowing, and she was constantly laughing and saying that she had always wanted to be a cook.

Most of the meat and fish brought back by the hunters and fishers, including Florimond and Cantor, was for smoking.

They had made grids under which they kept fires of dried, sweet-smelling grasses burning constantly.

With the assistance of Kouassi-Ba and Eloi Macollet, Angélique took charge of this part of the work. She spent whole days kneeling in grass stained by the blood of the game and offal, her sleeves rolled up, her hands filthy, cutting joints of meat, some of it previously boned by old Macollet, into thin slices, which Kouassi-Ba placed over the fires. They had called a halt to all work in the mine in view of the urgency of their present situation, and the old Negro never left Angélique's side. As in days gone by, he talked ceaselessly to her, calling up his memories of the past, telling her of his adventures with Count Peyrac on the Mediterranean and in the Sudan, all the period in her husband's life she had only been able to guess at.

'He was not happy without Madame,' the old Negro would say. 'Oh yes, his work, the mine, the gold, his travels, bartering with the sultans, the desert, yes, all that kept his mind happy enough. . . . But as for women, it was no good. . . .'

'Hm . . . I find it hard to believe that.'

'Oh but yes, believe me, Madame! The women he had – it was just physical. As far as his heart was concerned, nothing.'

She listened as her friend Kouassi-Ba rambled on, while her hands, as skilled as when she had run the Red Mask Restaurant, cut the meat and sliced it, deftly deboning a leg or a shoulder, or cutting through ribs with an accurately placed stroke of her carving knife.

Eloi Macollet watched her out of the corner of his eye. He would have liked to have criticized her, but he found no occasion to do so.

'I dunno. Anyone would think you'd spent your entire life in a wigwam.'

Head bowed, eyes reddened with smoke and hands with blood, Angélique allowed nothing to distract her from her task. Every pile of well-smoked slices that went into one of the birch-bark and plaited grass baskets represented one meal more, every basket filled meant one more day they could survive. . . .

Does, stags, roebucks were dragged across the prairie as they fell, and the sharp knives swiftly got to work on them.

There was even a bear which Florimond had killed by leaping on to its back and plunging his knife in it. The first time he had missed the nape of the neck and had struck again farther forward, severing the carotid artery.

'I never heard of anyone killing a bear that way,' said Nicolas Perrot. Florimond never did things in the usual way. But he got away with it with only a torn doublet and a scratch from one of the bear's claws.

Angélique placed a cool dressing on his still smooth chest as Florimond told her of his exploit in detail while devouring a wing of roast turkey. Florimond's prodigious strength had already turned him into something of a legend. The American colonists liked superlatives, and Florimond was by way of becoming 'the strongest young man in North America'. As she looked proudly at him, Angélique remembered how frail he had been as a small child.

They melted the bear-grease down to make lamps, and they tanned the hide to make an extra bedcover for the winter.

Although late, winter was now coming on fast. Occasionally a harsh gust of wind from out of the blue would sweep over the trees, ruffling their tops and tearing off the last reddish-brown leaves. The forest had turned from red to pink, from pink to mauve, and was now grey. The rounded tops of the Appalachians, thick with pines and firs, seemed now to be clad in sombre hues, a brownish-violet tone that accentuated their undulating line.

The forest no longer smelled of blackberries and wild life. The fur-bearing animals, bears, foxes and marmots were beginning to take to their lairs; all that remained was the smell of mushrooms and moss, of dead leaves and bark; the first tang of winter was in the air.

Every evening more and more migratory birds, especially ducks and geese, settled on the lakes and pools. Throughout the day the sky was dark with them, and they showed every symptom of noisy panic, the panic of laggards trying to make up for lost time. It was impossible to chase them off the prairies any more, and one day, Angélique, armed with a stick, had to defend Honorine from the attack of a huge, white, black and grey barnacle-goose.

As she considered the body of the bird she carried back by the neck to Madame Jonas for the next meal, she thought how useful some goose fat would be if anyone were sick during the winter; it could be used to make poultices for the lungs, ointments for burns, and she thought too how good it would be to be able to eat some tasty game as a change from pemmican. Could they not catch some of the water fowl swarming before their eyes, and pot them against the bleak days ahead . . .? But how could she do it? She thought carefully. She had an abundance of bear-fat. Slowly it occurred to her that she might cover each bird with a layer of grease following the method used for preserving goose in the Charentes and Perigord regions back in France.

Joffrey de Peyrac approved the idea, and confirmed that the fat would protect the birds from deterioration by contact with the air. As a further precaution, he advised smoking the meat lightly beforehand. For containers they prepared the bladders of female moose and bears, which hunters were accustomed to use for this purpose since they were very capacious. They made a special little hut for smoking the birds quickly and filled it with juniper wood.

Every evening a party of men armed with sticks went down to the lakeside and made great slaughter among the birds, for man can protect his own life only by taking the lives of animals.

Green, violet, red, dazzling white, crested and glittering heads were shattered in a great flurry of feathers. The three women sat close by plucking, plucking till their fingers were raw, gutting the birds, trussing them, cutting off their heads and feet. The children ran backwards and forwards, arranging the prepared birds on the grids in the little hut. The following morning they took them out, duly smoked, and after boning stored them in the precious bladders, or, when there were none of these left, in bowls made of bark, wood or wicker-work. They were then covered with hot fat. When there was nothing more left to put them in, they even sewed them up in little doeskin bags.

The children had gathered so much juniper wood that their fingers were pricked all over, while Angélique no longer dared to look at her hands. They were hideous, rough-skinned, blackened and cut.

The smell of smoked meat and frying that hung about the narrow valley mingled with the scent of freshly cut wood.

A low-hanging, heavy cloud spread out across the lake, carrying to the farthest shores the scent of sap, of resin, of grasses and thorn-bushes, the scent of blood and the pungent smell of the meat of wild animals.

There were men working there. . . .

The handful of Indians still travelling down the Appalachian trail, sniffed the unaccustomed smell on the air and headed towards the camp.

They were nomads, travelling without baggage, solitary families seeking some lake where they could fish for beaver during the winter. They followed the crest of the hills above the lake and before disappearing over the other side of the cliff, peered curiously through the black-clad conifers, staring at the encampment on the Silver Lake, as it rang with the sound of axes on tree-trunks, blue beneath the pall of smoke that rose from the grids in the little hut.

Were the Palefaces attempting to stay here during the winter? they asked themselves. There were too many of them. They must be mad! They would die! The place was taboo. And they had some strange animals with them that wandered along the shore. They weren't moose, they weren't bison. . . . They too would have to eat. And what would they eat in winter? The Indians took fright and made off swiftly: no good would come of this. . . .

Then one morning Angélique, still busy cutting meat, felt a hand fall heavily on her shoulder. Lifting her eyes she recognized Mopuntook, the Sagamore of the Metallaks.

Looking as magnificent as ever, and still half naked in spite of the intense cold, he made signs to her to get up and follow him.

First he took her down to the shore of the first lake, touched the sand, tasted the water near the bank several times and likewise that of a little watercourse that formed a pool there before flowing down into the lake. Like some types of rock crystal which, although transparent, retain an amber tint, the crystal-clear water looked brown. It was water from the marshes, what is called humic water, that is, water that has filtered through humus.

It was wonderful water for washing clothes.

Angélique gathered that Mopuntook was asking her whether she was satisfied with the quality of the local water. She nodded her head several times to show that she was.

Then he led her farther off, took her up the hill and down the other side, stopping as they reached each pond, stream or spring.

'Ware! Ware!' he said, meaning water. This was one Abenaki word she could hardly help learning from him!

Farther on they encountered some very clear water that had a strong taste of limestone. Bad water. Angélique shook her head and made as if to spit the water out again, to indicate that it was undrinkable. You only had to look at it to see that this was true.

Mopuntook gave his approval in no uncertain terms. The Paleface woman had taste. They continued on their walk and came across red-coloured ferruginous water, cloudy water that did not look appetizing but tasted good.

Then, late in the afternoon, he revealed to her an almost invisible spring in the heart of a little clearing; the water gushed from it and disappeared almost immediately without a tremor, absorbed by the spongy ground, a silent, uninterrupted offering that came from the earth like an everlastingly sweet sorrow, a spring with a flavour of verdure. It brought the taste of leaves to one's tongue, spring was born again, in the mingled flavours of watercress, sage and mint. The charm of this spring made Angélique lose all sense of time.

At the beginning of their excursion, she had tried to make Mopuntook understand that she could not stray too far from the outpost. But later she had to abandon her attempt for they had gone round in so many circles through the forest that she feared she would get lost if she left his side.

Night was falling when she reappeared hard on the heels of the big red man. She was exhausted.

Once again, they had been anxiously searching for the Countess of Peyrac.

Mopuntook strutted about, exceedingly pleased with his day of water-prospecting and delighted that Angélique had shown such a gift for recognizing good water. Dignified and yet familiar, he placed a protective arm round the Count's shoulders, who was none too pleased, and told him how happy he was.

The white woman, he explained, was naturally enough, like all other women, somewhat obstinate, and a trifle inclined to suggest that a man did not know what he was about, but she did know about spring water and could distinguish different varieties by their taste. This was a great gift, a blessed gift. He, the local chief of near-by Lake Umbagog, hoped that the Palefaces would remain beside the Silver Lake for a long time, and that the Appalachian trail would be reopened, the trail the Indians used to follow when they traded between the great river in the north and the shores of the Atlantic.

It turned out that the day had been well spent.

And indeed, the following day, some Metallak Indians appeared saying that it would be a good idea if the Palefaces joined with them in a last big hunt before the winter set in. The Palefaces would bring their guns, their gunpowder and ammunition, in exchange for which help they would be given their share of the animals that were taken.

The moose or elk were beginning to head down from Canada towards the milder regions of Maine. When Mopuntook had returned from Wapassou he had had to chide his Indians, and reproach them for their idleness at a time when game was temporarily more abundant again, pointing out to them that it was their indolence which was the cause of the famine that yearly decimated their ranks. They always reckoned to have enough provisions, but no one ever had enough provisions to last the whole long winter through. Furthermore Mopuntook had had a dream: the Manitou had told him to organize a last great drive and to invite the Palefaces from the Silver Lake who had stood up to the fierce Iroquois and had got away alive with their hair still on their heads, through the skill of their tongues and of their magic! And it certainly took skill to persuade an Iroquois to abandon his plans for revenge. The Palefaces had paid the blood-money by setting fire to all their stores. There followed an inventory of the many splendid goods that had been sacrificed to the flames, a list the Metallak Indians recited like a litany, savouring every word. A hundred bales of furs, brandy, scarlet blankets, etc., etc. The Man of Thunder was not a Paleface like the others. He had special powers. Better make a friend of him. Mopuntook and his people, the tribes around Lake Umbagog, and their neighbours, would take him under their protection.

Nicolas Perrot, Florimond, Cantor and one of the Englishmen went off with the Indians for four or five days to the west, to organize the biggest hunt of the year, while the others concentrated all their efforts on finishing work on the outpost.

When the hunting party returned from Lake Umbagog towards the end of the first week of November, they were faced with a new spate of work. Then at last they reckoned that their food supplies were adequate. With luck, an early spring and a few good catches in the traps they would lay in the snow, and they would get through the winter. Eloi Macollet nodded, with new confidence:

'Maybe we shan't have to eat one another after all.'

'Whatever are you talking about! What an idea!'

'It's happened, you know, my good lady.'

And he was scarcely joking.

When Angélique heard him, she was suddenly seized with apprehension. She wavered between a feeling of well-being that the beauty of this deserted hidden spot gave her and a natural fear when she considered the ordeal that awaited them and how ill-prepared they were to face it. These men and a handful of women crowded together in so small a space with inadequate food supplies, no medicine, living in total, oppressive isolation, in a closed circle, and above all the children, frailer than the rest, must all somehow survive the winter.

CHAPTER 39

JOFFREY DE PEYRAC had said nothing when he saw Angélique take on the hard task of smoking the meat. She had a feeling he was watching her from a distance and was determined to prove herself up to the task.

'Does he imagine I am useless and that I am going to stand around with my arms folded?'

They had a whole year to catch up! That was what he had said, wasn't it? And right now they owned scarcely more than the clothes on their backs.

To help him survive, to help him triumph, what secret delight it would be to her to do that, after such a long time when she had been unable to serve him.

The thought of toiling for him and thus making some kind of amends for her past disloyalty, made Angélique's eyes bright with pleasure. And the hardest of tasks seemed easy to her.

There are some things the passage of time alone can prove, and among these is faithfulness in love. She was determined to tear down the wall of suspicion that sometimes seemed to haunt Joffrey de Peyrac in his dealings with her. She would prove to him that he was all in all to her and that she would in no way limit his freedom as a man nor become a burden to him, any more than she would force him to abandon his work and the goal he had set himself.

The fear that he might one day regret taking her with him or even finding her again appalled her. During this time the work going on at the camp had separated them again; and when she was far from him she was miserable. The menfolk huddled as best they could beneath rude bark shelters built in Indian style, while a bigger wigwam had been built for the women and children with a rough little chimney at one end. This provided warm shelter enough but Angélique once more began to dream that she was alone again, desperately seeking her lost love across the world, or she would imagine him rejecting her with that remote look he had worn on board the *Gouldsboro*.

So she worked like a slave. And every time she had a spare moment she would run into the woods with the children to gather sticks. They had not enough firewood and she knew from experience that there is nothing worse on a winter morning than being unable to light a fire.

They made haste to gather up all the branches and twigs that had fallen on the ground and made piles of them in the shed with the log supply.

By now the tops of the highest mountains were sprinkled with snow and the wind was dry and icy.

But the glowing colours of the larch-trees lent colour to the landscape. Russet and rose, like flames or feathers, their delicate tufts danced against a leaden sky. Their furry needles floated down and the undergrowth beneath them was covered with a deep yellow carpet as soft as sand.

Angélique and the children trod noiselessly over it.

Gathering wood had always been a task that Angélique enjoyed. Back at her father's château when she was a little girl, her aunt Pulchérie used to say that it was the only task she would gladly do. She was able to gather enormous bundles of sticks very quickly and carry them tirelessly. The first time Peyrac's men had seen her coming back from the woods, like a forest on the march, bent double like an old woman under her load with the little band of children behind her, they had stood open-mouthed, not knowing what to say or do.

So perfectly did she perform every task she undertook that any interference seemed out of place and they refrained from comment. But they talked it over among themselves, still without reaching any conclusion. They could see that she was a woman who had worked hard during her life, who had turned her hand to all manner of tasks, a woman who was deterred by nothing, but she was also a great lady used to being waited on, used to giving orders, accustomed to enjoying herself – they had seen her at the feast of Katarunk! – but somehow, she didn't like mixing business with pleasure.

And if, during those tough days of frenzied work that preceded the first winter at Wapassou, one of the men were to come up to her to give her a hand, more often than not she would send him packing.

'No no, my lad, you've got other more urgent things to do! If I need you, I'll call you.'

Joffrey de Peyrac was watching her too. He had seen her bustling about the fires in the smoke-room with an almost professional competence. He had watched her skin does and bucks, gut them, break bones, pluck wildfowl, melt down nauseating pans of fat, lift the cauldrons from the fire; and every task her delicate, elegant little hands seemed to perform with almost miraculous skill combined with the energy of a man accustomed to the heaviest physical work.

With mingled astonishment and respect he discovered how exceedingly strong and capable she was, how she knew a great deal about innumerable matters for which her education and above all the gilded life of luxury he had given her in Toulouse certainly had not prepared her.

And when a feeling of anger occasionally swept over him, almost forcing him to go over to her and snatch the butcher's knife she handled with such dexterity, or the heavy cauldron she would move with a single twist of her back, or the load of dead wood that bent her double, he was aware of the full depth of the anguish he felt when he remembered their years of separation.

For this was the other woman, 'the stranger', the woman who had learned to live without him, this was the woman she was showing him now, and he almost resented the fact that she was so strong, so unshakeable, and that she had learnt so much during her separation from him.

He remembered the words she had shouted at him one day aboard the *Gouldsboro*: 'and how would you have hoped to find me? Peevish, silly, useless? Would you rather I had learnt nothing from the life I was left to face? ...'

Yes, it was true that he had not reckoned with the full strength of Angélique's personality and what she would make of it when left to her own resources. He told himself that he still had much to learn about women through this particular one, and his heart was torn between admiration and jealousy.

Angélique was not totally unaware of this weakness of his. She had enough subtlety to see why he felt as he did and it almost gave her pleasure, for he was so strong, so superior, he towered so high above her that she felt a little reassured to know that he could suffer, that he was vulnerable. As she went by she gave him a look that was both gently ironical and tender, but also held something inscrutable that caused him pain.

'Don't be anxious,' she said, shaking her head with a smile, 'I like working like this, and . . . I've known worse slavery than gathering firewood for love of you....'

And he felt as if a sharp blade had been driven into his heart. How could she still be the only woman capable of making him suffer, blasé as he was, and merely by being herself?

Truth to tell, he had no reason to reproach her. There was no sign of false humility, no provocativeness in her attitude. But she had acquired these qualities far from him. And this fact tormented him with a fierce desire to get his own back. On her account he had made up his mind even more firmly to triumph over every obstacle that stood in his way, and such was his passion to overcome his environment that he communicated it to his men along with his conviction that nothing could prevail against him.

Wapassou seethed with activity like an ants' nest.

Peyrac was busy on all fronts, directing the carpenters and masons, advising the tanners and joiners, and it was no rare sight to see him take the woodcutter's long axe in his hands and fell a tree with a few strong, well-aimed strokes, as if pitting himself against refractory nature in order to vanquish it in single combat.

So, without the communication of speech, this period of work consolidated the bond between Angélique and her husband, through the things they learnt about themselves, through the things that remained unvowed, and through the things they sensed about one another. Peyrac guessed Angélique's anxieties. He had noticed that when she grew over-tired she was subject to a depression that made everything look black.

It was at times like these that the vision of Cain in the tempest haunted her again.

And what if God really were against them, she asked herself? What if they really were outcasts? . . . What if they had been already condemned, wherever they might go, the two of them? What was the point of struggling? And she would remember that look of hatred she had felt coming from some creature lurking in the bushes beside the lake, that look she had felt the day she had bathed, that look that had driven a poisoned shaft into her heart. . . . It was a memory that often came back to her, and she would stop at the edge of the trees as she returned from the woods, and scan every inch of her surroundings.

There were some weird constructions at the foot of the two hills on the left, huge upended pieces of timber and wheels that stood out like instruments of torture, nightmare shapes against the bare sides of the mountain where the shadows made gaping holes and patches of raw, freshly exposed ground. The mountain top was capped with a little crown of forest from which, night and day, a thin line of smoke rose up, as from a censer. She knew that in actual fact they were only charcoal burners' huts, with rounded clay tops, that kept elder and birchwood constantly at combustion point to produce the charcoal the miners needed for their work.

The dwelling in which they were all going to shut themselves up as if in the Ark rose out of the ground at the far extremity of the promontory, and now its roof with its white shingles and three tall stone chimneys was erected and ready.

There was another matter that vaguely troubled Angélique. In spite of the good qualities in them that she had begun to appreciate, Peyrac's companions remained rough men, not easy to get on with, in fact not at all reassuring. When they were all shut up together in the fort, and were living at such close quarters, what would be the result of the clash of divergent characters, the hardships and the lack of women? Would not the atmosphere become unbearable?

When she had led her men through the Poitou wars, she remembered that the peasants had hated any man they suspected of being her lover, like La Morinière or Baron du Croisset. . . .

The situation here was similar. Perhaps the hostility the men felt towards their leader's wife might develop into a feeling of rancour. Angélique knew full well that her husband held her at a distance in front of the other men in order not to awaken jealousy in their solitary hearts.

Madame Jonas thought about these things too and was worried about Elvire, who was of an age to attract men's attention. Up till now the men had treated her with respect, but what might happen when they were all shut up together and they began to feel bored?

One evening Joffrey de Peyrac took Angélique's arm and led her down to the lakeside. The setting sun was reflected like rubies in the calm waters and the dry chilly air was pleasant.

'You seem worried, my love. I can see it in your face. Tell me what it's all about!'

With a trace of embarrassment she told him of the fears that occasionally assailed her. First and foremost, she wondered whether ill-fortune or bad luck might not turn out to be too strong for them.

It was not that she feared hunger, cold or hard work. Her life at Monteloup had not been very different during the winter from the life they expected here. Isolation, hard work, and the fear of possible raids by bandits, just as they feared the Indians or the French here, had created the same atmosphere of insecurity and alarm.

No, it was not that. . . . She liked Wapassou. . . .

He sensed what it was she was trying to explain.

'You are frightened that there is a curse on me, aren't you? But, my love, there is no curse. There never was a curse. On the contrary, there was only incompatibility between those who have lagged behind in the

256

paths of ignorance and myself, to whom God has seen fit to reveal hitherto untrodden ways. And even if it brought persecution upon me, I shall never regret the fact that He gave me this grace. I have come to this land to make use of my gifts. Is there anything in that which could possibly displease my Creator? No. So don't be superstitious and mistrustful of God. For that is where Evil would lie. . . .'

From under his doublet he drew the little golden cross he had taken from the neck of the dead Abenaki brave.

'Look at this. . . . What do you see?'

'It's a cross,' she replied.

'As far as I'm concerned, what strikes me is the fact that it's gold. . . . It was because I saw a large number of these little trinkets, crosses and other emblems, round the necks of the natives that I decided to explore this area. The only explanation that anyone could offer was that these jewels had been given to the river tribes by sailors from Saint-Malo who had put into port along the coast, and this explanation did not satisfy me. Our Breton people are not so generous as that, and a copper cross would have been a perfectly acceptable gift. These crosses must have been made here, which proved that there must be gold and silver somewhere in the area where the greedy Spaniards had found nothing, accustomed as they were to Inca and Aztec treasures. In fact there was very little visible gold, in the form of nuggets that can be washed from a stream, but there may be a great deal of invisible gold. The crosses spoke the truth, and I found it. As you see, I was guided by the cross. Wapassou is the richest of all the mines, but I have others scattered all over Maine. Now that I know that the Canadian Government has its eye on me, I must make haste to bring my work to fruition. . . . I would have liked to install you more comfortably in Katarunk, but by coming here we have saved time. All we have to do is get through this winter, and it will be tough. Here, our one and only enemy is nature. But it is from nature that I shall draw my strength. In the old days I possessed money without strength, and I need strength in order to have the right to live. I shall find it easier to acquire it in the New World than in the Old.'

Then, as they walked slowly along the edge of the lake, he clasped her close and went on:

'Listen to me, my love, we're all gallows-birds here, and that is precisely why we shall survive. I chose my men because I know that they appreciate the value of patience. Prison, the galley, captivity, they reached the depths of abjection with the dregs of humanity, and that, if anything, is a school of patience. . . . And what if they do have to face long days of snow often with an empty belly? They can all do it. They have all come through worse things than that. . . . What do cold, hunger and cramped quarters mean to them? They have known worse. . . . Perhaps you are frightened that the children won't stand up to it, but if we make sure that their essential requirements are met and if they feel themselves surrounded by affection, they won't suffer. Children are fantastically tough when their hearts are at rest.

'I have no qualms about your friends the Jonases either. . . . They know all about patience too. They waited for years for their sons to return, then one day they realized that they would never see them again. And they survived. What about Elvire? I agreed to bring this young woman with us because she begged me to. And I know why. She couldn't stand the sight of her companions from La Rochelle any more, for she felt that they had been the cause of her husband's death by involving him in the mutiny I had to crush and in which he was killed. She will get over it better with us than she would in Gouldsboro. I think it was for similar reasons the Jonases wanted to leave the coast and come with us too. I welcomed their company, for I hoped they would be companions for you with whom you could discuss all the little things that make up your day. And Elvire's children are playmates for Honorine, and will help her to feel less lonely now that I have monopolized you.'

'Thank you for thinking of all these things; I am indeed happy to have friends and to see Honorine playing happily with Bartholomew and Thomas, whom she already knew back in La Rochelle. But I am beginning to realize that as far as you are concerned, having brought children and above all womenfolk with you can only be a source of embarrassment and difficulty.'

'On the contrary, it might turn out to be a good thing,' Peyrac replied gaily. 'The presence of women often has an excellent influence on men's minds. It is up to you ladies to prove that true.'

'Are you never afraid of anything?'

'I enjoy taking risks.'

'But don't you think that these men, who themselves have no women, might not in the end grow jealous of you who have me, or begin to lust after Elvire who is young and pretty, and that that might lead to conflicts and fights among them? Elvire is beginning to feel disturbed and frightened at the thought that she might become the object of their attentions once we are all shut up in this little outpost for months on end.'

'Has she had any reason to complain of any of them?'

'I don't think so.'

'Then tell her from me not to worry. My men have been warned. Hanging would be the mildest punishment they would be liable to if they dared show the slightest disrespect to any of the women here.'

'You'd do that!' Angélique exclaimed, looking at him in horror.

'Indeed I would! Did I show the slightest hesitation, on board ship, in hanging the Moor Abdullah who tried to rape Bertille Bercelot. And yet he was a faithful servant of mine, a servant whose devotion I miss greatly. But discipline comes first, and this my men know. My dear, here we are still on board a ship. As we followed the trail we were still on board ship. That is to say that I am the only master here. I have the right to do what I like. I have the right of life or death over my men, the right to reward or to punish, and also the right to do what I like with my life, even to have the loveliest woman in the world as my wife.'

And laughing, he kissed her.

'Have no fears, my little Mother Abbess! ... Women sometimes have odd ideas about the true nature of men. You have lived too long among depraved, idle, vicious men with no feeling in their hearts, impotent men seeking a cure for their incapacities in an endless series of sexual adventures, or among brutes with thought for nothing but the satisfaction of their instincts. But sea-going men are of a different stamp. If they were unable to do without women, they would never go to sea. For them passion and voluptuousness are replaced by adventure, the will-o'-the-wisp of fortune, of discovery, that is their dream and the means to attain it. ... There are men for whom a well-loved task can occupy both heart and senses. For them women are a luxury, very pleasant of course, but never capable of fixing the course of their lives. There is more than that for us here, my love, as I said before! Don't forget what it is that binds us all together. We are all gallows-birds, even the Huguenots who were condemned to ignomy by the Jesuits and the King of France. And as for the others! ... Each one of them has his secret. ... In prison you learn to do without women too.

'Sometimes the love of liberty replaces all other loves. It is a much stronger, a much more burning passion than anyone thinks. ... It can become a man's sole pre-occupation. And it always makes him a nobler creature....'

Angélique listened as he spoke, moved by the fact that this man, whose customary tone was so often caustic, should suddenly speak so seriously to her, in his desire to fortify her heart and spirit before their ordeal, and that he should reveal to her another aspect of life which she had never envisaged, the outcome of his own suffering and meditation.

Night had fallen around them, hard and clear, although there was no moon. The sky had an almost oriental luminosity. It seemed to be spangled with stars, so tiny overhead, yet in the shimmering waters of the lake their trembling reflections looked like strings of pearls.

Angélique shook her head humbly.

'I too was a captive,' she said, 'but it seems to me that I never learnt the kind of patience you are talking about. Far from it, I am all of a tremble – I can no longer bear constraint. And as for doing without your love....'

Joffrey de Peyrac burst out laughing.

'You! You are different, my love, quite different! You are of another stamp. You are a living spring that gushes out to bring freshness and delight to the earth. ... Patience, little spring, one day you will travel down more peaceful valleys, and delight them with your charm and beauty. Patience, I shall catch and hold you in your madness, and guard you jealously for fear that you might get lost or go astray. I am beginning to know you. You can't be left alone for very long. Here you are, after only a few days' separation, a few days sleeping away from me, and you are already no longer quite yourself. But the roof is finished and I have asked the carpenters to make a big handsome bed for us to sleep in. Soon you will be in my arms again. Then things will look brighter, won't they? ...'

The following day they moved back into the fort.

CHAPTER 40

THAT BED! Angélique looked at it almost fearfully, the first evening she and her husband entered the tiny, low-ceilinged cubby-hole that was to be their bedroom. The bed seemed to fill the entire room. It was vast and solid with a dark walnut frame, that had been stripped of its bark and squared up, and for all its rusticity it had a regal look. Covered with furs, it was the resting place of a Viking Prince.

The new wood still gave off a fresh, aromatic smell, and across its dark graining ran the pink lines the axes had left as they cut.

Standing before this bed, torn from the forest whose scent and whose poetry it had brought with it, before this proffered couch, that spoke of health-giving rest and nights of love, Angélique began to feel anxious and a little dismayed. And she stood looking at it, standing beside it biting her lips.

A new phase of her life was about to begin, the one she had dreamed of for so long.

But as she stood on the verge she recoiled, ready to take flight like a frightened doe. The life that was beginning for her now was the life she would lead, day after day, night after night beside her husband, because she was his wife. And it was something to which she was no longer accustomed. She had always led a roving life where love was concerned, and even recently, since that day not so long ago, scarcely three months back, when he had won her again on board the *Gouldsboro*, their busy lives of travel had scarcely enabled them to be more to one another than casual lovers, making the most of chance opportunities.

And even in the old days in Toulouse, even if occasionally they had slept together, they had nevertheless had their own private suites of rooms, vast and sumptuous, in which, according to how they felt, they could retire alone or welcome each other.

Here they would have nothing but this tiny refuge, this bed of moss and lichen, a single place of refuge for both of them, where their bodies would lie close, intertwined in love or sleep, evening after evening, night after night.

This was something new to both of them!

Angélique realized that for the first time in her life she would be living a true married life....

And her perplexity could be seen on her face as Peyrac, smiling, watched her out of the corner of his eye, as he slowly removed his jerkin, standing before the fire.

He, the pirate of sea and ocean, the great lord of oriental palaces, he, even more a vagrant than she, selecting his pleasures according to his whim and his fortune, he had wanted it thus: to be alone with her in this one room, in this one bed. He had an urgent need of her presence, to be sure that he held her captive, to prevent her from escaping him ever again.

As a man who had studied human nature and women in particular, he was even more conscious than Angélique of the fragile bonds that united them.

They had been married a long time ago, their lasting feelings for each other had been fed on memories, while between them lay the chasm of what was almost another life, which they had lived apart.

The firmest bond that had survived the disaster of the past, was it not, after all, their physical attraction for each other? It was these glowing embers that must be blown on again and he had waited impatiently for the time to come when he knew her to be entirely his, in the eyes of everyone, when he would be able to display his possession of her and his rights over her through their cohabitation. If he wanted to win her again, he must keep her close to him, closely dependent on him. But he sensed the complex feelings that troubled Angélique, and came towards her, reciting the lines of Homer:

'... "Why so suspicious, Woman? ... The Gods have not willed it that we should have spent the days of our youth together, but neither have they prevented us from coming to the threshold of old age together. ... We can still recognize one another. ... This bed that I built with my hands, think you that I know not its secret? This we share, you and I alone, we who have slept in it together. ..." Thus spoke Ulysses on his return from a long voyage where he found Penelope with the white arms. ...'

Count Peyrac, his chest bared and brown, bent over Angélique.

He clasped her tight in his arms and, caressing her restive brow, murmured soft, reassuring words into her ear as he had done when they had first made love.

CHAPTER 41

ALL THROUGHOUT this late autumn, the harsh American land seemed to have signed a pact with the bold men of Wapassou. It was as if it wanted to give them, who had sacrificed everything they possessed, a saving reprieve. When winter came at last they were ready.

It came after this blessed remission. It came with a soft, abundant unfolding.

The snow began to fall.

It fell for several days, without a moment's interruption. The world became blind and deaf, stifled in white, heavy draperies that enveloped it like a shroud.

The trees, the earth and the heavens vanished. Only one thing remained real, the silent snow, as it drifted slowly down unruffled by the slightest breath of wind. Higher and higher it rose, until it covered the sleeping earth.

So they shut themselves up in the outpost to live out the long days ahead in which warmth and food were to become the two most important things in life.

Peyrac added a third, no less essential, he considered, to their well-being – work.

An underground passageway leading out of the main room enabled them to reach the workshop. No one would be lacking in work, so no one would have time to feel the winter weighing him down with its whiteness: there would be more than enough work for everyone.

For the women, it was simple – the provision of food and warmth.

Those were their guiding principles.

No one needed to tell them what to do and they succeeded in sharing out their tasks with diligence and efficiency. This was yet another of Angélique's gifts.

She worked as hard as the others, without appearing to be directing everything, and yet it was she who was the driving spirit.

She was in fact the mistress, but claimed neither title nor prerogatives. She knew instinctively that her time would come. But it went without saying that her task was to serve the others and to do everything in her power to keep those who had been entrusted to her happy and healthy. And still Joffrey watched her.

Food and warmth – the kitchen fires – and then came tidiness.

Without order and cleanliness life would become unbearable in this overcrowded burrow.

From early in the morning their heather brooms would come into action.

Before that they would already have rekindled the fires, laid sticks and logs across the fire-dogs, and hung the cooking-pots to boil in the five fireplaces.

The respite allowed them before winter began had enabled them to enlarge the outpost considerably. On entering the door you came into a narrow room where outdoor clothes and snow-covered boots were to be left. Here they were hung to drip and only afterwards brought to dry into the main room.

At the end of the main room stood a chimney across one corner with a single hearth, beside the swinging bails where the men had their mattresses; this was the one especially set aside for the vital task of drying and it gave off clouds of steam smelling of wet leather and fur.

People tended to sit round the central chimney where soups and stews hung simmering. This huge fireplace had been built of round pebbles on the same pattern as the one at Katarunk whose convenience Angélique had already learnt to appreciate.

This one also consisted of four hearths, two of them facing forward and to the right into the big hall, while the other two served to warm Angélique's and her husband's room on one side, and on the other, to the left, the huge room screened off with planks of wood where slept the Jonases and the children, watched over by Elvire. The third, raised room, set on a spur of the rocky promontory on which the outpost had been built, or rather in which it had been excavated, was the bedroom set aside for the Count and Countess.

It was reached from the main room by four steps and a platform about half-way up, where Angélique kept the bowls, boxes and baskets directly necessary in the kitchen or for serving meals.

The heavy oak door hung on leather hinges opened with difficulty, reluctantly as it were. It was necessary to stoop to pass through it. The ceiling was low and there was only one tiny parchment-covered window. All the rest of the room was made of black oak, with the beams squared up and placed so close to one another that they gave an impression of massiveness and intimacy. The fireplace was at the far end.

On the right a door led into a cubby-hole that had been fitted out for steam baths. This was where Angélique enjoyed the best of her moments of relaxation and could satisfy her passion for hot water. At the Court of Miracles she had often been taken to task for this weakness, but she had not mended her ways!

Angélique immediately fell in love with this dark hideout half buried in the rock, half covered by the black overhanging branches of the fir-trees that brushed lightly against the shingle roof.

Behind the main room there was a kind of shelter under the rock face that served as a storehouse and cellar. Here beer was brewed, soap made, and the washing done. Here the pig, the spoilt child of the household, grunted away and was visited by those whose task it was to see that he grew fat and bring him scraps. Then there was the covered passage that led to the mysterious area of workshops and forges. Lead pipes ran along this underground passage bringing hot water heated by the mine furnaces to the women of the house, which they found a great boon.

Sometimes Angélique would call out:

'Run and make sure Eloi Macollet hasn't died! . . .'

For the old trapper had absolutely refused to shut himself up with the others, and had installed himself outside in the yard, like an old bear, in a wigwam that he had made with his own hands out of bark, with a fireplace in the middle inside a circle of stones. It was only when he refused to share their life with them that it was realized that he did not belong, in fact, to their party, but was merely a solitary old trapper who had come down from Mount Katahdin, following innumerable streams and rivers, and had halted one night at the outpost of Katarunk, when the Canadian army were camping there and Peyrac had just arrived. Why had he remained with them and followed them? None but he knew the answer to that. The old fellow had very definite ideas on that score, but he would never have confided them in anyone. In fact he had stayed because of Angélique. Macollet was a sceptic by nature. His compatriots in Quebec had told him that Angélique was most certainly the She-Devil of Acadia, and he remembered that his daughter-in-law in Levis believed in this story of a she-devil who would bring calamity to Acadia. So he told himself that his daughter-in-law's hair would stand on end under her bonnet when she learned that he had spent the whole winter with the woman they now suspected of being the She-Devil. Furthermore, he'd thought about this a lot, now! Demons and She-Devils, he knew all about such trash, for he'd explored all the forests of America. Well now! The woman they were accusing, she wasn't one of them. He'd have staked his life on that. She was simply a woman, an unusual one, a pretty, charming woman, who knew how to laugh, to eat well and even to get a bit tipsy on occasion. He had seen her very gay and a very great lady at one and the same time in Katarunk, and he would treasure that memory as one of the happiest moments of his life. There was no dishonour in helping a woman like that, he told himself. Not to mention the fact that these folk needed him, or they wouldn't get by. They had too many enemies; so Macollet was going to stay with them.

Macollet's insistence on sleeping outside was a great worry to Angélique. The day would come when no one could reach his hut and he might die without anyone knowing.

To please her, the staunchest among them would go across twice a day to see how the old man was getting on and to take him some hot soup. They always came back coughing from the smoke-laden atmosphere of the hut where Eloi Macollet, crouching in front of his fire, voluptuously smoked his white stone pipe and savoured his freedom.

CHAPTER 42

AND STILL the snow fell.

'What luck it was that it didn't come a week earlier,' some of them said.

'Luck! A miracle, you mean.'

The Catholics among them called it a miracle, the others, luck.

But they all saw it as a sign from Heaven, and never failed to quote it as evidence that they would all survive the ordeal.

'And it's not everyone that manages to survive!'

And they would call to mind earlier settlers.

Quite a number had died during the winter along the shores of America. More had died of hunger and illness than had been massacred by the savages – half the Pilgrim Fathers from Plymouth, for example, during that first winter after they disembarked from the *Mayflower* in New England in 1620. The *Mayflower* lay out in the roadstead, but what could the brine-sodden ship do, with no more fresh food on board than they had, save watch them die and speak to them of distant European shores. And in 1606 half the French of Monsieur de Monts and Monsieur Champlain, the first on the island in the middle of the Sainte-Croix river, the others not far from Gouldsboro, had died too. Half of every contingent that disembarked, that was the regular number quoted in the annals of famine. Occasionally more . . . But never less. . . .

They exchanged glances, wondering which of them would still be there in the spring.

And there was Jacques Cartier, who had wintered in the Saint Charles river beneath Quebec in 1535 with two ships. It was easy to imagine those two lost ships, with their sailors and their captains wearing their long beards over their old-fashioned frilly ruffs. They had sailed too far up the Saint Lawrence, and when winter came they slipped up the little Saint Charles river and took shelter under the cliff, and then the two ships were transformed into fortresses of ice, while inside the men died one after the other with bleeding gums. The Indian chief from Stadacome brought them a brew made of bark, which they drank, and recovered, and thus the remnant was saved.

And then there was the story of the Demoiselle. She was the niece of the Sieur de Robeval, who had come to Canada in 1590. The jealous wretch had abandoned her with her lover, Raoul de Ferland, on an island in the Gulf of Saint Lawrence, where they eventually died . . . stark staring mad. . . .

And there was the story of the foundation of Jamestown, where the people ate one another, and countless other stories as well. There is no end to the stories of famine in America.

The most tragic tale of all was the tale of Sir Walter Raleigh and the English on the island of Roanoke in Virginia. That was in 1587. The leader of the settlers, John White, had to go back to England to fetch help. When he reached the island again he found not a single trace of the settlers among whom had been his wife and his little daughter Virginia, the first white child to be born on American soil. For a whole year he scoured the sea, the coast, the forests, but he never found anyone. And what happened to those first settlers still remains a mystery.

As she listened to these tales, Angélique thought of every means she could adopt to ward off the spectre of famine and scurvy. She felt them to be haunted by the ancient dread of 'the land disease'. Innumerable shipwrecks, innumerable attempts to winter in desolate, unknown lands, had gone to build up the legend. For centuries men had gone to earth with salt pork and biscuits. They did not know what species of the surrounding hostile vegetation were edible, and they had planted nothing, for they did not have time!

And it was no business of sailors to plant crops. The earth was motionless, it went nowhere, it merely went to sleep beneath its white shroud; implacable and indifferent, it shrank, grew hard and died. It went away, leaving them there, these men with nothing. They had nothing. Not a bird, not an animal, not a leaf. Everything about them was inedible: stones, wood and snow. They had nothing, and the land disease slowly slid into their veins, gnawing away their lives, destroying their souls. Even the air they breathed became an enemy, stripped of all vitality by the frost. . . . It made them cough, then they died. . . .

And now it was the turn of Peyrac's people to face all that!

The very idea of Wapassou, set in the middle of nowhere, more than a hundred leagues from any inhabited place, inhabited, that is, by either Palefaces or Redskins, was madness! And these women among the men were a further challenge to fate. All these people to keep alive during the long period when nature all about them seemed completely dead; it was an interminable task. All these minds to keep sane among the phantasms born of solitude and the silent threat of limitless space . . . it was an impossible task.

But where there are deserts, there are also oases.

Where there are vast, cruel spaces, there are also havens of refuge.

Where there are sickness and discomfort, there are also nursing and medicine.

Where there are fear and fatigue, there are also consolation and rest.

Where there is solitude, there can also be welcome.

And this was what Angélique had decided she must stand for in the eyes of all those beneath her protection; she must always represent the opposite of what threatened.

She wanted to make it possible for the men to come home from their work in the evening and find the table laid and an appetizing smell already filling the main room. A line of bowls on the long central table represented a promise that their appetites would be satisfied. There was always a panful of scalding hot toddy standing beside the fire, and she would pour them a bowl while they waited. Even the smell of the hot toddy made them feel better and more willing to wait, and so did the sight of the wooden stools that had been placed before the fire to welcome them. They would remove their wet clothes, hang them before the fire at the back of the room, then return to sit down at the fireplace, and would exchange a few words with the ladies as they watched the meal being prepared.

The thing they missed more than anything else was tobacco. So rare a treat was it that the few puffs they were allowed to have in the evenings, either before or after their meal, became so important that the loss or breakage of a pipe assumed the proportions of a disaster.

Angélique had a kind of rack made beside the door where everyone left his precious pipe after use, and found it again in the evening after work like a reward. There were pipes of all shapes and sizes, little nose-warmers, long Dutch pipes, made of wood, of clay or even of stone. Eloi Macollet smoked a white stone peace-pipe, with two old scorched feathers on either side of it, a pipe the Mascoutins of Lake Illinois had given him when he had visited them in his youth, the first Paleface ever to do so.

During the day the men worked in the workshops or cleared the ground outside. Then in the evening they would all gather in the main room of the outpost, which had become a dormitory, a kitchen and a refectory.

They made mattresses from rushes and branches of fir-trees, throwing leather clothes and blankets on top. On the very first day Peyrac divided out the blankets and made sure that everyone had enough to keep warm. Then a certain number of exchanges took place between those who felt the cold and those whose native constitutions would have enabled them to sleep in a hole in the snow and still have sweet dreams.

Beds for the women and children were built in the bedrooms, of logs from which the bark had not been stripped.

The circumstances in which these people found themselves, brought together to survive a trying ordeal, obliged Angélique to consider what role she must play among them, what she could bring them – the basic essentials of life.

A series of tiny details revealed to her that, without being consciously aware of it, without admitting it even to themselves, they were pleased to find her there when they returned from their work and foregathered in the main room. So she gradually gave up the habit of spending the evenings with the Jonases in their room where she had grown accustomed to spend some quiet hours among her friends. Now she stayed among the menfolk.

She would sit on the little platform in front of 'her fireplace', where she prepared soothing drinks and medicine. She would strip the skin from a root, sort her herbs, tidy her little birch-bark pots full of ointment. She would sit a short distance from the others, and a little above them, in her little niche on the platform, not exactly with them and yet present. She never joined in their conversations but not an evening passed without her becoming involved.

'Madame la Comtesse, you know about these things, what do you think about what Clovis has just said?'

'What is it all about, my friends?'

'Well, you see, the stupid man claims . . .'

And they would tell her of their difficulty, forming a group around her, sitting in a familiar, friendly way on the wooden step. She was beginning to know them better through these conversations about this and that. And when some quarrel blew up at the far end of the room, she only had to lift her head and look in the direction of the disturbance for their voices to drop immediately.

She encouraged Madame Jonas and Elvire to join them in the main room, pointing out to them how much the men's morale was improved by their presence.

Madame Jonas treated them all alike as if they were small children, so that when she was not there they felt abandoned. They liked her round, friendly face and her comfortable laugh. She laughed at everything they told her like a mother full of admiration for her innumerable progeny. It encouraged them and kept them cheerful, without tempting them beyond the bounds of propriety or good humour.

Elvire, who was timid and gentle, occasionally became the butt of some friendly teasing. They teased her about her downcast eyes, and the look of fright that came over her whenever someone shouted or there was an argument, but she was sprightly and vivacious, and they respected her. She had been a baker's wife in La Rochelle and so was used to mixing with all kinds of people. They all seemed to get on well together. In the evenings after serving the supper, the women would settle themselves before the fire on the right and the men before the bigger one in the middle. The children would move about the room demanding a story here, there, listening wide-eyed, delighted with anything that came their way, and their presence helped to create the family atmosphere that men find so restful.

The children were happy at Wapassou. They had all they needed: warmth, entertainment, motherly laps in which they could hide their faces and crowds of friends to spoil them, to whittle toys for them, and tell them wonderful, horrific stories.

And when she saw the three little tots turning up their permanently grubby faces towards the tall figure of Joffrey de Peyrac, so full of confidence in the great lord who smiled down at them, Angélique would say to herself: 'That's what happiness means!'

She was able to watch her sons too, in this new intimacy, and discovered that they were very well informed and that their father, who taught them everything, expected high standards from them. The two lads had no time to stand about gaping. They worked down in the mine, in the laboratory, covered sheets of parchment with figures, and drew maps. Florimond was like his father in character, full of new ideas and avidly seeking after science and adventure. Cantor was different, harder to understand, although he seemed every bit as capable of being taught as was his older brother. The two brothers were great friends and would spend long hours talking together in English, finally coming to Angélique or their father to settle some point of disagreement. It was often upon religious or biblical matters, which they had been taught at Harvard, that they found themselves in dis-agreement, but they sometimes discussed more daring philosophical questions. Angélique would often hear the word Mississippi recur – for Florimond's great dream was to cross the China Sea which every navigator had been seeking since the discovery of America, and he thought that the great river a Canadian geographer and a Jesuit, Father Marquette, had recently discovered, might lead there. But Joffrey de Peyrac was not convinced and that worried Florimond.

CHAPTER 43

WITH EVERY day that passed Angélique became more and more glad to have the Jonases with them. They were folk who had not felt at all attracted by the delights of Indian life. The filth of the savages had sent shudders up the spine of the worthy Huguenot housewife. Her religion taught its daughters early in life that their attitude towards the Lord was to be manifested in an immaculate, carefully ironed coiffe, in a well-made bed, and in a neatly set table, and that untidiness was a sin.

Monsieur Jonas was an equally valuable member of the little community. His cheerfulness and his good nature played no small part in keeping a sense of proportion among its members. He had a way of drawing himself up and saying hum! hum! when he did not like something someone had said, that had the effect of halting the boldest of them in their tracks. He had taken the Protestants in hand, that is to say his own family and the three Englishmen, and on Sundays he would read the Bible to them in French, but in so solemn a voice that the Englishmen would listen, gripped by the religious awe demanded by this most puritanical of sects. Gradually the Catholics also acquired the habit of hanging about in the vicinity of the reader during the Sunday services.

After all, we all share the same Bible, they said, and there are some wonderful stories in it. . . .

Monsieur Jonas was equally welcome among the miners, for no one could rival him when it came to making the small precision instruments required in their work. He had brought his watchmaker's eyeglass from La Rochelle.

Everyone was dreadfully upset when, towards the end of November, the good man developed an abscess under one of his teeth that forced him to take to his bed. After trying various herbal drinks and poultices in vain, Angélique realized she would have to take drastic measures.

'I'll have to take the stump out, Monsieur Jonas or you'll get blood poisoning.'

Under her instructions he himself manufactured his own instruments of torture, a small pair of forceps, and a lever of the same size with a forked end. Angélique had never performed an operation like this before, but she had occasionally assisted Grand Mathieu, in Paris at the Pont-Neuf. This charlatan, in spite of the hullabaloo that accompanied him, his orchestra and the general uproar, was a skilful man. He had a light touch when it came to removing rotten teeth, and considered that the operation was more successful if he passed his forceps through some brandy before using them. He had noticed that wounds became infected much less frequently if he treated his instruments in this way or held them briefly in a flame. To be doubly sure Angélique did both. She dipped the instrument in alcohol then passed them through a flame.

Clovis from the Auvergne held the patient's head. He was the unfortunate watchmaker's usual partner in their work and it was in this capacity that she asked for his assistance, and also because his strength was Herculean.

After soaking the gum in a highly concentrated concoction of cloves, which deadened sensation, Angélique went straight to the root of the trouble with her forceps and lever. The tooth came out without undue pain nor did she have to make a second attempt. Master Jonas couldn't get over it.

'Well, I must say, you do have a light hand!' He looked at Angélique's supple, apparently frail wrists as if unable to believe his eyes. But woman's wrists as they were, they were capable of supporting the weight of heavy arms, mastering restive horses, and lifting weighty burdens. She would sometimes complain they were unduly thin. If one day she ever got to Quebec or one of the New England towns, she would buy some bracelets, but meanwhile her hands had found a new occupation, that of surgeon-barber.

'Your turn next, Master Clovis,' she said, holding out the forceps towards the blacksmith.

Clovis, already very pale and shaken by the operation he had just witnessed, made off in a hurry.

Thus it was that they all took to coming to her for dressings or medical attention, towards the end of each morning. Angélique had had a little shelf fixed in the angle of one of the fireplaces and on this she placed everything she needed. She had requisitioned a small cauldron which she used for brewing herbs and other mixtures. Yann Le Couennec had made her a lightweight poplar-wood box in which she kept her medicines. She had to be prepared for accidents, fevers, or the insidious approach of illness. Once and for all Angélique had decided that trouble must be dealt with at its source. And although she had what she needed to treat a simple cold, a sore or a burn, if she were faced with inflammation of the lungs through a chill, or an arm that had become infected and swollen from an untreated cut, the resources of her pharmacopoeia would prove insufficient. So if anyone gave the slightest cough, he found himself condemned to a concoction of fir-tree buds, with a hot brick to keep his feet warm, nor was there a single wound that she would not insist on washing with plenty of water before placing a dressing on it soaked in brandy. The tiniest scratch was watched over with the greatest possible care. She had to keep her eye on the self-coddlers and the 'he-men' – those who concealed what was wrong with them in order not to have to go through the agonies of having it dressed, and those who resorted to a dirty pen-knife to remove a splinter or lance a whitlow.

They soon realized that very little escaped her.

'Master Clovis, a sledgehammer fell on your foot not long since.'

'Who told you?'

'I can see that you are limping.'

'No I'm not. And in any case it doesn't hurt.'

'That's as may be, but let me see your foot.'

'Never on your life.'

'Show it me, please.'

She had a certain very firm way of speaking that left no escape for even the most pigheaded of them.

The blacksmith grumbled but took his shoe off, revealing a swollen, blue foot and a crushed big toe. Angélique immediately made him soak it in a decoction of chestnut-bark, wrapped it in birch-bark and insisted, in spite of his protestations, that he should raise his bad leg on a stool as he sat to keep the weight off it.

They all rapidly came to show her the respect mingled with a tinge of fear which is due to all those capable of easing suffering . . . or of dispensing it. Once in her hands, it was better to remain docile, for it was not easy to gain her sympathy, to get round her, and it was necessary to do exactly what she wanted.

So, little by little, their initial suspicion of her wore off. It was not so much her lancet and her potions that they had feared with a woman like Angélique in their midst, but seeing her so beautiful, many of them had thought: 'There'll be trouble here . . .'. Things had in fact turned out quite differently, without any of them having time to realize just how. Where she was concerned, all the men were treated exactly the same. And when she opened an abscess with a flick of a blade, or poked a swab soaked in goodness knows what down their throats, they all felt like little boys, and lost all inclination to show off.

On the days when Count Peyrac did not retire to his room with one or other of his followers, to talk over his plans away from the general hubbub, he would sit at the far end of the long table and spread out his maps or plans over which Florimond, Cantor, Porguani, and Kouassi-Ba would pore. . . . The two groups of men would exchange remarks:

'None of you is going to die,' Joffrey de Peyrac said, 'beware the man who dies! I'll have something to say to him about that!'

It took the men some time before they smiled at his joke, for they took it all very seriously. The mere thought that their chief might call them to account in the next world would certainly prevent some of them from allowing themselves to die.

There was an indefinable complicity between Peyrac and his men, indestructible bonds that took root in the secrets they shared. Angélique felt certain that Joffrey knew everything there was to know about their lives and about their thoughts. They were bound to their chief by the confidences and avowals which he had never sought, but which he had been alone in receiving.

Angélique began to realize that this bond would never be broken by any piece of pettiness, or by any 'woman trouble'.

The centre of these men's lives was the workshop, the mine and the laboratory.

Coming from that part of the outpost they could hear strange sounds, smell strange smells, and sometimes there were clouds of steam and smoke. . . .

'Far better not to know what they're up to,' said Madame Jonas, intimidated.

Angélique, on the other hand, sought pretexts for going there. She would say she needed a mortar in which to crush some roots, or a bit of sulphur for an ointment she was making.

It was in a similar setting – forges, crushed stones and creaking wheels – that she had begun to discover the man she had married and to love him.

She stood silent in a corner, looking around her with keen interest. This was the other side of these men's lives, their own private world, and she found Kouassi-Ba there, holding some hot coals in his hands. Clovis, the gnome from Auvergne, had taken on the stature of a spirit of the nether regions as he went about his business in the red glow of the fires, and the Englishman, pale and dumb, seemed less wretched as he poured glistening lead with the gesture of a priestly figure, looking as if he were taking part in some ancient, solemn rite.

They were a mixed group of men from all four corners of the globe, forming a heterogeneous group united by their faith in their chosen leader. He alone could control them, and for this he needed an iron hand and constant vigilance.

Angélique too had once led peasants into battle, but they had been men lacking sophistication, simple, limited folk, easy to dominate.

These men on the other hand were sensitive, hot-headed, a very different proposition. She had already felt that many of them hated women, while others, like Clovis, were frightened of being despised by her for their coarse manners, and would wantonly behave still more coarsely. 'We didn't go off to the ends of the earth to find ourselves still forced to mind our p's and q's for a *marquise*!'

There was something daunting about all these men.

'But there is something daunting about me too,' Angélique told herself one morning. 'I have done unspeakable things! There are terrifying things in my past too. . . . I too have killed. . . . I too have fled. . . .'

And she saw herself again, dagger in hand, as she slit the throat of the Great Coerse, King of the Beggars, and had visions of herself wandering barefoot, covered with mud, through the streets of Paris, in company with a band of thieves; she saw herself again lying like a prostitute in the bed of the Master-at-arms of the Chatelet. That memory came one morning while she had been treating the carpenter Jacques Vignot for a wound on his hand. The carpenter, a Parisian with a sharp tongue, was swearing foully, secretly hoping to shock her.

Then suddenly in her annoyance she had cut him short with a single well chosen word, from the very depths of the slang of the Paris underworld. He looked at her aghast, scarcely able to believe his eyes and ears. To have heard a word like that pass such lovely, respectable lips. . . . Something happened to him that had not happened for years, to him, a carpenter from Paris and a filibuster by vocation. He blushed. And she grew pale on account of all the memories that had flooded back to her at that moment.

A look of recognition passed between the pale face and the red one, an admission that they both 'belonged'.

Then Angélique took charge once more.

'You see, my lad,' she went on with perfect composure, 'if you go on talking like that, we'll all begin to sling the lingo. . . . Perhaps you might try to remember that you are in Monsieur de Peyrac's service here, and not working for the Great Coerse.'

'Certainly, Madame la Comtesse,' the man replied humbly.

From then on he was more careful. Occasionally he would throw a puzzled glance in Angélique's direction, then quickly think the better of it. No, why attempt to understand? She was the chief's woman, what matter whether wife or mistress? If there were things she sought to forget, that was her right. And it was his too! It was not always a good thing to meet someone who reminded you of your past in the way they spoke or acted. She would sometimes call him Monsieur Vignot, and this gave him a feeling of importance. It was then that he realized that he had in fact been an honest man and that if he had had dealings with a band of thieves, it had only been in an attempt to rescue his wife and children from penury.

He had nevertheless been condemned to work as a galley slave. . . .

Angélique did not discuss with her husband the difficulties that arose between her and the more unruly of the men. She felt it was up to her to get on as best she could with them.

But often, of an evening in their room, as they talked over the day before going to bed, she would question him about his companions, and bit by bit she got to know about each one of them, and was able to imagine what their lives had been, even their childhood. . . .

And on their side, they grew more open with her, and would reveal things about themselves to her as they sat beside the gallery.

Where men were concerned her judgement was particularly sound. Experience had taught her that there was no great difference between one man and another, be he prince or serf. She had been able to lay a friendly hand on the solitude of a king, win the affection of churlish old curmudgeons like Maître Bourgus or Savary, and had softened the hearts of many a dangerous bandit as well as that of Philippe du Plessis. She infinitely preferred to face the malice of a man like Clovis or the touchiness of the Chilean miner, than to have to deal with the sophisticated underhand criminals at the court of Versailles. Here everything was in the open. Open and simple like wood, meat, cold, or maize broth. Life itself and all human contacts here had a rustic flavour she found invigorating. If there was any trouble in the offing it never dragged on for a long time. Angélique saw to that. It was her task to incise all wounds. In her own mind she enjoyed dividing the men into three groups, 'the Innocents', 'the Foreigners' and 'the Trouble-makers'.

CHAPTER 44

THE 'INNOCENTS' were those who had pure souls and showed good-will. She was particularly fond of young Yann le Couennec and treated him like a son. He was obliging and diligent, and always managed to find time to shape pieces of wood into things the ladies asked him for, paddles for the washing, scrubbing-boards or pastry-boards, carving dishes with a well-shaped runnel for catching the blood, or little flat squares of hickory wood on which to flatten the griddle-cakes of maize flour before putting them in front of the fire to cook. Once the winter had set in he carved bowls and jugs for them, and every day would add little ornaments to them, garlands or posies of flowers. He carved twisted roots, giving them heads like dragons, and taught Florimond and Cantor how to use a chisel, which they managed very well.

Count Peyrac had bought him from the Berbers who were using his services while holding him captive on their galleys. On looking over the slave-gang with the Moroccan captain who was transporting him to Saleh, he had noticed this obviously Celtic young man and had realized that he was about to die. Peyrac had paid a good price for him, in spite of the obsequious protestations of the Arab Reis that he could refuse nothing to the man who had won the confidence of the great Sultan of Morocco. Peyrac had had the young man nursed back to health and would have helped him to return to France had not the young Breton begged to be allowed to remain in his service. His great dream was to travel to America and settle there.

Born among the great forests of Huelgoat, in the Armorican penin-sula, he had learnt the trade of carpenter along with that of wood-cutter and charcoal-burner, and had likewise learned a bit about making clogs. He was more a man of the woods than of the sea. His reason for becoming a sailor was that the sea is the natural place for a Breton to go when he leaves his forests and his marshland, and also that it was no longer possible for him to remain in the country. When he was a child his father had been hanged for poaching by the lord of the land on which they lived. The poor man had only caught a hare in his snare to make Christmas a bit jollier for his children, who were all too often reduced to feeding on buckwheat broth. But the old laws of serfdom had not allowed him to escape and he had been hanged.

When Yann had become a man he had killed the gamekeeper

responsible for his father's condemnation. One evening he had turned the corner of a path beneath the blue green vault of the oaks and chestnuts and there, between two vast falls of granite, he had found himself face to face with a man dressed in livery, embroidered with the arms of his overlord. He had raised his axe and struck the man down, throwing his body to the bottom of a near-by torrent that swirled over the rocks, hollowing them out with its eddying waters. Then he had left the country. He often forgot what had happened. And when he remembered it, it was to congratulate himself on what he had done. Now he was no longer a slave. He was older than his laughing boyish face suggested; he must have been about thirty.

Another Innocent, that is to say a trusted friend in Angélique's eyes, a friend who would never prove false, was the man from Malta, Enrico Enzi. He was a mixture of Turkish, Greek, and Venetian, with something of the French Crusader in him, and the semitic background which the people of the island of Malta owe to their Phoenician origins. He was of medium height, if anything on the short side, and was handsome, almost beardless, with a dark olive-coloured skin and as muscular and supple as a fish that can strike a deadly blow with its tail. The Count had taken him on in Malta when he was still only a lad of fifteen, diving for coral and placing firebrands under the hulls of the Great Turk's galleys, all in the name of religion. This naked orphan child was an ardent defender of Christianity, and the Knights of Malta made full use of his great dexterity and astonishing ability to remain under water for a length of time that the most skilled Maltese divers considered a record. Single-handed he had given more trouble to the Crescent and to the Sublime Porte than many a renowned knight. And what did he receive in exchange? The assurance that he would go to Heaven.

He also obtained some pleasure from these exhausting expeditions down into the cold green depths of the sea. And he was delighted by the fury of the turbanned Moslems and the admiration of his brother divers, with their limbs roughened by the salt water and their lungs enlarged by their lengthy stays under water. If this kind of life satisfied the part of him descended from the Crusader, to whom he owed his blue eyes, the Venetian and Semite parts of him grew weary of it in the end. Where was this wretched life going to lead him? When would he become rich? When would he find some underwater treasure which he would be allowed to keep for himself? ...

For him too, the masked pirate had come at the right moment, the man they called the invincible lover of Justice, the Rescator, whose keen gaze, one morning, on the quayside of Valetta, had lighted on the child sitting in the shade of a wall.

'Are you Enrico, the boy who swims farther, deeper and for longer than any of the others? Would you like to come on board my ship and become a member of my team of divers?' asked the Rescator.

Taken aback the lad shook his head energetically.

'I don't want to leave Malta and my friends.'

'It's Malta that will abandon you, my boy. Malta will abandon you in favour of others when you have grown sick within you and are no longer useful to her. As for me, if you serve me well, I shall never abandon you.'

The boy stood up slowly. He was small and thin, and looked about thirteen. He came over and looked up at Peyrac's face, as he spoke.

'I know you. You are Rescator. Those who work for you don't regret it, that I know.'

'That's true. I came here specially for you today because I need you.'

The Maltese boy's eyes grew round in his thin face which was the colour of boxwood.

'That can't be true. No one has ever said that to me before. No one has ever needed *me*.'

Then he shouted angrily:

'If I set sail with you it will be on condition that I can disembark at any time, wherever you are, and that you will give me enough money to return to Malta.'

'All right, I accept your bargain, because I need you,' Peyrac repeated.

'I am incapable of being a slave to any man. It is only danger that attracts me.'

'You'll get more of that than you bargained for.'

'I am a good Catholic; will you expect me to fight against the Christian galleys?'

'You won't have to, provided the Knights don't attack me. And there is no reason why they should since I have made treaties with them.'

'All right, then!'

So Enrico embarked there and then without any other baggage than the cotton loincloth he wore round his hips. He had changed greatly during the ten years he had spent on board Count Peyrac's ships. Apart from his skill as a mine-layer, able to sabotage ships, he was extremely gifted at wrestling, throwing a knife, and shooting, which made him much sought after in boarding fights. He was a lithe, ferocious demon who struck down everything round him. He had never asked to return to Malta.

When Joffrey de Peyrac left the Mediterranean he took Enrico with him to the Caribbean and it was thanks to his team of Maltese divers, of whom Enzi was the leader, that he had been able to plan his most unusual but extremely lucrative enterprise, recovering treasure from the Spanish galleons that had been sunk by the French buccaneers.

The young man from Malta was now rich. The Count had made him a present of the three most beautiful gold vases they had found during his work in the Caribbean and he had continued to draw a fixed salary as a member of the crew and to share in all the booty. So Joffrey de Peyrac had shown no little surprise when, at his request for volunteers to set off by land into the back country, he had seen the frog-man step forward who, for the past ten years that he had worked for him, had never sought to stray farther than a hundred yards from a beach or from a seaside town into the interior.

'Enrico, do you think forests, mountains and marshlands will suit you? You are a son of the Mediterranean. You will feel the cold.'

'The cold,' Enrico replied scathingly, 'who knows more about cold than I do? He who has not dived as deep as I have into the ocean knows nothing of the cold of the shroud of death. My lord, there is no one who has had as much experience of cold as I.'

'And you won't be able to dive any more either. The gold I am seeking is under the earth, not in the sea this time.'

'What do I care, provided I get my share?' Enrico replied in an off-hand manner, which he sometimes allowed himself to adopt in his capacity as a very old friend of his esteemed master. 'And then there are lakes,' he added with a laugh, 'a large number of lakes, from what I am told. I could always do some diving to get you some fish.'

Then he drew closer and added softly in the Sardinian dialect which Peyrac understood:

'It is good that I should accompany you, you my master and my father, for if I do not come who will warn you of the threats that lie heavy about you? For I am a cross between a siren and an albatross, and I can see the invisible arrow that awaits you in those woods. If I knew how to pray I would stay here by the sea and pray for you. But I am bad at praying, for I believe more in the Devil than in the Madonna. So you see the only thing I can do is to come with you. And my knife will always be swift enough to come to your defence.'

Peyrac smiled as he looked at the little brown-skinned man, now older but still as fiery and eager as ever, raising his head and staring at him as he had done ten years before on that sunlit quayside in Valetta. He replied in Italian:

'All right. Come then, I need you.'

And yet it was he who had shown the greatest suspicion of Angélique ever since the *Gouldsboro* days, staring fiercely after her, and muttering bitter comments and incantations. And it was he who had shown more jealousy than anyone, fearing that his master's passion for this woman might alter the lofty image Enrico had created of him. He had never known a man who had not been diminished in stature by his obsession with a woman. Up till now he had not seen any woman bring the Count under her sway. But with this one everything was different. He watched her anxiously, ready to take amiss everything she said or did. It had partly been to keep an eye on her that he had wanted to accompany them into the forest, and partly to protect little Honorine who had been entrusted to him on board the *Gouldsboro* by a sign from his Sicilian friend who had died there.

Angélique had found this out during the long journey, when Enrico would constantly appear from nowhere looking like a martyr fulfilling a secret vow, and would make himself useful to her and Honorine by bringing them water or doing his best to amuse the little girl and satisfy her whims. At first she was surprised, for she knew that Enrico did not like her, then at last she understood, and her affection for him was born. On his side he found out that this disturbing young woman knew the port of Valetta very well, that she had been received by the Grand Master of the Knights of Malta, that she had even been as far as Crete, that in short she had 'knocked about' all over the Mediterranean. He began to understand what his master found so attractive in her and, guessing the bonds that united them, bowed to the inevitable. Angélique kept an eye on him, for his health was not very good. The biting cold made him turn green, and the dry air so irritated his mucous membranes which were accustomed to the damp air of the seaside, that he coughed frequently and suffered from nosebleeds. This agile fellow, half-man, half-fish, lured to the heart of the forest, who had a swarthy, lined complexion with large eyes of unfathomable expression, which made him look older than his twenty-five years, was undoubtedly the most skilful and industrious of all the men. He was skilled with knots and ropes like all seafaring men, wove baskets and nets, and, under Eloi Macollet's direction, took up the manufacture of snowshoes. This he would do of an evening in the company of the carpenter Jacques Vignot and the dumb Englishman. Everyone needed two pairs, one spare. When the rope ran out they used animal gut as the Indians did. Joffrey de Peyrac also made use of Enrico in his workshop in the preparation of chemicals. As a child in Malta he had always been intrigued by this kind of thing. Valetta was full of Arab scientists, and the grubby little boys used to climb up the Moucharaby window grilles to watch them at work in their laboratories full of retorts, preparing their explosive, pyrotechnic mixtures. Enrico had made several varieties of Greek fire with the Count after obtaining the recipe by stealth. Here at Wapassou they were also seeking to contrive a means of producing a smokescreen to screen artillery fire or some kind of tear-gas. He reckoned that the sulphur that they used was not as good as that found on the Island of Vulcano in the Tyrrhenian Sea, between Sicily and Naples. Their experiments almost made them cough their lungs out, but they continued them all the same.

The person for whom Angélique most feared the rigours of the winter was dear old Kouassi-Ba.

But Kouassi-Ba had braved everything. He rose above his race and his condition of life. He was the pagan god of the cupellation of gold, bending his dark face over containers of bone ash in which liquid gold shone irridescent. The secrets of the earth dwelt within him and little mattered to him beyond this enchanted toil which had left its stamp upon him since his childhood days, deep, deep down in the gold-mines of the Sudan, where he had descended the pit shafts by pressing his back and the soles of his feet against the sides and working his way down for what had seemed an eternity. In his country, gold was offered up to the devil. His devotion to the depths of the earth and to gold was closely linked with his devotion to his master. To aid him, to save him, to serve him, and to watch over his sons, was in his eyes, inseparable from the working of gold. He was serious, powerful, calm, childlike and wise.

He had a wide knowledge of metals and mines. He learnt it all under the guidance of Peyrac, assimilated it all, and mingled it with the intuitive insight he possessed as a son of the depths of the earth. He impressed the white men who came to work with him. He had given lectures in the University of Palermo and at Saleh in Morocco, and the great doctors in their ermine cloaks and learned Arabs had listened with great respect to this black slave. Nothing could ruffle him. His profound, gentle resignation before the forces of nature was the only thing that marked him out as one of the sons of Ham. His hair had grown completely white now and the deep furrows across his face showed his African heredity, for he was many years younger than the

Count but the sons of Ham grow old early and swiftly. Nothing ruffled him and yet he was sensitive to everything. Angélique found his presence a real comfort, and when he sat down before the fire she felt that among them sat a wise, good man, a man of considerable stature, who brought among their civilized passions an element of ancient, primitive simplicity. Opposing currents grew calm, as they do when the bar has been crossed, and the water in the lagoons stretches out, calm beneath the gently swaying palm-trees.

There were others for whom Angélique felt friendship untinged with apprehension; one was the Piedmontese, Porguani, for ever diligent, eloquent and scrupulously discreet, and Lymon White, the dumb Englishman about whom they in fact knew nothing, but on whom they felt they could count, along with Octave Malaprade the cook from Bordeaux. She and Malaprade had that immediate understanding of one another that is characteristic of fellow-professionals as far as cooking and restaurants are concerned. (For she had once run the Red Mask Tavern and the chocolate shop in the Faubourg Saint-Honoré.) His experience was manifest in everything he said. And she had no doubt that this sea-cook with his threadbare coat, whom she had seen so valiantly managing on board the *Gouldsboro* amidst the dancing upturned pots and the billows of salt water that filled them at regular intervals as they lurched about in the storm, was an authentic *maître d'hôtel* in the same class as Vatel or Audiger.

Why was it that she imagined him, as she watched him stirring their maize gruel or briskly carving some game, not merely wearing the chef's white hat, but rather clothed in the powdered wig and frogged jacket of an officer of the King's domestic staff, officiating with rolled-up sleeves amid the bustle of a court feast?

Once the time was past when he had had to lend a hand with the felling of trees and the building of the refuge, he had taken up his position once more beside the cooking-pots. He left Madame Jonas and Elvire to do the rough work, like peeling the vegetables, but he himself would taste the humblest soup and check the seasoning with religious care.

From time to time he would give free rein to his fantasies and talk about exotic menus, boasting that he would make them a Royal caper sauce, crayfish soup with Sauterne, and chocolate profiterolles.

Everyone drew round him to listen.

Angélique would vie with him, recalling recipes for *pieds de mouton à la lyonnaise* and individually served sorbets. These were tales of the Thousand and One Nights to help to pass the long evenings.

283

Joffrey de Peyrac would listen carefully to all that Angélique said, for it intrigued him.

'Once when I had to prepare a very special meal for thirty people . . .'

'When I used to go to the Paris market to choose my wine-casks . . .'

The ladies were on the best of terms with Octave Malaprade.

CHAPTER 45

THE 'STRANGERS' were the Spaniards and the other Englishmen. These men sat at the same table as the others, shared the same work and the same dangers, showed the same courage and the same patience, and yet somehow they remained strangers. It was as if they had just arrived and were just about to leave again, as if they were only there for a short time, as if they really had nothing to do with the others among whom, nevertheless, they lived day by day.

The five Spanish artificers and their leader Don Juan Alvarez were of precisely the same stamp, sombre, haughty and sober. No one could have reproached them for being difficult, nor for sowing discord. They carried out the orders and performed the tasks they were given. They paid scrupulous attention to their own arms and to those for which they were responsible, worked very ably at the forge and down the mine. They were all crack marksmen, trained in jungle and sea warfare. They had been members of the soldiery that his Most Catholic Majesty of Spain had placed on the gold-laden galleons to defend them against pirates. They had all taken part in hazardous expeditions through the hot, humid, snake-infested forests, or up in the Andes where the mountain-tops rose so high that they had to drag themselves along on all fours with blood flowing from their ears and noses. They had all fallen into the hands of the Indians, as their scars and permanently broken health bore witness, and were all firm in their hatred of the Redskin. These soldiers spoke only to one another and said what they had to say only to their immediate superior, Don Alvarez, who in turn would only speak to Count Peyrac. Even in the friendly bosom of this winter-bound community, they preserved the withdrawn attitude of mercenaries in a strange land. Angélique did not know how they had come to find themselves in Count Peyrac's service.

It was even more difficult to care for their health than to help the blacksmith from Auvergne. She often noticed Don Alvarez limping, and saw that Juan Carillo grew pale with pain when something disagreed with his stomach, but she could not see herself ordering the tall Castillian señor with the distant, haughty look to remove his boots, nor imagine herself asking the fierce, taciturn Carillo about the state of his digestion. It was unthinkable!

So she limited her activities to sending herbal drinks containing mint and absinth to Juan Carillo. Octave Malaprade used to take them over to him and make sure he drank them. The cook did not smoke, so he gave his tobacco to the young Andalusian mercenary, in exchange for which the young man would occasionally pass some remark about the weather. Coming from him, this was a great sign of sociability.

As for Don Juan Alvarez, she had not yet found a way of establishing contact with him and prevailing on him to put linseed-flour poultices on his rheumaticky joints to ease their ache. Blast these proud men and their lordly moorish education! They despised women, and wanted to shut them up behind bars to be kept there for two purposes only, to pray and to bear children. Don Alvarez was indeed a worthy subject of his sovereign Philip IV, who had been burnt to death by a brazier which no one was able to move for reasons of etiquette.

What a mummified, brutal, austere, mystical civilization; and yet it had given birth to those prodigious conquistadors who, in less than fifty years, between 1513, when Balboa crossed the Isthmus of Panama and discovered the Pacific, and 1547, when Orellana travelled the full length of the Amazon in the Andes down to the Atlantic ocean, had conquered the greater part of a vast continent, and had absorbed and brought beneath their yoke three brilliant Indian civilizations, the Aztec, the Mayan and the Inca.

Joffrey de Peyrac would sometimes talk to them in Spanish:

'Thanks to the four of you,' he said, 'Spain will be represented in the conquest of North America. Your compatriots lost heart when they didn't find any golden objects in the Algonquin and Abenaki villages. What was the point of coming from a race of miners, as the people from the Iberian peninsula has always been, just to end up as looters. Because you have followed me, you alone will be able to re-establish your links with your ancestors who used to extract silver and copper and gold from the bowels of the earth.'

As they listened to him the fiery eyes of the Spaniards would suddenly glow with human warmth and they seemed happy.

The 'Troublemakers' were four in number, Angélique reckoned.

These were O'Connell, Vignot, the Hispano-Peruvian miner, and the blacksmith from Auvergne, Clovis.

She was not anxious about the Parisian Jacques Vignot. He was somewhat loud-mouthed and partial to drink, but he was amenable, and a kindly fellow at heart; provided you tickled his vanity by taking special notice of him from time to time, he showed himself willing enough and not a bad chap. Eventually she came to trust him a great deal. She needed him as an ally, for with his bantering ways and quick repartee and his assertiveness he could change the whole mood of the group.

O'Connell was only dangerous because of his violent nature and his persecution complex. He was indeed a persecuted man, and no one could change the fact. He was persecuted by the British because he was Catholic, and by the French because he was British. He had been the one who had taken the burning of the fort of Katarunk with all its valuable contents hardest. They should have found some other way out, he said, without burning Katarunk, he could never forgive them that. He was furious with them all.

Angélique did not know how to take him. His sombre face, his threatening growl, his permanent rancour weighed heavy on her heart, the more so because she understood his chagrin. One day she would ask her husband what the Irish were like, and he might be able to help her along the difficult path towards reaching some under-standing with this son of the green Erin.

The Hispano-Peruvian miner Sorrino was no trouble provided she ignored him, without, however, altogether forgetting his existence. He would never forgive Angélique for having taken him for an Indian when they first arrived, and equally he would never have forgiven her had she first taken him for a Spaniard. But above all he resented being treated as a half-caste.

Inside him there was a permanent battlefield where two irrecon-cilable enemies fought it out, an Indian Quechua from the Andes and a Spaniard of Castille, a mercenary of Pizzaro, enemies who were only reconciled for as long as it took to look down with scorn on this creature of mixed blood that he was, staining the noble land of the Incas by his presence. Count Peyrac had managed to make him see that the two races he represented had equally strong vocations to work in mines, and that thus his mixed blood, by linking the two heredities and their gifts, was exactly what was needed for the creation of the most remarkably knowledgeable mining specialist in Peru. His pre-diction turned out to be correct, for whenever this man put his mind to his work, he became at peace with himself. All she had to do was to leave him at his forge and in between times to avoid speaking to him, while treating him with consideration.

So the most dangerous among them remained the unruly Clovis, whose chief characteristics were his violence, his suspicious nature and his fierce egoism. Angélique felt that he liked none of them. He was one of those that could bite the hand that had fed or saved him. And occasionally Angélique wondered whether her husband had thought carefully enough before accepting as a volunteer on his expedition this troublesome man who was so hard to get on with. Of course, he was a good blacksmith, skilled at every kind of lockmaking and gunsmith's work. He was a real servant of Vulcan, dark, stocky, always sweating, his face for ever shadowed with beard like a layer of soot. He shoed horses better than anyone else, but however valuable this talent was, it did not make them forget his coarse and quarrelsome nature. He loathed women and was the only one who talked bawdy in an attempt to shock the prudish ears of Madame Jonas and Elvire. He had been uncommonly insolent to Angélique on occasion, so the war she waged against him was just as bitter as his was against her.

But the two of them were at least agreed on one point: that no hint of their conflicts should reach Count Peyrac's ears. She was frightened of bothering her husband, and he was frightened of being hanged. During the past three years in which he had been working for Monsieur de Peyrac he had had time to learn that when his chief said something he meant it. And he had the good sense to restrain himself in front of Peyrac. His companions reproached him for being underhand, and he would have considered himself dishonoured had he made the slightest effort to get on better with them or indeed with anyone.

One evening Angélique handed him a garment with a hole in it.

'Here is a needle and some wool, Master Clovis. Mend it for me quickly, would you.'

The blacksmith protested, not before making sure that the Count was nowhere in the offing.

'That's your job, woman.'

'No, sailors know how to sew, it's part of their job.'

'But why me? You're the one who mends other people's togs.'

'That's as may be, but you need to do penance.'

Her argument was on target. Clovis looked at her for a moment, with a garment in one hand and his needle in the other, then set about the job without a word. The man who shared his stool with him,

Jacques Vignot, heard him mutter several times: 'Do penance! Do penance! That's a new one! ...'

He would often say something the meaning of which remained a mystery to Angélique and the others.

'Damn me!' he would say, with a toss of his shaggy black head, 'what was the point of my carrying my chains to Sainte Foy de Conques if this was where it was going to get me?'

On another occasion, hearing the sound of a violent altercation out-side, Angélique went out just in time to catch Clovis brandishing a log above the head of an Indian. As he swung his missile to strike a more effective blow, Angélique just had time to seize her pistol and to shoot in their direction. The log shattered and fell from the man's hands, and he fell over backwards on to the icy ground. Angélique rushed forward to stop the Indian, who had seized his knife and was about to remove Clovis's shaggy scalp. But seeing his aggressor on the ground, the Indian calmed down.

The noise of the shot brought everyone rushing outside. This time it was hard to cover up the incident. The Count came running to the scene taking it in in one glance.

'What happened?' he asked the blacksmith who was picking him-self up again, deathly pale.

'She ... she tried to kill me,' he stammered, pointing to Angélique. 'She was within three inches of blowing out my brains.'

'What a pity I didn't!' said Angélique with a laugh. 'You silly fool, I didn't try to kill you, I only tried to stop you doing something stupid that would have cost you your life. Do you think you would have been able to avoid the Indian's knife if you had struck him? I fired at the log and not at you. One log's as good as another! If I had really wanted to kill you, I would have done so, believe me.'

But Clovis shook his head. His pock-marked face was livid beneath his unshaved beard. He really had been badly frightened and was still convinced that Angélique had tried to kill him, and that it was only a matter of luck that he was still alive. He had been convinced for a long time that this terrible woman would surely kill him, either with her scalpel, or her lancet, or by casting some spell on him. But with a pistol, that was the limit!

'I don't believe you,' he growled. 'You just didn't aim properly. Women don't know how to aim. ...'

'You fool,' said the Count in anger. 'Do you want to do it again so that you can see that if Madame la Comtesse had really wanted to hit you you wouldn't be here any more? Go on, pick up that log, and lift it up, and you can see whether what they told you about the marksmanship at Sakoos Ford was correct or not. Pick up the log.'

The blacksmith refused categorically to do so. But Yann the Breton confidently volunteered to do so himself. He had been beside Angélique when she had stopped Pont-Briand. He raised the log and Angélique, who had positioned herself by the door of the house, fired and the log splintered. Everyone applauded, and they asked her to do it again. Don Alvarez woke from his dream and asked to see her handle a match-lock musket, then one with a flintlock. She lifted the heavy weapon without the slightest difficulty and they all stood amazed at her strength, and began to feel proud of having her among them.

CHAPTER 46

WHEN IT was as cold as this at Wapassou, how could they begin to imagine what it must be like in the towns that lay still farther north?

Three towns . . . three small townships in the middle of nowhere on the banks of the Saint Lawrence. Ships could only reach them again in the spring. The great wall of ice had closed around them making them prisoners of the white steppes, prisoners of silence, and of the vast, bleak, empty spaces.

There was Montreal on its island at the foot of its small extinct volcano.

Then Trois-Rivières, frozen in among the ramifications of its ice-packed delta.

And the queen of them all, Quebec on its rock. Three townships, crowned with the white diadems of smoke that rose ceaselessly, in a long, calm trail from their chimneys into the ice-pink morning and evening skies.

Three lost towns.

How the fires crackled in the hearths to save them from death!

The fires blazed so cheerfully that people forgot death, and silence, and the wild. The cities were thronged with people, who gossiped, plotted, intrigued, fought the whole winter through, with their tongues in the drawing-rooms, throwing stools in the bars, violently, secretly, cordially among friends, cousins, the people of Canada.

And they prayed a lot too, went endlessly to confession, meditated, and dreamed as they looked out towards the incredibly white Lauren-tian mountains, or the grey forest-clad horizon towards the south.

They dreamed of their departure. To the sea, to Europe, to the west, to furs or savages. Hither or thither. They dreamed of setting out, always of setting out. When would the time come to set out again?

They made love too, secretly, on the sly; and even married couples felt remorse afterwards, because of the eyes of the Jesuits that weighed on *all* their consciences.

They drank a lot. That was their only pleasure. Brandy, still more brandy. Brandy made from apples, plums, or wheat, transparent brandy with a strong bouquet, boiled in their own stills.

The winter streets reeked with the smell of brandy, of wood fires, of bacon soup and smoked eels.

The winter days were heavy with the smell of incense at Masses and Vespers, and the parchment smell of leather-bound books brought over from Europe to be endlessly thumbed and re-read in the chimney corner.

The winter nights crackled with frost and the windows seemed about to burst.

Patterns of hoar frost clung to the panes.

It was in these towns that the news broke and was spread about:

The strangers from Katarunk whom everyone thought had been massacred by the Iroquois were alive! The beautiful woman from the heart of the forest who had appeared on horseback near the source of the Kennebec was still alive!

The She-Devil was still alive!

Triumph and terror!

Jubilation among those who believed in the powers of hell.

'For do you think, my brothers, that the Devil would take the trouble to send one of his minions here on earth for her to be sent up in smoke after a mere skirmish with a few Iroquois? . . . Oh no! The Devil is more powerful than that! He has not caused enough trouble in Acadia yet for us to be able to say whether he will win or lose.'

And the proof was that the She-Devil was still there although Katarunk had burned down.

Loménie repeated that he himself had seen the ashes of Katarunk.

But the man who had brought the transcendent item of news was quite definite about it. He assured them that the strangers were not dead but living in the mountains at a place called Wapassou on the Silver Lake.

And who would ever doubt the man who brought this news? He could see everything from a distance. He was a saint. He had seen that the strangers had escaped the Iroquois, without even having to fight them, and that this was indeed a proof that they were hounds of hell.

If it was not God who saved them by some miracle then it could only have been the Devil.

And God could not have come to the rescue of people who did not set up a cross, who practised heresy, and did not partake of the sacraments.

Therefore it must be the Devil!

Monsieur de Loménie must have been out of his mind.

The She-Devil had beguiled him, they said, as she had Pont-Briand, whom they had seen wandering through the streets of Quebec looking dejected and haggard, and talking of a woman of unsurpassed beauty he had met in the depths of the forest....

Riding a horse....

As if such a thing were possible. White women did not exist in the depths of the forest. Those who saw her astride a horse must have been mistaken. It was undoubtedly a unicorn. Some of the men who had been in the ravine when she had first appeared against the moonlit sky, claimed that they saw the single pointed horn. People besieged them with questions, begging them to remember what they had seen; they were mobbed, all those who had been on Monsieur de Loménie's expedition that autumn, who had met the black, masked figure and the woman whose name no one yet dared to speak aloud: the She-Devil, who was already called the Lady of the Silver Lake.

And now what was going to happen?

His Grace the Bishop ordered processions and fasts. He went to see Sister Madeleine the visionary in her convent, then paid a visit to the Governor of Canada, Monsieur de Frontenac, where he met Monsieur de Loménie and Monsieur d'Arreboust, the pious syndic of the City of Quebec, and several other people including many of the Jesuits.

The candles burned for many a long hour at the windows of the castle on the Rock.

And the Saint Lawrence river lay like a vast white plain under the moon.

CHAPTER 47

A SMALL family of Indians had come to Wapassou and settled about one league from the outpost, beside a lake, to fish for beaver. They were often seen roaming about the neighbourhood.

The fight between Clovis and one of the Indians had been over the latter's sister, a rather pretty wild creature with long plaits whose teeth flashed white when she laughed, and who made no secret of what she expected from the 'Normans' who had a reputation for enjoying the pleasures of love. There was another girl too who seemed shyer but was no less forthcoming when it came to arranging assignations.

It was astonishing how little the men took advantage of these easy-going neighbours. Young Yann, Jacques Vignot and one of the Englishmen were the only ones to do so, and they were only rarely absent from the fort.

It even turned out that the dispute between Clovis and the Indian was in no way concerned with amorous dealings but with the fact that the girl, while wandering round the outpost, had stolen some tobacco and a knife from him.

Angélique remembered what her husband had told her once. Sea-faring folk were chaste. He himself, when he had to, was capable of living for a long time without a woman, and had been therefore able to distinguish the men he should take with him. They had followed Peyrac because he had promised them gold. The attractions of adventure and success were a sufficient substitute for a life of pleasure. Women were part of the booty, and the battle had not yet been won. Later they would see! They had an instinctive wariness of becoming sentimentally attached for fear that it might lead them along the path to slavery, and this fear helped them to overcome their natural desires.

Angélique thought too of Nicolas Perrot, who had left his wife and child at home three years back to live as a trapper and wander over the earth.

A short time before the snow had fallen he had set off towards the south in an attempt to reach a little trading post run by a Dutchman at the mouth of the Kennebec in the hope of bringing back some essential foodstuffs, such as salt, sugar, flour, and a little oil. . . .

The man who took the greatest interest in the pretty Indian girls was, believe it or not, old Macollet. There was much coming and going between his smoky wigwam and the Indians', regardless of the weather. He was a fine one, old Macollet! And he enjoyed sitting in front of an Indian fire to have a chat, too.

The chief of this tribe was something of a medicine man. He would bring Angélique roots, herbs and resin. Once she had got over her initial fright when she had seen him one fine morning standing behind her with arm upraised – as a sign of peace, although he was so muffled up in fur that he looked like a bear – they had become great friends.

She was beginning to be able to speak to him in his own language, and was very proud of the fact since she had been told that the native languages were very difficult to learn. The French missionaries claimed that it took years to acquire them, and even the trappers never seemed to encourage newcomers to make a start. You had to belong to the country, they would explain. But Joffrey de Peyrac had quickly become familiar with these tongues and had explained to Angélique that the difficulties were only superficial, and that those who found them difficult lacked perception.

He himself had very soon seen that most of the neighbouring tribes spoke dialects that stemmed from the same source, probably owing their origins to the language of the Incas or the Quechuas of Peru. This was how his half-caste miner had been able to understand them as soon as he arrived in North America.

The Iroquois, the Algonquins, the Hurons and the Abenakis were all cousins where language was concerned, the only differences being of accent and intonation, or in a few common words like water or child, and again simply because according to the tribe you came from a certain word was given a different interpretation. For example, the word for spring or liquid could be used for water or, when they were referring to a child, they might use the word for young, small, or son.

The root of the word gave the general meaning. Detail was added by suffixes and prefixes, and the roots themselves were relatively small in number. So, with about five hundred root words you could cope with any situation in spite of the apparent variety of languages.

Once her husband had given her this key, Angélique was surprised at the progress she made.

Of course it would be a long time before she spoke well, and she would continue to amuse the Indians who burst into peals of laughter at her every mistake. First she must listen carefully. Then she would acquire the accent and the tonal qualities of their speech, especially the particular way they had of articulating a word in their throats without moving the muscles of their faces, which made it impossible for an Indian speaking in anger to utter his word with anything but an impassive face. On the other hand, when they were not talking, they would pull a great number of faces and roar with laughter at every opportunity. Eventually Angélique found that there were only sixteen sounds, but that they were each four times longer than in the European languages or on occasion twice as quick, so that the rhythm of utterance had eight variants more than in French or English and that it was this that conveyed the finer shades of meaning.

But meanwhile, although perfection was still a long way off, everyone at Wapassou practised hard and those who knew more corrected the others. Angélique managed pretty well with her old Sachem of the Beaver Wigwam and he, either through indifference or because he was a serene old man, did not pull her up each time she made a mistake, so that when she spoke to him she would launch out into long speeches which greatly amused Joffrey de Peyrac whenever he overheard her conversations with the red-feathered medicine man.

Everything about her delighted him, her vivacity, her love of life, and her courage. And now it was he who could no longer keep his eyes off her.

At the start he had thought 'it all depends on her'. Wapassou would be their moment of truth. And he was astonished to see how she had managed to gather around her all these hostile vagabonds, who by now had all found a place for her in their hearts as mother, sister, friend or sovereign.

One evening Joffrey de Peyrac asked Angélique to fetch Elvire so that he might speak to her privately, and asked her to accompany the girl when she came to their small room. For lack of anywhere else to go to be out of hearing when he needed to speak privately to some-one, this room had been named 'the captain's cabin on the poop deck', and the fact of having to climb a few steps to it completed the illusion.

The furniture included a rustic armchair covered in fur in which the Count would sit. The man he had summoned remained standing, his head almost touching the ceiling, particularly if he was on the tall side.

When the interview was a friendly one, Joffrey de Peyrac would get him to sit down on the hearthstone in front of him, and would call for a pint of beer and two goblets.

Often of an evening he would retire there with one or other of the men, and they appreciated this moment of privacy with him, far from the crowd. Here they could explain things to him, make com-plaints and receive orders which, where necessary, helped them to get things straight again.

It was in a great state of agitation that poor Elvire walked trembling up the five steps that led to 'the poop'.

Angélique's presence reassured her a little, but she was suffering agonies for she was a very scrupulous person and lived permanently with the feeling that she had done something wrong.

Once the heavy door had fallen to, the noise from the main room grew faint. All that could be heard in the snug little room was the crackling of the fire and the occasional rustle of the fir-trees outside as the wind brushed them against the roof.

The Count sat down. The young woman remained standing and Angélique, standing behind her, saw her narrow shoulders grow taut and her delicate neck bow itself. The poor girl did not know what to do as the Count looked her up and down darkly with an indulgent smile playing about his lips.

There was not a woman who would not be moved by the warmth and the tension of his glance.

'Elvire, my child, my lovely child,' he said gently, 'listen calmly to what I have to say.'

'Have I done something wrong, my lord?' she stammered, twisting her apron in her hands.

'I told you to listen to me calmly and without fear. . . . Please don't worry. I have nothing but praise for you and your sweetness. But you are nevertheless responsible for something which may give rise to serious consequences.'

'I? . . . Oh, my lord!'

'Yes, you, in spite of your discretion and your modesty, for you nevertheless have lovely, melting eyes and pink cheeks.'

Elvire, more and more disconcerted, stared at him uncomprehending.

'I have noticed that one of my men is paying court to you. Now tell me truthfully whether his attentions are causing you annoyance, and if you want him to stop, or whether he has said things that have gone further than you would have liked.'

And as she remained silent, he went on:

'Here in this fort there are only three women and you are the only one without a husband. I gave the strictest orders where you were concerned. So I must know whether my orders have been obeyed. Well, come on, answer me! Are you pestered by the court that has been paid to you for some time now? You know who I am talking about, don't you?'

This time she lowered her head and blushed as she nodded.

'Octave Malaprade,' he said.

There was a pause, that gave them time to picture the cook, with his pleasant figure and deferential smile.

Then he took one of his few remaining cigars from one of the pockets of his doublet, and bending down towards the fire, lit it at a burning log.

He leant back in his chair, puffed at his cigar and went on gently:

'If he has disobeyed my orders he will be hanged.'

Elvire gave a cry and hid her face.

'Hanged! . . . Oh, my lord! Oh no, the poor boy! Not for that! Not on my account! I am not worthy . . .'

'Women are queens in these matters. Did you not know that, my pretty girl?'

And he looked at her again with his inimitable smile that turned up the corners of his handsome mouth in that slightly caustic and winning manner that Angélique knew so well.

'Did you not know that women are queens?' he insisted.

'No, my lord, I did not,' she replied naïvely.

She was shaking from head to foot but the fear she had felt for Malaprade gave her the strength to gather her thoughts in the defence of the man whom she felt to be threatened.

'My lord . . . I swear to you, I swear on oath . . . that he never said or did anything to make me blush. It was just that I felt . . . I thought . . . that he . . .'

'You love him? . . .' It was scarcely a question.

She broke off, and looked around her wildly.

'No, I . . . I don't know.'

'You lost your husband three months ago aboard the *Gouldsboro*.'

She stared at him, stupefied.

'My husband?'

'Did you love him?'

He was hustling her, forcing her to examine herself, and his piercing eyes caught her childish glance and forced her to look at him.

'Did you love your husband?'

'Yes . . . of course. That is, I . . . I don't know any more.'

Once again he looked away and puffed at his cigar in silence. She made no move, but had stopped trembling, and stood staring at him, her arms at her sides.

Then he went on, still calm.

'Octave Malaprade came and spoke to me earlier. He loves you. Realizing that I would not fail to notice how he felt, he decided to come to me first and tell me about it. . . . This is what he told me to tell you about him and his past.'

'Five years ago in Bordeaux, where he ran a well-known hotel, he killed his wife and her lover when he stumbled on them together. Then, not knowing how he would escape the consequences of his action, nor how to hide the evidence of his double crime from the inevitable investigation, he carved the two bodies up, burned some of them and managed to get the remainder on to the slaughterhouse garbage heap.'

Angélique smothered a cry and bit her lips.

Elvire staggered back.

She seemed thunderstruck.

Peyrac went on smoking and watching her with interest.

'After this,' he went on, 'he waited some time, then made his escape to Spain. It was there that he made himself known to me on board my ship and I took him on.'

There followed a long silence.

Then suddenly the young woman from La Rochelle straightened up, and standing erect, seemed to be looking at something outside of herself.

'Monsieur le Comte' . . . she said at last in a voice that had grown firm and clearer, a voice they had not heard before. 'I hope Monsieur le Comte will forgive me if I seem somewhat insensitive. But these are the thoughts that come to my mind. I think that this man committed murder in a jealous rage, that he was taken by surprise, and that afterwards, he found himself alone and lost, facing this horrible thing and not knowing how to get out of it. He did what he could to save his own life. What happened to him was a misfortune, an accident, like an illness that suddenly strikes you down.'

She took a deep breath.

'But no sickness like that would stop me loving him,' she said passionately. 'What you have just told me has made me aware of my own feelings. Your questions helped me to see straight within myself. Yes, I was very fond of my departed husband . . . I must have been . . . since I married him . . . once. But I never felt for him what I feel for this man now. You can say what you like about him. As far as I am concerned I feel that he has remained a good, honourable and fine man in spite of everything. I know him well enough by now to feel sure that he is unhappy.'

She fell silent, then added dreamily:

'He sustained me along the way during the storm, that night we arrived at Wapassou, and I shall never forget it. . . .'

Joffrey de Peyrac looked kindly at her.

'Good. Good,' he said. 'I hoped that would be your answer. There is strength in your soul, little Elvire, and your heart is noble. You are clear-headed and do not allow yourself to be influenced by sentimentality, which would be quite understandable but which would be misplaced under the circumstances. You are right in thinking that Malaprade is reliable, courageous and capable. This . . . accident as you call it has marked him for life. It has made him more mature and has given another dimension to his life which until then had been pretty run-of-the-mill, although he had known a high degree of success which had been very flattering to him in his profession as a chef. Then when he lost everything he could well have gone to pieces. But he survived and did his best to put together the broken pieces of his life. Some might consider that justice has not been satisfied, and that I grant them. But his victims were not people of much character and I have never urged him to feel remorse or a need for expiation. That happens by itself, day by day, through one's memories. But I did encourage him to become what you now consider he is, a good man, with fine feelings, but also full of grit and clear-sightedness, which were qualities he lacked before this disaster. He will love you dearly and well.'

The young woman stood with joined hands, drinking in his words.

'But let me continue,' he went on. 'I will give you both a dowry, so that the early years of your married life will be easy.'

'He has a right to a considerable share of the fortune we shall extract from the Silver Lake mine. But in addition as a personal gift from myself I intend to give him enough money to open an inn or a restaurant wherever he would like to, in New England for instance or even New Spain if he feels like it. And we shall look after the education of your two oldest sons to make sure that they are well placed later on. . . .'

'Oh, my lord,' she cried, 'oh, how can I ever say . . . oh, my lord, bless you. . . .'

And she fell to her knees beside him, her face streaming with tears.

'He knows all the tricks,' thought Angélique. 'He could have any woman on earth at his knees. In spite of the fact that she is in love with another man, that girl there would be perfectly prepared to give herself to him as a token of her esteem and gratitude. A prince's right . . .'

Joffrey de Peyrac bent down kindly towards the girl as she knelt there, shattered. He made her lift her head and looked straight into her tear-filled eyes, brimming over with gratitude.

'You must not cry, my young friend. You have borne quite unjustifiable hardship with courage. And as for the man you love, I know that he has atoned for what he did. And now it is only right that we should try to put things right again. Life is a good deal kinder than men. It makes us suffer, but it has its rewards. . . .'

298

'Yes, oh yes, my lord, I understand. . . . I understand what you are saying.'

Her voice was thin and rent with sobs.

'When I was in La Rochelle, I was just an ordinary woman. . . . I never used to think about anything. Now I can see that I hadn't any life at all . . . but you have taught me, my lord, you have taught me and now I am different. I have understood so much since . . . since I have lived among you,' she said timidly. 'How I like Wapassou, how I like your house, my lord! We shall not leave it. No, never! We shall remain here, he and I, to serve you . . .'

He interrupted her with an indulgent gesture.

'Calm down, now! It is too late this evening to make plans. First you need to rest. All this has been a shock to you. Now dry your eyes, you mustn't let him see you've been crying, otherwise he will think you don't want him and will go and put a bullet through his head before I even have time to reassure him. They're an impulsive lot, those chaps from Bordeaux. . . . But I would advise you not to give him your answer till tomorrow. Go off to your room now, for it will be a good idea for you to think over your decision for a night, and one night of doubt and meditation won't be too much for him to bear. He will appreciate the value of your feelings all the more for it. I'll just tell him that you've asked for time to think.'

She listened obediently to him.

'And then I will ask the two of you to go on living as you have in the past, to all intents and purposes like mere friends. We are about to enter the worst of the winter, and it's no time for love-making. There are difficult days ahead of us, from which we must all come out alive, and in good morale. You do understand, don't you?'

She nodded her head gravely.

'When the spring comes, we shall go down to Gouldsboro, and there the Pastor can marry you . . . or the Priest, whichever you prefer.'

'Oh, it's true, I am a Huguenot and he is a Papist,' she exclaimed, remembering the fact with horror.

'If you've only just realized the fact now, it seems to me that the barrier between you is not that great. Peace now! Peace on earth to men of goodwill. . . . There's something that concerns us all. Good night!'

Angélique escorted the young woman back to the door of her room and kissed her before she left her.

Most of the men had retired behind the big curtain that had been sewn together from skins which hid their two-storey dormitory.

As she walked back through the room she heard a clatter of saucepans and kitchen utensils and realized that they had slipped from poor Malaprade's shaking hands.

The cook was pale and looked at her like a wounded spaniel.

Angélique took pity on him, and, going over to where he stood, hurriedly whispered, 'She loves you!'

CHAPTER 48

THE FOLLOWING day Elvire herself went to find Malaprade and as it was fine the two of them walked down to the lakeside where they spent a long time walking up and down the path beside the water.

When they returned they looked radiant and were holding hands.

A small party to celebrate their engagement was planned for them at which everyone was on their best behaviour. If Malaprade was subjected to any of the customary jokes from his friends, at least they were out of earshot of the womenfolk.

He was transfigured.

His happiness gave pleasure to everyone.

But in spite of everything it was some time before Angélique found she could forget what Peyrac had revealed about the chef. It had upset her more than it had Elvire, probably because she was less innocent. It reminded her of her own sordid memories. And in the evenings, as she sat before the fire in her little room, she could not help thinking about what he had said.

Two lovers dismembered by a cook's knife. Hands stained with blood, fear, his brow dripping with sweat, the loneliness of a hunted animal.

Angélique's thoughts drifted on.

Bill-hooks slicing at men's necks as they slept; that head of a man from whom she had sought vengeance, which a peasant stood holding up before her by the hair, with blood dripping from it, in which she felt she could have washed her white fingers with delight.

That feeling of hatred, those reactions of an implacable yet terrified animal, that utter abjection of a creature dragged through its own filth and degradation, these she had confessed to the Prior of the Abbey of Nieul and he had given her absolution.

But how could anyone wipe out the marks, the painful traces of events like these? As she knelt before the fire in her room, her delicate profile leaned forward, her skin continued to creep, and she felt vaguely sick. She understood Malaprade. Especially what had happened to him afterwards: that nameless terror, his whole being shaken as in a tempest, his horror of himself.

She threw some wood on to the fire to give her trembling fingers something to do. She thought that Elvire had been very brave; she possessed the courage of a pure soul, of someone who 'doesn't know'.

'It's not easy to get them to talk, those little Huguenot girls,' Joffrey de Peyrac told himself, thinking of Elvire. 'But they're easier to deal with than this one.'

And he watched Angélique as she knelt a few paces from him, so far away, so distant, that she was not even aware that he was looking at her.

Of all 'his men', she was the person who had least to confide in him. There were so many things he did not know that he had to be careful not to hurt her. He must wait till she came to him for comfort.

'She is a woman. Woman was not made for hell, whatever they say. She retains a feeling of shame for all the despicable, abject things she does. . . . She was not made to live in darkness and disorder, but to dwell in light and harmony. . . . Don't go on suffering so far from me, my little soul, I know your weakness. You have been struck down by life, and there is no shame in that. It is the human lot. The important thing is to know how to recover. In the old days women, children, peasants, partisans, the ordinary man, all weak people had a defender. He was the knight. It was the knight's role to fight battles for the poor, to take up their cause, to pay blood-money for those whose wrists and souls were delicate. It was the knight's role to defend the man who had not been born to fight himself, whose role in life was not to deal with crime, blood, blows and misfortune. But things have changed, and there are no knights any more. Everyone fights for himself. Women defend themselves with tooth and claw, and as for the common man, he does what Malaprade did, he succumbs to fear and panic. The ordinary man was born to lead a gentle life. And when the day comes when he is brought face to face with life, passion, evil, he panics, he is not ready, it has never occurred to him that this sort of thing could ever happen to him. In his fear a man of this type is capable of doing anything, terrible things, unthinkable things. The only thing he is really aware of is the loneliness of the sinner. I can just see that respectable man, well thought of in his town, his brow covered with sweat as he dissected the still warm limbs of two people he had known and no doubt loved, and I must admit that the thought of it fills me more with pity than with horror.

301

'Poor artisan! Where is your defender? Where is the man who will stand up for your rights?

'A man who was born a gentleman in those times seemed to have the inborn gift of being able to face risk, death, the very worst that can happen on earth, springing from the infirmity of the world.

'That is what a conscientious artisan like Malaprade lacks. Had he been a gentleman he would not have murdered those who flouted him, he would never have given way to his blind, demented rage. He would have had his wife locked up for life in a convent and would have fought a duel with the lover, in broad daylight, and would have killed him, but without running the risk of being sent to prison or being hanged, since a knight was immune from the charge of murder when it took place in open combat. But the days of knighthood are gone, the knights themselves abuse their advantages and privileges by extortion, and Cardinal Richelieu has put an end to it all by forbidding duelling.

'What sort of a world should I bring my sons up to face? A world in which cunning and patience are indisputably the chief weapons. But for all that it has gone underground, force still remains indispensable.'

As he discoursed within himself, Peyrac in his turn had wandered so far that it was Angélique who suddenly realized the fact and looked up at him.

She looked at him as he sat there, turning towards the flames his heavily lined face in which the eyes and lips seemed the only living part, for the wind, the sun and the sea had turned the skin of his face into a hard leather-like mask. He no longer wore a beard, for he said that the Indians didn't like men with beards. And he advised his men to do likewise so as not to worry the natives, in whose eyes the sight of tousled hair on the face was as unbearable as some obscenity. And if the trappers did not make sacrifice of their beards, it was through laziness and a feeling that it didn't matter, coupled with a lack of understanding. They would have been wiser to do so. For they were all aware that the admirable Father Breboeuf had been horribly martyred because he bore two stigmata which the Indians found intolerable: he was bald and he wore a beard.

Joffrey de Peyrac always sensed this kind of thing, which stemmed from the respect he felt for whomsoever he was speaking to, a respect that guided his intuition.

Angélique drew closer and laid her forehead against his knees.

'How do you always manage to remain unmoved, and never to be frightened?' she asked. 'It seems as if, whatever happens to you, you are incapable of feeling a low cowardliness, of feeling disgusted with yourself. . . . Even when you faced the stake, even when faced with torture. . . . How do you do it? Have you always been a man, ever since your childhood? . . .'

So he told her of the thoughts that had gone through his head: that they were facing a time that lacked honour or dignity, a time in which human beings could do nothing but hide, masking themselves from the reigning forces beneath an appearance of docility, or fighting it out alone and to the bitter end, no matter what their strength was. It was not surprising if there were defeats. It was already quite a lot to be alive. And since she had mentioned childhood he remembered the fact that he had come to grips with terror at a very early age, for he had been only three when the Catholic soldiers had slashed his cheek with their swords and hurled him from the windows of a burning château. It had been then, in the primitive innocence of childhood, that he had felt the mythical shock of Evil, that he had known every fear rolled into one. But having survived this, he had never again felt fear, although it was true that he had grown to a man's stature, that is to say that he had felt ready to face anything. And he had not minded occasionally being brought face to face with the monster. 'There you are, terror,' he would say, 'there you are, massacre. There you are, hideous face of fear. Well may you strike me down, but never hope to frighten me again. . . .'

He went on to say that she should not feel ashamed of the failures she had encountered during the terrible tribulations that had assailed her, for she was a woman, and it was men, who had failed in their roles as guides and protectors, who were responsible for making her feel as she did.

'It's an old battle: man's temptation to use brute force or temporal power to sweep aside the things that stand against him, to use constraint to stifle the lesson of his spirit. . . .'

And he, although a man himself, had he not fallen victim to this too? For a single man cannot always triumph over an overpowerful coalition. There is a time for everything, a time for a mud-laden tide, that rises irresistibly. . . .

'Our century had turned its back on the Christian doctrine which was its strength, had abandoned itself to an uncontrolled desire for domination. . . . Domination at all costs, coming from every point of the horizon: the Kings, the Nations, the Church. . . . We are not out of this stage yet, and he who does not wish to be crushed has no option but to dominate also. But beneath this avalanche of heavy stones, the spirit must live nevertheless, and make its way. . . .'

He stroked his smooth brow with a pensive hand. And she sat with closed eyes, huddling up to his warmth and his strength. She remembered the words of the little Arab doctor who had been Joffrey de Peyrac's friend and who had told her that he was the greatest scientist of his age and that for this reason he would always be persecuted. . . . 'For indeed, this age refuses to harken to the lesson of the spirit.'

CHAPTER 49

WHEN THEY lay down together Joffrey de Peyrac liked to watch the firelight grow slowly dimmer in the silent room where the only sounds were their sighs of love and the gentle crackling of the flames.

By their pink or golden glow he loved to discover the languid curves of his wife and the flesh tints of her delicately scented skin.

And when it was very cold and his hand had to feel beneath the furs to uncover the secrets of this body, in the half-light nothing remained visible but her astonishing head of golden hair spread out like a sheet of phosphorescent seaweed that glinted mysteriously as her lovely head moved softly from side to side in surrender.

Angélique was the only woman from whom he felt unable to abstract himself, to detach himself. Even during the most intimately pleasurable moments she always remained present. This fact astonished him since he had held many women in his arms and had never hesitated to forget about them once his male egoism had been satisfied, for he had always been more concerned with the physical satisfaction he could obtain from them than to satisfy their feelings, although he was always prepared to fob them off with a few amiable protestations.

But with Angélique he could never forget that it was she he held in his arms and that it was she whom he could weary, enrapture, bring to ecstasy, and that it was her body that he bent to his will, and her proud lips that opened, vanquished, beneath his.

He was always acutely aware of her.

It might have been a habit he had developed in the early days of their love-making. She had been so young and so frightened that he had had to remain aware of her every reaction in order to win her over. But the magic went on.

It was as if Angélique's sensuality remained for ever linked with something secret and spiritual within her, something that informed the utmost gesture of surrender of which her beautiful body was capable.

And it occurred to him to wonder, full of scepticism and surprise, if she were not restoring to him the heady emotions of youth which a man tends to forget as he grows more familiar with the pleasures of the flesh. It was a certain concern, a certain doubt, a solicitude for his partner, and beyond that those heavenly reaches of pleasure in which he was fully conscious of their being two people experiencing together an irresistible and almost magical communion. These were moments of rapture, of ecstasy, of weakness, of unrestrained abandon, and in their mutual fulfilment, swooning, he tasted the taste of death and of life eternal....

She was the only woman who made him feel like this and he was delighted to perceive her understanding of a man's pleasure. She knew exactly when to do certain things, and when to stop. And when she herself had been sent plunging into the abyss of pleasure, blinded and dead to the world, still her hands, her body, and her lips went on following him, knowing when to offer themselves, when to clasp him, when to release him, guided by those mysterious laws that Eve has handed down to her daughters.

She remained present to him because, even while he possessed her body, he was never quite sure of possessing her entirely, never sure that she might not yet escape him.

He knew that she no longer had in her the natural docility of a young girl. She had left that behind her, by the wayside, replacing it with a clear-headed independence, and self-awareness.

Where love was concerned, she had her good and her bad days. There were days when, from the very way she smiled, he could see that she was easy, and days when, without any apparent change in her behaviour, he felt that she was refusing him, that she was distant. He interpreted this as a change in the climate of her feelings.

Then, when evening came, he would delight in trying to discover by what means he could overcome her prickly mood, how to make her warm to him, and fan the slumbering flames.

More often than not he would respect this woman's withdrawal from him, this irrational need to escape from him, to put a distance between them, which was mostly only a sign of physical tiredness but occasionally submission to invisible orders, an indication of squalls in the offing, just as a strong wind often foretells the coming of a storm, or some obscure psychological disturbance or some approaching danger, all of which acted like an imperative call to alertness and attention.

He would let her relax and fall asleep. Sleep would dispel these phantasms and in the course of the night something would change within her or without, he never knew which, and when she woke she would have changed. Then it would be she who drew close to him.

Dawn, that half-waking state of the indeterminate hours that precede the day, brought an audacity to Angélique which she would never have had when fully awake. She became gayer and less anxious.

She would become a cajoling siren, and would slide up to him, and through the early dawn light he could see the brightness of her sea-green eyes close to him, and the flash of her teeth as she smiled.

He would feel the soft silk of her hair fall like rain upon him, and the light offering of her lovely lips in numberless kisses.

With all the skill of an oriental slave girl bent on sparing her lord and master any kind of trouble, she would stimulate his desire, leaving him powerless to defend himself.

'Was it in Moulay Ismael's harem you learnt all these tricks, Madame? Are you trying to get me to forget the concubines who once used to wait upon me?'

'Yes . . . I know their methods. . . . May it please the lord my sultan to trust in me.'

And she would kiss his lips passionately, then his eyes and the whole of his beloved face, and he would give in, and give himself to her, letting her dispense pleasure to him with all the skill she knew.

'What a charming lover you are, my Lady Abbess,' he would say again.

And he would run his hand over her supple hips, clasping them in his embrace, and when she finally collapsed across him in ecstasy, he never tired of looking at her as she lay there in a heap, with half-closed eyes, through which he could see a faint glimmer, while from her parted lips came the almost imperceptible sound of her panting breath.

It was like a sweet death. She would expire far from him, in some unknown place, and this very distance between them was a homage to him.

He was overjoyed to see her so deeply affected. The woman who would be born of this winter, of this hard life in the fort, of these weary nights surrounded by frost and darkness, but which for them were taken up by their new intimacy, the woman who would emerge from this pilgrimage to the frontiers of life that a long winter in the north represents, with famine for a companion and all the latent threats that hung about them, that woman would be a woman of his shaping.

The day would come when the agonies of the past left no more traces.

He was looking after her. And when delight had accomplished its joyous task within her, a hymn of gratitude would rise to her lips and she would whisper softly: 'Oh, my love, my master.... You alone....'

It was not so long since that night during the storm on board the *Gouldsboro* when she had tremblingly given herself up to him.

The moment she had so feared since the night of Plessis had come, and nothing very terrible had happened. Nothing but the feeling of being in a dream, a feeling of infinity as the ship rocked to and fro, lifting her up on the wings of a new-born delight.

Here it was the nocturnal hollow of woods and winter, the slumbrousness of this rustic bed that smelt of resin and moss.

Another dream, heavy with silence, scarce troubled by the distant cries of coyotes or wolves. A moment lived outside of time. A sweet journey. A dream come to life, the vague dream that men have in which they seek refuge in the depths of some lair, there to sleep in the warmth of love.

She would sometimes waken, and, scarce daring to breathe, savour the wonderful sensation of fulfilment.

He had not been able to give her the palace or the house he had dreamed of.

But there was the bed.

The bed! The night!

Before, when they had lived in Toulouse, they had not slept together much at night. They had had all day in which to make love and long, delicious siestas.

But here, in this wild, rustic existence, they lived as did the poor and needy. They only had the nights.

She breathed deeply, beside his tranquil strength. Sometimes she would waken and watch him sleep, close to her, and alive. She envied him his male insensitivity that allowed him to be so calm, whereas women allowed their imaginations to dominate their bodies.

The ashes glowed deep red in the hearth, casting hardly a shadow on the beams.

The room was plunged in darkness smelling of burnt wood.

She could see nothing, but could hear his regular breathing beside her and she delighted in it.

All her feelings of nostalgia, all her roving fancies led back to him. And he was her husband, he would never leave her again!

She put out one hand to touch him, to recognize him, and was moved by the unexpected ruggedness of his angular body. And he instinctively drew her towards him in his sleep, close against his powerful chest, streaked with scars. He had scars all over his body, she ran her finger over them. How many times had his life been in peril and his flesh tortured? Of those terrible hours, nothing remained save these marks inscribed, about which he cared not at all. Many of them had already disappeared.

'You said once that each of these scars bears the name of a different cause for which your blood was spilled . . .'

'It would be more accurate to say that they are the signatures of my enemies, as many as they are diverse. You ask which are the worst? The ones left by the King of France's executioner. He stretched out my game leg for me and got it to work again, but he left me with something wrong in the nerves of my left arm, something I become aware of sometimes, especially when I have to fire.

'And the best scars? Those I got when duelling or fighting round the Mediterranean. They are good with their swords there, and swords make good, clean cuts. That deep hole in my side? That was a bullet that got me in the Caribbean, Spanish or French, I don't remember any more. That recent scar there on my forehead, that you looked after so tenderly for me with your pretty hands, that was an Abenaki tomahawk, commissioned by New France. Possibly the first of a long line.'

'Don't, my love! You frighten me.'

'And you, my lovely warrior, you show me your battle scars.'

But Angélique drew the sheet and all the furs up around her to hide herself.

'Never! Men's scars are marks of glory. They enhance their prestige and tell the tale of their exploits. But those on women are errors, blunders, they are the marks that life has left on them, a sign that they were doing things they had no business to be doing. . . . A sign of failure. . . .'

'Show me.'

'No, there's only the place where they branded me with the fleur-de-lis.'

One evening he managed to grasp one of Angélique's delicate ankles and turn it towards the light to examine the violet-coloured scar she still had after her flight from Morocco.

She had to tell him about it. It had happened in the desert. She had been bitten by a snake. Colin Paturel had cut into her flesh with his knife and then had cauterized the wound. . . . It had been an agonizing operation and she had fainted. And after that? . . . Well, Colin had carried her on his back for many days. There were only the two of them left, for the others had all died on the way.

She always hesitated to call up memories of Colin Paturel. As if Joffrey could have known! But he certainly knew. And he had a way of clasping her close to him, and watching her closely, which frightened her a little.

And even if the memory of her wandering through Morocco was still, in spite of the suffering involved, surrounded by an aura of beauty because of the magic of the uncomplicated love that Colin had given her, she no longer could understand how she could have given herself to him.

All the delight she had felt in the arms of her erstwhile lovers now seemed, as she tried to call it to mind, to be unimportant.

It had been pleasant, that was all. But in the context of her present discoveries, what she had felt then now seemed incomplete.

She did not know to what she could attribute this resurgence of pleasure when she was in his arms. She would discover herself anew each time like a stranger, as she surrendered to these multifarious revelations that left her amazed and stunned.

Then she would feel delight flood through her whole being, mingling sensations of strength and languor, and the pleasure she felt was like a shrill note, that vibrated, long and strident, through her body.

When she had regained her composure after a short sleep, she would sometimes reproach herself for being too sensual.

The Calvinist indoctrination she had undergone among the Protestants of La Rochelle, would come back to her, bringing a hot flush to her cheeks.

He would watch her out of the corner of his eye, as she dressed somewhat severely, and donned her white linen coif into which she tucked all her lovely hair very tight so that not a single strand showed, as if by these rather belated scruples she could wipe out or make reparation for the excessive sensuality of their love-making during the night.

She did not realize that this liberation, that this blossoming of all her senses was utterly and completely normal.

She was thirty-seven.

She did not know that women reach the peak of enjoyment in their mature years. The young girl's uncomplicated appetite for the sports of love is succeeded by all the refinements of discovery.

Few are those who know this or understand it.

It doesn't take a hundred years to awaken the Sleeping Beauty, but it does take quite a few.

Then the time comes when this uninstructed body becomes a sanctuary. And from then on the eternal rites can take place in all their magic. And it is obvious at a glance.

Few men can mistake that look.

It is the age when woman often reaches the peak of her beauty.

For that same process of completion that, beneath the pressures of life, has enriched her personality, now seems to work upon her outward form and to transfigure her movements, her voice and her bearing.

She is herself now, finished, in full possession of all her riches, charm, beauty, femininity, emotion and intuition. And she is still young. . . .

A formidable combination indeed, and one which, provided she has retained all its constituent elements, makes her, at this age, the most dangerous creature of love imaginable.

That was how Lieutenant Pont-Briand saw her, when Angélique appeared to him at the lakeside, one cold clear morning, when, after chasing madly across country for several days, he reached Wapassou.

CHAPTER 50

THE LAKE was frozen, and entirely snow-covered, a smooth, spotless plain. Lieutenant Pont-Briand strode roughly across it destroying the velvety surface of the sumptuous white carpet with the tracks of his round snowshoes. He staggered forward heavily, with staring eyes. He had just caught sight of Angélique. It was her! She really was still alive. And he was coming to her as he had dreamed for so long.

Angélique was standing on the path at the lakeside and she watched the strange figure coming towards her, hardly believing her eyes.

A crisp blue-tinted brightness, characteristic of certain winter mornings, still bathed the segment of land where the fort stood hidden, encircled by forest and cliffs.

The sky was neither gold nor silver nor pink nor blue, but a colourless, watery, transparent shade, and on the horizon, where the cliffs began to drop towards the waterfalls, there were trails of lilac-coloured clouds. Towards the west at treetop level there were sudden streaks of pink, reflections of the rising sun, which was about to come over the opposite horizon but had not yet crossed the line of the black fir-trees.

The half-glimpsed mountains seemed very far off and inaccessible, with their tops lost in a pure, icy dream. Bit by bit the sunshine began to fall across the lake and the lieutenant's silhouette stood out hard and black, outlined by the light, while his long shadow spread out beside him over the snow.

'Who can it be?' Angélique wondered.

Her heart was anxious, and although a sure intuition had already told her who it was, she nevertheless asked herself the question.

Another figure, farther off, all muffled in furs, came into sight through the cold shadows at the tip of the lake.

'Frenchmen? Heavens! Are there many more of them?'

The Canadian lieutenant crossed the lake like a man hypnotized.

To his mind, exhausted by two weeks of journeying under appalling conditions, the fact that she was the first person he saw as he approached Count Peyrac's retreat was a manifest sign of his success.

It was as if she had been waiting for him! As if she had never ceased to hope that she might see him appear, in her loneliness and helplessness among these brutish creatures in the depths of a barbarous forest. That was what he imagined.

As he drew near, he had a flash of lucidity: 'After all, she's only a woman. Probably as disappointing as the others. So what's all the fuss about?'

Then almost immediately he was dazzled once more, but a hundred times more than before, since now his vision had become flesh and blood before his eyes. Then joy welled up within him, dispelling all his doubts and weariness. 'It was worth it, yes, it was worth it a hundred times over!'

Angélique watched him, speechless, hardly believing her eyes, for it seemed impossible that this dead, frozen landscape should bring travellers their way.

He stood looking at her, his arms hanging at his sides. Although he had halted, he staggered, for he had walked so far and so quickly that when he stopped he grew giddy and found it hard to keep his feet.

The rays of the sun trembled at the tips of the trees, casting long spangled shafts of light into the sky. The sun was about to appear, and as it crept up it made the whole landscape sparkle.

'So beautiful,' thought Pont-Briand, 'so beautiful, my God, so beautiful.'

So it had not been a dream.

She really was as lovely as he remembered her, and seemed to radiate beauty, more dazzling still than the morning light.

In the shadow of the thick hood that covered her head, her lips stood out red like some jewel in their brilliance, while her cheeks were pink like wild roses. These two delicate colours, pale pink and scarlet, were like the sweetness of spring in bud, brightening her flesh and lending to her Madonna-like face, with its harmonious, almost hieratic lines, all the freshness of youth. A wisp of pale gold hair strayed across her forehead.

Her eyes like pools of green water looked grave and intimidating as they watched him, trying to fathom him. She was standing in judgement on him and seemed to see beyond him, with a look that was a hundred years old.

The look of five generations of fairies in an unchangingly youthful body.

She was a creature who knew everything, who understood everything, who possessed all manner of powers, and a body skilled in all manner of seduction.

She was a sorceress, a goddess, a fairy.

Yes, she was indeed the Woman. Or possibly the She-Devil!

The man who had come to Pont-Briand in his fort at Saint Anne, on the Saint Francis river, had warned him about her. It was he who had pushed him into this crazy escapade. 'If she is really as lovely as you say, she must be a snare laid by the Devil....'

He stood looking at her.

Angélique's eyebrows had grown pale in the sunshine and as she puckered them slightly they cast a shadow, like a passing cloud, over her clear green eyes, giving them the tint of deep sea-water, suddenly almost dark.

She hesitated as she recognized him.

The cold was intense, petrifying. The water vapour that escaped from between her lips was transformed by the sunshine into a delicate, evanescent halo round her head. Once the first ecstatic moments had gone by, Pont-Briand experienced a sensation of fear which his weak physical state made it impossible for him to overcome.

He spoke in a brusque gruff voice:

'Greetings to you, Madame. Do you not recognize me?'

'Of course! You are Lieutenant Pont-Briand.'

He gave a shudder, for the sound of her voice was like the echo of his memories and it moved him deeply.

'Where have you come from?' she asked.

'From up there,' he replied pointing northwards. 'Three weeks of blizzards and uninterrupted snowfall. It's a miracle my Huron and I weren't buried alive.'

Then she realized that she was failing in all the laws of hospitality imperative in that harsh climate. When a traveller, after wandering through this white waste, with the sound of no human voice save the echo of his own among the trees, or in the hollows of ice-bound cliffs, or across the windswept plains, reaches a blessed haven from which rises the life-giving sign of a wreath of smoke, he must be welcomed, warmed and fed, since he has escaped from the hostility of nature and rejoined the race of men. Hospitality demands it.

'But you are exhausted,' she cried. 'Come into the fort, quick. Are you able to walk as far as that?'

'After walking so many miles, I think I can manage those few paces. Salvation is near. But what am I saying? It is here. For the mere sight of you gives me back my strength....'

And he endeavoured to smile.

The sentries, musket in hand, came towards them. The two Spaniards stood on either side of the French lieutenant, making signs to him to find out whether he was alone. Just to be sure, one of them went off in the direction from which the travellers had come.

The Huron came up with them, limping.

'He fell down a cliff,' said Pont-Briand. 'I had to carry him for two days.'

Angélique went ahead, walking without snowshoes on the hard-packed snow of the path.

The fort was flooded with sunshine now, and then from afar off they could hear the sound of voices, the noise of hammering, and the roaring of the forge.

The children were playing and shouting happily in the open and sliding on the frozen puddles.

The men all came rushing up to have a look at the new arrivals.

No sooner had they set eyes on them than there was a general move back, and they made as if to seize their weapons. 'The French!'

'They are alone,' Angélique said, and sent someone to fetch Count Peyrac.

Pont-Briand removed his snowshoes and leant them against the outside wall. Then he put down his musket which slipped and fell; he had not the strength to pick it up again.

He clattered heavily down the steps behind Angélique and into the main room of the little outpost. The only two windows had just been opened and the sun was beginning to creep in, but the air was still heavy with smoke and the smell of hot soup, and so warm that Pont-Briand felt he was entering Paradise.

He collapsed on to a bench beside the table. As for the Indian, he crept like a sick dog to the hearth and crouched there against the chimneypiece. Their leather clothes were stiff with frost.

Angélique swiftly built up the two fires, and threw some green stones into one of them to heat them for a steam bath.

The cooking-pots were already boiling, for they had been simmering all night ready for the first meal of the day.

'You are lucky. Today we have salt pork in the pot, with peas and onions. We are celebrating the first day of sunshine after the storm.'

She leant forward to remove the lid from the pot, and her movement showed her full hips beneath the folds of her short cloak. He grew giddy and faint. So it was really true! She was alive, she was here! He had not dreamed of her in vain! . . .

Angélique filled a ladle and gave him a goblet of brandy, then she served the Huron.

'We haven't much to offer you. All our supplies were burned at Katarunk. No doubt you heard about that.'

'Yes. I saw the ashes.'

He listened to her melodious voice, forgetting to eat, as he devoured her with his eyes. 'The man's even madder than last time,' she said to herself resignedly. 'Come on, eat up,' she urged him.

He did as he was told and began to eat slowly and deliberately, in a state of bliss.

The others were watching them from the doorway, looking suspiciously at the intruder, while the Spaniard stood guard over him with his musket at the ready.

Pont-Briand heard nothing and saw nothing but Angélique. He had paid dearly enough for this moment. . . .

'The fort was burned down, but you managed to escape,' he said.

'How did you get away from the Iroquois? In Quebec, the news that you were still alive caused a sensation. . . .'

'They can't have been too pleased either, can they? Our death-warrant had been signed in spite of Monsieur de Loménie.'

She was defying him, her eyes glowing dark. . . .

'How beautiful she is,' he said to himself.

Angélique had thrown her cloak down on a stool, together with a bunch of a kind of blackish boxwood she had been picking that morning by the lake at the edge of the forest.

Pont-Briand admired her slender waist, freed now from the heavy cloak, and the nobility of her bearing from which her plain clothes did not detract.

'She's a Queen!' he thought. 'She would stand head and shoulders above all the others in the drawing-rooms of Quebec! Whatever is she doing in the depths of the woods like this? She must be got out of here....'

The sight of her set his blood boiling. Exhausted as he was, she roused his desire. And just as the first time he had caught sight of her beneath the trees, he felt a sharp shock, something leap within him, a feeling of attraction mingled with fear, something absolutely new. Even half-dead as he was, he could not help wanting her.

Gradually the warmth of the room penetrated his body, while the food began to ease the pains in his stomach, and he gave way, weak as he was, to the gentle yet overwhelming tension of his body, making no attempt to control it, but rather welcoming it as a token of life and rebirth after the hardships through which he had passed.

This woman had an undeniable erotic power over him. It had certainly been worth his while to come, to have risked death on the way, and what if she were a She-Devil? What did it matter?

'Who would want to see you dead?' he protested, trying to stretch his chapped lips into a playful smile. 'Even I wouldn't, even after the charming way you sniped at me the first time we met.'

Angélique saw him again trying to cross the ford and splashing in the water, and the memory of it made her laugh. This fresh, spontaneous laugh finished Pont-Briand. As she approached him to remove his plate, he seized her by the wrist.

'I adore you,' he said in a muffled voice.

Her laughter ceased abruptly and she broke away from him with an expression of annoyance.

Joffrey de Peyrac had just appeared in the room.

'Ah, there you are, Monsieur de Pont-Briand,' he said in a tone that showed not the slightest astonishment.

It was as if he had been expecting him.

The lieutenant hoisted his tall frame off his seat, not without difficulty.

'Please don't get up. You must be feeling weak. Have you come from the Saint Lawrence? It takes an uncommon amount of courage to set off at this time of the year through the deserted back country . . . but of course, you are a Canadian.'

Pont-Briand fumbled in his jacket pocket to find his pipe, and the Count handed him some tobacco. The Huron, his eyes half-closed, had already filled his.

Angélique brought each man a lighted splint.

315

A few puffs seemed to revive the lieutenant, who began to describe all the difficulties he had encountered during the journey. They had lost their way several times during blizzards.

'And what urgent task brought you on this journey, all alone, at this time of the year?' the Count asked. 'And so far from your base. You have some mission to fulfil?'

Pont-Briand seems not to have heard him, then he started as if awakened from a dream, and stared uncomprehendingly at Peyrac.

'What do you mean?'

'What I said. Is it chance that brings you here?'

'Indeed not.'

'So you intended to make for our outpost, and join us here?'

'Yes indeed.'

'And why?'

Once again Pont-Briand gave a start, seemed to wake up, and for the first time he appeared really to see the man he was talking to and to realize who he was. He made no reply.

'I think the man's sleepy,' Angélique murmured. 'When he's had a good rest he will tell us why he has come.'

But Count Peyrac was pressing.

'But why? Do you bear some message for us? No? Then why this journey all alone at such a dangerous time of the year?'

Pont-Briand looked all round the room, then ran his hand several times over his brow. Then he gave this strange reply:

'Because I had to, Monsieur, I had to.'

CHAPTER 51

EVENING CAME – it grew dark so early. Lieutenant Pont-Briand seemed like a new man. His tongue had been unloosed again and he kept the company entertained by tales and news from New France.

His skin had regained its normal colouring, and he was talking about Quebec where he had been recently, about a ball that had been held there, and about a play they had put on at the Jesuit College.

Angélique sat listening to him with parted lips, for she found him interesting and he told his stories well. Moreover she felt a devouring curiosity about the things he spoke of, the towns, the three cities of the north, Quebec, Trois-Rivières and Montreal.

She burst out laughing several times, in amusement at his gay stories, and Pont-Briand was unable to resist casting a glance at her, the passion of which he tried hard to control. He had regained some degree of elementary caution. He did not remember having heard her laugh before in that throaty way which sent shudders through the very roots of his hair. Count Peyrac had not asked him again why he had come, which was something he would have found very hard to explain. Thus it was that part of him was chatting merrily with the assembled company while the other still lived through the dark torments of the past month, when at first he had thought her dead and life had seemed to him so desolate that he had even lost his taste for tobacco.

Never had the days seemed longer to him. He saw himself again, tramping up and down the ramparts of his fort, looking out towards the horizon as if a female figure might have risen up there, or lost in contemplation of the motionless river, whose noise had been stilled by its shell of ice.

He had brutally driven away the Indian girl with whom he had been living for the past two years, and as she was the daughter of a local chief, this had caused trouble.

But little did he care.

And then suddenly the news had come, no one knew how, that the foreigners from Katarunk were not dead, had not been killed by the Iroquois. They were all alive and in the mountains! And the women? Yes, the women too! Of course they must have been under the Devil's protection, to have escaped from a trap like that. . . . Then Pont-Briand had grown still more uncontrollable. He wanted to live again, to become as he had been before. He had tried other Indian women, young ones, abandoned ones.

But he would send them all away, disgusted by their shiny, greasy skins. He dreamt of a luminous, fresh skin, with a sweet, pungent scent, a scent you noticed suddenly, with some movement or gesture, a scent that rose to your nostrils and made you giddy.

One thing which he had found most attractive about the Indian girls when he had first arrived in Canada, their absence of body hair, now put him off like some abnormality. He dreamed of a mound of fleecy hair, standing out in sharp contrast with the surrounding white skin. Unless of course she removed it as the great ladies did. But how could she remain a great lady in that wild forest land where her formidable husband had taken her?

There had never been any white women living in the woods.

This was the first time and it was madness. Immoral. Everyone in

317

Quebec was talking about it, and right up the river as far as Montreal.

Monsieur de Loménie could remind them as much as he liked of the fact that when Monsieur de Maisonneuve and his men had gone up to the Island of Montreal to found Marieville, Mademoiselle Mance who accompanied them had found herself in a similar situation, in fact even more scandalous than Madame de Peyrac's, but nobody listened to him. They merely replied that Monsieur de Maisonneuve had an invisible legion of angels and saints on his side, and a couple of very visible chaplains, and that he himself had erected a cross on Mount-Royal, whereas the Peyracs were accompanied by godless, debauched and heretical men among whom she, no doubt, chose her lovers.

Furthermore the women of Montreal, who incidentally lived under the individual and special protection of the Blessed Virgin, and the threefold protection of the Holy Family, had never left the banks of the river. . . .

Pont-Briand knew what they were saying. When he had been to Quebec on business, he had appeared before the Grand Council and had been questioned by Monsignor Laval, by the Jesuits, and in private by Governor Frontenac. He told them all that she was the loveliest woman in the world, and that yes, indeed, he could not hide the fact, she had bewitched him. And his descriptions growing more and more lyrical as he went on, he succeeded in creating an atmosphere of hysteria around the unknown woman. People watched him go by in the streets with mixed feelings of horror and envy. 'Look at the state she has got him in! . . . Good heavens! How could she do that, with a single look!'

His state did not improve. He dreamed of her constantly. Sometimes it was the sound of her voice that came back to him, sometimes the perfect line of her knee that he had glimpsed when he had entered the cottage without knocking at the door.

He dreamed of that knee, smooth and white like marble, and imagined himself caressing it, pressing down on it to part her glorious legs . . . and he would lie tossing on his bed and moaning.

And now he was at Wapassou, right beside her, and he felt even more acutely the mixture of desire and fear that had haunted him for so long.

Beads of sweat pearled on his brow. He had talked a great deal that evening, talked brilliantly, but his glass was empty and no one seemed to be filling it again. The men were beginning to go off to bed. . . .

It was after a visit he had received in his fort at Saint-Anne that he had decided to set off and find her. Before that it had never occurred to him. To set out on a journey at the beginning of an already hard winter would have been foolish, and moreover he had his outpost to run. But the man who had come to see him had banished all his fears, even those he had had about arriving alone and unarmed among these dubious people. . . .

And that evening, as he had sat alone at the wooden table, he had felt that he was among strangers, among enemies. In a flash he had noticed that there was no crucifix, no gathering for prayers. And outside, they had erected no cross. He heard them talking English and Spanish. The Father was right! They were miscreants and godless men, possibly even dangerous heretics. He looked round again.

She was no longer there, for she had retired. And behind that closed door she would sleep beside old Scarface, perhaps even give herself to him.

Pont-Briand began to die a thousand deaths. What he had undertaken was sheer madness. She would elude him. She was somehow different . . . inaccessible. . . .

And then he heard the echoes of a reassuring voice: 'If you succeed in snatching this woman from an immoral life, it would be a good work that would count towards your redemption. You alone are capable of bringing this about.'

To which he had replied sharply:

'And what if she is a demon, a real demon?'

'My prayers will protect you.'

The man who had come to see him wore a black robe, and a crucifix made of wood and copper across his chest. Just above the figure on the crucifix, there was a glitter of rubies. The man stooped slightly as he stood, for he was still recovering from a wound in his side that the Iroquois had given him in the recent skirmishes near Katarunk. He had very handsome dark blue eyes, deep-set beneath bushy eyebrows, and a curly reddish-brown beard that hid a pleasant, gentle mouth. His face was often compared with that of Christ.

He was of medium height and strong. Pont-Briand did not like him. He was frightened of him, as he was of all Jesuits, who are too intelligent and want to deprive you of all the pleasures of this life.

The man's hand, mutilated by Iroquois torture, filled the lieutenant with repulsion, although he had never felt the same way about the infirmities of his trapper friends like L'Aubignière, in spite of the fact that they had been subjected to the same ordeal.

He was astonished to receive a visit from Father Orgeval whom he suspected of despising him for his rough ways.

But the priest had been most charming, saying that he knew that Pont-Briand was madly in love with the foreign woman he had met in the upper Kennebec.

He showed no sign of being shocked, on the contrary! God had possibly inspired this worthy man, a Christian and a Frenchman into the bargain, to help put an end to the dangers that threatened Acadia and New France, by the encroachment of Count Peyrac, renegade and traitor, who was in the service of the English.

'Do you know then, who he is, Father, and where he is from?'

'I shall soon know. I have sent my agents out in every direction, even to Europe.'

'Was it you, Father, who encouraged Maudreuil to scalp the Iroquois chiefs at Katarunk?'

'Maudreuil had made a vow. He is a pure child. Our Lady appeared to him by way of recompense for his victory.'

'How did Peyrac manage to escape from the vengeance of those demons?'

'Some diabolical machination on his part. There is no other possible explanation. You can see for yourself that we must get rid of him, otherwise his presence will contaminate our land. And you can help us....'

'I very much doubt,' he went on, 'whether the woman he calls his wife is in fact so in the eyes of God. She is probably some unfortunate creature he has seduced and corrupted.

'If he is vanquished, the woman will be yours.'

There was no doubt that Father Orgeval had never uttered these last words, but Pont-Briand had never ceased to hear them ringing clearly through his head all the time the priest spoke.

'And what if she is really a She-Devil?'

'My prayers will protect you.'

The calm assurance of the Jesuit had won the officer over, and after handing over his outpost to his sergeant he had set off towards the south-east, accompanied by a single Huron.

In fact he was not really frightened of her being a demon, but just occasionally the love he felt for her was so strong that a shadow of a suspicion crossed his mind, a fear that he might in fact be bewitched.

Since his mission was under the protection of the celestial powers, he told himself from time to time that after all, there might be something rather exciting about making love to a demon.

He threw himself down on the mattress they had put out for him, but it was a long time before he fell asleep.

Father Orgeval's ingratiating voice went on reassuring him as he lay half-asleep.

'Believe me, she will welcome you as a saviour. I have heard that the man who calls himself her husband still leads and has always led the life of a libertine. He has brought the few families that make up a small Indian tribe in the region of Wapassou to live near by, so that he can have the Indian girls at his disposal, and although he has a white woman whom everyone says is most attractive with him there, he often visits these other girls and corrupts them. As far as these things are concerned, this buccaneer, it would appear, has always done exactly as he liked . . . and the unfortunate creatures who have become attached to him are to be pitied. . . .'

Father Orgeval always knew everything very quickly, and in spite of distance; he knew everything there was to know about everyone. Tell-tale indications, guesswork and a knowledge of psychology had something to do with his redoubtable gift.

His glance could pierce the secrets of a man's conscience. Many a time had he stopped a man in the street, and said to him: 'Go to confession quickly, you have just committed a sin of the flesh. . . .'

Whenever he was known to be in Quebec, men returning from visits to their mistresses would go to fantastic lengths to avoid running into him in some narrow street of the city. Furthermore he was said to be a protégé of the Pope and the King of France, and it was rumoured that the Jesuit Superior in Quebec, Father Maubeuge himself, had occasionally to bow to his decisions.

With such guarantees behind him, what fears need Pont-Briand have for his soul, his career, or the success of his love-affair? He had God and the Church on his side.

He fell asleep exhausted, but determined to triumph.

CHAPTER 52

On Angélique's return from the lakeside she entered the main room of the outpost. Then she had a good look at the leaves she had just picked, which had cost her many a scratched finger, not to mention the pain of the biting cold. They were from the bearberry, a small bushy plant with evergreen leaves. Its fruit, the arbutus-berry,

321

is precious, and its leaves likewise possess health-giving and diuretic qualities. Angélique hoped that it would help to cure Sam Holton's stone in the kidney. Poor Sam Holton, so timid and shy, it was just his bad luck to find himself suffering from this painful complaint. The brown girls from the beaver wigwam were in no way involved, for Sam was a chaste man and had never been seen making his way over to the other side of the mountain. But he had mistaken his symptoms for those attributed to the darts of Venus and Angélique had anxiously watched him wasting away, visibly in pain, without being able to find out from him what it was all about.

In the end the Count had to intervene. Forced to admit what was wrong, the puritanical Englishman had made his confession under the seal of silence. He thought he was being punished for some lapse in his youth, and Angélique had to arrange to treat him without his realizing that she knew. Fortunately she had remembered the bearberry bushes she had seen along the path by the lake where Pont-Briand had surprised her. She had brought some back then and today had returned to pick more.

She took her little cooking-pot, filled it with water and hung it up over the fire.

At this hour of the afternoon she was alone in the big room, and the door stood open, for the sun was shining brightly outside.

Count Peyrac had gone off with five or six men to the far end of the three lakes, near the waterfalls, to examine the damage caused to the Chilean mill by the pressure of the ice.

They would certainly not be back before nightfall.

The others were working in the mine or carrying out measurements upon the cliffs.

Eloi Macollet was tinkering about with something or other in the stable.

Monsieur Jonas had gone with the Count.

Immediately after lunch Angélique with her two women friends and the children had gone down to the lakeside to pick bearberry leaves. She wanted to make a highly concentrated drink from them, in the hope that it would dissolve the stones that were tormenting the unfortunate Englishman.

As soon as the basket was full, the children had urged her to go a little farther along the lake to a piece of sloping ground where they could toboggan down the packed snow, sitting on the dried animal skins which they used as sledges. Madame Jonas and Elvire went with them and Angélique returned to the outpost to prepare the medicinal brew.

The leaves had not been picked under ideal conditions, but there was nothing she could do about that! She had to manage as best she could.

She would add some beard of maize and some couch-grass roots.

She threw the stripped leaves into the boiling water, then cut up her couch-grass root, softened it a little in another container, threw away the first water, put it on to boil again, and finally pounded the fibres in her little lead mortar. Once again she put it on to boil, until the liquid had been reduced by half. She added this to the pot full of bearberry with the beard of maize. The concoction now looked blackish and unappetizing. Her only hope was that it would be effective. Angélique was not sure how much she should give Sam Holton, and had to trust her intuition and the memories of what she had learned from Savary and the sorceress Mélusine.

What a pity it was that she had left her recipe book in La Rochelle.

As she stood up she literally bumped into Lieutenant Pont-Briand, who had been standing right behind her. He must have come into the room without her hearing him.

'Oh! you!' she exclaimed. 'You are worse than an Indian! Worse than Sagamore Mopuntook or the old chief of the Beaver Wigwam; I tread on his feet every time he turns up here. I shall never get used to the way people have in this country of creeping up noiselessly on you.'

'The Indians appreciate the gift I have of moving about the way they do, which is something fairly rare among Palefaces.'

'You're a deceitful fellow,' said Angélique, sternly.

'It's risky to trust appearances. . . .'

Pont-Briand had not deliberately surprised her, for his silent tread had become second nature to him. But it certainly was unexpected in such a colossus whose gestures were so clumsy. On the other hand he had undoubtedly reckoned with the fact that she would be alone in the big room at that time and that he must approach her now or never.

He had watched her from the threshold, as she stood surrounded by medicinal vapours, handling her herbs and cooking-pots with an expression of concentration that made her big, gentle lips take on a look of severity.

This was an expression he had not seen on her before and, as she stood there in the glow of the fire, amid her utensils and the hot, dark liquid, she caused him no small feeling of anxiety. Pont-Briand approached her, his heart beating a tattoo.

'Is there anything you want?' Angélique asked as she began to tidy her utensils.

'Yes, you know there is . . .'

'Please explain . . .'

'You are surely not unaware, Madame, that you have inspired me with a devouring passion.' He was panting with emotion. 'It was on your account that I came here . . .' And he tried to explain his aspirations to her, how for the first time in his life he had met a woman who appeared worthy of love. . . . Yes, of love. . . . Purified of its coarsest aspects. . . . He repeated the astonishing word love to himself, and it made him feel like weeping.

'You are stupid,' she replied indulgently. 'Yes! Yes! you are! Believe me. But what does it matter anyway?' she replied impatiently. 'Has it ever occurred to you, sir, that I was not born into this world to satisfy your military nostalgia when you happened to feel sentimental. I have a husband, and children, and you must realize that the only part you have to play in my life is that of a guest whom I have welcomed as a friend. But if you continue to behave in this way you will lose my friendship.'

She turned her back on him to indicate that he should not persist, and that she considered the matter closed.

She did not like his type of man, fairly commonly found among officers, the colossus with feet of clay. Their only qualities lie in the strictly masculine domain of war, but in the presence of women their clumsiness is only equalled by their fatuousness. They are convinced of their own irresistibility, and consider that any woman who has been fortunate enough to catch their fancy must inevitably belong to them, and they fail to understand why the women do not always respond.

Pont-Briand was no exception to this rule. He would not take no for an answer, and the urgency of the desire that tormented him as he stood so close to Angélique made him almost eloquent. He told her that he needed her. That she was not like other women. That he had never stopped dreaming about her, her beauty, her laughter, that she was like a light that shone through the night. . . . She could not rebuff him, it was impossible. . . . He might die tomorrow. . . . But before being roasted alive by the Iroquois, let her at least grant him the delights of her white skin. He had not tasted white skin for so long. These Indian women had no souls. They stank. . . . Oh for a white woman again. . . .

'And so you have chosen me to satisfy your need for some white skin again, have you?' Angélique asked, unable to restrain her mirth at his clumsiness and naïvety. 'I don't know whether I should regard it as flattering...'

Pont-Briand grew scarlet as she mocked him.

'I didn't mean that...'

'Monsieur, you are a bore.'

Pont-Briand looked like a child who had been rebuked. All the gentleness he had felt in her had been transformed into needle-sharp points. He could not understand it.

He could never give her up. He had never been able to control his sensuality, and was utterly blinded by his imperious need to take her in his arms and make her his by force. As he looked over Angélique's shoulder he noticed a half-open door and a big wooden bed.

His hunger for her, and the uniqueness of this opportunity, made him cast all restraint to the winds.

'Listen, my love, we are alone. Come with me into that room. I shall be quick, I promise. But afterwards, you'll see! You will understand then that we must love each other. You are the only woman in the world to have ever made me feel as I do now. You must be mine.'

Angélique, who was picking up her coat to leave the room and cut the interview short, looked at him speechless, as if he were out of his mind.

She did not have time to give him the curt reply she had intended for he threw his arms round her and pressed his lips to hers. She was unable to disengage herself immediately, for he was very strong and in a frenzy of passion. His lips forced hers open and this contact, reminding her as it did of other beastly men with slobbering mouths who had forced and sullied her, made her feel sick and filled with a sudden deadly rage.

At last she wrenched herself free and, grabbing a poker from behind her where it stood propped against the chimney, she brought it down with all her strength on the lieutenant's head. The blow on Pont-Briand's skull made a dull thud. He saw stars, staggered, and fell all of a heap into a world of star-spangled blackness.

When he came round he found himself lying on a bench. His head ached but he became immediately aware of the soft cushion upon which it lay. It was Angélique's lap. He looked up and saw a face bending over him with an expression of concern. She was dabbing a wound on his head, which she had laid on her knees, and he could feel the warmth of her body through her woollen clothes. He was very close to her bosom, and felt an urge to turn his head towards her soft, warm belly and hide his face in it like a child, but he resisted the temptation.

He had done enough stupid things already for one day. So he closed his eyes and gave a deep sigh.

'Well?' she asked, 'how do you feel?'

'Pretty awful. You've got some strength in that arm of yours.'

'You're not the first drunk I've had to deal with. . . .'

'I wasn't drunk.'

'Yes you were.'

'Then it must have been your sensuous beauty that went to my head. . . .'

'Don't start raving again, you poor man.'

Angélique felt a certain remorse at having dealt with him so harshly. A slap on the face would have been enough. . . .

But she had been unable to restrain herself.

'What's all this crazy notion of yours to go and get enamoured of me?' she asked reproachfully. 'Prudence alone ought to have stopped you. Did it not occur to you that my husband might take umbrage at your behaviour?'

'Your husband? Pooh! People say he isn't really your husband!'

'Yes he is. That I swear on the heads of my two sons.'

'Then I hate him even more. It's not fair that he is the only one who is allowed to love you.'

'The laws of exclusivity were instituted by our Holy Mother the Church herself.'

'They are iniquitous and unjust laws.'

'Tell that to the Pope. . . .'

Sulking and miserable, Pont-Briand felt completely sober once more. My oath! She had almost killed him! But at the same time, with mingled admiration for her and pity for himself, he began to tell himself once more that she really was an exceptional person, and he would have liked to have prolonged their quarrel in order to be able to remain pressed up against her bosom, breathing in the close perfume of her breasts and her arms.

But Angélique stood up, and helped him to rise to a seated position. He was unsteady on his feet and, realizing that all was finally over, he felt a great weariness and unhappiness flood over him.

'Monsieur de Pont-Briand?'

'Yes, my love.'

He looked up at her. She was examining him with a serious, motherly look.

326

'Do you perhaps not drink too much? Or do you chew some of those Indian grasses that are said to be narcotic?'

'Why do you ask me that?'

'Because you are not behaving normally.'

He gave a short laugh:

'How could you expect me to behave normally when the loveliest woman in all the world has just hit me over the head?'

'No, I mean before that ... ever since you got here.'

She looked at him in perplexity. Pont-Briand was one of those people who display mingled naïvety, pride and an immeasurable degree of indulgence towards their own passions.

This type of man is of low intelligence, and easily hypnotized by ideas he fails to understand, or by others of greater willpower. Hypnotized? A suspicion crossed her mind but she was unable to define it.

'What is the matter?' she went on in a friendly manner. 'Tell me?'

'But you know,' he moaned, 'I am in love with you.'

She shook her head.

'No! Not enough to behave in such an idiotic way. What else is wrong?'

He did not reply, and laid two fingers on his temple with an expression of suffering. Then suddenly he felt like crying. He was beginning to understand what had happened to him.

He had indeed been tormented with love for her, ever since he had met her, but since when was it that the feeling had grown intolerable? Had it not become intolerable since the Jesuit's visit? It was as if his voice had never ceased to hammer through his head: 'Go on . . . go on . . . the woman will be for you.' And in the depths of the night, those blue eyes, as brilliant as sapphires, never left him. He was beginning to understand. He had been sent to perform a task in which he was a mere instrument. He had been sent to ruin the woman he loved by degrading her, and to ruin Peyrac through her.

And now that he had failed, he found himself stripped of everything. Poor fool. A poor, lost fool.

Either way, he was lost. Even if he had succeeded. Especially if he had succeeded. He had been sent to his death. . . . He suddenly realized in a flash that he had only a few more hours to live....

'I am leaving,' he said as he stood up, with a haggard look.

He staggered over to the recess where he had slept, picked up his mittens, his jacket and his fur cap, put them on and came back carrying his haversack.

327

'Let me put some food in it,' said Angélique, disturbed at the idea that he was about to spend many long days alone with his Huron in the wilds of an ice-bound, hostile nature.

He watched her, caring little, and his mind was filled with bitter thoughts. Failure lay everywhere, before him and behind him. In the harsh light that had suddenly flooded his mind, various incidents came back to him and he realized that he had never really appealed to women as he had once imagined. Things would always end in scenes in which they told him he was being a pest and that they had had enough of him. Whereas a man like Joffrey de Peyrac for example was never a pest! A new wave of anger began to surge up within him.

As he reached the threshold he felt he wanted to take revenge on all womankind by attacking this one, and wounding her who had inflicted so many wounds on him. He spun round.

'Do you love your husband?' he asked.

'Yes, of course I do,' she murmured in surprise.

He burst into a peal of sardonic laughter.

'Well, that's your bad luck. Because it doesn't stop him going off and seducing the Indian girls. There are a couple of them out there in the forest whom he fetched here specially so that he could have a bit of fun with them when he grew tired of kissing you. How silly you are not to enjoy yourself with anyone who comes along, and to keep yourself for that rake who is busy deceiving you. You may not know about it, but the whole of Canada does. . . . And the men here laugh about it and make fun of you! . . .'

As if summoned by some invisible signal, the Huron appeared at his side and set off behind him.

CHAPTER 53

'HE'S GONE,' Angélique told the others on their return. And she looked away.

Joffrey de Peyrac came up to her. As he was accustomed to do after any fairly long absence, he took her hand and kissed the tips of her fingers.

But she evaded this furtive token of homage.

'Gone!' Malaprade exclaimed indignantly. 'With night about to fall and a blizzard threatening! And without saying good-bye to anyone! Whatever got into him? He's crazy! I must say, these Canadians are a mad lot. . . .'

Angélique set about the tasks of the evening. She called Florimond to her and quietly asked him to take the cup of herb tea over to Sam Holton. She had put some molasses into it and a little sugar to make the medicine drinkable, and Florimond was to encourage the Englishman to drink it while prattling on to him about anything that came into his head in order to calm his suspicions. Then she helped Madame Jonas set the bowls on the table and hung out the wet coats in front of the second fire.

She did everything she had to do with diligence and apparent calm, but her mind was in a turmoil.

The hours that had passed since Pont-Briand's departure had wrought havoc within her.

Her mind no longer dwelt on the lieutenant's declarations, but rather on the poison dart he had hurled at her as he stood, about to depart, on the threshold, a dart whose venom had slowly seeped through her veins.

At first Angéique had shrugged her shoulders when she heard Pont-Briand tell her that her husband had been deceiving her with the Indian girls in the small neighbouring camp. Then suddenly her day-to-day life had seemed to take on a new turn, and she asked herself, as a sudden flush rose to her cheeks, if after all, the idea was all that implausible. It had never crossed her mind that Joffrey might have been amusing himself with the Indian girls, although the Count paid frequent visits to the chief of the tribe, and she had noticed the way the two girls Argeti and Wannipa behaved when they were near him. They gave him the glad eye and he answered them gaily in their own language, chucking them under the chin and giving them presents of beads, as if they were spoilt children. Was it not possible that all these innocent exchanges were intended to cloak a dubious familiarity the significance of which had escaped her?

She had always been somewhat naïve when it came to detecting intrigues, and in this kind of misadventure those most involved were always the last to be informed.

After Pont-Briand had left, she had gone to the store to fetch some beads with which she intended to make a necklace for Honorine to give her at Christmas.

But her hands were feverish; she made no progress with what she was trying to do and from time to time she shrugged her shoulders as if to shake off some unwanted thought.

329

And the idea grew within her. She began to feel the sensation of separation from her husband which she always felt whenever she thought of all the unknown facets of his character. His independence had always been an important element in his make-up. Was he to renounce it because he had found a wife again whom he had managed to do without for fifteen years? After all he was the master, the one and only master on board, as he had occasionally declared.

He had always been free, with a freedom that went beyond scruples. He feared neither sin nor hell. His self-discipline was based on other laws. . . .

Then suddenly she felt so dreadful that she got up, dropped her work, and ran off towards the wood as if in flight.

The snow made it impossible for her to go far. She could not even walk for miles through the woods to calm her state of agitation. She was a prisoner. So she returned and began to exhort herself to be reasonable.

'That's life,' she told herself, repeating without realizing it the disenchanted phrase used by poor girls who have reached the limits of their courage and see that they cannot win.

'That's life for you, you see!' the Polak, her friend at the Court of Miracles used to say to her ten times a day. 'Men are like that.'

Men do not have the same conception of love as women. A woman's way of loving is full of illusions, of dreams, of unreasonable sentimental aspirations.

What had she imagined? She had thought that behind their caresses lay bonds forged anew, something that could only exist between him and her, that this feast of their senses was the evidence that their two bodies had chosen each other, that they could never grow tired of each other or be separated, a symbol of a loftier harmony between their hearts and their minds.

She had believed in an impossible miracle. That harmony was so rare. And what had once been granted to them could no longer exist since they had both changed so much in the years of their separation. She could hardly accuse Joffrey of failing to do something he had probably never intended to do. And was it not unreasonable to call his philandering with the savage girls unfaithfulness.

She must hide her bitter disillusionment. He would tire of a jealous, possessive wife. But for her, the light had gone out, and she wondered how she would manage to carry on.

The most detailed of arguments were as nothing before a certain precise vision that tormented her. She saw him laughing with the savages, caressing their tiny breasts, finding pleasure in penetrating their supple bodies with their strong, primitive smell, and these visions made Angélique shudder, for they hurt her physically as well as wounding her pride.

This was something that men never understood — a woman's pride. She could be hurt but she was also sullied. Impossible to explain why, but that was how it was! And they did not realize....

The children had come home squealing shrilly after their walk and their games. They told her all about their adventures. They had sledged down the hill at a fantastic speed, had seen the footprints of a white hare, and Madame Jonas had fallen into a snowdrift. It had been very hard to get her out. They were all more or less soaked, and she had to remove their shoes and their clothes, put their coats to dry, wrap the children in blankets, and put them in front of the fire with bowls of hot soup.

Honorine's cheeks were as red as lady-apples, and she was very excited.

'I sledge fastest, Mummy! Listen, Mummy...'

'Yes, I'm listening,' Angélique replied, her mind elsewhere.

She had begun to think about Pont-Briand again. There was something about him that reminded her of the red-headed ogre who had been put to guard her in the château of Plessis-Bellière, where the King had held her prisoner. What was his name again? She could not remember. He too had grown mad with desire for her and had been scarcely more subtle than Pont-Briand in expressing his feelings. Every evening he used to come and knock at her door and make a thorough nuisance of himself....

She had always felt sure that it was he who had fathered Honorine, that night of the rape. And Pont-Briand reminded her of him. This memory alone sent a spasm of revulsion surging up into her throat.

When the men returned later they were ferociously hungry and were given a meal of dried meat and maize griddle-cakes.

Angélique burnt her fingers as she turned the griddle-cakes over in the ashes.

'What a silly I am!' she exclaimed, her eyes shining with tears she was unable to contain.

Apart from this incident, she managed to carry out her tasks throughout the evening without faltering. She lit the lamps one by one, a job she enjoyed. The light from the oil lamps was reddish and dim. It was a soft, mysterious light, a light that made them all instinctively speak more softly.

But all the same Angélique dreamed of having candles, which were more elegant and gave a whiter, stronger light.

'You ought to make us some candle moulds,' she said to the blacksmith. 'We could fill them with beeswax, although it isn't easy to come by in the forest here.'

'The missionary who was on the banks of the Kennebec, Father Orgeval,' said Eloi Macollet, 'I know he used to make green candles with vegetable wax he got from some berries the Indians used to bring him.'

'Oh! That's very interesting.'

She talked for a while with the old trapper then went off to put Honorine to bed, who was exhausted. She helped serve at table and eventually felt quite pleased that she had managed not to show how wretched she felt.

Was Joffrey de Peyrac taken in? At times he seemed to look at her inquisitively, but he could not guess what she was going through and she would say nothing to him. No! nothing. She had made up her mind about that.

But when the time came to go to their room Angélique felt panic-stricken. How she regretted that evening that they did not live in a vast château where she would have been able to retire to her rooms under pretext of a headache in order to escape his presence as well as his embraces.

Once in the room she knelt down before the hearth and rekindled the fire with feverish gestures. She wished it was very dark so that Joffrey could not see her face.

The whole of that evening she had been playing an unbearable part. Gone were all her good resolutions. In fact they were of no use.

Once in bed she lay as close to the edge as she could, turning her back on him and feigning sleep.

But this evening he did not, as she had hoped, pay any attention to her weariness.

She felt his hand on her naked shoulder and, not daring to arouse his suspicions by any unusual behaviour, she turned towards him and forced herself to put her arms round his neck.

Oh, why did she need him so much! Never had she been able to forget him, and the love she felt for him was woven into the very fabric of her being. What would become of her if she found she could not accept things as they were. She must do her utmost to prevent him growing suspicious.

'You're far away, darling, aren't you?'

Leaning over her, he interrupted his caresses as he questioned her gently. She cursed herself for having found herself unable to respond to him.

'You're a long way off, aren't you?'

She felt that he was watching her, and began to panic. He would not allow her to remain silent. He persisted in his questions.

'What's wrong? You were not yourself this evening. What's happening? Tell me....'

She blurted out:

'Is it true that you go to see the Indian girls? Is it true that they are your mistresses?'

He did not reply immediately.

'Whoever put such a ridiculous idea into your head?' he asked at last. 'It was Pont-Briand, wasn't it? He considered himself on sufficiently good terms with you to give you that kind of warning, did he? Don't imagine that I haven't noticed his passion for you. He tried to make up to you, didn't he? Did you listen to him?'

His fingers suddenly tightened about her arm until he hurt her.

'Did you encourage him? Did you flirt with him?'

'Me flirt with that boor?' Angélique cried with a shudder. 'I would rather I were as ugly as the seven deadly sins if it would save me from men like him. ... Do you imagine that a woman is always to blame whenever some stupid fool tries to make advances to her? And what about you? You knew Pont-Briand would make up to me and you went off on purpose just to see how I would behave, just to make sure I wasn't going to jump at the first man to make advances to me, as no doubt you imagine I did during the fifteen years I spent alone, always alone, and so much alone. Oh, I hate you, you don't trust me!'

'Neither do you me, so it seems! What have the Indian girls got to do with all this?'

Angélique's anger had evaporated.

'Oh, I suppose he said that just to hurt me, to take revenge on me because I would have nothing to do with him.'

'Did he try to take you in his arms? Did he try to kiss you?'

In the darkness she could not see Peyrac's face but she guessed that it must look far from reassuring. She made light of what had happened.

'He went on, so I was a bit ... er ... rough with him. He realized it was no good and so he left....'

Joffrey de Peyrac was breathing very hard.

333

So Pont-Briand had tried to kiss her, now he was sure of it. He had laid his lips on hers with all the brutality of a trooper.

He himself was not free of responsibility in all this. Although he had not gone off on purpose, as Angélique accused him of doing, had he not unconsciously taken advantage of the situation created by Pont-Briand's arrival? Had he not allowed events to take their course and made use of the situation as an experiment? But you must not experiment with the heart and feelings of a woman as you can with retorts, stills and inert minerals. It was true that he sometimes had secret doubts about her, and now he was paying for them.

'Is it true?' she murmured, in a plaintive, unfamiliar voice. 'Is it true that you go to see the Indian girls?'

'No, my love,' he replied with grave insistence. 'Whatever would I want Indian girls for when I've got you?'

She gave a brief sigh and seemed to relax. Joffrey de Peyrac was furious.

Wherever did Pont-Briand dig up such a horrible idea? Were people gossiping about them in Canada? Who was?

He leaned over Angélique to try to clasp her to him again.

But although she felt easier about his alleged infidelity, she still felt remote from him.

She tried to take a grip on herself but she had been too upset throughout the day. She had abandoned too many hopes to find it possible to muster them all once more. And above all she had summoned up too many memories, too many repulsive faces. . . . Among others, the face of Montadour who looked like Pont-Briand. . . . There, she had remembered his name again, the name of the red-headed ogre . . . Montadour . . . Montadour. . . .

And when her husband sought to take her in his arms again she grew rigid.

Peyrac felt a furious desire to strangle Pont-Briand and all military men with him. What had happened was no unimportant skirmish which an experienced woman could take in her stride, as he had at first thought.

The incident had reopened old wounds which were scarce healed and he was all too bitterly aware of the rancour she probably felt towards him. It was one of those brief moments when a man and a woman confront each other, with all their opposing forces bristling, in a kind of incurably fierce hatred. She was unwilling to submit to him, while he on his side felt he must vanquish her to make her his again, for, if they were not able to come together again this evening, Angélique's allusive and somewhat mysterious nature ran the risk of becoming still more distant from him and escaping from him altogether.

He felt her delicate hands push spasmodically against his shoulders to thrust him away from her, and he clasped her all the more closely, incapable of letting her go and leaving her alone. For even if Angélique's mind was wandering far from him in a desert of solitude, her body lay there close to his lips, and Peyrac was under the spell of her beauty although her body recoiled under his kisses; he was both annoyed by the way she shrank back, and at the same time found his desire for her all the greater.

Desire, which has always been the driving force behind man's need to conquer woman, can occasionally be an embarrassment. It weighed heavy on his loins, encouraging him to acts of violence which he had difficulty in controlling.

In addition he was spurred on by the thought of all those who had touched her and possessed her. He was a man who had seen a great deal of life, and he was very much aware of one of the reasons men found her so attractive, which was something that left those who had known her, in the biblical sense of the term, with an incurable longing. The fact was that she was marvellously made for love. She was one of those women of whose bodily perfections the Master of the *Art of Love* had written 'they possess the key to multiple pleasure', those daughters of Venus whose embrace is warm and close and whose instinctive skill is the equal of their natural endowments. He had discovered this the very first time they had made love. 'She's a little wanton who doesn't know it yet,' he had thought to himself in amusement, surprised at finding such perfection in her virgin body as he had by no means always encountered in the most accomplished courtesans.

This wonderful body, created for man and his pleasure, had kept its powers intact, and fifteen years later Peyrac had been surprised and delighted to experience the same marvellous sensations once more.

And that night on the Atlantic, he had realized that once again he would become her slave, as before, as had all the others, for he could not tire of her or forget her.

But if her body was intact, something else had been damaged. And Peyrac cursed life that had hurt her so, and all the memories that rose up on occasion, creating an impenetrable barrier between him and her. These were the thoughts that flashed through his head while every fibre of his body tensed itself in an irresistible desire to possess her, as he tried to draw her to him and overpower her. Never had he felt so fiercely, so jealously that she was his, and that for nothing in the world was he prepared to leave her outside himself, to abandon her to others, to herself, to her thoughts and her memories.

He had to take her almost by force.

But as soon as he had begun to possess her, his anger and violence abated. It was not just to satisfy his own desire that he had, that evening, taken advantage somewhat roughly of his marital rights. He must take her with him on a journey to Cythera, for when they came back together the shadows that loomed over them now would have vanished.

There is no more magical remedy to rancour, doubts, or distressful notions than a successful trip for two to the island of love.

He knew how to bide his time. There would be no egoistic haste, no embarkation during the storm.

A shaman he had known in the East Indies during some of his earliest travels through those countries where the art of love is taught in the temples had told him the two greatest virtues of the perfect lover, which are patience and self-control, for women are slow to reach the peaks of pleasure. When a man is strongly attracted to a woman this often involves a certain sacrifice on his part, but surely he is amply rewarded by that marvellous awakening of a quiescent body?

As soon as he felt her relax a little, and begin to heave and tremble less, as if blinded, he began to stimulate her gently. He had clasped her lovely legs around him which was already a position of greater surrender, of greater dependence, and he could hear her heart thudding irregularly against his chest. The heart of a small, terrified animal. So from time to time he sought the freshness of her lips in a light, comforting kiss. And in spite of the yoke of pleasure that thrilled him to the very marrow of his bones and sent great shudders down his spine, he did not let himself go.

Never, never would he leave her alone again by the wayside. She was his wife, his child, part of his very flesh.

And Angélique, her heart tormented with anger and uncontrollable rancour, began to grow aware of him leaning over her with attentive curiosity. His presence within her did her good, like a soothing balm that radiated gently through her limbs to the very depths of her body. Tempted to give herself up to this feeling of well-being, she stilled the noisy voices in her mind that prevented her enjoying it. But, scarcely had she begun to achieve this, than the voices would start their noisy cackle again and the delicate sensations would vanish.

She rolled her head from side to side with impatience.

Then he withdrew from her and it was as if she had been stripped of everything, the agony of the void was enough to make her cry out, and she felt empty, and tense in her painful appeal to him; she herself moved towards him and his return brought her such relief that she clasped him to keep him where he was and he felt the light touch of her fingers on his hips, on his loins, a great delight to feel her eagerness once more.

'Don't leave me,' she moaned. 'Don't leave me . . . forgive me but don't leave me . . .'

'I shan't leave you . . .'

'Be patient . . . please, be patient . . .'

'Don't be anxious, I couldn't be better as things are . . . you're so wonderful, my love, I could spend my life here! Now be quiet, and don't think of anything.'

But he continued to torment her by moving away from her, and seemed to want to prolong her anticipation. As he leaned over her in trembling expectation he scarcely brushed her with some insidious, burning caress, which did not satisfy her but awakened all kinds of new sensations in her body, some sweet, some agonizing in their intensity, while uncontrollable shudders coursed through her body, sweeping in great waves to the very tips of her nails and the roots of her hair! How could she have felt so rebellious this evening? What had men done to her in days gone by? Ah, please let him not leave her now, please let him not grow weary. . . .

And she began to grow impatient with her own body, not because it was insensitive, but because it was contrary and refused to submit and remained obstinately unwilling to capitulate. Joffrey calmed her with a word. He never grew weary, for she was as dear to him as his own life and he was constantly aware, like a dart within him, of the strength of his attachment to her, while the joy of triumph began to spread through his veins. For now he could see that she was entirely taken up with the voluptuous struggle going on within her, which he stirred up ceaselessly. Those gentle spasms that ran over the surface of her satiny skin, that twitching of her lips and throat as she gasped for breath, then suddenly he caught a glint of her little white teeth clenched, this was the sign that she had ceased to be alone, and that once again he had led her on to those luminous strands, far from the icy chasm. And he laughed as he saw her suddenly place the back of one hand over her mouth to stifle a moan. Women are so sweetly modest. . . . In the midst of the most blinding ecstasy, the slightest sound, a mere rustle or creaking puts them on the alert. . . . They are terrified of being surprised, of betraying their abandon.

337

Yes, they are strange, fugitive, difficult creatures, but what rapture to captivate them, to tear them from themselves and to bring them, half-dead with delight, to the forbidden shores. With Angélique he experienced indescribable sensations, for she gave him back a hundred-fold everything he lavished on her. And Angélique lay there, wanting to beg for mercy, and yet not wanting to, for he knew how to move her in a thousand different ways and she was defenceless before his skill as a lover; then at last she joined with him in the deep, powerful wave of love that swept them both up towards the peaks of their mutual delight. She was filled with adoration for him and entirely absorbed with the promise that rose within her and whose fulfilment she now cried out for. He spared her no longer, for now they shared the same passion and haste to reach the shores of the enchanted isle.

Swept along by an irresistible and violent tide, the two of them gained the shore and, closely intertwined, were driven together up on to the golden sands; he, suddenly aggressive in all the tension of the final onslaught, while she collapsed, languid, in an endless, delicious, ecstatic release....

And they were astonished, when they opened their eyes, to find that there was neither golden sand nor blue sea ... Cythera ... Land of lovers! It can be reached from any clime!

Peyrac raised himself on one elbow, while she lay there, still far away, with a dreamy expression on her face and the dying glimmer from the fire glowed beneath her half-closed eyelids.

He saw her lick the back of her hand in a reflex action, where she had bitten it earlier on, and this animal gesture moved him once again.

Man wants a woman to be either a sinner or an angel. A sinner to give him pleasure, and an angel so that she can love him with un-swerving devotion. But the eternal feminine foils his plans, since for her there is neither sinner nor saint. She is Eve!

Eve our saviour!

He twisted her long hair about his neck and laid one hand on her warm belly. This night might well bear new fruit....

He did not reproach himself for his imprudence. You cannot always be prudent when it is a question of saving something essential that exists between two hearts, and she herself had made it clear what she wanted at the crucial moment.

'Well now, what about these savages?' Peyrac murmured.

338

She gave a start, laughed softly, and turned her head towards him in a languid gesture of submission.

'How could I have thought such a thing about you? I can't imagine . . .'

'You little silly, is it as easy as that to fool you in matters of the heart? And you actually suffered torments because of it? Have you so little faith in your power over me? Whatever do you imagine I'd see in Indian girls? I don't deny that those smelly little grass-snakes can on occasion be quite fun, but what could they possibly offer me when I have you? My goodness, do you take me for the god Pan or one of his cloven-footed acolytes? Where and when do you imagine that I find time to make love with anyone other than you? Lord, how stupid women are!'

Dawn was still a long way off when Count Peyrac rose noiselessly from his bed. He dressed, buckled on his sword, lighted a dark-lantern, and slipped out of the room and crossed the big room to the alcove where Porguani the Italian slept. After a rapid confabulation in low voices, he returned to the big room, and lifted up some of the curtains and fur screens behind which his companions lay stretched in a deep sleep. Having found the man he sought, he shook him gently to waken him. Florimond opened one eye and, by the light of the lantern, saw his father's face smiling warmly at him.

'Get up, my boy,' said the Count, 'and come with me. I want to teach you what a debt of honour is.'

CHAPTER 54

ANGÉLIQUE stretched languorously, astonished that day should have followed so swiftly upon night. She had slept the whole night through without waking.

An indefinable feeling of joy flooded through her hazy mind and weighed down her limbs.

Then she remembered. First she had felt doubt and fear, had known black thoughts and distress, and then it had all evaporated in Joffrey de Peyrac's arms. He had refused to allow her to fight on alone, and had forced her to take refuge in him, and it had been wonderful. . . .

Her hand hurt her. She looked at it in astonishment, saw that it

339

was wounded and remembered what had happened. She had bitten it to stifle her moans as they had made love.

Then, half laughing, she curled up beneath the furs. Snuggling down into the warmth of the bed, she thought about some of the things she had done and said during the night. The movements people make, the words they utter almost without hearing them in the mystery of the shadows and the ebullience of pleasure, words that later make you blush. . . .

What was it he had said to her during the night? 'You are so perfect in the ways that matter, my love! I could spend my life here. . . .'

Remembering his words, she smiled and ran her hand over the empty place in the bed beside her where he had lain.

Thus it is that in the life of a couple, these nights of purple and gold stand out as landmarks in their lives, and these nights mark them secretly, sometimes even more permanently than the noisy events of their days.

When Angélique joined her friends in the big room, full of remorse at being so late to take up her household tasks, she learned that Monsieur de Peyrac had left the fort, early that morning, accompanied by Florimond. They had donned snowshoes and taken enough food for a longish journey.

'Did he say which way he was heading?' asked Angélique, surprised at his decision to set off without revealing anything to her.

Madame Jonas shook her head, but in spite of her denials, Angélique had the impression that the good lady had her suspicions about this unexpected expedition. She looked away and glanced knowingly at her niece.

Angélique questioned Signor Porguani, but he knew as little as the others. Monsieur de Peyrac had come to him very early that morning to tell him that he would be away for a few days, in spite of the cold.

'Did he say nothing else?' Angélique cried in alarm.

'No, he just wanted to borrow my sword. . . .'

She felt herself grow pale, and stared at the Italian. She decided to say no more, and went off. Everyone set about their work and the day passed like all the others of that quiet, hard winter. Nobody mentioned Monsieur de Peyrac's departure.

CHAPTER 55

THE CHASE that Count Peyrac and his son had embarked on demanded superhuman efforts of them, for Pont-Briand had set off half a day earlier and was himself hurrying.

They began to walk through part of the nights, when the air was so cold that it sometimes felt as hard as steel, as if it would crush them. They would bivouac as the moon began to wane, warm themselves up and sleep for a few hours, then would set off again as the sun rose. Fortunately, the tracks they followed remained fresh, the snow hard and the weather set fair.

The stars twinkled with particular brilliance, and with the help of his sextant the Count twice took the risk of leaving the trail left by those who went before them and cutting across country by another route that saved them several hours' walk. He and his men had made a very accurate survey of the region during the preceding year, and he knew by heart all the maps they had drawn up from the data they had obtained, including all that was relevant concerning tracks, portages and accessible routes which they had learnt from the Indians and the trappers. These maps, which Florimond, who was a good hand with a pen, brush and measuring instruments, had helped to make, were as important during the winter as they were during the fall, and explained the apparent imprudence with which they both, as newcomers to the country, had nevertheless set off on a journey that could have been considered sheer madness at this time of the year.

The irregular yet monotonous contours of the deceptive landscape beneath its uniform covering of snow and ice, its many pitfalls and its rare good points, all these were indelibly inscribed in his memory and in that of his young son. Nevertheless Florimond had shown a certain anxiety when, one moonlit night, they had left the visible trail that headed straight across a broad plain and cut across the plateau that rose up beside the plain, thus avoiding a long detour. This plateau was traversed by deep rifts, hidden beneath snow-laden trees, into which they could easily have fallen, but when dawn came, and they slid down from the heights, they found the bivouac where the Canadian lieutenant and the Huron had camped, and the hot ashes were evidence that the two men had only just departed. Then Florimond pushed back his fur cap and gave an admiring whistle.

'Father, I must admit that there were times when I felt that we were lost!'

'And why should we have been? Was it not you yourself who discovered that short cut? My son, never doubt figures or the stars. . . . They are the only things that NEVER lie. . . .'

After a short rest they set off again. They spoke little, conserving their strength for the almost superhuman efforts of the long walk, their feet clad in snowshoes made of rope, which were clumsy and impeded every step, and not adequate to keep them permanently on the surface of the soft, powdery snow. Each time a foot sank beneath the surface crust they had to lift it out by raising their knee, and, taking a further step, feel the snow give again under their weight. Florimond kept muttering about it, saying that someone ought to invent another way of walking on snow. The image he had of his father moving steadily and indefatigably forward must have been very like that which Lieutenant Pont-Briand had of him at that very moment. He strode on, a dark, implacable avenger, wtihout manifesting the slightest sign of weariness, and gave the impression that nature in all her ferocity, recognizing her master, had effaced herself, prostrate at his feet. The forest that seemed impenetrable from a distance had now been left behind, and the plain they thought they would never reach, they were now crossing and were almost at the farther side.

Florimond's muscles ached. He had thought himself young and strong, but now he realized how feeble his arms were when, in a space of twenty minutes, he was obliged to make the same muscular effort ten times to haul himself up out of a snowdrift by clutching the branches of a fir-tree. This was the fault of all that time he had wasted learning Hebrew and Latin in that grotto of prayer at Harvard. Enough to get a man completely out of training and make him lose the faculty of moving about in a land of ice. And meanwhile his father was moving forward exactly like a space-devouring machine, and if Florimond had ever in the arrogance of youth had any doubts about the toughness of a man like Peyrac, now he was finding out the answer the hard way.

'He is killing me,' he thought anxiously. 'If this goes on much longer I shall have to give up.'

He began to wonder how long his pride would enable him to carry on without admitting he was exhausted. He kept giving himself time-limits and was delighted when Peyrac said: 'Let's stop for a minute,' for the suggestion reached him just as he was about to fall to his knees. So he had the satisfaction of saying in an offhand way, although he sounded a bit breathless:

'Do we need to stop, Father? If you want to go on I can . . . still . . . perfectly well . . . go on a bit farther. . . .'

But Peyrac shook his head, said nothing, and recovered his breath with a kind of inner concentration that Florimond attempted to copy.

Truth to tell, as they sped on their way, the Count was scarcely aware of the feats he was performing. His strength and tenacity had been put to the test many a time, and his furious desire to catch up with his rival helped him to make light of the toughest stretches of the journey.

Like the man to whom he was giving chase, Angélique's image never left his mind. She spurred him on to greater speed, and kindled a fire in his heart that seemed to render him insensitive to the biting cold. And the thoughts that filled his mind kept him so busy that he crossed valley and mountains almost without being aware of the fact. Angélique's face shone like a vision before him in which he kept on discovering new charms. He had no sooner left her than she became still more powerfully present to his imagination. No sooner had the last reverberations of their voluptuous delights died down, than the mere memory of her asleep, as he had left her that morning in the cold light of dawn, with her head thrown back and her eyes closed, sent desire coursing through his limbs once more. This was yet another of Angélique's gifts; she could delight and utterly satisfy the man who desired her, yet he would never tire of her, so that no sooner had he left her side, than his desire and longing to be with her again, to look at her, to touch her and to make love to her once more fired his blood. She was for ever new. She fulfilled all hopes and never disappointed. And every time, it was like a new discovery that left one full of delight and enchantment. The freer he felt to enjoy her during the night, the less he felt able to deprive himself of this satisfaction.

The closer he lived to her, in the day-to-day life of the fort which they shared intimately, where he could see her living her life without pretence or dissimulation, the more her hold over him increased, through the charm of her whole personality. And the more it astonished him, for he had expected rather to be disappointed in her.

That she should have such powers, was this not something so strange that he ought perhaps to be a little wary of it? Of what secret craft, what fairy gifts given to her in her cradle, powers derived from a hidden, magic source, was she possessed?

Here he was, beginning to talk like the men of his century, who were so prone to attribute anything that they did not understand to a miracle.

From the very moment she had first set foot on American soil, all kinds of things had taken on a new dimension.

And the Canadians already saw her as the incarnation of the demoniacal vision that terrified them, a woman rising up over Acadia to bring about its downfall. . . .

Resist as he might, Joffrey de Peyrac was tempted to recognize the fact that Angélique, whom he had found again after fifteen years of absence, possessed extraordinary powers.

And if he himself could come to believe such things, he had to face the fact that, in these arid lands where the main, primitive, natural currents are more evident, a woman such as she was, because she had exceptional gifts, would, from her very appearance, come to be regarded with suspicion, even to the point of becoming a myth or a legend.

This was a common phenomenon in a land of mirages, a land where there were so many strange manifestations; sparks, coming from no one knew where, ran crackling over body or clothes, causing painful shocks; coloured lights appeared in the sky like some mysterious firework display; the sun hung for hours on end in the gathering darkness, then would suddenly vanish into the night. . . . The Canadians saw in these manifestations the appearance of burning canoes, bearing the souls of their dead, trappers or missionaries who had been tortured by the Iroquois, while the Puritan English would see a planet come to announce some terrible punishment for their sins, and they would begin to fast and pray. . . .

In such a continent, brutal and austere as it was, where truth was received with sharp directness, it was natural and inevitable that the aura that surrounded Angélique should arouse uncontrollably strong feeling. It was natural, he told himself, that once her pretty foot had lighted on the shore, her name should be on the lips of everyone from New England to Quebec, from the Great Lakes of the West to the Island of the Gulf of Saint Lawrence in the East, and indeed from the Valley of the Mohawks among the Iroquois, right over to the Nipissing and the Nadessioux along the frozen shores of the Bay of Saint James. But, although he understood the reason for these emotional extravagances, he fully recognized their dangers.

His work in the New World was made still more difficult now by this added conflict of which Angélique was the centre.

And with the insight of a heart that loves, he had immediately realized that Pont-Briand's arrival at Wapassou was the result of some plot, possibly still unformulated, but of far greater import than the amorous passion of this one man. Pont-Briand's wild wooing was nothing but a skirmish, a pretext, the advance-guard of something much more powerful, much more hostile, which, by attacking the privileged 'aura' of his wife, sought to work his ruin through her.

In placing her at his side he had exposed her to attack. He had revealed her, no doubt to a world as yet unready for this revelation, a world that would do its utmost to reject her at all costs.

From the moment when he had taken her hand, and had said to the people assembled on the beach at Gouldsboro: 'I present to you my wife, Countess Peyrac,' he had drawn her out of the shadows where, all alone, with the wiles, as it were, of a hunted creature, she had endeavoured to remain hidden; he had exposed her once again to the gaze of men, which could convey only love or hatred; for no one remained indifferent towards her.

Peyrac caught himself scanning the still whiteness, the frozen, blandly inhuman landscape, as if he could see his enemies gathering there, their faces still hidden, but implacable. By pressing on as he was doing, he was falling into the enemy trap; he was doing what he was expected to do, but nothing would stop him, for, at the heart of all these threats lay a woman who was his by inalienable right, a woman whom he knew to be fragile, in all the vulnerability of her womanhood, a woman he had to defend fiercely and unswervingly. . . .

'Father! Father!'

'What is it?'

'Nothing,' Florimond replied, his mind numbed with fatigue.

Seeing the face the Count turned towards him, with a gaze as hard as steel, the poor boy could not pluck up the courage to admit that his feet felt like lead. His father was the only person who sometimes put him out of countenance. And at the same time he could not help admiring this giant of a man, standing against the sombre, lowering sky, all grey and gold in the setting sun — his silver temples, his scar-lined face, which was sometimes forbidding. This was the man he had set out to seek across the ocean, the man who had not disappointed him, his father.

Count Peyrac set off again, unmindful of the hardships of the way. He was content to overcome them by the reflexes of his body that had been trained to endure the harshest fatigues, and his thoughts took up their monologue again, concerning the mysterious 'someone' who was bent on attacking him and her.

He did not yet know. Was it some dark earthly power, or some spiritual one, did it concern the defence of an idea, some mystical concept, or some sordid self-interest: was it some mass movement or the hostility of a single individual who stood as a symbol for all the others?

What was certain was that Angélique's presence, which had increased their mutual strength, had also marked them out to these destructive, negative forces, these forces that sometimes remain sleeping and neutral, only to be awakened in all their ferocity by some sudden extreme provocation.

And was not Angélique, so beautiful, so alive, a provocation, a challenge in herself?

Even if he were able to outwit his enemies, he knew that they would seek his downfall on her account. . . . It was almost as if he had entered into the mind of his unknown enemy and could guess his thoughts. . . .

He was forced to stop. And Florimond made the most of the halt to get his breath again and mop his brow.

Peyrac's brows puckered as he pondered over what he had just discovered. When Angélique had arrived in the New World she had stirred a most powerful enemy into action against her.

'Right,' he said between his teeth. 'We'll see.'

The words did not pass his lips, for they were so stiff with cold that they scarcely moved.

CHAPTER 56

THAT EVENING they again came upon a shelter that Pont-Briand had used. Beneath the thick branches of a pine-tree, protected by walls of driven snow, the ground, scarcely damp, was covered with dried moss, earth and pine-needles, and still bore the black traces of a fire. The area had been thickly carpeted with branches, and others had been woven into the archway over the camp so closely that the smoke from the fire Peyrac and Florimond lit could scarcely find a way through them. Peyrac cut a larger opening with his cutlass while Florimond huddled on the ground coughing, his eyes streaming from the smoke. He had not yet acquired the endurance of the Indians, who live almost permanently in a pungent, smoke-laden atmosphere and whose eyes seem to suffer no harm; even in the summer they light fires to protect them from mosquitoes and sandflies. But after a while the fire burned bright and clear, in this natural shelter afforded by the forest. There was no risk of the branches catching fire because of the snow piled up outside. Some of the needles were singed and crackled around the air hole as the flames occasionally licked it, and this created a pleasant aromatic smell. There was just room for the two of them to sit with their sacks, one on either side of it. It soon grew warm and Florimond's teeth stopped chattering, and he stopped grumbling and wiping his nose. As the blood began to flow again through his frozen fingers and toes he felt acute pain, but he resisted the temptation to grimace, for it would have been unworthy of a trapper to complain of such a thing when he was preparing himself to undergo torture at the hand of the Iroquois one day. The Count had placed a little lead pot of snow on the fire, and the water quickly boiled. After soaking some hips in it for a while he added a good measure of rum, which he had come to prefer to brandy from his Caribbean days, and a few lumps of crystallized sugar. The mere smell of the scalding drink brought Florimond to life again, and once he had drunk some he felt positively gay. In silence father and son devoured some maize biscuits, and, as a special treat, some slices of fat bacon and smoked meat. Then they ate dried fruit, some of the sour berries that Angélique occasionally handed out as solemnly as if they were nuggets of gold.

From time to time a heavy drop of water fell with a dull thud on to their thick clothes; it came from pieces of ice sticking to the pine-needles above them, which gradually melted in the warmth of the fire.

The difficulty was to keep enough wood under shelter to feed the vital flames. They could not use the dry fir cones that lay at the foot of the tree, for they made an infernal crackle, sent sparks flying in all directions, and burnt too quickly. With a few strokes of his hatchet Florimond had cut a bundle of wood from the lower branches of the neighbouring trees. The wood they brought in from outside was wet and sizzled, but gave off an even heat and no more than a tolerable amount of smoke. Florimond told himself that in the days when he used to dream about his father as he listened to the tales of old Pascalou in their house at Beautreillis,[1] he had felt his father closer to him than he did now that he was actually with him. And yet his meeting with him several years before had been very similar to what he had dreamed. In New England he had found a man of the sea, a great lord and a scientist who would teach him all he knew, and this was what he sought even more than his heart sought a father's love. When the Jesuits, with whom he had boarded for a time near Paris,

[1] See *Angélique and the King*.

347

had given a decidedly chilly reception to the wonderful inventions of Master Florimond, he could console himself by saying: 'My father knows much more than any of these . . . fools', and it was true. And if, now that they were actually face to face, Florimond sometimes felt paralysed and dumb with confusion, although he had been admitted to the intimacy of King Louis XIV and had looked down on such eminent professors, it was because he felt himself overwhelmed by the force of personality of this father whose great knowledge he discovered a little more of with every day that passed, not to mention his experience, and his exceptional physical endurance. Joffrey de Peyrac felt that his son thought of him less as a father than as a mentor, for when Florimond had set out to seek him he had been just on fourteen, and beginning to feel the need of someone he could confidently follow. Finding, among those who claimed this position, nothing but sophistry and fickleness, evasion, ignorance and superstition, he had fled from them all.

Whenever he looked at Florimond, Count Peyrac felt that he was looking back at the image of his own youth, as if faithfully reflected in a mirror. He saw in him the same admirable egotism of the lovers of Science and Adventure which renders them insensible to everything that does not contribute to the satisfaction of their consuming passion. Away with the affections of this world! . . . He remembered how he himself had left home at the age of fifteen, limping and jibed at for his ugliness and his uneven gait, to set off round the world. Had he given even a moment's thought to the mother he left behind him and who watched him set off, her only son whom she had snatched from the clutches of death?

Florimond was of the same stamp. He had the same easy-going emotional attitudes, which would enable him to reach the goals he set himself without allowing himself to be distracted. The only way he could be mortally wounded was by being denied the pursuit of knowledge, which his avid mind demanded. He sought the satisfactions of the mind much more than those of the heart.

As he reflected on his son's character, Peyrac thought that, once he had grown to be a man, and had finally broken away from his family, he might at times show himself insensitive or even hard. And that the more because he did not have to overcome his father's handicap of a scarred face and a deformed body. His good looks would smooth many a path for him. . . .

'Father,' Florimond said softly, 'you are much stronger than I am, you know. How did you become so tough?'

'A long life, my son, in which I have never had time to allow my muscles to grow rusty.'

'That's just the trouble,' Florimond cried. 'How could I train to walk and run in Boston where our only relaxation consisted of reading books in Hebrew?'

'Do you regret all you learned during those few months as a boarder?'

'I suppose not; I managed to read the book of Exodus in the original and my Greek came on a lot from studying Plato.'

'Good, and now in the school you're going to attend under my direction, you will have the opportunity to strengthen your body as well as your mind. Are you complaining that the training has not been tough enough today?'

'Heavens no,' Florimond exclaimed, for he was stiff from his head to his feet.

The Count curled up on the other side of the fire, leaning on his haversack. All about them the forest lay in an icy silence, punctuated by a myriad crackling sounds which they were unable to explain and which made them jump.

'You are stronger than I am, Father,' Florimond repeated.

The past few days had been a lesson for his easily satisfied vanity.

'Not in all ways, my lad. Your heart is untrammelled and serene. Your insensitivity protects you like armour and it will enable you to undertake certain things which I can no longer face since my heart is captive.'

'Do you mean that love makes one weaker?' asked Florimond.

'No, but being responsible for the loves of others is a fearful restriction on one's freedom, or what we call freedom during the springtime of our lives. You see, love, like all new knowledge, enriches us, but it is written in the Bible: 'He that increaseth knowledge increaseth sorrow.' Do not be impatient to possess everything, Florimond. But do not renounce anything that life has to offer you for fear that it may bring you suffering. The foolish thing is to want to own EVERYTHING at one and the same time. The art of living consists in replacing one strength by another. A young man enjoys his freedom, but an adult is capable of loving and it is a wonderful experience.'

'Do you think I shall ever experience it?'

'Experience what?'

'The love you're talking of.'

'It has to be deserved, my son, and it has to be paid for.'

'I expect so . . . and others have to pay for it too,' said Florimond, rubbing his aching shins.

Count Peyrac gave a hearty laugh. Florimond and he always

understood each other without having to spell everything out. Florimond laughed too and gave him a knowing look.

'You are more cheerful, Father, since you brought our mother back to us.'

'And you are gayer too, my son.'

They fell silent, thinking vague thoughts that included a vision of Angélique's face, thoughts that slowly crystallized around the man Peyrac was pursuing, the man who had come among them to do them wrong, like a wolf.

'Father, do you know who Lieutenant de Pont-Briand reminds me of,' Florimond said suddenly. 'He's more refined, less vulgar, I know, but he's the same sort of man all the same. It's a ghastly thought that he's just like Captain Montadour.'[1]

'And who was this Captain Montadour?'

'He was the swine whom the King set to guard our château with his militiamen, and who used to insult my mother by the very way he looked at her. Many a time I felt like running him through. But I was only a child and I could do nothing to defend her. There were far too many soldiers and they were far too powerful. . . . The King himself wanted to bring about mother's downfall and force her to surrender. . . .'

He lapsed into silence and drew around him the folds of his heavy cloak with its wolfskin lining. His silence lasted so long that Joffrey de Peyrac thought he had fallen asleep, but the lad suddenly went on:

'You say that my heart is still closed and insensitive, but that's where you're wrong, Father.'

'Really? . . . Are you in love by any chance?'

'Not in the way you mean it. But I have a wound in my heart that gives me very little peace, and for some time now I have been tormented with a terrible hatred. There it is! I hate the men who killed my little brother Charles-Henri. He was someone I loved. . . .'

He raised himself on one elbow and his eyes glistened feverishly as he held his face out towards the brightness of the flames.

'Yes, I was wrong,' the Count thought. 'His heart is alive.'

Florimond went on to explain.

'He was my half-brother, the son my mother had by Marshal du Plessis-Bellière.'

'I know.'

'He was an adorable child and I loved him. I am sure it was Montadour who killed him with his own hands to take vengeance on my

[1] *Angélique in Revolt.*

350

mother because she would have nothing of him. He was a man rather like that Pont-Briand who was strutting around a few days ago, pleased with his fine presence, and his jovial smile. . . . Exactly the same conceit! And when I think of Montadour, I begin to hate all swash-buckling ribald Frenchmen with their self-satisfied smiles. And yet I am French myself. Sometimes I feel angry with my mother for not having allowed me to take my little brother away with me on my horse; I could have saved his life. Of course he was very young. I don't know whether I could have saved him. When I think back, I see that I was only a child myself . . . I didn't think so at the time, but I was nothing but a bare-handed child . . . in spite of my sword. And my mother was even more defenceless. I could do nothing to defend her, to tear her away from her cruel tormentors. All I could do was to set off to find you. And now I have found you and we are both strong, you her husband and I her son. But it is too late, they had time to finish their cowardly work. And nothing can ever bring little Charles-Henri to life again. . . .'

'Yes, one day he may come alive again for you in a way.'

'How do you mean?'

'The day when you have a son yourself.'

Florimond stared at his father in surprise and gave a sigh.

'That's true! You are right to remind me of that. Thank you, Father!'

He closed his eyes and seemed weary. All the time he had been talking, he had spoken slowly in short phrases, as if little by little he were uncovering the truth he had not hitherto wanted to face. And for the Count too, it had been the lifting of one corner of the mysterious veil that hung over Angélique's unknown and cruel life that she had spent far from him. She never spoke of her child Charles-Henri. Out of tact towards him, no doubt, possibly also out of fear. But did her mother's heart bleed any the less for him than Florimond's?

Shame, anguish and a feeling of helplessness seared the young man's heart and Joffrey de Peyrac felt that they shared the same anger, as men who had been insulted, which had filled him ever since they had left the Fort of Wapassou to pursue Pont-Briand.

Their anger was almost of the same kind, the anger of wounded love, and took its roots in the same ancient, corrosive sources of a past in which both of them, the child and the man, had been rejected, betrayed and defeated. He leaned towards his son in an attempt to lighten the unbearable burden on his young heart, and to turn him from his bitterness towards action.

351

'You cannot always escape the harsh laws of trial and defeat, my lad,' he said. 'But the wheel goes on turning, and now, as you yourself have just said, we are strong, the two of us, and reunited. Now the moment of vengeance has at last come for you and me, my son. . . . Now at last we can reply to those insults, stand up for the weak, and give back the blows we have received. Tomorrow when we kill this man, we shall be avenging Charles-Henri; we shall be avenging your mother's humiliation. Tomorrow, when we kill him, we shall be killing Montadour. . . .'

CHAPTER 57

IT WAS IN the vicinity of Lake Megantic that they met.

During those winter days, when a thick crystalline veil about as deep as a child is high hovers over the surface of the lake, betraying the presence of the waters sleeping beneath the ice, no human cry could ring out in this region that was not immediately lost amid the infinite indifference of the plain. The trees, standing out dead above the frozen waters, are so many pillars of pure crystal, raising their branches hung with cut glass which the brightness of the air, rather than the pale sunshine, seems to set shimmering with flashing stars. These ice-covered giants stand alone in the kingdom of lakes, rivers, channels and marshland which the snow hides beneath a deceptive carpet of spotless velvet.

When summer and autumn come again, the Canadian gentlemen and their savages will set off once more from this land of waterways towards the south to add to their collection of scalps or indulgences in New England, saving their souls and their trade by spilling the blood of heretics. The brown, transparent course of the Chaudière brings them this far without any difficulty. Then, before making their way down the other side of the mountains, they halt and pray, singing hymns with their chaplains round vast camp fires.

Thus it was that when Lieutenant Pont-Briand picked out the Lake Megantic region from the top of a rock, in all its pale, shimmering desolation, so familiar to his Canadian eyes, the band of fear around his heart loosened a little and he breathed more freely. Now his own country, his land of Canada was near. The area was peopled with memories for him, for it was not so long since he had been there with Count Loménie, on the occasion of their return from the disastrous expedition to Fort Katarunk.

352

Yes, disastrous, he repeated to himself firmly, for it was his meeting with the people of Katarunk that had destroyed his peace of mind.

But not for anything on earth would he have missed that meeting. What he had felt ever since for this one woman had so enriched his life that the thought that he was henceforth to be deprived of it filled him with misery. No longer to be able to dream of her, no longer to be able to compare her with others the better to savour her beauty, to contemplate her and to adore her. In truth an inexplicable folly, but one that had meant much to him, and without which he felt himself incapable of survival, for, without her, life lost all its savour. She had become too much a part of his life during the past month. 'I shall go back,' he cried in despair. 'No, I can never give her up, never . . . never. . . . It is she I want. . . . I cannot die without possessing her. . . . If she was not to be mine, then why did she cross my path. . . .' And he kept on telling himself that her flesh had the savour of ripe fruit, sweet and full-flavoured, and that it would feed him, body and soul. He kept on thinking, not of the moment when he had taken her mouth by force, an action of which he felt ashamed, but of the moment at which he had regained consciousness and found his head lying on her knees against the motherly curves of her bosom. More than any gesture of consent might have done, the care and commiseration she had shown for him at that moment stirred him to the depths, so that he alternated between feelings of weakness and exaltation.

In his imagination he saw again the changed look that had come into her eyes, gentle and profound. He had felt the indulgence in her glance, of which he had felt unworthy, but which had been balm to his heart, and had heard her fascinating voice:

'Come now, what's wrong . . . You are not your usual self, Monsieur de Pont-Briand. . . .'

Furthermore, he knew that she was right. He had noticed it the moment she had looked at him with those wonderful eyes, eyes that seemed to see beyond him, eyes that had sensed something abnormal about him. He had known that he was the victim of a frightening will, that clung to him, that held his mind in thrall, that he could never throw off by his own unaided strength. In any case, the evil arranged in advance had in fact come about. He had played his part in it, but he had failed in his objective, and now he would be rejected and abandoned by everyone. He had left the camp staggering, briefly freed from the obsession of his thoughts by the blow he had received on the head, but the effect had very soon worn off and he had continued on his way haunted by the same fixed ideas as usual.

It was more an impression he had of her than a vision, like a sprite walking beside him, but one that had ceased to be entirely sexual and had been transformed into a more friendly, ethereal presence, more sympathetic to his distress, a presence he would talk to on occasion, softly.

'You, Madame . . . perhaps you could save me from him who directs and enslaves me. You might be able to help me to shake him off. . . . But, no, alas! that's impossible. He is stronger than you. . . . He possesses the very essence of Strength. . . . We can do nothing, can we? He is stronger than any of us.'

Sometimes he thought he could see the folds of her dress through the blueish branches of the trees. But they were always hazy and imprecise. Whereas the eyes he could see clearly were not those of the woman he loved, but blue eyes, gentle and smiling, yet strong and implacable. The voice he heard was warm and persuasive: 'The woman will be yours' . . . Pont-Briand burst into strident laughter that echoed through the petrified forest and across the pale valleys, and the Huron behind him looked askance at him with eyes like pools of black water. The lieutenant was muttering to himself and tittering.

'No, the woman will never be mine, Father . . . and you knew that before you sent me, you who know everything . . . oh Father! But it was worthwhile being tempted, wasn't it? And it was one way to attack the man you want to get rid of! The way to strike Peyrac in the heart! . . .'

Then, addressing the blue eyes:

'Why you, Father? And why me?'

He continued muttering as he plodded rhythmically on, his feet shod with snowshoes.

Another fear lurked within him as he continued his mad race. Had he reasoned things out, he might have told himself that Peyrac would not follow him, for he would never dare to set out across country at this time of the year. Only a man who had made many journeys in the area, as he himself had done, would risk such a thing. But something told him that Count Peyrac was capable of anything, and he thought of him as in magical alliance with the elements, a huge black figure moving swiftly on where ordinary men would flounder, overwhelmed and lost almost before they had set out.

How could he have been so crazy, so mad to have dared to defy such a man? He must have been out of his mind!

He had now reached the boundaries of Maine and stood looking down on the desolate region of Lake Megantic. It would take him another good week or even two to reach his fort, his friends, and safety! But by the relief he felt at having finished this first stretch of the journey, he had implicitly recognized that all the land that lay behind him to the south of the Appalachians already belonged to the man who had said: 'I shall make Maine my kingdom.' He recognized that he had reached the boundaries of Count Peyrac's land. Already he accepted the fact that these disputed territories lay under the sway of a conqueror who had taken their virginity, had penetrated on horseback to the very heart of the forests and the wild lakes, and had settled there, resolved to impose his law and economic prosperity. The fort of Wapassou, buried in the heart of the black rocks, was like a warship that had cast anchor, and the anchor was already embedded in the soil. It would be no easy matter to hoist it. The man who had cast it was not there by mere chance; he knew what he was about and he knew what he wanted. So true was this that all along the way Pont-Briand had been unable to escape the feeling that once he had reached Megantic he would escape Peyrac, since he would be outside his territory. And now here he was.

At last he had arrived, and stood leaning against a tree, grown insensitive in the transient death that winter brings, whilst the living man sighed convulsively, mingling hope with despair.

A few steps more and he would plunge down into the glistening mists of the plain, would be lost among the white shadows, would be hidden, gradually hidden from sight, and Peyrac would no longer be able to catch him. Still fleeing, he would reach the Saint Lawrence and the wooden fort, then the few villages built of stone around the pointed church tower, and a vast farm-house which he could enter and sit down beside the monumental hearth to eat a gargantuan hunk of salt pork washed down with burning brandy. But above all he would be safe, there in Canada....

But he would have lost the most precious part of himself, his dream torn to shreds on the branches of the dead trees, slashed to ribbons along the white trail....

He shook himself and gave an angry snort, sending the snow flying about him, like a moose whose weight had brought it down in a snowdrift, and who was unable to extricate itself again. He clung to the prosaic vision of an elm-wood bowl full of pea soup and salt pork, placed on his knees beside the great fireplace. But even that had a bitter taste after the happiness he had glimpsed. For at Wapassou also he had sat beside the fire, with a cheering bowl of hot soup, and a goblet of brandy in his hand, but then she had been there, just a few paces off, leaning over the glowing fire with her strong, golden arms. He had devoured her with his eyes, and her mere presence had made the fire glow brighter, the food taste better, and for a moment he had known complete happiness.

He trudged heavily down the deserted, icy hillside, every step taking him a little farther from his impossible hopes, and, since he had neither the strength to renounce them nor was he able to accept their consequences, he felt himself to be the unhappiest of men. As he followed the line of the little valley that led down to the lakeside, the Indian touched his arm and pointed to something above them, just before the valley opened out into the plain. He saw dark shapes moving, and this sudden movement in a landscape that had hitherto been gripped in an icy paralysis made him shudder. For so long nothing had moved around him. The rhythm was now broken, and the shapes immediately seemed hostile to him.

'Bears?' he murmured.

Then almost immediately he shrugged his shoulders, thinking what a fool he was. Bears sleep in the winter. He had not encountered a single non-hibernating creature throughout his entire journey. During some of the colder winter months even wolves, foxes and caribou are seen so rarely that all living creatures seem to have disappeared for ever, as if seeking to leave the winter in complete control.

'Indians? . . .'

But what would Indians be doing in these parts at this time of the year? They too go to earth in their birch-bark wigwams, and nibble at their stocks of food. The time had not yet arrived when hunger would force them out on to the frozen trails to hunt the rutting deer, and save their wretched lives by catching some scarce and skinny piece of game.

'So they must be men,' said Pont-Briand aloud.

Palefaces! Trappers! Suddenly he shut his eyes and stood still, for he heard the hollow tolling of the bell of doom within him, and he knew who it was.

A deep sigh passed his lips, and a cloud of white vapour circled his head, rising slowly into the cold air as if his soul were already leaving his body.

A shudder of fear shook him convulsively from head to foot. Then he took a hold on himself again. What was he coming to, he, a soldier who had found little else than battles and dead men on his path through life!

356

He drew himself up to his full height and, with a vague smile on his lips, watched impassively as Count Peyrac and his son came down towards him.

CHAPTER 58

As HE WATCHED them come towards him, strange dark figures across the snow-smothered valley, Pont-Briand looked less at Count Peyrac's silhouette than at that of the young lad behind him.

He had not taken much notice of him at Wapassou. Now he noticed that the young man was the very image of his father, but that there was something about his features, above all about his expression, it might have been his smile, that reminded him irresistibly of Angélique's face. And seeing this young man as the evidence of their union, the living proof that the woman he had been dreaming of belonged to another, that she was bound to this other man and to this child by bonds of which he, Pont-Briand, could never begin to imagine the strength, he saw the measure of his loneliness. The lad was not yet as tall as his father, but already his movements had a hidden, confident force that commanded respect, and on his smooth face, with its young, red lips sparkling through the furs, he saw evidence of a strong, rational willpower which was not easily moved.

They were both coming towards him to kill him. And they would kill him.

Pont-Briand thought of the son he would never have, the son he had perhaps had; but he had never concerned himself with the children he might have fathered. A sombre jealousy stirred within him that made him hate the man that came towards him, the man who came to seek justice, the man who possessed everything that he lacked. A wife, a son. He was about to shoulder his musket to fire on them and kill them both. Then he despised himself for having had a thought unworthy of a gentleman. In any case, he felt sure that the Count, who was watching him closely, would have been quicker on the draw than he. His reputation as a shot had reached Canada through the stories of sailors who had heard them from bands of pirates, or even directly from the pirates themselves, who told up and down the Saint Lawrence the tales of their battles and who had many a time mentioned the name of their most dreaded enemy.

Why hadn't this man Peyrac stayed at sea? Pont-Briand thought.

He would have given his entire fortune not to have to face him now. From the first day they had met, the Count's personality had disturbed him, and he had resented the fact that Monsieur de Loménie had been so prompt to befriend the disquieting stranger. Had he felt a presentiment that he would die by Peyrac's hand? Had Pont-Briand really been willing to examine himself, he would have seen that what distressed him above all was the fact that he was so much less of a man than Peyrac.

They stood looking at each other in silence, motionless, at a distance of a few paces. Pont-Briand showed no sign of surprise, and asked no questions. He would have considered it unworthy of him to indulge in any such display.

'Sir,' said Peyrac, 'you know why I am here?'

And as the lieutenant remained impassive, he went on:

'You tried to steal my wife from me, and I have come to call you to account. I am the injured party, therefore I have the choice of arms.'

Pont-Briand murmured:

'What arms?'

'The sword. You are a gentleman...'

'I do not have a sword.'

'Here is one.'

And he threw him the sword he had borrowed from Porguani and drew his own from its scabbard.

'This ground does not seem to me to be very suitable for an encounter,' he continued, looking around him. 'The snow is soft and deep here, and once we had removed our snowshoes, we should not be able to stand. So we had better go down to the lakeside where the ground is harder. While we fight my son will keep an eye on your Indian, in case, not knowing our code of honour, he makes any attempt to come to your rescue by attacking me treacherously. Warn him that, if he makes the slightest attempt to do this, my son will shoot him down without pity.'

Down at the lakeside the snow formed an icy crust, all corrugated and crackling under their boots. Taking his lead from Count Peyrac, Pont-Briand put down his haversack, his musket, his powder horn and his pistols, unbuckled his broad belt and removed his fur-lined cloak. He also removed a sleeveless leather jerkin which he wore over a woollen shirt. Then he took this off too, and the cold stung his bare flesh. Peyrac had done likewise. Then Pont-Briand came and stood before him.

He looked at the sun as it sank towards the horizon and disappeared

358

into the mist, an immense pink, cotton-wool sun that suddenly cast a saffron yellow light over the endless white wastes. Shadows of which there had been no hint during the day now stretched out at the foot of the trees, thin and blue and as lively as snakes. Night was falling.

Pont-Briand devoured it all with his eyes. The scene he was living through seemed unreal, and he would have liked to break away from it. . . . Was it true that he was about to die? The feeling of rage that swept over him revived his confidence. He was no good with a sword, that he knew, but at least the snow would be on his side. Peyrac was not used to fighting in snow. Megantic would not betray a Canadian from New France. Pont-Briand straightened up and said in bantering tones:

'You know, you're tough customers, you and your family! . . . Madame de Peyrac has already knocked me out cold with a poker.'

'A poker, really?' Peyrac replied, delighted. 'Ah, the jade!'

'Well may you laugh!' Pont-Briand retorted bitterly. 'One of these days you'll have less to laugh about for he will take her away from you, that I warrant.'

'He? Who? Who are you talking about?' the Count asked briskly, taking his guard with a frown.

'You know as well as I do!'

'But still . . . I'd like to hear you name him. Speak up!'

The French lieutenant looked around at the frozen landscape as if some invisible spirits could hear him.

'No,' he replied panting, 'no, I shall not tell you. He is powerful, and he might harm me.'

'Meanwhile I'm the one who's going to harm you, that's for sure.'

'What do I care! I shall say nothing, I shall not betray him. I don't want him to abandon me.'

And he gave a kind of sob.

'I want him to pray for me when I am in Purgatory!'

Despair overcame him again. He saw himself alone, naked and frozen in this landscape that foreshadowed the limbo where his soul would soon begin its wanderings.

'It was he who made me do it,' he cried. 'Had it not been for him, I would never have done what I did. I would never have hurled myself headlong upon your sword. . . . But he will win all the same. He is the stronger. . . . His weapons are those of the other world. . . . He will strike you down. . . . He will separate you from the woman you love. He can't stand love. . . . He will separate her from you, you'll see!'

359

At first he had been shouting, then his voice had grown weaker, and hoarse, while his dilated pupils stared fixedly ahead.

Then, very softly, with poignant intensity, he repeated several times: 'You'll see! You'll see!'

He kissed the medallions he wore round his neck and took his guard.

CHAPTER 59

JOFFREY DE PEYRAC and Florimond had been gone too long. Angélique's anxiety had grown into a terrible fear. She did her best to remain calm, but her face looked drawn. She could not sleep at nights, and when occasionally she did fall asleep, she would wake again very soon with a start, listening for the slightest sound, any crackling of the ice by which she hoped to identify approaching footsteps, or any sound of whispering voices. But the whistling wind merely heralded the unleashing of the storm that would make her husband and son lose their way and would engulf them for ever. During the day she could not resist the impulse to go to the door at least twenty times to look for them, or to walk down to the lakeside and wander along the shore, hoping that some miracle would bring two distant figures from out of the forest. At last she could stand the strain no longer, and she broke down.

It happened one evening when a purplish blue sky had settled low over the landscape, swallowing up what was left of the light. By three o'clock it was already dark, and a tempestuous wind arose, that sent the snow swirling in white flurries on the frontiers of darkness. Those who had gone out into the compound to fetch some tools or close a gate were knocked over by the wind and had to seek shelter on all fours. In spite of themselves and in spite of the firmly shut doors, they all listened to the frenzied wailing of the winter night, as the furious elements strove to destroy the world, and a sense of the frailty of the human lot crept into their hearts. They put the children to bed early and ate their evening meal before the usual time.

The men ate their food in silence, grim-faced and anxious.

Angélique felt she could stand no more. She felt that her self-control was about to give way. She began to pace up and down the room, wringing her hands, pressing them against her mouth to hold back her plaints, then crossing them convulsively as she murmured:

'My God! My God! . . .' After a few moments the men looked up and became aware of her agitation and her despair. At first they were amazed, then dismayed and moved at the fact that she, who had taken her place so well above them, and had become the great lady from whom they had sought help, assistance or counsel, who had even taken them to task, should show herself capable of weakness and fear.

'Mother, dear Mother!' Cantor murmured, leaping up from his chair and rushing over to embrace her.

They all sprang immediately to their feet and surrounded her, over-whelming her with rough protestations.

'You mustn't worry, Madame la Comtesse.'

'After all, what do you imagine could happen to them?'

'It's unreasonable to fret about so little!'

'They're tough, those two, believe you me, they know all about living rough!'

'I've seen Monsieur le Comte at it!'

'Even during a blizzard, if you've got a good bark shelter, there is nothing to worry about.'

'I am pretty sure there is an Algonquin village on the way, too. . . .'

No one mentioned on what way! They had known right from the start that the Count had set off towards the north, in hot pursuit of a man who had wronged him. That was the law! And there were quite a number among them who would have liked to have had a go at Lieutenant Pont-Briand themselves. . . . Angélique nevertheless felt that not one of these rough men had the slightest doubts about her, nor about the manner in which she had dealt with the Frenchman's atten-tions. In their little community, nothing could be kept hidden. And if no one had actually witnessed her scene with Pont-Briand, they all guessed what had happened in essence. Pont-Briand had told her of his feeling for her, she had put him in his place and then the Count, when he had learned of what had happened, had set off to kill him. This was as it should be. But now here was this anguished woman wringing her hands and looking from one to the other in the hope that they could offer her some comfort. And they felt overwhelmed and obscurely involved in the unspeakable action of this Canadian who had dared to do what they would never have allowed themselves to do even in their thoughts.

'He had to go, Madame,' said Jacques Vignot, 'but you'll see, he'll be back.'

'He'll come back! He'll come back!' they chanted as if repeating some spell.

Angélique became aware of the warmth in their hearts and suddenly burst into tears on old Macollet's shoulder, for he happened to be there that evening. He always seemed to be there when you needed him, like an old tree that could never be uprooted by the wildest of storms. He clasped her firmly to him and said:

'Go on then, go on, have a good cry! It will do you good.'

But the others were absolutely thunderstruck.

Strangely enough it was the blacksmith from Auvergne, who earlier had stood aside from the others with a furious expression on his face, who found the right words to comfort her.

'What have you to fear? He's with Florimond!'

Angélique raised her head and looked hopefully at him.

'That's true! You're right, Clovis! He is with Florimond! And Florimond never gets lost, does he?'

'No, never; we always say here that that boy must have swallowed a compass when he was little.'

And they began to feel better when they saw her wipe her eyes and attempt a wan smile. So they drew closer round her and talked to her in a simple, friendly way. Don Alvarez, always so solemn, showed her his black boxwood rosary beads, and gave her to understand that he prayed ardently every day for the return of Count Peyrac and his son.

At such a display of sincere, open friendship, Angélique began to cry again, unable to control herself.

Madame Jonas took her by the shoulders, and said:

'Come with me, my angel, my love, you've had about enough! You must lie down and rest otherwise you will be the one who looks like a ghost when they reach home hale and hearty.'

Angélique had never realized just how kind Madame Jonas could be. The good lady supported her all the way to her room, helped her to undress, and put her to bed after warming the sheets with two good hot stones, then brought her a sedative drink, keeping up an endless prattle all the while.

Bit by bit Angélique grew calm again. The fact that she had shared her anxiety made it weigh less heavy on her, and Madame Jonas gave her no time to dwell on it.

'Men are tough, my dear. We can't begin to imagine just how tough. ... We women, we look at things from a distance, and make mountains out of them. ... They take things like cold, snow and great distances in their stride, provided they don't go on for too long. Men are tough-skinned, hot-blooded, and cool-headed. Have you ever seen Monsieur le Comte show the slightest sign of fatigue or fear? . . . I never have!'

'I know,' Angélique replied, as she sipped her drink, 'but he could get lost, especially in this blizzard.'

'Get lost? It would surprise me if those two ever got lost! Isn't Monsieur le Rescator the best pilot of the seven seas? The wide open spaces are not very different from the sea, and the stars are always there for those who know how to read the skies. Monsieur Porguani told me that Monsieur le Comte took his sextant with him.'

'Oh, did he!' Angélique replied, reassured by this piece of news. But she grew gloomy again and went on:

'But what about during a blizzard, and at night? And all this infernal snow that hides the tracks and obscures the stars.'

'They will have taken shelter in some hole, or in an Indian wigwam where they'll wait till the end of the storm. When day comes they'll find out where they are. Monsieur le Comte is not a scientist for nothing and Florimond never gets lost.'

'Yes, that's true, there's Florimond,' Angélique repeated with a trace of a smile.

She closed her eyes, Madame Jonas took her bowl from her hands, puffed up her pillows and plaited her hair to make her feel more comfortable.

'How can I ever thank you,' the young woman murmured as a wonderful feeling of sleepiness stole over her.

'It's only right that we should look after you a little, my poor angel, you who have been supporting us all,' said the worthy lady with emotion.

That evening Angélique discovered the place she occupied in the hearts of all the people of Wapassou.

And in exchange for all the courage, the help, the patience, the good humour and the gaiety she had given them, now they took care of her. She was one of them.

'The men say that if Monsieur le Comte doesn't get back tomorrow, they will organize an expedition to meet him,' Madame Jonas added.

'But they don't even know which way he went...'

'They've a fair idea. He set off northwards, after Pont-Briand.'

Angélique opened her eyes again and stared at the worthy lady's red face, then she buried her face in her hands in despair.

'It's all my fault,' she wailed. 'What did I ever do to make a man in his right mind think he could come and insult my husband under his own roof? Madame Jonas, tell me truly I beg you, tell me; did you ever see anything in my behaviour that could possibly have encouraged Lieutenant Pont-Briand to show any lack of respect towards me?'

'No, I didn't, and don't you start blaming yourself for it. . . . I know you of old, my friend, I saw the way you lived in La Rochelle and on board ship, with or without your husband. There, like everywhere else, there were always men who would say that you behaved with great decorum and others who would not. It's not your fault if you are too beautiful! Only it leads to misunderstandings.'

'Oh! my husband will always be the same!' Angélique cried. 'What does he care about the agonies I go through? He follows his own impulses, his own code of honour. He went off without even telling me . . . and if he . . .'

'You wouldn't love him as much if he were different. If he were more staid, you might well have a quieter time of it, but believe you me, you wouldn't love him as much as you do. You are extremely lucky! If you had the choice, you wouldn't have anyone else, that I am sure, and neither would he, however awkward he may find it at times to be married to you. . . . There now, I've managed to make you laugh. You see, my love, anyone who has a treasure always attracts envy. You mustn't be surprised if people try to destroy what you have. It takes courage to defend it like everything else. I know what I am talking about! And now, that's enough chatter. I shall stay with you tonight and if you wake up and can't get to sleep again, we'll have a little chat.'

Before they fell asleep they listened to the wind whistling, the beams creaking, trees splintering and crashing to the ground, the howling of the storm suddenly stifled by the suffocating gag of the powdered snowdrifts. They could feel the snow piling up outside.

'We shall be buried tomorrow,' Madame Jonas said.

At last they fell asleep, then woke again, talked together quietly for a bit about La Rochelle and the people on the *Gouldsboro* and about all the little things that must be quickly done.

'I must ask Clovis to make us a second iron,' said Madame Jonas, 'only he's so difficult!'

'But he's the only one who can make those irons that seem both heavy and light at the same time. You never have to use the bellows on the embers.'

Morning came soundlessly. The world, exhausted, scarce dared come to life again. In the rooms of the fort, the day dawned grey, for snow had piled up right across the window-panes. But no sooner had they drawn the door open, not without some difficulty, than a glorious winter day, all pearly and gold, burst upon them. Nature was smiling in the brightness of a virginal beauty that was almost excessive, so pure and white was the snow, so satiny blue the sky, so golden the sun, and so perfect the soft lines of the trees looking like tall candles, motionless ghosts, turrets of clouds, with an occasional dome of branches bowed down like those of a tree in spring beneath a profusion of heavy, velvety blossom.

'We mustn't touch it, it's too pretty,' Honorine shouted, then almost immediately dashed out on to the white carpet and rolled delightedly over it.

The men set to work with shovels to clear the entrance. At some points where the wind had blown particularly strongly, the snow was piled as high as the roof. They fought through impalpable, crystalline clouds of snow, intangible icy vapours, they struggled in the midst of the soft, insinuating invasion, and their breath formed little translucid clouds over the surface of the buried earth.

Angélique, who was affected more by the iridescent beauty of the countryside than by the mortal threat it represented, decided that on such a day there could be no mourning and no despair. They would come back!

So she set about her work serenely, doing her best not to allow her imagination to run wild.

Towards the middle of the morning a shout brought her out of the house where she saw everyone pointing to the cliff from which huge sheets of snow were breaking away.

'An avalanche...'

'But who's causing the avalanche, who?' shrieked Jacques Vignot. 'Look, Madame. It's them!'

Then they made out two human figures on the steep black cliff face, clambering slowly down from one rock to another, clinging to the branches of small trees and bushes as they went.

'It's them!'

The men cheered and threw their fur caps into the air. Then they ran with floundering steps towards the foot of the mountain, but it proved impossible to make any progress without snowshoes, and they had to abandon the idea of going to meet the two travellers. It seemed an interminable time before they appeared in the vicinity of the fort.

Then at last they hove into view, close by and alive.

Angélique acted as if she was out of her mind. She had gone back into the fort, come out again, then gone in again. She paced round and round the room, and at last, remembering what it was she had come in for, grabbed the bottle of brandy that was kept under lock and key in a chest, and once again rushed to the door.

Joffrey de Peyrac had just reached it too and their eyes met. He was half smiling and his face, black and unshaven, seemed more emaciated, almost grimacing with the pale lines of the scars he bore, while his shining, sombre eyes fastened upon her almost feverishly. Now he was really looking at her.

He looked at her, indifferent to those all about him, as if she were the only woman in the world. And for her he seemed to rise up like the sun without which she could never survive, and she saw only him. Vignot had to take the bottle from her hands.

'Have a drink, Monsieur le Comte,' he said, pouring a tot into a goblet and handing it to his master.

'Good idea,' Peyrac replied.

He drank the draught of brandy in a single gulp, walked somewhat stiffly with a slight limp over towards the fire and sat down on a stool.

Then Angélique ran to join him and knelt down at his feet.

Or rather it would be fairer to say that she fell to her knees before him, for her happiness at this moment had made her strangely weak. She had intended to remove his boots, but when her hands came into contact with the solid reality of his muscular legs through the cloth of his breeches that had become stiff with ice, once again she almost swooned. She did not know whether it was through joy, through love or through the terrible fear of the thought that so dear a person might one day be taken from her, but her mind was, as it were, struck by a revelation, and she lost all awareness of her surroundings, so that she existed only in him and with him. She threw her arms round his knees, clasping him tight as she gazed at him with her big luminous eyes that trickled with silent tears, as if she would never weary of looking on the face of this man, whose unique features had never ceased to haunt her life since the day when she had first set eyes on them.

And he leaned forward a little and examined her intently.

It only took a moment. Just an exchange of glances. But it was enough for those who witnessed the scene never to forget the impression it made on them. And yet not one of them could have said what it was that had impressed them most at that moment, the adoration Angélique manifested as she kneeled before the Count or the warmth of love that lit his imperious face, the face of the man they were accustomed to think of as untouched by human weakness, even invulnerable.

A feeling of contentment and a vague nostalgia gripped their hearts, while a sudden reticence made them lower their eyes.

Every one of them, as they stood there with their sad memories, their dreams and their feelings of disillusion, seemed to see at that moment, as if in a flash, something appear between them, illuminating these two people as they reached out towards each other, the face of Love itself.

Count Peyrac laid his two hands gently on Angélique's shoulders to bring her back to herself again, and turned towards the men standing motionless beside him.

'Greetings, my friends,' he said in his hoarse voice that was muted with weariness. 'I am delighted to see you again.'

'So are we, Monsieur le Comte,' they replied in a schoolboy chorus.

Their minds were still hazy and the time that had elapsed seemed twice as long as it really had been. Silence fell again, and Elvire brushed aside a tear as she clasped Malaprade's hand where he stood beside her.

'What about me! What about me!' Florimond called out. 'I am half dead and no one's taking the slightest notice of me.'

They all turned round and burst out laughing.

Florimond, covered with snow, and with icicles hanging in a fringe round his hat, had collapsed against the door.

The Count gave his son a look of affectionate understanding.

'Give him a hand. He's exhausted!'

'You won't catch me coming with you again,' Florimond growled. 'You won't catch me ...'

They realized that the poor boy was in fact literally frozen and utterly exhausted.

Cantor and Jacques Vignot picked him up and carried him over to his bed, where they removed his clothes and boots, while Angélique ran over to examine him.

'Poor little lad!' she said as she kissed him.

She rubbed him over from head to foot with brandy, then sat at his bedside and thoroughly massaged his rigid calves with her lovely hands.

He fell asleep blissfully like a child, as Madame Jonas hustled about preparing a glass of toddy for everyone.

CHAPTER 60

'So you killed him, did you?' Angélique said as soon as she found herself alone with her husband in the cubby-hole that had become their bedroom. . . . 'So you killed him? You risked your life to do a crazy thing like that! Just because a man made advances to me! Do you call that a sensible thing to do, Monsieur de Peyrac?'

The Count had thrown himself down on the bed, and his exhausted limbs lay spreadeagled across it. He looked Angélique ironically up and down as she stormed at him.

'Pont-Briand came from up there in the north,' she went on, leaning over him. 'What are they going to do in Canada when they hear about this? They will try to take their revenge on you, they will denounce the treaties . . .'

'The treaties were broken a long time ago,' said Peyrac, 'no sooner had the ink dried than they condemned us to death.' He half sat up and, taking her by the hair above her forehead, he gently turned her head so that she looked him full in the face.

'Now listen to me, my love. There is one thing that is by no means about to die in me. And that is the urgent need I have of you, and it is perfectly natural that I should want you to belong to me alone and entirely to me. You can call it jealousy if you like, what matter! Neither you nor I has reached an age when our desires grow calm – far from it. Never again shall I leave you to struggle unaided in the face of temptation. . . .'

'Did you really think that I might have been seduced by a man like him?'

'No, I didn't. But I have a feeling that there could be bolder men than him. One man's weakness is another man's strength. You must realize that defending one's honour in these wild places is a matter of life and death! Now you are my life, and I shall kill anyone who tries to take you from me. . . . There now! It had to be said. . . .'

And as she leaned over him he clasped her suddenly to him and began to kiss her passionately with his lips all dried and cracked by the cold.

Florimond was telling Cantor all about it.

'I thought I'd die. Father keeps going along the trail as well as a Redskin or a Canadian.'

'Was it swords or pistols?'

'Swords. It was marvellous. Father knows all the feints and a lunge you'd have to be an acrobat to do properly, believe me. . . . The other chap put up a good show. He wasn't all that good, but he was quick off the mark and stuck it out a long time.'

'And . . . is he dead?'

'Course he's dead. You can't escape a thrust like that! Went right through his forehead!'

Florimond collapsed on to his bed again, his eyes shining.

'Now, a sword, that's the weapon of a gentleman. Here in this land of clodhoppers, no one knows what a sword is any more. They fight with tomahawks and axes like the Indians, or with muskets like mercenaries. We really must remember the sword. It's the shaft of noble souls! Oh to be a cuckold one day and to be able to have a good duel.'

CHAPTER 61

ONE DAY when Florimond was better again, he went up into the loft and with an air of great mystery picked out a huge pumpkin as yellow as the sun. Then with a well sharpened knife he cut out eyes, a nose, and a great curved smiling mouth.

He made a hole in the top, hollowed out the soft pulp and fixed a candle inside. Then he hid his work of art away in a dark corner.

Christmas was nearly upon them.

They must have a party, so they decided to hold it on the feast of the Epiphany. After the reverence of Christmas, custom had it that they should make merry for Epiphany, that they should have a feast after crowning the man they had chosen to be the happy king for that single evening; and that they should follow the example of the Three Kings and give one another presents.

In preparation for this event they all competed to see who could show most ingenuity.

Elvire went off to the edge of the forest to pick holly branches covered in red berries. It was no light task to disentangle the holly from the bushes and cut enough of it. Octave Malaprade went with her to lend a hand. Then he helped her arrange it in three great lead mortars borrowed from the workshops for the occasion. It looked magnificent, and when they stood back to take in the general effect, and admired the shiny green leaves with their glittering red berries in the great dark bowls at either end of the table, they looked at each other and smiled, full of serene and gentle joy.

All the joy and peace of a real Christmastide seemed to fill their hearts, and they held hands shyly.

Something had changed since Count Peyrac had returned from his expedition to the north, more precisely since they had seen Angélique kneeling before him and clasping him in her arms with a look they would never forget.

'If one could love like that, it would be worth taking a wife . . . yes it would be worth it,' old Macollet had said a little later with a nod. And all the others around him had nodded too as they puffed at their pipes. They had discovered that true love really did exist.

It was not for them of course, for they were outcasts; they were unlucky, it would never happen to them.

But it did happen to some people. . . .

Something to make life more beautiful, something to dream about.

They also felt that they no longer depended on a single leader, but on the comforting authority of a married couple. And the childish need for security that so many of these rough men still felt from their early unhappy fears, was satisfied at last.

So there really was a Christmas spirit in the camp. No task seemed too heavy, everything was done cheerfully. They laughed on the slightest pretext and caught themselves humming or whistling snatches of old refrains.

The everlasting boiled maize and smoked meat were eaten cheerfully with many a joke during happy mealtimes kept warm with good-humoured conversation. They were all good friends, good companions, they understood one another, and supported one another. Let anyone who sought to harm them come and try!

Preparations for the feast were a great secret.

Wonderful smells began to tickle their nostrils.

Giving honour where honour was due, first and foremost would come the thousand-and-one tasty possibilities offered by his lordship the pig, who had been sacrificed at last.

The day of the sacrifice was invested with almost ancient solemnity, and gave scope for meditation on the significance which attached in the old days to the prosaic operation of 'bleeding' the pig. Some god well-disposed to man must have smiled on the pig, an insufficiently appreciated animal, for everything in it is not only edible but delicious.

By way of a treat, they had immediately eaten the trotters, the head and the offal, variously seasoned, but they kept the more delectable portions for the night of the feast. At this point Nicolas Perrot arrived back from the south, and the mere sight of his good friendly face was a boon to them all. He told them of the little trading post on the banks of the Kennebec where he had obtained stores; it was run by a tough, silent Dutchman who lived alone, except for two English assistants, on an island in the middle of the river, which had turned as grey as a snake and was full of drift ice.

He had brought back sugar, salt, wheat-flour, sunflower-seed oil, seal-oil, prunes, peas, and dried pumpkins, also blankets, three pairs of linen sheets and some woollen cloth to make clothes. He had loaded all this on to a sledge which he and his Panis slave had pushed for endless miles.

Angélique locked the precious food supplies up in a wooden chest that Joffrey de Peyrac had had made for her with a lock and key and which had been placed in their room.

She sometimes got up in the middle of the night to check that everything was there.

Madame Jonas would have liked to bake a ham in a piecrust, and they had had to decide whether some of Angélique's meagre stocks of wheat-flour that she had kept hidden away should be used for this purpose or whether it should be used to make the traditional Christmas pie.

They decided to make the pie, with a bean hidden in it for the ritual drawing of lots to choose the king.

The ham, all pink and flavoured with juniper berries would be delicious on its own.

Angélique herself made the pastry for the pie, her sleeves rolled up over her strong arms; she added a pinch of salt, some yeast from the beer and some pork fat.

Never since her childhood had she joined in the preparations for a feast with so much joy and delight.

The dough, a friendly, familiar substance to her since the days of the Inn of the Red Mask, responded to the touch of her fingers. The ghosts of the poet Crotte, of Maître Bourgus, of Flipot and de Linot hovered about her.

Here, nothing could harm her any more. She was protected from everything. From everything . . . far, far away in the midst of the forest.

And she stopped to listen, with a smile, to the utter silence of the snow lying heavily upon them.

This was the fulfilment of a very old dream she used often to have: a dream that she was making cakes, surrounded by children looking up at her.

The children watched her as she bustled to and fro, their eyes sparkling. They cheered every time the great wooden rolling pin in Angélique's fingers pressed more vigorously on the dough, stretching the pale disc farther and farther across the polished table, lightening it and thinning it out, while the air was full of a subtle aroma of baking, all warm and heady.

It was stiflingly hot beside the big fire in the main room and whenever she left off kneading it, the dough began to rise and take on scrumptious shapes.

Angélique allowed the children to stay beside her while she prepared the pie. Honorine drew diamonds and squares all over the big soft round crust, sticking out her tongue; then Bartholomew sprinkled sunflower-seed oil over it, for Angélique had noticed that the oil extracted from the black seeds of the huge flower produced a lovely golden glaze, every bit as attractive as that produced by egg yolk, which was not available. Then finally Thomas's innocent little fingers slipped the bean inside. Closely watched by the band of children, which Florimond and Cantor had unashamedly joined, Angélique placed the pie in the oven they had built between the two fires in the big chimney. It was the best oven she had ever known. She made first-class *gratin* dishes in it and nothing ever caught. The children were given the task of watching the fires, as they sniffed the delectable smell that in no time began to filter through the cracks in the cast-iron door.

But when the moment came to take the pie out of the oven she sent them all packing, for she wanted it to be a complete surprise for Epiphany evening.

Shouting with delight and impatience they took refuge in the dark cellar under the rock face where Jacques Vignot was busy brewing beer.

'We are not allowed to see the pie, Jacques . . . you can't imagine how pretty everything will be! . . . The pie's as big as the sun. . . .'

Yes, it was, as big and shiny and crisp as a sun, with a sheen on its golden brown crust throwing the well-risen criss-cross squares into relief.

In other words, it was a masterpiece!

Angélique placed the pie on top of a pyramid she had made from a gridiron with its feet decked in holly and three bitter-apples in sumptuous shades of greenish gold, flame and pale yellow.

This arrangement in the middle of the table was probably not as elegant and sumptuous as those that Madame de Plessis-Bellière used to create surrounded by all her glittering silver when she received guests in her house at Beautreillis, but it was very impressive.

The table was draped in white to the floor. Two pairs of sheets had been commandeered for the occasion, so thoroughly ironed that it was impossible to see where they had been folded.

For several hours before the solemn festivities began, everyone was sent off to the workshops, the loft or even the stables.

Eloi Macollet invited the children into his hut so that they would not become too impatient. This was an added thrill since Macollet's hideout was a place of mystery they had been dying to see but had never been allowed to enter.

When, later that evening, the hunting horn was sounded, and Florimond and Cantor rang a peal on the cowbells, the children of the Silver Lake rushed over to the house, running, slipping and stumbling over on the frozen snow, and stopped on the threshold, as dazzled and delighted as any other children the world over.

'Oh!'

The room was a-glitter with a thousand lights and the table that occupied the centre of the room groaned beneath a pile of treasures and knick-knacks. It was hard to say which was best, the wonderful sight before them or the delicious smells of the fried black pudding and all the sweetmeats.

The three tiny tots of the Silver Lake stood on the threshold, their eyes shining like stars in their faces red with the cold.

Honorine was no longer a little girl weighed down with a secret load of shame.

The little Protestant boys forgot the incomprehensible tragedies that had torn them from their native land of France and made orphans of them.

Like all children at Christmas time, they knew a moment of complete happiness.

The others had to take them by the hand to bring them into the room.

On the table, on either side of the strange, monumental construction holding the pie, stood two birds decked in all their feathers.

Malaprade, the creator of this masterpiece, had shaped them out of some of the potted meats and smoked game, and not all their feathers belonged to them. They owed quite a few to other species of their feathered friends.

But the effect was striking.

Red and blue plumes mingled with black and white, some formed crests on the birds' heads, and others hung in fan-like tails, creating two birds of some mythical species, all the more impressive for being unknown.

The original beaks had been covered with gold dust and glittered proudly, and the eyes were made of pieces of jet.

Octave Malaprade nodded his head with a smile of satisfaction, for he could not remember ever having presented a piece so successfully in the days he had plied his trade in Bordeaux.

The princely birds lay on a bed of sweet-smelling courgettes, the whole set upon two dark red dishes which heightened the effect of sumptuousness.

The same shimmering red, that glowed like dying embers, had been used to colour the large plates set before each guest.

This unusual set of porcelain came from the miners' den, and was a gift of the servants of Vulcan. Some of them had fashioned the plates in clay and Joffrey de Peyrac had worked out the formula for the enamel made with lead oxide.

The others had decorated them, and then the Epiphany plates had been baked in the oven used for assaying gold which Kouassi-Ba and Clovis kept burning fiercely with their bellows.

Now they lay red and gleaming on the white table-cloths, while beside each one lay a more modest white wood bowl for bread, and a little pewter saucer holding nuts, sweets and dried fruits to nibble.

It was Florimond who had made the two great soup tureens with handles in the shape of wolves' heads. Madame Manigault would not have missed her Palissy china here.

There was not a single empty space down the full length of the long table, while dishes of black and white puddings lay steaming at either end.

They had had to place the goblets and other drinking vessels on a serving table. A barrel of claret which Nicholas Perrot had brought back, stood on wooden supports beside one of brandy and one of rum.

Another lower table was weighed down with piles of gifts which the king of the evening would distribute to them all later.

And the hollowed-out pumpkin that Florimond had prepared hung from the beams above, with a lighted candle inside, and a great luminous smile on its face. He introduced it to the children as Miss Pumpkin.

CHAPTER 62

It was little Bartholomew who got the bean, and he chose Honorine as his Queen.

Florimond's hand that had slipped beneath the white cloth to divide out the pieces of pie might have helped out fortune a little. But why this unworthy suspicion? Fortune was kind enough anyway to do what all expected of it and to favour the children.

Angélique was delighted that it was Bartholomew. He was a sweet child. He still squinted a little and had a mass of straight hair hanging down over his eyes.

Pink with delight, he took the precious silver crown from Count Peyrac's hands, and placed the other crown himself on Honorine's head, who had grown red with excitement and for a moment looked as if she was about to hurl the insignia of her embarrassing royalty violently to the ground. But pride and pleasure won the day.

Their chairs stood a little above the level of the rest and they presided side by side over the banquet table.

The solid silver crowns sparkled on their innocent heads. Honorine's hair hung over her shoulders, like a cape of coppery sheen, as if it too was made of some precious metal, and with her regal posture, and her head held high on her slender white, softly rounded neck, she looked quite a beauty.

Honorine was so happy and so utterly convinced of the importance of her destiny that she would have thought it beneath her dignity to glance at her mother. But she knew that her mother was looking at her. And her joy lay like a halo round her head while compliments, laughter and jokes swirled about her like incense.

Each time she lifted her cup to her lips everyone cried: 'The Queen is drinking! The Queen is drinking!'

Angélique's eyes were glued to Honorine, and throughout the whole evening she never ceased to think that all she had once gone through was insignificant compared with the happiness of this child.

She was unable to take her eyes off her, so lovely was she.

That evening everyone had put on his best clothes, and Monsieur Jonas, Porguani, and Don Alvarez among others were wearing elegant wigs; where had they come from?

Count Peyrac was wearing the dark red clothes he had worn the day he had faced the Iroquois on the hills below Katarunk. He had left Katarunk wearing these best clothes, and his lace cravat and cuffs. In fact they were his only clothes and he kept them folded away in a chest. The rest of the time he wore borrowed clothes, mostly Porguani's, for he was his height. He was accustomed to a considerable personal elegance and this he had always maintained throughout the many different occupations he had pursued, although he seemed in no way to mind having to dress in leather and coarse woollen garments this winter. But that evening, dressed in his lordly livery, the matchless nobility of his presence impressed itself once again upon Angélique. His bearing was one of sombre, princely distinction.

He had returned from the kingdom of the dead.

Beneath his hat of crimson silk edged with feathers, his hair fell black and straight on to his shoulders, except for the silvery glitter that stood out against suntanned temples.

Angélique had put on a lace collar over her dress and skilfully dressed her hair, for it was her only adornment. With that and a few feathers and a brooch borrowed from Madame Jonas she might have been about to attend a reception at Versailles.

The ladies had exchanged a fair number of their possessions. Madame Jonas was wearing a beautiful red and green satin square and a pair of earrings belonging to her niece, who did not want to wear them herself because she was still in mourning.

Elvire wore a pearl-grey dress of Angélique's and Angélique had helped her to dress her hair beautifully.

Monsieur Jonas's high-crowned black hat was decorated with one silver buckle which he had borrowed from a pair of shoes no one was wearing, and the buckle from the other made a brooch for Elvire.

Even old Eloi Macollet had dressed for the occasion: when he had first appeared no one had recognized the mild, sprightly old man with the white curls of his powdered wig peeping out from under a round beaver hat of the finest quality, trimmed with gold braid around the edge, and wearing a lace jabot, a flowered waistcoat and a snuff-coloured jerkin.

'We helped him to dress,' said the children.

It was difficult to imagine all these preparations going on in the confined space of the trapper's tiny wigwam.

But even if it bordered on the miraculous, the result was there for all to see.

Eloi sat down amidst applause and exclamations of admiration. He sipped his wine with half-closed eyes and wondered what his bitch of a daughter-in-law would have said if she had seen him dressed up in all his finery for the feast.

What particularly delighted them about their appearance was the fact that it had taken an extraordinary degree of ingenuity to make them look so civilized. And it was true that, had anybody arrived suddenly through the snow that night, he would have stood on the threshold struck dumb with amazement to see such a gathering in the depths of the woods. Dazzled by the light, the sound of music and of singing, the laughter and all the elegance, he might well have thought himself the victim of some fairy-tale vision, a vision that would fade and vanish away at the first light of dawn.

As the sons of the lord of the manor, Florimond and Cantor waited on everyone with the help of Yann, who had been valet to a naval officer before turning buccaneer.

'Don't forget that I was a pageboy at the King of France's table,' said Florimond, holding a plate aloft on his outstretched palm. His life of adventure had not made him forget the skills he had acquired in his exacting apprenticeship. He made a wonderful job of carving the geese and the ham, apeing Monsieur Duchesne and the senior officers of the King's table all the time. They spoke of the Sovereign, Louis XIV, and of Versailles and all its splendour, which delighted the French Canadians among them and impressed the English and the Spaniards.

Cantor poured the drinks. First it was wine, then brandy and rum to help them digest their nourishing food. After the meagre rations they had been living on this was a feast indeed. They would not think about the morrow.

Then suddenly Sam Holton began to speak. He called to mind the time when he had been a little boy, living at Saco Bay in New England, in a rough log cabin. Their every-day diet consisted of barley broth and cod, but at Christmas they killed the pig and their mother brought out her stocks of bilberries. They would set off for the 'meeting house', their church, some four leagues away, the men, armed with muskets, surrounding the women and children. As they passed their neighbours' houses more and more people came out and joined them, and thus they walked through the icy forest singing hymns as they went. One year as they were returning from the service, they were set upon by a war party of Abenakis who killed them all except Sam, who was ten at the time and had immediately sought refuge at the top of a fir-tree.

Afterwards he had made his way to Springfield, his teeth chattering all the way. Since then none of his Christmases were worth remembering, except the one he was enjoying today at Wapassou.

Thus spoke Sam Holton in excellent French that was almost poetic.

This was his Epiphany gift to the assembled company, who listened to him in a religious and delighted silence, is spite of the tragic end of his tale.

They all felt that they had witnessed one of those miracles that so often seemed to occur around Christmas time.

After thanking the narrator and congratulating him warmly, they began to distribute the gifts, and here too there was good reason for merriment.

Who had carved all those wooden toys for the children? There was a windmill for Thomas, a spinning top for Bartholomew and a doll with bright red cheeks for Honorine; the body and limbs were made of straw which had been covered with a silk dress embroidered in tiny red knots that made it look most striking. Angélique had seen Elvire sewing at the dress. But where had she managed to find the silk and thread for it?

Angélique smiled at her and also at the artists who had shown such skill with the gouge: Yann, Cantor and old Eloi.

With Florimond's help they had also, at Angélique's suggestion, carved a set of chessmen, and made a board from wood of two colours; they had also constructed a draughtboard and draughts and a dice box made of bark for the backgammon players.

The peace of the long winter evenings was assured.

But there were many other unexpected things that seemed to appear at a wave of some magic wand. The young King and his Queen proudly called out the names that Elvire or Yann or Jacques Vignot whispered to them while Florimond spun around to hand each present to its recipient.

Angélique received two pairs of finely sewn gloves to protect her hands from the work she had to do. And in a tiny silver box she found a Neapolitan cameo showing the profile of a goddess in pure white on a pinkish red shell background. She glanced at Cantor, for she knew that this cameo had been his talisman ever since his childhood days on the Mediterranean, and he had parted with it to give it to her.

'I made the little silver box and the crowns for the King and Queen,' said Florimond, slightly jealous of the loving look Angélique had given his younger brother.

In spite of his adult stature he received his full share of kisses.

Honorine was examining her doll guardedly.

She had never been very keen on little girls' games and Angélique feared she might react in a way that would upset the creators of the toy they had conceived with such love. But after a few moments' consideration, Honorine cradled the doll in her arms in a capable manner, and everyone smiled with pleasure while Angélique gave a sigh of relief.

With her other hand Honorine counted out the pile of new treasures that would soon go to swell those already in her precious box which she had brought with her from La Rochelle: the necklaces of beads her mother had made filled her with delight and she strung them round her arms, and her neck, and decorated her silver crown with them and and her young partner's as well.

In a silver box she found still more sweets which Angélique had made from caraway-seed paste mixed with some of her jealously guarded stocks of honey.

There were many silver objects among the gifts, wrought by skilful hands in the hidden depths of the forge with silver wrested from the earth. This was a foretaste of the mineral wealth of Wapassou that was beginning to come forth from the darkness and glitter in all its purity!

When their exclamations and expressions of astonishment had come to an end, they reminded Count Peyrac that he had said he had two surprises in store for them.

He had to admit that as far as the first was concerned, only those who had lived in Mediterranean lands would be capable of appreciating its value.

It was a little bag containing some powdered coffee. There were shouts of pleasure interrupted by protests from those who disliked the dark concoction. How, asked the Englishman and the Canadians, for once in agreement, how was it possible to enjoy drinking this bitter mud? You'd have to be at least as barbarous as the Turks. But those who liked the divine brew changed places with the others and formed a tight group round the Count in order not to miss anything of the ceremony of its preparation.

While Kouassi-Ba brought in the cups on a copper tray which had survived several disasters and which Angélique had thought was lost, the Count distributed twists of Virginia tobacco of the finest quality to the other men.

Florimond handed round their pipes and held out a burning brand to the well-filled bowls.

379

He did not like coffee. He preferred chocolate, he said . . . with a knowing wink at Angélique.

Cantor on the other hand enjoyed the smell, which reminded him of his childhood expeditions on the Mediterranean with his father, of the places where they had put into port, of the fights they had seen and of Palermo where he had studied with the Jesuits, in the shadow of ancient mosques and Norman palaces.

Angélique was delighted and clapped her hands for joy.

Her love of coffee might be childish but her husband's announcement had made her eyes shine and her face glow with pleasure.

What with Cantor, Enrico Enzi, Porguani, the Spaniards and the Peruvian, there were plenty of them crowding round Count Peyrac.

'Do you remember the old Turk in Crete who used to make the most marvellous coffee?' Peyrac asked Enzi.

Angélique sniffed in the evocative aroma and as always there were phantom memories in the curling blue smoke – the slave-market in Crete, the carnival figures dressed in turbans and long robes; and she lived again the violent emotions she had felt at the time – terror at first, then an intoxicating sense of relief as she stood beside the masked man who had bought her. . . .

She drank her scalding coffee. Yes, my lord Rescator, it was you! How could I have failed to guess? And she cursed the ironies of fate that had played such a trick on her.

'You were furious with me, weren't you, for not recognizing you?' she whispered, leaning towards him.

And as they sat very close to each other at the end of the big table, lost in the depths of the woodlands of the New World, they exchanged tender glances and thought that all was well.

CHAPTER 63

'SOME OF you know what is going to happen now,' said Count Peyrac standing up. 'As far as the others are concerned, it will come as a real surprise. But I think that you will all be equally delighted, for you all deserve to be.'

The Italian Porguani and Clovis had gone off to the workshops. As they made their way slowly back out of the darkness, the others saw that they were carrying a kind of wooden stretcher so heavily laden that their muscles bulged with the effort. The object on the stretcher glittered dully, and when they came closer a kind of rough block became visible, giving out a cold, mysterious light. The two bearers laid the stretcher down at the end of the table in front of Peyrac.

It was gold.

The block on the stretcher was made up of several gold bars piled on top of one another.

'Here is the result of our labours. During these past winter months we have been busy assaying the gold we had mined during the summer. Each gold bar contains three avoirdupois pounds of gold, or 1,700 ounces. This is the first share I intend to give to each of you on this Epiphany night. The results have exceeded all our hopes. Just think, we have produced a hundred and fifty thousand pounds worth of gold, in other words more than the total annual budget of Canada. This is a considerable result when you consider that last century the Medici family, which was the richest in the world, possessed no more than a hundred pounds of gold in their coffers. We have obtained half as much again in less than two years. We are richer than the Medici, and next year, when we have enlarged our fort, and made sure it is well armed and well defended, when we have brought a band of mercenaries up the Kennebec with canons and supplies, we shall be able to devote ourselves peacefully to our work and to producing still more gold.

'According to the contract we have all signed, a quarter of the production will be regularly shared out among you, my first companions, thus enabling each of you to build up a private fortune. With the rest I shall improve and enlarge our outposts, pay our mercenaries, equip our ships, etc., and in this way we shall all be linked by the power of gold and of the silver, an important by-product, and our power will grow.

'We shall add ships to our fleet for trading purposes, for Gouldsboro is one of its home ports. And we can establish warehouses along the Kennebec and the Penobscot.

'We shall be able to open other mines of which some of you could take over the ownership if you are prepared to face a hard time at first as you begin to exploit them. . . . The country of Maine, a land of forests and rivers, and also a land with an open sea coast looking out on to an ocean teeming with fish, is a land that has remained wild up till now, although it has been claimed by many nations who have not exploited it. Maine, the land of hidden gold and silver, will become our kingdom because we alone have discovered the secret of its wealth.

'Do you regret coming with me?'

'No! No! my lord,' said a few voices choked with emotion. But most of them were speechless.

Kouassi-Ba went the rounds like one of the three kings, and with his black hand distributed a gold bar to each of the men.

They hardly dared to touch them.

Their eyes, a trifle hazy from alcohol and tobacco smoke, stared at the softly shining bars and found it impossible to look away. They looked at the shining gold as if gazing into a crystal ball, and saw in it the fulfilment of their dearest dreams, their most impossible ambitions. Angélique felt a chill of fear. Gold corrupts. Once already her happiness had been destroyed by gold. Might these men not lose their heads faced with the dazzling temptations of riches? She looked at her husband. He was like a magician observing the passion he had stirred up.

Would these men whom he had formed in his own image in the course of their daily labours disappoint him and succumb to the irrational myths which seem to have dominated mankind from the time of its remote beginnings?

A feeling of oppression came over Angélique, troubling her earlier joy.

'Gold! Always gold!' she murmured. 'I'm frightened! It was in the name of gold that they cursed you before!'

He gave her a sidelong glance.

'You mustn't fear gold and its powers,' he said. 'There is nothing on earth that can degrade a man unless he wants to be degraded. But man would like to see himself as a pure spirit, like God, and when he takes stock of the material side of his nature, he accuses matter. He does not want to admit his earthy nature . . . and that is why he alternates between cursing and idolizing everything that fascinates him most in the created world: gold, women, science, or wealth. . . . Whereas what he should do is simply to come to terms with them. For him who loves the spirit, the spirit exists in all material things.'

Jacques Vignot the carpenter turned the gold ingot round in his fingers and looked at it dubiously.

'As far as I'm concerned for the time being I ask nothing more than to be here. I've got a good job, with plenty to look forward to at the end, and no police spies after me. . . . But all the same it's good to hold a thing like this in your hands. I've seen so many of them. . . .'

'You'll feel less awed by it when you go to Boston and see it transformed into good hard cash. Then you'll know what to do with it,' said Peyrac.

'A whole purseful of crowns?' Vignot asked, looking at him in perplexity.

'Two, or even three. . . . You've got a thousand pounds' worth in your hands there.'

'I say, my friends, what a spree we'll have, what drinks all round!' the carpenter exclaimed, thumping his neighbours' shoulders.

Everyone began to talk at once, some making plans, some doing complicated calculations in an atmosphere of excitement that made their voices shrill.

Madame Jonas stood up to clear the table, for she felt it was improper to mix such beautiful gold with the remains of a meal, however good it was.

She and her husband had each been given a gold bar, in other words, 3,400 ounces, while Elvire had one of her own and one for her two little boys.

Old Eloi lifted his and waved it in the air.

'You have made a mistake, Monsieur le Comte. I am not one of your men. I just happened to come along and I stayed. You don't owe me anything.'

'You are the labourer of the eleventh hour, you old pirate,' Joffrey de Peyrac replied. 'Do you know your Bible? Yes you do. Well then, think of what it says and hang on to what people offer you. You can get yourself a new canoe and enough goods to barter for two years, so you can come back with all the furs in the west. All your rivals will choke with jealousy. . . .'

The old trapper opened his eyes wide in astonishment and burst out laughing, then began to dream out loud, describing how he would plunder the rivers up-country.

Then they all looked at one another in embarrassment, and after a moment's consultation they said:

'What shall we do with all this gold? Monsieur le Comte, until the time comes for each man to go his own way, and we go off to the cities, would you keep the gold here, Monsieur le Comte, with you? You are not frightened of gold, but it is too much for us, and if we kept it under our pillows we would never get to sleep.'

'Agreed,' said Peyrac with a laugh, 'but take a good look at it tonight. It's your handiwork and a gift from God who made the world.'

CHAPTER 64

IT WAS AT that moment that Angélique thought she heard a call.

Above the noise of the singing, the twanging chords of the guitar and the ritornellos of the creaky hurdy-gurdy played by Madame Jonas, she heard a voice calling:

'Help! Help!'

But since it was a physical impossibility, she immediately realized that the voice had come from within her. Then almost immediately there was a knock on the door.

Angélique sprang to her feet.

'What's wrong?' Joffrey asked, grasping her hand, surprised at her sudden reaction.

'Someone knocked at the door.'

'Knocked at the door? You must be dreaming, my love.'

The singers fell silent and turned towards them.

'What's the matter?'

'Someone knocked.'

'Someone knocked!' Nicolas Perrot burst out in an offhand way that was not at all like him and was no doubt due to over-copious liberations. 'Whoever would be knocking at our door on a night like this? Only spirits or French Canadians would dare to be out in weather like this!'

They fell silent and stared uncertainly at one another.

Spirits!

They felt their isolation as human beings, hidden away in all this snow in the depths of winter as if they were at the bottom of a crevasse.

Winter clasped them fiercely in its icy grip and, now that the fire burnt less brightly, they became aware of the penetrating, deadly cold that strove persistently to find a way in through the tiniest cracks, and they could hear the soft, endless whistling of the wind skimming over the frozen snow outside and compassing them about like some evil incantation.

They knew that at this time of the year no one would ever dare to attempt to reach them. So who could be knocking at their door on this glacial, windy night?

Spirits!

Angélique thought she heard more knocks.

'Can't you hear?' said Angélique with a start.

But this time the sounds were not as clear as before, and as she looked at the utterly incredulous faces around her, she began to wonder whether she had not been suffering from some illusion.

'It might have been a branch in the wind, tapping the walls,' she murmured.

'But we would have heard it too . . .'

Joffrey de Peyrac rose to his feet too and went over to the door.

'Be careful, Father,' Florimond shouted, running after him.

Standing in front of his father, it was he who opened the first door. Then, at the end of the corridor that served as an entrance hall, he turned the handle of the second door which the snow had blocked so that he had to tug hard at it to pull it inwards.

The cold came whistling into the room with a swirl of powdery snow.

Florimond held his pistol at the ready and threw himself to one side of the door.

From a distance Angélique and the others leaned forward but could only make out a vague shimmer of light through which the snow swirled as the wind spun it off the ground. Unexpected moonlight had burst through the clouds, and this explained the glow outside, which shone with a kind of phosphorescence in the doorway.

'There's no one there,' said Florimond. 'And it's terribly cold,' he added, pushing the door to again.

He came back into the main room and closed the second door. There was a general sense of relief.

It was better to go on feeling nice and warm in their burrow than to think about what was going on outside.

The gust of freezing air had swept through the room like a deadly wave, sweeping the clouds of tobacco smoke into a long trail, so that they could only see one another through long ribbons of white smoke that twisted and wound round their faces.

The lamp and candle flames had been blown almost flat in the icy blast and some had gone out and gave off thick, unpleasant-smelling wreaths of smoke.

'I think that all this excellent wine has disturbed your judgement a little,' said Peyrac. And the sound of his voice dispelled their unease.

Angélique alone remained hesitant.

'And what if there's someone out there dying in the snow? Far or near, I don't know,' she thought.

And she looked anxiously about her, counting her friends. All her loved ones were present, safe beneath her watchful eye.

Joffrey de Peyrac clasped her round the waist as if to reassure her. He looked down at her, silently questioning. But she slipped away from him.

After a certain over-indulgence in good food and 'warming' drinks, people would accuse her of hearing voices.

But the incident put an end to the festivities.

The children were already half asleep. They were carried off to bed with all their toys, and Miss Pumpkin was seated on a stool beside them to watch over them with her scarlet, slightly macabre smile. For a time Bartholomew, Thomas and Honorine did their best to keep their eyes open to see whether Miss Pumpkin's eyes and smile would be the first to go out.

But their struggle was of short duration and they fell asleep in the gentle glow of the magic pumpkin.

The others tidied up the big room, and then suddenly they all felt very tired and longed to sleep like weary animals.

Angélique tried to find an excuse to go and have a look around outside. She would never have been able to sleep easy if she went on thinking that some human being might have lost his way and was dying in the snow just a few paces from their shelter.

She said she was going to take four pieces of sugar to the horses, for they too deserved a bit of a treat on Epiphany night.

No one paid any attention to her.

Never mind then! She slipped on her thick leather leggings beneath her skirt, donned her fur boots, and threw a cloak lined with wolfskin over her shoulders. This, and a pair of heavy gloves would suffice for a brief look round outside.

Eloi Macollet was standing in front of the second door, likewise fully dressed over his party clothes, and was lighting a dark lantern.

'Are you off to your hut?' she asked him.

'No, I am coming with you, Madame, since you're bent on seeing what's going on outside.

CHAPTER 65

THEY HAD no need of the lantern.

Once out of the narrow trench that had been cut between two walls of ice from the threshold up to the hard surface of the yard, the moonlight was quite bright enough.

Dark clouds scudded across the sky, occasionally covering the dazzling moon. Even so, earlier in the evening the clouds had been low enough to bring snow, which had piled up to about a hand's depth and lay all floury in the intense cold and crunching beneath their feet.

As they emerged, they were met by flying wind-driven snow, which could do as much damage as finely powdered abrasive metal.

It struck their clothes with a noise like sand and burned the skin of their faces. They held their heads low and stumbled across to the stables, but as they walked Angélique took as much in as she could, trying to uncover the secrets lurking in the shadows of this unusually bright night.

Visibility extended quite a distance, right to the far end of the nearest lake.

The countryside lay shrouded in the powdered snow which the wind was stirring up from the ground, and seemed to appear through a dazzling mist that blurred its contours. It was like diamond dust forming a swirling halo round the tops of the trees, a nimbus over the curve of the hills, making the edge of the lake stand out beneath its great expanse of smooth icy snow, in which the moon was reflected, making it look more like a Silver Lake than ever.

An endless high-pitched whistling and hissing made up the ill-tempered music of this night landscape abandoned to the rigours of the northern winter.

Angélique's eyes began to stream with tears which immediately froze and stuck to her eyelashes, as she vainly tried to see she knew not what.

Then suddenly a white ghost loomed up at the far end of the lake, a transparent spectre that waved its arms, then, after turning right round, vanished as if it had been dissolved by the implacable whirling wind; then more floating shapes, then nothing.

387

The young woman and the old man stood in stupefaction at the end of the promontory.

'Did you see it this time, did you see it, Eloi?' Angélique shouted.

The old trapper nodded.

'They must be spirits,' he stammered. 'Nicolas Perrot said so. Spirits . . . only spirits could be out in this weather. . . .'

'No, you're raving . . . they may be people.'

And she began to cough, for the frozen air choked her as it entered her lungs. They had to stand nose to nose as they spoke and shout to hear what they were saying.

'Human beings, I tell you . . . human beings, and they'll die. . . .'

They returned to the fort in all possible haste. Their report caused general consternation. No one was very clear-headed and it would be quite a while before they were. Most of the men were already half undressed, and they groped around to find their jackets and trousers and put them on again.

Angélique did her best to convince them that she had seen someone at the other end of the lake, but old Macollet kept on repeating obstinately:

'They're spirits, I tell you. . . . After all, they do exist. . . . And it's not the first time I've seen 'em, either . . .'

'I've seen them too,' 'So have I' some of the men chimed in.

Angélique stamped her foot and shouted louder than they, in order to stem the spate of tales about ghosts and apparitions that was beginning to break out.

'That's enough! I am telling you that these are people! And what about the shout I heard? And the bangs on the door?'

'Yes, exactly! What about the shouts and the bangs, Madame? If they came from human beings that you saw just then at the end of the lake, how could you have heard them here, inside the house, more than a mile away?'

'It's just the sort of thing spirits do; they go wandering around and tapping at people's doors, and scaring the life out of everyone around Christmas time,' said Master Jonas, lifting a sententious finger. 'All we can do is to snuggle down and say our prayers.'

Angélique ran her hand over her brow which was so cold that it seemed to be made of hard, insensitive wood.

What was she to believe, what was she to think? Even if what she had heard could have been a hallucination, what she had seen was definitely not.

Count Peyrac emerged from his room, to which he had retired. He walked down the steps from the platform that led into the big room and asked what all the fuss was about.

'We saw . . . something, out there at the end of the lake,' Angélique explained.

'It was ghosts,' Macollet affirmed. . . . 'I am sure they were souls in torment, because I could see the woods through their bodies.'

Angélique did not know what to say for she herself had had the same impression that they were transparent.

'Was it eddies of snow caught up by the wind,' asked Peyrac.

But this time Angélique and Macollet were in complete agreement.

'No! No! It was . . . something else.'

Joffrey de Payrae scanned his wife's face attentively.

She had a lost look about her that he sometimes noticed when something had seized upon her inwardly.

Then she would seem far away, entirely preoccupied by questions as yet unspoken, questions to which she and she alone must find the answer. He was beginning to know her, and knew that she was extremely sensitive to different phenomena which, although they had physical manifestations, were none the less inexplicable. For his part, he was perfectly willing to accept the fact that people could transmit messages and calls for help by some invisible means, for he had witnessed some disturbing examples of this during his travels.

The Count remained thoughtful.

Nicolas Perrot also shared his doubts, and he looked at Angélique with the same shrewd, puzzled gaze as that of his leader, then suddenly stood up:

'We must go and see,' he decided. Then with a questioning tilt of his chin towards Angélique he added: 'That is what you would have us do, isn't it, Madame? Yes? Well, if that's what you want, let's go . . .'

'All right,' said Peyrac, making up his mind. 'After all, the worst that can happen to us is a rather unpleasant walk, and then, my love, you will have a clear conscience, won't you?'

Clovis from Auvergne made his refusal to participate clear with a gesture.

'Me go chasing after ghosts? Never,' he cried, taking refuge under his blankets. And the disbeliever crossed himself several times.

So they left behind those troubled with a superstitious dread, which was, after all, understandable enough.

Angélique and her husband, followed by Nicolas Perrot, the two Spaniards, Jacques Vignot, Florimond and Cantor, went down to the lakeside carrying lanterns. They had considered it pointless to disturb Porguani, who had already gone to bed in his glory-hole near the workshops, and Eloi Macollet followed them at a distance muttering to himself and clutching his rosary beads inside one of his jacket pockets.

From time to time the moon hid behind the clouds.

The snow was so hard that snowshoes were unnecessary.

Their little group set off along the right-hand shore of the lake. Walking was by no means easy, and no one spoke. The only sounds came from the crunching of their boots and moccasins on the snow, and the hoarse, irregular sound of their breathing which seemed to be amplified by the freezing air.

When they reached the end of the lake they called a halt.

'Well, this was the place,' said Angélique looking around.

Everything seemed so peaceful, so utterly peaceful, that their earlier anxiety now seemed groundless.

Even the wind had dropped a little, and was now only blowing at ground level, lifting the newly fallen snow and rearranging it in little waves and tiny soft mounds.

During the summer months, the sound of the waterfalls as they fell from one lake to the level of the next could be heard from this point. But on this winter night there was utter, stony silence, apart from the low murmur of the wind.

If they went on a little farther they would see the waterfalls, now solid ice, frozen stiff as they foamed over the brink, like the great pipes of an organ made of glass.

Everything was still and sleeping.

'Let's look around,' said Peyrac.

They spread out, casting the round beams from their lanterns over the ground.

But the carpet of snow was untrodden.

Angélique, numb with cold, almost began to reproach herself. When she woke tomorrow, once the wine was out of her system, she would laugh at her own foolishness, and for a while would have to suffer the jibes of those around her. Then she felt a sudden, urgent desire to find *something*; so strongly did the feeling take hold of her again that she continued her search with renewed energy, stumbling into trees and bushes, and tripping into hidden hollows.

They gathered together again shortly and decided to return to the fort.

But Angélique felt as if an invisible hand was upon her, drawing her back. She could not bring herself to leave the spot and she let the others go on ahead.

She regretted the fact that Nicolas Perrot's Panis Indian had not come with them, for he could smell out things like a hunting dog. But he was too frightened of the spirits of darkness, and even his master would have been unable to persuade him to go.

One last time Angélique's eyes scanned the ground from the lakeside to the edge of the forest.

'There's a kind of heap over there . . .'

At that moment the moon came out in all its splendour, and a shaft of silver light, shining down through the branches, touched the snowy mound. She almost gave a cry.

The diffused brightness, by creating new shadows and outlining afresh the ridges and furrows of the ground, had given her a fleeting glimpse of two outstretched human forms.

She had seen them, yes, *seen* them beneath that gently curving white shroud, seen the hump of a head and the curve of a back.

And there, did that not look like an outstretched arm?

She rushed towards the place with thumping heart. It was half dark there again now. It was only rocks and low bushes covered with snow . . .

But nevertheless she fell to her knees and began to scrabble frantically at the snow. She found something, she knew not what, but it gradually appeared as her frozen fingers tugged at it, and it was neither leaves nor earth nor . . . what? What would one expect to find beneath the snow?

She removed her glove so that she could feel what it was: it was a piece of cloth!

So she began to tug and tug. Then something stiff and heavy appeared, a human arm.

As she continued, she released a shoulder, raised a whole torso from which the snow slid off easily, for only a thin layer covered it. Just thick enough to have hidden from them the body of the man who had collapsed there in exhaustion.

She lifted her lantern and shone it around her.

There were others.

She could see them clearly now.

How ever could they have passed by so close earlier on without seeing them?

She returned to her task and managed to get the first body out and to drag it away from under the trees, clutching at the man's rigid clothes with her bare, agonizing fingers.

She had been breathing so quickly with emotion that her throat burned, and she no longer had the strength to shout.

Fortunately someone called her, close by; it was the Count who had retraced his steps.

'Where are you?'

'Here,' she replied, 'come quick, they are here!'

'Good God,' he exclaimed.

And he saw her emerge from the shadows of the trees half carrying a black, inert form on her back.

CHAPTER 66

THEY GOT eight of them out. Vague shapes beneath the icy shell of their cloaks, their mittens and their blankets.

They were inert, but still supple.

'They're alive. They must have collapsed here less than an hour ago, and been covered up by the thin sprinkling of snow the wind is blowing.'

'Who are they?' Vignot asked.

'Who do you expect?' Macollet replied.

'You heard what Perrot said; they're not spirits, so they can only be French Canadians wandering around in the wilds at this time of the year.'

Only one of them was completely stiff like a tree-trunk. This was the man Jacques Vignot was carrying.

'Weighs as much as a dead donkey, this one does,' growled Vignot as he dragged himself along the path. 'That's a corpse you've got there, my lad! No doubt about it. You've a dead man on your back, Jacques, my friend!'

As the sweat froze on his face it formed a viscous mask. Pagan as he was, in his exhaustion, Jacques Vignot began to think about Jesus carrying his cross.

This was the night of Epiphany.

A night that was like no other.

Back at the fort it looked as if there was not an inch to spare in the big room. It was crammed with people. Those who had remained behind looked at the others in horror. More and more of them kept on coming in, and both the men who had been found and their discoverers had the same ghostly look, covered with snow as they were, with their eyebrows and chins hoary with frost.

They were all icy spectres with glistening eyes, some of whom seemed still to be looking across at the shades of the nether regions.

Jacques Vignot unloaded his corpse straight on to the table, where the stiff, hard body fell among the plates and some of the gold bars with a dull thud. The poor man was exhausted, puffing and blowing like a sea-lion, and shaking his blue fingers.

They laid the limpest of them on the floor, but sat the others on benches, for they seemed to be coming round.

As far as they could tell from examining their faces, grown yellowish-white in the cold, there were five Europeans and three natives. They were Frenchmen as Nicolas Perrot had predicted, and all wore beards.

The ice was beginning to melt from their beards and fell on the ground with a tinkle like broken glass. They slipped some glasses of brandy between their lips, which the men swallowed, and they began to breathe louder and deeper. They had been immobile, dangerously asleep in the cold of the night beneath a covering of snow for something under two hours.

Yet one of them was indeed dead. The man on the table.

Nicolas Perrot went up to him and lifted the woollen cap that hid the dead man's face.

He gave a stifled cry.

'God Almighty! Holy Mother! What a shame!'

And he crossed himself.

The others drew close too, recognized the dead man and recoiled with a stifled cry. Fear, horror, and superstitious dread filled their hearts. For they had realized that this man whose face they had just looked upon, a face grown motionless as stone, was dead, guessed he had been dead for a long time, for at least three weeks, on the distant shores of Lake Megantic.

It was Lieutenant Pont-Briand!

They all turned towards Count Peyrac, who came forward, with puckered brow and without showing any sign of emotion, examined the face with its closed eyes and marble-like skin sticking to the bones.

He managed to raise the man's hood with one finger, revealing a black star on his temple. The wound had bled very little because of the cold.

He nodded. Yes, this was the man he had killed with the point of his sword. The eyes which he had himself closed, as for an opponent who had fought fair, had never opened again.

The dead man was merely a three-weeks-old corpse kept intact by the frost, up in the branches of a tree where the Huron had placed it.

This was a traditional method of burial in the winter, to protect the corpse from foxes and wolves until the earth appeared once more and made it possible to dig a grave.

'The dead man . . .' whispered Madame Jonas, leaning towards Angélique as she busied herself building up the fires and reheating some of the soup and the meat.

'Well?'

'It's Monsieur de Pont-Briand.'

Angélique gave a start and stood up. She was standing beside the raised fireplace and could see right across the room, which presented a strange sight with everyone standing motionless round the table looking at the rigid corpse as it lay there among the remnants of the feast and the gold bars that still glistened on the table.

'Yes, Lieutenant Pont-Briand,' said a strange voice forcefully.

One of the newcomers staggered to his feet, revealing a white face still bearing the marks of his terrible ordeal. His eyes burned, unnaturally big and staring.

'Yes, Pont-Briand, whom you murdered, and in whose name we have come to seek justice, Monsieur de Peyrac.'

Joffrey looked at him calmly.

'How is it you know me, Monsieur?'

'I am Count Loménie-Chambord,' the voice replied. 'Do you not recognize me? I met you at Katarunk.'

Nicolas Perrot, who had been away when Lieutenant Pont-Briand had visited the fort, was unable to understand what it was all about and looked first at one then at another.

'No, it can't be,' he cried, rushing over to Count Peyrac and grasping him impulsively by the doublet, a gesture he would never have dared to make had he not been in a state of great agitation. 'Was it you who killed this man? . . . But he was my friend, my brother . . . and it was you, you who killed him! . . . No, it's not true.'

'Yes it is,' said one of the other arrivals in a weak voice. 'That's the kind of monster you serve, Nicolas! He won't show the slightest compunction about killing one of your countrymen if it happens to suit him. . . .'

Joffrey de Peyrac, who, up till then, had remained impassive amidst the agitation of the crowd, seemed suddenly to be seized with violent anger, especially when he saw the look of distress in his good friend Perrot's eyes.

'Yes, I did kill him,' he replied in a thick, hoarse voice. 'But Nicolas Perrot is my friend; don't you attempt to separate him from me.'

His black eyes flashed and grew terrible.

'You hypocrites! You hypocrites! You know why I killed him. So why do you pretend to be indignant? And why do you accuse me of committing some crime, when all I did was to avenge my honour that had been flouted! Has not one of you got a gentleman's blood in his veins?

'Did you not know that this man had designs on my wife? That he came here to try to seduce her . . . to appropriate her, to take her away from me? He came here to steal her from me and to outrage her under my own roof. . . . And was I expected to tolerate this treachery? Was I to allow him to go unpunished for what he did? If he was crazy enough to want to try such a thing, let him pay for his craziness! That is the law! We fought a duel according to all the proper rules, and he is dead. And let it here be known that anyone who dares to covet my wife will be dealt with in exactly the same way, no matter what his race or nation?'

His voice broke in the midst of the petrified silence. Their eyes went from him, standing erect in his magnificent scarlet clothes, to the woman in the flickering firelight, who appeared to them in all her beauty with a halo of golden hair about her face, and wtih her brilliant sea-green eyes that held at that moment a trace of fear. . . . The Frenchmen who had not met her before seemed to tremble with the impact of her presence. She was indeed as lovely as they had been told, the Lady of the Silver Lake! The sight of her subdued their anxiety, and they gazed at her as if stunned for a long time. Then one of them ran his hand over his brow.

'God in heaven!' he murmured. 'What a fool the man was!'

Then, turning towards Loménie:

'You were right . . .'

There was not one of them who did not know that Pont-Briand had been in love with the foreign woman from the woods. He had been half out of his mind about her. . . .

Nicolas Perrot bowed his head.

'If that was how it was, you had to do it, my lord. You had to. . . . I beg your pardon on my friend's behalf!'

He removed his fur cap and stood with bowed head before the corpse.

Could one conceive of a people more terrible and extremist than these Canadians? Peyrac thought to himself. He pictured them fighting their way through the snows of winter, white as a shroud, bearing the stiff corpse of the friend who must be avenged. . . .

'What else do you wish of me now, gentlemen of New France?' he went on aloud, speaking in bitter tones. 'You wanted Katarunk to be burnt down, and that's done: you achieved what you wanted. You wanted my name to be wiped from North America or for me to incur the everlasting hatred of the Iroquois, or at least that I should take sides with you in your battle again them. But your plans miscarried.'

'Sir, I never went back on the promises I made you in Katarunk,' Loménie protested.

'If it wasn't you it was your brethren Maudreuil, and especially the Jesuit who was on the Kennebec and was unwilling to accept the agreements you made with me, a stranger. It was he who egged Maudreuil and the Patsuiketts on, although, for appearance's sake, the Government of New France did not want to be mixed up in that particular crime.'

'You are wrong. Our wish to make an alliance with you was sincere, and to prove it, let me tell you that as soon as Monsieur de Frontenac learned that you were still alive, in spite of the bitter weather, he sent me out with a message to you containing new proposals.'

'Do you mean to tell me that when you left Quebec on this occasion you had no hostile intent towards me?'

'No, indeed! And as you see, there are very few of us.'

The Count glanced at the four exhausted men and the three Indians who, in spite of the attention they were receiving, did not seem to be recovering.

'What happened to you, then?'

'It's hard to explain. We are quite used to these winter expeditions. All went well till we reached Lake Megantic, where we found the traces of your duel and the body of this unfortunate man. And ever since then ill luck seems to have dogged our footsteps as we carried the corpse with us. It was as if an evil spell were hounding us down as we drew nearer....'

'Wapassou is a place of taboo.'

'Our Indians knew that, and they were frightened. They seemed to grow weaker and we ourselves felt as if we were growing feebler with every day that passed. The strongest had to carry the weakest. It would have been impossible to turn back, for we should have faced certain death. In the end our only hope was to reach your outpost in spite of everything. But after the tremendous effort it cost us to negotiate the waterfalls, we collapsed from exhaustion and lost consciousness. ... But how did you discover us in time?'

No one replied to his question, for the atmosphere was still somewhat uneasy, and when the people of Wapassou remembered what it
was that had brought them out of their retreat to go to the assistance
of these lost men, a shudder ran down their spines.

'But how did you manage to find us?' one of the Frenchmen repeated, looking at them somewhat suspiciously.

'It's Epiphany night!' Peyrac replied with a caustic smile. And he
stared enigmatically at the man who had spoken.

'Things don't always turn out as we would like them to,' he went
on. 'I believe you when you say you left Quebec with the intention
of joining me here in all . . . neutrality, shall I say? But on your way
you were distressed to find your friend dead, and began to feel more
aggressive and vengeful towards me. But winter is a more terrible
enemy than I am, and in the end, you were quite glad that I was here
to save you from it. There is no doubt about it; our encounters seem
always fated to have something equivocal about them. Am I to consider you as prisoners, hostages, because you had plans to seek vengeance against me, or as my guests, on account of your original intentions?'

Once again the little group of Frenchmen seemed to consult one
another in a glance and one of them, a fine figure of a man with a
certain distinction, began to speak.

'Allow me to introduce myself. I am the Duke of Arreboust, first
syndic of the city of Quebec, and I confirm what Monsieur de Loménie
has just told you. We were instructed by Governor Frontenac to visit
you with all peaceful intent. He wished to put a suggestion to you
which . . . but perhaps we could talk of this a little later,' said the
unfortunate duke, rubbing his numb fingers into which the blood was
just beginning to flow again and which must have been hurting him
dreadfully.

He glanced at the corpse of the Canadian officer lying there, already
showing the signs of the work of the icy winds and frost, in the midst of
the glitter of gold, a sombre, shattering symbol of the vanity of this
world's goods.

'In view of the circumstances that forced you to kill this man, we
are willing to grant that this did not constitute an act of hostility towards New France, although we cannot but deplore such brutality.
Monsieur de Loménie and I have spent many years in the close-knit
communities of the early colonial times, and we are well aware of the
fact that strict discipline is needed to hold the demon of lust in check,
but there is always prayer . . .'

397

'I am not running a convent!' said Peyrac. 'As far as I'm concerned, there's gunpowder and a rope . . . and a sword for gentlemen.'

'There is no holiness in you.'

'No, there isn't! God forbid!'

They stiffened, as if to seize their weapons, scandalized by his violent, paradoxical reply. He too was just as everyone had said he was: a black devil, standing beside his mate, setting them at defiance with his grimacing face and sparkling eyes.

The tension between them rose until it was almost unbearable.

Angélique came down the steps from the platform and walked over to them.

'Come and sit by the fire, gentlemen,' she said in her calm, musical voice. 'You are exhausted. . . .'

And seeing that Count Loménie was near collapse, she put her arm round him and supported him across the room.

'What should we do with the corpse?' whispered Jacques Vignot in Peyrac's ear.

Peyrac signalled to them to carry it outside into the cold, into the frosty darkness of the night.

There was nothing else they could do. That was where the dead belonged.

PART IV

The Threat

CHAPTER 67

WAS IT the fact that she had had too little sleep, or overexcitement due to the events of the evening, or the cold which had grown still more oppressively intense, until nature itself seemed almost to be cracking under its marble grip?

Although fully awake Angélique found herself quite incapable of movement.

She dared not stir for fear of feeling a great shudder run through her. She could just make out a thick layer of frost on the tiny panes of fish-skin over the narrow window, which let in a meagre, almost non-existent light.

Enough, however, for her to see that it was already late. Normally, when they got up it was still completely dark, but this morning no one had yet stirred.

Angélique kept on telling herself that she must get up and light the fire, but as the minutes crept by she found herself sinking back into a kind of torpor from which she felt she would never have the strength to wrest herself.

Because the thought had occurred to her several weeks earlier, the morning after a particular night of love, it crossed her mind again that she might be pregnant. The prospect shook her from her lethargy and she hesitated between a feeling of depression and the vague sensation of contentment that most women feel when a new life makes its appearance in their existence.

But she shook her head. No, it was not that.

It was something else.

A feeling of apprehension, almost of fear hung over the fort, and it was the first time she had felt it since their arrival at Wapassou.

Then she remembered.

There were strangers beneath their roof.

She felt no regret at having saved their lives, but with them a threat had entered the house.

She rose noiselessly in order not to awaken her husband, who lay sleeping beside her, breathing regularly in his usual peaceful way.

When she had put on her long woollen leggings over her

underclothes, then her fustian dress, her sleeveless, fur-lined leather jacket and her cloak, she began to feel better.

Each week some further garment was added to their accoutrement. Madame Jonas said that by the end of the winter, all three ladies would be wearing so many clothes that they would look more as if they were rolling than walking.

As was her custom, Angélique buckled on the leather belt that held her pistol holster on the right and two scabbards on the left, one for a dagger the other for a knife. Essential odds and ends were constantly being added to it as well – pieces of string, gloves, mitts, purses. . . .

Once everything was ready Angélique felt prepared to face the world again, and to respond to all that was required of her. And God only knew there was plenty of that!

She felt comfortable in her clothes that were adaptable to all her activities.

For going outside she would throw a coat over her shoulders, and was glad to keep it on inside in the mornings, too, until the fires were alight.

She usually put her hair up in a tight knot on top of her head and tucked it under a narrow coif with the edges slightly turned back around her face, after the fashion of the wives of the great burghers in La Rochelle.

This headdress showed off the pure, oval lines of her face to perfection, although it made her features look a trifle severe. A face framed by a white coif is exposed and bare. It can hide nothing. There is an extraordinarily open quality, a kind of bold directness in those ancient portraits of women with their smooth brows and temples tightly encircled by a hennin.

Angélique had the sort of face that could stand such an austere headdress. And she found it comfortable too, knowing her hair to be protected from the black smoke of the fires and from the dust. Occasionally she would wear, in addition to the coif, a dark brown felt hat with a lilac-coloured feather. The feather having been spoilt by the sharp wind, she had replaced it with a ribbon of coarse black silk to which she had given a touch of brightness by adding a silver buckle at the front.

The brim of this hat was not too wide to prevent her drawing the great fur-lined hood of her coat up over it when it snowed.

Indoors she wore chamois leather slippers over her shoes, cut and sewed in the native fashion, and these she found very warm. For outdoor wear she would don a pair of leather leggings that came to just below the knee and a pair of heavy boots.

There was no gainsaying that all these items of clothing were not exactly the height of elegance; they were what the circumstances demanded. When spring came, that would be the time to take a look at her figure in the mirror.

There was still occasion, on feast days, for the ladies to show that they had not forgotten their more elegant ways.

And every day clean bands, spotlessly laundered and starched, and occasionally a little lace collar, would grace the ladies' necks and relieve the austerity of their dress.

This, with their immaculate starched coifs, was their one and only vanity.

As Angélique was just about to leave her room someone else was preparing to knock at the door, so that when she opened the door she found herself face to face with a man standing on the other side.

Eloi Macollet's face, with its sharp lines that seemed to have been carved out of knotty wood, with the black slit of his toothless mouth and his scarlet cap pulled down once more over the scalping marks on his forehead, was not the kind of a face a person at all nervous could encounter in the shadows without giving a start.

Angélique jumped.

The old man had almost fallen on her and from close up she had seen his little eyes shining like fire-flies.

It was unusual to see him inside the fort at this early hour of the morning.

She opened her mouth to greet him, but he pursed his lips against his raised index finger as a sign for her to remain quiet. Then, setting off on tiptoe with all the grace of a gnome, he made his way towards the door, beckoning to her to follow him.

At the far end of the big room some of the men were stretching and yawning. The main fire was not yet alight.

Angélique drew her cloak around her to face the early morning cold with the air as clear as sapphire.

'What is it, Macollet?'

Still he motioned to her to say nothing as he made his way up through the snow trench, still moving as if he were walking on eggs, with his knees bent and held apart. The frozen snow made strange crackling noises beneath their feet.

There was no other sound.

In the east a glimmer of pink and gold was creeping up the sky and little by little the world emerged in a petrified mass from the blue of the night.

There was a particularly strong smell of smoke. It was the very smell of those translucent, frozen dawns, the only smell of life, for it betrayed the presence of human beings, who had taken refuge in some fort or hut.

The smoke filtered slowly in thick wreaths through the cracks in the birch-bark and from the rounded top of Macollet's wigwam.

Angélique had almost to get on hands and knees to creep inside after the old man. It was hard to see anything in the smoky darkness. The embers were not bright enough to lighten the hut, which was fairly big but chock-a-block with all kinds of miscellaneous objects. All Angélique could make out was the three savages huddled around the fire, and their immobility at once struck her as strange.

'Do you see?' muttered the old man.

'No, that's the trouble, I can see nothing,' Angélique replied, beginning to cough with the smoke that tickled her throat.

'Wait a minute, I'll light up . . .'

And he struggled with a little horn lantern.

Angélique looked apprehensively at the Indians lying huddled beneath their blankets.

'What's the matter with them? Are they dead?'

'No . . . worse!'

At last he managed to strike a light.

Macollet seized one of the Hurons unceremoniously by his top-knot, lifting up his head to expose his face to the full glare of the lantern light.

The Indian made no objection, for he seemed inert and unaware of what was happening. His breath came in hot gusts from his tight, fever-parched lips, which had turned a hideous, livid colour. His skin looked very dark, red in fact, and was covered in purple blotches.

'It's smallpox!' said Eloi Macollet.

All the ancestral terror that this terrible affliction inspired could be heard in the old man's words and in the flash of his eyes as he glanced up at her from under his bushy eyebrows.

Smallpox! The dread smallpox. . . .

Angélique felt a shudder run down her spine. She was unable to utter a sound.

She turned wide-eyed towards Eloi Macollet and they stood there looking at each other in silence.

At last the old man whispered.

'That was why they collapsed in the snow that night. They already had it! The red plague!'

'What will happen?' she said in a whisper.

'They will die. The Indians have no resistance to a filthy disease like that . . . and as for us . . . we'll die too . . . not all of us, of course. You can recover, as long as you don't mind a face that looks as if someone's taken pot shots at it!'

He released the head of the Indian, who gave a long moan then relapsed into his former motionless prostration.

Angelique ran back to the outpost, stumbling as she went. She must find Joffrey before she began to think, otherwise she would be seized with panic. Then she knew she would only have one thought, to seize Honorine and rush with her, screaming into the icy forest.

As she entered the main room, Cantor was busy lighting the fires and Yann le Couennec was sweeping the hearth to help him.

They greeted her in a cheerful, friendly way, and as she looked at them the truth was borne in upon her in all its terrible, overwhelming reality.

They were all going to die.

Only one of them would survive, Clovis from Auvergne. He had already had smallpox and had recovered from it.

He would bury them one after the other . . . bury them? In fact he would have to lay them beneath blocks of ice, and wait for the spring before he could bury them. And he himself might go mad!

Her room seemed to her a last refuge and the man asleep before her in the bed, so full of health and strength, seemed like the last rampart between her and death.

Only a few moments earlier there had been nothing but happiness around her. A rustic, hidden, secret happiness, a happiness quite out of the ordinary, but nevertheless happiness, since they possessed the most precious gift of all – life, exultant life.

And now death had slipped in among them like a fog, like smoke seeping and flowing along the ground, and it was useless to shut all the doors, for it could get in anywhere.

She called softly:

'Joffrey. Joffrey!'

She no longer dared to touch him for fear of contaminating him.

And yet, as he opened his eyes, dark and lively and smiling, and they lighted on her, she found herself hoping against hope that he would be able to defend her from this danger too.

'What is it, my angel?'

'Monsieur de Loménie's Hurons have got smallpox . . .'

She admired him for giving no start of surprise, he rose without undue haste, saying nothing, and she handed him his clothes. Only he did not have a good stretch as he often did when he woke, like a great cat preparing to face the world. He said nothing.

There was nothing to say and he knew that she was not the sort of woman to delude herself about their situation, nor one to seek useless words of comfort.

But she sensed that he was thinking. Then finally he said:

'Smallpox? I'd be surprised. It would have to be a result of an epidemic brought with them from Quebec. But illnesses like that always arrive with the ships in the spring. If there haven't been any cases of smallpox in Quebec since the autumn, in other words since the Saint Lawrence has been icebound, it can't be smallpox . . .'

His reasoning seemed correct, even obvious. She began to breathe more freely, and the colour returned to her cheeks.

Before they left the room he laid a hand on her shoulder for a moment and, giving her a firm squeeze, bade her take courage.

CHAPTER 68

WHEN HE reached the wigwam, Joffrey de Peyrac examined the sick Hurons with great care. They were disturbing enough to look at, for they were the colour of molten lead, and when he lifted their eyelids he could see that their eyes were bloodshot. Their breathing was still strident, almost like a whistle, and they were unconscious.

'They were more or less in this state yesterday evening when we found them under the snow,' Macollet explained, 'and when I brought them in here I thought their stupor was due to the cold.'

'What's your opinion, Macollet?' Peyrac asked. 'It's hard to say, isn't it? They've got the symptoms of smallpox, that I can't deny, but I don't see any of the typical smallpox spots on their bodies yet. Nothing but these red blotches . . .'

The trapper nodded thoughtfully. They'd just have to wait and see! There was nothing else they could do.

Speaking in low voices, the three of them discussed what precautions they should take and what orders to give. Macollet said that he would look after the Hurons. In his experience, alcohol protected people from epidemics and infection.

So he would settle down to it in his wigwam with a keg of brandy.

The old man admitted with many a nod that even the worst situations have their bright side. He would drink brandy and rinse his mouth out with it frequently, and clean his hands with it when he had touched the savages.

They would put up a little hut beside his wigwam in which he would change his clothes before entering the fort.

'Don't you worry about me, I was with the Montagnais and the Hurons at the time of the great smallpox epidemic that decimated them in 1662. I went from one village to the next and found nothing but corpses. And I survived. I'll give these fellers here some herb tea and keep the fire going. And after that, well, we'll see!'

'I'll fetch you some food and some herbs for the tea,' said Angélique.

Her tread was firmer as she walked back to the fort. She must remain completely calm. The day had dawned now, all pink and cold and serene.

As she entered the main room she found herself face to face with the most authentic specimen of a Jesuit anyone could have imagined within a distance of a hundred leagues.

He was a priest of medium height, on the plump side, with a good-natured expression superimposed on the more sombre lines of his face. He had laughing eyes, a bald forehead, and a thick beard. His soutane, his black robe, were of good, solid drugget, and he wore a black leather belt from which hung several small items, a knife, a purse. . . . Across his chest hung a largish black crucifix tipped on the corners with copper, and held in place by a silk cord. His neck was rather fat and overflowed a straight hard collar, lined with white cloth.

'Allow me to introduce myself,' he said. 'I am Father Masserat of the Company of Jesus.'

His sudden appearance at such a time made Angélique think she was having hallucinations. She took several steps back and had to lean against the wall for support.

'But wherever did you come from?' she stammered.

'From that bed, Madame,' he replied, pointing towards the far end of the room, 'from that bed where you yourself tucked me in so carefully yesterday evening.'

Then she realized that he was one of the men they had saved the night before from a certain death beneath the snow. Was this not the very man she had discovered first and roughly dragged out of the snow?

Beneath his cloak stiff with frost she had not realized there was a soutane.

'Yes, it's me,' he said, as if following her train of thought.

'You carried me on your back, Madame. I was aware of it, but I was too paralysed with cold to introduce myself at the time and to thank you.'

His eyes continued to smile, but when she examined him carefully she could see that behind their gaiety lay all the crafty reserve of a peasant.

Angélique ran her hands distractedly over her face.

'Oh Father, how can you ever forgive me! I had absolutely no idea we had a Jesuit among our guests . . . and I have just received a terrible piece of news.'

She drew closer to him and whispered:

'We fear that your Hurons may have smallpox.'

Father Masserat's cheerful face changed colour.

'Good God!' he said turning white.

Such an exclamation from his lips was an indication that he had received a considerable shock.

'Where are they?'

'In old Macollet's wigwam.' And as he made to go outside, she added:

'Wait a minute! You mustn't go out like that, Father! It's terribly cold.'

And she seized the great black high-collared coat which he had laid across one corner of the table, and threw it round his shoulders, wrapping it about him to keep him warm.

She would never have acted in this way in other circumstances, had she, for instance, been introduced to the worthy Jesuit in some drawing-room.

But she was distracted with worry, and was acting without thinking, feeling intensely her responsibility for keeping everyone well, so much so that she feared that the Jesuit might be more prone to the infection if he caught cold. She handed him his hat as well and he strode off.

Angélique decided that she must have a hot drink to help her take a grip on herself again, so she went over to the fireplace, poured a little boiling water into a wooden bowl and took the bottle of apple-jack from the table.

Some of the men were finishing their soup, which they had reheated themselves, while some of them dipped pieces of cold maize griddle-cake into their brimming bowls of apple-jack.

But so well disciplined were they that not one of them had even thought of cutting himself a piece of fat bacon or ham, since these provisions were distributed in the mornings only by Madame Jonas, who herself took orders from Octave Malaprade who was responsible for the stores. And Madame Jonas was nowhere to be seen.

'Has no one seen Madame Jonas yet?' Angélique asked them.

They shook their heads.

The presence of strangers sitting at the end of the table made them feel uncomfortable. One of them was the man who had introduced himself as the Duke of Arreboust.

He was a big, stout man, greying at the temples, and he looked every inch a gentleman. He had taken the trouble to shave. With him was a tall young man with an austere look.

But Angélique's thoughts were elsewhere and she did not even notice them.

She was worried by the fact that Madame Jonas had not appeared, for she was always the first up and took it upon herself to light the fires and bring the pots to the boil.

There was no sign of Monsieur Jonas either, nor of Elvire.

Had they been struck down already? And what about the children?

She refrained from going to find out what had happened to them before she had taken the precautions Count Peyrac had recommended, and gone back to her room, changed her outer clothes, which she exposed to the icy air, along with the dress she had worn the previous evening for the feast of the Epiphany, changed her coif and rubbed her hands and rinsed her mouth out with brandy.

Then, with beating heart, she went and scratched on the Jonases' door, and was relieved to hear their voices reply.

The children were up and dressed and playing in a corner, but the three adults from La Rochelle were sitting stiffly on three stools, looking towards her with pale, sad faces.

'Do you know?' they murmured.

'Yes indeed!'

'What is to become of us?'

'But how is it that you know already?' Angélique asked.

'Oh, we noticed it almost as soon as you brought them back last night.'

'You might have said something earlier.'

'What for? There's nothing we can do.'

'We could have taken the necessary precautions at once. . . .'

Monsieur Jonas looked at her uncomprehendingly.

'Precautions?'

'But . . . what is it you are talking about?' Angélique cried.

'About the Jesuit, of course!'

'I had a feeling he was a Jesuit last night,' Madame Jonas explained, 'there was something about him and his beard that made me feel uneasy although he was as stiff with cold as the others. But this morning when I saw him, as I went into the main room, all black from head to foot in his soutane, with his collar and his crucifix, I thought I was going to faint. I've still got the shudders. . . .'

'We have something worse than the Jesuit father among us,' said Angélique sadly.

And she explained the situation to them.

Isolation was the best way of preventing the spread of infection. The Jonases must remain with the children in their own two rooms until further notice.

Food would be brought in to them, which they would prepare for themselves and for the children. They would be able to take the air by climbing out of their window at the back of the house, for the snow was high enough to be almost level with the window ledge.

By taking these precautions it was just possible that they might be spared the terrible scourge.

She returned to the big room to find a group of men standing round one of the beds at the end of the room, near the men's dormitory.

She went over and saw Count Loménie's face scarlet on his pillow. He was already unconscious.

CHAPTER 69

ONE OF the Hurons died that evening, after making his confession and receiving the last sacraments from Father Masserat.

'But at least the comfort of the last rites of the Church are available to us,' said Nicolas Perrot. 'And that doesn't happen very often when people die in the back country during winter.'

They had moved Count Loménie up into one of the lofts.

The chimney-stack passed through the loft and gave it some warmth, and they brought up a brazier and left the trapdoor open.

But for fear of the house catching fire, which is the great dread of all who live in winter quarters, there had to be someone permanently at the sick man's bedside. This was necessary for other reasons too, for he was very agitated and kept on trying to get up. He needed to be given drinks, have his forehead bathed, and be constantly covered up. Angélique asked Clovis to help her, not that he showed any special aptitude as a nurse, but because he was the only one who had had smallpox and could therefore approach the sick man with impunity.

Angélique put on the skin gloves she had been given the previous evening in order to tend the unfortunate Count. She was not convinced that this precaution would be adequate, but decided to leave the gloves near the bed and to put them on again whenever she came back.

She spent the rest of the day boiling up huge quantities of water into which she put every medicinal root and leaf she could lay hands on.

In addition, she had to take over Madame Jonas's and Elvire's tasks, and when Count Peyrac realized this he put two men at her disposal.

He kept an eye on everything.

He continued his work in the workshops as usual, but visited Count Loménie several times and likewise Eloi Macollet in his wigwam, who was coping philosophically with the sick men as he smoked pipe after pipe and drank glass after glass of brandy.

When he returned that evening from his last visit, he was accompanied by the Jesuit father and informed them of the death of the first of the Hurons.

Supper was on the table, and they sat down to eat, although several of them had a lump in their throats.

No one had thought to remove the Christmas holly decorations. Although it had happened so recently, the happy feast of Epiphany seemed already far away. If they came out of this alive they would remember that happy day.

They all kept a close watch on one another's faces for the slightest sign of impending illness. The first to be examined were of course the three strangers, the Jesuit father, the Duke of Arreboust and the very tall young man who never opened his mouth except to eat, and there was general relief when they were all seen to be enjoying their food, since by now they too might normally have been expected to be struck down by smallpox.

They talked about the practice current in the East, of protecting people from the illness by scratching the skin with the point of a knife or a broken razor blade and rubbing in some of the matter from an unhealed pustule of someone who had recovered from smallpox. Some of these survivors had turned it into a veritable business by keeping some of their pustules going for years on end, and travelling from town to town offering people the chance of protection against the sickness.

But here in America the conditions for this prophylactic treatment were not available, since only Clovis had had smallpox already, and his pustules had long since dried up; and the Huron had died before the characteristic pustules had appeared. . . .

These discussions at table took what was left of Angélique's appetite away, for even before this she had had to force herself to swallow the little she had eaten.

As was to be expected on a day like this, the children, finding themselves freed of their customary strict supervision because the adults were fully occupied by their worries, followed the natural instinct of their age and got up to an unpredictable piece of mischief.

A sudden terrible cry rang out from the Jonases' room, and Angélique, who was the first to reach it, found Elvire in sobs and Monsieur and Madame Jonas dumb with horror. They pointed to something, or rather someone in a corner whom at first she did not recognize.

It was Honorine.

The little girl, taking advantage of the rare miracle which had diverted the grown-ups' attention from her, had decided to do her hair in the Iroquois style and had persuaded young Thomas to help her.

It had been no easy task and in spite of the simultaneous use of a pair of scissors and a razor it had taken the two children a good hour to cut off Honorine's thick head of hair, leaving just the central topknot rising gloriously from the middle of her skull.

When at last Elvire, who had eventually grown anxious at finding them so quiet, discovered what they had been up to, they were trying to examine the result by leaning over a piece of armour for lack of a mirror.

The young woman's screams and the horrified exclamations of the Jonases, followed by Angélique's bursting into the room, froze them with dismay in their corner, where the two tiny creatures sat wide-eyed and staring. They were disconcerted but by no means aware that they had done something silly.

'We've not finished yet,' said Thomas. 'I'm just putting the feathers in.'

Angélique collapsed on to a stool and laughed till her sides ached.

Honorine's little round face with the great red topknot sticking up from it was really too funny for words.

Her laughter was partly due to the fact that she was overwrought, but what else could she do? There are days when devils seem to have special permission to torment human beings, and if you let them, they dominate you and drive you mad.

She tried to explain to Elvire, who was still weeping and was shocked by Angélique's reaction to the disaster, that too many terrible things were going on that day for them to attach any great importance to this trivial occurrence, which was a mere childish prank.

And it was a miracle that Honorine had not had her ears snicked or been badly cut, as she might well have been. Perhaps young Thomas had the makings of a barber in him yet!

Monsieur and Madame Jonas suggested grave penalties – they should be made to go without bread and cheese. But here again Angélique intervened. Not that day, and especially not by depriving them of bread and cheese.

By now she had grown serious again and she went up to the two naughty little mites, pointing out to them severely that they had been very disobedient in borrowing a pair of scissors and a razor without asking permission. But she refrained from giving them both a good slap for fear of contagion.

The little monsters had certainly picked the right day for their escapade.

They were both sent off packing to bed in the dark, as their only punishment, but one which they would certainly feel and which could do them nothing but good.

Back in the big room Angélique told everyone the story of what Honorine had done; it brought laughter to the lips of all and immediately made the atmosphere less tense. They all felt that this way of cocking a snook at bad luck might perhaps ward off the evil spirits. Honorine had made it quite clear from her actions that she was in no way concerned about smallpox. She had other irons in the fire.

All this might well put off, perhaps even completely hoodwink, the spirits of darkness, which do not always show any very great subtlety in their understanding of human reactions.

Another thing that brought them comfort was the discovery of bread and cheese in the Canadians' baggage.

Three of the men had gone back to the far end of the lake to dig out the remainder of the Frenchmen's equipment from the ice and snow, and, together with the customary dried meat and smoked bacon, maize-flour and tobacco and adequate stocks of brandy, they had found half a large cheese and a whole loaf of wheat bread, all of it as hard as rock.

But all that was needed was to put the bread in the oven for a minute and place the cheese beside the hearth to make them as good as fresh again. The bread was warm and the cheese soft, but not unduly so, and its smell was delicious.

The Frenchmen insisted on sharing out their victuals among their hosts, for these items were their staple diet in Quebec, whereas the forest dwellers never saw such things.

Some mumbled something about possible contagion from the food, but their greed got the better of them. Angélique hesitated for a moment then decided that it didn't matter. She made the sign of the cross on the pieces of bread and cheese to exorcize the evil spirits and sent some to the two children in disgrace, whose sobs were calmed by the offering.

CHAPTER 70

THE MEN of Fort Wapassou had taken the news of the threat that hung over them very coolly. Their fatalistic attitude held a good measure of true Christian feeling, of resignation to the will of God.

Angélique did not possess that kind of resignation. She loved life passionately, all the more so since it seemed to her to be only recently that she had known it in all its fullness.

And she did not want Honorine or her sons to be cut off in the pride of youth from all it had to offer. The death of any of the children or the young men would be a crime for which she would feel responsible.

But there are times when a person must be prepared to sacrifice his life, for himself and for those around him, to admit that the sword may fall at any moment, and to give himself up without pointless revolt to the common lot of mankind.

'And so we walk with life and death as our companions – each has its own importance – we should not be afraid of death. . . .'

Who was it that had uttered those splendid words? It was Colin Paturel, the king of the slaves in Meknes, a Norman, a simple sailor, a man of the same type as those here gathered together as captives of winter in a strange land. . . .

All these men had narrowly escaped death on many an occasion, not only death in the battles into which they had been drawn by their thirst for adventure, but death from illness and epidemic as well.

Most of them had come unscathed out of at least one epidemic, if not two – plague in the east, yellow fever in the ports of Africa, smallpox everywhere at all times, scurvy, gangrene, and fevers – and others had been condemned to die of hunger, of thirst or as the result of torture. . . .

The survivors had come unscathed out of all these disasters, more and more convinced of their own immunity on each occasion.

It was the same in every battle they had fought.

If your name was not on the bullet, you were all right.

If it was, good night! Your time had come.

When Joffrey de Peyrac decided to sit up for part of the night with Count Loménie, and leave the blacksmith to take over again later, Angélique felt no anxiety on his behalf. She felt him to be immune to illness. And it was this calm certainty of victory that turned out in the end to be the best panacea of all. On the eighth day, the last of the Hurons died wasted with fever and covered with red blotches.

But still there were no pustules.

At dawn on the following day, when she came to relieve Clovis, who had been sitting up with the sick man all night, Angélique found him almost unconscious, his breathing shallow, his face as red as the metal in his own forge, altogether in much worse shape than the sick man he was looking after.

Angélique stood looking at him for a long while, then she fell to her knees crying: 'Praise be to God!'

Clovis never forgave her that. They could say what they liked! There was no doubt about it at all; Madame la Comtesse had been really delighted to see him ill!

She hadn't even done anything to help him. She had simply said 'Praise be to God!' And then she had left him and run off telling everyone: 'Clovis is ill. Isn't it wonderful! . . .'

He had heard her with his own ears.

And she had hugged the first person she had met, who happened to be Nicolas Perrot.

No one was able to persuade Clovis of the fact that what had so delighted Angélique, when she had seen him, struck down like the others although he had already had smallpox, was the fact that at last they could be absolutely certain that the present epidemic was not smallpox!

It was a virulent form of measles, and many of them caught it, but it was nothing like as serious as smallpox.

415

The Hurons had died, but, as the Canadians said, they died of almost anything. An ordinary cold would bring them to death's door. They had become a delicate race since they had come into contact with the Palefaces. Their protective spirits seemed to have abandoned them and many of them attributed their decline and the downfall of their race to the fact that they had been baptized.

They seemed to have no resistance to infectious fevers.

During the following weeks, the sickness absorbed all the energies of the inhabitants of Wapassou.

All their loves, their hates and their plans were shelved until *afterwards*. But first of all they had to get through this red tunnel where their enemy, death, lurked in the shadows. Until the last man was back on his feet again, pale and unsteady as he began his convalescence and joined them at the common table, and they raised their glasses to welcome him back among them, death could still strike; they had to fight it foot to foot, force the fever back inch by inch, overcome their weakness, their relapses, help one another to pass the crisis, clasp a sick man in their arms as he struggled feverishly, and hold him there for hours on end, as in the hollow of a wave or on its crest, and bring him down to the other side at last, exhausted, covered in sweat, and out, to lie on the shores of life. Then Angélique would examine the inert body. The man would lie as if dead, the thin breath separating life from death was imperceptible, but Angélique would know that the worst was over and that he would live. In order to be quite sure, she would lay a hand on his brow again, from which the burning pulsation of fever was slowly departing like a storm, then, reassured, she would cover him up carefully to make certain that he did not catch a chill, and make her way to the next sick bed.

The sight of a sick man overcoming his illness would give her added strength to carry on, and seeing him put up a good fight filled her with sympathy and esteem for him. Gratitude too. At least he had not abandoned her, had not disowned her, had not allowed her to be vanquished, in spite of her ridiculously inadequate weapons.

'Don't leave me. Don't leave me,' the man would say. 'I can't do it all myself, you must help me.'

And ever afterwards there existed between them a feeling of having fought a battle together, a battle of life and death.

When men are ill they tend to give in too easily. Sickness is an enemy that readily overcomes them because it is repugnant to them and they are unwilling to face up to it. Angélique shook them out of this state and forced them to measure the strength of their adversary and plan their campaign against it. She would explain to them:

'Tomorrow you are going to feel very ill. Don't call me every five minutes because I can't look after everyone at once for several hours on end. . . . I shall leave a jug of herb tea and a cup beside you, all you have to do is to drink, but please do it. When you find yourself face to face with someone who wants to harm you, you draw your knife, you don't wait for someone else to do it for you. . . .'

She seemed to be letting them get on with things as best they could, but they always felt that she was there. She would go by, casting no more than a brief glance at them, but her smile said 'Bravo, you are not letting me down', and this made them feel better as they lay aching and half-delirious, longing to let go in their misery. And whenever necessary she would spend long hours beside their beds, without showing any signs of impatience or discouragement.

At first the three women took it in turns to be on night-watch. Joffrey de Peyrac would often take over the unpleasant hours around dawn, but he realized that Angélique's mere presence seemed to possess healing properties. He would have liked to spare her this inhuman burden of fatigue which little by little began to make her features drawn and to etch rings under her eyes. It was lack of sleep she found most trying, and yet it seemed to her that were she to spend a whole night without going to see *her* invalids, she would find them all dead or dying in the morning. So she forced herself to do the rounds at least once every night, and would go from one bed to the next, examining them all. She would straighten their covers, lay a hand on their feverish brows, help them sip something to drink, and speak a few comforting words to them.

Through their sickness they would hear her voice, savour its inflections, as sweet as balm, like a caress intended for them alone, and when she leaned further over them, so that she blotted out the diffuse light from fire or lantern, their senses, both numbed and sharpened as they so often are by a fever, delighted in her womanly scent and in the glimpse they caught over the top of her bodice of the dazzling curves of her breasts, a furtive delight, more nostalgic than lascivious, for she had become to them a warm, maternal figure who gave them back the distant, delicious and never-to-be-forgotten security of their childhood.

One night, Loménie-Chambord thought he was going to die. In his mind his whole past life faded into dimness. He stood in another world, on the other side of the door he had never dared to push open. On the other side of the door through which he just never dared to pass.

417

They were among the damned. Through the trap-door he could hear the sounds of voices, he caught the smell of cooking; it all came to him as a confused hum and the familiar sounds took on a new character, a new meaning. They seemed to possess a new pungency, the savour of life itself. A life he had never tasted. For he had only touched life with the tips of his fingers. Not even that, he had only touched it with a gloved hand. And now that he was about to die, his whole being had acquired an acute, although diffuse, carnal awareness. And he, who had spent his days longing for the day when death would reunite him with God, found himself regretting the loss of the rough, material world so much that tears began to flow from his eyes. He seemed to be stifling and felt alone. And he began to long for Madame de Peyrac to come up into the dark loft as if she were a saving angel. When she came, she saw in a glance all that he had been going through, and spoke to him seriously in calm, reassuring tones: 'You are feeling ill because you are about to reach a crisis. . . . After that you will get better. . . . Have confidence, it will be unpleasant, but you will get through it. . . . If you were in any danger, I would know, for I have had long experience of sick and wounded men. . . . You are not in any danger.'

He had believed her at once and already his breathing seemed easier. She had wrapped him in a blanket and helped him to get up, then had supported him as far as the chair where she had made him sit down, placing him beside the wall so that he ran no risk of falling. He could still feel the pressure of her firm arm supporting him in his weakness.

'Now keep still and don't move.'

Then she had changed his damp sheets, shaken up his mattress which had been flattened by the weight of his feverish body, aired the blankets and remade the bed with clean sheets, all of which she did in a series of firm, neat movements so harmonious in their liveliness that he felt no weariness at the sight of her; then she had helped him back into bed again and he remembered how good the clean sheets had felt. Finally she had sat down beside his bed, and as he gave himself up to the numbing effect of the fever, she laid her hand on his damp brow, her hand that was like a talisman, a precious pledge, an indomitable force that barred the way to phantasms, her hand that was like a surety, a promise, calmly attentive, a light to watch over him. . . . A heart keeping watch. He had fallen asleep like a child and had woken later to find himself weak but better, cured, in fact!

When he came down from his attic and took his place at the common table, they celebrated his recovery like that of the others. The outpost was so small that it made it hard to treat the Frenchmen as prisoners. After ministering to them like new-born babies, it was hardly possible for Angélique to treat them differently now and not to look after them during their convalescence. . . .

There was a time towards the end of January when more than half the inhabitants of the outpost were in bed. The illness was at its peak for about three weeks.

Joffrey de Peyrac caught it too, quite badly, but he was up and about again sooner than the others. He had a very high fever for several days during which time he was almost unconscious.

Angélique watched over him and was astonished to find that she was not more anxious. As he lay there rigid, it was as if some indestructible force still emanated from him, as if his illness was unable to abase him or make him pitiful.

When she thought back, Angélique realized that he had never inspired pity, even when he had stood in the forecourt of Notre-Dame, a human wreck wearing nothing but a shirt, with a rope around his neck, in all the abjection of his tortured body, even there he had seemed stronger than those around him. And it was the hateful, stupid crowd, and the hysterical, half-crazed monks, that one might have been tempted to pity. As for his strength, nothing and no one could ever take it from him.

Of the men they had saved on Epiphany night, Father Masserat was the only one not to develop measles and he was able to give Angélique invaluable help. He was tireless and always willing, cheerfully taking on the most unpleasant tasks, thus sparing her the really heavy work, for she found it exhausting to be constantly lifting these inert men, some of whom were exceptionally athletic specimens of humanity, like Jacques Vignot, the blacksmith, and the Englishman. The Jesuit father would grasp his man as if he were a doll, turn the mattress and remake the bed; then, when the man was safely back in bed again, he would feed him some soup on a spoon with all the patience of a nursemaid. Like many of his cloth, he had nursed savages during epidemics, and had sometimes been the only man left on his feet in a whole village, as he went from hut to hut. He told them humorously that things had a habit of working out badly in such situations, for the savages would accuse him just like children of trying to starve them to death by giving them nothing but broth to eat and keeping all the meat and vegetables for himself, and as he remained in good health, before he knew where he was, they were holding him responsible for their misfortunes.

Times of calamity favour the medicine-men, who are quick to inform their people that the gods are full of wrath because the villages have welcomed the Black Robe. . . . So no sooner had his patients regained some of their strength than he had to take flight into the woods to save himself from death. The priest always had a story to tell to keep his patient interested, and he would entertain the children and keep them company, playing with them during their convalescence, and paying no heed to the three Huguenots who sat huddled in a corner of their room, not daring to move for fear that the worst might happen. . . .

When the patients gave him a few moments' respite, he would tie an oilcloth apron round his squat, square frame and go off to the cellars to brew beer, to make soap or even to scrub the dirty clothes.

And when Angélique, in confusion, tried to stop him, he countered her objections with a kind of passive resistance characteristic of the Jesuits.

How could they, after all this, remain enemies?

After all, they were all in the same boat, and for months on end the howling gales outside kept them shut up together with their crazy hostility, and turned them all, men and women, into one fraternity bent on fighting the winter.

Thus it was that they were able to discuss the matters left in abeyance ever since Epiphany night without passion or animosity.

As soon as Monsieur de Loménie was well again, he made no secret of the fact that he had been sent by Monsieur de Frontenac to ask for Peyrac's help in financing an expedition that was to explore the course of the great Mississippi river, which, they felt certain, must flow out into the China Sea. He wanted to put his right-hand man, Monsieur Robert Cavelier de la Salle, who was the tall, coldly austere young man who had come with them to Fort Wapassou, in charge of the expedition. The gold ingots among which they had laid Pont-Briand that first evening had not escaped his eye. Then he had been as sick as a dog. But no sooner had he recovered than he had tackled Loménie and d'Arreboust and urged them to do their utmost to seek some satisfactory arrangement with the master of Wapassou.

'Are you really as rich as people say?' the Knight of Malta asked the Count.

'I am, and I shall become still richer as I continue the work I have come here to do.'

Florimond was in a great state of excitement, as it had been his secret ambition to explore the Mississippi and discover the China Sea ever since he was a small boy, or so he claimed. He was an accomplished cartographer, and lost himself in contemplation of the still undiscovered areas of the maps he drew and over which he would pore endlessly, for ever making calculations and working out new possibilities.

As soon as he learned of Monsieur de la Salle's intentions, he never left his side. De la Salle was a cold man who appeared much younger than his years and who had behind him considerable and varied experience. He was as touchy as a stripling, insisting sometimes on being addressed as Monsieur de la Salle, at others as Cavelier, when it happened to cross his mind that Canada was being conquered and built up by the common man. He had only recently been created a noble, and in case Angélique had any doubts about the fact, which was something it had never occurred to her to have, he showed her his letters from the King. 'To our dearly beloved Robert Cavelier de la Salle, in recognition of the good and praiseworthy report we have received concerning good services rendered in the land of Canada ...'

The new peer's coat of arms consisted of a greyhound courant on a field sable surmounted by a mullet of eight points gold. But besides this, he possessed an undoubted fund of erudition, unfailing courage and all the tenacity of a visionary. Convinced that he would one day become the discoverer of the famed China passage, which was the dream of every daring young man who had ever set out towards the west across the Sea of Darkness during the previous century, he was impatient of the fact that he had not yet reached his goal . . . and was not already back from it! Florimond understood him well: 'I feel certain that the huge river the Indians call Father of the Waters will lead straight to China without our having to leave our canoes. Don't you think it does, Father?'

No, Joffrey de Peyrac did not think it did and greeted his son's enthusiasm with an expression of scepticism that worried the lad but failed to discourage him.

Angélique grieved for Florimond, for as an admiring mother, whose heart was touched by his youthful enthusiasm, she would gladly have given him the China Sea on a plate, while on the other hand her devoted confidence in her husband's scientific genius gave her no room for hope. Joffrey de Peyrac was the first to admit that his doubts were not based on anything very precise.

'In fact,' Florimond said, 'your scepticism is not based on calculations.'

'No, it isn't! Knowing as little as we do at the present moment, it would be hard to make any calculations. . . .'

'So the best thing would be to go and see for oneself. . . .'
'Yes indeed. . . .'

'I think it would be a good idea to allow Florimond to go off on this expedition with all these crazy fanatics,' he told Angélique one evening. 'Through his association with them he will learn the value of the opposing qualities: good organization and a sound scientific training are often every bit as effective as genius. He will also be able to fulfil his ambitions to go exploring with a group of men whom nothing will deter and who will undoubtedly never show more ingenuity than when face to face with some difficult or even desperate situation. That is where the French excel, and Florimond, who is as well endowed with this particular quality as any Frenchman alive, can develop it at his leisure, without having his enthusiasm damped by the dourer and more prudent mentality of the Anglo-Saxons.

'Furthermore, if they are successful, my position in North America will be established. If they fail, I shall nevertheless have financed the expedition and saved Monsieur de Frontenac from having to dip into the public purse. Out of gratitude – and he is an honest man, and a Gascon into the bargain – he will then do his best to make sure that my position remains tenable here on the borders of his colony.

'If I make this loan without any kind of security, at least I will gain a moral advantage from it, and our elder son will receive an invaluable training, not to mention all the plans, notes and information he will bring back to me about the subsoil of the areas they cross. This is something that Cavelier, in spite of a certain competence, could never do. On that score, Florimond is already much more knowledgeable than he is. . . .'

CHAPTER 71

WHEN HE learned of his father's decision, Florimond acted with all the spontaneity of youth and ran to his father and embraced him, then knelt down and kissed his hand. The storm had raged almost without a break for two months, and had been followed by heavy snowfalls, ruling out any question of setting off immediately on a long journey. Having obtained the necessary funds from Peyrac, Cavelier de la Salle did not intend to return to Quebec, but rather to set off west towards Lake Champlain and make his way from there up to

Montreal. In the region of Marieville there was a domain with a small manor house which the local inhabitants had nicknamed 'China' on account of the innumerable times their landlord had harped on his plans. This would be the base from which they would plan the expedition, buy goods for bartering, and weapons and canoes. Then they would set off towards the great lakes and Cataraconi, on the first stage of their journey. Peyrac would give his son a few of the gold ingots and a letter of credit to a man called Lemoyne, who was a merchant in Marieville in the vicinity of Montreal, and who would deliver its equivalent in supplies.

'What!' Cavelier exclaimed. 'You're not telling me that that old bandit is capable of minting coinage from pure gold?'

'He's done it often enough before,' said the Duke of Arreboust. 'Do you think he'd be as rich as he is if it weren't for the fact that he's always going off to Orange to trade with the English? Canadian paper money is worth nothing compared with the gold of those gentlemen! Look!'

And from his fob pocket he produced a gold coin and threw it down on the table.

'That's a coin we found on an English prisoner the Abenakis sold us in Montreal last autumn. Have a look at what is written round the picture of James II: King of England, Duke of Normandy, of Brittany and ... King of France! Do you see that? King of France! As if we hadn't won back Aquitaine, Maine and Anjou over three hundred years ago with Saint Joan of Arc. . . . But no, they won't give up. And they have called one of the new provinces they intend to colonize Maine, on the grounds that the Queen of England was once Queen of Maine in France. That's the kind of gold a man like Lemoyne had the temerity to accept as payment. Frankly insulting I call it.'

'You must not worry about that, Sir,' said Peyrac with a smile, 'as long as the English confine themselves to a few words struck on their coins to claim their sovereignty over France, it's no great matter. Nor should you seek to inquire what Canadians like Lemoyne or Le Ber are up to when they go off into the woods; such men are the cornerstones of your colony, not only because they were first to settle here, but because they are the boldest, the strongest and the richest men we have.'

Father Masserat withdrew his little briar pipe, which was a great source of pleasure to him, from his mouth.

'They are very pious people too, devoted to the Church, and they say that one of the Le Ber girls is going to become a nun. . . .'

'May their sins be pardoned!' Peyrac exclaimed. 'And as for their trading and bartering, have no fears about that, Monsieur de la Salle.'

Angélique held out her hand towards the coin Monsieur d'Arreboust had thrown down.

'May I have it?'

'Of course, Madame ... if it gives you pleasure. ... But what will you do with it?'

'Keep it as a talisman, perhaps.'

She tossed the piece up and down in her hand.

It was a perfectly ordinary coin, about the same weight as a gold Louis. But she liked the fact that it was not completely round, and thought its old English inscription held a strange charm. The coin epitomized many things: gold, England, France, the age-old enmity between the two countries that continued unabated into the depths of the forests of the New World. She tried to visualize the bewilderment of the poor English Puritan snatched away from the familiar shores around Casco Bay and his cod fishing and dragged off by feathered Indians to the dreadful Papist fur-traders of the Saint Lawrence.

'He could not understand why we were so angry,' Arreboust went on to explain. 'And we thrust the coin we had found in his fob pocket under his nose and said "King of France!" "Ah, yes," he replied. "Why not?" He had always seen that written on his coins. ... As a matter of fact, it so happens it was Madame Le Ber who bought the man in the hope of making a valet out of him. She hopes to convert him soon too.'

'You see!' said Father Masserat benignly.

In this atmosphere of plans to make and tales to tell the long evenings became friendly gatherings once more. They tried not to talk too loud so as not to disturb those who were ill, and were delighted whenever a new convalescent was able to join them once more.

Angélique would take Honorine on her knees and rock her till she fell asleep, or she would strip a handful of roots, but she was all ears to what was going on. There was no doubt about it; these Canadians could carry an audience with them into the past as well as the future; they had the gift of bringing a whole world, a veritable saga, to life with one or two anecdotes.

That evening they talked about the Lemoyne family and the Le Bers, who, as poor artisans or farm-hands hiring out their labour to some tight-fisted farmer, had grown weary of this life of slavery and had come over to Canada with the first ships. They had been given a hoe, a sickle and a musket, and had married some of the King's girls.

They had had four, five, ten, twelve children, all of them healthy, strong and unbiddable. They had soon abandoned their sickles and, in spite of Monsieur de Maisonneuve's remonstrances, had gone off to buy furs from the Indians, moving always farther and farther west. They discovered huge lakes, waterfalls, the sources of unknown rivers, and more and more Indian tribes. They too claimed that there was no such thing as a China Sea and that the continent just went on and on, and they would argue with that crazy man Cavelier de la Salle over a tankard of good cider. Apple cider from their Norman apple-trees which had eventually succeeded in establishing themselves in their Canadian field, thanks to the care lavished on them by the women-folk. They came back rich men, with mountains of soft, splendid furs over which they would run their fingers mutilated by Iroquois torture.

Now their sons accompanied them on the waterways of the high country, and their daughters dressed in lace and satin like the ladies of Paris. They made gifts to the Church....

Then it was Monsieur de Loménie's turn to evoke the early days of the City of Montreal, when the Iroquois used to come into their gardens at night and hide among the mustard leaves where they could listen to the Palefaces' voices. And woe betide anyone who stirred abroad on those nights . . . for Marieville or Montreal had neither rampart nor palisade to protect it, since its founder wanted the Indians to be able to have free access to them without any kind of hindrance, as brothers visit brothers. And they took full advantage of their opportunities. Many a time did Mother Bourgeoys's nuns look up as they knelt in prayer to see a hideous Iroquois face pressed up against the window looking at them....

The priest talked about the early mission stations, Macollet about his first voyages, Cavelier about the Mississippi and d'Arreboust about the early days of Quebec.

And such was the power of suggestion in their voices, against the crackling of the fire and the ceaseless raging of the storm outside, or the deathly silence of the drifting ribbons of snow, so varied were their recollections, the graphic evocation of scenes they had lived through, that Angélique felt she would never tire of listening to them.

'Of the twelve Jesuits I have known working with the Iroquois, ten of them died a martyr's death,' Macollet said proudly. 'And they won't be the last, believe me.'

Father Masserat painted a picture of the violet-coloured cliffs of

425

Georgian Bay, as the tinkling of a bell rang across it from a mission station lost among the trees and the tall grasses, and the wooden forts that rose up here and there, all smelling of the same smell – smoke, salted meat, furs and brandy.

This was the other side of the picture Angélique had been given at the Court and in Paris. In the drawing-rooms everyone loved to hear stories of the Jesuits and the salvation of Canada, and ladies would throw their rings and ear clips into the horribly mutilated hands of some martyr who, after a series of incredible adventures, had been brought back from Canada by ship. Many a great lady had become a benefactress of distant charities.

Some of them had even come to America to offer their services in person, for instance Madame de Guermont, Madame d'Aurole and, the most famous of all, Madame de la Pagerie, who had founded the Ursuline convent in Quebec.

Angélique had such a way of looking at the Jesuit father that he eventually found himself talking for her alone. For all these tales of the past fascinated her.

She had begun to discover an entirely new world, and Versailles with its petty intrigues now seemed far away, as indeed did the kingdom of France with its persecutions, its wretchedness, and the inescapable weight of its past lying heavy upon it, in comparison with these new lives, and the zest of a people out to take the world by storm. Oh liberty!

It seemed as if in Angélique's eyes they had been 'chosen and sent out into the world', that they were of a different breed, who, without knowing it, had been granted the grace of freedom. And when she questioned them or burst out laughing as they related some tragicomic episode such as any saga abounds in, d'Arreboust and Loménie would look at her without realizing that their austere faces wore an ecstatic expression. 'Oh! if only they could see her in Quebec,' they thought, 'beside those cantankerous women who never stop grumbling about their lot. . . . The whole city would be at her feet. . . . Oh, but what are we doing, thinking thoughts like these!'

Then suddenly their eyes would meet the ironical gaze of Father Masserat.

What they could not guess was that Angélique, partly unconsciously and because she sensed in them possible enemies, a potential source of danger, did not hesitate to make the fullest use of her charm. So how could they have failed to succumb in advance? There are certain gestures, certain looks, certain ways of smiling, invisible to others and of no particular consequence but which, by their simple air of confidence, compel the friendship of a man.

Angélique had an instinctive and a well tried knowledge of these methods.

Joffrey de Peyrac noticed it too, but said nothing. Angélique's cleverness, her feminine tricks, all her womanly ways, delighted him as if he were looking at a work of art, perfectly executed. He was sometimes frankly amused by the spectacle, for every day he saw the French gentlemen drawing nearer and nearer to their downfall, not excepting the Jesuit, even though he considered himself a hard man to get the better of.

There were other times when Peyrac ground his teeth, for she seemed to him to be playing a dangerous game and he was perspicacious enough to realize that Count Loménie was decidedly attractive to his wife. It could well be that one of these days something a little more than friendship might develop between the two of them. But he did not interfere, for he realized that there was nothing in Angélique's behaviour to anger a husband in love with her, and that any attempt to transform or constrain a person as warm and spontaneous as she was, a charmer to her very bones, would be pointless, almost criminal. She had reigned at Versailles, over princes . . . and she had kept the same imperious, irresistible charm of those born to stand above others, for the power to charm also confers a kind of royalty upon those who possess it.

CHAPTER 72

RIGHT FROM the start, as a hostess conscious of her obligations towards her guests, Angélique had suggested to Father Masserat that he might like to use one of the small rooms to say his daily Mass.

The Jesuit had been grateful for the suggestion, although, as he had explained to her, the rule of Saint Ignatius did not require him to say Mass every day. Jesuits only had to say two Masses a week and these need not be in public.

They had no obligations to hear confessions, or even to officiate at the request of the faithful.

The only thing they could not refuse was extreme unction, in cases of evident danger of death.

And as for their duties towards God, the communion of the Mass could be replaced by the communion of the Spirit. They were the vanguard of Christ's army, and were granted the liberty of action appropriate to trail-blazers, and the necessary freedom from rigid rules and discipline.

He was nevertheless delighted to be able to say Mass at Wapassou, for as an isolated missionary he found the Holy Sacrifice a source of comfort. He had brought with him a plain wooden box covered in black leather and studded with nails, that contained a chalice, a paten, some altar-cruets, a ciborium, several vestments, a missal and a Bible.

All this had been a gift from a benefactress, the Duchess of Aiguillon.

Nicolas Perrot, the Spaniards and Yann le Couennec went to Mass every day and were obviously pleased to be able to practise their faith.

But Father Masserat was less pleased. Although he was extremely obliging in their day-to-day life, he had no vocation for secular pastoral work. He had come to America for the Indians, and the Whites did not interest him.

Moreover he was a remarkable theologian, and a very learned man, and was fascinated by the splendour of God, about whom he was discovering more and more as he meditated further upon Him, while the rough piety of the humble, unlettered man who dared to attempt to converse with his Creator, irritated him considerably. He came near to deploring the fact that God had Himself given him the right to do so.

Like many of his order, he preferred solitude, a private communing with the divine mystery. And he would frown when, by the dim light of his two candles, on either side of his makeshift altar, he caught sight of one of the Spanish soldiers, or the young Breton, or even Perrot, leaning heavily against the door jamb as he stood, arms crossed, with his shaggy head of hair piously bowed.

He must not forget that Saint Ignatius was a Spaniard!

Father Masserat made a great effort to be patient with the compatriots of the founder of his order. The young Breton served Mass for him piously, and to all who gathered there in the shadows he would distribute the bread of life, the small white Host.

They would make their way towards the secret sounds in the dawn, in some far corner of the house, towards the shadow making the ritual gestures, towards the tinkle of paten and chalice, as if approaching a hidden spring, which they had heard babbling through the forest.

Father Masserat reminded himself that there were heretics no more than a few paces away, who were unable to look upon a crucifix without going into epileptic convulsions, and who at the very same moment were making their culpable prayers.

The women were beginning to move about in the kitchen, chopping kindling wood and striking a light from their tinder box. He could hear the crackling of flames and the rattle of pots being hung up over the fire, and the sound of pouring water.

Then men yawning as they awoke.

Occasionally a child's high-pitched voice would rise shrilly, only to be suddenly interrupted on its highest note, no doubt because some-one had said: 'Shush!'

From still closer in the workshops he could hear still louder noises; the sound of tools being placed on the bench, the whistle of a forge bellows being started up, and the murmur of grave, sober voices also exchanging the ritual responses of their rite in their own strange terms.

There was a huge Negro, jovial and intimidating, so learned that he left a man gasping, a half-caste with a fanatical look, 'a man of Mediterranean stock who resembled him and knew all about the bottom of the sea, a wan creature who seemed to be dumb, a coarse brute from Auvergne and two young men as handsome as arch-angels....

He could hear the sound of stones, rocks and earth being crushed and sifted, and could smell the smell of fire, of steel and of sulphur.

Father Masserat told himself that he would have a most interesting report to make about it all when he returned to Quebec.

CHAPTER 73

ANGÉLIQUE had taken on the task of keeping all the guns clean, of examining them and making sure that they worked properly, and of polishing them until they glistened. This was a task she performed with such minute care, and with all the skill of an old hand who was more than a bit fussy about these things, that the trappers, even those who clung most jealously to their favourite weapons, handed them over to her without a qualm. They had got into the habit of asking her to 'overhaul' their guns as if she were a professional gunsmith, and even Clovis trusted her with his old poacher's cross-bow from which he re-fused to be parted.

One morning d'Arreboust, de Loménie, de la Salle and Father

Masserat himself found her sitting in the midst of a whole arsenal, so absorbed in her task that she forgot to greet them. In fascination they watched her small, delicate, feminine hands handling the heavy gun butts or tracing the line of a faulty barrel, as she examined the mysteries of a pan reeking of gunpowder, cold oil and burned metal, with all the loving attention a mother lavishes upon a new-born babe.

Angélique was sorry that Honorine was not there to help her this time, as she usually was, but the little girl was still ill. Her temperature was only just beginning to go down. Normally when Angélique cleaned the guns Honorine always came and sat beside her, and her little fingers seemed to make the same gestures as hers, as if she were every bit as familiar with the handling of weapons as her mother. She had been brought up in the midst of weapons.

Spread before her on the table were all kinds of hooks, rods, awls, bowls of pure oil she had filtered out herself, various waxes, in fact all manner of things she had made herself and which she alone knew how to use. The gentlemen from Quebec watched her as she worked, scraping, polishing, examining this and that, frowning occasionally and muttering to herself. They could not understand it. When at last she raised her head, she caught sight of them and gave them an absent-minded smile.

'Good morning to you. Have you eaten yet? How are you all? Monsieur de Loménie, have you ever seen a more handsome weapon than this gun from Saxony?'

Florimond came in, greeted those present and said:

'My mother is the best shot in all the American colonies, would you like to see?'

After several days of stormy weather, today it was fine and bright and they set off for the shooting range they had made by the cliffs. Florimond carried two flint-lock muskets, one matchlock gun and two pistols. He wanted his mother to give a complete demonstration of her gifts and since she wanted to check the weapons anyway, she gladly fell in with his suggestion. She could feel the weight of each of these muskets in her very muscles, and seemed to know in advance just how it would feel against her shoulder, how much it would recoil, how much it was likely to bruise.

'No woman could ever raise a thing like that!' said Monsieur d'Arreboust as he watched her seize the Saxon musket.

But she raised it without apparent difficulty.

She took aim, head on one side, right foot forward, then, after admitting that the weapon was in fact heavy, that she would lean against the kind of parapet they used for training, she took up a half-kneeling position, and her whole body from her hips to her shoulders seemed to express concentration. Her position revealed no sign of tension, but rather a deep, complete calm. She had the gift of switching in a few seconds from great vivacity of movement to this state that was almost like sleep, in which her heart beat slower and her breathing grew almost imperceptible. And in the keen light of winter, with the sparkle of frost all round her, her cheek, pink with the cold and shaded by a half-closed eyelid, seemed to tilt in a gesture of surrender.

The shot rang out.

The smoke rose slowly, twisting like a white snake from the end of the gun barrel. The feather they had placed a hundred yards away had vanished.

'What do you say to that?' Florimond exclaimed.

They stammered out their praise.

'You are envious! And I don't wonder either!' the young man went on, but Angélique just laughed.

She liked the sensation of power that ran through her whole body as the gun obeyed her command. This seemed to be a gift she had been given. And she might never have known it had not circumstances placed weapons in her hands. As she rode back and forth through the forest of Nieul she had discovered this inborn understanding between her and these cruel objects of steel and wood. She forgot that they had been made to kill, forgot that they did kill. She forgot the fact that life and death lay at the end of their trajectory. And although it might seem strange, she sometimes thought that all the attention she had given to this art, all the calm and concentration it had demanded of her, all the tenacity she had shown in order to become a skilful shot, had greatly helped her in her times of misfortune not to lose her reason entirely. Arms had kept her safe from everything.

Arms were holy and good things. The weak of this world needed arms in a time without faith or conscience. She loved them.

She went on talking about the guns, and she began to wonder what was upsetting Loménie-Chambord and giving his handsome face an almost pained expression. Eventually she left them, and went off with her son, who carried all the guns in his arms. They were talking animatedly together.

Count Loménie and Monsieur d'Arreboust exchanged glances.

Father Masserat looked away and drew a Prayer Book from one of the pockets of his soutane, while Cavelier stared at all three of them, rubbing his icy hands together, for he had forgotten his gloves.

'Well, one thing's certain,' he said with a grin, 'that woman shoots like a wizard . . . or should I say a "She-Devil"?'

He thrust his hands into his jacket pockets and stalked off, affected and proud in his indifference.

He was almost enjoying seeing these edifying gentlemen in so embarrassing a position. And he, better than anyone else, was able to guess the kind of theological and mystical torments that rent their souls. He was used to these matters of conscience.

He had been a Jesuit himself for ten years.

'Yes indeed!' said Monsieur d'Arreboust, 'that is in fact what we are here for. Is she a She-Devil or is she not? Does she constitute a danger or does she not? That is all we have to decide. Asking Count Peyrac to finance the Mississippi expedition was only a pretext! We could not trust your judgement, Loménie. We needed an outside opinion, so they chose me to come, and Father Masserat as well. I must admit, my dear Loménie, that I felt certain that you had been misled and circumvented. But now, what are we going to do?'

The Duke of Arreboust cleared his throat. First he looked at the flaxen-coloured sky, deceptively mild looking, then at the wooden outpost a short distance from them, half-buried under the snow, surrounded by its cliffs, and the long white stretch of the lakes.

Seeing that Father Masserat did not appear to be listening, he continued to address his words to Monsieur de Loménie.

'So you see, it had to come. We came, we saw. . . . We saw,' he repeated half to himself. 'And what does Father Masserat of the society of Jesus think about it all? Father Masserat is busy pretending he doesn't understand. And do you know why, my dear Loménie? Because it's all beyond him. Yes, for he has already made up his mind about it. While we were allowing ourselves to be lulled in that deceptively pleasant atmosphere, he had already made up his mind. He had stopped asking himself the question that is now tormenting all of us, a question that appears almost insane: WHO IS SHE? . . . Who is she? A She-Devil? A seductress? A witch? Is she harmless? Or is she plotting against us? He is perfectly happy, for his dialectic has at least enabled him to see black on white that the matter is beyond him, and that he cannot – no, above all he must not commit the imprudence of getting mixed up in any of it. So he dives into his breviary! Father Masserat, tell me now, am I wrong to put it like that?'

Monsieur d'Arreboust's voice had gradually risen higher and higher with emotion: it hung for a couple of seconds in the crystal-clear air, then died away ironically with a short echo. Father Masserat looked up in astonishment at his two friends and gave a brief, amiable smile.

One would never know whether d'Arreboust had hit the nail on the head or whether, on the contrary, the Jesuit considered his attack a harmless joke, or whether in fact he had heard nothing at all, for his thoughts were often far away. He turned back to his Prayer Book and wandered off quietly, moving his lips as he read.

Monsieur d'Arreboust shrugged his shoulders in a gesture of defeat. 'That's the Jesuits for you,' he said. 'Compared with them, Pontius Pilate was an altar boy!'

'But it's really up to Father Masserat to settle the matter,' Loménie decided, 'for although I am in orders, I have neither the qualifications nor the training of a Jesuit. And they are trained as they are so that they can judge, with the light of the Holy Spirit, situations that are too complex for a simple layman. After all, that is what Father Masserat came here for!'

'He won't say anything, and you know it,' replied d'Arreboust in disillusioned tones. 'He has already found a good reason to remain silent, and he will keep it to himself with all the rest.'

'Is that in itself not sufficient proof that we have nothing to fear from these people? Had Father Masserat judged them to be suspect, or considered that they constituted a real danger for the souls of our colony, and the security of our missions, he would have said something, he would have opposed the agreement we are making.'

'You may be right. But it's also possible that he may have decided he is not strong enough to oppose us, that we would not listen to him because we are already under the influence of our hostess. He may be waiting till we reach Quebec before firing the powder keg, and saying that the whole affair smells of brimstone and damnation, and that we must exterminate all these criminals down to the last man, unless we want to perish along with the whole cause of Catholic Canada. Then we would look pretty fools, and guilty ones at that. The Jesuits would become saviours, with Father Orgeval and Saint Michael the Archangel. . . .'

'How is one to tell whether a person who doesn't behave in any outlandish way is in fact a sorceress or a demon?' Loménie asked thoughtfully. 'She is very beautiful, and indeed her beauty could be regarded as suspect from the fact that it is not . . . ordinary. But is beauty ever ordinary?'

'Witches can't cry,' said Monsieur d'Arreboust. 'Have you ever seen her cry?'

'No,' replied Loménie, moved, in spite of himself, by the image it conjured up, 'but I would not necessarily have seen her if she had . . .'

'They also say that witches float if you throw them into the water. But it's a bit difficult for us to try any test of that kind on Madame de Peyrac.'

And he gave an uneasy smile as he looked around.

'Not enough water, it's all frozen,' he murmured.

Count Loménie looked at him stupefied, for he had never known him indulge in this kind of sick humour before.

Monsieur d'Arreboust begged his forgiveness, saying that the rigours of the climate and his own anxiety had made him bitter. He would take advantage of the fine spell to go for a short walk.

Loménie said that he would withdraw to pray to God and seek his advice.

The Duke went off towards the lake.

He found walking difficult for the compound was nothing but a network of icy paths, narrow tracks cut with a spade or a pick, as intricate and twisting as a mole's burrow, some leading to the frozen fountain, some to Macollet's wigwam, some to the workshops, the stables, the shooting range or games area, and some leading nowhere in particular, that is to say towards the impenetrable forest.

After much slithering and slipping, the chief syndic of Quebec managed to reach the lakeside, where it was possible to walk up and down the banks as long as the snow was hard. Little by little an ice-packed path had been formed here, and on fine days like this one, figures could be seen walking slowly up and down in the sunshine, following this rough path towards new horizons, then turning back when they reached the far end of the lake and came up against the insurmountable barrier of snowdrifts. When the Duke reached the end of the lake he grew thoughtful as he looked at the place where he had nearly died. He remembered the feeling of weakness and resignation he had experienced as he collapsed exhausted into the snow, and the oppressive feeling of cold as the night air bore down on his chest like a huge slab of cold stone, and he had thought: please let it be quick! The last sensation he remembered was a kind of burning at his temples when he had realized that snow was falling on his face and that his features had already stiffened into an icy mask and would never move again.

He was unable to explain this deathly drowsiness to which they had succumbed any more than he knew how it was they had come to be saved and brought back to life again. It all seemed to be part of the place itself, of this forbidden land. And Peyrac had had the audacity to settle here.

It must be that as you approached Wapassou you entered a strange zone full of subtle, hidden snares. He found himself unable to explain it and yet it was his duty to do so, at least to take a look around. Those had been the instructions he had been given in Quebec.

He remembered how unexpected, how little in keeping with Monsieur de Loménie's very guarded nature had been the enthusiasm he had shown for the people of Katarunk. He spoke with considerable warmth and esteem of the adventurers he had been sent out to destroy by force and whom he now felt proud to rank among his friends. He had been delighted to hear that they were still alive when everyone else had thought it an excellent way out for them to have perished at the hands of the Iroquois, and, although he did not speak about Madame de Peyrac in the extreme terms used by Lieutenant Pont-Briand, it had been clear on several occasions that he would not hear a word against her.

And Frontenac was only too happy to take his part. But then Frontenac was a hot-headed man, who enjoyed paradoxical situations, like women, and who detested the Jesuits; and his appointment as Governor of Canada had been intended more as a disgrace than an honour. For Louis XIV had never forgiven him for having the audacity to pay court to Madame de Montespan.

But he was a good politician when it came to running a country, and had immediately trusted the new arrival, Peyrac, whom others had denounced to him as an enemy of New France, because Peyrac, like himself, bore a Gascon name, and also because he had taken the trouble to find out a few things about him. Count Peyrac was rich. The idea had come to him to ask for tangible proof of his friendship towards New France. . . . So he had sent Loménie and the ambitious Cavelier to make contact with him.

Monsieur d'Arreboust and Father Masserat had been instructed to go too with a special brief from the Bishop to try to get to the bottom of the suspicions that hung over the newcomers. And above all to make up his mind whether or not the woman with them, about whom so much, too much, had been said, was in fact a She-Devil or not.

So there it was! And here they were stuck at Wapassou, where nothing had turned out as they had anticipated. A veritable hornets' nest.

'Witchcraft! Witchcraft!' whispered the light wind, which was as keen as a knife edge in spite of the relative warmth of the day.

He, Jean-François d'Arreboust, who, along with Father Masserat, had been sent with Count Loménie to keep an eye on him and also to form their own opinions about Count and Countess Peyrac, he, a sober, pious man, a man who led a well-ordered, modest life, bent on saving his own soul and doing good to others and the colony, he had seen nothing, and suspected nothing.

He had awoken from his sleep of death and had begun to live in a different way, without even thinking about it, and this was something that had never happened to him before in all his life.

He had eaten, drunk and smoked in an atmosphere of tranquillity and warmth, where they had talked together, discussing their memories and their dreams, and had quickened in the glow of those green eyes that transformed the world around them. 'But at that moment, Monsieur d'Arreboust, when the Mascoutins were about to scalp you, did you not feel any fear, did you not feel that the game was up?'

'No,' he had replied, drawing himself up, 'everything seems so simple when you are about to face your God.'

He had never realized till that day that he was a hero.

Neither had the others.

He was a modest man, but it did him good to realize that he had a valiant soul and that his heart was in the right place, and that he deserved a woman's admiration.

He had forgotten, completely forgotten, that she was the woman whom the others, back in Quebec, suspected of being the She-Devil of Acadia, she, the very same woman with whom he had had such charming, gay conversations.

Until this morning!

Seeing her there with weapons in her hands, he had felt a kind of shock.

Perhaps it was that weapons called to mind the idea of danger, and the fear he had felt at the unexpected sight of this woman with her lovely hands handling guns and using them with such unnerving skill, had woven itself into all the fears that lurk deep down in the heart of man: the fear of women, the fear of being seduced, the fear of witches. Then he had remembered all the things that people had said, had remembered Father Orgeval's opinion. Loménie-Chambord had felt the same sense of shock, of that he was sure. And possibly Father Masserat too. But where he was concerned, they would never know.

Monsieur d'Arreboust gave a shudder as he drew the folds of his cloak round his mouth.

'So you see what's happened to us, without our even being aware of it,' he told himself. 'It's happened, I am sure of it. I feel anxious and unhappy and unable to pray. For the past hour now I have been unable to stop thinking about her, to stop thinking about women, about love ... ABOUT MY WIFE!'

He could see his wife in his imagination, that irreproachably modest woman, in all sorts of incongruous, lubricious postures she had never been known to adopt, even in the early days of their married life, when through defence and duty he had honoured her in haste and afterwards reproached himself for the satisfaction he had obtained from his shameful action. He also called to mind the bawdy comment made by one of his friends, a rather loose-living young man, who had told him on the occasion of some ball, that Madame d'Arreboust, his wife, had such pretty little breasts and that it must be great fun to be married to her.

He disliked, in fact heartily disliked this kind of comment. For love and marriage distracted him from his vocation of piety. Had becoming a Jesuit not involved such long and difficult study, he would have joined the order, but after giving up the idea of a religious life he had married to please his parents. Then, once they were dead, he had finally abandoned the idea of giving them a grandson as heir. Why this vain conceit to perpetuate one's name? It was better to offer one's fortune to God. It so happened that his wife shared his views, for she too would have liked to become a nun, so they got on very well together. Their dream was to offer themselves to God in some great work, and Canada had fulfilled all their expectations and their plans for a life of sacrifice. . . .

Monsieur d'Arreboust gave a sigh, for at last the wicked visions were beginning to fade, and he managed to visualize his wife again other than as a lubricious courtesan.

He saw her now as she was most familiar to him, praying in the half-darkness of some chapel or oratory, with her head bowed and tilted slightly to one side just as he had seen Madame de Peyrac tilt hers this morning over the breech-bolt of the musket. This gesture had always moved him; without realizing it he associated it with the idea of a woman letting her head fall on to a man's shoulder, and it always stirred a feeling of tenderness within him. Madame d'Arreboust was *petite* and scarcely reached his shoulder. In the early days of their marriage he had called her 'little one' in an attempt to promote conjugal familiarity, but he had noticed that she did not like it, for, in fact, she was bold, energetic, of extremely robust health, with something unbending about her that the passing years had accentuated.

What a shame! How sad!

She could have been a delightful, gay woman, but she had striven too much after perfection. In repudiating her own body, she had grown entirely spiritual, indulging in great flights of mysticism.

'It is all the fault of this Lady of the Silver Lake that I have grown full of regret, of languor and of uncertainty. It is because of the laughter of a happy woman, because of the way she looks at a man, one man only, and the way that man puts his arm round her, and the way the door closes on them both in the evening. . . . It is because of this woman's dependence on the man she loves that I have begun to suffer.

'For my wife is no longer dependent on me. I mean scarcely more to her than her spiritual director, Father Orgeval; less, in fact, for I am more like a spiritual director whose only concern is with figures and business. When we meet once a year, after the arrival of the first ships, bringing mail from France, we discuss the state of our fortune, and decide to which good works we shall give the income from our farms. My wife owes me nothing, not even solicitude. She has given herself entirely to God.

'She is a holy soul, and an example to the community of Montreal!

'She has pretty little breasts. . . . They are still very pretty. . . . Dear Lord, why am I thinking about these things? Whatever am I doing in this accursed place? Whatever shall I tell them in Quebec? If we ever get back to Quebec. . . . Will the man with the sardonic face ever let us go? After all, we are his prisoners. . . . He could always . . . But what's that coming across the lake? It looks like . . .'

Monsieur d'Arreboust shaded his eyes with his hand.

CHAPTER 74

THEY ALWAYS travel in pairs, these winter wayfarers.

Death would dog the heels of a man who travelled alone.

A pair, a Frenchman and an Indian. It was just like a Frenchman to conceive the preposterous notion of braving cold, snow, storms, and the wide-open spaces devoid of all human life. And it was just like an Indian to follow him; for the Palefaces, with their relentless argumentation, have the power to dispel the chilly-faced snow demons that whistle through the leafless branches.

Looking identical beneath their fur-lined, leather-fringed hoods, and walking in the same cumbersome manner because of their snowshoes, the Frenchman and the Indian came on across the lake. Their shadows were short, for it was midday. As they drew closer, Jean-François d'Arreboust thought he recognized a familiar face, but before he had been able to place the man and remember his name, he experienced an unpleasant sensation, as if his whole being recoiled before an intruder.

He could not bring himself to hail the man, and watched him approaching with a feeling of suspicion, almost hostility. He felt like shouting out: 'What have you come here for? Why have you come to disturb the peace of this place where everyone is happy? Go away!'

The people in the fort had seen the new arrivals, and Florimond and Yann le Couennec came down to the lakeside, muskets in hand.

As the Frenchman came forward he held his head high and slightly thrown back, like a man seeking to catch all the light he could under his half-closed eyelids. And as he drew closer, d'Arreboust realized why. The traveller was blind, his eyes burned by the reflection of the light on the snow – one of the most terrible afflictions suffered on these winter expeditions.

His eyelids were red and swollen and covered with leprous-looking white crusts. He was hideous to behold. He shouted:

'Is there someone there? I can just make you out, but I cannot see you clearly. . . .'

The Indian beside him clutched his gun and looked darkly at the weapons trained on him.

'Who are you? Where are you from?' asked d'Arreboust.

'I am Pacific Jusserand, from Sorel, but I have just come from Norridgewock on the Kennebec, and I have a letter for Count Loménie-Chambord from Father Orgeval. . . .'

Then he added:

'Are you going to shoot me? I have done nothing wrong. I am a Frenchman speaking French like the rest of you.'

He was greatly hampered by being half-blind, and must have felt himself entirely at the mercy of the men he was addressing, incapable as he was even of seeing whether their reaction to him was one of welcome or not. D'Arreboust had at last recognized him as someone he had often met in Quebec, and who for the past four years had been Father Orgeval's right-hand man.

His first reaction was to feel as if he had swallowed something unpleasant, something bitter, but charity won the day and he hastened to say:

'You unfortunate man, what a state you're in!'

Then he turned towards Florimond:

'This man is in the service of Father Orgeval and his mission.'

'I have a feeling this servant came to Katarunk.' The young man exclaimed, wrinkling up his nose.

'Don't shoot me,' the man repeated, turning his face here and there in the direction of the voices, 'I am not an enemy. I have simply come with a message for Count Loménie.'

'And why should you fear that we might shoot you on sight?' Florimond asked. 'Or have you got something on your conscience that you've done against the master and owner of this fort, Count Peyrac?'

Visibly embarrassed, the man gave no reply. He tried to walk towards the shadows he could apparently just make out, but stumbled on the sloping bank at the lakeside.

Then d'Arrebout took him by the arm to help him along the path to the fort.

Count Loménie-Chambord turned the letter over in his hand. It was thick and had been folded in the middle and sealed with a dark wax seal stamped with the arms of Sebastian Orgeval, and it would undoubtedly cause him pain, that he knew; so he temporized and did not open it immediately but questioned the man Monsieur d'Arrebout had seated down on a bench. He was one of a group of pious men and young lads who offered their services to the missionaries for a year or more in order to obtain indulgences. This man, Pacific Jusserand, had been working for Father Orgeval now for four years.

'How did Father Orgeval know I was at Fort Wapassou?' the Knight of Malta inquired.

The man turned his fierce-looking swollen face towards him and replied proudly:

'You are well aware of the fact that Father Orgeval knows everything. The angels tell him.'

Angélique cleaned the burns on his swollen eyelids and laid cooling compresses on them. Then she gave him some soup and some brandy, and he ate, with his eyes bandaged, sitting very upright and looking disdainful.

He was a man whom Angélique immediately felt to be very odd and disquieting. He had answered all her questions, in fact everything she had said to him, in monosyllables, and only showed any liveliness when

440

his master, Father Orgeval, was mentioned. She was to learn later that Father Orgeval, who was himself a remarkably urbane priest, seemed deliberately to surround himself with uncouth, unsociable men, through whom he seemed to project the sombre, tormented side of his nature, which otherwise remained hidden. Father Le Guirande and Father Louis Paul Maraicher were men of this stamp, who played an important part in his struggle to preserve Acadia and the great territory of Maine for the Catholic church and the King of France. It is a noteworthy fact that these two priests and Pacific Jusserand all died violent deaths as the result of this struggle.

And it was later a question whether the man who 'knew everything' had not been the first to 'see' what would inevitably happen when he wrote to Loménie-Chambord in the following terms to put him on his guard:

'My dear friend,' the letter ran. 'I have learned that you have reached the place called Wapassou, where Peyrac and his band sought refuge after the Katarunk disaster. I trust that the courage you have shown in making your way to him in spite of the winter conditions, will not remain unrewarded. Nevertheless I am writing to beseech you to show no sign of weakness with regard to the decisions you have to take. I tremble lest you succumb to I know not what subtle arguments and false impression of virtue that these adventurers have contrived to make in order to insinuate themselves among us and destroy our cause. When I saw you in Quebec you were prepared to take Monsieur de Peyrac's protestations of friendship as evidence of his loyalty, but since then he has killed Pont-Briand, one of our men, and has made still further inroads upon the territory of New France.

'You claimed that you saw in him a man of great ability, whose sole concern was to develop the resources of an uncultivated land. But, for the benefit of what King does he work? For the glory of what religions?. . . Furthermore, the presence of a woman in these regions did not seem to have had any effect on you, at least not in the way that I had hoped.

'You claimed to see in them no more than a married couple like any other, or rather more exemplary than others, and you spoke in glowing terms of the quality of the feeling you had sensed between them, that united them in bonds of unfaltering love.

'Well then, so be it; I grant you this and will speak now of this feeling.

'Let us consider the artful charm that consists in dressing up evil to look like good, an old trick which you seem to have fallen for in your somewhat naïve straightforwardness.

'You told me over and over again that what you admired about this man was the fact that he was free, truly free.

'But has it not been said that Satanism is bound up entirely with the problem of liberty?

'According to Saint Thomas, did not Satan go so far as to seek to become God? But Satan wanted to hold *his honour and his happiness* from himself alone. THAT IS HIS CERTAIN AND DISTINCTIVE HALLMARK. I do not know whether you realize just to what extent this feeling of love, which you recognize between two people who have openly separated themselves from God even to the point where they will give succour to the enemies of their native religion, can be distorted, can actually become an insult to God. No creature should ever adore another, but should only adore God. Corrupt love is not love at all.

'And this is precisely where, in the last resort, lies the most terrible and serious threat of all that I believed I discerned since these people disembarked in the vicinity of our frontiers, nay, in French Acadia itself.

'For by holding up a deceptive model, they lead simple souls astray, and cause them to aspire to a state of happiness which is not of this world and which we can only attain in God through death.

'And here I am seized with a terrible anxiety, for suppose it is precisely by means of this gentleness, this tenderness that moves you, that the She-Devil is laying her most subtle traps?

'What if evil were showing its most tempting face in the learning that so impresses you in this man? All the theologians are agreed that *God left the Evil One his power over Knowledge, the Flesh, Women and Riches.* And that is why the Church in its wisdom and its prudence, refuses to grant women power or influence, since any society that gave women such right would be handing itself over to *all that Woman represents,* that is to say *the Flesh.* And from that point on, downfall is close, and relapse into the blindest paganism.

'The flesh and idolatry, those are the dangers that await the spirit seduced by the graces of the opposite sex, *no matter what these moral or physical graces may be,* that I would emphasize. In your admiration for Madame de Peyrac, in which I thought I discerned a certain nostalgia, how big a part does concupiscence play? Did Pont-Briand not lose his head and then his life on this account? I must

442

therefore remind you that to dwell on earthly delights is to turn away from the one and only goal at which we should be aiming – our personal salvation in conjunction with the salvation of the world – is to obstruct the blossoming of the soul, which, in order to reach God, must free itself from the bonds of the flesh.

'Re-read the fifth chapter of Saint Paul's epistle to the Galatians, and you will find matter for meditation:

' "Brethren, this I say then, walk in the Spirit, and ye shall not fulfil the lust of the flesh. For the flesh lusteth against the Spirit, and the Spirit against the flesh: and these are contrary the one to the other: . . . Now the works of the flesh are manifest, which are these: adultery, fornication, uncleanness, lasciviousness, idolatry, witchcraft, hatred, variance, emulations, wrath, strife, seditions, heresies, envyings, murders, drunkenness, revellings, and such like. . . . Remember that they that are Christ's have crucified the flesh with the affections and lusts . . ."

'What could I possibly add to the words of the Great Apostle?

'So I shall conclude by saying: My dear brother, I beg you, yes, I beg you to deliver us from the danger that Count Peyrac represents for us, for Canada, and for the souls of whom we have charge.

'He is by no means the first adventurer nor the first heretic to disembark on these shores, but I have a strong feeling that unless we immediately make it impossible for him to do any more harm, on account of him, on account of them, I shall see all my work in Acadia crumble before my eyes, and they will bring about my defeat and my death. I see it, I feel it.'

'Oh my God, what is to become of me?' poor Loménie cried out almost aloud, holding his head in his two hands.

His heart was breaking, tormented as he was by the dilemma Father Orgeval had placed him in.

He laid his fingers on the letter as if seeking to blot out from his sight the words that lay there, each of which cruelly rent his sensitive soul.

He did not question himself, did not attempt to think whether he still had a choice, whether it were not possible to find some other way out of a situation of which he no longer had control.

What really horrified him was the gulf that seemed to be opening up between him and his dearest friend, and he was seized with panic at the thought of no longer finding him there, ever present, strong, and wise at his side, in this arid life.

'Do not leave me, my friend, try to understand. My brother, my father,' he begged, 'my Father, my Father!'

Then, reproaching himself for not addressing his prayers to God, he went on: 'Oh my God, do not separate me from my friend. Enlighten both our hearts so that we may each come to understand the other better, so that we may never know the terrible agony of considering one another as strangers....

'My God, show us your truth . . .' But it was not as simple as that! One had to suffer. He looked up and saw Angélique standing a few paces from him. So there she is, he told himself. The woman whom Father Orgeval seeks to destroy at all costs.

She was looking into a bowl, then leaning over the pot to take some water.

She stood up again, and glanced towards Count Loménie, then, seeing his face, came towards him.

'You seem sad, Monsieur de Loménie.'

Her deep voice with its soft inflection made him shudder and a great wave began to surge through him, ready to break in a childlike sob.

'Yes . . . I am sad . . . very sad. . . .' And he looked at her standing there before him. . . . And he felt abashed, won over, already vanquished by her, while the harsh voice within him scourged him mercilessly.

'The time is not come for us to deliver ourselves up to woman and all she represents, that is to say the flesh. . . .'

'The flesh?' Yes, possibly, he thought, but also the heart. . . . All the kindness and tenderness that lies in a woman's heart, without which the world would be but a cold battlefield.

And he saw her once more as she had supported him in her arms when he had been ill.

Angélique was more susceptible to Count Loménie-Chambord's charm than she would admit. He was a gentle and most courageous man, and his appearance gave a true picture of his character. There was nothing false about him. He looked like the officer he was, of soldierly bearing and capable of carrying through any warlike task, while his serious, grey eyes revealed a chivalrous heart. Further acquaintance with him would never be a disappointing experience. A certain hesitancy in his manner did not stem from any faint-heartedness, but rather from his scrupulous conscientiousness, his desire to remain loyal to his friends, or to those whom it was his duty to defend and to serve.

444

He was one of those men whom women seek to protect from the machinations of other women or overpowering friends, for he was the kind of man of whose sensitivity and loyalty people are often tempted to take advantage.

That was what Father Orgeval was doing, she felt certain. She had felt like saying to Loménie, as he sat there with the letter with its proud handwriting as yet untouched: 'Don't read it, I beg you. Don't touch it. . . .'

But his whole life was involved, the lifelong friendship between Count Loménie and Father Orgeval, and that was something that Angélique had no part in yet.

The Knight of Malta rose heavily to his feet as if prostrate with grief, and walked away with bowed head.

CHAPTER 75

THE THOUGHT of Father Orgeval – he could almost have said his presence – never left him throughout the day. It followed him like a shadow, exhorting him quietly but insistently. But as night fell, the voice began to change, and took on a tragic, almost childish tone as it murmured: 'Do not abandon me. Do not betray me in my struggle. . . .'

It was the voice of Sebastian d'Orgeval as he had been as a youth in the Jesuit College where they had first become friends.

Because Count Loménie-Chambord was now a man of forty-two, a man not lacking in experience of the world, he could not entirely delude himself about the impulses that drove his friend Orgeval to wage so secret and virulent a war against the newcomers.

There were certain memories that helped to explain his intransigence. For he, Loménie, had never known, as Sebastian d'Orgeval had, the dark loveless wastes of an orphaned childhood.

He had had an agreeable, attentive mother, even if she had been a trifle worldly, who had never lost interest in the young lad she had sent as a pupil to the Jesuits, nor in the Knight of Malta he was later to become. She wrote to him often, and when he was a child she used to send him some extraordinary gifts which sometimes caused him embarrassment, and sometimes delighted him: a posy of early spring flowers, a Venetian knife studded with precious stones, an oyster-shell medallion containing a lock of his hair, pots of jam, and for his fourteenth birthday a complete musketeer's outfit with a thoroughbred horse. . . . The Jesuit fathers considered it all a bit frivolous. Just like a mother!

He also had two sisters, one of whom had become a nun. They were gay, sprightly and spontaneous. When his mother had died ten years earlier, Loménie had wept for her as a lost friend. He kept in touch with his sisters, who were very fond of him and were greatly loved in return.

That evening at Wapassou, in the cubby-hole where the Italian Porguani slept, he carefully re-read the letter from the Jesuit, and when he fell asleep he felt as if he were impregnated with the bitter, underlying feeling of disgust that he sensed behind the words on the paper, and of which he alone knew the origin.

Was he asleep or only half awake as he conjured up that night he had lived through with his friend when they had both been children?

Sebastian had been the victim of what had happened, but he himself had been unconsciously involved, as he slept like an angel, his head wreathed in curls, while in the shadows beside him, as in some terrible nightmare, the reality of which he later sought to deny, Sebastian had come to grips with Woman.

That night the children had been sent to sleep in the outbuildings, for a bishop and his retinue had arrived unexpectedly at the school. So the boys had settled down in the straw to sleep. Orgeval had gone to the far end of the barn, for he did not like to mix with the others, when suddenly in the shadows there appeared A WOMAN AS LOVELY AS THE NIGHT, looking at him with an equivocal smile, a smile that burnt him like fire and set him all a-tremble.

'Get thee behind me, Satan!' the young man breathed, but he felt that his lips would not obey him properly, and he felt under his clothes for a little iron bell, engraved with the image of Saint Ignatius, which, when you shook it, had the power of dispelling diabolical apparitions. But the apparition herself had a laugh like the silvery bell, and she whispered: 'Don't be frightened, my cherub,' as she laid her hand on his body, and did things to him which he found impossible to resist, and he had let himself be swept away by an unknown physical force whose violence had utterly overwhelmed him. He had accepted her lascivious caresses, had accepted everything, and had done what she expected of him, giving himself up to it in a kind of mad horror. . . .

When they awoke later he had said:

'You saw, didn't you? You saw?'

Orgeval shook his neighbour, young Loménie. But he did not

remember anything very clearly, for he was an innocent, healthy child who slept like an angel.

But he did remember having seen a woman, he had some recollection of noises, scents and disturbing movements. All this he had sensed through his innocent sleep. But such was the distress and the despair of the older boy that he told all to his friend, who did not understand it very well. But what young Loménie would never forget was the sight of those blue eyes through which flashed despair and fury alternately, the eyes of the boy he so admired, and he would never forget the trembling of the youth's body that had been ravished and overcome by the irresistible forces of lust. He had talked to him till dawn, trying to console him with the inadequate words of a child: 'Don't let it upset you. . . . We'll tell the Father Superior. . . . It's not your fault. It was the woman's fault.'

But they had said nothing. Or rather, they had not managed to make themselves understood. . . .

No sooner had they begun to speak than they had been interrupted . . .

'Don't worry, children, it was no apparition you saw but one of our greatest benefactresses. It is she who provides the money – and a great deal of it is needed – for needy pupils like yourself, d'Orgeval, and she has the privilege of being able to come unannounced to visit her protégés – "privilegiae mulieres sapientes" – it is a very ancient rule which many Christian teaching communities have adopted, which proves that we have nothing to hide, neither by night, nor by day . . .'

'But . . .'

They were dismayed. Were the fathers dupes? Or was it they who had dreamed it all?

In the end they had forgotten the episode, and had silenced their fragile spirits which felt more reassured in the light of day.

Later Count Loménie's school friend became Father Orgeval and he had now reached the peak of a brilliant career. In the full flower of his manhood, the serenity of his priestly life, the equilibrium brought about by mortification, and a body which, after a lifetime of denial had grown insensitive to cold, hunger and torture, could he not now smile at these memories, these slightly hazy dreams?

Twice, three times, Loménie-Chambord awoke from a sleep full of nausea, and wiped the cold sweat from his brow. He heard the sounds of the night around Wapassou and felt reassured. Then he slipped back into an anxious state of torpor in which he saw the She-Devil in the guise of the nocturnal seductress whose face he had conjured up from the description given him by his friend, with black serpents entwined in her hair and fire flashing from eyes that had become mere slits. She was riding a unicorn and laying waste the snow-covered land of Acadia. Towards the end of the night he noticed a change come over his vision; now the She-Devil had golden hair and emerald-green eyes. . . .

Father Orgeval, when he had taken holy orders and had returned to the world after his fifteen-year-long novitiate, had never been found wanting in perceptiveness.

He saw into men's souls, foresaw events and situations about to arise, and would even make prophecies and give warnings that appeared to have no foundation. He would refer to them almost casually but, however improbably, they would shortly afterwards turn out to have been right. . . .

On every occasion when the Knight of Malta had had the good fortune to confess himself to this great Jesuit, he had always come away feeling a better man, believing that he knew himself more intimately and felt surer of the direction his life was taking. He could fully understand why people fought for a place in his confessional, and would queue for hours on end in the tiny, freezing chapel of the old mission station on the Saint Charles river, where Orgeval went whenever he came to Quebec.

There was nothing to suggest that he was not a man entirely to be relied upon.

Loménie was a sensible, observant man, one who had made the most of his experience of community life in the colonies. Many a time had he seen how patient, tenacious and incredibly cunning some women could be, and had realized that it was not always easy to unmask them.

So he resolved to be more prudent and severe and, after seeking advice from Monsieur d'Arreboust, to try and unmask the diabolical side of Angélique, if there was one.

CHAPTER 76

NIGHT CLOSED in again, a night that lasted for six days. Snow and wind joined forces and seized the outpost in their clutch, so that not a glimmer of light could penetrate the snow-clogged windows. They found it impossible even to open the door on some days, while the wind blew the smoke in great gusts into the room, making them choke, for it was impossible to get rid of it. But the fort stood firm, their hideout at Wapassou remained a sure place of shelter in spite of the terrible battering it received from the wind, which, from time to time, made the roof creak. The two black oak roof beams, well squared and solidly joined with a kind of mortar, did not give way.

They all huddled together in the warmth of their refuge.

It was during the course of this long night that one of the horses, the black stallion, was torn to pieces by the wolves.

Joffrey de Peyrac then decided that he would have to kill the mare, Wallis. The stable and the outhouses had been demolished and there was no longer any shelter for the animals. There was neither forage nor food for them, and the humans were beginning to go hungry.

Joffrey de Peyrac reproached himself for having hesitated to kill the animals, hoping for some impossible miracle. He knew that the stocks of meat were growing dangerously low and, even had they been able to hunt every day, it was very unlikely that the game they caught would have sufficed to keep them going. And now their chance of survival had been still further reduced by the loss of the black stallion.

Angélique said nothing.

The urgency of their situation altered their sense of values. They had all fought for the lives of those horses; bringing them into the back country had assumed a symbolical meaning, and keeping them alive had seemed of overwhelming importance to them all.

But now it was a question of saving men's lives, and it was no longer the existence of horses in the upper Kennebec that was at stake, but the very existence of Peyrac and his men.

No one said anything. There is a great bitterness in undeserved failure. They had failed to carry through their intentions to the end, but Angélique kept on telling herself that one cannot expect everything to be successful and that it is impossible to reach a desired goal without sacrificing something by the wayside.

Her bitterness was dispelled, and in its place she felt a great wave of excitement when she realized she would be able to give her invalids and her convalescents some good, stimulating meat broth; and for several days the abundance of fresh meat, and the smell of grilling steak so stimulated their tired stomachs, that it made them happy in a mildly hysterical way, and helped them gather strength and to bide their time in patience.

449

Little had Angélique ever thought that she would one day eat horse meat. Members of the nobility found it inconceivable to think of a horse in the same terms as domestic animals destined for the slaughter-house, bullocks, sheep or calves. . . .

For the horse was their friend, from their earliest childhood, the companion of their walks, their journeys and their warfare.

In normal times she would have viewed the idea of eating horse meat with as much horror as the idea of cannibalism.

It was possible to sense the differences of background of the members of the little community by their different reactions. The Canadians, the English peasants, the seamen and even the young men like Flori-mond and Cantor never blenched. They felt sorry that they had all gone to so much pains to bring the horses as far as this, and that they now were forced to kill them. But later they would bring others, they would start again.

They did not feel this inner recoil that the noblemen among them felt, for whom horses were like an integral part of themselves. The age of chivalry was well and truly dead, and a new race of men was being born.

These were matters that Angélique thought about later, for just then she was far too weary to indulge in any such digressions. What she saw at the time was that Honorine's cheeks grew plump again, that everyone revived and she began to understand the Indians' deification of food, how a gathering round a fire between friends to 'have a feast' is akin to a veritable religious ceremony.

CHAPTER 77

ANGÉLIQUE looked at the gold ingot in her hand.

It was hers.

Count Peyrac had given it to her, just as he had to the others, to one of 'his men'.

She wanted to carry out an idea that had been dear to her heart for some time now.

Having promised a whole bundle of candles to all the Saints in Heaven if they escaped the smallpox, she now decided to offer her gold ingot to the sanctuary of Saint Anne of Beaupré of which the Canadians often spoke.

It had been built by Breton sailors who had been saved from shipwreck on the banks of the Saint Lawrence, and it was said that numerous miracles occurred there.

As she entered the big room that afternoon Angélique reckoned that the moment had come, for Monsieur d'Arreboust and Monsieur de Loménie were sitting alone at the table, reading their missals.

Angélique walked over to them and handed them the ingot as she told them of her intentions.

She would like the gold to be used by the priests of the parish and place of pilgrimage as they thought fit, either to purchase chasubles or other priestly vestments to make the services more beautiful, or to build a path, a crucifix, or a main altar of carved wood covered in gold leaf. All she asked in return was that her name should be engraved on a white marble plaque, beside the hundreds of other ex-votos, on the church wall, in memory of her thanksgiving to heaven that had preserved them from the terrible illness.

The two gentlemen leaped to their feet and backed away so precipitately that Monsieur d'Arreboust knocked a chair over.

They looked down in horror at the gold as it lay glimmering softly on the table before them.

'Impossible,' the Duke stammered. 'They would never accept this gold in Quebec, especially when they knew where it had come from and who had given it.'

'What do you mean?'

'His Grace the Bishop would undoubtedly prefer to burn down the sanctuary or have it exorcized. . . .'

'But . . .'

'This gold is accursed.'

'I don't understand you,' said Angélique. 'You didn't make all this fuss about accepting the gold my husband gave you for the Mississippi expedition. I even seem to remember that you came here especially to ask for it.'

'That's not the same.'

'But why not?'

'But from your hands! . . . Just think! . . . They would stone us for it.'

She looked at them in silence, unable to believe that they had gone mad. It was something worse.

'Madame,' said Loménie, with averted gaze, 'I greatly regret that I have to carry out the unpleasant task of telling you that certain rumours have begun to circulate about you, rumours that have grown and divided our fellow citizens in Quebec and indeed those in the whole of Canada. Certain people were surprised at your arrival, and more so at your exploits, and have grown anxious, thinking that they saw certain coincidences ...'

Angélique's gaze fastened upon him made his admissions none the easier.

She already had an inkling what it was he was trying to say, but it all seemed to her so preposterous that she preferred to leave him floundering, and not come to his assistance. One thing was certain, and that was that she was beginning to grow angry.

She had not expected them to show extravagant gratitude, but all the same!

Were they not going a little too far, these pious soldiers? She had nursed them in their illness. She served them at all hours of the day or night. Now she was weary, she was exhausted.

At this very moment, the muscles of her back and her arms ached, for she had been hacking at the ice outside the door which had become like a skating rink. Monsieur Jonas had slipped over on it this morning and had sprained his ankle quite badly. So, to prevent the same thing happening again, Angélique had worked for two hours without a break, then covered the patch with ashes and clinker. And this was the moment they had chosen to hurl these insulting, imbecilic accusations at her, with their suggestion that she possessed diabolical powers.

D'Arreboust, seeing that Loménie was in trouble, snapped out: 'They suspect you of being the incarnation of the She-Devil of Acadia. Have you ever heard of this prediction?'

'Yes I have! I understand it's a vision one of your nuns had, in which it was revealed to her that a She-Devil was seeking the damnation of the souls of Acadia. These are things that happen,' Angélique went on with a trace of a smile.

'And so you think that I possess all the qualifications necessary to play this part?'

'Madame, we cannot, alas, make light of these unhappy combinations of circumstances,' Loménie sighed. 'Fate dictated that Monsieur de Peyrac should settle in Acadia at the time of the prediction, and this made a disturbing impression. And it was known in Canada that he was accompanied by a woman whose description seemed to correspond to that given by the nun who had had the vision, so their suspicions fell on you.'

In spite of herself Angélique was beginning to feel anxious.

When she saw the two gentlemen recoil she had immediately realized that there was something serious afoot. She had not been entirely in the dark. She had heard of the vision. Nicolas Perrot had referred to it. . . . And she guessed that people might well have made comparisons. But she had never thought that things would reach this pitch of seriousness.

But now she saw what was happening. The beast was on the prowl, and she could hear its heavy tread. . . .

THE INQUISITION!

The monster that lay in wait for her in America was not nature as yet untamed, but still the same enemy, perhaps even more virulent than in the old world. For she was fully aware that in the Spanish territories the Inquisition had been lighting, one after the other, the most gigantic autos-da-fé in the whole of history. Indians had been burned by the million for showing themselves unwilling to serve the servants of the Church.

Back in France she had been persecuted because she was a young, beautiful, much loved woman who was valiant and different from the others. . . . Here they shouted 'She-Devil' at her as they had once shouted 'Sorcerer' at Peyrac.

In America everything is more clear-cut. Men's passions stand out clearly, are easily exacerbated. She would have to learn to face this myth, repudiate it and overcome it, and she felt as if some evil spirit really had slipped into her home.

But things must be faced up to, even evil spirits.

'Explain yourself, Monsieur de Loménie,' she said in a voice that sounded different. 'You are not going to tell me that in Quebec there are people of standing, people of breeding, who believe this story, who seriously believe that I could be . . . the incarnation of the demon woman whose coming has been foretold?'

'Alas! the facts appear to be against you,' cried Loménie with a gesture of despair. 'You disembarked at the very spot described in the vision. You were seen riding on horseback into the very territory that the nun said was threatened by the She-Devil. . . . And you are . . . very beautiful, Madame. Everyone who had ever seen you has testified to that. . . . So you see, it was his Grace the Bishop's duty to find out more about you. . . .'

'You surely are not going to tell me that the Ecclesiastical authorities attach any importance to this kind of tittle-tattle . . . and especially not to its interpretation?' exclaimed Angélique.

'Yes they do, Madame! His Grace was unable to do otherwise than take the reports from Father Orgeval, and from Brother Mark on the

Saint John river, seriously. Furthermore, the chaplain to the Ursulines of Quebec, Monsieur de Jorras, has testified to the mental health and stability of Sister Madeleine, whose father confessor he has been for many years. And Father de Maubeuge, the Superior of the Jesuits, is equally convinced of the fact that your arrival is an irrefutable sign of impending calamity. . . .'

Angélique stared at him, her eyes wide with horror.

'But why?' she cried. 'Why are all these priests against me?'

Joffrey de Peyrac, who had just come in from the workshop, heard her cry.

For him it seemed to be a symbolic cry. The cry of an outraged woman. Outraged, and rejected for so many centuries.

'But why? . . . Why are all these priests against me?'

He stood there in the shadows, making no move to come forward.

She had to defend herself.

For so many centuries the Church had had a misogynist outlook and had rejected Woman, that it was high time somebody protested.

And it was only right that the woman to protest should be the most lovely, the most 'womanly' woman the earth had ever borne.

He stood motionless and unseen, watching her from a distance with pride and great tenderness, as she stood there so lovely in her surprise, with indignation rising bit by bit within her, touching her cheeks with red and setting her green eyes ablaze.

The Duke of Arreboust alone noticed Peyrac's presence, he saw the flash of his smile as he watched Angélique, and the Duke's heart was torn with jealousy.

'That man Peyrac possesses a treasure here, and he knows it,' he told himself. 'He knows it. . . . My wife has never belonged to me. . . .'

Bitter words rose to his lips, while venom filled his heart, and he felt like spitting out his loathing in violent words of denunciation, in an attempt to humble this triumphant love, yet at one and the same time he realized that anything he might say would undoubtedlly come from some tainted source in the depths of his own being.

He remained silent.

Loménie went on courageously and conscientiously.

He drew a letter from his doublet, and opened it with an expression of distress on his face.

'I have here, Madame, the exact terms of the prophecy. Some of the descriptions of the countryside are disturbing. And recently a Recollect friar, Brother Mark, who is chaplain to Monsieur de Vauvenart, on the Saint John, recognized beyond a shadow of doubt the spot where you recently disembarked, Madame, with Monsieur de Peyrac.'

Angélique snatched the paper unceremoniously from his hands and began to read.

The visionary first described the place to which she had been taken in her dream.

CHAPTER 78

I WAS standing on the seashore. There were trees growing right down to the edge of the sand. . . . The beach had a pink sheen. On my left stood an outpost built of wood, with a high palisade, and a turret with a flag on it. . . . The bay was crowded with islands like sleeping monsters. . . . At the top of the beach, below the cliffs, stood some houses built of light wood. . . . And in the bay two ships lay at anchor. . . . At the far end of the beach, some distance away, perhaps a mile or two, there was another hamlet of small huts surrounded by roses. I could hear the screeching of seagulls and cormorants. . . .

Angélique's heart began to thud irregularly. Later she was to reproach herself for this emotional reaction, for she could well have noticed certain details in the letter that would have enabled her immediately to refute the accusations that had been made against her. One day she would remember this document, and would understand everything that had happened. But by then, it would be almost too late. . . .

At present what struck her above all was the details that identified the place as Gouldsboro, and she felt a wave of powerless rage mounting within her.

Then suddenly an extremely beautiful woman rose up out of the sea and I knew she was a She-Devil. She remained there, suspended above the water, in which her body was reflected, and I found it unbearable to look at her because she was a woman. . . . And I saw her as the symbol of the evil within me, a miserable sinner. . . . Then suddenly a creature loomed up over the horizon which I first took to be a demon, but as it galloped swiftly towards me I realized that it was a unicorn whose long pointed horn glittered like crystal in the light of the setting sun. The She-Devil leapt astride the animal and bounded off through the air.

455

Then I saw Acadia spread out like a vast plain viewed from the sky above. I knew it was Acadia. Demons were holding it by the four corners and shaking it violently like a blanket. The She-Devil flew over it on her unicorn, setting it alight. . . . And while this vision persisted I remember that I had the feeling that in one corner of the picture stood a black, grimacing demon, apparently watching over the dazzling demoniacal creature, and I was filled with a terrible fear that he was Lucifer himself. . . .

I was watching it all, in despair, for I saw that this spelled disaster for the dear land we have taken under our protection, when everything seemed to grow calm again.

Another woman crossed the sky. I could not tell whether it was Our Lady or one of the Saints under whose protection our people lie. But her appearance seemed to calm the She-Devil, who retreated before her as if afraid. . . .

Then I saw a kind of furry monster emerge from the undergrowth, hurl itself upon her and tear her to pieces, while a young archangel with a dazzling sword rose up into the heavens. . . .

Angélique folded up the sheets of paper.

She stood there a moment, waiting for her fear mingled with irritation to evaporate.

This was nothing but a collection of arrant nonsense, the ravings of a cloistered nun. And to think that intelligent men could take it all seriously!

Everyone knew that convents were full of visionaries. And yet there was something about the story that made her fear that it contained some grain of truth. So, instead of protesting, at first she remained thoughtful.

'If it is true,' she murmured at last, 'that the places described here seem to correspond to Gouldsboro, I grant that the priests could well draw a disturbing interpretation from the arrival of a woman and horses on those shores. By my arrival, in fact! . . . But how is one to refute it? The symbolism of images hides so many different truths, as you know. I do not find all these coincidences convincing. For instance, your visionary never says whether the She-Devil was dark or fair? And that seems strange after so detailed a description of the landscape.'

'Yes indeed. But Sister Madeleine told us herself that the apparition rose out of the water with the light shining behind it and that she could not see the woman's features.'

'That was very convenient,' said Angélique. 'But how can she claim that the woman was so beautiful, if she was unable to see her face?'

'She was talking mainly about the beauty of her body. She emphasized that. The woman's body appeared to her so astonishingly beautiful that this holy maid was greatly struck by it and found it quite disturbing. . . .'

'I am perfectly prepared to believe you on that score, but it seems to me to offer inadequate grounds for doing me the honour of suggesting that I am the incarnation of this vision. No one can claim to have seen me rising naked out of the water . . .'

She broke off suddenly and grew very pale. She had just remembered the little blue lake where she had swum during their journey across country. And she remembered the sudden fear she had felt, as if someone had been spying on her through the trees.

So it was true! Someone had seen her! She stared desperately at Loménie and d'Arreboust, and their expressions told her that they were thinking the same as her. So they knew. . . . Someone had seen her and had revealed the fact. . . .

She seized Loménie-Chambord's wrist, holding it in a vice-like grip.

'Who saw me? Who saw me when I went swimming in the lake?' Her eyes flashed and the unfortunate Knight of Malta looked away.

'That I cannot tell you, Madame! But you are right in thinking that you were seen, and this only added to the fears people had begun to have about the vision.'

Angélique was beginning to feel a sense of panic. So she had not been imagining things when she had felt so uneasy and frightened by that lake, in spite of the fact that it appeared deserted.

'Who saw me?' she repeated with clenched teeth.

But he shook his head, determined not to reply. She let go his wrist. After all, what did it matter! For a long time she had thought that she had been mistaken, or that the feeling she had experienced had merely been fear, perhaps that the Iroquois had been watching her, possibly Outakke himself; but now it appeared that it had been one of the French Canadians, some soldier or officer or trapper who had been wandering about in the forest! So the legend had taken shape. Everything fitted. She had been seen 'naked, rising up out of the water . . .' what a catastrophe!

She was seized with fury again and brought her fist down hard on the table.

'The devil take you,' she said between her clenched teeth, 'you, your King, your nuns and your priests. Is there nowhere on earth remote

457

enough for me to be spared this kind of rubbish? Do you have to be everywhere, spreading confusion, under the pretext of saving souls or serving the King? Do you have to raise your heads everywhere to prevent honest men living in peace? Or even washing themselves in peace? Fifty thousand lakes? There are fifty thousand lakes in this land! And I was unable to pick a single one of them in which to cool myself during a heatwave, without one of your men being there to spy on me and to represent what he had seen as something out of the Apocalypse.

'Because some ill-bred boor thinks that he too has had a celestial vision, you all fall into line, and hail the fact as evidence that this man has been warned of the dangers threatening New France because a woman bathed in a lake. . . . And who was it who guided me, when the idea came to me to go out and look for you in the snow where you lay dying? If it was the Devil my master, he must have a very soft spot for you, since it was your lives I saved. We nursed you, we shared the last of our food with you, we were forced to kill our last horse. . . .

'Then, as if it were not enough for your Hurons to have given us all their filthy disease, to have accepted our care and our hospitality, and to have shared our remaining food with us, to have received a promise of help for Monsieur de la Salle's expedition, you are now busy asking yourselves whether we are not in league with Satan, whether I am not the prophesied She-Devil. . . . Just when are you going to grow up?' she said, in a voice full of scorn, almost pitying.

'Through the fault of the people who rule you, you have shown yourselves today to be cowardly, stupid and ungrateful. . . . I don't want to see you any more. Get out of my house!'

And she repeated more calmly but every bit as coldly:

'Get out! Get out of my house!'

The two men rose to their feet, and with bowed heads, walked towards the door.

CHAPTER 79

THEY WERE greeted outside by a wan, violet-coloured evening light, and the cold air cut them like a blade. They stumbled off across the icy ground, and stopped at the lakeside, where they stood looking at the horizon that lowered dark yet livid with the last light of day.

It was an extraordinary situation for men of their age and stamp to find themselves, at this hour of the night, with the wind whistling across the snow, as completely abandoned as orphans.

They were beginning to realize that if they lost the friendship of Madame de Peyrac, their lives would indeed become unbearable.

'We did not deserve this,' said Loménie in lugubrious tones.

'No. . . . But I understand her anger. I am damned if I enjoyed telling her all this tittle-tattle and wounding her as we did. She is an adorable young woman and we have received nothing but kindness from her.'

'She is right, Loménie! We are ungrateful wretches! And it's all the fault of those Jesuits. They so stuffed our minds with all their nonsense that we have ceased to be men.'

'Good heavens!' said Loménie, stupefied. 'I always thought you were a devoted supporter of the Company of Jesus. Almost one of them yourself! Are you and your wife not an example which . . .'

'The Jesuits have stolen my wife from me,' said the Duke. 'I did not know she belonged to me. And they took advantage of this to take her from me. I might just as well not exist. They have made a eunuch of me, in the service of the Church. . . . A highly desirable state to be in, in their eyes, for they regard marriage, even Christian marriage, as sinful. It was the Lady of the Silver Lake who made me realize all this. She is so beautiful, so very much a woman.

'I like her fiery spirit, and the warmth of her personality. . . . She is a woman you could take in your arms. . . .'

He gave a cough, for he had spoken very loud and the icy air rasped at his lungs.

'Understand me, you at least, my friend, for no one in Quebec will understand me when I set the cat among the pigeons. The Lady of the Silver Lake belongs to Peyrac and to him alone. She was made to be taken in a man's arms. . . . That is what I said. She was made for that man's arms. And that is a good thing! That is right! That's what I'm trying to say.'

'You're delirious, old chap, you're not yourself, you know.'

'You may be right, or possibly the fact is that I am becoming myself again. For were we not once ardent, full of joy, a trifle gay, men full of faith in God and in life, a life we put behind us when we ceased to be young, beneath a confused mass of rules and regulations that are incompatible with truth. Now Peyrac is a man who has never disowned his own nature. He has stood like a rock in the midst of a life full of base actions. I envy Peyrac, not only because he is the husband of that woman, but because he is a man who has never repudiated himself.

Never in all his life,' d'Arreboust repeated emphatically. 'Even though it might bring about his death, he has never repudiated himself at any stage of his life. Youth is the most difficult stage, for it is then that one comes under influences that can never be shaken off, because one imagines that they have their basis in one's own will.

'Do you still suspect her of being a She-Devil?' he asked, pointing fiercely at Loménie, whose teeth were chattering with cold.

'No, and I never did. You may remember that in Quebec I was the one who refused to listen to all the scandalmongers, and everyone shouted me down, and accused me of having fallen under her spell. And you were the first . . .'

'Yes, that's true, forgive me! Now I understand. God in Heaven! I am dying of cold! Let's go in quickly and offer our excuses to the charming lady we have so gravely offended.'

CHAPTER 80

'WERE YOU frightened I would stop feeding you?' Angélique asked when she saw them standing behind her in a contrite attitude.

'Hurled into the outer darkness, amidst weeping and gnashing of teeth,' quoted Count Loménie, 'and into the bitter cold,' he added with a pitiful smile.

When they had left her, Angélique had slowly regained her calm. At first she had been hurt and anxious, but her sense of humour had gradually got the better of her, and the thought that her arrival in America had so bemused the superstitious Canadians, that she had become mixed up in their visions, made her smile in spite of herself. The embarrassment of the Bishop's plenipotentiaries had brought her some measure of revenge. Poor Loménie had been in a terrible state, and as for d'Arreboust, she had been unable to see clearly what it was that had made him so furious, whether it was his dislike of having to talk matters over with a supposed servant of Lucifer, or the fact that he had had to play the inquisitor in front of her. She was inclined to think that it was the latter. They had all got to know one another well during the past few weeks, so when she saw them standing behind her looking so abashed, she was inclined to show them indulgence.

The Knight of Malta explained that he understood how upset she must be, and he begged her to forgive him for having been so clumsy in his approach. She had misunderstood them. They had never intended to suggest that they suspected her of being in league with the infernal legions, but merely wanted to warn her of the dangerous situation that existed. . . . Their compatriots were quite wrong about it, and they would make this quite clear on their return to Quebec.

Angélique gave them her hand to kiss and forgave them.

'She is a very great lady,' Duke d'Arreboust said. 'I'll swear she has been received in all the salons of Paris and even at Court, just from the way she holds out her hand.'

During her lively exchange with the two gentlemen, Angélique had not noticed her husband's presence. And he had slipped silently away. He waited for her to mention the incident but she said nothing. On reflection, she considered the matter not worth mentioning. Not yet! Later, perhaps, if it looked like assuming proportions that might harm them. She feared Peyrac's reactions where she was involved, and in any case, the discussion she had had with the two Canadian representatives had gained her and Joffrey two certain allies. Two people of considerable influence in Canada had been forced to take her side.

Father Masserat seemed in no way hostile, and as for Cavelier de la Salle, he had his money. Little did he care whether it came from the Devil or from Providence. The only thing that mattered to him was the fulfilment of his own plans. He was a hard, materialistic man, entirely absorbed in his own affairs, and it was difficult to imagine how such a cold, enterprising young man had been able to think for as long as ten years that he had a religious vocation.

As long as Angélique felt hersuf surrounded by friends in the fort, she was not afraid. It was a very different situation from the one Joffrey de Peyrac had had to face when he had been accused of being a sorcerer, in a land where the authority of the King and the Inquisition could find its way everywhere, even into his own palace.

She was free! She was gradually beginning to understand the full meaning of the word when she looked out across the snow-covered mountains, in all their untrodden, indomitable splendour. This was a land without a prince, a land under no royal suzerainty, a land that cared nothing for the rights of the King of France or the King of England.

It was too big for the handful of men trying to appropriate it. In the fort, Angélique felt even more strongly that the only master on whom they all depended was Joffrey de Peyrac, and that he possessed both the power and the force to defend her against anyone. He had promised her that when the spring came he would bring twenty or thirty mercenaries to Wapassou, which would give them a garrison three times stronger than the most heavily defended French establishment. These men would build a fort which, according to the plans they had drawn up, promised to be the most handsome and best conceived in the whole of North America.

Angélique enjoyed looking over the plans with her husband and sons. She helped to plan the living quarters, arranging separate quarters for married couples, a common dining-room, and also a large room next to the shop in which the Indians could assemble, and spit and belch to their hearts' content. . . . There would be a garden, a kitchen garden and stables. . . .

During the month of March the weather improved sufficiently for various groups of men to set off. But of course they still ran the risk of being caught in the soft snow that came with the end of winter, sometimes even thicker than in the winter itself, and heavy, wet and treacherous.

Nicolas Perrot set off towards the south to the mission station at Norridgewock, escorting Pacific Jusserand whose eyes were not sufficiently healed for him to be able to travel unaccompanied. The Indian who had come with him was detailed to accompany d'Arreboust, Loménie and Father Masserat back to Quebec.

The group of men who had the longest distance to cover, since they were heading west, towards Lake Champlain, was that consisting of Cavelier de la Salle, Florimond, Yann le Couennec and a young Indian from the small neighbouring tribe who had asked to join them. The distribution of rations caused considerable difficulties. They needed salted meat, smoked meat, maize-flour and brandy. . . . If everyone was given sufficient for several weeks' travel, the inhabitants of the fort would find themselves with almost nothing left, so they had to trust in providence to put some game along their route.

When the day came for them to leave, Angélique stood on the threshold with a goblet and a jug of brandy in her hand, for everyone to drink a 'stirrup-cup' – although they were not in fact travelling on horseback! They carried their snowshoes strapped to their backs, for the snow was still resilient and firm enough to enable them to walk for quite a while without putting them on.

The dry, cold spell continued, thawing a little but not too much. The travellers considered it decidedly promising. If the weather stayed like this for another six days, they would be out of danger. . . .

Florimond kissed his mother without any show of emotion, nor did he even show too much youthful enthusiasm and excitement at the idea of going away. He was quite calm. He checked over his instruments and the maps he was taking one last time with his father, and they exchanged a few words. Florimond seemed older than either Cavelier de la Salle or the Breton. No one could describe what it was about him, but they all felt that, if the need arose, it was to him his companions would all turn.

As Florimond turned his dark eyes to the distance, measuring up nature before doing battle with it, then set off walking in the direction of the lake, Angélique felt her heart tighten within her, from admiration and joy. From satisfaction too.

A new Joffrey de Peyrac was setting out into the world. . . .

Some time before these departures, Octave Malaprade and Elvire had taken advantage of the presence of Father Masserat to get married. At first the Jesuit had refused point-blank to agree to any union between a good Catholic and a notorious Protestant. After that he made a little speech to Malaprade, reminding him that marriage is a sacrament which husband and wife administer to each other, and that the participation of a priest is in no way obligatory, except in so much as it concerns his placing his signature as a witness in the state archives.

If he had grasped the situation correctly, Monsieur de Peyrac was the representative officer of their nation, and as for a divine blessing, there was nothing to prevent a married couple who sought to have their promises hallowed, from receiving it in the same way as any other members of a religious gathering when they attended a service.

Malaprade was quick on the uptake. He said he had understood and went off without saying any more. But the following morning the little cubby-hole where Father Masserat said Mass seemed strangely full, containing as it did almost the entire population of the fort in their best clothes, and when the priest turned round to bless the assembled company, he failed to notice two humble figures kneeling side by side, who, from that day on, each wore a gold ring.

So Octave Malaprade and Elvire were married before God and before men, and their own quarters were made for them up in the loft.

When Monsieur de Frontenac's envoys reached Quebec they were welcomed as if they had returned from the dead, for they had been believed long since frozen in the snow or assassinated by Count Peyrac.

It was as if they had come back from hell to say the least, and people surrounded them, horrified and respectful. The grave Duke of Arreboust caused considerable dismay by behaving in an unusually jovial manner and saying things which, to say the least of it, everyone found incredible.

'The harm is done,' he said. 'I'm in love. I'm in love with the Lady of the Silver Lake!'

Monsieur de Loménie-Chambord still clung to his earlier opinions. In spite of the revelations of the visionary, in spite of Pont-Briand's death that shocked everyone, he still continued to regard the strangers from Wapassou as friends.

He spent a whole day with the Governor in the Château Saint-Louis. Then he went to a Jesuit house to make a retreat.

When Pont-Briand's death was mentioned, he replied:

'He deserved it.'

D'Arreboust talked a great deal about his adventures and his sojourn among the 'dangerous heretics' – describing each one of these almost legendary characters, the tall, learned Peyrac, the miners holding gold ingots in their blackened hands – and when he got on to the subject of HER beauty, it was hard to stop him.

'I'm in love with her,' he would repeat with childish obstinacy.

A report of all these goings-on reached Montreal, and his wife, whose outlook was somewhat altered by pique, wrote to him in the following vein:

'I have received some unfortunate reports concerning you. . . . I, who love you. . . .'

To which he replied:

'No, you do not love me, Madame, and I do not love you either. . . .

Never before had so many messengers, at this time of the year, shod in snowshoes, had to cover the fifty leagues between the two cities. Never had the word 'love' been so often heard in Quebec and Montreal, brushing through Trois-Rivières as it passed, where no one had any idea of what the fuss was all about, and never had so much time been spent in discussions about the meaning of this very basic human sentiment.

Monsieur d'Arreboust was fully aware of the fact that something had changed within him, but where people failed to follow him was when he claimed that the change was not for the worse. He seemed rather proud of his scandalous statements, and Frontenac, delighted, roared with laughter. The Governor hoped that the negotiations he had begun with Count Peyrac would continue, and the Duke and he congratulated each other as they stood in one of the high-ceilinged rooms of the castle before a roaring log fire, on the charm of beautiful women and the pleasures and the disadvantages of love; for Frontenac had left behind in France a brilliant, flighty and forgetful wife whom he loved dearly.

Passionate discussions, heady dreams, grandiose projects were the things that kept their hearts aglow, warmed their spirits, and helped these Canadians to get through the last months of winter. For this was the time of famine, when the cold wore down resistance, and even in the cities people grew weary through lack of food, and exhausted from their struggle against the cruel cold. They feared lest they could not hold out until the arrival of the first ships from France. And they knew that in the bleak, bare countryside, death would sweep over the land like a terrible blizzard. The garrisons of the distant outposts buried those who had died of scurvy, and in the more improvident native villages, the missionaries had to gnaw their caribou-skin belts. Whole villages, driven by famine, would set out towards some refuge and fall dead by the wayside along the white trails. Others merely waited for death, wrapped in their red and blue bartered blankets, beside the dying embers....

When at the beginning of April there was a further prolonged fall of heavy, icy snow, Monsieur le Colonel de Castel-Morgeat, the military governor, who was one of the irreconcilable enemies of the men of Wapassou, went around Quebec saying with a sardonic smile on his face that there was no longer any point in discussing their merits or demerits, for by now they would certainly all be dead, out there in the woods, with their womenfolk, their children and their horses.

CHAPTER 81

LITTLE BY little Angélique felt herself overwhelmed by a great weariness.

She would first feel it in the morning. No sooner had she opened her eyes, feeling perfectly lucid and keen to make a start to the day, than she felt as if her body had turned to lead as it lay in the hollow of the mattress like a wreck stranded on the shore. And yet there was nothing wrong with her. It seemed to come from within, although by now she knew that she was not pregnant. But something seemed to have given way inside her which she had not the strength to put together again. 'I am tired,' she would tell herself in astonishment. It never helped to go on lying there, on the contrary. She merely grew heavier and more apathetic, like a log with a mind, wide awake and longing to get up and do things, but in fact quite incapable of moving.

She missed Florimond. He was always so gay, so even-tempered, with that lack of self-pity that was characteristic of his father. If he did show any traces of it, he would make a joke of the matter, like the day when he had shouted: 'What about me? What about me?' when no one had taken any notice of him and he was about to collapse with exhaustion. And even then he had made them all laugh by taking it lightly. He had a very French temperament, possessing that popular gift which is to be found in all circles, even in the antechamber of the King himself, namely, the more uncomfortable or thorny a given situation is, the more one jokes about it. She had no anxiety on his behalf. She might well have had, like all mothers, if she had had the strength to consider the matter, but she was so weary that she laid this particular worry on one side. The food situation caused her far more anxiety as their stocks grew smaller with every day that passed. They could scarcely swallow the insipid maize gruel any more, and once again they had completely run out of salt, while the meat was so tough that it required a great deal of chewing.

'I am tired,' Angélique repeated.

And occasionally she would say it out loud as if comforting herself by this confidential information which she dared tell to no one else.

With a supreme effort she would get out of bed. Every movement seemed to exhaust her but by the time she was dressed after a thorough wash, with her coif carefully arranged, her numerous skirts and fur-lined clothes carefully adjusted, and the holster of her favourite pistol resting on one hip, she began to feel better. Her weariness had almost left her, but on the other hand, until she had had something to eat, she felt so much on edge that she avoided talking to anyone, for fear of bursting into a tirade of reproaches or imprecations. This had in fact happened on two or three occasions, once at Honorine who had spent the rest of the day weeping, for she was easily brought to tears at that time, once against Cantor, who had sulked with her ever since, and once against Clovis who had spat on the ground, and she had almost flown at him like some termagant. Then afterwards they had made it up. After all, you had to make allowances for the fact that bodies were vulnerable, and minds, deprived of physical support, were fallible. She felt a constant sense of annoyance with herself, as if she had been guilty of something, as if she had some lapse to reproach herself with. One evening she told her husband how she felt as she lay at his side, resting her head against his shoulder.

'It's just hunger, little lady,' he said, gently stroking her cramped,

466

aching stomach. 'When you are able to eat your fill, life will look brighter again.'

'But what about you, you never complain, you are always as even-tempered as ever. . . . How do you manage it?'

'My old carcass has been toughened in the fire.'

And he clasped her to him as if to instil into her some of the manly strength of his indomitable body. She curled her legs around his, and put her arms round him, and fell asleep with her head resting on his firm chest.

'I sometimes feel,' she told him one day, 'that woman really did come from man's side, just as the child came from the woman.'

She was often plagued with intolerable headaches. Then the following day snow would fall in great sheets. Because of this snow that fell in enormous quantities but did not freeze, Nicolas Perrot did not get back till the end of March. In spite of his snowshoes, he had several times been almost buried with his Redskin in the snowdrifts. When he reached the Norridgewock mission he had only found one of Father Orgeval's assistants there, Father de Guérande, to whose care he had committed Pacific Jusserand. He had half thought of making his way farther south as far as the Dutchman's trading post, but in view of the bad weather that would have prolonged his journey, and the uncertainty of spring which, as soon as the thaw set in, would render all the trails and river impassable, he had decided to return to Wapassou. He suggested they organize a big hunt. So some of the men accompanied him westwards as far as Lake Umbagog, in the domain of Mopuntook. This was the time of the year when the natives, driven by hunger and the need to find skins for trading, began to hunt in groups again. The rutting deer which were beginning to fill the icy woods with their noisy cry, were easy prey, although they had grown thin after the rigours of the winter and fights with their rivals. There was also the possibility of running into a herd of does, or of killing a bear asleep in its lair which they had noted in the autumn, and they would use sticks to kill the beavers liberated by the melting ice on the ponds and waterways. As far as the Indians were concerned, the arrival of the white hunters was welcome, for they carried with them stocks of gunpowder and shot. Nicolas Perrot decided that in order to leave more food behind at the fort, each man would take only a small supply of suet, flour, Indian corn and dried meat, pounded up with herbs. Just enough for them to eat a little twice a day during the journey, by mixing a pinch of all these ingredients in their palms as the Indians did. He worked out just how much they would need for a six-day trip.

467

'And supposing you are delayed by storms or by the thaw?' asked Angélique, to whom these provisions seemed totally inadequate.

'Then we'll hunt! The birds are beginning to move about again in the undergrowth. There are white partridges, polar curlews and even the occasional Labrador goose. There are hares too. . . . Don't worry about us, Madame. That was how we used to fight in the days of Monsieur de Tracy. A hundred-and-twenty leagues in the depths of winter, right across to the Iroquois villages in the valley of the Mohawks. Unfortunately, in the heat of the battle, we set fire to the Iroquois grainstores without thinking of the fact that we had no supplies for the return journey.'

'So what happened?'

'A lot died,' said Nicolas philosophically.

He loaded himself up with his powder flask, his cartridge belt, his Indian knife in its sheath all sewn with beads and porcupine quills, his flask of brandy, his axe and his tomahawk, his tinder box with its long stick of tinder, his pipe, the pouch in which he kept flints and the one containing tobacco, his leather-fringed coat and his red woollen cloak, and finally his multicoloured belt which ran five times round his waist; then he set off, an indefatigable trekker through the woods, with a heavy, flat-footed gait on account of his snowshoes, at the head of his little band of men.

He forgot his bag of food on the table and Angélique had to shout after them.

But they were already far off on the other side of the lake and signalled to her that it didn't matter.

They set off through the undergrowth, through a soft white universe of trees weighed down with snow that stood all round them, like lush pyramids, dripping candles, pale ghosts; and as they went by they left a long trail of a myriad dazzling particles of snow hanging in the air.

There were only a few men left at the outpost now with the women and children, and even these found the food-stocks inadequate.

Once again Cantor had been furious with his father for refusing to allow him to join the hunting party, as he had refused to allow him to go off with Florimond. Angélique agreed with her husband, who considered that the lad, who had been ill, was not strong enough to face the long walk to Lake Umbagog. And this was without reckoning with the fact that when they arrived there they might well find the Indian tribes decimated by famine, or discover that they had set off southwards in a hopeless bid to flee the deadly clutches of winter. Peyrac comforted his younger son by telling him that they needed someone strong at the outpost to attend to the traps. So the lad would set off courageously every morning, sometimes returning with a hare, sometimes empty-handed. It was difficult to bait the traps, and in spite of his determined efforts, Cantor was quickly tired. He used to return home with such an appetite that any skinny piece of game he brought back with him he would have been capable of eating alone and unaided. Then he fell ill again and no one attended to the traps.

The Indians from the little beaver camp had come several times to beg for maize which they felt they had to give them. In exchange they offered a little beaver meat. Then one day, they packed up all their things and disappeared.

Joffrey de Peyrac apart, those who had remained at the fort were either ill or weak. There were two of the Spaniards, including Juan Alvarez who never left his bed, the dumb Englishman, Enrico Enzi, who never stopped shivering, and Monsieur Jonas and Kouassi-Ba, who were considered too old to take part in the hunt. These two still seemed hale and hearty, and did most of the heavy work, like chopping firewood, clearing the snow, breaking the ice, and mending anything that could be mended.

Clovis should have gone with the hunters but the day before they left he had suffered a serious attack of lead poisoning.

It was Kouassi-Ba who noticed just in time that the blacksmith had a swollen tongue and was complaining of a strange, sweet taste in his mouth. On entering the little penthouse where Clovis usually carried out his metallurgical work, the Negro noticed that Clovis, no doubt because he was feeling the cold, had blocked up all the gaps and cracks in the walls to keep the cold out. Unfortunately it also kept the air out, and he had not considered that harmful gases from the process of cupellation would stagnate in the enclosed space. Kouassi-Ba immediately informed Count Peyrac of what had happened and they gave the man a calming brew to allay the terrible colic pains that had begun to grip his stomach. But the best medicine for this kind of poisoning was something they lacked altogether, namely milk. They had not set eyes on a drop of milk ever since they had landed in America – in fact, ever since they had left La Rochelle, if you did not count the small quantity of goat-milk reserved for the children on board the *Gouldsboro*. Failing this, the miners knew that the entrails of a rabbit, pounded and eaten raw, especially the liver and the heart, could prove efficacious. But where would they obtain these? Cantor set out to look in the traps and found two white hares.

Angélique was so delighted that she began to understand why the French-Canadians thought their land was full of miracles.

As soon as he had taken the mixture Count Peyrac himself prepared and gave to him, the blacksmith began to feel better and it was clear that he was out of danger. But he had to keep to his bed for a long time, permanently shivering beneath his blankets, although he was kept always surrounded with heated stones.

Angélique no longer had the strength to lift him.

'It's just as well it's you, Clovis. You're old enough and ugly enough to stand up for yourself, for I can do no more.'

But Clovis refused to be tended by Madame Jonas or Elvire, and moaned miserably that he wanted Angélique.

'I want her to look after me, HER, HER,' he would say. 'It's not the same with you others. There's something about her hands that gets you better....'

So Angélique simply had to go and sit at his bedside from time to time and talk to him a little so that he did not undermine his strength with his own gloomy thoughts.

'What will you do with the gold you have earned working for Monsieur de Peyrac?' she asked him one day.

And so strange was his reply that at first she thought his mind was wandering.

'When I have collected enough gold, I shall bury it at the bottom of the sea, in a creek I know on Mount Desert Island in Gouldsboro Bay; then I shall set off for Granada in the heart of South America. I have heard that you can find emeralds there as big as stones. So I shall find some of those. And then I shall go to the East Indies where they say there are rubies, sapphires and diamonds, and, if necessary, I shall tear them from the eyes of the idols in the temples. And when I have got all the precious stones I need, I shall pick up my gold and make a dress for little Foy from Conques. I shall make her a crown, and some slippers studded with gems, far more beautiful than any she has ever had before....'

Angélique, at a loss, asked who was this Foy of Conques. Some old flame? Or had they once been betrothed?

Clovis darted a scandalized, furious glance at her.

'What, Madame, have you never heard of Saint Foy of Conques? It's the greatest sanctuary in all the world. Don't you know about it?'

Angélique admitted that she was unforgivable and that her lapse of memory must be due to her tiredness. Of course she had heard tell of the sanctuary of Conques-en-Rouergue, in the mountains of

Auvergne. There, in a fortified church, in a shrine of pure gold, a single tooth and a few hairs from the head of the little Roman martyr of the second century had been preserved, for she had the reputation of performing many miracles, particularly by her intercession on behalf of prisoners and by helping them to make good their escape.

'Three times I carried my chains to her,' said Clovis proudly, 'the heaviest chains you ever saw. The first set from the prison at Aurignac, then from the keep of Mancousset and the others from that filthy hole of a prison in the bishopric of Riom.'

'Did you escape?' asked the children, drawing near.

'Yes indeed! And in a spectacular way too, thanks to the help of the little Saint. . . .'

Whenever Angélique was called away, Honorine would take charge of the sick man and would hold his great black paw in her tiny hands as she had seen her mother do.

During the course of the winter Angélique had noticed how well her daughter managed to get on with all their most difficult companions. She liked Jacques Vignot and Clovis best, and was so forthcoming with them and so full of solicitude that in the end they were won over.

'Why do you like me so much?' the carpenter asked the little girl one day.

'Because you shout very loud and say a lot of naughty words!'

Honorine was looking thin and pale, and showing signs of sickliness. Her hair was slow to grow again and Angélique had visions of her being bald for the rest of her life. Twenty times a day she would glance anxiously at the child. She noticed that her daughter would often curl up her lips in a grimace over her swollen gums and she trembled for fear that the child might be developing that terrible scourge of winter, scurvy, the land sickness.

She knew, as did her husband, that the only way of avoiding this illness was to eat fresh fruit and vegetables, but the ground was covered with snow.

CHAPTER 82

PEYRAC SENSED his wife's profound lassitude. She seemed less gay, spoke little, striving only to keep essentials going, remaining active only in so far as it was necessary to keep up day-to-day life, her own health and the health of those in her care. Her anxiety for her daughter and her son, for those who were sick and those whose resistance she felt to be low and on the point of breaking, and for her husband too – those were her sole concerns in life, and they were sapping her strength.

When he lay down beside her at night the total abandon of her delightful body woke his desire, but although he knew she would have been perfectly prepared to accept his advances, she seemed nevertheless absent from him and this she could not help. It was a natural lack of contact, inevitable in a woman tormented by worry, a woman kept in a state of constant anxiety by the threats that surrounded her. For even when she slept – a heavy, exhausted sleep – he sensed that she was on the qui vive.

She remained constantly aware of everything that was going on around her: the storm that howled outside, the cold that grew daily more intense. From the moment she awoke her cares were ever-present. The foodstuffs were diminishing, Honorine was growing pale, Cantor had been coughing for the past three days, Madame Jonas was growing thinner and seemed less cheerful, the hunters had not come back yet and seemed to have vanished into the frozen cotton-wool world of the snow-bound forest, and still the spring refused to come.

She was both absent and indifferent, absent yet present. She was scrupulously present wherever she had something to defend, but absent to anything that did not concern their survival. And as he thought about it, he came to admire her instinctive submission as a woman to the natural law of the world. He recognized in this woman who lay resting beside him, pale and weary, distant yet anxious, apathetic yet on the alert, the present unease of the earth, of the whole of nature, that was using up its final reserves in order to survive the tail end of winter. Gathering them together too, in order to survive the sudden onslaught of spring. It was the time of death before rebirth. The trees died, animals died, exhausted by their struggle, men died, empty-handed after eating their last mouthful of maize, only a few days from the fulfilment of their hopes; they died while in the woods the indomitable buds began to burst through the mummified branches, and all these living creatures gave up the ghost. . . .

Without realizing it, Angélique had adjusted her own rhythm to this supreme struggle. She must avoid all wastage. In Iroquois communities, it was the women who organized the collection of food for the winter months, who decided when to move if the land grew arid, who knew when to fight if the survival of their community depended on it. The men would say: 'We men, we were created for the present, for action.

472

We fight wars, we do not take decisions about them. . . . It's the women who know about that. . . .'

He would lean over her with a feeling almost of reverence and stroke her soft hair, murmuring words of comfort. They were both calculating how long it would take the hunters to get back with some fresh game, they were dividing up the remaining food once again in their minds, and deciding to give Clovis a bit more, for he was slow to get well. . . . And should they allow old Eloi Macollet to go off as he wanted to and break the ice on the ponds in order to fish up some beaver or anything else that came to hand? He might get lost, or fall ill, in spite of his toughness, for he was very old. . . .

Angélique would often sit with Honorine on her knees beside the fire and watch the dancing flames. The child, habitually so active, now sought refuge with her, and sat huddled up in the warmth of her mother's arms, as they clasped her against the breasts that had suckled her. From time to time Angélique would tell her some story or hum a tune. But they might equally well remain silent, and they passed many a pleasant hour together in a kind of vegetative retreat from the world which had a quality of intimacy which they both enjoyed. Angélique had ceased to feel guilty, and no longer reproached herself, for their situation necessitated a lack of action which at other times she would have found unnatural. It was in fact a sign of sound mental health that she was able to accept herself as she was, as a lesser person, or even an unhappy one, when circumstances justified it, without feeling any anxiety, without seeking to make excuses, without attempting to defend herself. There is a measure of pride in an attitude that refuses to acknowledge human weakness. Her stomach was a cold, yearning hollow within her, and her head buzzed. She often felt sickened by the sheer monotony of the food, and was tempted to give her share to the children, but she forced herself to swallow what she had been allotted. She had to accept the fact that, in spite of her desire to cope with everything, she had not the same physical strength as Count Peyrac. Nothing ever seemed to affect him, and his zest for life and calm acceptance of everything was neither feigned nor forced. He too had to withdraw into himself like everyone else, in order to face cold and hunger, but in his case the process seemed to take place within him, whereas with the others it was evident from their behaviour; they were out of sorts, or weary, or visibly weaker. One of the Spaniards like him and the Englishmen stood up to it well too.

Angélique was well aware of the fact that her anxiety was wearing away her resistance. But no one can entirely change their nature. In her time she had fought like a man, faced with crippling loneliness and borne down by a burden that was often heavier than a woman could properly bear; but now she could accept her role as a woman in this ordeal, and could lean on her man. Peyrac's mere presence kept them all alive.

And yet a change had come over him which she did not notice at first, but which she remembered later with considerable emotion. From being their master, he had become their servant, and spared himself nothing in his effort to help these enfeebled, imperilled people in his care. Because he knew he was already asking a lot of them to survive, he demanded less of them in other respects. So, for example, he would help Madame Jonas to hang the heavy cooking-pots over the fire, to carry buckets of water, and would himself change the dressings of the injured or tend the sick to spare Angélique the constant burden of this work. He would dispel Cantor's ill-humour with friendly banter, and with the warm pressure of a hand on a shoulder would arrest stupid, unpremeditated quarrels as they broke out, and would keep the children happy by taking them into the forge or the laboratory, where work had slowed down considerably, to show them some magic that delighted them. Normally the children were not allowed in the workshops but now they became welcome visitors.

He went off with Lymon White or Cantor to collect whatever was in the traps, and one day Angélique saw him on his return skin a muskrat with a casual flick of the wrist. A few calm words from him sufficed to help Elvire fight against a feeling of depression that caused her to doubt her new love and brought on feelings of remorse. Malaprade's absence distressed her terribly, and she felt sure that the Lord, to punish her for having been so easily consoled after her first husband's death, would take her second from her.

'Don't think about anything as long as you are still hungry,' Peyrac told her, 'and don't confuse great and majestic thoughts about God with phantasms caused by your stomach cramps. Hunger is a bad counsellor. It attacks your self-esteem and degrades you. It makes us all self-centred and reduces us to abject solitude. So stand firm. Your husband will come back, and you will eat together again.'

By paying careful attention to their movements they sustained their flagging bodies. They all moved about rather like automata, slowly and carefully. Once the essential tasks of the day were over, Peyrac advised them to go to bed and sleep, for an old proverb says that he who sleeps forgets his hunger. And here again he was to be seen carrying hot stones to warm the beds of those who had forgotten to provide for themselves. He would get up during the night to keep the fires going.

One day he said to Angélique: 'Let's have the little girl in our bed to help to keep her warm.'

He had noticed that Angélique seemed more and more worried with every evening that passed at the idea of leaving Honorine to struggle on alone in her little bed against the black hostility of the night. The temperature would fall so low that their bodies, weakened as they were, found it hard to keep warm. When dawn came they were all shivering beneath their blankets. Honorine was so delighted to be sleeping between her father and mother that the colour returned to her cheeks. The wind might howl outside, but Honorine slept on between them like a happy baby animal.

Whenever the weather was fine, the colonists of Wapassou forced themselves to take a short turn outside, then quickly returned to the warmth of the outpost. It took them a long time to warm up again. Honorine's hands were permanently white and frozen, and Angélique would make her soak them in hot water, and she herself and the other women as well would warm themselves up in this way. They developed a great affection for wood, the ever-faithful wood, that burnt on tirelessly in the grate, but Count Peyrac was constantly on the lookout for any risk of fire. The others had grown less vigilant out of weariness, so he redoubled his watchfulness, and would make a tour of inspection of each room every evening, even going outside with a lantern to make sure that nothing obstructed the edges of the chimneys, so that no spark risked falling on the shingle roof. All this was specially important once the snow began to melt.

Then suddenly it grew very warm, and the atmosphere became moist and saturated with water vapour like a hothouse. Their exhausted bodies were suddenly covered with sweat and throughout the day they removed more and more of their fur-lined garments, and opened doors and windows, and put out the fire in the chimneys, only to light them again promptly in the evenings as the blazing sun fell over the horizon, plunging the world anew into icy darkness.

By day the snow had begun to melt away with a never-ending, subterranean trickle of running water. It was like waterlogged cotton wool, like the pith of an elder-tree swollen with water. It slithered off the trees in great heavy dollops. In two days the immaculate white forest had become grey, then black, shining with a myriad glistening drops of water. But it would take a good deal longer for the deep

475

snowdrifts round the house to vanish, and the ground to be cleared of the icy layer of snow over six feet deep which had gradually accumulated during the winter. At night it would freeze again and become as hard as marble, while icicles, hanging from the edge of the roof, snapped off and crashed down like fragments of breaking glass.

The only immediate result of the sudden heat was to spoil their last stocks of preserved meat which had been kept as long as it was frozen in the loft. As soon as it occurred to them that the heat might spoil their remaining meat, Angélique immediately climbed the ladder to the loft where they had hung some joints of game and horsemeat, with their last ham and their last piece of salt pork; a sickening smell told her immediately what had happened. Even the smoked meat seemed to have been spoiled and in addition, all sorts of tiny creatures, which one might have thought dead or asleep, such as mice, rats, and squirrels, had suddenly appeared from every corner of the loft and were nibbling away at the provisions, thus rendering uneatable anything they might still have made use of. Too depressed by this disaster to say anything about it, Angélique, with the help of her two assistants, Kouassi-Ba and Madame Jonas, sorted out everything that did not look too unpleasant from among the stinking remains. The rest they threw out as carrion, which might possibly attract jackals and wolves. These, however, were not edible game, and their approach merely constituted a danger. The pieces of meat they had managed to retrieve were boiled for a long time, and they all ignored the somewhat unpleasant smell of the soup as they swallowed the last remains of their winter stocks as dutifully as anyone could have wished. At a time of famine food is something to be savoured in solitude, and it was common to see certain members of the community going off to some corner with their bowls so that they could concentrate on the business of eating without being distracted. They no longer sat round the big table. The Spaniards, ever frugal, tightened their leather belts and never complained, but their weather-beaten faces took on the colour of yellow ivory beneath their curly black beards.

Angélique could not forgive herself for having forgotten about the meat in the loft.

'I should have thought about it,' she repeated. 'It would have been so easy to put what we still had down in the cellar between two blocks of ice. . . .'

'I should have remembered it too,' said Peyrac, in an attempt to cheer his wife up. 'You see, my love, that our privations have affected me too,' he said to Angélique with a smile, 'because I completely forgot how the sudden change of temperature was bound to affect our food supplies.'

'But you weren't there! You went off very early that morning with Cantor to see what was in the traps while the snow was still hard. No, I am the one responsible for this unpardonable oversight.'

And she ran her hand across her brow.

'My head aches so. Do you think that means it's going to snow again?'

They looked up into a dazzling blue sky and shuddered as they noticed a flock of rooks circling in the clear air.

The presence of these dark birds was as certain a sign of snow as Angélique's headache.

And the very next day snow fell again, preceded by a new flight of black birds, dark, exuberant messengers, winged horses drawing the chariot of immaculate swirling drapery across the sky, and once again the earth was buffeted with pallid, icy squalls.

The arrival of spring had been set back. The snowfall was followed by several days of white fog, and after that, several days in which the sky hung grey at the edge of the forest. A cold mist covered the land, hiding the grey, wan tree-trunks. Now the snow fell as sleet, in tiny pieces as hard as glass which they could hear pattering against the wooden walls and the skins stretched across the windows.

They had only enough food now for two more days. Every morning each man received his portion but Angélique was delighted to find that she felt no desire to eat hers. She laid her bowl to one side on the hearth. It would be one meal more for Honorine. She stood in front of the fire, her arms hanging limp at her side, and dreamily watched the flames. Her head was full of vague ideas, unconnected with one another, but each one distinct in itself. She felt neither despair nor anxiety. They would not die, they would survive, of that she felt certain! They must simply wait and not give in. Wasn't something about to happen? Spring was on the way. One day it would be there and the animals would begin to run again in the emerald green undergrowth, and along river-banks bright with flowers. Then the big rivers would begin to flow again, and the little red canoes paddled by the Indians and the trappers would begin to move up and down the waters, loaded with merchandise, as life-giving as the blood flowing in one's veins. Only they must wait, and when she stood quite still like this, she felt less cold and empty. She did not know what it was she was expecting, but it was already on its way,

477

nearer than anyone thought. It was coming closer and was in fact, quite close now.

She stiffened, and listened hard. 'THERE IS SOMEONE OUTSIDE!'

There was no sound but of the wind whistling round the house, and yet Angélique knew, she felt certain that *there was someone outside*!

She wrapped her cloak about her and staggered over towards the door. No one noticed her go out.

No one saw her go.

Outside, the flying snow stung her face, and although it was the middle of the morning, it was as dark as at sunset. The wind had plastered the two icy walls that rose up on either side of the door with a shaggy coat of snow. Beyond that, nothing was visible except an endless vista of grey fog. Angélique looked up.

Human figures stood there above her, leaning down and watching her. They were Indians. The squalls of snow made them look blurred and unreal, but she recognized them immediately from their plumes. They were Iroquois. But the most extraordinary and terrifying thing about them was the fact that, apart from a strip of loin-cloth between their legs, *they were completely naked.*

CHAPTER 83

THEY WERE naked. They stood looking down at her in the biting wind that flattened their top-knots of hair and feathers to one side of their heads, and tore at the fringes of their loin-cloths. They stood there staring down into the hole, watching the Paleface woman who had just issued from it with a certain curiosity, while the wind whistled furiously about them. Yet they were not shivering, and their black eyes sparkled, quite undismayed. Then Madame Jonas came out too, and, losing no time with words, signalled vehemently to the newcomers to enter the house.

'Come on in, young men, and hurry. You'll make us freeze to look at you! You must be crazy to be going around naked in weather like this!'

They immediately understood her dumb show, burst out laughing and leapt down into the hollow pathway where they greeted the two women with raised hand and open palm. Then one by one they entered the outpost.

There were six of them, led by Tahoutaguete, the chief of the

Oneiouts, with the hideous, pock-marked face. They disdained to look at the pitiful creatures, bundled up in their clothes and furs, staring wide-eyed at them. Their stolid figures, smeared all over with grease, shone like polished yellow marble.

Peyrac came forward and Tahoutaguete held out both hands to give him a wampum necklace made of several bands of leather sewn with the symbolic design of tiny mauve and white beads.

'Outakke sent me here, the great chief of the Five Nations. This necklace contains his word. He says he remembers you and all the riches you gave to the souls of the great chiefs. . . . He sends you this necklace because he wants you to remain his friend. Outakke is waiting for you. . . .'

By now Peyrac understood enough of the Iroquois language to be able to translate what he said and thank him himself.

Then the Iroquois with the pock-marked face turned towards Angélique and handed her a wampum necklace too. She hesitated to take it, not knowing whether protocol would allow the inclusion of a woman in the solemnity of an alliance, but Tahoutaguete insisted, saying:

'Take it, Kawa! This necklace bears the words of the women of our tribe. The Council of Mothers gathered together at the time of the April moon and said: "Hear us. The-Man-who-listens-to-the-Universe, the Man of Thunder, is about to perish with his tribe, for he gave our dead chiefs all his foodstocks to wipe out the shame of their deaths. If he dies, of what use will our alliance with him be, and all it has cost us? If he dies, he will take with him all the treasures of his mind and his heart, and we shall have lost a friend of our race. If his children die, his wife will curse us. If his wife dies, he will curse us, for he will remember that it was his wife who saved the life of Outakke, and Outakke will have allowed her to perish. No, neither he nor his wife nor his children must die. This shall not be. We shall each of us offer a handful of our own food supplies to preserve the life of Kawa, the Paleface woman, who herself saved the life of Outakke, our hero, our chief. Without him, we should have been orphans. Without her, we should all have been orphans. Our children will no doubt cry out more often that they are hungry. Two or three times more often, no doubt. But what matter? . . . Hunger is a pain that gets better when spring arrives, but the loss of a friend is a pain that never gets better." Take it in your hands, woman, for this necklace is an offering from our tribes to Kawa the Woman-Mother, who took the Five Nations in her arms when she saved Outakke's life at a time when the treachery of enemy nations had condemned him. There, do you see, there is a picture of the women sitting in council, and that is you, and those are the handfuls of beans they have sent you so that you and your children may eat your fill.'

As he spoke he made a sign, and one of his followers went across and opened the door; six other naked Indians who had waited outside – WHO HAD WAITED OUTSIDE! – came in, carrying heavy sacks made of sewn skins. Tahoutaguete untied one of the sacks and a shimmering pile of beans ran out on to the wooden table. At this time the Old World was just beginning to grow familiar with the bean, since the first explorers had brought it back from South America during the last century.

The beans ran out of the skin bags and made a goodly pile on the table.

They had never seen such wonderful beans!

These had grown and ripened on the shores of the six great Iroquois lakes, and on the sunny slopes of the valley of the Mohawks, and the burst pods, all gold and honey-coloured, mingled with the dark gleam of the beans themselves. Some were of the type found especially on the shores of Lake Cayuga, rosy-red, veined with white; then there were those that the Mohawks of the east cultivate in the region of Orange, which were almost round and brilliant black with a violet sheen; then there were others longer than these, smooth and pink like shingle in a river-bed, and others that were delicately curved, coffee-coloured with strange purple spots, and others of a dazzling white. From beneath these shining husks came a delightful vegetable smell as if throughout the dark winter months they had kept locked up within them some of the pure hillside air from the time they had been picked, before the autumn had reddened the elm and the shad-berry bushes, while the marrows and pumpkins were still pale beneath their velvety leaves, and the maize stood wrapped in acid green, and the air was so pure, so dry and so hot in the hollow of the valley of the Mohawks, through which no river now flows, so hot that the bean pods there ripen more quickly than anywhere else and burst like pomegranates from their shells.

The children crept up to the edge of the table, and buried their hands in the pile of beans and laughed delightedly as they let them run through their fingers. Angélique's eyes went from the pile to the wampum necklace then to the stolid faces of the savages who had covered a hundred leagues across the icy waste dragging sledges loaded with these gifts from the Five Nations. She did not know what to say, for she felt so moved that her eyes were full of tears before this unexpected, in-explicable action, more moved in fact by gratitude than by her joy and relief at the reprieve they had brought with them.

'Our thanks go to the Iroquois nation,' said Joffrey de Peyrac gravely, and his voice seemed quiet and husky, as if he too now felt that he could give way to his weariness. 'Here, in the same place where you have just handed over your gift, Tahoutaguete, I shall place gifts for you to take back to your brothers. But no matter how precious these gifts are, they could never be as priceless as these! For it is our lives you have brought us in those skin bags, and each one of these beans,' he said, 'represents a heartbeat which we owe to you.'

'Can we put the pot on to boil?' asked Madame Jonas.

'Yes, let's make a hot-pot,' the fearsome Tahoutaguete agreed, for he had keen hearing and he seemed to have some scraps of knowledge of French.

So they all sat down forthwith, the naked, leathery Iroquois and the Europeans with their white faces, muffled up to their noses, men, women and children, round the big black cast-iron cooking-pot.

Angélique held the pot still while Madame Jonas filled it with water and Tahoutaguete carefully added several measures of beans.

Joffrey de Peyrac himself added their last piece of bear fat and Eloi Macollet suggested they might add a pinch of wood ash to make the contents cook more quickly. Since they had neither salt nor small berries from the woods to add, they put a few scented leaves in and hung the pot on the hook over the fire, while the children piled up sticks and logs round its soot-blackened base. Then everyone sat down solemnly. The fire was so hot that soon the soup was boiling furiously. They all sat on the ground, some on bearskins which they had thrown down, some on the hearthstones and some almost among the ashes. As the children leaned towards the stewpot they were already drinking in the delectable smell.

The Indians accepted some Virginia tobacco and filled their pipes which they had drawn from their belts, but disdainfully refused any brandy.

'Do you think we could have faced the demon of winter as you saw us do,' said Tahoutaguete to Peyrac, 'if we had been accustomed to drink that poison the Palefaces have brought here to steal our souls?'

'What force is it, what god enables you to face the winter like that, without even covering your bodies as we Palefaces are forced to do?' the Count asked.

'It is Oranda,' the Indian replied gravely, 'it is not a god. It is

481

everywhere – in the grain of maize that feeds you, in the air that surrounds you, the air you breathe, and in the vast spaces of the sky.'

'Do you think they came all the way from the Iroquois country dressed like that?' Angélique whispered to the old trapper Eloi in private, as he helped her put out the wooden bowls for the feast they were about to eat.

'Heavens no!' the old man replied with a shrug of his shoulders. 'There are limits even so to their endurance and their blasted sorcery! But they're the very devil of chaps for play-acting so they prepared their little effect. They will have stowed their fur-lined clothes and blankets and supplies in some hideout not far from here, then, after doing their special breathing exercises, they came along just as they were to give us the surprise of our lives. You've got to admit, it's quite something. I've seen them hang out like that outside in winter for two days and two nights....'

As she dipped her great wooden ladle into the soup, which was chestnut coloured and smelt a trifle like chestnuts but with something lighter and more unusual about it, Angélique felt like some priestess filled with a quasi-mystical joy.

She filled the bowls one by one as they held them out to her and the words the Iroquois had spoken still rang in her ears.

'This is for you, Woman-Mother, who held the Five Nations in your arms when you held Outakke....'

They are lyrical and superstitious people, these Iroquois, but they have the courage to express things that we Palefaces would never dare to face. . . . And they have the courage to do things which we, a Christian people, would never even think of doing....

So excited was she that she no longer felt how weak she was. She put one portion of the beans into a small pot and took it off to her room, leaving it among the ashes beside the fire, on the hearthstone. Then she laid her necklace of shells that the Council of Mothers had given her across a stool, and went back to join the others. She did not eat with them, but helped Honorine to eat her plate of soup, then put her to bed, all sleepy from the new food which she had been able to eat to her heart's content. After warming the bed, she tucked the little girl in, and watched over her lovingly as she fell into a deep, restful sleep at last.

Tahoutaguete, calculating his effect, had, towards the end of the meal drawn from a kind of haversack about a bushel of rice, a dwarf rice with long thin grains, so transparent that it almost looked like some mineral.

'That's what they harvest from the water in the oat-grass area, near Lake Superior,' said Eloi Macollet. 'But they never get enough to feed many ...'

'But enough to save their lives,' said Tahoutaguete.

And he told Macollet he was an ignoramus. He explained that this was not a food but a medicine. He told Count Peyrac that he should spread out some of the grains on a large dish, and keep them in a warm place well moistened with water. As soon as the little green shoot appeared the Palefaces need only eat a single mouthful of the rice to cure them of the sickness from which they so often died. And the Redskin tapped his filthy finger on his magnificent, regular, gleaming-white teeth that had never known the ravages of scurvy.

'If I understand you aright, this rice will protect us from scurvy,' said Peyrac. 'Come to think of it, it's obvious; for the little shoot, however tiny, is something fresh and growing that will preserve us from the deficiency diseases of the winter. But is so little really enough?' Nevertheless, he took the Iroquois at his word and together they got up to prepare some of the rice as he had been advised.

'Let us give thanks to God,' Madame Jonas concluded as she put away the plates.

And Monsieur Jonas went off to fetch his Prayer Book.

CHAPTER 84

WHEN SHE saw that everyone had eaten their fill, and had either fallen asleep or was on the point of doing so, Angélique slipped away to her own room. Already the sound of the wind outside did not seem so relentless. The room was redolent of the scent of stewed beans which had been simmering by the fire. She poked the fire a little to bring more light into the room, then sat down and took the wampum necklace on her knees. She ran her fingers over the tight-packed, satin-smooth shells, the work of many a patient hour. At first she had not appreciated the value of these wampum necklaces, and had been astonished to see these pieces of leather sewn with beads being exchanged to stop the course of wars, and re-establish peace; in the eyes of the natives they represented a treasure still more precious than their hundred pounds of gold had once been to the Medici family. The tribes that possessed a large number of these necklaces was considered rich, and when defeated, they had to give them away, being impoverished thereby.

Now Angélique saw these pieces of limestone tumbled by the waves, worn down by the sand, subtly coloured by nature's glorious alchemy, these mysterious fragments, ground and pierced by the secret skill of some craftsman, sorted by the fingers of little girls, assembled by the women's hands, and finally carried religiously aloft on the hands of the men, as the highest form of expression of the American Redskin. These interlaced bands of leather and beads were the very heart of the people, their history recorded and handed down, for they had no written language. Angélique examined the picture of five women sitting on either side of a hieratic figure intended to represent herself. Beads were scattered everywhere, represented as dark-blue stars on the white background. The band was edged with a line of mauve beads, with a further narrow white band outside it. It was a masterpiece, long and wide, with evenly cut leather fringes hanging down both sides.

One day she would be envied for possessing this token of esteem from the Iroquois. She ran it back and forth through her hands, delighting in it; then when her enthusiasm and fervour were sated, she turned her mind to more earthly considerations.

First she poured herself a bowl of steaming soup, and began to eat it slowly, clasping the bowl tight to her, with half-closed eyes, dreaming of the valley of the Mohawks which she would visit one day, presided over by the three gods – maize, pumpkin and bean....

The air was clear in that valley, and the light rose-pink. A smell of smoke hung about it from the innumerable villages with their long houses. She could visualize the long houses on the summit of the hills, strange houses that Nicolas Perrot had described to her, in which lived ten or fifteen whole families, and she saw them, row upon row, with their rounded rooftops with plumes of smoke rising from the different chimneys, as they glistened like gilded shrines in the light of the setting sun beneath the dark gold covering of their walls made of heads of corn hung up to dry.

She imagined smells of the countryside too from the crops spread out across the hillsides, and surrounded by woods lighter and less dense than those of the north. Without ever having seen it, she guessed that there must be quite a difference between the fertile valley of the Iroquois with its yellow-skinned, serious-minded people, and the eroded, wild plainlands, cleft with valleys and escarpments like so many traps, a land where nothing would grow, the land of the mocking, red Abenakis.

Joffrey de Peyrac opened the door and saw her sitting there alone, quietly eating with her wampum necklace across her knees and her eyes closed.

'You were hungry, my love!'

He gazed tenderly at her, thinking that she was like no other woman, and that everything she did carried the hallmark of her charm. She would have been unable to explain even to him why it was she felt so happy. He could read it in her eyes. She had come to life again.

Far away, over the icy waters, a group of strangers, of enemies, of savages had become aware of her, and she had come to life in their primitive hearts.

'They called me Kawa. What does it mean?' she asked.

'Superior woman, woman above all other women,' he murmured. 'Woman, Fixed Star.'

PART V

Spring

CHAPTER 85

'LOOK, MOTHER, the first flower!'

Cantor's voice rang out through the fresh, clear evening air. Angélique heard him through the open window of her room where she was sweeping the dead ashes out of the fireplace.

She gave a start.

'What did you say?'

Cantor looked in at her with a beaming smile.

'The first flower! Here, under the windows!'

Angélique rushed out, calling the children as she went.

'Honorine! Thomas! Bartholomew! Come quick! Come and see the first flower.'

It was a spring crocus, that had forced its way pure and white through the muddy earth. Its translucent petals showed the merest glimmer of a carefully guarded golden pistil.

'Great heavens! Isn't it wonderful?' said Angélique, falling to her knees on the damp ground.

And they all stood in delight at the miracle. The little flower had come through at the very edge of the snow.

From that day on they found a large number of them. Whenever they shovelled away the wet snow they would find a whole host of pale yellow stalks, ready to burst into flower, which by the following day would turn a sturdy green in the sun, while the calyx gradually turned mauve or white.

There were flowers even at the edge of the roof, where a few violets had sprouted from a fragment of moss and bloomed there, bowing in the sunshine, with a constant stream of water from the melting snow rushing around them.

It was the end of April.

The sun was hot and the thaw came swiftly. Without waiting for the snow to disappear from beneath the trees, they went into the forest to slit the bark of a number of maple trees and collect the sweet-tasting maple syrup.

This Eloi Macollet boiled up in a pot to produce a kind of liquid honey which the children adored.

In the forest the snow had become all dingy. It was covered with

489

blackish moss, bits of broken branches and rotten fir cones rejected by the squirrels. There was a constant pattering as of light rain as it thawed, and the squirrels leapt from branch to branch.

Many of the trees and bushes showed livid wounds where they had been gashed by the teeth of starving hares or does. The intense cold had split some of them, some had snapped beneath the weight of snow, while others, growing on the sheltered side of hills or in cold, shady hollows, were almost flattened by great blocks of ice accumulated on their tops, which refused to melt.

But already the hazel-tree was thrusting forth its catkins like furry green caterpillars, and they danced in the wind, spreading their pollen, which coloured the snow beneath them yellow. The birch-tree which, only the day before, had been a lifeless ivory skeleton, was now covered with mauve and grey pendants, which formed a curtain of fringes. The elms, spreading like huge fans, had put on their emerald veils; and then the hunters had returned, bringing with them the smoked meat of two stags and half a moose, as well as the stuffed entrails of a bear, a delicious gift from Mopuntook who had promised to visit them soon. They dared not sow any seed yet for there was not sufficient land uncovered and the fear of frost or further snowfalls was not entirely behind them. But with every day that passed spring was winning the battle.

The solid frozen lake had begun by looking like a big, smudged mirror; then water had covered the ice, dividing it up into translucent islands.

One of the things about the spring that particularly delighted Angélique was the sound of the waters come to life again. At first it had been no more than a soft whisper, born of the great winter silence, then had begun the incoherent sobbing of the waterfalls, and now the whole of nature rang with the sound of rushing waters, which filled the nights with a tremendous, uninterrupted rumbling.

By the time the summer came it would no longer be audible, for the leaves would deaden the noise. But now in her new-found freedom, the wanton abandon of the first thaw, nature, unkempt and naked, disarrayed and ugly, still half-buried beneath her snowy shroud, bellowed, wild and unchecked, to the clear sky above.

Angélique thought: 'Spring is here!'

Dawn came earlier, and in the evening the sun lingered on the threshold and they no longer needed to light the candles.

The sound of running water encircled the outpost and its lakes in a magic ring.

'The trappers and their Indians have gone by to the east . . .' reported the Panis slave one day. He spent many hours splashing about on his snowshoes, keeping a constant watch on what was going on in the neighbourhood.

He had caught sight of them heading towards the Kennebec. The trappers were off again towards the south, stumbling into snowdrifts, negotiating the icy slush, the holes in the ground and the broken, rotten branches, as they went off to take the English villages by surprise.

Who they were, no one knew, for they ignored the outpost. Perhaps they had orders to do so. . . . The people of the Silver Lake were busy in the pale sunlight, getting their strength back and rebuilding their palisade. A great many things had been broken or crushed, and the fences and the roof were threatening to collapse; bit by bit as the earth was uncovered, it assumed the appearance of a battlefield. The men turned their thin, pale faces towards the sun, and blinked their tired eyes, letting the sunlight stream over their skin, as if it were the water of the spring of eternal youth. And the three children sometimes stood motionless in the warmth of the sun like so many baby chicks.

At first Angélique took things gradually.

Tomorrow she would do something about her chapped, roughened hands, and would wash her face in the water of the first rains, and she and Madame Jonas would spring-clean the house. But today she intended to sit quietly with Honorine on her knee, as she had done when they had been hungry and worn out. She would wait until her strength returned and rose in her like sap in a tree. The big effort they had made deserved a time of convalescence. She had always tended to ask too much of herself, and experience had taught her that a victory won could be dearly paid for in subsequent days. . . . Once in Paris she had almost committed suicide, just as she had been on the point of winning through. . . .

Conscious of her delicate state of health, she took things quietly, doing only what she had to, without haste, and putting off till the morrow all the urgent tasks that clamoured for attention.

First she must go up into the mountains, along the river-beds and the shores of the lakes to find flowers, plants, bushes, and roots, with which to fill all the boxes and jars in her medicine chest. She would not let a single one escape her! She would track them down where they hid in the tiniest crannies in the rock. She would pick even the unfamiliar ones and discover their secrets.

She swore to herself that never would she go through another winter as difficult as this, with no other standby, very often, than boiled water and goose or bear fat to treat the sick. She would fill the loft with sweet-smelling plants. She would fill her shelves with pot after pot and box after box of them, all clearly labelled in bright colours. People would come to Fort Wapassou from twenty leagues around to be cured. . . .

Then one day she set off with Honorine on her expedition to discover the spring, the flowers and the herbal remedies.

Among the yellowish, matted grasses, flattened by the snow, violets blinked their pale eyes, dazzled by the sun. The mountain primrose raised its pink crown, and the white ranunculus spread its corolla, so delicate that a mere whisper of wind would scatter its petals. The anemone hepatica, known in Poitou as 'the-daughter-before-the mother', since the flower emerges before the leaves from the soot-black leaf-mould, shed a blue glow through the pale, lime-green undergrowth.

On the rocky slopes they found the tiny coltsfoot (*tussilago farfara*), with its multitude of yellow tufts, growing side by side with crocuses and snowdrops. All these fragile, unprotected flowers trembled at the edge of the snow in a wind that was still unpleasantly cold. Angélique strode briskly from hillside to valley, happy to find herself walking again on the springy ground and nothing daunted by mud and swamp. On flower-picking days she took the other children with her too and asked for help from Elvire or one of the young men at the outpost, since the job was one that had to be done quickly. Samples could be picked only when it was dry and sunny, towards the middle of the day, and the evening dew must be avoided, since the slightest dampness spoilt the delicate petals and deprived them of their healing virtues. There was a lot of coltsfoot, which made an excellent, reliable remedy for sore throats and mouth ulcers. Violets, the aristocrats of the pharmacopea were harder to find; they too were used for coughs and colds. An infusion of violets was the treatment of princesses, a concoction of coltsfoot was the peasant remedy.

Honorine enjoyed looking after the violets and put them away to dry in the loft with every possible care. Her mother had told her that they would make a sweet-tasting syrup out of them for children who coughed and disliked being nursed. Dandelions were springing up everywhere through the still yellow grass, and the children set off with little knives to dig up the soft white roots which they ate in the evening after cleaning them and tossing them in a little birch vinegar. Later when the roots turned a reddish colour Angélique dried and preserved some of them. She slit the rhizomes of wood avens (Herb-Bennet, *geum urbanus*) down their length; it was a curious, timid little flower, with a long black woody root containing a bitter juice, excellent for stomach-ache, and the rhizome of the sweet flag (*acorus calamus*), the aromatic rush that grows at the edge of swampy land. She grated the roots of the great burdock (*arctium lappa*) otherwise known as burweed, used in her native province in France for curing patches of falling hair. She was not quite sure she had identified it correctly, for very minor differences made the New World version of a familiar flower difficult to recognize, and she turned some specimens over and over in her hands for some time before making up her mind.

One day Honorine brought her a small bunch of a tiny bell-like flower that looked rather like heather, except that it was soft and fresh. The delicate spidery leaves were greyish green and the little bell-like flowers pink. Angélique eventually identified it as fumitory (*fumaria officinalis*), known as earth-gall or widow's weeds, no one quite knew why. She knew that you could make a cleaning liquid for the skin from it, and that if you boiled the flowers in water, the resultant milky liquid removed excessive traces of suntanning from the skin. As an eye lotion it made the eyes clear and sparkling, and as an infusion stimulated the appetite. Finally, it also had the reputation of curing scurvy.

Honorine was congratulated on her excellent find and Sam Holton the Englishman, who was a man of some learning, quoted Shakespeare as having described King Lear as 'crown'd with rank fumiter and furrow-weeds . . .'

Whenever she set off to look for plants rather than to gather them, Angélique would go with Honorine and no one else.

Now that the winter was over, Honorine had stopped being a child like the others, concerned only with fires and food and getting up to mischief, and once again she had become her mother's companion. There was a strange depth of understanding between them when it came to firearms or flowers. Honorine had stamina. She followed Angélique wherever she went, often covering about twice as much ground because of the way she ran hither and thither, looking at everything. To make quite sure she would not lose her in the wild woods, Angélique tied a little bell round her wrist, so that wherever she went, its happy sound revealed her position.

'Don't hamper yourself with the child, Madame, leave her with us . . .' Elvire would sometimes say in an attempt to be helpful.

But Angélique shook her head.

Honorine was no trouble to her. She would not have enjoyed going all alone to look at nature in bloom; the treasures of the spring were made to be shared.

They would kneel together before some flower they had discovered, and talk in a patch of sunlight with the breeze still blowing cold across the snow. The forest had turned to pale gold, and was decked with catkins, grey, golden, pink, mauve and green. As they climbed higher into the hills amid the black fir trees they discovered larches standing as in a thin green mist.

Angélique found herself so much at one with the countryside that she sometimes felt so happy she would seize Honorine in her arms and kiss her ecstatically, and dance hither and thither with her, while the child's laughter echoed over and over again across the untamed landscape.

CHAPTER 86

THE BEARS were waking from their winter sleep. One day Honorine discovered a tiny black, friendly ball of fur in a hollow. Angélique heard the mother bear growl and the noise of snapping branches as it blundered towards them. She arrived just in time to kill the fearsome beast rearing up on its hind legs to terrify the intruders. A well-aimed shot into its red, gaping mouth stopped it in its tracks.

Honorine was sad to see the mother bear killed, and the sweet little bear cub left an orphan.

'She was defending her baby just as I had to defend you,' Angélique told her. 'She had her claws and her great strength and I had my pistol.'

They brought the bear cub back to the fort and fed it on maple syrup and maize gruel, for it was already weaned of its mother's milk.

In Honorine's eyes, it was the loveliest pet in creation, and she loved it more passionately than anything else. It was only with considerable difficulty that she could be persuaded to allow her playmates Bartholomew and Thomas to come anywhere near it.

The cub, which was given the name of Lancelot, after the hero of some stories the children were told, caused a spot of bother between Cantor and Honorine.

As soon as the fine weather had returned, Cantor had also gone off into the hills with a very specific object in view. He was looking for an animal he hated, a nasty, sly animal that had devoured almost all the hares and rabbits caught in the traps during the winter, while he dragged himself, exhausted, from one trap to another in the hope of finding some scrap of meat to take home for them to eat. They all knew who the culprit was, the hated pirate of the forest, the glutton or wolverine, an animal quite different from any other woodland creature. It was as cruel as the ermine or the weasel, and belonged to the same family, but it was bigger than a beaver.

Cantor discovered his sworn enemy, a female, and killed her, but brought back the pup with him, a little bundle of bristling hair about the size of a cat, already curling its lips back aggressively over its pointed teeth.

'You're a fool to land yourself with that one, me lad,' said Eloi Macollet, frowning at Cantor's find, 'it's nothing but badness and deceit, that is. The meanest critter in the forest. The Indians say that devils take refuge inside it, and they won't enter any valley where they know there's a wolverine's lair. They won't come here any more.'

'Well, we'll be all the quieter for that!' Cantor replied, and kept the animal.

He called it by its English name, Wolverine. Wolverine bared its fangs at poor Lancelot and terrified him. One day he got at the cub and bit him, and Honorine was so angry that the whole outpost knew about it. She went off to look for a stick, a knife, a hatchet – anything to kill Wolverine with. After putting his pet out of harm's way, Cantor made fun of the little girl's fury.

'Now I know who it is I want to scalp,' said Honorine. 'It's Cantor! . . .' Cantor's mirth redoubled and he went off calling her 'Miss Beaver', the nickname he had given her because he said her eyes were like a beaver's.

'He called me Miss Beaver,' Honorine wailed, bursting into tears at this final insult.

Angélique managed to cheer her up by pointing out that beavers were delightful animals, and that there was nothing to get cross about, and she took her and Lancelot off to see the new denizens of the pool on the other side of the mountain, which were making as much noise as a gang of lumberjacks, felling trees and busily constructing their rounded lodges.

'You see, beavers are pretty, and you are as pretty as they are.'

Honorine so much enjoyed watching the beavers, supple and lively, diving and swimming in the clear water, that she began to feel more cheerful.

But the quarrel between her and her half-brother had not been settled, and it flared up again about the Old Man of the Mountain. It took very little to rekindle the fires of war between the taciturn youth and the touchy little girl. Towards the west, the cliffs around Wapassou stuck out at one point in a long, rocky, jagged projection that looked like the profile of an old Indian or an old man with a vaguely piratical air. Particularly when the setting sun picked out the figure in coppery lights, the likeness was striking. Everyone admired the effect, and saw the Old Man with a grumpy expression in the mornings and a sardonic grin in the evenings.

Honorine was the only one who could not see the face. She stared wide-eyed, trying to make out the different landmarks they pointed out to her, but if she said she could see what they meant, it was without conviction, merely to stop the others from making fun of her. For in fact she could see nothing.

Cantor never lost an opportunity of teasing her about this, and told her that she was not even a beaver, but more like a mole, while Honorine stared darkly at the mountainside vainly seeking among the trees and the rocks this vision of the Old Man that had been denied her and set her apart from those who could see it.

Once again that morning Cantor baited her, and once again she flew at him, hammering him with her fists, and crying so loud that Joffrey de Peyrac himself rushed to the scene.

'What's going on?'

'Everybody wishes I were dead,' said Honorine in tears, 'and I haven't even got any weapons to defend myself.'

The Count smiled and knelt down in front of the child, stroking her wet cheeks, and promised that if she calmed down he would make her a pistol all her own which would fire small lead shot and with a silver butt she could use as a tomahawk.

Then he took her by the hand and together they went off to the workshops.

Angélique turned to Cantor, who had watched the scene sulkily.

'Don't go on at her about the Old Man of the Mountain. If she can't see it, what does it matter? You're just humiliating her.'

'She's stupid and lazy.'

'No she isn't. She's only four. When will you grow up, Cantor? It's so silly of you to quarrel with a child of her age.'

'Everyone spoils her and makes a fuss of her,' Cantor replied obstinately.

And he strode off muttering to himself:

496

'Let the others become slaves to that little bastard. You won't catch me!'

Angélique was cut to the heart. She alone had heard what he said, and the words had indeed been intended for her. She stood rooted to the ground, as if paralysed by some sudden pain, then she went off to her room and shut herself in. Her first reaction had been to slap Cantor's face, to shake him violently and . . . yes, she would have been quite capable of knocking him out. She was in an absolute fury at the arrogant, coarse behaviour of this bit of a lad whom everyone loved and cared for, who had a father who taught him patiently, who had friends, almost servants, full of deference, for he was the master's son and knew his rights, and yet who still dared to play the part of the wronged child in front of her.

He had been a secret thorn in her flesh throughout all the winter months, for in spite of the happy times she had had talking to her sons, laughing or singing with them, while Cantor played his guitar, when he became gay and good company, she had never ceased to feel a certain reticence in him, and little by little a kind of hidden animosity. Far from healing this wound, time seemed to be making it worse, because Cantor's feelings were smothered up, unavowed, and she did not know whether he held it against her that she had been separated from them for so long, which would have been ridiculous, or whether, judging her with childish strictness, he found it impossible to accept the fact that during her separation from their father she had led so free a life. No doubt it was a bit of both, and Angélique had felt she could not begin to explain to her sons that fifteen years of 'widowhood' had been some justification for the liberties she had taken, which in any case had generally been imposed on her by the life she led.

'Youth is single-minded and must grow more mature before it can understand certain things,' thought Angélique. She had given herself this excuse for remaining silent, but she could no longer hide from herself the fact that she had chosen the easy way out.

For Angélique knew perfectly well that youth can understand anything provided it is properly explained, and that it was she who had not felt sufficiently mature to undertake the task of explanation.

She had not had the courage to go back over her terrible past and especially not in front of her two sons. She had been frightened of their reactions, but frightened above all of her own. For she knew full well that youth contains the best of everything: sound judgement, warm heart and an unfailing sense of justice. She had treated them as children and not as the young men of fifteen and seventeen that

497

they were. She had not taken them into her confidence, and now Cantor was returning her lack of trust with the hostility of a wounded heart.

Things were simpler with Florimond. He just accepted things as they were. He was more easy-going, more detached than his brother. From the King's antechamber down to the holds of ships he had seen so much! All he really cared about was that he should win through unscathed to his goal.

She could almost have sworn that he had already had some experience in matters of love.

His younger brother was less adaptable, had a less easy-going nature, and took everything seriously. Angélique asked herself whether she had not been right to keep him at a certain distance, whether he might not have become still more difficult had she taken him into her confidence.

She thought it over carefully, and could not make up her mind, as she paced round and round her room, calling him a silly fool, an ungracious lout, a heartless wretch, and longing to tell him to go away ... that she did not want to see him again, if this was how he felt, and that there was not much point in God having reunited them all if this was how things were! ... Then she grew calmer again, for she began to realize that he was still only a child, her child, and that it was therefore her duty to attempt to untie the knot of bitterness that was making life with him so difficult at the moment. . . . But would it not in fact be better for him to go away? He loathed Honorine. He had found his mother again, but it had been too late. There were some things you could never make up for. . . . He could have gone off with Florimond and he had in fact asked permission to do so, but his father had replied that he was not yet ready. . . .

Angélique blamed herself for not having asked her husband why he had come to this decision, since then she would have been able to discuss the matter with Cantor, in an attempt to lift him out of the gloom into which he had sunk.

There are, it is true, some things in life which, once they have happened, can never be altered, but at least one can establish some contact. One can try. . . . Now Cantor was here, and she could not reach him, she could not see how she was going to approach him, for she felt that whatever means she used he would treat her as an enemy.

And yet she must do something! He would end up by making Honorine miserable. A child of only four! How many of them knew that this American spring for the fourth time recalled her shameful birth in the sorceress's cave in the heart of the Druidic forest? Angélique alone knew this fact and she had dared tell no one.

She sat down on her bed. Cantor must go; it seemed inevitable. Should he be sent to Gouldsboro on some mission? Possibly. He enjoyed travelling. Then all of a sudden she feared that Cantor might never forgive being exiled on her account and Honorine's, and that once and for all she would lose any possibility of establishing contact with her son.

She really did not know what to decide, and she left the decision to fate, for it was quite beyond her.

From the pocket in her belt she took the English gold piece which she kept there as a talisman. If it came up heads, the side with the royal effigy on it, she would talk to her husband about Cantor's insolence and discuss with him the advisability of sending the boy away. But if it was tails, the side depicting the arms of Great Britain and the outrageous inscription 'King of France', she would go forthwith and find Cantor, and explain everything to him.

She threw the coin in the air.

It was tails.

CHAPTER 87

CANTOR, WHO was busy doing something or other at the forge, saw his mother coming towards him and immediately got to his feet, for his conscience was not easy.

'Come with me into the woods,' she said to him.

She spoke in a tone that brooked no reply. And he followed her, feeling decidedly uneasy, for she seemed extremely determined.

It was a clear spring day, but the air was fresh, almost cold, since it had rained the day before. The waterlogged ground had a violet hue seen through the first timid blades of grass.

The wind itself was fresh and cool. The undergrowth was blue and gold. The buds on the maple-trees looked like pink tulips, as yet unopened.

Angélique walked swiftly. She knew every track, every furrow, and although she did not exactly know where she was heading and her mind was elsewhere, she did not get lost. Cantor found it hard to keep up with her and felt very clumsy as he slid stealthily between branches tipped with the green of their first leaves.

From time to time Angélique would speak:

'I say, there's spurge olive growing in that ravine. We must come back here in the autumn, because you always find that mushrooms grow under them,' or else:

'The white laurel is just about to bloom. . . . What's that smell? . . . Ah! valerian.'

She did not stop, but walked on, looking up a little, her eyes alert, catching the slightest trace of perfume, and, seeing her treading so lightly before him, as if the branches moved aside to let her pass, he thought that she looked like a fairy. . . .

They reached the top of the mountain and the rough ground opened out at their feet while the wind murmured through the pine wood. The pine-trees were covered with yellow-gold and green-gold buds, and the firs were cherry red, the spruces pink and the larch-trees lilac-coloured, while a delicious, balmy scent rose up like incense.

Angélique stopped at the edge of the plateau, and looked out towards the horizon. Below them lay the sacred river, winding through the valley towards the east.

Angélique turned towards Cantor.

'You may not like her,' she said, 'but a child, whoever it is, wherever it comes from, whoever its father and mother are, remains a child, and taking advantage of another's weakness is always a cowardly way to behave.'

He was a bit breathless; the words reached him and he could not reply to them. . . . A child, a cowardly way to behave. . . . 'If the blood of the knights your forefathers has not taught you that, then it's my business to remind you of it today.'

And Angélique continued walking. She climbed down the hill a little, heading along a path that followed the line of the river half-way down the hill, falling slowly into the valley.

'When you were born,' she went on, 'it was the day your father was burned in effigy in the Place de la Grève. But I thought he was dead. . . . When I took you back to the Temple, a tiny creature in my arms, it was Candlemas Day and I remember that the whole of Paris smelt of lemon fritters, which orphan children sell throughout the streets on that day. I was twenty. You see, I wasn't much older than you are now. When I reached the courtyard of the Temple I heard a baby crying and saw Florimond being chased by some older boys who were throwing stones and snow at him and shouting: 'Sorcerer's brat! Sorcerer's brat! Show us your horns!'

Cantor stopped dead in his tracks and grew red while he clenched his fists in fury.

'Oh!' he exclaimed, 'why wasn't I there! Why wasn't I there!'

'But you were there,' said Angélique with a laugh, 'the trouble was you were only a few days old.'

And she looked at him, still laughing, as if she were making fun of him.

'Well may you clench your fists today, Cantor, but your fist at that time was no bigger than a walnut!'

And she laughed again, for she could just see that tiny, pink baby fist waving in the air.

But her laugh echoed in a strange, bitter way through the woods, and he looked at her in perplexity, as an indefinable ache began to grow inside him. Angélique stopped laughing and seemed to grow serious again.

'You're pleased to be alive, aren't you, Cantor?'

'Yes,' he stammered.

'It wasn't easy to keep you alive. I'll tell you about it one day, if you like. Incidentally, you never thought about that, did you? You never asked yourself how it was that you were still alive, you, the son of a sorcerer, condemned to death even before you were born? You don't remember it? Then, what do you care? You are here, you are alive. It's not your business to ask what your twenty-year-old mother may have done, indeed had to do, to preserve that treasure you still have there in that strong chest of yours, your life!' And she almost struck him with her fist, at once delicate and strong, over his heart. He recoiled in dismay and stood staring at her, his eyes like limpid water, so much like hers, as if he was seeing her for the first time.

Then Angélique began to walk down the path again. Now they could hear the sound of water in the river and the noise of trees stirring in the wind. The alders, the poplars and the willows along the banks were covered in long leaves that rustled softly in the breeze, and they could see that here the spring was further advanced, for the grass in the hollows had grown thick and tall.

Angélique realized that she was no longer angry with her son. The lad had a lost look that showed her that he had never given a thought to everything she had just said. But of course not! He too was only a child.

She had been wrong not to speak of these things earlier, at any rate about the memories that concerned him.

It would have made him more indulgent, less intolerant. Children like to be told about things they cannot remember themselves. These tales help to fill that agonizing void in their memories.

They like to be guided through the world of primitive sensations, so often incoherent, which make up their own memories. Cantor, for lack of a guide, had been forced to judge by appearances.

When he had grown older, he had suffered from jealousy, knowing his mother to have been unfaithful, finding that she had fallen from the pedestal on which he had placed her during the innocent years of his earliest childhood.

The hardest things of all still remained to be done . . . to be said. And Angélique's mind kept on turning back to Honorine, who must be protected from unjust resentment.

They were about to reach the fields at the edge of the water.

She turned to face him.

'I have already told you that you should never try to crush the weak. And I repeat what I said. As far as I am concerned, hate me if you like. But not her. She never asked to be born. But there again, you would be wrong to judge me on that score! When you don't know what happened, it is wrong to let your heart fill with bitterness, and what's more, it's stupid.'

She was staring fixedly at him and bit by bit he saw his mother's eyes turn sea-green and fill with a glow of detestation and hostility that frightened him, since he thought it was aimed at him.

'You are only a child,' she went on. . . . 'But soon you will be a man . . . . A man,' she repeated dreamily. . . . 'You will go to war, my son, and you will fight, fight fiercely, to the bitter end. . . . And that is good. A man should not be afraid to kill. . . . Then you will enter cities as a conqueror, you will celebrate your victory, you will get drunk, and you will enjoy women. . . . And are you going to worry about your victims afterwards. . . . No! That's war, isn't it! Are you going to worry about whether they die of shame? Whether they jump down the nearest well? No, of course not, for that's war! And after all, it's not as terrible as all that, let me tell you! "When the army's on the loose, women lose their honour. . . ." It was old Rebecca who used to say that. Now tell me, what would you think a woman ought to do when she finds she's bearing a child conceived in war? . . . What do you think she can do? Kill it? . . . Kill herself? . . . Every now and then it happens that a woman gives birth to a child like this, and brings it up, and loves it, and tries to make sure that it has a happy life, because it's a child. Do you understand? Do you understand? . . .'

And yet again she repeated: 'Do you understand?' looking him straight in the face.

Then her eyes wandered across the valley again, as it lay before them, gently murmuring.

'Never mind,' she thought, 'never mind if he doesn't understand, if he is in fact as hard as rock! So much the worse for him; let him go away, let him become a man, a heartless brute.... Let him go away. I have done what I can! ...' She waited a moment then stole a glance towards him, and saw that his lips were trembling.

'If that's how it was,' he said, his voice thick in his throat, 'if that's really how it was, oh, Mother, please forgive me! Forgive me! ... I didn't know....'

She had not expected this reaction, and she clasped his head wildly to her breast, while she stroked his hair, repeating over and over again:

'Calm yourself! It's nothing! ... Calm yourself, my little one.' Just as she had done when he was a child. And she remembered how fine and soft his hair had been then, whereas now it had grown so thick and bushy.

'Calm down, now,' she repeated. 'Please, Cantor, the past has no right to make us suffer. We are safe, Cantor. We are together again, all of us who were born to belong to one another, whom fate had separated. That is the only thing that matters to me! So don't cry any more.'

Slowly he grew calm again. Her quiet voice, her gentle firm hand eased the tension, refused to allow him to feel remorse, by repeating over and over again that the gift of life was the only thing that mattered, and that for her, to be surrounded by those she loved, as she was at present, was heaven, and that her joy at having found her son Cantor again, when she had thought him dead and had wept so long for him, largely compensated for the often prickly side of his character.... Then he gave a sort of smile, and sniffed, still without daring to lift his head. And she clasped him to her heart, desperately conscious that this was her son, born of her flesh, and that there was still a great deal she could do for him, for a long time yet, through the mystery of parenthood that bound them together, for which there was no substitute.

He drew away from her; before getting up he looked at her with a sudden serious look, a look that altered his appearance, and made him seem several years older.

'Forgive me,' he repeated.

And she had a sudden intuition that it was the man in him asking her forgiveness in the name of all men.

She took his face between her hands.

503

'Yes, I forgive you,' she said softly, 'I forgive you.'

Then as he stood up, she began to laugh.

'Isn't it ridiculous? . . . You're half a head taller than I am.'

CHAPTER 88

As THEY stood there, still deeply moved and seeking to regain their calm, Angélique thought she still heard the echo of Cantor's sobbing ring through the forest.

This was an incomprehensible phenomenon. She thought at first it was the effect of emotion upon her, but bit by bit she began to realize that, however surprising, it was a real sound she heard, for the sobs were drawing nearer instead of vanishing into the distance. Soon she heard whimpering voices as well.

'Can you hear it too?' she asked her son, turning towards him. He had raised his head.

He nodded, and instinctively drew her into the cover of a clump of trees.

The sound of voices and weeping in a deserted place like this! Nicolas Perrot would have said that it could only be souls in torment or else . . .

'Sshh,' said Cantor.

The voices drew nearer and they could clearly make out the sound of several people walking through the grass.

An Indian came into sight round the bend of the river, walking along its bank. He was a tall man, the colour of red clay, but disfigured by his red and white war paint and his greasy topknot surmounted by pieces of fur and feathers and porcupine quills. He was carrying a musket. The blanket over his shoulders seemed to be weighted down with water, for it had rained that morning. The Indian had travelled a long way, and must have walked without a break, even during the heavy shower. He came on slowly but regularly, with his head bowed and a look of weariness as he followed the river-bank.

He had almost reached the little clump of trees behind which Angélique and her son were hiding, and they, knowing how keen the Indians' sense of smell is, feared lest he smell them out, but already other people had appeared at the edge of the clearing.

There was another Indian, then a white woman, with tattered clothes, unkempt hair and mud-caked face, leaning on the Indian.

Then followed another woman, after a short gap. She was carrying a child of about two in her arms, and it was his wails they had heard. His mother was utterly exhausted and looked like a sleep-walker. Then followed two Indians, one of them carrying a little boy of about five or six, the other a girl who looked a bit older and had fallen asleep unless it was that she was half-dead. Then came a white man dragging another one behind him, both of them in rags, their shirts torn, their faces and arms covered in scratches, then a child of twelve with a dazed expression, loaded like a donkey with a hetero- geneous collection of parcels and various objects crowned by a tin jug.

Then finally, bringing up the rear, and looking as if he was driving the whole band before him, came a strange, solemn Indian, balancing his hatchet in one hand and his tomahawk in the other.

This strange, pitiful procession filed past Angélique and Cantor without taking the slightest notice of them. Even the Indians seemed weary.

Then suddenly the young woman carrying the child fell to her knees. The Indian with the musket retraced his steps and struck her hard between the shoulder blades with the butt of his gun. The child let out a series of piercing screams and the Indian, suddenly incensed, caught him by one leg, held him out at arm's length, and threw him into the river.

Angélique gave a cry.

'Cantor! Quick!'

Cantor leapt out from among the trees, crossed the grass in a couple of bounds and dived into the water beneath the astonished gaze of the little group. Angélique came out from the trees too with her hand on the butt of her pistol, fully aware of the fact that, where the Abenakis or Iroquois were concerned, the slightest incident could easily develop into a massacre. But it was equally likely that all would be well; it was just a matter of luck and diplomacy.

'Greetings to you,' she said, addressing the chief, 'are you not the great Sachem Scacho of the Etchemins?'

She had been able to tell what tribe he came from by the way his bear-tooth necklace was made and from the vermillion porcupine quills stuck in his hair. He replied:

'No! But I am a relative of his, Quandequina.'

'Praise be to God!' thought Angélique.

She had been almost right!

Meanwhile Cantor clambered out of the water, dripping wet and

505

holding the child, who was choking and spluttering but had not been long enough in the river to lose consciousness.

The child's blue eyes were filled with terror and his fear had made him dumb. His mother seized him and clasped him wildly to her, and there they sat, with their teeth chattering, trembling so violently that they would have been quite incapable of standing. But they remained silent, their animal fear making them incapable of speech.

'They are English,' said Cantor, removing his shirt to squeeze the water out of it. 'This band of Abenakis must have taken them prisoner in the south.'

The Etchemins, faced with this unexpected intervention, had hurriedly grouped themselves round their prisoners, where they stood suspiciously waiting for a word from their chief to determine how they should react to this encounter. The fact that the white woman who had just come out of the woods spoke their language made a favourable impression on them.

'So you know our language, do you, woman?' the chief asked, as if unwilling to believe his own ears.

'I am trying to learn it; may not a woman speak the language of the True Men?'

This was the name the Abenakis liked to call themselves by. The Children of Dawn, but also the True Men. The only true men. The others, all the others, including the Algonquins and the Iroquois, were nothing but mongrels. The chief seemed to appreciate the fact that she understood this subtlety, and also that she was conscious of the honour it represented to speak their language. His anger began to evaporate.

Through the silence broken only by the rustle of leaves, the song of birds and the chattering of teeth, they looked at one another and summed one another up.

At that moment one of the Englishmen, the wounded one, whose comrade had set him down on the ground, touched the edge of Angélique's skirt.

'You? You French?'

'Yes,' Cantor replied, 'we are French.'

The poor wretches immediately rushed up to them and fell at their feet, beseeching them:

'Buy us! Pray, buy us!'

They clutched at Angélique and Cantor with their icy hands. They were livid, and their faces were battered and bruised where branches had struck them as they walked through the forest. The men had several days' growth of beard.

The Indians looked at them in scorn.

Raising her voice above the wails and supplications, Angélique endeavoured to persuade the Indian chief to come as far as the fort with them, where valiant warriors like them would find rest, tobacco and sagamite, but the Indians shook their heads. They were in a hurry, they said, to reach the Saint Francis river and thence their village on the banks of the Saint Lawrence. Later they would take their prisoners on to Montreal, where they would get a good price for them. And in any case were the Palefaces of Fort Wapassou not friends of the English? Black Robe had told them it was so!

Their looks became menacing, and Angélique took the precaution of leaning against the trunk of a tree and noticed that Cantor was doing likewise. A blow on the head from behind with a tomahawk was the sort of thing that all too readily happened. As she retreated with the wretched group of English prisoners still clinging to her, Angélique went on talking, aided by Cantor, half in French, half in Abenaki. She spoke to them of Piksarett, of Mopuntook and of old Massasswa with whom the Man of Thunder had made an alliance.

Once again their curiosity was aroused.

'Is it true that the Man of Thunder made the mountain explode?' they asked. 'Is it true that the Iroquois fled before him?'

Angélique replied:

'Yes, the Man of Thunder did make the mountain explode. But the Iroquois did not take fright. The Iroquois made an alliance with the Man of Thunder, for he had paid the blood-money, more blood-money than anyone had ever paid before. . . .'

'Is it true,' asked the Abenakis, 'that among the gifts given to the Iroquois there were beads as red as blood, as yellow as gold, and as transparent as the sap that flows from a tree, beads unknown to other traders?'

'Yes, it is true, come to the fort and you will see. . . .'

Rain was beginning to patter softly down on the leaves.

A thin cry came from among them, rather like the mewing of a cat. . . . Angélique and Cantor showed such surprise that the Indians burst out laughing. Delighted to be able to astonish the Palefaces in their turn, one of them put his hand into a kind of bag slung round his shoulders and drew out a tiny red, naked creature which he held up by its feet and which immediately began to bawl with all the energy of a cross-tempered babe.

Then one of the women, tears streaming down her face, turned to Cantor, who she realized could understand English and spoke:

'She says it's her child and that it was born in the forest six days ago. . . .'

'Heavens,' Angélique murmured. 'We really must persuade the Indians to come to the fort so that we can attend to these poor people.'

Finally, after promises of still more beads, tobacco and ammunition for their muskets, as well as indescribably beautiful blankets, the Indians were persuaded to come.

As they made their way back to the fort, Cantor supported the wounded man, who told the tale of their adventures.

They all lived in a tiny hamlet in the interior, and were 'frontiersmen' as the coastal dwellers called them. Their village, called Biddeford, was situated in the Lake Sebago region. The fort housed about thirty families within its palisade, but a few of the more independent farmers, like the Williams family, had settled outside. He, Daugherty, and his son, young Samuel, worked as hired hands for the Williamses. One morning when the two of them arrived for work, they no sooner opened the door of the house than a band of Abenakis rushed out of the forest, where they must have been lying hiding during the night, waiting for precisely such an occasion to get into the house.

In the twinkling of an eye the savages had overpowered everyone in the house, and snatched the children from their beds, which explained why the poor little creatures were barefoot and dressed in nothing but shifts, like Mistress Williams herself, who had only just got up. The Indians took whatever they could lay hands on in the way of clothes, utensils, and food, and rushed everyone off to the forest, into which they plunged with their captives; the whole raid had taken place so swiftly and so silently that no one in the fort or in the village had noticed a thing. It would in fact have been difficult to see anything, as there was so much mist that morning that visibility was down to about ten paces.

Then the nightmare march had begun for the unfortunates. The Indians, keen to get away as fast as possible from the scene of their misdeeds, harried them and forced them on. The farmer, who only had one shoe on – he had been in process of putting on his stockings when the savages seized him – had given the stockings to his wife who was barefoot. On seeing this, one of the savages who realized that the woman was expecting a baby at any moment, and would never be able to walk in a mere pair of stockings, gave her a pair of moose-skin slippers. Williams hurt his bare foot on a thorn. . . . The following day they had reached the banks of Androscoggin river, where the savages built a couple of rafts on which to cross the river. . . . Then, since they were now some distance from any English settlements, the Indians consented to slow up a little. Williams's foot was swelling . . . and he had to be helped along. Then Mistress Williams had felt the first pangs of childbirth. . . .

The voice of the poor hired hand, Phileas Daugherty, rose and fell in an endless litany as he told his tale of woe, for it was a great relief at last to be able to tell their story to a sympathetic listener.

Meanwhile the rain came on harder, making the going still more difficult through the wet clay.

As they came in sight of Fort Wapassou and skirted the lakes, a squall began to blow, tearing at the birch-trees, and soaking the party with water as they went by.

CHAPTER 89

AT LAST Angélique and her Indian guests entered the well-armed main room and, while Joffrey de Peyrac, who immediately grasped the situation, welcomed the Indians with great deference, Angélique was able to devote her attention to their prisoners. They put Mistress Williams into Madame Jonas's bed, well warmed beforehand, and once she had been washed, and suitably tended, the wretched woman began to get a bit of colour back into her chalk-white face. The other woman, whose child of two had been thrown into the river, still sat shivering on a bench, and when Angélique tried to take her off into one of the bedrooms to remove her soaking clothes the Sachem Quandequina refused to allow her to move. According to Abenaki custom he who first lays a hand on a prisoner thereby becomes his master and owner, and the prisoner must obey him under pain of the severest penalties. The young woman and her son therefore belonged to Quandequina, who did not appear to be a particularly soft-hearted master.

'That man Quandequina is as difficult and unpleasant as they come,' Angélique whispered to Nicolas Perrot, drawing him aside. 'You're a trapper, you try to persuade him to let me care for the poor woman.'

She felt considerable indignation at Perrot's indifference to the fate of all these people, especially the women. Although he was a good man, he was above all a Canadian, and as far as he was concerned the English heretics were not the sort of people you had to worry about.

But seeing Angélique's eyes fill with a mixture of disappointment and horror, he tried to justify himself.

509

'These women are not to be pitied as much as all that, Madame. We know the Indians will treat them like servants, but you need not fear for their honour. Indians never ravish their women prisoners[1] in the way Europeans do. They reckon that a woman taken against her will brings down misfortune upon a wigwam, and I think that they also find white women somewhat repugnant. If these English women and their children do as they're told, they won't be badly treated. And if they have the good fortune to be bought by some worthy family in Montreal they will be baptized and their souls will be saved. These English folk are lucky to be snatched from their heresies.' He also reminded her of the fact that the Canadians had suffered greatly at the hands of the Iroquois, who also kidnapped white men, but that in their case it was for the purpose of inflicting terrible tortures, which the Abenakis, who were allies of the French, never did.

After this explanation, he went and persuaded Quandequina to allow his prisoner to rest and eat, since, if she were to die on the way, there would be no point to his expedition, apart from the acquisition of a few clothes and cooking-pots which he would have had to trundle for several hundred miles.

Quandequina, deep in the delights of Virginia tobacco, agreed to his suggestions.

The young woman was one of Mistress Williams's sisters. She normally lived in the outpost of Biddeford but as her husband had gone to Portland for a few days, she and her little boy had gone to stay with her sister. Whatever would poor James Darwin say when he came back and found no one at home? She wept incessantly. With Elvire's help, Angélique made her take a steam bath, gave her some clean clothes to wear and did her hair for her. And at last she gave a wan smile when she saw her little boy, warm and well fed, fall asleep in her arms.

She was petrified for the child, since during the entire journey he had never stopped crying loudly, and this had so exasperated the Indians that they had twice been on the point of killing him in order to be rid of him, and on this last occasion, had it not been for Cantor's intervention, he would certainly not have survived. She kissed Angélique's hands and went on begging her to buy them from the Abenakis. Then at last she fell asleep beside her sister. Madame Jonas came in to ask

[1] During the seventeenth century the Indians continued to show respect to women, but this gradually disappeared under the example of the Pale-faces and the influence of brandy. Towards the end of the seventeenth century many Indians were perfectly prepared to rape white women.

Angélique's advice as to whether Farmer Williams's foot should be bandaged or whether he should be given herb tea to drink. Meanwhile he had it soaking in a basin of water to which had been added some friars balsam and some comfrey. Angélique immediately saw that she would have to use her lancet, to prevent his swollen leg from becoming gangrenous, and the Indians watched her, full of admiration, as she unhesitatingly plied the little shining scalpel which Master Jonas had made for her for use in delicate operations.

The savages were pleased with their welcome, and Farmer Williams's master thanked Angélique for performing an operation on his prisoner which would enable him to walk.

From time to time the newborn baby let out a wail from the bag where one of the Indians had put it, for all the world like a skinned hare ready for his dinner. And it took great diplomacy on Angélique's part before they handed over the tiny creature. Then at last she was able to take it away and wash it, laying it on its mother's bed.

'Praise be to God, it's a daughter! She will live. . . . Girls have greater resistance than boys. . . .'

She rubbed its delicate skin with sunflower-seed oil, bound it up in a napkin and put it to its mother's breast. Fortunately the poor woman had a little milk. She told of the terrible time they had had crossing the forests at such breakneck speed, what with the cold, their hunger, their fear and their aching feet. Madame Jonas who, like all good traders from La Rochelle, knew English, translated what she said.

The English woman told them how, when she had felt the first pains of childbirth, she had thought her last hour had come. But the Indians had shown some humanity, and had built a little hut for her to shelter in, and, leaving her to the care of her husband and her sister, had taken the children off to some distance away. After the birth, which had taken place without undue difficulty, they had seemed delighted at the event, and had even celebrated it by dancing and letting out blood-curdling shrieks. They had decided to remain where they were for a day to give the woman some rest, and during that day they had constructed a kind of stretcher from branches. Then for the following two days her husband and the white farmhand had carried her on this, but after that, they had been so exhausted, especially Williams, whose foot had become infected, that they were unable to carry her any more. The Indians would not carry the stretcher, considering it beneath their dignity. When they began to discuss whether they should abandon the woman and child in the forest after killing them with a stroke of the tomahawk, Mistress Williams, for all her exhaustion, managed to summon up enough strength to walk, and so their terrible ordeal went on.

Here they thought they were in heaven, but tomorrow the trek would begin again.

Angélique was horrified at the thought of leaving these white women to the mercy of the savages. She spoke to her husband about the possibility of saving them from this sad fate; Count Peyrac had already suggested buying the prisoners from the Abenakis, and had found them intractable. They gladly accepted the gifts offered them for having agreed to stop at the fort, and when several more handfuls of pearls, six knives and a blanket for each of them had been added, they agreed to stay on for another day to give their prisoners time to recover.

But they were bent on making a glorious entry into their village, driving before them their prisoners daubed in bright colours, amidst shouts of joy, and regarded it as unthinkable to return empty-handed from so perilous an expedition. Furthermore, they had Canadian friends in Montreal who would welcome their contribution to the salvation of souls for the Frenchmen's paradise.

And they would get a good price for them too, for the French were very generous when it came to winning souls for their faith. No doubt because there were so few of them, they needed to have all the invisible forces on their side. And there were plenty of these: the saints, angels, the souls of their dead, the souls of converts. . . . That was why the French-Canadians would triumph over the Iroquois and the English in spite of their small numbers. Quandequina could not possibly betray them by depriving them of these souls which they needed so badly. Was Peyrac willing to give an undertaking that he would have these 'Yenngli' baptized by Black Robe? No? Then why this pointless discussion?

By nightfall Angélique was beginning to have a certain understanding, if not indulgence, for the Spanish conquerors who had burned large numbers of Redskins at the stake. There must, she thought, have been moments when there was some excuse for their behaviour.

Angélique would have gladly fought them over this issue, but in spite of everyone's reluctance to hand the whites back to the savages, Peyrac felt he could not run the risk of a war against New France and the Abenakis for a handful of English farm labourers.

Eventually Angélique, sick at heart, was forced to agree. She still had much to learn about America.

Angélique spent the following morning at the bedside of the little

English girl. Even with all the care they were lavishing upon her, they were not at all sure that she would live. Her mother had no illusions about the state of her oldest daughter, who was called Rose-Ann, and she looked on pathetically as Angélique came and went.

She must have understood what Angélique was saying to Madame Jonas, as they discussed the intransigence of the savages who would not relinquish their prisoners, and as she thought of the cold nights they would have to face in the forest with the sick girl when they set off again, tears trickled down the face of the Puritan farmer's wife.

'My daughter will die,' she murmured.

During that afternoon, Angélique saw the Indian who owned little Rose-Ann sitting beside the fire smoking his pipe.

She came and sat down opposite him.

'Have you ever seen the mountain explode?' she asked him. 'Have you ever seen the green caterpillar come down from the sky, and the stars falling like rain?'

The man seemed interested. That is to say, his eyes moved slightly in the slit between his eyelids. Angélique had learned to interpret these signs and was not unduly discouraged by his impassive face.

'The Iroquois saw all this. And they fell to their face on the ground.'

The Indian whose name was Squanto took the stem of his pipe from between his lips and leaned forward.

'If you saw it too, you alone,' Angélique went on, 'and if you were able to tell your people about it, you would not need any prisoner for them to congratulate you and show interest in you. . . . On the contrary! Believe me, a sight like that, for you alone, is well worth the sale of your captive to us! And in any case, you know she is going to die! So what about it?'

These enticements nearly caused Squanto to come to blows with the other Indians, who were jealous of the fact that he alone was to witness the magic spectacle. But they were unwilling to give up their own prisoners, although it was a terrible temptation! Joffrey de Peyrac sorted things out by saying that, if Squanto was to be the only one to see the sight, they could nevertheless hear what went on and tell the others what they had heard. Squanto would tell them what he had seen, and it would not be a bad thing either for the Canadians to know what was going on at Wapassou.

As dusk fell they went off with Squanto to the other side of the mountain, where he saw the cliff burst open, rend itself, spewing forth half the mountainside with a terrifying roar. And when night came, three or four fireworks they managed to set off in spite of the damp, put the finishing touches to his astonishment. He returned to his brothers with an expression on his face like Moses coming down from Sinai.

'Yes, I saw the stars fall from the sky!'

The following day at dawn Mistress Williams embraced her unconscious child, who she knew would now recover but whom, she also knew, she would doubtless never see again.

She gave Angélique a description of the house at Brunswick, on the River Androscoggin where the child's grandparents lived, adding that one day they might manage to take her there.

Then clasping her new baby to her bosom, she set off courageously behind her fearsome guards.

Angélique watched the little group as it set off in the gentle rain. Patches of mist and fog hung over the surface of the lakes, and the tops of the trees were lost in swathes of watery clouds.

The Indians and their captives set off along the lakeside; there were the children, carried by their masters, Samuel Daugherty, the twelve-year-old boy still laden like a pack animal, and the hired hand supporting Farmer Williams, who was still limping.

The women were now more warmly dressed and better shod, and carried their babies. Angélique had drugged Cornelius, the child who never stopped crying, to keep him quiet, and had given some more of the potion to his mother in a flask.

The two captive women held their heads high and strode on valiantly in an attempt to keep up with the swift tread of the Indians, in order not to bring down their wrath upon them.

The little group gradually disappeared into the green forest, as if vanishing into a world where all was hazy, shifting and watery. . . .

CHAPTER 90

AS THE season wore on, Indians began to arrive from all directions to begin trading. They entered the outpost as if it belonged to them, threw their furs down on the table and made themselves comfortable on the beds with their peace pipes and their muddy moccasins, calling for brandy and handling everything within reach. They were the despair of Madame Jonas.

Even the most phlegmatic members of the Wapassou community seemed to be infected with the passion for furs. Peyrac kept on repeating that he wanted none of it and that any profit that might be made out of fur trading was nothing but a snare and a delusion. He also knew that, where the French-Canadians were concerned, two things were sacred in this world – the Cross and the monopoly of the beaver trade, and he saw no point in bringing down the wrath of the Government of Quebec upon his head by engaging in trade for which he had no need. But it was difficult to keep right out of the bartering business, for it was a kind of sickness, characteristic of the land and the spring. It disturbed everyone like a seasonal illness.

How could anyone resist the fascination of these rich, warm furs, their incomparable softness, the immaculate ermine, the midnight splendour of otter, the grey, mauve or blue smoothness of mink or silver fox, and especially the burnished golden fur of the beaver, perfect medallions sometimes as much as ten inches wide, or the black bearskins, wolfskins, pinkish weasels and striped skunks. . . .

Among the Canadian trappers who arrived was Romain de l'Aubignière, laden with furs he had collected in the high country on the far bank of the Saint Lawrence. He and his companions had risked the journey to Peyrac's outpost without the knowledge of their compatriots, for they wanted him to sell their furs in the English and Dutch cities, which they themselves were unable to do without being accused of treason. But they knew they would get twice as much for them by this means, and that in exchange they would be able to buy hardware from the English at half the cost and of far better quality than anything obtainable in Canada.

The Count agreed to act as their go-between in exchange for their support and goodwill when the occasion arose.

After L'Aubignière's visit, old Eloi Macollet could hold out no longer. Surrounded by all this familiar-smelling fur, he was like an old war-horse that hears the sound of fife and drum.

He stripped bark off some birch trees, bound it together with hoops, sewed it, glued it together, plugged up the cracks, then, when his little canoe was finished, he put it on his head and set off in search of some waterway which would take him down to the Saint Francis river and from there to the country of the Outaouais. Angélique and the children accompanied him as far as they could and waved a long farewell as he steered his canoe with brisk strokes of the paddle through the rapids and eddies.

The English girl, Rose-Ann, had recovered. She was a tall, frail pallid child who seemed overwhelmed by Honorine's exuberance. Honorine referred patronizingly to her as 'the little girl' although Rose-Ann was twice her age. But they made friends at last and spent

515

hours concocting strange mixtures to give their dolls to eat, which Lancelot disposed of afterwards.

Angélique noticed that Cantor had stopped provoking Honorine and was kind to her at times. He would go off roaming in the mountains all day long and sometimes even at night, with his little dark furry wolverine at his heels. His father did not interfere. Cantor brought back strange tales of his nocturnal wanderings and promised Honorine that one night he would take her to watch a pair of wolves playing with their cubs in the moonlight.

He had grown more talkative, and generally more communicative.

'I like wolves,' he said; 'they are sensitive, intelligent creatures. Dogs are fierce, but wolves aren't. They merely defend themselves. Dogs have men to rely on, wolves haven't. They know they are alone and friendless.'

Tepees began to spring up around the outpost with their lazy curls of smoke, the shouts of children, and the barking of dogs.

One day the magnificent Piksarett arrived. He came striding along the edge of the lake, alone, proudly shaking the headdress of crow feathers intertwined with strings of beads that graced his topknot.

He came smiling into the compound, casting haughty glances about him. He did not appear to notice the commotion his arrival had caused, but walked straight up to the men who happened to be in the compound with Elvire and Angélique. He raised a hand in a cordial greeting, then held out to Vignot the carpenter a handful of what they at first took to be furs, but were more like rather dirty rats tails.

'Would you like some "Yenngli" scalps? . . . Englishmen's scalps?'

Elvire lifted a hand to her mouth, feeling sick, and ran away.

'Do you want some "Yenngli" scalps?' the Indian repeated. 'They are whole scalps! I cut them myself in Jamestown, from the heads of those loathsome coyotes who killed Our Lord Jesus. . . . So hang them on your door if you are good Christians!'

And the big Abenaki burst out laughing at the horrified expressions on their faces, then turned on his heel and stalked off just as he had come, full of arrogance, holding his hideous trophies out at arm's length.

Towards the beginning of June, there was a rumour that an armed band of men was coming up the Kennebec in canoes. Things had been too quiet for some time. They sometimes laughed when they remembered how they had imagined things were going to be once they had shut themselves up in the fort for the winter. They had thought they would see no one for months on end, for who would dare to cross the terrible deserted wastes? But these French-Canadians dared everything, that they had learned during the winter. They had certainly not lacked visitors!

And now that they had strength to spare and had plenty of gunpowder and shot made in the mine, they asked nothing better than to receive still more visits....

But soon, from certain details mentioned by the Indians who had brought them this news, it appeared that the men on their way were mercenaries recruited by Curt Ritz, Peyrac's right-hand man whom he had left in New England for this purpose.

Now they had a different reason to be excited, and Nicolas Perrot set out as a courier while the others pressed on with the construction of quarters to lodge the new contingent. A few days later Nicolas Perrot's Panis slave appeared.

'They're here! They're here!'

Dropping everything, the men of Wapassou and the Indians ran down to the shores of the lake. As they reached the far end of the third lake, the first man was just emerging from the leafy hole where the waters plunged over the waterfall. He appeared, clad in a steel breastplate, square, Germanic, with coarse hair and blue eyes beneath his bushy eyebrows, the perfect picture of a mercenary from the battlefields of Europe, disembarking with heavy tread for the first time on the shores of the New World. They surrounded him and greeted him warmly, and he replied in German.

More and more of them kept on arriving, with Perrot as their guide. There were about thirty in all, Englishmen, Swedes, Germans, French, and Swiss.

Joffrey de Peyrac noticed immediately that Curt Ritz was not among them, but his lieutenant and faithful friend introduced himself. He was a nobleman from the French-speaking part of Switzerland, called Marcel Autine. He greeted Count Peyrac and handed him a bulky envelope in which, he said, would be found an explanation of his commander's absence. He himself had taken charge of the men and was glad to have arrived safely. He told them also that a sailing ship had come up the river with them, and that others would come on later. Food had already been brought up, and each man carried a small barrel of brandy or wine, with which to celebrate their arrival. When Peyrac asked him whether Ritz was ill or had been wounded, he gave an evasive reply, saying that the explanation would be found in the letter and that, if the Count so wished, they could discuss the matter later.

517

The Count agreed, realizing that it was preferable not to spoil the excitement of the arrival.

Back at Wapassou, long trestle tables had been set up to greet the newcomers, and they feasted in the open air under the gaze of the astonished Indians. Angélique went from one to the other, serving them all with food, or sitting beside them to ask them questions and exchange a few words with each of them. Her heart was wild with joy.

'We have won through! We have won through!'

And she exchanged long knowing glances with the old inhabitants of Wapassou as she went by, shaking them warmly by the hand. She would have liked to kiss them all, even Clovis, and she wept as she thanked them. She remembered what her husband had said before they had shut themselves up in the fort for the winter. What he had given her to understand as he had looked darkly at her with his flashing eyes – that the outcome of the winter would depend on each and every one of them.

And the winter was over.

And they were all there still. Every man, woman, and even child in Wapassou had proved their worth. They had remained true to themselves and to the man who had wagered that they would come through. And now victory was theirs; they had triumphed.

For thirty men spelt strength in this New World where most forts could only boast five or six soldiers at most. What nation could now prevail against the fort on the Silver Lake? Tomorrow the mercenaries would set to work felling trees and building impassable ramparts. They had won.

This land of America where they had disembarked, deceptive in its emptiness, in what did its challenge consist? Six thousand Canadians in the north, two hundred thousand Englishmen in the south, strung out along the banks and mouths of the big rivers, two hundred thousand pro-English Elorquois in the west, and about as many Abenakis, Algonquins and Hurons in the east, supporting the French.

Very little, in fact, for the country was vast and its inhabitants weakened by perpetual quarrels amongst themselves.

That was why sixty resolute people constituted an unbeatable force, since the spirit behind them was what counted. The French-Canadians had already proved this, for, although thirty times less numerous than their adversaries, they had succeeded in terrorizing the whole of North America right down to New York, and might soon succeed in doing so as far as the China Sea.

Today Joffrey de Peyrac had won his liberty and his independence!

And as the moon rose in the sky they began to make merry. The Indians had been given their share too, and joined in the general uproar.

The revelry continued well into the night, with drinking and singing and dancing to the sound of Cantor's guitar and the frenzied music of a newly arrived Irish fiddler. And from the Indian encampment the beat of drums and tortoiseshell bells rang out in unison with the farandoles, the bourrees and the tarantellas which Enrico Enzi danced while juggling with a set of knives.

The three women of Wapassou could hardly complain of a shortage of partners. That evening Angélique and Elvire danced every regional dance from France and even Madame Jonas was prevailed upon to dance a rigadoon. The cliffs echoed strangely with laughter and singing, music and clapping, while the moon made its way slowly over the three lakes.

Shortly after midnight Angélique went back to the outpost, for her husband had sent a message that he wished to see her. She found him in their room with a kind of tooled leather bag, which had arrived along with the mercenaries' luggage, and which, when they opened it, revealed a heavenly pale-blue satin dress, with a collar of silver filigree work, which he had ordered to be sent from Gouldsboro, together with a richly trimmed velvet costume for himself.

Angélique donned the new dress almost shyly, and when they both appeared on the threshold of the outpost, and stood on the promontory, a great shout of acclamation rose from the prairie where the men and the Indians had assembled.

And in the shout there were pride, contentment, the exaltation of success, and also the love of many hearts for the couple who stood there, turned towards their companions with a smile that made up for all their hardships. . . .

By the light of the moon, Angélique's dress looked like silver, and her hair, hanging loose on her shoulders, was of pale gold.

'By Jove!' said one of the Frenchmen, who had struck up a friendship with Jacques Vignot, 'talk of a princess! If I'd been told you had such a vision here! . . .'

'She's not a princess,' the carpenter replied disdainfully, 'she's a queen!'

And he turned towards Angélique, who was coming towards them, her hand resting on Joffrey de Peyrac's wrist.

'Our Queen!' he muttered. 'The Queen of the Silver Lake'.

CHAPTER 91

THAT NIGHT in Joffrey de Peyrac's arms she tasted love with a feeling of gaiety and a lightness of heart which, it seemed to her, she had not experienced since her youth. And he could see from her smile that she was at last freed from all the tensions which for so long had inhibited her spontaneity.

Birds were beginning to sing outside in the trees, and the darkness was growing paler. At the lakeside a few fires were still burning, and men were sitting around them smoking their pipes. The sounds of forest and water came to them through the little window.

This rustic bed welcomed their joy in one another. This bed had been the ship that had taken them to the far shore of winter. She had slept so close to him that she could sometimes feel his breath on her cheek, while the scent of his skin pursued her in her dreams, and in the morning she only had to part her lips to feel the movement of his tongue against hers. These were little things, but they spelt warmth and tenderness, and from this lovers' sleep had come her healing.

Now they had found the thread again and taken up the communion that had been interrupted fifteen years before by the fires of the Inquisition and the King of France's rejection of them.

On the following day Joffrey de Peyrac read the letter which came from Master Berne. The merchant of La Rochelle sent him news of the Gouldsboro colony and of the manner in which they had spent the winter. On the whole, all had gone well, but recently they had been plagued by a buccaneer known as Gold Beard who was pursuing his piratical activities in Frenchman Bay. Harassed on all sides, he had taken refuge among the Gouldsboro islands and it was he who had kidnapped – heaven only knew why – the man named Curt Ritz who had just disembarked with his men at the port.

In spite of this setback, Manigault and Berne had encouraged the mercenaries, who had just arrived from New England in one of the Count's small ships, to continue on their way as planned to the Upper Kennebec, since Monsieur de Peyrac might well be in need of their support. But they both hoped that Monsieur de Peyrac would be able to come to Gouldsboro soon to deal with the pirate and various other matters.

Berne had added a postscript to say that his wife, Abigail, was well but expecting a child in the summer, that she was somewhat alarmed at the prospect, and greatly hoped that Madame de Peyrac could be with her when her time came. If Madame de Peyrac found it possible to accompany her husband on his visit to Gouldsboro, they would all be delighted. . . .

The Count remained thoughtful for some time.

'What can all this mean?' he asked himself. He was thinking of the kidnapping of Ritz the German. Although pirates were fairly frequently seen in the region, it seemed to him that there was something odd about this particular kidnapping. He talked to Marcel Autine to find out exactly how it had taken place. It all seemed very mysterious. Curt Ritz had gone off for a short walk along the shore one evening, and later some Indians came and informed Autine that they had seen some of Gold Beard's sailors leap on him, knock him out, and carry him off in their longboat.

Suddenly Joffrey de Peyrac announced that he was going to Gouldsboro.

Suddenly their daily life at Wapassou was turned topsy-turvy. Peyrac apparently had no intention of leaving Angélique behind, and she could not quite see how she could be away for at least two months. She would have liked to watch the construction of the new fort, and in any case, would it not be imprudent to leave all these people on their own?

She also had to store away all the food supplies brought up by river, then carried up to the mine. And there were herbs to pick for medicines, and jam to make. . . .

On the other hand she was tempted by the idea of seeing Gouldsboro again and her friends . . . of talking to Abigail, and seeing Séverine and Lauriet and little Charles-Henri again; and finally, the thought of seeing the sea again and eating oysters and lobsters. . . .

'I wouldn't dream of leaving you behind, my love,' said Peyrac, 'I can't live without you now.'

'But what about Wapassou?'

Joffrey de Peyrac said that Wapassou was in excellent hands. Those who already knew the place would see to it that the newcomers were made welcome, that room was made for them, the discipline of 'the ship' was instilled into them. He had complete confidence in the good influence of the Jonases and the Malaprades on the others, and in Marcel Autine, who, although from a French-speaking canton of Switzerland, also spoke fluent German, Italian, Spanish and English. He would delegate his own powers to the Italian Porguani, whose loyalty, diligence and energy he had always admired. This handsome dark-eyed bachelor remained a mystery to Angélique, but she knew that her husband's trust was not misplaced.

They would take the hotheads with them – Vignot, Clovis, O'Connel and Cantor. But Peyrac persuaded Angélique to leave Honorine behind, for, in spite of the apparent casualness of Berne's reference to the pirate on the loose in Frenchman Bay and in the vicinity of Gouldsboro, things might become a little difficult. Peyrac was in no mood to allow anyone to kidnap a man he had taken on in New York during his first trip to America and who ever since had served him with devotion.

On the other hand, the inland fort seemed to him well protected against anything untoward. The palisade was rising rapidly, and their well-armed garrison could hold out against any Canadian, Iroquois or Abenaki intruders who might seek to harm them. You never knew what might get into these people, but trouble seemed unlikely, for in Quebec the Governor was busy preparing Cavelier's expedition, now made possible by Peyrac's generosity, the Iroquois had proved their goodwill and the Abenakis were heading south, utterly absorbed in the business of fur trading.

Angélique was a trifle anxious and somewhat upset at the idea of leaving her daughter behind, for she had never been separated from her. But fortunately Honorine took it well. She had plenty to do with her bear cub and all the changes connected with the arrival of the mercenaries. She was losing one of her friends in the person of little Rose-Ann, whom they were going to take with them in an attempt to restore her to her English grandparents. But she still had her two inseparable friends, Bartholomew and Thomas, and Elvire and Malaprade were more than happy to take charge of her during her parents' absence.

CHAPTER 92

EVENING WAS falling over Wapassou, another evening of peace amidst the exuberance of nature. The triumphant tide of leaves and grasses crept over the earth, and a green glow seemed to fill the earth, from the lakes themselves up to the sky.

Joffrey de Peyrac passed his arm round Angélique's waist, and, clasping her to him, drew her away into the forest. They crossed the

Indian encampment and followed the left bank of the lake towards the pine wood. They strode on swiftly, briskly, in step with each other.

As soon as they had crossed the summit of the hill, the world grew silent again, the only sound being the wind in the branches. The ground was rocky and covered with moss, and they crossed it without difficulty, automatically following a familiar path which led to a sheer drop down to the plain and looked out on to the distant mountains. Once again the mountains had changed colour, and a kind of blue haze covered their summits, broken in places by the pale-green patch of some clearing or the grassy banks of a stream tumbling through a little valley.

The forest was now decked in all its summer finery, of a sumptuous emerald green. A light mist, as impalpable as steel dust, blurred the contours of the land with its heavy dampness. But on all sides the sun's rays flashed back from the shimmering waters of a myriad lakes. They stopped.

This was their last evening in these parts. Tomorrow they would set off again to trek as far as the Kennebec, where they would embark in small boats and canoes and travel down the river to the ocean.

So before setting out Joffrey de Peyrac and Angélique took pleasure in looking out over their land in the fading light of evening.

'I have been happy here,' said Angélique. And in her heart she savoured the fragile word, 'happiness', for when danger and difficulty are shared, that is happiness too.

A mysterious ferment can suddenly mingle with the heavy dough of everyday life, and then that intangible thing called happiness is with you and will not leave you.

She stood there drawing the scent-laden air into her lungs.

'My little love, my companion,' he said to himself, devouring her with his eyes. 'You have shared my life, and I never saw you weaken. . . . There is no pettiness in you. . . . Once you have taken on a task, you carry it fairly on your shoulders. . . .'

They were happy, for they had triumphed over the winter, and had broken down the barriers that lay between them.

'I must gain a year,' Peyrac had said.

And it already seemed as if their enemies had grown less implacable. Only one remained.

Their thoughts were running on the same lines, while their eyes rested on the distant forestland that softly merged into a dark haze.

'I fear that priest,' said Angélique softly. 'I cannot help feeling that he must have prophetic powers, a mind that is everywhere at once.

From the very depths of the forest he seems to see everything, to know everything. He knew immediately that we represented the very opposite of everything he himself stands for.'

'Yes! For I claim gold and riches, he claims the cross and a life of sacrifice. I am on the side of the impious, the heretics, the rebels, and he is on the side of the righteous and the docile. And what is worse, I adore you and revere you, a woman.

'Charming woman at my side, my life, my joy and my flesh. . . . And that is what he hates most. . . . For I love you, Woman, you eternal temptress, the mother of all evil. I am on the side of creation while he is on the side of the Creator. Now I can see that there can be no reconciliation between us. The choice is between him and us. He has sprung to the defence of Indian Christianity. And he will fight to the death! Oh yes, I understand him. . . . For him it is a case of fighting for the very meaning of his own existence, the fabric of his life. And he will fight to the death, and give no quarter. All right then, I too shall fight. . . . I must accept the world as it is, and fight for the ungodly, for the heretics, for gold, and for the created world. . . . And for the woman who has been given to me to be my companion.'

And as he uttered these words a thought flashed through his mind so poignant that it almost hurt him physically.

'And what if that were the way,' he thought, 'what if the dagger with which he seeks to strike me down were the woman who has been given as my companion?'

And Pont-Briand's hoarse, panting voice rang in his ears:

'He will separate you, you will see! You will see! . . . He hates love. . . .'

At that moment Joffrey de Peyrac, the man of reason and Cartesian experimentation, suddenly felt frightened of the invisible, hidden magical forces that might be used to turn Angélique's heart away from him. And if her heart were to cease loving him, his strength and his life would trickle away like blood, and he could not survive.

'It's a strange thing,' he thought, 'when I arrived here in the autumn I was not frightened. I did not know whether the days we would spend together would reveal her to me as something of a disappointment or whether, on the contrary, they would draw us closer together, but I felt no fear. . . . Whereas now, things are not the same.'

Today he was learning the meaning of fear. He looked at her, trying to imagine what he would feel if one day that sweet, tender glance began to burn with love for some stranger. . . . And he felt such pain at the thought that Angélique saw him shudder and looked at him in astonishment.

At that moment a soft musical wail rose up behind them, from the top of the black cliff above them. It was a wailing that grew and trembled on the air and died away again, to be taken up once more on a single note, prolonging itself indefinitely in a cry of ecstasy mingled with sorrow.

'Listen,' said Angélique, 'it's the howling of the baby wolves!'

And she visualized them as Cantor had described them, the six little wolf cubs seated on either side of the he-wolf, with their round, pink noses straining forward in an effort to imitate their father, while he stretched out his tragic head like an arrow pointed at the moon.

'It's the song of the forest,' Angélique murmured. 'I don't know whether I'm right, but I think I agree with Cantor; I like the wolves too.'

He was looking at her intently, savouring every inflection of her voice, every word she uttered.

'It's a strange thing,' he told himself. 'I used to love her passionately, and yet for years I managed to live without her, to enjoy life, even to find pleasure in other women. . . . But now I could no longer do it. . . . If she were taken from me it would be as if part of me were torn away. . . . I could no longer live without her now. . . . And how did all this come to pass? . . . I don't even know. . . .'

At the mere thought that someone might try to steal her from him, not through death but in a more subtle fashion, he clenched his fists; for if, by betraying him, she ever fell from the pedestal on which he had placed her, this creature of beauty and light, he would fall with her, struck to the core of his vital being, drunk with fury and vengeance, to the point where he would undoubtedly forget all other human considerations and all wisdom. Through her, the arrows that struck him would all be poisoned darts.

Frowning, he clasped her hand tight in his, while she stood there wrapped in the nostalgic poetry of the wolves' chorus. Then Peyrac looked away from her into the dark undergrowth as if his keen eyes had discerned some hidden enemy.

Then it happened. A glimmer appeared on the southern horizon, grew bigger and bigger as it rose above the trees and mountains until it formed an immense oval ring of light in which there was outlined a giant draped figure; the draperies turned first pink then green and were superimposed on one another in a kind of fluted spiral, which, as it began to disintegrate, rained down a shower of brilliant flashing lights.

'What is it?' Angélique asked in astonishment.

'The aurora borealis,' Peyrac replied.

And he went on to explain that the phenomenon, whose cause was still unknown, occurred frequently in these latitudes at this time of the year. Angélique, who had been transfixed by the sight, began to breathe again.

'It frightened me, I thought for a moment that we were witnessing some celestial vision, we too. . . . It would have. . . . That's to say, I should have been greatly perturbed!'

And they both laughed.

Count Peyrac leaned forward and drew the folds of his cloak around her, for a sudden chill seemed to be rising from the ravine. He wrapped it carefully around her, running his hand several times over her shoulders, then, taking her cool cheeks between his hands, he kissed her mouth long and passionately. The darting lights in the sky illuminated them from time to time as they stood there, while the pink and green rain streamed across the darkling sky.

Then they stood in silence, filled with the indescribable sensation of being two people united, as friends and lovers, face to face with life, so deeply aware of the value of what had been given them that they fully understood the jealousy of others.

From time to time a sense of anxiety stole over them and Peyrac clasped Angélique to him.

As they looked towards the south, they both thought of a lone man, taking a brief rest on a bed of branches. On the stroke of midnight, he would rise and set off through the high-pitched hum of sandflies, to kneel in his little shanty with its beaten earth floor, before an altar with its ever-burning red lamp. To the right of the altar stood a banner with a red heart in each corner and a sword in the middle. And in the middle of the altar, beneath the cross, lay the musket of the Holy War.

The cross was made of wood.

Joffrey de Peyrac felt calmer now. He was even beginning to feel curious to know what form the fight would take, this secret, obstinate fight that had begun between them and this man, before they had ever even met.

Peyrac was himself familiar with every kind of fighting, and yet he had the impression that the fight that was to come would be no common one.

One hope remained. Where there is antagonism, there is always a meeting point, some possibility of contact....

And on both sides the stakes were so high that they would surely be granted this grace.

'God's will be done,' he murmured.